BEARS OF BRIDGETOWN

RAGE OF LIONS BOOK SEVEN

MATT BARRON

BLADE OF TRUTH PUBLISHING COMPANY

To my friends at Caffissimo,

*With thanks for the many, many cups of coffee and bottles of water.
You fuel the writing machine.*

God bless you all.

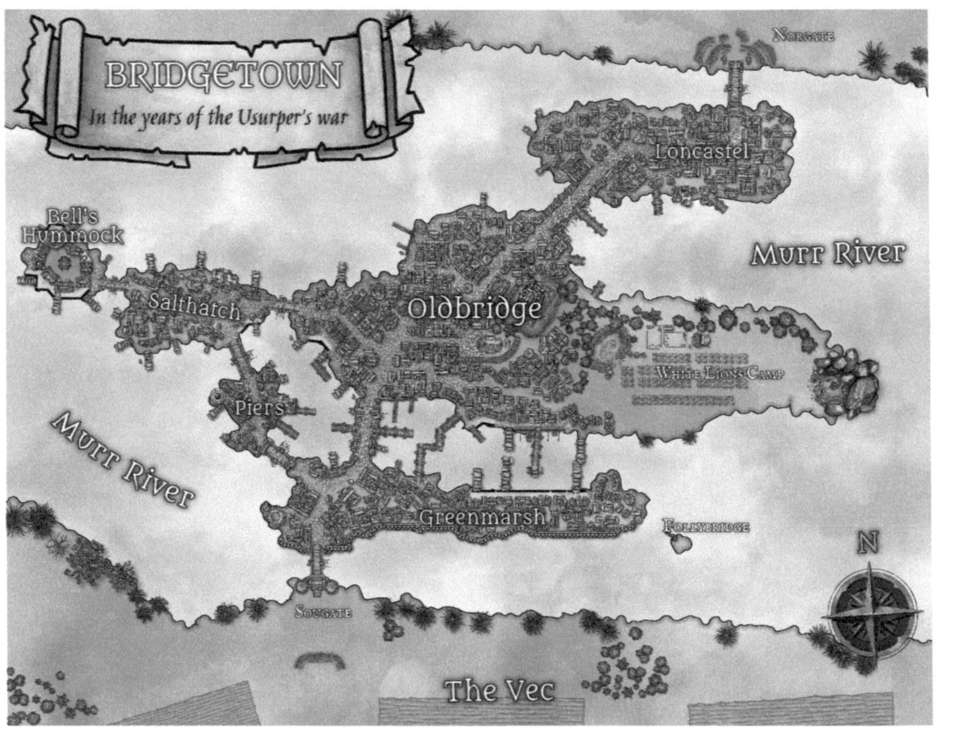

BRIDGETOWN
In the years of the Usurper's war
Norgate
Loncastel
Bell's Hummock
Murr River
Salthatch
Oldbridge
White Lions Camp
Piers
Murr River
Greenmarsh
Follybridge
Sougate
N
The Vec

Salt Sea
NORTH TO QUENLAND
SALTMARSHES
AZURE MOUNTAINS
Fallenhill
WESTERN GRASSLANDS
Ruined Castle
Inverel
Greycastle
Ramat River
Rallong Lake
DWELTFORD
RHALES
Hawkspurr
Halling Pass
Pennysworth
Brotta's Emerald
Ongatta
UNKNOWN
DENAY
River Dwelt
WESTERN REACH
THE GRAND KINGDOM
Tassasim
Ocean
Ashfield
Griffith
UPLAND
DESERT
Rose Garabost
Tachra
RADENGON
BEYOND DWELT
Murr River
Upper Murr
Rapids
BRIDGETOWN
Aubrey
Sobridge
Eden Bay
Longshepherds
THE GRAND KINGDOM, THE VEC,
& THE UNEXPLORED WEST
in the 3rd year of the Kingslayer's Usurpation.
Sunbury
BY SOLFT OF LOWER OTNEY
SCHOLAR
Trachester
THE VEC
UPDATED FROM THE JOURNAL OF BORROSOD THE PILGRIM
SOUTH TO MASNIA

PROLOGUE

"Welcome to my little niche in God's great kingdom. Never mind the smell—it's peculiar, but you'll soon get used to it."

Cerulean cocked an eyebrow at his host's assertion, and his upper lip twitched, as if to sneer of its own accord. The "smell" was in fact a mixture of unpleasant aromas, although predominantly made of charcoal smoke, brine, and fish guts going to rot. It was precisely what the Inquisition's man expected a dockside smokehouse to smell like, and that was what most prompted his distaste. He drew his fingertips along the rough wooden planks of the wall, pulling them away and studying the oily, sooty residue left upon them. Every surface in the tiny room was suffused with the deposits and Cerulean was certain that in short order his own clothes and hair, likely even his skin, would become infested with the distinctive odor.

One might as well hang a sign and leave a herald's announcement everywhere he goes, the spy of the Church's Silent Hand thought as he allowed himself to be ushered further into the dimly lit refuge.

While it was pungent, it was not the unpleasantness of the smell that troubled Cerulean. He could gladly endure any amount of mere discomfort for the Inquisition's purposes. What displeased him was that once it had become infused in his person, sticking to his clothes, skin and hair, the distinctive aroma would undermine all attempts at disguise and subterfuge. Enemies would not have to "look" for him; they would be able to simply follow the smell. He would need to find different lodgings, and soon, certainly before he could begin his mission in earnest.

"I know it seems humble," his host went on, taking one of the room's two rough-made wooden stools, each no more than a stump with the bark stripped away. He gestured for Cerulean to have the other. "Still, it's truly ideal for our purposes. As a fish-mock—that's what they call the trade here on the Murr—I can keep an eye on all the river traffic and an ear to all the gossip. Most of it's drivel, as you can imagine, but no one looks askance when I ask questions, and the fishwives see more than they know."

Cerulean nodded as he took the offered seat, letting the other man prattle on for a short while. He knew the inner pressure to speak openly, if only once, which a life of silence induced. He had even fallen victim to the urge himself in recent years and still regretted the amount he had divulged to someone who should not have outlived the conversation.

"Yes, in all, this little bolthole has allowed me to be most effective, and I do not doubt it will serve you just as well, Master," the false fish-mock concluded, and, at last, he stopped speaking. Cerulean could feel the man's earnest gaze upon him, hopeful for some response to his report. For his part, the minstrel spy kept his eyes roaming over the little room, as if there were a myriad of tiny details all around which he was trying to absorb. In truth, he had summed up the man and his little hut within heartbeats of entering, but keeping underlings uncomfortable was a tactic of the order, from the least informer like this one to the Master's Bench in the Vault Above the Pit. The fish smoker was left to study his guest a moment longer until Cerulean could hear the man shifting his weight in nervousness, as if he was about to spring off his little seat.

"You say you have been effective," the minstrel said suddenly, at exactly the moment before the man's nerves caused him to speak again. It was such a perfectly timed interdiction that the "fish-mock" actually blinked with surprise, his mouth half open.

"'Most effective,' you say, in fact. I take it you have some evidence of this 'most effectiveness'?"

"I have much, but surely you would say the silencing of the Vardian Sacrist was my most recent triumph."

"'Triumph'?" Cerulean repeated, still not looking at his underling.

"Wouldn't you think so?" the man asked, clearly proud enough of his work that he was ready to defend its value to a superior. "The man was sermonizing day and night, condemning King Daven Marcus and urging on the forces of rebellion. The king's men had been chasing him all over the bridges for nigh on a season. And this was no penny prophet. He was an adjunct of the cathedral, cousin to the previous patriarch. His sermons were starting to be published in pamphlets. Bridgetown is more than two thirds merchant class and guildsmen. They can all read. Even their wives and many a shoreman have letters enough for that kind of firebrand simplicity. He was a threat to the throne."

"And you silenced him?" Cerulean asked in a tone that should have made it clear he saw no reason for the man's pride in the story.

"I did," the fish-mock continued eagerly, apparently missing the hint. "The seditious mongrel was hiding down on the docks—not here, but on Bell's Hummock, the next island upriver. But the docklands are all one folk, really, and whatever is muttered under one bridge is heard under them all. Once I knew where he was, it was only a matter of having a dagger put to him one night for mere coppers. Simplicity itself, in fact."

Put to him for mere coppers? Cerulean repeated the words in his thoughts and then drew in a sighing breath that was cut short by the room's stench. He had no doubt this fool had done the job himself, regardless of his boast that he had hired another. Likely he had pocketed the money and considered it a clever lurk. Cerulean shook his head slowly. Time to put this pointless interview to an end.

"You do not approve, Master Bluebird?" the man asked, apparently surprised he was not receiving more praise for his report.

"Dead in the shadows is meaningless," Cerulean said, and he finally turned to face his host. "I doubt a week goes by that some poor fool doesn't find himself on the wrong end of a dockside knife. Hardly a triumph."

"What would you have done, then?" the fish-mock demanded, and Cerulean cocked an eyebrow again. The man at least had the sense to look somewhat fearful at this point, ducking his head and adding more humbly, "If you would be so kind as to instruct me, Master."

"You knew where he was," Cerulean explained, as if his subordinate was a child in a classroom. "You could have had him followed, for days if necessary. He might have led you to co-conspirators, sympathizers, others who have doubtless been assisting him."

The fish-mock's face fell as he clearly realized the obvious utility of Cerulean's plan. He swallowed visibly, doubtless feeling the chill of his confidence turning to doubt.

"I wouldn't think he had many folk about him," the riverside agent stammered out rapidly. "I think we can trust that any such as he did have will have fled without his inspiration to rally around."

"Quite probably you are right. They have now escaped to resurface only God knows where, doing yet more mischief," Cerulean said pleasantly, then narrowed his eyes in a cold glare. "The Silent Hand of Mother Church does not doubt or trust. We are always certain. Not only should you have waited to make sure you had all of his fellow heretics, but even until they escorted this street preacher to his place on whatever corner they found for his next sermon. You should have had five or ten jackanapeses ready to infiltrate the crowd—the kind of rowdies always up for rash action—sent them in to make a fuss, turn the rabble into a brawl, with specific orders to 'put a dagger' to each of the firebrand's closest confidantes. Then, in the midst of the chaos, our painful heretic cries out in anguish, collapses in a fit and dies. Before sundown, a pamphlet circulates saying that the renegade sacrist has been felled by God for his apostate beliefs and that the latest riot, which threatened the peace and commerce of all of Bridgetown, was put down by Daven Marcus' loyal knights, bringing their longswords to bear in the defense of Bridgetown's steadfast citizenry."

As Cerulean's words went on the fish-mock's eyes grew wide. He looked down at his own hands in disbelief, shaking his head.

"How?" he muttered, then looked up again at his disdainful superior. "How was I supposed to engineer all that?"

"If you could not, then you should have done nothing," Cerulean chided. "Were you not taught that often no action is the best possible action? There is a long list of names and titles given to the order by ignorant fools and heretical enemies, but the only one we own for ourselves is the Silent Hand. We are to be all but unknown. The mystery is our greatest power."

"But no one knows it was me, I swear."

"That is not enough. Any fool will guess. It's not enough to hide our involvement; we must also make it so that the low folk understand it the way they should. Mother Church has many enemies. It is not enough that they merely die. They must be seen to die because God himself has ordained their deaths. Their passing must sometimes come as from holy writ, in an ecclesiastical court, and sometimes it must come as from on high, by the quiet, unseen hand of God Himself. *We* are that unseen Silent Hand."

"I never considered," the fish-mock said, shaking his head in wonder. "I...I suppose...I suppose I only thought to have something worthy to report."

"Of course," Cerulean said gently, smiling like a kindly uncle, to relieve the man's fear of rebuke. Inwardly he was impressed with the swiftness of the man's insight, and his humility to accept his failure. Nevertheless, the consequences of his disappointing action would be dire enough. At least he would have had one good confession to take with him into the afterlife. As the riverside informer drew in a relaxing breath, thinking himself to have survived with only a quiet correction, Cerulean began to tap out a simple rhythm with the fingers of his right hand. The common beat of numerous folk songs, some of which Cerulean had penned himself, it would be familiar to every patron in any tavern or bawdy house from the forests of Quenland to the southern-most princedoms of the Vec. The fish-mock looked down at Cerulean's fingers, hearing the deceptively common rhythm as the minstrel began to improvise a song to the beat. He sang softly, almost inaudibly, in a language that had not been spoken by any living nation in over a millennium. There was a rumor that the tower builders themselves had spoken in this tongue before they were scattered abroad, divided and confused. Wherever it came from, Cerulean was adept in its use in song, and while his audience of one would not understand the words, their meaning would penetrate to his very soul and the fish-mock would do what he was told.

"Tomorrow you will be overjoyed," Cerulean sang in the mystic language to the enthralled man. "You have received word that your long-estranged brother from Tathra is coming to visit you. You will invite your neighbors to drink a toast with you to his coming. So overjoyed will you be that you will dance foolishly along the dockside and in a tragic end, fall into the water to drown before any can rescue you. When your brother arrives in several days' time, he will learn the sorrowful news that you have passed, but not before you had registered a legitimate will with the Conclave factors, bequeathing your property in the main to him as a gesture of reconciliation between you."

Cerulean stopped singing and a moment later let the beat lapse. The other man blinked as if awakening and then looked alarmed.

"Sorry, Master," he said with fearful urgency. "I thought I heard music or singing."

"Some ribalds returning late from a taphouse, I think," Cerulean told him with a dismissive wave in the direction of the smokehouse's door. "They went by at a distance."

"Oh, of course."

"Well, for now I think we will have at least one good use for your bolthole, being upon the docks," Cerulean said, his manner becoming much lighter and more friendly. The fish-mock visibly relaxed and even risked a fresh, though hesitant, smile. The minstrel returned it and nodded. "I shan't lodge here though. Better we not risk being seen together in the coming days. Suspicions might be raised."

"Yes, good thinking," the underling agreed, as if his word were of any value, his contribution to Cerulean's plans more than that of a walking corpse. The minstrel agent was not typically given to being this wasteful with resources, even with ones as inept as this docksider had proven himself to be, but the speed of recent events was forcing him to move more quickly than he usually liked. Besides, he had better tools arriving in Bridgetown in the coming days, and all he needed of this fool was his hut for a temporary storage space.

"We will speak again later about your further place in the order's plans," the minstrel said, lying to the doomed man. "For now, though, I want to hear all you know about this."

Cerulean pulled a single gold coin from his pouch, holding it up to the meagre light of the room's rushlights. With foreign writing on one side and a foreign ruler on the other, it was not much larger than the length of a single finger joint.

"Masnian gold?" the fish-mock said, confidence returning to his smile once more. "That I *can* tell some true tales about."

CHAPTER 1

"*Seven* guilders on the coin! My Caius says we should expect nine at the least. It's extortionation!" Lady Spindle declared in clear disbelief. Clothed in a linen overdress and pale green silk shift, her fine attire and improving manners made it easy to forget that she was still peasant-born and knife-edged at the core. The half mask of black lace on the right side of her face still concealed the ugly scars of her former life.

"Money changers are not known to be generous at the best of times, My Lady," Marquis Consort Farringdon replied. "My father used to say that foreign coin was only ever worth half its value because the banks or the money changers will ever take the other half for themselves."

"And that is in the best of times," Archduchess Amelia added from behind a linen kerchief that she had taken to holding to her mouth most of the time since arriving in Bridgetown. With droplets of lavender oil soaked into the cloth, as well as some perfuming flower scents, it was better for her pregnant nose and stomach than the miasma of dockside reek that pervaded the river town—a mix of swamp water murk, pitch-tarred ropes and boat boards, and fish of every kind the great Murr River could provide. Against this concoction the handkerchief was a poor bulwark, but it gave some relief, and in the moments when it failed, it allowed her some cover to spit out the bile from her stomach with the dignity of a high peer rather than as a fishwife squatting upon the docks with a mouthful of chew as she scaled the day's catch. Even so, her fine dress, in gold and grey and sewn for her by Spindle's expert hand, would have to be washed before she could face wearing it again, even after only an hour or two on the docklands.

"You wait 'til Dalflitch gets here," Spindle continued. "One smile and these'll be fallin' over themselves to give her a dozen guilders on the gold piece. You watch."

"Then let us pray Lady Dalflitch is not delayed too much longer," Amelia replied. "And in the meantime, let us remember that we are a noble household with new wealth and new power. Let us at least try to project a little ancient dignity."

Recognizing the implicit chastisement in the archduchess's gentle words, Lady Spindle bowed her head, smiling decorously as she had learned from her new tutor in upper class manners. Amelia watched, finding the change almost as unfathomable as the bestial transformation of Redlander *brakkis effar*. Behind her lace mask and new poise, Lady Spindle, the Lace Fang, was becoming almost indistinguishable in dignity from any other well-born lady-in-waiting, lapses in speech notwithstanding.

"Of course, once the lady does reach us, she will bring with her several thousand more souls for us to house," Farringdon added as he stood aside like a steward and gestured for his wife to lead the way into the dockside warehouse where many of the archduchess's forces were sheltering while better lodgings were found.

The militia's Lion Banner Company had only been in Bridgetown mere days, and already their presence seemed to be stretching the unique municipality to its limits. In any other city of the Grand Kingdom, a newly arrived army would camp in the farms and fields on the fringes of the settlement easily enough, but Bridgetown had no such facilities to offer. True to its name, the town was literally built upon bridges between a handful of islands protruding through the surface of the widening Murr River. Initially, the town had been no more than the serfdom of a local earl's castle, occupying the island in the middle of what was then merely two long stretches of ancient stone bridge. As the settlement grew, with space so limited, the bridge itself was built upon and extended, with docks and wharfs hanging off pylons and footings so that now more than half the town's businesses and dwellings were conducted on wood hanging over the flow of the mighty river. There were Bridgetown folk, it was said, who lived their entire lives never setting foot upon earth. While she might not have believed it, as Archduchess Amelia looked around the bustling riverside community which dwarfed the impressive docklands of her hometown of Dweltford, she could understand why some would. In every direction the bustling waterway was crowded with all manner of watercraft. Rivermen with the agility of acrobats leapt from gunwale to jetty and back, or vaulted with their long poles, seeming to hang in the air like gulls as they arced over the busy water. Even as she took one glance backward, Amelia saw a man spring from his own narrow lighter over the bows of a rowboat, landing upon a broader barge on the far side, there to embrace another fellow like a long-lost friend. The pole vaulter was so adroit, he never even risked losing his straw hat, let alone fearing a dunk in the filthy river.

Ushered into the warehouse, the stink of the dockside was added to by the yet more pungent odor of men and women in cramped conditions. Amelia was, not for the first time, forced to spit bile as her uneasy stomach turned in revulsion. Little more than a barn with some heavily built shelves towards the back, the warehouse was occupied by hundreds of White Lions Militia sweating in the hot, cramped air of late summer, the shade of the building doing nothing to cool the crowded atmosphere. Pressed in, with no more for most of them than a patch of floor to rest upon, nonetheless there was an unmistakable order to the sweaty chaos. Militiamen sat on the floor in their lines, groups of ten together, while their junior officers were clearly visible, keeping order. A distinct aisle down the middle of the building was being maintained, with folk moving up and down the space, carrying water, victuals and laundry. Some men diced or played cards in their little squads, while others moved back and forth carrying orders to and from their superiors. The process of assessing the losses and wounded from the aborted campaign in Aubrey was continuing, not to mention the quartermaster merchants looking out to replace damaged equipment.

Now that I have coin again, there are many empty purses that need to dip into my coffers, Amelia thought, not resentful, for once, but rather thankful that she had at least some wealth with which to honor her debts—especially to these loyal men, who had encamped the summer against multiple armies and faced bitter odds with iron discipline and courage. *Lions indeed.*

"We must find Sergeant Markas," she said quietly to Spindle, and her lady-in-waiting was about to start off down the aisle to seek the company's banner sergeant when some of the men nearest to the warehouse's open barn door noticed the arrival of the ducal party. Amelia's intention was to consult quickly with Banner Sergeant Markas and make sure no new issues had arisen before she met with Bridgetown's recently risen ruler, the Baroness Penelope, to discuss the longer-term disposition of her men. This warehouse was barely acceptable as a stop-gap measure. She would absolutely not have them housed like this for a prolonged period, as if they were livestock, or worse, convicts. Now she watched as the word was passed, and more and more heads turned to look at her. "Her Grace" was the whisper that flowed backward through the warehouse, stilling the mutter of other conversations. She was astonished as, beginning with the ones nearest and following the whispered revelation, the entire warehouse was soon on their feet, standing as one before her. Beginning with the faces nearest, whenever she met someone's eyes, they bowed their heads, tugging the forelock in the gesture of respect every lowborn man and woman owed to a peer.

"Good Reachermen," Amelia whispered, tears in her eyes for this gesture of respect. Crowded in like termites in a mound and they still made the effort to honor her. She was astonished when a line first, distinguished as a halberdier or pikeman by the lion's claw symbol on his spaulder, stepped boldly into the aisle before her and saluted as if she were any other officer of the militia.

"We ain't broken, Your Grace," the man declared proudly. As he lowered his saluting hand, Amelia could see that the bottom part of his undershirt sleeve on that side had been recently ripped away, doubtless to have made a bandage. The line first continued his protestation. "We know we took a kickin', Your Grace, but true to God, we ain't broken. You just give us the word and we'll go give 'em back ten-fold what they gave us! Just give the word."

Many men near him added their assent, nodding vigorously and muttering "aye," until they were no longer muttering. Amelia felt like a deer startled by hunters as around her the acclamation grew.

"Three cheers for Her Grace!" someone shouted, and the huzzahs rang out. Then they became a chant, "Amelia! Lioness!" On and on it went, rolling up the warehouse like a tidal flow of sound, and Amelia felt her cheeks reddening. The chant was still continuing when Sergeant Markas rushed up the narrow aisle through the crowd, attended by a corporal Amelia did not know and a drummer boy who she did recognize as one of the lads who had attended her during the evacuation from Cattlefields during the final days of the Aubrey Campaign. Markas tugged his forelock and bowed his head. Amelia tried to speak to him, but the cheering and chanting made it impossible to be heard. Seeing her inability to communicate, Markas tapped the drummer on the shoulder and the boy hefted his drum around on its baldric to sit in front of himself. Then he lifted his sticks high over his head, and as if he thought to hammer the instrument down into the very earth beneath him, drummed out a mighty beat, calling for silence. Even with his earnest pounding, the signal beat barely penetrated the chanting, and Amelia suspected that those nearest began to fall silent not because they could hear the drumbeat command, but because they could see the lad's vigorous efforts for themselves. Slowly, but inexorably, the chant died down. Even so, all the militia present still looked to her with earnest faces, and

Amelia knew she could not speak with Markas now without first addressing her loyal men-at-arms.

"Good Reachermen, true lions," she shouted, knowing there was little chance her voice would reach all the way to the back of the space, but trusting the word would be repeated and passed. "We will return to Aubrey, and we will end the oppression of our people there."

The chant started up again at that point, but a diligent order and swift repeat of the beat for silence stilled it.

"But first we owe a debt here. I will pay your wages and then we will repay the baroness for her aid to us, helping us to escape that..." Amelia paused. What was she to call it? A trap? Certain defeat? She could not tarnish her Lions' pride with such terms. "Helping us to escape that disadvantageous position. We will help the Baroness of Bridgetown to defend her home and then we will go back and take Aubrey out of the hands of the Veckanders who exploit her. In the meantime, I must speak with your sergeant and see to finding you better quarters. Lions so bold as you deserve better than to be lodged like a herd of cattle going to market."

Amelia looked to Markas as she stopped speaking and he took the signal. Before more cheers or the chant could be taken up, he was bellowing orders in a rough voice that would definitely carry from one end of the warehouse to the other.

"Right, enough o' this disorder! Back to your fallen-out doings. Corporals and line firsts, see to discipline."

Inducing an almost disappointed air, as if the Lions had thought they would march immediately from their cheering acclamation to a renewed fight for the fallen town of Aubrey, the junior officers finally managed to settle the militiamen to their previous state of controlled boredom.

"Fighting spirit is still firm it seems, Banner Sergeant," Farringdon observed quietly.

"Indeed so, My Lord Knight Captain," Markas answered, saluting formally.

"But not for long, if lions are kept like livestock," Amelia observed. Markas nodded solemnly.

"Frustration and indolence are the enemies of discipline and fighting spirit, true enough, Your Grace, but we've got ourselves a pretty deep store of both at the moment. We won't run out tomorrow, I promise." Markas looked to Farringdon. "I reckon the knight commander's lancers have it worser than us in the short term."

"That is true, Banner Sergeant," Farringdon agreed. "We tried walking the mounts on the dockside, but it's nothing like a proper run, with grass to crop and fresh water to drink."

At present, the lancer company's horses were still being housed on the barges that had been used to transport them, which was even worse than mere poor stabling. Mucking a barge was a significantly more difficult task than a regular stables, and the motion of the water, not to mention the miasmas, were as much a threat to the beasts' stomachs and lungs as they were to any person not born to the riverside. As eager as Amelia was to get her people better situated, she knew that the lancers were likely to lose many of their mounts altogether to sickness if they were not soon disembarked permanently from their river barges.

"I am not insensible to the needs of your fine horses, Knight Captain," Amelia told her husband, "But these are the heroes of the Reach, and better lodgings for them are not to be delayed."

"I would not ask it to be otherwise," Farringdon replied graciously but with an earnest tone that made it clear he agreed with her. Neither Sergeant Markas nor Lady Spindle so much as blinked at the assertion. There were many nobles, north and south of the Murr River, who valued their horses more highly than whole villages of peasants, but their liege lady would never be such a noble and would never suffer such to be her husband either. Every militiaman in the warehouse, from Markas down to the least Claw or Fang, knew they were beloved sons of the Lioness. They were her pride in more ways than one.

"I will bring these issues to the baroness' attention when I meet with her at noon," Amelia said. "Now before I go, tell me all our needs so that I can make them plain to our hostess."

"Yes, Your Grace," Markas said readily, and he began to list the many needs and problems that a force of thousands of men-at-arms afoot generated, and which of these the Lions needed first.

CHAPTER 2

B irdsong greeted the dawn, enlivening the air above the waving fields of grain and the nearby village as the Gryphon Banner Company camp awakened. The sweet trills of swallows and the magpies' harsh cries were blasted to momentary silence as drummer boys amongst the tents and campfires gave the morning their own greeting—the dawn beat, awakening the camp to the day's duties.

Baron Prentice Ash, Knight Commander of the Western Reach and leader of the Gryphon Banner, was already long awake and returning to the camp with Dahyoor, the exiled fey man who had become his squire, of sorts. "Of sorts" because it was in most respects a ridiculous reversal of the typical noble and squire relationship, which was very like an apprenticeship to knighthood. There was nothing Prentice could teach Dahyoor about horses. The knight commander was a poor horseman even by Grand Kingdom standards. By the standards of the mountain and plains riders of the Wind Rising fey, he was worse than an infant. *Palpolon* they called him—saddlebags, and poorly secured ones at that. However, while Dahyoor the "squire" exceeded his master's riding skills by leagues, he nonetheless respected Prentice as a war leader and because the knight commander had done the one thing for Dahyoor that the fey man had never imagined might happen—he had given him a place in the company. By making Dahyoor his squire, Prentice had taken away the fey rider's shame of exile. For Prentice it was pure practicality. He had to deal with the fey as his prickly allies, and Dahyoor was the perfect advisor for such a situation. And keeping him close meant Prentice's own horses were cared for by an expert. For Dahyoor, it meant the difference between being half a man and being made whole. Nonetheless, the fey squire was still a typical example of his people—wiry and tanned from the sun, hair the color of the ripe wheat, and never dressing in more than buckskin trousers and a sleeveless tunic. When they rode to war, his kin would also wear stiff corselets of layers of linen, sewn with bright-colored patterns, but Dahyoor had no such garment, as near as Prentice knew. The knight commander assumed he had been forced to give it up when he was exiled by his people.

"I will go to the horses," Dahyoor told Prentice without so much as a by-your-leave. Such was the way of the fey. They shared almost none of the manners or mores of Kingdom folk. They neither saluted nor bowed, said no "pleases" and no "thank yous." Despite trying to teach his "squire" the proper forms, so far Prentice counted all his efforts as failures. He nodded to Dahyoor as the fey left him and shook his head with a smile.

"Something amuses you at this early hour, good husband," a female voice called, and Prentice looked to see his wife Righteous approaching, wearing only her linen underdress and a shawl of deep green wool about her shoulders. The weather was not yet autumnal, but his wife insisted that breastfeeding made her feel chilled, even in the summer heat. Her sleep-tangled, strawberry blonde hair fell to one side, and in her arms was one of their newborn twins.

"My sweet, you are the very picture of motherhood," Prentice told her and kissed her cheek. Then he bent down to kiss the forehead of the baby, who turned out to be their daughter.

"Rather I was a picture of motherhood that slept," Righteous said sourly. "This'un stirred just as you left the tent and she ain't settled since. I fed her twice and she still wants me walking her about."

"High strung, like her mother," Prentice teased, and his wife's green eyes narrowed upon him.

"Say that again when I've put her down. We'll see how high strung I am then," she told him. He chuckled quietly. In all his life, from its greatest glories to his worst injuries and sufferings, nothing pleased him like his wife, and now, family.

"Is her brother still asleep?"

"Not bloody likely," Righteous assured him, casting her eyes back in the direction of their tent. "He was quiet awhile but not long enough. He's with the wetnurse now, not that I like it."

"It is typical for noblewomen, you know, and Emma is a sweet thing," Prentice told her, not for the first time. He knew his wife hated sharing the breastfeeding duties for her two children with a wetnurse, but it was indeed common for women of rank to do so, and while they were on the march with half the Reach's armies, it was also necessary. Even so, Righteous had screwed up her nose and looked ready to express her distaste once again when a fresh signal was beaten out by a drummer nearby, and the infant stirred in her arms. She held her daughter up close and comforted her through the disruptive noise.

"They need their names, husband," Righteous said as she rocked her babe back and forth. Prentice sighed and nodded, recognizing his obligation to his children. Since his return from the headwaters of the Murr, he had added this duty to the many others that were the lot of a commander. However important his militiamen's needs were, though, this could no longer be held off. Children needed their names. In truth, his reluctance came not from business but from not wanting to face an ugly reality. Most Kingdom folk, most folk around the world, he supposed, drew names first from their own families—a tradition both Prentice and his wife would find challenging, for different reasons.

"What do you want for her?" he asked Righteous, nodding at the daughter in her arms.

"Well, I never knew my ma's name," she answered. "The workhouse I ran away from said I was orphaned at about six of age and they never told me nothing about who bore me. So, I don't got any names that are close to my heart like that. What of you?"

"My mother lives, but she and I were never close."

In truth, almost as soon as he had been weaned, Prentice had been handed over to tutors and instructors to make him into the perfect candidate for the Academy at Ashfield so he could become a knight of the Church. Prentice looked straight into his wife's eyes and saw a plaintiveness there. It was clear she had been thinking this question over and had a suggestion.

"Can we name her Amelia, do you think?" she asked softly. "Little Amy Ash, she could be called. Do you think her grace would permit that?"

"I think the archduchess would be flattered and honored," Prentice said truthfully. It pleased him that his wife wanted to honor the most significant woman in both their lives. They might be estranged by time and circumstances from their own mothers, but the Lioness had become the young mother to the whole Reach, and they were Reacherfolk now. He smiled at his wife, and she nodded down at their daughter Amelia.

"We'll have to get her named proper at a church when we get to Bridgetown. I ain't want to wait later than that. Her and him." Righteous looked back in the direction of their tent once more. "What's he to be named?"

"Gant," Prentice said without hesitation, naming his friend, lost in battle on the same river flowing mere leagues south of where they camped.

"It's a good, honorable name," Righteous agreed, nodding. "And a proper memoriam, I'd say."

Prentice hugged mother and daughter together and enjoyed the morning as the sun crested the horizon, illuminating the world around them. A line of militiamen marched past on their way to relieve the night's picquets, but their line first discretely chose not to disturb the parents and child with a command to salute. In fact, it was a polite, feminine cough that disrupted their moment of peace. They stepped apart to see a young woman wearing a full wimple and veil, so that her eyes were the only part of her face that was visible, and garbed in an undyed linen dress, waiting patiently nearby.

"With respect, My Lady," the girl addressed Righteous, but the new baroness tutted almost immediately.

"The baron is here," Righteous said, her normal voice shifting to a more formal tone unfamiliar to her husband, her speech becoming courtlier. "You beg his indulgence first."

"Sorry, My Lady," the girl said, curtseying. "My Lord Baron Ash, if I may speak with your wife."

Prentice gave a nod, bemused by this extreme level of formality. The young woman addressed Righteous again.

"My Lady, Lady Dalflitch respectfully...requests your...presence," she said, clearly working to remember the exact wording of her message. "At your early...convent?"

"At my lady's *earliest convenience*," Prentice corrected gently, and the girl nodded.

"As you say, My Lord."

Righteous's expression was as po-faced as a churchman's, but her eyes glittered with amusement as she cast a glance at her husband before giving the maiden her answer.

"You may inform Lady Dalflitch that I am at my family's business, but will attend her within the half hour," the new baroness said. The girl accepted the message with another curtsey and withdrew to give her mistress Lady Righteous's answer. When she was gone, Righteous looked to Prentice and he smirked.

"Does she have to repeat your words exactly?" he asked.

"It's Dalflitch's idea," Righteous confirmed.

"So you are all to talk like queens and princesses?"

"Yes we are, husband," the baroness replied, her voice slipping back into her more casual accent and vernacular once more. "We need the practice. All us Lace Fangs can talk like fishwives and milkmaids. We don't need practice at that. But we needs be ready to not shame her grace before we can take a proper place in her chamber. Our behavior reflects upon the archduchess."

Prentice nodded, smiling in amusement. "And having the maids dressed like anonymous neophyte nuns? I take it that is Dalflitch's idea as well?"

"Cunning, I tell you, husband," Righteous said vehemently. "These trainee Fangs, they don't show their faces or their hair in the common sight now. That's the mystery they are until they become like us, proper Lace Fangs."

Righteous tapped at the brawler's brand under her eye. Since the children had been born, she had taken to not wearing her lace half-mask but had made it clear that when she returned to her duties as the archduchess's bodyguard, the mask would return with her.

"And in the meantime," Righteous went on, adjusting her baby's weight to her other arm. "If we send them out without their covers, they can move about unknown like, listening at doors and windows, carrying secret messages, all sorts of canny, back-alley stuff, because no one will know their true faces under the veils. In 'mufti,' Dalflitch calls it."

"Cunning indeed," Prentice said, appreciating the breadth of Lady Dalflitch's plans for protecting Archduchess Amelia and the Western Reach from the shadows. Just as he had built their liege an effective fighting force, so Dalflitch was working to build a spy network out of the ruins of the smuggling community of the Reach, broken and burned by Redlander infiltration. Masked women, trained to defend themselves and to pose as any other woman, from the lowest born to the highest, would make the perfect anonymous go-betweens, connecting loyal spies with their spymaster.

"I had best let you go to your meeting, my love," Prentice said, kissing his wife once more, this time upon the lips.

"And you?" she said. "You off to lead the march on Bridgetown?"

"It is near, but Daven Marcus still has a loyal army between us and the gates. It will be a battle."

"Go. Win. Come back to me," she told him and then turned to take their daughter Amy back to the tent so she could be handed off to the wetnurse and her mother and father could prepare for another day of marching and fighting on behalf of the Western Reach.

CHAPTER 3

"Well, there she is—Bridgetown the bitch," declared Guillam, scar-faced corporal of the Gryphon Banner's Roarsmen. His rough features were a chaotic mix of judicial convict brands and powder burns, more disfigurements than clear skin. Nevertheless, he grinned brazenly as he looked back to his fellow officers while they all stared down from their hilltop vantage at the town on islands in the river below them.

"You should call her a sow, Corporal," Lyrach, a line first under Guillam's command, corrected.

"What's that, junior?"

"A female bear is a sow, not a bitch," Lyrach explained.

"What's a female bear got to do wif' it?" Guillam demanded, too confused to care that he was being corrected by an underling. For a long moment, no one answered his question.

"The bear is the heraldic beast of Bridgetown," Knight Commander Prentice explained at last, his expression almost absentminded as he surveyed the town and the ground between it and his company's position.

"Alright, Bridgetown the sow, then," Guillam conceded, as if losing a pointless argument over cups in a tavern. "I don't see what difference it much makes..."

"Shut up, Guillam," said Sergeant Gennet, standing beside the knight commander, with the other senior corporal, Porth, on his far side. Guillam saluted, but his expression showed he was far from chastened. Serious-minded and devoted to his role, Prentice could feel Gennet's presence beside him, ready to take orders or give his own impression of the situation, whichever was required. Along with these highest ranked men of the Gryphon Banner, Prentice had Dahyoor present, standing a step behind the officer cadre, holding the reins of the commander's two horses. Also there, standing a little apart, Chaplain Whilte was resting upon his staff, as quiet and solitary as a man at prayer. Like Prentice, the sergeant and corporals all wore their Reach-blue brigandines and steel armor pieces, their respective specializations in the company marked by the embossed symbols on their left pauldrons. Soon as he could, Prentice wanted to make sure to add a dragonfly medallion to the armor of every man who had traveled west with him and fought at the far mountain lake of the Verdant fey. Whilte had only his cassock, plain and humble.

Prentice realized that he was growing to feel comfortable amongst this group of men who followed his commands almost without question. Even the fey war leader Benjamin, who was sitting upon his mountain pony several paces farther away, felt like less of an outsider now. He still would not dismount for something as insignificant as pre-battle counsel, but Prentice was at least becoming confident that the fey ally would follow his instructions and raise any objections openly rather than the pure insubordination that had characterized their earlier relationship.

"What have we in store for us, would you say?" he asked, inviting his men into his thoughts about the day's coming conflict. Every other man turned his eyes on the fields once more and gave them their full attention.

"It's all meadowlands, now that we're past the tilled crops," Gennet said first, describing the open fields between themselves and the town.

"So, we can bet all that pretty-looking grass near the river'll be boggy and wet, 'specially if it's still green so late in summer. Men in plates'll sink up to their thighs, or could do," Porth added, completing his sergeants thought.

"The enemy will do his best to push us into that, first chance he gets," Lyrach agreed, and all eyes turned to the east northeast where the encamped army of Denay loyalists could be seen no more than two leagues from the riverside barbican of Bridgetown's north gate. "For sure they probably already have all the firm ground scouted and sentinelled. Astride the Great Bridge Road like that, they'll sweep down on our flank as we march to the gatehouse, shove us into the bog and nibble at our trapped sides while we swim in muck until we surrender from pure exhaustion."

Prentice nodded. He had much the same sense of the ground. Having merged his smaller expeditionary force with the impressive company of new recruits that his wife and Lady Dalflitch had been leading, Prentice had inherited their mission, which was to link up with the Lion Banner Company led by Archduchess Amelia and Knight Captain Marquis Farringdon to defend Bridgetown and to lift the siege by the Usurper Daven Marcus's forces. The word he had was that the army beneath his hill was currently led not by the kingslayer himself, but by his most loyal nobleman, Duke Robant. Daven Marcus was leading a separate army, currently locked in a prolonged campaign in the north of the Grand Kingdom.

So, the regicidal mongrel has two armies, and so do we, Prentice thought. *But our two are here and only one of his. It would be an ideal strategic situation, except for the fact that we really have three armies, not two.*

The knight commander had ordered his smaller force of campaign veterans to join the larger body of new recruits, but at the moment they were simply a handful of cohorts tacked on, not properly integrated into the company order. The recruits were armed and trained but not really tested. Prentice knew almost none of their junior officers by name or sight, and though he was sure the dutiful Gennet was doing his best to commit faces to memory, he too had to be floundering somewhat. The knight commander knew what to expect from his veterans, and they knew what to expect from him. The recruits were a more unsure quality—like untempered steel. He expected they were ready for the fire, but a battle like this would be a true test.

"How many would you say they have?" he asked, looking again at Duke Robant's camp.

"Not as many as we do, that's for sure," Guillam declared confidently. The others nodded, but ultimately they turned to Lyrach to let him render the final opinion. Each of Prentice's officers could count, but only the young line first, who had formerly been a squire, had sufficient numbers to do large calculations quickly.

"By the tents, the fires, and the livestock, I'd guess somewhere closer to two thousand than one," Lyrach said carefully.

"Two thousand? That means we've got 'em at two to one, don't it?" Guillam asked, confident of a gambler's read of the odds, even if his mathematics were not up to the actual numbers.

"That's the look of it," Gennet agreed. "Always assuming they haven't fetched themselves up some new cannon or other thing of war we ain't seen yet. Seems every second battle of this war one side or tuther is turning out a new war-beast or secret engine of destruction."

Everyone nodded or grimaced in response to that observation. Only Prentice showed no emotion. He just stared at the prospective battlefield and cursed the circumstances inwardly—not because he was afraid of the coming combat. As his men had said, the numbers were on their side, the ground made it reasonably easy to pick threat from safety, and even his raw recruits were trained to fight Grand Kingdom knights in open fields like this. And despite Gennet's misgivings, he was not afraid of the sudden intervention of a new tactic or tool of war. All warfare was based on clever twists, new turns in the path to battle that the enemy did not expect. There was no point fearing what he could not define and thus could in no way prepare for. He had enough to worry about as it was. No, what made the knight commander want to curse was the opportunity they were about to miss.

"If only we had a pathway to the knight captain's ear or the archduchess herself," he said quietly. "If we were properly integrated and could tell the Lion Banner what we were about, we could encircle that force and annihilate it outright. Cut Daven Marcus' total army in half."

"Annihilate, My Lord Knight Commander?" Brother Whilte called, clearly uncomfortable with the brutal term.

"As an army, good Chaplain," Prentice explained readily. "The men themselves would be prisoners, not corpses."

He looked askance at the religious man who was a former knight himself. Whilte should have readily taken Prentice's meaning. The hope would not have been for a massacre but a decisive victory. Since their march west, the chaplain had more and more taken on a role as a kind of conscience for the company, as well as a voice to explain the knight commander's thinking, especially at times like this. Recognizing the value of Whilte's intervention, Prentice turned to his underlings.

"We are more than strong enough, both in numbers and man-for-man," he told them. "I have no doubt we will see the inside of Bridgetown's gatehouse before noon. Our enemy has not even committed himself fully to the siege yet. There are no trenches, no siege engines, none of the Usurpers bronze puppies emplaced. My regret is not for our strength but for the missed opportunity. We will win, but the enemy will comfortably withdraw to reform for battle another day. If we could come at them over this field while the Lion Banner sallied from the town and swept around them to the east, we could catch them between hammer and anvil, as it were. With such an advantage of numbers we would be able to force them into surrender, take prisoners, and strip them of weapons and harness. Half of Daven Marcus' army would be gone in a single day's work."

"In the jaws of the wolf, my old sponsor used to say," Lyrach reflected, nodding as he and the others turned their gaze once more on the field below them. Sneers and tuts made it clear they now recognized the disappointment this field represented.

"We could send fast riders to the town," Porth suggested half-heartedly, rubbing his stubbled chin and casting a glance at Benjamin on his horse.

Prentice shook his head. "It would not work," he said.

"You don't trust our 'friends'?" Guillam asked provocatively, giving Dahyoor a sly look. The fey man only snorted once derisively. Prentice looked from his squire to Benjamin and then to Guillam.

"I would trust our friends to get their whole *keshiyaa* down to the gatehouse before Duke Robant even heard they were out in the open," he told the corporal. "What I do not trust is that they would be heard by the right ears once they arrived. Our allies may still not fully trust us, but it isn't as if our folk much trust *them*, is it?"

Prentice did not bother pursuing the matter any further. He knew that the opportunity was here, but there were too many other factors he did not know for sure. There had been great commanders in antiquity whom he had studied who would have taken the risk, gambling that the prize was worthy. At some time soon, the Lions of the Western Reach were going to face the army of the Usurper in open combat somewhere on the sacred lands of the Grand Kingdom itself. But as much as he could see the value of springing to the first part of that fight now, he also knew it was not his decision to make. He had been out of contact with his liege for virtually an entire summer now. He had no idea what plans she had, what alliances she was fostering. Even an easy victory now could prove a political disaster for the archduchess, and there was no guarantee of an easy victory here.

The truth was that he could commit the Gryphons to a full attack, trusting that Amelia or Farringdon would equally see and desire the opportunity, but even if they did, they almost certainly would not be swift enough to prevent Robant from seeing the danger as well. The enemy duke could simply withdraw up the road once he saw the numbers against him, and Prentice's company would be bloodied, possibly badly, with nothing to show for it but a few captured tents. Whichever way he poured the water from the bucket, it still slipped through his fingers. He shook his head and put the whole matter out of his thoughts.

"Here is our strategy," he told them and then unfolded the specifics of his battle plan—where each cohort would march and how to respond to the likely enemy actions. When he was sure that the sergeant and corporals understood the instructions they would have to take to their junior officers, Prentice cocked a head in Benjamin's direction.

"What do you see, Benjamin," he called. "Is there a ride for the *keshiyaa* to the gatehouse of Bridgetown? A swift battle ride? Reach that ground and deny it to the enemy?"

Like his kinsman Dahyoor, Benjamin was contemptuous that he was even being asked such simple questions. When the Gryphons began to march for the gates, Prentice was sure Robant would send knights ahorse to block their path or slow them down so that the rest of his men-at-arms could charge at the company's flanks. If Prentice could send the fey horse archers ahead to secure the ground in front of the gates, the loyalist army would not be able to cut off his company's path. The Gryphons would be able to make a fighting march straight to the town.

"We have seen this ground," Benjamin said simply.

"Riders in coats of steel will likely try to take the ground from you," Prentice added.

"Anteaters," was Benjamin's response, referencing the spiny animal that made burrows under bushes and hedgerows. Even against full steel harness, the best armor the Grand Kingdom could provide, fey arrows had an uncanny knack for finding seams and gaps. The horse archers would pepper the enemy with so many shafts they would resemble the spiky little animals.

"Then we have a plan," Prentice declared. "Everyone to your places in the order and I will see you all later inside Bridgetown, the sow."

Smirking as they saluted, the cadre fell out to their duties, Benjamin wheeling his mount to return to his own warband. Only Brother Whilte lingered a moment.

"Where would you have me march, Prentice?" he asked, only using Prentice's given name now that they were in relative privacy. "With the standard or back with the luggage? Or somewhere else entirely?"

Prentice looked at the man who had once been his sworn enemy and gave him a wry smile.

"You are our only healer at present, Brother," he said, and he clapped his hand on Whilte's shoulder. "I trust God to direct you to the place you are best suited."

"You know there's a good chance I won't be doing miracles in every battle," Whilte responded, only half joking. Mere days ago, the chaplain's prayerful presence had miraculously turned aside a flash flood that threatened to engulf the entire company. The militia had taken to calling him the Moses of the Lions.

"Then I trust to your best judgement," Prentice told him. "Just as you trust to mine."

With that, Prentice nodded to Dahyoor and mounted up on his horse, Boots, while the fey squire threw himself bareback onto the knight commander's other mount, Dusty.

CHAPTER 4

Armed with Sergeant Markas's reports, Amelia made quick progress through the other warehouses and one stock yard, where the rest of her militiamen sweltered, before heading to her appointed meeting with the baroness. Although there were no more spontaneous chants in her name, nonetheless she was welcomed with smiles and affirmations at every stop.

"Far from home, but truly amongst friends," she said to her husband, and he smiled, nodding in agreement. In the days since they had arrived in Bridgetown, Farringdon had taken to not wearing his armor, and today he had only a belted surcoat over his undershirt, not even bothering with a doublet in the heat. To Amelia's eye his face looked thinner, his cheekbones sharper, and his limbs had a new, rangy character, like the muscular limbs of laborer yeomen, who lived hard lives of strong exertion and little rest. She was sure this was a mark of the hard days riding and fighting that he had undertaken in Aubrey. Any of the softness of youth or wealth that the former prince had once retained was now sloughed away to reveal a true frontiersman underneath—a Reacherman. His injured eye at least had returned to its previous clarity, and that pleased Amelia most of all.

No sooner had the archduchess and her entourage left the Piers Island docks and turned onto the main road—the crooked spine of the town called Great Bridge Road—than they were accosted by two men in the heraldic colors of Bridgetown—orange and gold chevroned stripes bright upon their tabards. Each man wielded a staff of ash wood, polished almost to the sheen of fine ivory, a sign of their authority, and they did not hesitate to use the rods to make their way through the press of the crowd.

"Archduchess Amelia, Lioness of the Reach," one called out as he sighted her, and the heralds pushed their way past a pair of tinkers who carried a pole hung with a dozen or more pots and pans on their shoulders. The heralds' authoritative shoves set the whole mass of metal jangling like a discordant instrument, and one of the tinkers cursed under his breath but watchfully, lest he draw an ireful kiss from one of the pale wooden rods.

"Your Grace, if we may interrupt your journey, we come with word from our lady, Baroness Penelope of Bridgetown," one of the heralds said as both men executed bows of exacting precision right there in the street. Each held his staff upright in his right hand, right foot back a half step, left hand sweeping forward and out, daring any of the press of the crowd to bump into it. Heads down, the bright and formal pair waited politely to be acknowledged. Around them the market-day-like press of the crowd flowed out of the way, like water around a rock in the river.

"Gentles, you are well come, doubly if you bring word from your liege," Amelia told them, matching her formality to theirs. "Rise, please, and give your message. We were just on our way to attend to the baroness' invitation. Your word must be urgent if it could not wait even that long."

If the message was urgent, the heralds gave no sign, standing from their impressive bows and taking a moment to adjust themselves into upright perfection before speaking further. With a glance at each other, perhaps to confirm that each was properly presented, the one who had been speaking thus far nodded to his fellow and that herald began the message.

"It had been the Baroness Penelope's pleasure to receive you near to the cathedral after prayer, thereupon to discuss certain matters of state," the man pronounced, his clipped speech clearly heard over the clamor of traders and livestock. Indeed, much of the nearby street stopped its day's business to listen in. The small crowd would have a curious tale of high-born activity to share with friends or family this night. "With her apologies, the baroness must ask you to meet her elsewhere."

Amelia nodded and waited for the new location, but the heralds said nothing. She blinked, wondering why they might not be giving it. After she gave Farringdon a quick glance, he leaned in and whispered.

"I think they are leaving you a discrete space in which to express your displeasure."

"What?"

"They are letting you get angry, if you want to," he said a little louder. Amelia shook her head. She was no stranger to courtly etiquette, and she certainly knew many a high-ranking peer of the realm who might take umbrage at being directed about by a slightly lower noble, but to leave her a gap in the message to make a fuss about it was a step too far towards nonsense for her taste.

"Please, good heralds, where would the baroness have me meet her?" she pressed. If the messengers were surprised or relieved that they would not be on the receiving end of vented anger, their expressions did not reveal it.

"My lady awaits your pleasure at Norgate, atop the barbican, if you would be so kind," the first herald declared.

"We will be there directly," Amelia told them, and they accepted her word with another bow. Then they stood silent, eyes on the archduchess and her companions, though not meeting her grace's own eyes, expressions still unreadable.

What now? she thought. This time it was Spindle who came to her rescue with the correct insight.

"Gentlemen, her grace will need your escort to her appointment," the Lace Fang said, her speech as formal as the heralds'. "Step lively and make the way clear ahead of you for us to follow."

They nodded and turned on their heels, loudly calling for the crowd on the street to make way for the Archduchess of the Western Reach, using their staves wherever mere loud voices were insufficient. Amelia felt she had to step lively as well or risk losing them in the crowd. Even so, as she followed in their wake, like a net trawled behind a pair of fishing boats, on either side merchants and tradesmen, goodwives and fishwives, tugged their forelocks or bowed or curtseyed at her passage.

"It's going to be like a courtly procession from one end of the town to the other," she said quietly behind her linen kerchief.

"Indeed, my love," Farringdon said quietly, standing close by her and shielding her from anything low hanging from the sides of the densely built houses, like tradesman's signs or drying washing. "By the time we reach the baroness, it will be a rare citizen of Bridgetown who does not know Amelia of the Western Reach by sight."

Amelia allowed herself a smirk and reached for her husband's hand.

"Was it just me, Marquis, or was that really as *very* courtly as it felt?"

"Courtly in the extreme, Your Grace," Farringdon agreed, smiling at her and sharing her amusement.

"Why?"

Farringdon only shook his head. Amelia looked to Spindle.

"And you, My Lady?" she asked, speaking slightly louder but not so much, she hoped, as to be heard by the vanguarding heralds. "What do you say? Why are we being feted with such manners?"

"You are the archduchess," Spindle said imperiously. "Sovereign in your own realm."

"And that is explanation enough?"

"It is all the explanation I require," the lady-in-waiting pronounced, and it was all Amelia could do not to giggle. It was still hard to reconcile this new Spindle, as fixated on courtly manners as her chaperone Matron Bettina had once been, with the knife-fighting seamstress she had first met not more than half a decade ago.

"I won't always need someone to remind me of my manners, will I?" she mused. "I'm fairly certain I'm rather talented in that regard. Surely, I am beyond the need of instructors by now?"

Farringdon lifted her fingers to his lips and gave them a gentle kiss.

"You have many things weighing upon your mind, my love, not least of which are your loyal retainers and your coming child and heir. Let some of us handle these lesser matters for you, just for a time."

"Is that a command from my husband?" she whispered. "Or a request from the knight captain."

"Whichever one will work, my wife, My Liege, Lioness."

CHAPTER 5

The main thoroughfare of Bridgetown ran through the entire town, from southern riverbank bank to north, twisting and turning somewhat, but especially over the main ancient bridges that predated the settlement's first founding—yet another curious artifact of a previous era. Some said those structures dated from the Bright Age itself, before the mountain was thrown into the sea. If that was true, they truly were a wonder, having had to survive the inundation of waters which that long past calamity had wreaked upon the world. Under her feet, Amelia could not tell she was not walking on solid ground, even though she could make out occasional glimpses of the river in the tiny, alley-like gaps between the densely built houses on either side. The structure must have been mighty indeed, for not only did it suspend numerous other jetties and piers from its pylons, but even with houses densely packed three and four stories high down both sides, nevertheless the thoroughfare itself, Great Bridge Road, was easily fifteen paces wide. Few if any of her hometown's streets were so broad or open to the sky, and all of those were built upon solid ground. So many were the arts of the ancients that were lost with the fall of that Bright Age.

Amelia noted a fortified house ahead, more like a keep than a gatehouse, broad across the whole road, under which the cobbled way passed through three large arches. As if it was a fine colonnade, the brick of each arch rested on carved marble columns that must surely have been more decorative than structural. Even from a distance, the wear and pockmarks of damage that centuries of passing traders and emigres had worn in the ornamental stone could easily be seen. The crowds were already thinning as Amelia's escort led her through the left arch, and in the cool shadows beneath, she blinked at the sudden change of brightness. Her vision adjusted in time for her to notice a tariff-taker's booth, made of grimy, aged wood that was so colored with moss or algae that its boards looked only yesterday to have come from the side of a wrecked boat. Inside the booth, a disinterested bailiff lounged on a stool, head leaned back against the wall. At the herald's approach he almost fell from his stool and gripped at the booth's side to pull himself upright before tugging his forelock to the highborn passersby.

The siege has robbed you of your trade as well, has it tariff-taker? Amelia mused, realizing that with the north gate sealed against Duke Robant's army, there would be no trade coming through the gate from the Grand Kingdom. Doubtless, the man's dockland comrades would be doing brisk business still with all the town's river trade, but for now this man's post was a mere hidden formality. He might as well sleep through his days.

Expecting to turn aside to some door or inner portico under the arches, Amelia was surprised to see the twinned heralds march straight out the other side of the undercroft passage and back into bright sunlight. She was puzzling about it when she heard their boots thump upon wood. She looked down to realize the ancient bridge had come to an end, but the river had one last channel left to cross. For whatever reason, the mighty stone span ceased at this point, and Great Bridge Road became a wood- and brick-crossing over water, no different in artifice to any other bridge in the world. It had also narrowed significantly. Amelia looked behind her at the keep that she had assumed was the gatehouse and realized that it must mark the end point of the ancient bridges. Perhaps the archaic structures had not survived the mountain's fall as well as she imagined.

Walking along the final wooden span toward a significantly less impressive fortification on the actual north bank of the Murr, the now absent crowds of townsfolk and traders were supplanted by men-at-arms, mainly in the orange and gold of their town. Many were leaning over the edge of the bridge, apparently watching happenings in the fields to the north. Even those who were not did not take up too much space, and none inhibited the herald's march.

So many bridges and how many islands? Amelia thought. *The river here must be ten times wider than at Aubrey.* Broad as the Murr was for most of its course, it was surely more like a flowing lake than a river here at Bridgetown. And yet this was where the waters were crossed.

"Good heralds, is that where the baroness is?" she called and pointed to the approaching end of the wooden bridge.

"Indeed, Your Grace, the Norgate Barbican," one responded with the air of a man too polite to be annoyed at having to repeat himself.

"Barbican is true spoken," Farringdon said quietly. "It is smaller even than the gatehouse in Dweltford. How long can it stand once Robant decides to make a concerted effort to claim it?"

Amelia was not surprised her husband shared her misgivings. Dweltford's gatehouse was larger and sturdier than this, and it had fallen in less than an hour when her forces took her town back from the rebel, Duggan. Of course, Dweltford's barbican had fallen to Prentice Ash's military cunning, not brute force. Even so, Duke Robant was also no fool in the ways of war.

"Perhaps the plan is to defend in depth," Amelia said, using a phrase she had read about but only vaguely felt she understood.

"If it is, then they've left too many men cluttering up the bridge for a swift retreat," Farringdon added.

They had now reached the rear of the diminutive fortified building, and as they did so, Amelia and her entourage drew closer to the heralds, so that the two escorts heard more of her conversation than she meant. One of them turned to her on the threshold of a doorway.

"If I may be so bold as to reassure you, Your Grace," he said, as indignant as his good manners allowed him to be. "The baroness is fully astute to matters of defense for her town. Although she has only recently taken over her father's seat, she is fully ready to accept the responsibilities. The gates of Bridgetown are strong and have never fallen in centuries, not even during the rebellion of the southern earls. Nevertheless, my lady is wise and not incautious, which is why she has turned out the full north militia to reinforce Norgate should there be an assault."

"Your speech is presumptuous, herald," Spindle said, offended on Amelia's behalf.

"If t'is, My Lady, then you have my apology. T'is fidelity to my mistress which drives my tongue."

Amelia gently touched Spindle's arm, discretely telling her to leave the matter. Far more concerning to the archduchess was the notion that the barely a hundred or so men-at-arms on the bridge were the entire north militia. Amelia knew already that the town divided its free levies into a northern and a southern contingent, and if this sparse crowd constituted half their town's total strength, then just how strong was Bridgetown? There had been many times more men chanting her name in just the one warehouse that morning.

Never mind Duke Robant, Amelia thought, shocked. *I could take the town for myself. Even if every man of their militia is worth five of mine, they would struggle to stop us.*

Looking at the men lounging on the bridge behind her, Amelia had no doubt they were not even man-for-man the equal of her White Lions, let alone superior. It was a troubling realization, and it comforted her to think that, in keeping with the spirit of the loyal herald's protestation, Baroness Penelope must recognize some of her town's vulnerability.

That is why she has sought this pact with me, no doubt, the archduchess told herself as she was ushered into a narrow, twisting stairwell and ascended the few levels to the barbican's parapet. She came out to the whip of an early afternoon breeze and a defensive rooftop, crowded with men-at-arms and engines of war set to defend. Amelia was still getting her bearings in this new crowd when a young female voice echoed in the open air.

"Lioness!" cried Baroness Penelope from the other side of the crowded space before the heralds could announce Amelia's arrival.

CHAPTER 6

Behind the merlons of the crenelated walls, the rooftop of the barbican was like a bubbling cauldron, filled to the brim and threatening to boil over at any moment. Men stood shoulder to shoulder, though only a few were in polished steel and heraldic colors. Most seemed to be patrician, likely ranking members of the town's guild conclave, although there was also more of the militia here, their tabards finer and brighter than the average man lounging on the bridge below. The crowd was pressed into any space not occupied by a pair of siege engines—large cauldrons suspended over iron firepans. Buckets were stacked like sentries beside each mighty pot's framework. If the barbican were to be assaulted, the firepans would be lit and the cauldrons filled with the buckets, lowered on ropes to the river beneath. Legends always told of hot oil cast upon enemies in sieges, but oil was expensive and boiling water was savage enough when it struck flesh. And best of all, on a bridge across a river, water was free and plentiful. For now, though, belying the otherwise battle-dressed folk standing beside them, the siege engines were inert and unready for any fight.

Amelia feared there would be no space for her on the crowded roof as she searched for the voice that had called her name. It reminded her of the one Forfeits Council she had ever attended in a hot and crowded tent years ago when the war had just begun. Before she could make anything more of her situation, the armored figures somehow managed to find space enough amongst themselves to draw back and form a small pathway from the tower door to the front battlement where a young woman beamed at her.

"My Lady, presenting Her Grace, the Archduchess Amelia of Dweltford and the Western Reach," one of the two heralds preceding Amelia declared formally. He and his partner looked ready to try for a similar bow to the one with which they had greeted Amelia, then realizing the august nature of the crowd around them seemed to think better of it. These were not mere yeoman townsfolk who might be shoved aside with a clout of the ash wood. "Archduchess Amelia, you are received by Lady Penelope, Baroness-elect of Bridgetown, daughter and heir of Earl John the Ninth."

Amelia pushed as swiftly down the narrow gap as she dared, fearful that a shove might knock one crowded man into another and so on until someone was toppled over the edge. She also had at least some compassion for the men who were squashing back against one another to make her this crowded corridor. Behind her she could feel both Farringdon and Spindle being pressed forward as the crowd closed behind them. The bare five to eight paces distance felt like a swim through thick mud, but soon enough Amelia was standing before her hostess, the youthful Baroness Penelope. The archduchess bobbed a polite curtsey, shallowly, for although the baroness was the ruling noble in this gathering, Amelia far exceeded her in rank. The baroness returned the gesture and Amelia took the moment to make the best swift assessment she could.

Seventeen, and you look it, was her first thought as she studied the young woman's face. Her dark hair was framed by a caul but without any veil hanging behind, so that it fell free in the back in an unladylike fashion. Her pleasant face was lightly sun-browned, with freckles on her nose and cheeks, and as she looked up from her curtsey, her dark brown eyes were bright and happy.

You look like a girl going to spring fair, Amelia thought. *Though not dressed like that.*

While Baroness Penelope's presentation was more rustic than was typical for a lady of her rank, her attire bordered on the outlandish. Whether she wore an overdress or bodice, Amelia could not say, because the woman's torso was clad in polished white steel, a breastplate of finest manufacture which, but for its size—fitted to a young woman's frame—would have suited any of the knights and men-at-arms that crowded the barbican roof. She added to this spaulders and rerebraces, so that her shoulders and upper arms were also clad in flashing steel. The lace-cuffed sleeves of a lady's typical underdress were next, and beneath the chauses of the breastplate, where men-at-arms might wear chain trews or other plates over leather breeches, a lady's skirt fell, the folds tucking neatly under the armor. The skirt was of the same striped orange and gold as the heralds' tabards.

"Does my appearance shock you, Your Grace?" the young baroness asked, and Amelia realized she had been staring, almost impolitely.

"My Lady, you are bright, like an angel of the sun, or a day star fallen to earth," Amelia said, fashioning the compliment out of reflex.

Lady Penelope laughed happily and the worthies around her nodded or murmured their approval, as was expected of polite courtiers the world over. "You are very kind, Your Grace," she said and then looked to the heralds. "You twins may withdraw. I think if we leave too many more bodies up here, we risk collapsing the roof beneath us."

"My Lady, the Norgate barbican has stood for centuries," one of the heralds began to protest, but the baroness cut him off.

"Then it would be a shame for it to fall on such a beautiful day, wouldn't you agree? Go, I will take charge of the rest of the introductions."

The man looked as if he might be about to protest further but thought better of it. The two executed hemmed-in bows once more and withdrew, pushing back through the crowd. Even when they had left, the press of bodies did not seem much diminished in

Amelia's eyes. She was surprised as the baroness leaned close and took her arm, almost conspiratorially.

"Silly, aren't they?" she whispered. "My father's men. Loyal and courteous to a fault. I call them the twins. Father always insisted on communicating through them." The baroness affected a masculine voice. "'Just because we dwell on the Grand Kingdom's frontier, little Penny, doesn't mean we forgo the niceties of our rank. We live near heretics and barbarians; we do not mimic them.'"

Amelia was surprised to hear Vec folk called barbarians, but perhaps the late baron had been speaking of Masnia, south of the Veckander lands. Or perhaps the Reachermen to the west, upriver.

"They seem very diligent as heralds," she said, keeping her voice quiet and her tone neutral.

"Oh, they are," the baroness agreed. "And they do nothing wrong, really, but it becomes tedious after a while. Can you imagine having formal messengers sent for every little instruction? 'M'lady Penelope, your august father bids you return to the earl's bedchamber, thereupon to retrieve the two dolls and one wooden ball which you have left behind after sleeping this night past in your mother's bed.'"

"Surely not," Amelia said reflexively, finding it hard to keep from smirking at the silliness of such a formal message for such a mundane task as having a child tidy up after themselves. Of course, most nobles of rank would never think of teaching a child that kind of responsibility, since there were servants to do all that for them, so perhaps there was some method to the late earl's "madness." As they were talking, she realized that the surprisingly charming young noblewoman had been slowly but deliberately leading her by the arm to the rampart walls, so that the pair of them now stood looking out over the Great Bridge Road, the fields that stretched away to the north, and the Grand Kingdom proper.

"Do not think me heartless, with my bright clothes," the baroness said next. "I know my father is only weeks dead, and I do mourn him. I prayed for his soul even this morning in the cathedral, though with our patriarch away, there are no services. Father was many months sick in bed, the illness eating him away until it was all he could do to even raise a smile. All my life he was a man of strength and broad mirth, and deep. He kept me the apple of his eye, his one child and the remaining joy of my lost mother. It broke my heart to see him wither, and I know it broke *his* to have to let me watch it. I am not glad that he is dead, not by any stroke, but I am pleased his pains are at an end."

Amelia had only met the girl, but this confession seemed sincere to her. It felt odd to be so swiftly brought into someone's confidence. Few nobles admitted to any weakness or pain, and virtually none on a first meeting, so far as the archduchess knew.

"Please, let me offer my condolences," she told the baroness. The young woman received the word with a nod and then looked out over the battlement to the north.

"The man my father was in his youth would never have suffered Daven Marcus' proud lackeys the way he was forced to in his sickbed," she declared. She bowed her head and Amelia watched her closely. "If I had been born to him a son, things would have been different. I tried to make up that lack, but the ways of the world are intractable, as you well know."

I do, Amelia thought, *but what do you know about what I know? Who do you think I am, that you speak to me like an old friend?*

"Father let my uncle run the town," the baroness continued, looking now toward Duke Robant's camp. "A good man, my uncle, but hidebound. Even more traditionalist than father. So, while he governed in my father's stead, he held me back, and the Usurpers dogs treated us like their private fiefdom—pillaging merchants to pay gambling debts, making affray after drinking sessions—that sort of thing. Once father was gone, I knew I could not wait for my accession. Those wastrels would have seized power 'for the good of all.' Uncle Forsle has not the will to resist them, and they would have had me married off before father was even in the ground. I had to put them off the bridges before they got the chance. As you can see, I have a few friends to help me in such matters."

The baroness cast a casual eye over the armored men in the crowd, smiling and receiving their smiles in return. Amelia noticed that every man-at-arms that was not in a militiaman's tabard was young, some younger even than the baroness.

"I know that you are no stranger to the speed with which a woman must act in this world run by men," Baroness Penelope said, and again Amelia wondered where the girl was learning all these facts about her that she took for granted. "That is why I am not taking the full time to give proper presentations and courtesies, the twins notwithstanding. I trust your retainers will forgive me for making them wait before meeting them formally, as mine must wait before being presented to yourself. If you look down, you will see why other matters must come first."

Blinking, Amelia realized that while she and the baroness had been standing some while at the parapet, she had not bothered to look down even once, so fixed was she on the baroness herself, or the duke's camp in the distance. Looking to the space in front of the gatehouse, Amelia held back a gasp of recognition. She did not know what she had expected to see. Given the calm of the crowd on the roof with her, she knew there was no assault happening. Nevertheless, she was surprised when she looked down and saw riders arrayed in the open ground in front of the gatehouse. Not Robant's men—knights on destriers as she might have feared—but ponies with fey archers on their backs, the lean riders brightly colored in their stiff, embroidered, glued-linen corselets.

"Benjamin?" she breathed, and a smile of hope lit her lips.

"So, you do know them?" Penelope asked her, and Amelia nodded readily.

Chapter 7

“They are allies of ours,” Amelia confirmed. “Fey riders.”

“Fey?” Baroness Penelope repeated, her tone one of pleasant disbelief, as if she thought she might be the butt of a good-natured jest.

Amelia did not confirm her words to the noblewoman for a moment, but turned to Farringdon and Spindle, sharing a smile with them. Since Prentice had led his mission into the west, with Benjamin and his warband accompanying them, the Western Reach had seen next to nothing of the fey.

“Is it Benjamin, do you think?” she asked her husband, and he leaned forward to see if he could spot some of the riders below. Farringdon smiled and nodded.

“They said they would always send him to us first, as their ambassador,” the marquis confirmed, then he bowed his head to the baroness, as an apology for speaking in her presence without formal introduction. For her part, Lady Penelope seemed not to notice, turning her attention back to the ground beneath them.

“They appeared not an hour of the candle past, crossing the open ground so swiftly we feared for a moment they were attacking us,” she explained.

“It was realized that it couldn’t be an attack, not with men armed like mere rangers,” said a young man on the baroness’s other side. Apparently having Farringdon speak out of turn had given the man the sense that he too could make his contribution, if he thought to.

"Is that who they are, Your Grace?" the baroness asked, "a company of rangers who go by the name of fey? Are we to let them in, on your honor?"

Amelia felt Farringdon twitch next to her, ready to answer the question, but managing to restrain himself.

"No, My Lady, if you will permit," Amelia said, looking out over the parapet again. She could see, perhaps a league up the road, a hundred or so knights ahorse were arraying for a charge. "These are most definitely fey, returned from antiquity to this current age, and if they do enter the town, you will see the truth of it."

The youthful knight on the other side of the baroness made a scoffing sound, with barely an effort to keep it low and at least somewhat polite. Baroness Penelope looked at him, but far from offended, she seemed to share the man-at-arms skepticism.

"If they are your allies, fey or no, could you say what it is they are doing?"

Amelia looked down again and then back to Farringdon. Beside him she saw Spindle, expression watchful, etiquette impeccable. Nonetheless, there was a glitter of hopeful pleasure in the lady-in-waiting's eyes that mirrored the archduchess's own emotions. She fixed her gaze back upon her husband.

"Knight Captain, what would *you* say they are doing?" she asked, formally inviting him into the conversation. Farringdon nodded to her and then turned to bow to the baroness.

"With your permission, My Lady," he asked, and the baroness acknowledged him. When she did, Farringdon gave the other men around them a swift sidelong glance before smiling broadly. "If I have to guess, Your Grace, I would say that the Knight Commander has sent them ahead to secure the ground in front of the gatehouse, so that he may march the rest of the militia here safely."

He nodded to the west, along the river, where a growing column could be seen tromping toward the bridge.

"If I am not mistaken, that is a blue and cream banner they are flying. I see a winged lion."

"A winged lion?" Lady Penelope asked rhetorically and around them the entire crowd shifted, as men strained to look westward to see what Farringdon had seen. Sure enough, there was a large force, marching over the fields at the line where the riverbank greenery faded to the yellow of the summer meadow hay waiting to be harvested.

"The Gryphon Banner Company, My Lady," Amelia explained, feeling her heart swell. There was only one such banner yet in the Western Reach, and if it was carried by the militia then it meant only one thing—Prentice's expeditionary force had returned from the west at last. Since leaving Aubrey in defeat, only learning that her husband was still alive had given Amelia greater joy. "The second half of my forces."

"The second half...?" the man at the baroness's opposite side repeated, more in awe than disbelief. "Just how many...?"

Amelia did not care to answer the young man's astonished curiosity. Instead, she studied the approaching force, working hard to estimate their numbers. They were still so far away that they were a single mass, like a dark, flat centipede with thousands of legs and a hide that occasionally flashed silver in the sunlight.

"Well, if your strange riders were sent to secure the gate ground for your militia, they had best hurry," the bold young man was saying, and it drew Amelia's attention away from the oncoming force momentarily. "Your colorful men on ponies are about to be driven off."

He was pointing straight north at a spot in the road now only half a league away, where about two hundred men-at-arms ahorse in full harness, their polished steel bright as mirrors, were arranging themselves into two tight lines to charge. The archduchess looked down once more at the fey and quickly counted to around a hundred.

"Two to one against us," she whispered thoughtfully.

"It would not matter if the odds were five to one in your favor," said the young man confidently. "Knights ahorse have no equal—certainly not mere rangers, whatever they call themselves."

"You might be surprised, sir," Farringdon responded, and the anonymous Bridgetown man-at-arms flashed him an odd, sullen look. Amelia wondered if he was the thin-skinned kind who took umbrage at every little disagreement, but when she noticed the man's distemper, Baroness Penelope smiled in a kindly fashion.

"My cousin has not received his spurs," she said in a light tone. "He is yet a squire and right hand to the leader of the Hopefuls."

She turned to her cousin directly.

"Wilforn, the man you are addressing is a Marquis, and if reports on the river are true, the Knight Captain of the Western Reach. Best you speak to him with respect."

Wilforn the squire turned and bowed unenthusiastically to Farringdon, who acknowledged the gesture.

"I have not heard of your deeds personally, Wilforn of Bridgetown," the marquis said. "Nevertheless, if you are one of those who liberated your mistress' town from the grip of Daven Marcus' forces, you are to be commended on the action. It was plainly done well and with regard to the wellbeing of the entire of Bridgetown."

Amelia smiled, watching her husband try to defuse the young man's prideful heart by treating him as he would any other knight on a first meeting. Kingdom knights showed respect when they met by each recounting tales of the other's high deeds or notable virtues. A handful of the men-at-arms amongst the crowd nodded or murmured approvingly at the display of tradition, but if young Wilforn recognized the marquis's efforts, it didn't show.

"I've never heard anything of you," the man said, almost churlishly. "Except that you were once a prince and gave it up."

"For love," Farringdon replied lightly, clearly refusing to let Wilforn's near insolence lure him into doing something rude himself. "And while I do have some worthy deeds to my name, I am afraid that in the Western Reach, my achievements are quite overshadowed by those of others, not the least being those of my liege and good lady wife herself."

He ended by nodding respectfully to Amelia, who let herself beam at him for a moment, then looked to the baroness who was watching the entire affair, rapt. When their eyes met, Penelope turned to her cousin and slapped her fingers lightly on his pauldron.

"See Wilforn, humility doesn't have to mean shame or weakness," she declared. It seemed the matter was one of long-standing contention between them. "And following a woman in war is no mean thing either!"

Ah, so that's where my example touches your life, My Lady, Amelia thought. She wondered how hard the young woman had had to work to persuade the men who served her, these "Hopefuls" she spoke of, to stand behind her rather than thinking to lead her. The archduchess remembered all the knights and noblemen who had thought to keep her from ruling her own land and felt for the first time a sense of the kinship which Baroness Penelope obviously thought existed between them.

A horn sounded from the Great Bridge Road and all eyes turned north to see the first hundred steel clad horsemen begin their charge, then the line behind them started as well, though slower. Behind them, another league still, a larger force, perhaps two or three hundred mounted knights, had begun to ride westward, doubtless to begin their assault on the Gryphon Company's main body.

"Your militia are going to find the ground held against them, when they get here Marquis," Wilforn said, his tone as churlish as ever. "Your man in charge of this company should have given the task to proper knights."

"We will see," Farringdon said with a tone of calm confidence.

"You are so sure?" the baroness asked him, obviously torn between her cousin's sour but sensible opinion and her respect for her new allies from the west, about whom she had heard legends but little else. Farringdon only directed his eyes north.

"I have been on the receiving end of what awaits this charge, My Lady," he said calmly. "I do not envy those men approaching."

Whether persuaded by Farringdon's confidence or simple curiosity, it felt as if everyone on the barbican roof leaned forward to watch the oncoming clash. The destriers had not even reached a full trot when the first thrum of bowstrings buzzed in the air. Amelia knew that fey horse archers loved nothing more than to attack the enemy on the run, staying out of bow or musket shot range themselves, launching their arrows and then turning full about. But that was when they were attacking. As she watched she learned that in defense they were somewhat different. Volley after volley was loosed swiftly, and the hum of the strings was like the pulse of a bee swarm heard on a whimsical wind. Five shots were in the air and the first was just landing when the fey riders, controlling their mounts with their feet alone, sprang to life, their warband splitting into two groups and riding aside of the now galloping knights and destriers.

"Scattered," Wilforn said with some satisfaction, but even as they watched, Amelia could see how wrong that assessment was. The two halves of the fey company had not run away, as if scared off, but had maintained their cohesion, continuing to shoot as they circled around the two enemy lines. Almost certainly Robant's men had been given the order to see these light horsemen off the field and then to turn west to support the main battle. As such, the knights in armor had not bothered to try to steer their mounts in the charge, only hammering straight toward the walls of the barbican and then reining themselves in, proud of their inexorable might. In the midst of the line, which had held its own cohesion reasonably well, one of the knights even stood in the stirrups and mockingly saluted those on the barbican.

"Fool," Farringdon muttered.

Amelia agreed with her husband. The saluting enemy who thought he had just demonstrated the invincible power of his fellows suddenly looked about as he realized he could hear cries of distress. During the charge, four or five knights had dropped out of each line, two felled by arrows completely, the other three with injuries or injured mounts. Hardly enough to rob the charge of its power. Now though, the fey had circled around and reformed on the road behind them. Where moments before the horse archers had been caught between the charge and the gatehouse, now they trapped the remaining knights between the closed gates and their own bows. The men who had dropped out of the line were the first to fall, twenty or so fey riders detaching to harry the wounded mercilessly. In seeming moments, the injured were down, although one urged his suffering mount to a valiant final effort, and he managed to fell one of the fey with his sword before he was swarmed and slain.

Surprised at the persistent and increasingly precise archery, the remaining knights seemed to hesitate, unsure how to respond. On their left one of their number called for a charge into the fields to break free, but only a handful followed him, and the detached group were swarmed as well. Only one of that number won free and was seen riding for the main force further west. The rest tried two charges at the main fey body, but the canny riders simply melted away and reformed elsewhere, loosing arrows all the time, and whittling down the number of knights. Amelia's thoughts of the buzz of bees were reinforced as she watched the entire fey company move like a swarm, splitting apart harmlessly when struck at and then reforming to strike and harry at will. In barely fifteen minutes of combat, the knightly force had been reduced to half their number and they had managed to remove only two fey men from the fight.

"They should muster and run straight for their camp now," Farringdon said. "It's the only safety they will find."

"They would have been best to have done that from the first," said someone unseen from nearby and several nodded in appreciation of the statement's wisdom. There was a momentary lull in the combat and then it seemed that whoever was left in charge of the knight company reached the same conclusion. Whipping their foam-bitted mounts to one last, exhausted effort, they formed up and ran, much less swiftly, for Duke Robant's camp, leaving over thirty of their comrades behind. The fey riders did not pursue them. Instead, they returned to the ground in front of the gatehouse, staking their claim over it as surely as if they had planted a banner and issued a written edict. On the way back, several stopped at the various bodies of the slain, horse and rider, and retrieved their arrows.

"What are they doing?" someone asked with a horrified tone. As the crowd watched, the victorious fey despatched the wounded—slender, double-bitted saddle axes rising and falling in clean chops after helmets had been wrenched away.

"Fey riders seldom take prisoners," Farringdon said solemnly and the sense of horror it spread over the crowd around them was heavy, like a blanket of hot summer air.

"How seldomly?" the baroness asked.

"I know of only once," the marquis told her and Amelia nodded, her own smile hardened to a grim line. Only two men were known to have ever been taken alive by the fey, and if God was kind to her, both were now advancing with the Gryphon Company to fully liberate Bridgetown from the Usurper's grip.

CHAPTER 8

"They will not sing songs about that one," Prentice muttered to himself, sitting in his saddle as he watched the rearguard finally march in column under the raised portcullis of the Bridgetown gatehouse. Shading his eyes, he looked up to gauge the time by the sun. It seemed like it was still barely midafternoon. He shook his head. No, this day's battle, if it could be called that, would inspire no epics.

While the fey had had their duel at the gates, the rest of the company had marched in a tight column, at full pace, with their supply train, wagons, and camp followers, protected in the middle of the formation. In the van and the rear, Prentice had divided his veteran cohorts so that the head and tail of the column, the most vulnerable, also had the best and most trustworthy men-at-arms. The rest, over three thousand trained but yet green, formed three sides of a square, protecting the non-combatants on all but the south, the riverbank side.

"You don't figure any danger from the river, Lord Commander?" Sergeant Gennet had asked as they marched earlier in the morning. "Some o' the rumors coming from the boat folks say that the Lions sprang some kind o' ambush on Veckanders at Aubrey by hiding amongst river grass, or something like."

"Benjamin's riders will be ahead of us," Prentice explained to his second-in-command. "They will spot any troops hidden riverside for us. And if *they* cannot, if by some twist of fate Robant can hide an ambuscade from even fey eyes, then we have worse problems than we even imagined."

"Ay, true enough. If they can hide from the canny folk, then we won't see 'em until we feel their steel at our throats."

Prentice hadn't thought it would be quite that bad, but as it happened, the long green river grass held no enemies, and the ones that did ride forth, perhaps five hundred knights in all, were grossly outnumbered. When they formed up to charge straight at the column's flank, the cohorts on the side turned in place and set to receive the charge, exactly as the Claw, Fang, and Roar doctrine their knight commander had devised required. For a time, Prentice feared Robant's force would be as foolish as other knights had been, under men like Liam or Sebastian, refusing to believe their sovereignty over the battlefield might be waning. Robant's men ahorse, for all their steel plates on man and mount, were vastly outmatched. If they had committed to the charge and melee, the Gryphon company would have chewed them to pieces, armor and all.

As it happened, it seemed these knights had learned caution, especially in the face of Roar-shot. Every time they began a charge, only a single volley of matchlock fire had been enough to make them veer away and circle back to reform. They were so reluctant to risk themselves against even the Roar, that the other ranks began to jeer them. With so little to fear, Prentice gave the order for the company to continue its movement in formation, the left flank cohorts ready to set to receive charge at an instant's command, and the Gryphons marched slowly but inexorably to the gate. The knights of Robant's force might as well have been an escort rather than an enemy, for all that they interfered with the journey. In the end, the knights withdrew their tiring mounts without a single serious engagement for the entire day.

"I suppose they had to learn some time," Prentice said, and shook his head again. If Duke Robant was even half the commander he seemed to be, Prentice had no doubt the man would be wracking his brain to develop a counterstrategy to the Lions. Whatever he came up with, it seemed likely the days of the Western Reach militia simply slaughtering knights like sheep were coming to an end.

"Begging your pardon, My Lord, but Corporal Guillam asks if you can come to him," said a militiaman, rushing up and saluting. Guillam was only a short distance away, commanding a detachment that had been set to police the bodies from the fey rider's engagement—the only true combat of the day, and still as one-sided as the rest. Prentice returned the salute and dismounted, squatting a few times to restore the blood to his legs after hours in the saddle. He was still a far distance from the kind of man-at-arms who might shift from mounted to unmounted combat with ease. Indeed, if he had his way, Prentice would never engage in any kind of hand-to-hand from horseback. He was a noble and was expected to ride into battle now, but he only ever wanted to fight on foot.

"What have we got, Corporal?" he asked as he approached Guillam, who was standing over the body of a fallen knight.

"Looks like we're not the only ones with spotty faces amongst our ranks," the corporal said, looking down at the armored body. The man's helmet had been removed, doubtless by the vengeful fey, but he had no axe-wound, unlike so many other corpses. Prentice looked around and saw a fallen horse nearby, a broken arrow shaft protruding through a gap in the plates on its neck, and other injuries on an exposed part of its flanks where arrows had struck, but been retrieved.

"Looks like he broke his neck when his horse reared and fell," Prentice said, assessing the scene and still unsure why Guillam might have called for him.

"That's what I figure, Knight Commander. I just thought you might like to take a closer look at his face."

Prentice studied the visage, blackening in places as the dead man's blood settled. Then he connected the corporal's first words with his own assessment and began to understand.

No, not a man, he thought. *A boy. Lucky to be sixteen if he was a day. Not too much older than Solomon.*

Prentice sighed and looked back up again.

"War cares nothing for age or rank," he said phlegmatically. "He is not the first squire to die before reaching his maturity."

"You think?" Guillam asked meaningfully and he nodded in the direction of the fallen horse once again. "That's his horse. He fell with a lance in his hand, but look at his saddle."

Prentice did as his man bid and noticed that the fallen horse's saddle had another weapon tied to it in a leather sheath—a longsword, the symbol of a full knight, as much as the set of gilded spurs on his heels, awarded to him on the day he acceded to his status. Prentice looked down at the dead man and quickly noted other details. Apart from the few fresh dents from the fall that killed him, the man's kit showed almost no signs of use. It was virtually new, as if this were literally the first time it had been worn. His spurs were bright and fresh as well. This youth had been hardly old enough even to be called a knight. Barely even a man yet. Prentice looked to Guillam, and the corporal nodded as they shared the realization.

"He's not even the youngest one, as I can tell," he said. "Course, it's not easy with all of 'em, what with the fey chopping faces and whatnot."

"Strip the bodies and gather the weapons," Prentice commanded. "Then get yourselves inside. I do not want anyone wandering around out here for a resentful enemy to bushwack."

Guillam and the men around him saluted their commander, and Prentice remounted Boots. Before he could ride away, the sergeant added one more thought for him.

"'Course, you know even when they're young like this, they can still kill a man well enough with sharp steel, Knight Commander. Your Solomon's a year shy of this one, at the least, and there's more'n a few Lions wouldn't want to face off 'gainst *him* in a fight. I figure if they want to put on the steel and ride at us hard, we're going to have to give 'em what for."

Prentice said nothing to that. What could he say? Bitter or not, Guillam had the truth of the matter. Nevertheless, it galled the knight commander. What youth that age could understand the sides of this war? That corpse would have ridden for glory and loyalty, and died for a monster, thrown like a clod of dirt against a wall of iron and fire, and a cloud of arrows. How many more young and naive fools were there in this war, dreaming of glory as they rode into death's waiting arms? He thought about all the refugees and other folk who were signed up in the White Lions. Were they any different? Then he thought of himself, and his wife, and all the other friends and foes who had been chained together and sent like so much livestock to be hacked apart by men like that dead lad had aspired to be.

It has always been bitter, brutal, and unjust, he told himself. *Perhaps it is only right that the peers start to drink deeply from that cup of wrath convicts know so well.*

He was ready to ride into Bridgetown at last, when Dahyoor approached on foot from the open fields to the west.

"There is a fire set, Knight Palpolon," the fey squire said. "Benjamin invites the elder to sit with him."

Dahyoor pointed back from where he had just come, and Prentice looked to see a small cadre of fey on horseback at one side of a campfire with two fey seated on their saddles beside it.

"Then I should go and see what Benjamin sees," Prentice said wearily, and he steered Boots toward the little meeting, knowing that it would be dishonorable in the feys' eyes, if he arrived at their meeting on foot.

CHAPTER 9

"The one with Benjamin is an elder, from amongst those who ride the southern Wind Rising paths," Dahyoor whispered as Prentice undid his saddle and hefted it from Boots's back. "They are the most unseen and curse the Serpent Witch with vehemence."

Don't we all? Prentice wondered drily but did not say. He still couldn't tell what kind of sense of humor the fey had, or even if they had much of one at all. Whatever jokes they did tell, he doubted that many were about the witch who had bound their people to slaughter and shattered a millennium old tradition of isolation.

"With vehemence?" he repeated to Dahyoor and his squire nodded.

It seemed to Prentice that the usually unflappable fey man was a little nervous, and it made the knight commander wonder what the full significance of this meeting was to be. With his saddle in his arms and the bags slung across his shoulder, Prentice went to the place around the fire which Dahyoor indicated. Using his saddlebags to prop up the leather, he arranged his saddle like a bench seat and sat upon it sideways. The two fey already sitting at the fire sat on their own saddles in the same fashion, the fey craftsmanship making the seats ideal for the purpose. When he was settled, Dahyoor sat cross legged on the grass at Prentice's left-hand side. Benjamin and the fey elder with him, who turned out to be a woman, watched silently, faces funereally serious. It might have felt unnerving, especially coupled with his squire's apparent disquiet, but Prentice found he was becoming accustomed to the stern, unwelcoming cast of fey manners. Without preamble, Benjamin turned to the elder and they appeared to share a moment of unspoken communication. Prentice watched every movement, every flicker of an expression or gesture closely, like prey alert for signs of a predator.

Benjamin appeared as he always did, though his corselet was more worn now, with many more of the colored threads of the embroidery worked loose or torn free. It would need repair, which Prentice imagined would happen in the coming winter, same as Kingdom folk, sitting around fires against the cold and repairing tools and equipment for the next working season. Would Benjamin repair his own armor, or would his wife do it? Was he even married? Prentice realized he had no idea. For all he knew, Benjamin was still too young by fey standards to even have a wife, or he could just as equally have a harem of twenty wives or concubines, each with their own enigmatic places in fey society.

Next to Benjamin, the elder was similarly dressed, although her embroidered body covering was not layered armor but rather a sleeveless buckskin jacket. The colors were also different, likely denoting the different clan or region from where the elder originated—the southernmost parts of the Azure Mountains, according to Dahyoor. As he noted her colors, Prentice also realized that she had the traditional scarf around her neck that fey wore in the mountains, and that Benjamin and his men had taken to wearing theirs again. During the ride west, the customary head or neck wear had been notably absent amongst the *keshiyaa*. Prentice wondered if that had been culturally significant, a sign of their presence in enemy territory perhaps, or if it was simply that the desert had been too hot and dry to wear something wrapped around one's throat.

At last, the two fey seemed to come to some understanding about who would speak, and the elder looked at Prentice, her eyes dark and inscrutable. By the wrinkles in the corners, she could well have been very old, but whether that meant the same age as a typical Grand Kingdom grandmother or centuries beyond count was anyone's guess.

"*Kreff*," she said simply at first, eyes fixed on Prentice. He set his expression to be equally as stern.

"Not so," he said, shaking his head once. "*Kreff enkreffra.*"

"I have not yet seen this," she answered, and that, at least, Prentice understood. She was reserving judgement. Her eyes ranged over him as he sat there and then became fixed on the hilt of his sword, with its handle of unicorn horn and silver lion's head, biting down on a tassel of unicorn's mane.

"With that you slew the finest of beasts," she said. "You carry that on the ride. You do not leave the blood of that death on the trail behind you."

Although the elder spoke these words as statements, there was the sense of a question to them, and Prentice thought she was demanding he justify himself. He looked down at the weapon on his belt and then drew it forth. There was a light intake of breath from everyone at the campfire, and out of the corner of his eye, Prentice was pretty sure several of the attendant riders had put their hands to their bows. He guessed that it was a significant but not irrevocable gesture to draw the blade, and that was good to his way of thinking. It would tell his allies how serious his next words were. He had no idea how an actual challenge would be delivered amongst the fey, or even if one legitimately could, but a challenge was not what he was about. He had no doubt that if he moved to attack the elder where she sat, he would die with arrows in his eye sockets. At this range no fey would miss. He laid the naked steel across his knees and rested the fingers of one hand on the edge while he kept the other hand on the hilt.

"This is the steel that spilled the blood of the unicorn," he said tersely, his own voice as hard as the metal in his hands. "And the stag, mighty and ancient. But I did not kill them. Their deaths came because of the Witch and the *imzuss*. And the treachery of the Untrue."

Untrue was the name which the Azure Mountains' fey gave to the Redlanders. As he used it, Prentice looked for any sign of recognition in the elder's expression, but she remained as unmoving as if carved in stone.

"The Serpent Witch bound the finest of beasts to her murderous will and by that binding took its life. I spilled its blood, to end its slavery. That blood, and its horn and its mane, I could not leave on the trail behind me, nor even with the herd. That was a blood debt that demanded to be carried. So, I carried this...death thing...into the west."

Prentice looked down at the blade, and both Benjamin and the elder followed his eyes.

"With this edge I claimed the debt from the Serpent Witch for my liege, for her people, and for the Wind Rising."

The elder looked up suddenly at that statement and then to Benjamin. Something about it plainly surprised her. Benjamin met her gaze in the same level, inexpressive fey fashion.

"What do you want for this?" she asked, and Prentice wondered if he had insulted her somehow. He hadn't meant to imply that they owed him anything. Wasn't he an elder of the fey now as well? Could he not act on their behalf?

"Nothing," he said. "I took her head, and the deluge washed her blood and body away to rot and feed the trees. I have taken all that I want. Benjamin has seen this."

"I have seen," Benjamin said, and Prentice was amazed to recognize just how much force the simple phrase had in fey society. Benjamin was vouchsafing Prentice's words with as much force as a man offering himself as a second in a judicial duel. Suddenly, something broke in the elder fey woman's reserve and she began to speak quickly in their native tongue, a tone of demand Prentice could recognize.

"What is it?" he whispered to Dahyoor.

"She is asking if you truly understand what you are saying," the squire translated, not as quietly. "But do not whisper at the fire, it is a sign of disrespect."

I wish someone had told me that before now, Prentice thought. He was about to ask if there was something he should say and do when the elder stood and stalked around the fire to stop before him. Benjamin had not stood, so Prentice knew this was not the end of the meeting. That was for the *keshkirae* to say, as it was his campfire. The elder drew a short knife from a sheath at her belt. It was a tool more than a weapon, and Prentice still had a hand on his sword hilt. Was everything between the fey a matter of life and death, or just when they had dealings with him? In truth Prentice had little fear she could kill him before he would her, but that wouldn't mean much once the archers started shooting from their saddles. The odds he would survive long enough to reach the gatehouse, even if Guillam's detachment saw and moved to intervene, were not good.

I could perhaps use her body as a shield, he thought as he watched the edge in her hand, muscles tense and ready to spring.

Instead of attacking, however, the elder reached her free hand up under the hair that hung loose at the back of her head. From amongst the straight fall, she drew out a slender plait that had been hidden there. Using the knife, she sawed off the little rope of hair and held it out for Prentice to take.

"This has been dipped in the blood of kin," she said simply.

Prentice was about to whisper to Dahyoor again, asking for guidance, but he remembered the recent advice. Instead, he took the plait, and holding it out from himself, he looked to his squire.

"How must I honor this?" he asked in full voice.

"If the witch was still alive, you would tie it into your hair, a symbol of carrying another's kin debt," Dahyoor explained. "Since she is dead, you tie it to your horse's mane. All her kin will recognize you now and what you have done for them."

Not knowing if even nodding was acceptable in fey culture, Prentice simply held the length of plait in his hand, the blonde hairs interspersed with the occasional strands of silver that characterized fey old age. He met the woman's eyes in their fashion and then lowered the plait to hook it around his sword hilt, the colors seeming dull next to the preternatural white of the unicorn mane tassel. The elder watched him do it and then, after another moment, stepped back. When she returned to her saddle, she sat again.

"I have seen," she said. "You are *kreff enkreffra*."

"We have seen," Benjamin added.

"We pass unseen," Prentice finished for them and for once there was a flash of a near smile on the elder's lips. Whether she was pleased or just amused to hear a *kreff*, a non-fey, make the declaration, he could not tell. Both respected fey at the fire repeated the credo after him though. Only Dahyoor did not speak. As one who had been put out of the camp for the dishonor of returning from a campaign without his horses, he had no place in fey culture anymore. If Prentice had not made him a squire, the knight commander suspected the fey man would have killed himself by now.

"What of this one beside you?" the elder asked. "He is outside the camp. Why do you drag him behind your horse?"

I assume that is another metaphor, Prentice thought. Dahyoor was a dour figure at the best of times, but no one in the White Lions had "dragged" him anywhere.

"I have given him a place beside my fire," Prentice said. The elder's brows rose at that, and there was a questioning expression in her eyes. Prentice did not give her a chance to form the question but went on to explain. "I am the *palpolon* elder, falling as much as riding. Whose camp would be better to redeem his blood debt? He rode and walked and took his share of the debt on our trail west. Benjamin has seen this."

"I have seen this," Benjamin agreed but with an uncertainty in his tone, as if he feared how the elder would respond.

Redeeming the shamed is new territory for your people, Prentice thought. *Do not worry. It is new territory for Kingdom folk too.*

The elder looked from Prentice to Dahyoor and then back again. Her stern expression seemed to be cracking a little, and Prentice was surprised when she stood from her saddle and waved at the fey still on their horses. For the first time Prentice realized that these ones wore scarves of the same colors as the elder. They were her escort, her closest confidantes most likely. Perhaps she had her own *keshiyaa*, just like Benjamin.

"*Palpolon*," she called to them, followed by a long string of fey speech Prentice had no hope of translating. The riders looked at her, astonished, and then burst out laughing, though not in a cruel or dismissive way, Prentice did not think. Then she sat once more, smiling broadly.

"An elder who falls as much as he rides, who walks and still leaves no debt on the trail behind him. This is something none before have seen," she said to him, her voice suddenly full of laughter. "But we have seen, *palpolon kreff enkreffra*."

"We have seen," Benjamin agreed. He stood and the elder stood with him. Thinking the meeting must be complete, Prentice stood as well, but he was surprised when the elder reached under her saddle and produced two leather bridles, while Benjamin pulled forth two folded cloths from his. Both of them stepped around the fire and presented their items as gifts to him.

"You have two children now," the elder said. "This we have seen. When we go, we will leave you two ponies from our herds."

Prentice received the bridles and then had a further thought. This was a lighter-hearted moment and he wanted to take a risk. He looked to Dahyoor.

"Stand," he said, and the fey squire rose to his feet, watchfully cautious of this break in protocol. Until now, the happier air of the meeting had even infected the fey exile, but his instinct to fear rejection surfaced immediately in his expression. Before he could say anything, Prentice handed him the two pieces of tack.

"Fey horses need a fey hand to guide them," he said. "You will keep these horses in trust for my children, riding them until they are ready. Then you will teach them the proper way to ride a fey mount."

Dahyoor's eyes widened in surprise, and the two others seemed equally astonished.

"A father usually keeps his children's horses for them in his herd," Benjamin said, for once being helpful rather than insulted by Prentice's breaking of protocol. The knight commander had a different idea. He looked to the elder.

"I would not insult your herds by making your ponies carry a big, steel-clad *palpolon kreff* like me," he said. "Fey ponies need to be ridden by fey and those who learn their ways."

The elder shook her head but did not stop smiling.

"Never has this been seen," she said. "But we have seen."

Prentice was glad that they recognized what he was doing. In everything but name, he was redeeming Dahyoor from the shame of his exile. Officially, the two ponies would belong to Prentice and his family, but in actuality they would be ridden by Dahyoor, and no fey would be able to despise him as a man afoot. As cousins, he noticed that Dahyoor and Benjamin shared the closest thing to wild exuberance he had seen in any fey. Then the *keshiyaa* leader stepped forward, holding out two pieces of cloth that he shook open to show were *treskarid* scarves, such as all fey wore—except Dahyoor, of course.

"You have two children now," he said, holding them out one in each hand. Prentice took them. "When we leave, we will leave these for them."

"Do I wear one? Or both?" he asked. Benjamin shook his head.

"They are for your children only," Dahyoor explained, his voice the lightest that Prentice could ever remember it sounding. "The pattern tells the story of the wearer's ancestors. You cannot wear one. You have no ancestors amongst the Wind Rising."

But my children do? Prentice thought and then he realized the answer. *He* was their ancestor amongst the fey. The scarves commemorated *his* story, as the fey knew it. He looked down at the weaving and picked out a pattern like mountains and another that was recognizable as a leaping lion. He wondered a moment if the unicorn or stag were in there somewhere and hoped they were not.

"I have seen this," he said. "And my children will see."

Both fey left then, taking their saddles up from the fire and returning to their horses. It was only once they were mounted up and riding, while Prentice wrestled with his own, heavier saddle and tack, that he realized the full import of what they had said.

They were leaving but for how long?

CHAPTER 10

"Thanks be to God that *reaching* the gates was not this difficult," Amelia heard her husband mutter as they together watched the awkward process of marching over four thousand armed men, their supplies and other bagatelle, into Bridgetown. From the first it was difficult, slowed by the presence of the town's own lackadaisical militia crowding the bridge right from the Norgate barbican. A strange moment of confrontation had ensued when the disorderly mob of orange and gold had been suddenly presented with the stone-faced column of cream and blue—steel-clad men of steely determination. Eventually, someone shouted from the gatehouse roof that way should be made, and the twins were sent for again, to guide the Gryphon Banner Company to lodgings.

"My Lady, can your town absorb yet more of us?" Amelia asked as she and Baroness Penelope rushed to get ahead of the newly arrived men-at-arms and provide them proper welcome. "Already I am sure the merchants on your docks would much rather be rid of our disruption."

Which was the archduchess's polite way of raising the notion of permanent lodgings, rather than mentioning that keeping her men shoved in storehouses was becoming a borderline insult. Descending the stairs, the two noblewomen had been rushing ahead of the crowd of Bridgetown worthies, and emerged on the side of the bridge right next to the Gryphon's second cohort, waiting in disciplined column. At first it had been a simple matter for the nobles to push along the beside them, since the Bridgetown militia was falling back and the Lions' column did not fully occupy the width of the span. However, as they hurried in nearly undignified fashion, someone in the column recognized Amelia for who she was, and a shout went up.

"The archduchess! Archduchess Amelia! Huzzah!"

Soon the lines were all shouting, and Amelia had to stop as the baroness ahead of her came to a halt and stared at the men beside them cheering their liege. Lady Penelope seemed almost enraptured by the scene, as if she were looking upon a natural wonder. Amelia did not see things the same way. She turned back to look for her husband and was pleased to see that he, in fact, was directly behind her. It made her smile; even in a crowd of allies, he would always contrive to be close by—not only her spouse but her most faithful defender as well.

"We need to stop them," she told him under the noise. "We come as friends, not an occupying army. We can't have them cheering me like a conquering queen. It will set the town alight with fear."

"I will pass the word immediately, Your Grace," Farringdon said, saluting her as if she were any other senior officer of her militia. He rushed away, bowing politely to the baroness as he passed her, and when he reached the front of the column there was a moment, then a new drumbeat began to echo through the cheers and a mighty voice was heard to bawl.

"Quiet in the lines! Beat for silence!"

It took a moment or two, but swiftly the drumbeat command dropped quiet upon the bridge, flowing back along the columns as each cohort in turn obeyed the order. Soon even the sound of the river flowing around the bridge's pylons below could be heard, along with the buzzing of insects.

"Such command," Amelia heard Lady Penelope say quietly.

"Where am I to send my force, My Lady?" she asked, and Penelope looked around her, blinking in the sunlight, as if emerging from a daze. Eventually her gaze fell upon her cousin Wilforn, some distance back in the press of Bridgetown noblemen now moved from massing upon the barbican to crowding the slender gap at the side of the bridge. If Amelia had feared to push one of the men off the roof, then she was certain the whole lot of them were now in danger of falling off the bridge. Nonetheless, the squire Wilforn shoved his way forward when his cousin called for him.

"Run to the twins and tell them to lead the Archduchess' militia...," Lady Penelope said and then hesitated. Her head whipped back and forth along the riverside, as if she were deciding which part of the seemingly overcrowded islands might conceal housing enough for an army of thousands. Then she smiled. "Have them lead the way to Runners Field, up near Great Dredgeman and the amphitheater."

"But that's the only open ground in the whole town," Wilforn objected as sullenly as he seemed to do everything else. "That's where the tourneys are held."

Amelia blinked at the interaction, then carefully fixed her eyes to look out over the river to the east, as if admiring the view. She did not want to risk embarrassing the baroness by appearing to notice the young man's insubordination.

"Her Grace's force needs somewhere to encamp," said Penelope quietly but with a terse tone. "And there hasn't been a tourney for a year or more."

"They just marched through plenty of fields ideal for the purpose," Wilforn retorted. "Why can't they camp out there?"

"Because we are not children playing castle together anymore, Wilforn!" the baroness answered him, and it was clear her patience was at an end, but rather than taking on a strong tone of command, her voice was acquiring something of her cousin's whine. "I am now Baroness-elect, and you are my bondsman. You have to do what I say and take *my* word to *my* heralds. Then you have to go and take the same message to the other Reach militiamen on Piers and lead them to Runners."

"Oh, of course, oh mighty cousin-elect." Wilforn executed a bow that managed to be at once both deep and disrespectful, then stalked away, hunch-shouldered.

"I'm sorry for that, Your Grace," the baroness said to Amelia, and the archduchess smiled politely.

"Not at all, My Lady," was all she said.

Penelope seemed genuinely flustered by her interaction with her cousin and she looked about, as if she thought she might have dropped something. Amelia gave her a moment to gather herself, but when it seemed like the uncertainty might overwhelm the younger woman completely, the archduchess felt compelled by compassion to act.

"Perhaps, My Lady, if I may be so bold, we could find a position from which to watch the Gryphon Banner Company enter the town," she said, stepping forward to take the baroness by the hand. "Perhaps out of the sun?"

The baroness blinked for a moment, looking from Amelia's hand on her own and back to her eyes.

"They are quite impressive in parade," the archduchess added. "Perhaps some of your closest confidantes might join us? I would suggest the undercroft of the greater gate keep there, to shield us from the brightness."

Amelia looked to the more significant fortification on the shore of the town's first island. Baroness Penelope nodded her relieved agreement, and so it was that Amelia and she, accompanied by Farringdon and two lesser nobles of Bridgetown—a baronet with sable black hair named Christmark and an elderly knight called Nencet—stood in the shade beside the lazy tariff-taker's booth and watched the Gryphon Banner Company march into Bridgetown.

"In truth, Your Grace, I confess I am surprised," Lady Penelope said somewhat later, having apparently reacquired some of her self-confidence. "I expected that the commander of your company here would have presented himself and his compliments by now."

Amelia smiled and looked to Farringdon, but her husband was busy giving some junior officers instructions about how to manage their cohorts' carrying pikes under the low roof without tangling them or smacking them against the overhead stones. When he was done, he looked back to see both noblewomen looking to him.

"I'm sorry, Your Grace, I didn't hear the question."

"The baroness was wondering why we have not had a presentation from the Gryphons' commander," Amelia explained.

"Well, I have heard from several of the veteran officers that the Knight Commander is indeed with the company," Farringdon said, adroitly responding to the unspoken question that Amelia most wanted answered. "But knowing Knight Commander Baron Ash, Your Grace, My Lady, I doubt we will see him until the very end. He will not come in until every one of his men and civil charges is safely bestowed within Bridgetown's walls. He is ever the first to the fight and the last to quit the field."

Amelia turned to look back to the baroness, to see how she felt about that answer. Poetics aside, every word Farringdon spoke was true.

"You aren't afraid it might be some slight, that he might be forcing you to wait?" Penelope asked, her brows knotted, as if she was trying to decipher a complex problem. In the light of her cousin's earlier sour unruliness, Amelia could well understand the young woman's uncertainty.

"Baron Ash's loyalty is unquestioned," she told the baroness sincerely. "It would be an insult to him and to all the men who have fallen at his side in my service to think otherwise. Every good liege should have a man like him at their command." She paused to look at her husband and even reached out to take his hand and squeeze it. "I am blessed to have more than one."

"*Baron* Ash?" Lady Penelope repeated, her troubled expression shifting to one of surprise. "I thought your militia leader was...oh, oh of course...because you are an *Arch*duchess."

"Your Grace, if we might present ourselves, with your permission" interrupted a sweet, feminine voice and the two ruling noblewomen turned to see Lady Dalflitch, accompanied by Baroness Righteous and an eccentric company of veiled nuns, swathed in plain homespun from head to toe. The two ladies of the archduchess's chamber were curtseying as they presented themselves, while the "nuns" stood politely in a line behind them, hands in their sleeves and even their faces hidden behind veils, their eyes alone visible. Behind them, other columns of the militia continued their march through the arched walkways, hobnail boots and steel harness raising a belligerent clatter. Almost certainly they were adding their own inadvertent bits of damage to the ancient stonework.

"Dalflitch, Righteous, I am overjoyed to see you both," Amelia told her two attendants. Then she cocked an eyebrow at the wimple-wearing women behind. "Have we acquired a convent lately?"

"Neophyte Lace Fangs, Your Grace," Dalflitch said smoothly as she rose. "This is to be their uniform until they attain their full status."

Amelia was astonished, and her eyes swept across the line of curiously dressed, obedient women. Apart from the color of their eyes and the fact that one or two were shorter or taller than the average, there was nothing to pick between them. They might as well have been five sets of triplets, and all identical to the others.

"You must unfold your reasoning, My Lady, but later, in my chamber," Amelia said, her voice momentarily lost to a rise in the clatter as horses and wagons began to pass, adding the wooden creak of their axles to the noise. "In the meantime, we must present you to our host."

She turned to Baroness Penelope.

"My Lady, may I present my ladies-in-waiting—Lady Dalflitch, wife of Sir Turley, Knight Castellan of Dweltford Castle, and seneschal of my purse and treasury."

Lady Dalfitch curtseyed again, this time to the baroness.

"And Baroness Righteous Ash, wife of Knight Commander Baron Ash, and first of the Lace Fangs, my bodyguard and close confidante."

"My Lady," Righteous said as she too curtseyed, perhaps a hair less smoothly than Dalflitch, but it would take a "professional's" eye to notice.

You've been practicing, haven't you, Righteous? Amelia thought and then she realized that the last time she had seen the Lace Fang, she had been heavily pregnant. Doubtless, the baroness looked lither and fluid in her movements from simple comparison.

For her part, Baroness Penelope received each woman's respects with a look of quiet awe, as if meeting heroic figures. She especially studied Righteous's mask on the left side of her face. For a moment Amelia imagined the baroness might even reach out and touch the simple accoutrement. She smirked when she thought what the old Righteous, the one first out of the training camps of the militia, might have thought of that presumption.

"Your Grace, I thought, I mean, I had heard that...," Penelope said, her eyes ranging up and down Righteous's form from the lace hem of her skirt to her hair under her coif and silver net. "Forgive me, but I have been told that your Lace Fangs wore trousers, after the fashion of men. 'Boyish and unlovely' was the phrase most used, if you will bear the insult repeated. But..."

Amelia watched and felt an old tension—the fear that her raised lady-in-waiting might take umbrage and turn an impolite conversation into a knife fight—arise in herself for the first time in years. Righteous had her eyes fixed on Baroness Penelope's, and Amelia was sure the old predator was still there, ready to throw down if fighting words were spoken.

"But they were more than mere insult," Penelope continued, meeting Righteous's gaze. "They were falsehoods from end-to-end. Utter lies. Baroness, forgive me that I ever gave them ear."

With that, the liege of Bridgetown reached out and took Righteous's hand, curtseying and bowing her head in a gesture of humble apology. When she looked up again, she held on a moment.

"It is my hope, Lady Righteous, that you and I might become close friends," she said earnestly. "And if it would please you, I would dearly love to take some instruction with the blade from you. I hear you are a master, and I have never had a woman instructor."

Amelia was astonished, and when she glanced at Dalflitch, the lady gave her a raised eyebrow to show she was just as surprised at the unexpected turn of events.

She is a peer now, Amelia thought, surprised at herself for not realizing the implication before this moment. For a long space she could not shake the image of the scruffy, wild-haired tomboy in striped trousers and gambeson who had demanded the ruler of the Reach command Prentice to marry her. That figure was nowhere in sight now as without even looking to her companions or liege for guidance, Righteous accepted the baroness's words politely.

"I don't know that I'm any kind of master—well mistress, I suppose—of the blade, Lady Penelope, but I would be well chuffed to give you some lessons of what I know. No doubt you'll be able to show me some fine tricks with steel as well, if you've had a lot of teachers."

"I wouldn't say a lot," Penelope said, "but I followed my father everywhere when I was little, to the marshalling yards and stables, and since he never had a son, many of his frustrated hopes found an outlet through me. I love swordplay most of all, and not in the manner of a fine lady who watches from the side and swoons for my suitor."

The baroness cast a surreptitious glance at Dalflitch and Amelia, clearly marking both as "fine ladies" of the type which she was not.

"Steel comes freely into men's hands, My Lady," Righteous said, with a slow and measured intonation, as if she were focused on saying the exact right thing and choosing each word with maximum care. "But sometimes it finds its way into a woman's hands, and we are rare enough birds that we should best flock together for each other's safety."

"Oh, well said, My Lady," Penelope declared, clapping her hands together. "Your companion Fang has gone ahead into town to secure your lodgings, but from your liege's reaction I suspect she will not know of all these...neophytes, did you call them?"

"Lady Dalflitch said," Righteous replied, giving credit where it was due. The enthusiastic baroness hardly even noticed.

"Then let us go find her before she lays money down on accommodations too small and must spend again on more spacious chambers."

Righteous did not agree but looked to Amelia for permission. Before the archduchess could say anything, Lady Penelope overrode any opinion she might have on the matter.

"You can spare her a few hours, can you not, Your Grace?"

"If it would suit you, My Lady," Amelia said politely. "We can accompany you, if that pleases."

"Oh, no need for that," the baroness replied with a nearly dismissive wave of her hand. "You can oversee your men and await the arrival of your Knight Commander, then come and we will have your rooms secured."

"As you say, My Lady," Amelia replied, but even before she had finished speaking, Baroness Penelope had taken Baroness Righteous by the arm and was escorting her into the main of Bridgetown, followed at a discrete distance by the dark haired, hawk-faced Baronet Christmark. That left the archduchess with only the older and clearly nonplussed Sir Nencet as guide and liaison. The last they heard of the baronesses's conversation was for Penelope to ask which type of blade Righteous most preferred to use.

"My Lady, beloved spouse," said Farringdon quietly, stepping closer and directing his words discreetly to Amelia and Dalflitch, "what precisely did we just witness?"

Amelia shook her head with a smile while Dalflitch maintained her poise, answering with perfect aplomb.

"Good Marquis, in the entire history of this venerable and storied Grand Kingdom, I do not think the words have ever been composed that might fully explain *what just happened*," she said with a calm that spoke louder than a raging sea storm. She met her liege lady's eyes and they both raised their brows in restrained surprise. "*Baroness* Righteous?"

"*Baroness* Righteous indeed!" Amelia agreed and she turned her attention on the cadre of neophytes shifting their weight slightly as they waited on the notice of their social betters. They were as inscrutable as they had been, but somehow the arch-duchess felt that they too recognized the inconceivable nature of the friendship they had just seen bud in the most unexpected soil. Somehow, their eyes seemed to reflect her own amusement and bemusement.

"Let us hope the Knight Commander is not too much longer in arriving," Amelia said, and she looked again to the marching columns, still saluting her dutifully as they passed. The middle of the company, with its supplies and civilian complement, had passed now. Surely Prentice would join them soon.

CHAPTER 11

B y the time Prentice's conference with the fey concluded, word had come to the archduchess that Baroness Penelope had obtained "the perfect lodging for her grace's entire household, even with her adjunct nunnery." Archduchess Amelia and her closest ladies had withdrawn to that location, and Farringdon remained behind to welcome Prentice and to escort him to her grace immediately.

"Adjunct nunnery?" Prentice asked the marquis.

"A joke on the new hopeful ladies-in-waiting," Farringdon explained. "Lady Penelope and Lady Righteous have become instant, fast friends, apparently. Perhaps some of your lady wife's playfulness is rubbing off upon the baroness of Bridgetown."

"What do you know about my lady wife's playfulness?" Prentice asked, cocking an eyebrow sternly.

"Only what my own goodwife shares in private tales, which I would never repeat in open hearing," Farringdon answered earnestly, not shrinking from the knight commander's apparent disapproval. "I would have no other way of knowing."

Prentice's suspicious expression broke with a smirk, and Farringdon returned that with a smile of his own.

"You are a more confident man than when I left, Marquis," Prentice said. "You have a better sense of yourself and your strength, I think."

Farringdon accepted the compliment with a nod.

"And you have been missed in your absence, Baron, and not just by your lovely family."

Prentice accepted that word with a nod of his own. Farringdon offered to lead the way to the archduchess's new lodgings, apologizing ahead of time if he got them lost on the way, and the knight commander accepted. First though, he made sure that Corporal Guillam's contingent knew where they were to go to rejoin the rest of the Gryphon Banner.

"Some field camp they got for us on an island," Guillam said.

"Tell Franken and Gennet I will come to the camp later tonight to inspect progress and to set out the duties for the next few days," Prentice told him.

"You sure your 'lady wife' ain't going to want you with her? First chance at a proper bed since we got back from the desert and the Verdants," Guillam asked with his impudent smile, lips smacking on his gums and his teeth half black from chew. "The knight captain said they missed you and all."

"I did not accept that cheek from the marquis, Corporal. What makes you think I will take it from you? Now that we are back, did you really want to keep digging trenches and midden pits?"

"No, My Lord." Guillam snapped a genuine salute, though his grin did not fade. Then he turned on his heel and gave orders to the rest of the militiamen waiting on him for them to march directly to the camp.

"It seems I'm not the only one with tales to tell from the summer just gone, Prentice," Farringdon said quietly when they were alone. He looked at Guillam's receding form on the bridge to indicate his meaning.

"Quite so, My Lord," Prentice agreed, smiling. "But first I must tell my tales to our liege. So, if you would lead the way."

They set off, leaving Bridgetown's Norgate entryway once again in the hands of its traditional militia.

As they had walked the bustling trade town's streets and bridges, Farringdon unfolded the story of Baroness Righteous's meeting with Baroness Penelope. After the two women had left the archduchess on the bridge, they found Lady Spindle, and like three goodwives assessing the day's catch for a fish supper or the best fruits to put in a pie, they had gone "shopping" for lodgings. They had lit upon a set of storied apartments, extensive and opulent, in the shadowed lee of one of the ancient bridges. Baroness Penelope had declared it perfect and insisted that it be prepared for the archduchess at once.

Apparently, a century previously this unusual location had been furnished for the mistress of the Vec prince of a city-state called Town Sobridge, not far from the Murr River. The unfaithful royal would tell his wife that he was off to tour his land's farms and villages, and then ride straight for Bridgetown, there to secretly spend as many days as he could in another woman's arms, despite the fact that his country and Bridgetown's were still officially enemies. So distracted was this prince by his love affair that when his lands were invaded by the prince of another city state called Eksdale, from farther to the south and west, he was in fact secretly here cheating on his wife and his people. By the time news of the invasion reached the unfaithful prince and he rode to his domain's defense, it was already too late. He was quickly slain in battle, and upon hearing of it, the mistress threw herself from the nearby bridge to drown in the river—a typical end to thwarted lovers in Bridgetown, it was said. Since that time, the large but-low roofed rooms where a prince and his doxy had played house together had become infamous and then forgotten. Officially the building's deed had been ceded to the previous noble family who ruled Bridgetown, and when Earl John had received his title from the late king, it became his. Until this moment, the Paramour's Chambers, as they were known, had languished unused for years.

"We'll have to rename it for Your Grace, of course," Baroness Penelope had said once she obtained the keys and informed a steward to see the place cleaned and made ready. Hours later, as the whole of the archduchess's close household arrived to attend her within, including Prentice and Farringdon at last, the place was not even half full. It still smelled of dust.

At one end was a brocade-curtained area where a large four posted bed was given a measure of privacy, along with a dresser lined with camphor wood to protect clothes from lice and other crawling pests. Two of the neophytes were at work there when the baron and marquis entered, unloading the few clothes which the archduchess had secured in the retreat from Aubrey, along with the expansion of her wardrobe brought from Dweltford with Lady Dalflitch. At the opposite end of the main apartment, other trainee Lace Fangs were working at a kind of makeshift kitchen, with a bench, a stove and even a device apparently designed to lift water in buckets from the river below. In whatever manner the mechanism had been supposed to work, time had corroded its wheels to the point of uselessness, and so wimpled young women were going back and forth through the yard to the river to fetch water, while others prepared bread dough to rise through the night or cut meat and vegetables for cooking. The liege lady of the Reach's new lodgings were a hive of activity, as if an entire noble household had been bestowed in a single room; yet for all the workshop-like busyness, and even with all Amelia's senior advisors present as well, along with the rich furnishings, the Paramour's Chambers did not feel crowded, let alone cramped. Through several doors, as well as down a short flight of steps, were other cells and closets where retainers and staff might sleep. There were probably bustling taphouses and even some boarding houses all over Bridgetown that could not boast such an amount of space. Whatever the man's other failings, the unfaithful past prince of Town Sobridge had not been stingy in the lodgings he had bestowed on his mistress.

By the time Prentice and Farringdon arrived, Lady Penelope had returned to the town's castle for her own evening meal and had promised to call first thing in the morning. The rest of the archduchess's close circle, what might have been called her court, from husband Farringdon to scholar Solft, were otherwise present. The mood was already full of joyous reuniors. The lord and lady of Fallenhill's two babes had been presented to their liege, and the archduchess had given her approval to their new-given names. The children were now bestowed in a pair of rooms on the floor below that had once been reserved for the mistress's favorite serving girl, safely being tended to by Emma their wetnurse.

"Baron Ash, your return, though delayed, is a genuine pleasure," Archduchess Amelia said as Prentice knelt before her while she sat in a throne-like chair at the head of the chamber's main table—a richly carved monolith with woodgrain stained a deep red color. Cherubs and satyrs danced around the table's legs, and vines laden with ripe grapes were carved into its edge. It was an overbearing piece of furniture that matched the opulence of the rest of the room. It was by no means the first time Prentice had knelt, bondsman fashion, to his liege, but this time did have the distinction of being the first when he might do it by right. Before, it had been a privilege she bestowed, justified by his diligent service in her name. Now, he did it as an anointed noble and true, sworn bondsman. From her expression, Prentice had the sense the archduchess recognized the significance of the moment as he did.

"Is Castellan Turley not with you, Your Grace?" he asked politely as he rose from his knee. Looking about at the many present, he could not see his old friend and it disappointed him. During the march into the west, Prentice had undertaken a small personal adventure of the foolish kind for which he had always chided Sir Turley, especially when they had both been convicts on a chain. Prentice had hoped to tell his friend that the man's larrikin ways had rubbed off. It would have to wait.

"Sir Turley remains behind in Dweltford at the seneschal's insistence," the archduchess explained. Prentice looked to Lady Dalflitch, seneschal of the archduchess's purse and treasury, and as it happened, wife to Sir Turley.

"I told him that as I was forced to travel with the new recruits to meet her grace in Aubrey, he would have to remain behind," she said. "He could not entrust the castle to a mere chief steward, especially not with the reputations of some of the *former* chief stewards."

"Was Sir Turley not formerly a chief steward?" Marquis Farringdon asked, more joking than genuinely puzzled.

"Yes," Dalflitch answered imperiously, "which only proves my point."

Everyone had chuckled at that, even the archduchess. As they relaxed, Prentice realized that, apart from Farringdon and himself, the only other men present were Master Solft, scholar and chronicler of the westward campaign, and Brother Whilte, chaplain of the White Lions. Both men had been standing discretely in the shadow of one of the mighty wooden pillars that held the heavy ceiling aloft. Apparently, there were yet more rooms above, some of which were for storage or staff.

"Brandy," the archduchess declared, and she looked to Dalflitch who nodded to nearby neophytes. "We must toast our reuniting and have drinks to tell our tales. You've not been back with us more than a handful of hours, Prentice, and already the rumors are flying. I had thought we would have a summer to boast of to you, but it seems you have trumped us yet again, if the words we have already received are true."

Two neophytes appeared carrying a tray of pewter cups and a silver carafe of decanted brandy, which they placed on the table and then bobbed politely to the archduchess. The two girls began to pour the brandy and distribute the cups. Prentice received his third, preceded only by his liege and her husband, but even that caused a moment of consternation for the two veiled maids. A marquis was of higher rank than a baron, so Farringdon should have been first on that account, as well as being husband to the ranking peer, but Prentice was knight commander and Farringdon was only knight captain. It was the kind of conundrum that could turn a herald or a steward's hair white, fearing to offend and almost certain to do so if either nobleman was of a prickly nature. Prentice received his cup with a gentle smile, which the girl did not notice, her eyes downcast as was appropriate to her place. He wondered if others noticed the girls' nervousness and looked for smiles like his. What he saw, though, was a noble peer seated at the table's head with her closest ladies-in-waiting standing nearby with all the dignity and reserve of a portrait. Even Righteous and Spindle, the former fish-out-of-water attendants, ladies only in name, not rank until recently, held themselves with a calm aloofness which would have shamed the infamous Matron Bettina at her most diffident.

"My Lady, I do not disapprove your plan of general anonymity," the archduchess said suddenly, looking to Dalflitch, "but I would have these maids unmasked when we are in private. I should get to know them all, I think. I do not like the idea of their veils becoming a double-edged sword, especially after what we have learned of our enemies' spies."

Prentice had already heard some of the stories of spies from his wife. While he had been in the west chasing a company of Church knights sworn to the Inquisition, other servants of the Silent Hand of the Church had been revealed in the Western Reach. Servants with supernatural abilities, by the accounts.

"As you say, Your Grace," Lady Dalflitch responded. "I would already have suggested such, but I wasn't sure whom you would admit into that confidence." She looked around the room at the other worthies, but her eyes stopped on Whilte and Solft. "With no insult implied."

"I think we can call this company trustworthy," Amelia said, her own eyes sweeping the gathered faces, also resting lastly and significantly upon Master Solft. "Even our scholar here has proven his reliability, I would say."

Solft and Whilte both appeared to accept the archduchess's word as a compliment, and they tugged their forelocks to her respectfully.

"You heard her grace's word, ladies," Dalflitch declared loudly, her normally charming voice suddenly stern and unyielding. "Fold back your veils in her presence and the presence of her approved guests."

"Begging your pardon, My Lady," the girl who poured the brandy asked as she turned her face covering back over her wimple to reveal a sun-browned maid of no more than sixteen, with hazel eyes and a pretty nose. "How shall we know who is approved?"

"You will know, Seskia, by the word or signal, which you will receive from me," Dalflitch informed the maid. "Or, in my absence, from Lady Spindle or Lady Righteous. Should we all be absent, only the archduchess herself has the right to give you that word. Do you understand?"

"Very good, My Lady," the girl answered.

"And should unpermitted company arrive, you must cover yourselves immediately and give word to your sisters."

All around the huge room, so vast that even with candles on every post and wall it was still awash with shadows, the neophytes flipped back their veils.

"Will it not be considered rude for your ladies to assess guests at her grace's chamber door?" Farringdon asked. "Even mere heralds might take umbrage at being vetted for status. Peers almost certainly will."

"The ladies-to-be of the archduchess' chamber are nothing if not discrete," Dalflitch said. By way of a demonstration of her meaning, she moved to the table and sat in the second chair down from her grace. Laying one palm flat upon the table, she covered her mouth with the other, giving two short, affected coughs that surely could barely have been heard in the far corners of the room. Nevertheless, every neophyte ceased whatever she was doing and immediately moved to form an orderly line down one side of the long table at the archduchess's left hand, heads lowered and hands clasped in front of themselves, as orderly as a military formation. Most surprising to Prentice was the fact that in the swift, silent reordering of the room, Lady Righteous and Lady Spindle had also redeployed themselves, one each at the archduchess's two shoulders, their hands inside the cuffs of their wing sleeves, ready no doubt to draw forth fighting daggers. Their lace-masked faces scanned the room with the watchfulness of a rowdy tavern's finest bouncers or the Lions' best sentinels.

"You militiamen have your drummers, Knight Commander, Knight Captain," Dalflitch said to Prentice and Farringdon in turn, having otherwise not shifted in her seat one fraction. "Ladies do not beat upon cowhide with sticks, so we must have gentler forms of communication."

Gentler or not, no one in the room, from the archduchess herself to the lowest of the neophytes, could doubt the effectiveness of the cadre which Dalfitch, Spindle, and Righteous were creating for their liege. Prentice found it oddly comforting, knowing that not all of Archduchess Amelia's safety rested on his shoulders anymore.

"I compliment you and your trainees, My Lady. Their order is most impressive," he said to Dalflitch with a bow. The lady accepted the praise and then with, another signal of the hand, this one so discrete that Prentice was not sure he really noticed it, the neophytes were dismissed to their previous duties. Spindle and Righteous kept their places but relaxed their postures.

"At least as good as most of those raw recruits we marched here with, eh Commander?" Whilte said quietly behind Prentice's shoulder, having taken advantage of the recent disruption in the room to move from his previous position. "I cannot help but wonder what the Lord Almighty might think of making what amounts to women-at-arms, though."

"I doubt God in Heaven thinks much less of it than he does of the purpose so many men-at-arms are put to," Prentice answered as quietly, and he looked Whilte in the eyes. "We are 'death-things,' remember."

Whilte nodded soberly. "Death things" was the translated title the fey of the far west had given to Prentice and to his sword, with its unicorn horn hilt and silver lion-head pommel. Before they could have any more private conversation in the archduchess's presence, however, their liege called everyone to sit at the table so that they might eat, drink, and exchange their stories of the past summer.

CHAPTER 12

"The fey are gone? For how long?"

"I cannot say, My Liege," Prentice reported honestly. As the candles burned lower and the plates and cutlery of their meal were being cleared away, Prentice had a chance to deliver his gravest news, at least as it related to the near future.

"If I may, Your Grace?" Master Solft asked from the far end of the long table. "I do not think the Wind Rising are withdrawing all their service, only meeting now to decide what form their service should take."

"I thought that had been determined already," Dalflitch said with a raised eyebrow, which seemed to make the scholar flinch, even in the diminishing candlelight.

"Forgive me, My Lady, but the ways of the fey are not so simple," the scholar answered, his hand hovering in the air halfway between the table and his face, as if it was trapped there while he decided if he should tug the forelock to her or not. Prentice had to wonder at it. Where was the adventurous man of learning, so passionate for discovery that it made him fearless? On the march, Solft had been heedless of enemy weapons and ancient curses alike, yet here he cringed back from a little polite disapproval. It was an odd juxtaposition.

"Although the fey lack many of the niceties of civilized society," Solft was explaining, "it would be a mistake to think of their social order as simple or unsophisticated. They have their own ways and their own priorities. Remember, if you will, that they have hidden themselves from us for a thousand years."

"From us, and amongst us," Archduchess Amelia added, and the scholar nodded readily. Ostensibly the fey had never been seen by mere mortals for a millennium, yet a pair was able to infiltrate Reach settlements so easily that they had nearly managed to assassinate the archduchess for the sake of a blood ritual.

"Quite so, Your Grace," Solft continued, placing both his palms flat on the tabletop. He drew in a deep breath as if to steel himself. "By what they have shared with me, their numbers are greater than we ever imagined, hidden in glades and valleys no one suspected could exist in the inhospitable mountains. As near as I can determine, they have no single rulership and rarely, if ever, gather to make decisions that govern their nation as a whole. Apparently, the elders' fire which Baron Prentice and Brother Whilte were invited to last year was the first such conference in their living memory."

That was news to Prentice, and when he looked to Whilte, he could see the chaplain was equally surprised.

"That is quite interesting, master scholar, but it still doesn't explain their retreating from our alliance," Archduchess Amelia said with no malice, only a clear concern. "What does it all mean?"

"Direct terms, Master Solft, to the point," Prentice encouraged, knowing the man's natural aversion to simplicity. Solft usually preferred either to be silent in thought or profuse in his enthusiasm for knowledge. Brevity was not one of the scholar's virtues. Solft accepted Prentice's admonition with a nod and then swallowed.

"Remembering that I know only in part, and that much of what I do know I understand only from the context of Benjamin's *keshiyaa*, as well as some time spent with Baron Prentice's squire, Dahyoor, a fey who is 'outside the camp,' as it were," he began, causing Lady Dalflitch to roll her eyes. Prentice seemed the only one to notice, though, and when his gaze met hers, she mouthed the words "to the point"? Prentice suppressed a grin.

"More swiftly to the point, Master, if you will," he said. "If her grace requires clarification, she is astute enough to ask for herself."

"Astute? Yes...," Solft said, losing his train of thought. "To the point. To the point...my point, Your Grace, is that they *are* coming back. At least I believe so. Much happened in the west, and some truly overwhelming discoveries were made. I believe...I am convinced...that Benjamin feels he must speak these discoveries to his people's elders so they can judge how it will impact the alliance."

"But you believe they will return?" the archduchess pressed. "More importantly, you are sure they will not become our foes again, regretting their dalliance with openness and returning to secrecy?"

"Of that I *am* convinced, Your Grace," Solft said, looking to Prentice to agree, which he did with a nod. "Many things happened in the west, and Benjamin's people saw much of them firsthand. The Redlander power over the waters is broken and there were victories and even miracles. If our places were reversed, Your Grace, I do not doubt you would want to hear a full accounting immediately, as evidenced by this very council. I think the Wind Rising will count themselves even more indebted to the Reach once Benjamin has spoken to his elders, but he must speak to them first."

"Why did they not tell us all this themselves before they left?" Dalflitch asked, her tone revealing her frustration. Her fingers were turning her cup in her hand, not one of the new signals but an unconscious gesture Prentice recognized as nervous thoughtfulness. "Why treat us as untrustworthy still? Why the secrecy between us if we are yet friends?"

Solft looked to Whilte and then to Prentice. Having spent a season either marching beside the fey or living under the fearful threat of their kinfolk's power, each man knew there was only one answer to the lady's question.

"They pass unseen," Prentice said. At first the archduchess, Dalflitch, and all the others around the table waited for him to say more. But all three men only nodded, as if Prentice's words said all that could be said.

"It is their way," Archduchess Amelia said at last, nodding to show that she at least partially understood. "Thank you, Master."

Solft seemed relieved to accept the archduchess's thanks and pull back from the center of the table's conversation. The archduchess herself looked thoughtfully at the wooden surface in front of her for a long moment, and then, as if she had just remembered something, lifted her eyes and took hold of her husband's hand.

"Friends," she said, but staring into Farringdon's eyes in the manner of love fresh between spouses. "Friends. Perhaps soon I will learn to stop waiting for pleasant days to share pleasant news. We have put our foot in the stirrup of business swiftly once again, and once again have stepped over our moments of joy. So, allow me to turn us back a moment. You have all heard or seen the baron and baroness' fine new heirs. The wetnurse's word is that both are hale and taking to milk readily, so we congratulate them and wish them a happy future as a family."

Everyone at the table gently banged their pewter cups upon the wood, applauding the happy parents. Prentice accepted their smiles and nods of congratulations. He could remember few times he had ever felt prouder, and looking to his wife, he could feel her pride as well, reflecting his back to him. Was there any marvel in all of life like a wife? His only regret was that Turley was not here to drink with them as they toasted his children's future. That thought brought Sir Gant and others passed to his mind, and he was forced to crush the rising memories of loss within him before they poisoned the joyous moment. The archduchess continued, looking at each guest at the table in turn.

"Now, I must tell you all publicly that soon the son and daughter of Fallenhill will, God willing, have a playmate and future liege to join them," the archduchess continued. She put her hand to her stomach significantly, making her meaning obvious. It was clear that Farringdon already knew about this announcement, and by her lack of surprise, it seemed Lady Spindle was also already privy to the news. For the rest of the table, even the normally exceptionally well-informed Lady Dalflitch, this revelation was fresh and yet more joyous. There was more banging of cups and cheerful smiles. Prentice found himself marveling at how his life had turned. Not only would his children be born with noble titles, but they would grow up with the heirs of one of the Grand Kingdom's highest ranked peers. He was so lost to the wonder of it in his thoughts that he almost missed the odd gesture Lady Dalflitch gave with her fingers, glancing as she did so at Righteous. Before he could decipher its likely meaning, his wife moved down the table and spoke to him quietly.

"Husband?" she said, her tone full of meaning and her eyes sweeping the table. Prentice did not understand her implication, but as he followed her look, he realized that the entire group had fallen silent. He had missed something, but what? He looked back to his wife.

"You have a duty," she said, nodding with a raised eyebrow towards the archduchess, holding her consort-husband's hand and also looking toward her knight commander. Suddenly, Prentice understood and nearly laughed out loud at his own mistake. He had only been a man of rank for just on two seasons now, barely half a year, and almost all of that had been spent riding and marching in the dust of campaign. He had never been a situation like this, where he was the next most senior man in the room after the nobles needing acclaim. It was his responsibility to toast the blessed couple. Suppressing a self-deprecating smile, he rose from his seat.

"My liege, Marquis Farringdon, I offer you my heartfelt congratulations," he began. "May your child come strong and healthy into this world, fair of features and auspicious of birth. May they be the first of many, until your joy of family overflows. And may God grant each of us the strength and wisdom to forge them a future, all our children born and yet to come—a future where they may be safe, prosperous and proud to remember us."

"Hear! Hear!" said Brother Whilte.

Prentice took up his cup.

"Stand with me, if you would," he said and waited while the rest of those seated raised themselves. When they had, he lifted his cup to the archduchess and her husband. "The coming heir of the Western Reach. The young lion."

"The young lion," they all toasted, but after they had drunk, the archduchess lifted her cup to them and added to the toast.

"To all the young lions," she said, and they all drank to that as well. As the council resumed their seats, the pleasure of the moment lifted their spirits, giving them fresh energy for the plans and tales of the summer past and winter coming. The cups were refilled, and the discussions went on into the night.

CHAPTER 13

"A tale of a miracle?" the archduchess asked, eyes wide and expression gentle as she looked once to Master Solft. Where Dalflitch had pinned the man in place like a hare shot through with an arrow, Archduchess Amelia was soothing the scholar's fears by encouraging him to be profuse in the tale. Solft's account of the battle in the far west was full of wonders including a night journey through passages in rock that magically appeared and disappeared, of a mighty dragonfly statue with beating wings of rainbow light, and most especially of the flood it caused when it fell. A mighty deluge, that nearly washed the men of the Gryphon Banner Company away and was held back only by the prayer of Brother Whilte with the light of his broken-spear staff. The chaplain was plainly embarrassed by Solft's account, ducking his head and looking away from the table, fearful of meeting anyone's eyes.

"It was no act of heroism, I assure you," he said, when he turned back and found the rapt listeners all looking to him. "We were all in desperate fear and certain it was to be our end. I cried out to God on behalf of the company, as my duty demanded, and He answered. No more than that. Do not make of me a Porlain."

Sacrist Porlain was the infamous glutton who had been chaplain to the previous Prince of Rhales. At the Battle of the Brook, when the angel confronted the first *brakkis effar*, the beastmen of the Redlander cult, exploding upon them like thunder and fire, Porlain had claimed that it was in answer to *his* prayer, that his panicked squeak for his own safety had summoned an angel of heaven to defend him, and to a lesser extent the prince he served. If Prince Mercad had survived that day, his claim to high holiness might have been more well received. As it was, the last word heard of the Sacrist Porlain was that an ecclesiastical court had tried him for heresy and found him guilty. What sentence he had received, Prentice did not know but could guess. It was little wonder that Brother Whilte was reticent about having miracles attributed to himself. Nevertheless, Prentice was convinced that the moment in the west had indeed been miraculous.

"Of the righteous man, the psalmist wrote 'surely in the floods of great waters, they will not come near to him,'" the knight commander recited, and Whilte nodded his head in humble acceptance. The two men shared the same religious education, but it had become easy for them to forget the fact since both had, in different ways, fallen out with the tradition that had trained them.

"Hear, hear," Marquis Farringdon said, banging his cup on the table, then raising it to Whilte in salute, downing it in a draft.

"Well, Master Scholar, as awe-inspiring as your account is, I think we who remained behind might have a story to equal it, or very nearly," Archduchess Amelia said, raising her cup to Solft, acknowledging him as the teller of the tale. Then she looked to Dalflitch.

"During the summer, this snide Brother Inxyphos of whom you spoke, Prentice, was not the only agent of the Church's Silent Hand whom we were forced to deal with. Others, like our friend Bluebird, were uncovered."

Prentice felt himself sit up straighter in his chair.

"The minstrel returned?" he asked, but Dalflitch shook her head.

"Not the man himself, but others like him. And some worse even."

"Though some of his influence had lingered, it turns out," the archduchess added cryptically, giving her husband another glance, this one more complex and difficult to read.

"Were many hurt?" Prentice asked, his lips downturned, expression hard. He was annoyed to realize that in pursuing Inxyphos and his company of Inquisition knights, he had not thought that the Inquisition might have other representatives at work in the Reach behind him. It was a lapse that did not please him.

"Some," Dalflitch said simply, and then, after receiving a nod of permission from their liege, she began to unfold the tale of hypnotic tricks played upon the archduchess and of mystical saboteurs that could change their bodies and faces, even their voices. She told how they had conspired to destroy the Reach's new company of cannons during its first battle, and as a result had slain Yentow Sent, all his cannoneers, and had almost slain the archduchess and Marquis Farringdon themselves.

"They could change their shape, you say?" Brother Whilte asked, his concerned tone making it clear what he thought of the news.

"Not like the goblins in fey tales, and not beast-man like, exactly either," Lady Righteous explained. "We never saw any become animals or that like. But they could mimic the face, the voice, so that you'd swear it was the same person. If I hadn't seen Flick's dead body beforehand, I would never have known it wasn't her."

"Another spoke to me in my own voice," Dalflitch said, and she shivered involuntarily, showing that the memory of the incident must trouble her still. "He, if such a one could be called a 'he' or a 'she,' planned to usurp me, use my influence to wreck her grace's household from the inside, I think."

"What happened to...it?" Whilte asked intently. Opposing sorcerous powers was one of the chaplain's main purviews, and Prentice expected he would want as much information as he could gather to help him in that regard if he now had to watch for mimicry amongst the shape-changing foes they faced.

"My husband took umbrage at the idea of my being replaced," Lady Dalflitch replied decorously. "He expressed his displeasure most clearly."

Prentice chuckled at her description. He had seen Sir Turley "take umbrage" himself at times, and the knight commander imagined that there hadn't been much left of the shape changer once Dalflitch's husband had "expressed his displeasure."

"So now we must keep watch for skin thieves, yet another monster out of legend," Prentice said letting his amusement fade.

"I have set everyone the task of keeping watch for any sign of other such figures, but will that be enough? Can it be? And what precisely do we look for?" The tumble of questions that poured from Dalflitch revealed the depth of her fears. Prentice had never seen the normally poised courtier so openly nervous or at a loss for what to do next.

"What say you, Master Solft," Prentice said, turning to their resident scholar and growing expert in all things mystical. "What do you know of skin thieves? Most especially, how are they stopped?"

The man of letters shook his head apologetically.

"Everything I know comes from fey tales, My Lord. I wouldn't know what to trust as true."

"Better anything we can test for ourselves, Master," Farringdon urged. "An unreliable possibility can be improved, refined. A reliable nothing remains nothing regardless of how trustworthy it is."

"Skin thieves are grumpkins," Solft said, holding his hands up as if to show that was literally all he had to say on the subject. "Even amongst ancient texts I have read that tell of other forms of fell craft, skin thievery is considered a virtual myth. It is a thing of the fey, and so as lost to us as they are."

"But the fey are lost no more," Lady Spindle said, making a rare contribution to the conversation. It caught Prentice's attention and troubled him. There was nothing in the courtly Lady Spindle that resembled the simple, brutalized, and scarred seamstress-doxy Tress, whom Prentice had first met in a cold, peat-roofed hut in ruined Fallenhill. And then on top of that, this woman wore a lace mask, originally to conceal the horror of her scars but now also to obscure her true identity. From Spindle, he looked to the others around the table and wondered how many he knew well enough to pick if they had been replaced by a shape-changing spy. The archduchess and Righteous—these were the only two he realized that he felt confident about, and even those, he had to concede, might take him too long to notice. Master Solft might only know fey tales of skin thieves, but like a man who fears he is drowning, Prentice felt the urge to seize any helpful possibility.

"I think we should all consider how we might detect this enemy, and please Master Solft, do whatever research you can think of to find out what has been written in the past. I know for a fact that there is at least one scriptorium of high repute here in Bridgetown. Go to them on the morrow and ask them for copies of whatever they have which you might think useful. If they must import others, then commission them to that as well. I will give you my letter of credit. No cost is too high in this."

"The archduchy will share that cost," Amelia said from her chair, and Lady Dalflitch nodded, accepting the statement as a command to the seneschal.

"Speak with me before you retire for the evening, Master," she said. "I will see you bestowed with a purse of Masnians to smooth the way for the baron's credit letter."

Solft looked from one noble to the next, blinking like a startled deer.

"It could take weeks to locate even a single useful text," he said plaintively.

"Then please begin first thing on the morrow," the archduchess urged and Solft tugged his forelock. "We will likely be here in town through the winter. You will have many weeks in which to conduct your researches. And in the meantime..."

She let her thought hang, incomplete. In the quiet, Prentice turned the problem over in his thoughts.

"In the meantime, Your Grace, I do not think we need to be too afraid," he said after a time, and all eyes at the table looked at him—most surprised but all attentive to hear what thinking backed his assertion. When his eyes met the archduchess's, she nodded for him to go on.

"Whatever way these folk have to change themselves, there cannot be too many of them, and I think they have probably expended themselves completely in the Reach, at least for now."

"How can you say that for certain?" Lady Dalflitch asked. Her tone was not argumentative, but there was skepticism in her expression, and Prentice did not blame her. She had had one of the closest encounters with the deadly mystics.

"Because two of them were revealed close in time, suggesting that they were rushing," Prentice explained. "We know that the one in Fallenhill had to have been in place for at least a year to have replaced Master Sent's journeyman and to sabotage the cannons during their construction. As far as we know, he made no effort to help Bluebird in his mission, certainly not enough to reveal his presence. If he was that cautious and patient by nature, then rushing to slay Righteous and our children was not in character. Likewise, using the Ragmother to replace yourself, Lady Dalflitch. It speaks of haste, a sense of urgency, as if they are running out of time."

"That seems a reasonable assumption, Knight Commander," said Farringdon. "But how does that point to them having no more nearby?"

"If they are so fearful that they will break from their hiding spots and rush to act, then why have others not done the same?" Prentice offered. "If they are willing to sacrifice a spy who has been hiding completely undetected for a year or more in Fallenhill, then why not sacrifice these others? If toppling the archduchess' house was their only intent, it would be no matter at all if they had, say, ten such skin thieves to send against us."

Dalflitch shivered again at that notion, and others around the table shook their heads sourly. The thought of a whole squad of such assassins was enough to terrify anyone. Nonetheless, Prentice could see that his reasoning was penetrating their fear. He kept explaining.

"Everyone here is surrounded day and night by armed men and many armed women. Could any one of us name them all on sight, let alone pick a fraud from true? If their intent is to cut the head off the lion, so to speak, and they have an endless supply of shape changers, then they would already have succeeded. You have guards at your side continually, Your Grace. Marquis Farringdon and I are surrounded by a horde of armed men. Since none of these has broken cover to assault us as the other two you discovered did, I think we can only assume they do not have so many to waste, as it were."

"One only risks the finest arrows on the best chances, you think?" Farringdon mused, and Prentice liked it as a good metaphor. "Thus, if they are not shooting, they must not have many such arrows left? Or any?"

"It is worth hoping," Prentice said.

"However many they do have, they must be saving them for a better chance than we have given them so far," the archduchess said. "So let us all fix our thoughts on this—we must not give them any better chances than they have already had."

Everyone around the table nodded, but solemnly, realizing that agreeing to their liege's command was not the same as fulfilling it. They would have to wrack their minds to devise protections against this new sorcerous threat.

"You truly think this is an art but one that only some can learn?" Whilte asked, apparently intrigued by the notion.

"Not every man or woman can do everything," Prentice answered simply. "You have all seen me try to ride a horse. All the effort in the world cannot overcome some deficiencies."

"You don't need to speak so lowly of yourself, husband," Righteous said, scowling at others in the room, daring those who were better on horseback to make any kind of comment.

"So, this is something which requires unusual talent, we think?" the archduchess mused, keeping the conversation on the task at hand.

"And likely no small amount of time to master," Prentice agreed. "I doubt this is a simple knack that someone of the right aptitude might grasp in a day's effort. This is not like catching a ball or even baking bread."

"Which means what, precisely?" she pressed.

"That for all we know, this power must be developed from childhood, trained for years—an apprenticeship more dire than the most brutal knight's preparation."

"Then we have cause to hope that even two slain and Bluebird hobbled might set our enemies back twenty years or more while they find and train replacements." The archduchess did not sound too hopeful as she said that, though.

"Unless these powers are a gift, like," said Lady Spindle and the whole table turned to the usually reticent Lace Fang.

"A gift?" Dalflitch repeated.

"From God," Spindle suggested with a delicate shrug. "Well, not from God, but as from something like to what the Redlanders pray to."

"Whatever devils receive the Redlanders' homage and whatever they return for that dread service, God does not give gifts like this to men," Whilte said with the force of a religious pronouncement. The chaplain might have been at odds with his religion, but none could doubt his *faith* in God had not diminished.

"Do we know for certain that the Inquisition still prays to the same God?" Prentice said, and he could feel the cold in his own tone. Now, worried expressions turned to horror.

"Oh, Baron Ash, surely we cannot..." Dalflitch began, but her words trailed away.

"But they are the Grand Kingdom's guardians against heresy," Amelia protested.

"Are they?" Prentice asked, certain he had finally found the one horrifying truth they had all been circling around, like blind folk grasping at the air, certain from the growling that there was a wild animal nearby. Now he had grasped the rabid dog by the tail and everyone in the room knew they were not safer for the achievement. They were now in more danger than ever.

"Have you more than mere supposition, Knight Commander?" Farringdon asked.

Prentice looked at Whilte, and it was clear the chaplain understood.

"Inxyphos," Whilte said, and Prentice agreed.

"The Inquisition's man in the west?" the archduchess asked.

"We saw him studying the Redlanders, the arts of their cult," Prentice said. "Like an initiate, participating in rituals that made beast-men and the slaughter needed to bind those ancient waters. Inxyphos had not gone to the *imzuss* to obliterate them, as we had. He was there to learn from them. We have all seen Redlander blood magicks, lost friends and even family to their madness. What servants of God want to learn such mysteries?"

"Are you saying, Baron, that you think these 'skin thieves,' if that is truly what they are, are from Redlander magick?" asked Solft, his voice and manner seeming stronger now that the question at hand was one of history or heresy. Society frightened him, it seemed, but magick and sorcery were mere academic concerns.

"Remember the smaller obelisk, Master," Prentice said, referring to an artifact they had found on the campaign. "We both thought it predated the Redlanders, that in fact the Blood Sect cult might have learned their powers from this earlier tradition, altered or corrupted by the passing of centuries. What if the Inquisition knows its arts from the same sources? What if their ruthless assaults on heresy are not to protect Mother Church, or not only, but to also guard their own power? We all know how faith can be twisted to serve other causes. We all remember Quellion's nonsense during the drought. How twisted might faith become if it hides in shadows for a thousand years? Men and women who call themselves the 'Silent Hand' might believe anything; how would we know what they think if they never speak?"

Prentice knew he was not being impartial as he offered these thoughts. His own resentment at the way the Inquisition had once abused him was bubbling up from the bottom of his heart where he usually kept it trapped and quiet. He decided to stop speaking before the frozen bitterness erupted into a raging flood-water. He already felt the fingers of his right hand—his main weapon hand—twitching ever so slightly. He pressed the palm flat to the table to bring it back under control.

"Well, it seems that your purpose is greater than any of us realized, Master Solft," the archduchess said, cracking the tense silence. "Do you think you can find out any of these secrets the Silent Hand has kept hidden from all the world? Are you that great a hunter of knowledge?"

There was a slight edge of plaintiveness to Archduchess Amelia's tone as she asked, not frightened but uncertain, and Prentice could tell she recognized the enormity of the task they were laying upon Solft's shoulders. The scholar himself also seemed aware as he soberly tugged his forelock.

"I will give you my every effort, Your Grace," he said. "The Paper House owes you that, at the least. I must warn you, though, even if the library of the scriptorium here is the most abundantly endowed in the entire world, they may have not a single reference or clue we can use. The Inquisition has had a millennium to hide their tracks, as we all know. I do have one notion, though."

"Then speak it, Master," the archduchess encouraged. "In this mood, even the slightest candle glow of light will be as welcome as the dawn's rays."

Solft paused and cast a glance at Prentice and Whilte. Then he looked back to the head of the table.

"The Inquisition has been a wildfire, raging through history and purging what it wants to hide from the forest of knowledge," he explained. Prentice caught Dalflitch's eye again as he looked over the table, and this time the lady seneschal was not troubled by Solft's long-windedness. She peered at his face in the dim can-dlelight, studying him as he would study an ancient document.

"It could easily be a waste of time looking for what they wanted to burn specifically," Solft continued. "We could kick through the ashes for years and never know which was the one tree they wanted destroyed. But if we look at all the different forests they burned, perhaps we could conjure their thinking from what they *did* burn and what they left."

Blank and bewildered faces contemplated the scholar's odd explanation until Farringdon's lit with the spark of understanding.

"By studying the targets they ignored, you mean to recognize what matters to them most," he declared.

"That will be where I set my beaters first," Solft agreed, mixing his metaphors. The Inquistion was a forest fire, and the scholar was now a noble on a hunt.

"Looking for the gaps in the tale," Prentice mused, building on the notion in his mind. "Find the parts of the tapestry that are torn, or obviously mended, to hide a hole where something else should be."

One more time, he and Dalflitch looked to one another, and they had a shared moment of unspoken revelation.

"That's how we can find them out," she said, and Prentice was sure she had realized what he had, as well. He remembered the night agents of the Inquisition had tried to lure him to an ambush by posing as White Lions. It had been the minor flaws in the way they carried themselves and wore their uniforms that had given them away, allowing him to survive and escape. The same solution would be an excellent start when dealing with skin thieves.

"Passwords; specific modes of dress; exacting manners," he said, eyes still on hers. She nodded.

"Baron Prentice and I have some notions, Your Grace," Dalflitch said, turning to her mistress.

"Well?" the archduchess asked when the seneschal was not forthcoming.

"I think we should each speak it to you separately, Your Grace," Dalflitch explained. "In private hearing. We may needs do many things this way from now on."

"You mistrust someone at this very table?" Farringdon asked, eyes flicking from Dalflitch to Prentice, and then around. He looked ready to seize his own blade and cut down the traitor in their midst. Then his glance returned to Prentice, and they could see in each other's expression the depth of the problem. Pretending to hunt out the traitor in their midst was exactly what the traitor would do. If a skin thief was already amongst them, it was too late.

"I think we will have to mistrust each other a great deal, in some ways, My Lord," Prentice said, hating to let the words out of his mouth. Never before could he remember feeling such companionship, such a sense of place, such unity of purpose as he shared with this group of people. They were as like a family to him as anything he had ever known, even since birth. And just the fact of the existence of skin thieves threatened to tear all of that apart. For the next short while, they would all have to work to create new bonds, stronger even than the ones they already shared, to keep what they had built from falling into rapid ruin. "We will have to mistrust and also to trust each other in our mistrust."

"Trust each other in our mistrust?" the archduchess repeated.

"We must accept the insult of proving and reproving ourselves to each other, over and over," Dalflitch explained. She had understood immediately. "It must be no offense to us that we even ask our spouses for a password, or watch even you, Your Grace, for a misplaced word or gesture. We will make no show of it. It will be our secret tree which we will burn forests to ash to hide. But it must be this way."

That was the somber thought which ended the council, with Solft resolved to find any hinted secrets of the powers of the Inquisition in ancient sources, while Dalflitch and Prentice were to develop the tiny details that a shape-changer would not know that would unmask them to the informed. It was a grim party, far from the joys of the earlier evening, that went to their beds that night. As they disrobed in their small room, Prentice and Righteous looked at each other. She pointed to a spot on his side where there was one of the ugliest of his scars.

"How did you get that?" she asked, and he could tell she was testing him. Was he her husband or a doppelganger?

"You tell me," he said. "You know that story already."

"Oh certainly," she answered. "Then you'll know the secret, too. If you're not you, then I'll have given somethin' away, won't I?"

"So, you don't trust me?" he asked. This could become a question that hung over them for the rest of their marriage.

"You don't trust me neither."

He stepped up to her and took her hands in his.

"I have had your edge to my throat more than once and never not trusted you," he said. "If you do it again, I will trust you again, because if you are not my Righteous then she is dead, and you will have stolen half the light out of my world already. Even if you cut me at that point, I will fight, and you will die first. However,..."

He paused and looked to the crib where the twins had been sleeping for a while, recently fed by the wetnurse.

"However, if you put an edge near either of them," Prentice continued. "Then there will not be enough pain in the whole world for you to suffer before you die, because my beautiful wife, already slain by your hand, would demand it of me. Take my wife and threaten our children, and I will send you crippled into the afterlife to face her wrath there."

He felt her shiver slightly through their hands, then she stepped up close, looking into his eyes and pressing herself against him.

"Oh, hells bells," she swore. "You're my Prentice. No mistake."

They kissed and took to their bed to share their first full intimate moment since their children's birth and his return. After, Prentice slept lightly in his wife's arms for the few hours he felt could afford. Even so, he still arose before dawn, and as the sunlight crested the eastern horizon, he was already out to assess the White Lions' new encampment in a place called Runners Field, unable to fully shake the fear that amongst eight thousand armed men, there might be one or two, or more, who had no fixed identity and who plotted his death.

Or worse, the death of those he loved.

CHAPTER 14

Runners Field was almost exactly what Prentice had imagined it would be—a flat, meadow-like expanse almost one and half leagues long and a third that distance across at its widest point. Tucked behind the hill on which the earl's castle stood, it was akin to a royal park—at one end the castle on its rise, at the other end a rocky bluff that rose even taller than the castle's turrets. From a distance, it looked as if there was a quarry carved out of the bluff's side, but there was no sign of masons or quarrymen at work there now. The only structure of any sort upon the field was on its north side near a stand of what looked and smelled like cedar in the early morning light. Not a building, per se, but the fences and lean-tos of a tilt yard and a list field to host jousts. It had been such a long time since Prentice had seen any kind of tourney arena that it had taken him awhile to recognize the fenced areas for what they were—that and the fact that as he approached on the path around the foot of the castle hill, the wooden structures were partially obscured by the sweeping array of white canvas, hundreds of tents in orderly rows, like an overnight bloom of uncannily regular wildflowers, all neat oblongs and equidistant campfires.

"Truth to say it's about as pretty a campsite as we've ever had," Sergeant Gennet declared when Prentice located him, awake on his bedroll near the Gryphon standard, just putting his boots on his feet. The White Lions' second company's second-in-command stood and joined his commander to give him the morning's reports. "And we never had this many in one place. We're a town to ourselves, almost, so I guess that makes you a alderman on top of all else."

"No, thank you, Sergeant," was all Prentice had said to that notion. If there was one "honor" he had no desire to receive, it was a position in civil government.

"Well, pretty as it is, Commander, it's got us some problems all the same," Gennet continued. "Food'll be alright as long as we can haul it along the river, but water's a different story. We're right at the most downriver of the whole town here. All their leavings is flowing in that water. Unless you go right out into the deeper channels, it's pretty mucky stuff. We take straight from the water's edge, and we'll have men coming down with the bloody-runs inside a week."

Camped beside the largest river in the land, and dysentery and fresh water are our greatest problems, Prentice thought, shaking his head in wonder.

"Course, the other end of the story's the same problem," said Gennet. "I set men with shovels to dig middens since we're going to be here too long for mere slit trenches, but they only got a couple of feet down before they struck wet mud and the holes started to fill with water. If we try to make proper midden pits here, I'm willing to bet they'll overflow once the winter floods hit the river. Our tents'll all be ankle deep in our own leavings, make no mistake."

"Filth in the water and filth in our camp," Prentice said with a nod, recognizing Gennet's concerns. He looked toward the southern riverbank and across a channel no more than a hundred paces wide to another island, little more than an outcrop. Upon that point, the water sprouted a profusion of spars and pylons, as if a giant bridge builder had spilled his scaffolding on the island and decided to just leave it there. On the other side from that outcrop was another channel and then the southern bank of the Murr, with its Vec lands, ruled by rebel princes and ostensibly an enemy still at war. Of course, if the Vec truly were at war and seeking to conquer Bridgetown, then that little island full of discarded lumber would be a perfect staging point. If the conflict had been serious at any time in the last hundred years or more, that small lump of stones rising out of the river would have been an important strongpoint. As Prentice's eyes left the water, he noticed a small company of yeomen in the shallows beside Runners Field.

"Who are they?" he asked as he watched the men bent over and carrying wicker baskets on their backs, while others hauled different-shaped baskets in and out of the water with long ropes.

"Cocklers—river shellfish fishers," Gennet told him. "Made a huge fuss when they found us here in the night. Kept waving their warrant pins at the sentries and saying they had the hereditary rights. Seems they feared we were going to do them out of their trade."

Sounds about right, Prentice thought. Eight thousand men suddenly raiding their traditional shellfish runs would destroy their livelihood overnight. It would take a generation for the industry to recover, if it ever did.

"Give instructions that we only eat what we pay for," he told Gennet. "No Lions are to go off fishing on their own, no exceptions."

"I'll pass it along, My Lord," the sergeant said. "But before I do, if I can, there's one other matter, and I'm sorry to say we are going to need you and probably the knight captain on this to get it resolved."

It was not normal for Gennet to be as sheepish as he sounded at this moment and Prentice wondered what it was that was embarrassing the normally unflappable militiaman.

"Do you want to tell me now, or should we fetch the marquis first?" Prentice asked, quite happy to facilitate Gennet's request. For his part, Prentice's willingness seemed only to embarrass the sergeant further.

"I...uh...I don't like to waste your time, you know that Commander. It's just that this is the first time we've had both banners together. We have sergeants and corporals, but what do we do if we aren't all singing the same hymn, as it were?"

Prentice nodded and smiled, clapping Gennet on the shoulder.

"You are exactly right, of course," he said.

Never before had both full banners of the White Lions, the Lion and the Gryphon, been encamped together. Each had its own corps of officers and its own hierarchy. That had always been the deliberate plan. Each banner was a small army unto itself. But when together there came the additional complication as to who was the more senior, who should take orders from whom, especially if two seemingly equal officers, say two sergeants, were at odds. It was a question of seniority, which also explained why Gennet was so reluctant to raise the matter. He would know, as all the men who had ever marched with Prentice should know, that the knight commander had little time for ambitious men who tried to improve their status through politicking or ingratiating themselves. Sycophants earned no favors from Baron Ash. Gennet would not have liked to seem like he was asking for his own prestige's sake.

"Rouse some drummers to take messages," Prentice told his sergeant. "We will want every sergeant and senior corporal here before the ninth hour of the day. Guillam and Porth will need to be promoted to full sergeants in short order as well. I will go to Knight Captain Marquis Farringdon and invite him along. We will get our pecking order sorted before we have a bunfight on our hands."

Gennet saluted and went off to gather drummer boys from the nearest cohorts, sending them to fetch the entire senior officer corps of the White Lions militia, a congregation that had never been gathered in all that company's short life so far.

We raised a sworn militia instead of knights to avoid exactly this question of jockeying for status and authority, he thought ruefully. *I may have been somewhat unfair on our peerage.*

Almost immediately that thought brought memories of the viciously ambitious nobles like Duggan and Liam to his mind, not to mention the regicidal Usurper himself.

"Well, we had better get this sorted before we reach that pass," he muttered to himself.

CHAPTER 15

Prentice had not expected to have to return the whole way to the archduchess's quarters to find Knight Captain Farringdon, but he was surprised when his quest was successful without even having to leave Runners Field. Heading west near the riverbank, aiming for the ancient path around the southern ridge of the castle's hill, Prentice was confronted by a train of horses, coming two abreast, with a rider on each right-hand mount leading the pair. The column trotted into the field and turned to their left to circle the encampment on the north side. Many of the riders did not even notice the solitary knight commander standing near the rushes, but those that did gave him the Lions' salute as they passed, and he returned it. None of them was in armor. In fact, most were stripped to their undershirts with the last of the lingering summer warmth in the morning, but some had their buffcoats on, and Prentice realized that these were Farringdon's lancers, moving their horses off the barges at last. The tiltyard and its attendant corrals would be an excellent place for the beasts to recover their health, at least until winter came and they needed better stabling once again.

"Ho there, My Lord Knight Commander," a voice called, and Prentice turned to see Farringdon arriving on his horse, accompanied by another rider in a sergeant's uniform. The pair of them appeared to be escorting several of the company's wagons in train. Prentice expected these would be carrying the weapons, armor, and equipment which the lancers were not bearing themselves while they transferred their mounts. Farringdon and his companion turned their horses aside, the sergeant pointing for the wagons to carry on, following the column. Once they had trotted over to Prentice, the knight captain dismounted, and the sergeant followed his example. Farringdon saluted Prentice like any other officer of the Lions, as did the other man, and the knight commander returned the respect.

"Knight Commander, if I may, this is my second-in-command, Sergeant Nunel of the Lancers," Farringdon introduced his man. "Nunel, this is the Lord Knight Commander, Baron Prentice Ash."

Having already saluted, Nunel bowed as he was introduced, which might have been a little presumptuous, since strictly only nobility had the right to bow to each other within the Grand Kingdom, but it was a breach that was far from uncommon, and knowing Nunel was a former Veckander mercenary, Prentice was happy to simply ignore it. He replied to the bow with the kind of benign nod he had seen a myriad of nobles use in his life.

"It is good to meet you, Sergeant Nunel," he told the man. "The knight captain and the archduchess speak highly of you. I look forward to seeing your skills demonstrated at training, in coming days."

Nunel was one of the names that had featured prominently in the tales of the Aubrey siege during the night before, as had Sedgewick and Markas, two men that Prentice knew well, or well enough. As he complimented Nunel however, he found himself unable to remember much about this particular man, other than that he was a skilled rider, brave in battle and, an odd detail to recall, that he was sweet on a washermaid and planned to wed her upon their return to Dweltford.

I hope your girl is the patient type, Prentice thought. *We will be here in Bridgetown until after winter at least, as far as we know.*

"A fine morning, is it not, My Lord?" Farringdon said, sucking in a lungful of the morning air, heady with the scent of the cedars and the flowing water, muck notwithstanding. "A fine morning and a lovely paddock. It's moments like this that a man might forget there even was a war, eh?"

"Except for the armed camp right in front of us?" Prentice said in a light-hearted tone. He smiled as he looked at the rows of tents sweeping away from them.

"Yes, well, there is that, I suppose," Farringdon agreed with sour amusement. Beside the marquis, Nunel lifted his hand up so that it would seem to block the bottom of his view, so that he could not see the tents anymore.

"I don't know," he said impudently. "Like this, all I can see is the bluff, the treetops and the bright morning sky. Quite picturesque, if you don't mind me saying so, My Lord Commander. The knight captain seems to have the right of it, looking like this."

Farringdon stood next to his sergeant, leaning his head over to follow the man's eyeline, and held his hand up in the same manner.

"Indeed so, Sergeant. Bucolic even," the knight captain agreed and then the pair looked at Prentice, smirking, as if daring him to object to their disagreement. Prentice shook his head with a smile.

"Sergeant Nunel, I have a man in my company—a corporal, though soon to be a sergeant. Guillam is his name," he said, a chuckle in his voice. "I think we should introduce you two. You would make a pair, no mistake."

Nunel accepted the comment, and Prentice turned to the knight captain more directly.

"In fact, if you will, Captain, I will require you both as soon as possible," he said. "I am calling a conference of all officers from both banners."

"Both banners?" Farringdon asked, eyebrows rising.

"Both. This is the first time we have had the entire militia together in one place. There are things that need to be put in order now, before they get out of hand. You know the tale of the mess Daven Marcus made of his march west just by not appointing a knight commander of his own."

"Disorder is death to an army," Nunel concurred sternly in the manner of a man quoting a written creed or philosophy. Given that the man was from the Vec, where small wars were endemic and philosophizing about military matters was a career in itself, Prentice expected he *was* probably quoting someone. It pleased Prentice to see that the man was not all laughter and japes but had some sense of the seriousness of their calling. This was no adventurous nobleman fighting wars as a hobby.

"It will take a short while to see the horses bestowed, I would think," Farringdon said. "We have no candles to burn, but will a rough half of one hour be convenient timing for you, My Lord Knight Commander?"

"One half of the hour then," Prentice agreed with a salute. "Go to, men of the Reach."

Farringdon and Nunel remounted and rode away with the last of the wagons, the heavy war vehicles with their thick, folded sides having already chewed a rutted, muddy path through the edge of Runners Field. Prentice watched the entire mass of men, animals, and carts rumble away, and then, just before turning back into the camp, he glanced back the way the column had come. There, under an enormous spreading fig tree, he saw three more riders, sitting abreast in the shade and watching the camp. At first, he thought they might be some of the lancers, but as his eyes adjusted to peering into the relative shade under the dense foliage, he saw that each of the three was wearing colors, and not Reacher blue and cream. One of them appeared to have a mail shirt with half sleeves over a white quilted arming doublet, while the other two wore doublet and hose under surcoats. All three had swords at their sides, but other than not being long enough to count as longswords, Prentice could make out nothing else about the weapons. Watching the three riders, he became convinced they were regarding him in return. They were too far off to make eye contact, and Prentice was about to hail them, when the one in mail put a hat on his head, broad brimmed, with a long feather plume like the ones Turley's wife bought for him. The man trotted into the full light, all the way to mere paces in front of where Prentice stood. As he approached, it surprised the knight commander to realize the man was much younger than expected, likely not even twenty years old. He looked down on Prentice with a marked sneer to his expression.

"Are you the captain of this mob?" he asked imperiously. "I was bid to find one dressed in armor such as you wear. Are you he?"

"I am Knight Commander of the Western Reach," Prentice said flatly. "Is that whom you seek?"

"Close enough," the man replied, and Prentice almost laughed at the youth's self-importance—like a young buck with his first horns, sure that he can sweep away the whole herd for the pick of the mating. It was the manner of a youth who had inherited his position in life and had yet to learn just how hard he might have to fight to hold it. There had been a time when Prentice would have resented such an entitled man-child, but now he had seen too much war and too much death to care about the arrogance of youth. War would sand the sharp edges of this twit soon enough, if he survived.

"If you were bid to find me, for what reason?" Prentice asked.

The young man puffed himself up in the saddle slightly, causing his mount to shift under him momentarily. The motion spoiled much of the dignity the youth was probably aiming for.

"My Lady, the Baroness Penelope of Bridgetown, bids the commanding captains of the militia out of the west to attend her, with their liege, at Sougate, as soon as they are able."

You could not sound more contemptuous if you wrote your message down with a pen dipped in venom and then spat it at me like a mouthful of chew, Prentice thought, more impressed than offended. In a society where those of higher rank despised those beneath them as a matter of course, this lad appeared to be a true master of the practice, and Prentice had suffered under the likes of the cruelhearted Baronet Liam in his time.

"Has word been sent to her grace, the archduchess, that she knows to attend?" he asked the disdainful messenger. "Or should I do that?"

"My Lady has dispatched the twins to summon your mistress," the young man said.

Summon? Prentice thought. He had a sudden thought of how his friend Sir Turley would respond to this disdainful young twit.

Boy's looking for a thick lip and a sore head, he heard Turley say in his mind. *Might take a tooth or two for good measure.*

That amusing notion made Prentice look to the young man's weapon once more, which he now saw was a kind of sidesword – a lighter civilian blade, not unknown in the Grand Kingdom but unusual since knights favored the longsword even in non-martial contexts. It was the main sign of their status, after all. This sidesword was even more unusual than Prentice was accustomed to, having its crossguard supplemented by a knucklebow, similar to but thinner than the White Lions Fangs' sword with its basket hilt.

The young man saw Prentice's eyes on his blade, and his disdainful cast took on a belligerent edge. His left hand went to the blade's scabbard, holding it ready for a sudden draw with his right. The gesture made Prentice blink in surprise. Did the fool really think he was about to make some kind of challenge to a duel? Disdainful *and* prickly, a nasty combination.

"Please tell your lady that I will fetch my horse and rush to attend both she and my liege. At Sougate you say?"

The man's tension relaxed slightly, and his frown turned surly and contemptuous once more.

"Do you know the way? Or do you need someone to lead you?"

Like a dog on a leash? Prentice thought, imagining the kind of lead this man would think to give.

"My thanks, but no," was all he said. He would have added more, but the arrogant young man had already wheeled his horse and started away. His two friends joined him and the three rode back into the town.

"Well then, I had best fetch my horse," Prentice said to himself as he also turned away, realizing that he would have to postpone his proposed conference of officers. He would also have to pass the condescending messenger's word to Knight Captain Farringdon. As he walked away, there was a loud cry and a splash, followed by laughter. By the riverside, one of the cocklers had fallen in the water, and his fellows laughed at him as he lay like a turtle on its back, splashing wildly as his heavy wicker basket made it hard for him to right himself.

CHAPTER 16

Amelia had not thought to sleep late, not when her husband rose in the pre-dawn to see to the lancers' animals. Nevertheless, she had rolled over, searching for a comfortable position for her changing body, and then awakened to find the sun was fully up and the Paramour's Chambers awash with the dazzling glory of morning light. As she blinked, she could see all the shutters pulled back and realized why the unusual apartment had seemed so dark the previous afternoon. All of the room's windows were on the eastern side, making the room dimmer and cooler in the evening but ablaze at this hour. No sooner had Amelia shifted her weight in the bed and begun to pull away her covers than a neophyte poked her head around the edge of the curtain.

"Are you in need of any assistance, Your Grace?" she asked politely.

"Just my chamber pot, thank you," Amelia answered then her head snapped up. "Wait. I do not know your name yet, do I girl?"

"No, Your Grace. I am Agatha," the neophyte replied and then ducked out, to return almost immediately with a porcelain bowl covered with a plain cloth. She came forward to the edge of the bed to place the pot on the floor, but Amelia reached out first and guided it to the bed.

"I do not think I need a groom of the stool just yet, Agatha," Amelia said, joking about the pitiable noble whose task it was to handle a king's chamber pot, especially in his advancing years, when the matters of the body were becoming more difficult for his aging frame. Despite the degrading task itself, the role was highly sought after, and grooms of the stool wielded astonishing influence in court, since they were the ones that kings trusted at their most vulnerable moments. Such men often became the closest thing an older king had to a true friend or companion. Their word in a king's ear could sway the course of history. What queens were expected to do with their ablutions and servants for the task, Amelia had never heard.

"Nevertheless, Agatha," Amelia went on, surveying the obedient-seeming girl before her. "I think we should get to know one another. I will make it a practice to know something of every member of my chamber, not just their faces. So, you may choose. Tell me either what it was your father did for a living or what the place you were born was like."

The girl blinked and swallowed. She was a small, almost birdlike figure, with dark eyes and sharp cheekbones that spoke of a life lived with only just enough food. Her body might well never become fat, no matter how much she ate. It simply would not know what to do with too much. Her small mouth pursed as she thought, and there was panic growing in her young expression.

"Please, Your Grace, Lady Dalflitch said I was to see to your morning ablutions and then send for others to help with your dressing." The girl made to leave, but Amelia caught her by the sleeve, surprising even herself with the speed of her move. She would not have believed she was awakened enough for such swiftness.

"You may go to your other duties when you have answered my question, Agatha," she said firmly but without malice, wondering if this was how Matron Bettina had felt when she had begun taking charge of Amelia's chamber years before. "You must learn that in all matters, unless you are speaking with a king, my word is law."

"Yes, Your Grace," Agatha responded, and she curtseyed, knuckling her forehead where her forelock would be if it were not hidden by her wimple. "My Da...my father...he was a riverman, born and raised, but I think you'd say he was a netmaker, if he had any trade at all. He mostly fished, like everyone on the Dwelt waters, but folk came from all up and down the river to have my Da make or repair their nets for them."

"He is gone?" Amelia asked.

"Two summers now, Your Grace," Agatha said, and the girl's voice caught in her throat a moment. "Right 'fore the drought hit us all so bad. I miss him, but I'm well glad he never lived to see the dry and how it ruined us riverfolk."

"You were very proud of him?"

The girl paused and risked looking the archduchess directly in the eyes a moment, perhaps suspicious that there might be some noble's trap in the question. Was someone so low-born allowed to be proud? Of anything? After a moment, the girl dared a hesitant nod.

"That is a good thing," Amelia said earnestly, hoping to encourage the young maid. "A child should be proud of her parents. I am only sorry for you that he did not live to see you on this path to becoming a fine lady. I am sure he would have been prouder of you than you could imagine."

Agatha's dark eyes went wide at such free praise, and she involuntarily straightened a little, which made Amelia smile.

"Now, young Agatha, go to and do the next duty Lady Dalflitch set for you. I will attend to my morning matters while you are away."

Agatha managed a flustered half-curtsey, half-stumble and backed out through the curtains. When she returned, she was accompanied by two other neophytes, who introduced themselves as Joan and Mathilda at the archduchess's insistence, while Agatha whisked away the now used chamber pot. A moment later Lady Spindle joined them, making the curtained "bedchamber" begin to feel a little crowded.

"Good morning, Your Grace. I trust you slept well?" said the masked lady-in-waiting, and Amelia felt sure there was a new level of formality in the seamstress's attitude. She cocked an eyebrow, but if Spindle saw it, she said nothing.

"Lady Dalflitch asked me to wish you a good morning on her…for her," Spindle continued, making the slip of forgetting the word behalf but covering reasonably smoothly.

Do not reach for it, Spindle's instructress in decorum had taught her. *If it doesn't feel natural, do not do it. Less with perfection is better than more with errors.*

"She didn't want to do it herself?" Amelia asked of Dalflitch, standing and allowing the two neophytes to help her out of her underdress.

"The lady seneschal apologizes, but she has turned herself immediately to writing notes of commerce to various merchants and money changers here in Bridgetown. I believe she is of a mind to fetch your gold that rate of ten to twelve silvers to the Masnian that I spoke of."

"She'll be lucky," one of the two neophytes muttered as she and her partner lifted a fresh linen shift over Amelia's head and arms. When the stiff but finely woven cloth fell from her face, the archduchess could see the panicked look in the second maid's expression, while the one who had made the comment was stricken, clearly aware of her breach of protocol. Amelia deliberately set her face to her courtly expression—neutral of all emotions—but Spindle, in her duty as most senior lady-in-waiting present, whirled on the young woman.

"This is not a milking shed, young Mathilda. You will keep your tongue in your head and your thoughts to yourself. If, by some miracle twist in God's great plan for the world your opinion comes to be necessary, her grace will ask it of you, but don't hold your breath waiting. Now, pack you off until you prove you can keep to your place. Send Agatha back in. She has shown herself useful, at least."

It was hardly the worst dressing down Amelia had ever witnessed, but the maid Mathilda turned to leave, head down and shoulders slumped, as if the weight of the world rested upon them.

Count yourself lucky Spindle didn't go after you with one of her "stickers" girl, Amelia thought. *Time was when your superior would have cut you, given you a handy scar, just to reinforce the lesson.*

Even as she that thought, though, it occurred to Amelia that there was another side to the incident.

"Wait, Mathilda," she said as the girl put her hand to the curtain. "Why did you say that?"

"I'm sorry, Your Grace," Mathilda answered sincerely, and she turned and bobbed with a face full of grief, as if she expected to be dismissed forever on the basis of this one mistake.

I'm a noblewoman, girl, not a tyrant, Amelia thought.

"Do not apologize to me," the archduchess told the obviously nervous neophyte. "It was Lady Spindle, your superior, whom your behavior embarrassed. Apologize to her, but later. It is not fitting that your personal business be conducted now. In the meantime, answer my question and explain why you said what you said."

"I don't know, Your Grace," Mathilda answered with a shrug.

"Yes, you do," Amelia insisted. "Tell me."

"Well...I mean...it's like Lady Spindle said. It's like milkmaid's gossip, is all. Won't that just waste your time?"

"Let me worry about what wastes my time when I speak to you. What prompted your words?"

"This mornin' I was down fetching water and there was all the dawn-time trades out and about. Some baker's boy offered me a taste of the bread off his basket, but when he learned I was your maid, he was off."

"You were speaking with baker's boys in the street?" Spindle demanded, but Mathilda shook her head vehemently, her speech slipping to the vernacular as her fear of disapproval grew.

"I wasn't playin' fancy for kisses or nothin' like that," she insisted. "It was just the usual beck and call of a mornin' street like. Baker's boys, butchers, and such. I got eggs for the archduchess' breakfast cakes from a hettie, but she was the only one willing to do trade with us. The rest, they all steered away. The hen keeper, she explained that the militia comin' to town's got everyone in a stir. They want the war to go away and business to get back to usual. Daven Marcus' knights were bad enough, but they were just fifty or so actually in the town, and what's left of them's shut behind gates. We brung near on eight thousand men-at-arms into town. Townsfolk're afeared of us, least that was the word. That's all I meant, Your Grace."

Amelia considered the girl's words carefully. They made perfect sense, and she was not surprised that tradesfolk were steering clear of her household, at least for now. That would likely change, once word began to circulate of the amount of gold coin the archduchess was ready to spend, especially once her militiamen's backpay was delivered to them. Such would be the task to which Dalflitch had so readily set herself this morning.

"Mathilda, Lady Spindle will likely want to hear an apology from you at a later time," Amelia told the maid. "In the meanwhile, go now to Lady Dalflitch, wherever she is writing her letters, and tell her what you just told me. Also, you are to tell her that I say you have a good pair of ears in your head. Do you understand?"

Mathilda tried to nod, but either fear or growing wisdom caused her to stop and shake her head instead.

"Can you repeat my words to Lady Dalflitch, at least?" Amelia pressed.

"I can do that," Mathilda agreed.

"Then that is enough. Go, do what I have said, and send Agatha in to replace you as you were told."

"Yes, Your Grace." Mathilda curtseyed again and withdrew.

Amelia looked at Spindle, who cocked the eyebrow not covered by her lace mask.

"We have to start with someone," Amelia said to her, and the lady-in-waiting accepted that without question. When Agatha returned, she joined Joan in helping their liege lady to dress for the day.

CHAPTER 17

B y the time Amelia was dressed, a message had been delivered from the baroness of Bridgetown, asking that they should meet at a place called Sougate.

"She doesn't hesitate to summon you about, does she?" Righteous commented with a smirk and a baby in her arms. She had just arrived from tending to her children, wetnurse Emma in tow, who was bearing the other bundle. Emma was a plump, buxom woman who seemed as overawed as the neophytes to find herself in the august company of the archduchess's chamber but never actually let her attention wander far from the infants in her care, so it seemed to matter little to her where she was.

"She is the liege lady of the town," Dalflitch said. As her lady's seneschal, it was she who had actually received the heralds' invitation and presented it to Amelia.

"So? Her grace is ruler of an entire frontier, isn't she?" Righteous retorted, swaying back and forth as she rocked her son gently.

"Do we know where this Sougate is?" Amelia interposed herself into the ladies' conversation, uninterested in another round of which noble owed what respect to whom. Such was the endless fascination of the courts of Rhales and Denay, and the archduchess was becoming thoroughly sick of it all, like a child who had outgrown the simple toys of their infancy and was ready to seek out the toys that would prepare them for their adulthood—the practice swords, the first sewing needles or darning spindles. She was in Bridgetown to pay back the help she had received from the baroness in evacuating her men by training up the town's militia to the Lions' standard. Then she wanted to go home and govern her land in strength and peace.

"I would guess it to be the opposite to Norgate, Your Grace," Dalflitch said, making the obvious seem politic by her tone. "I suppose we step onto the Great Bridge Road and turn south."

Amelia smiled and nodded, then said that she would do exactly that. A short discussion arose as to who would be best to escort her. Since they were all together once more, both Spindle and Righteous were eager to return to their jobs as bodyguards, but it was decided that since there was little known threat at this time, best would be that one Lace Fang would accompany the archduchess, with two neophytes as well, to give the trainees experience with being watchful in public. Lady Dalflitch begged leave to return to her seneschal duties, since the changing of the money was an expensive and complex business.

"For now, the two main chests of gold are held in Master Welburne's strongroom and watched by his most loyal men," the lady-in-waiting explained. "As secure as any place that is not a royal treasury, but so much coin in one location is a temptation to thieves that only grows. The faster we disperse it to pay our debts, the better. With your permission, Your Grace, I mean to send letters to all our creditors in Dweltford so that they may send men to collect their shares from here during the winter."

"Do not forget our militia and their pay," Amelia insisted.

"Without question, Your Grace."

A further swift discussion about whether tending to newborn babies or sewing the finishes to the archduchess's new clothing was more important ended in a tie, and Lady Spindle deferred to Lady Righteous's rank as a bladeswoman, meaning that it was the new mother Lace Fang who stepped out as Archduchess Amelia's escort to the opposite end of town from the previous day—the bastion of Sougate.

"Of course, you knew it would have to be you," Amelia had said to her lady as they made their way through the midmorning crowds on Great Bridge Road. "No matter what *we* wanted, your new best friend, the baroness, would expect me to bring you along."

"As you say, Your Grace," Righteous replied, eyes searching the crowd like a huntress strafing a herd with her predatory gaze. With her black lace mask in place, she was once again a deadly Lace Fang, undiminished by the gentility of motherhood.

If anything, she might be all the more deadly for it, Amelia thought, though she was not exactly sure what gave her that impression. Perhaps it was just such a long while since she had experienced Righteous's oversight.

"Is she a worthy friend, do you think?" Amelia asked Righteous.

"It's not for me to say, Your Grace," Righteous replied, taking note of something in the crowd and looking back to give a signal to the trailing neophytes, walking two paces behind the archduchess. One of the two moved swiftly forward to take up a position slightly ahead. Amelia had no idea why at first, but the crowd shifted suddenly and three bleary-eyed men, clearly half-drunk despite the early hour, came into view, sitting on upturned barrels out in front of a taphouse. One of them spotted Righteous and then Amelia and slapped his friends' shoulders for their attention. Another of the trio whistled his crass appreciation when the leading neophyte escort stepped naturally into their line of sight. She paused to look at them, and one of the men, taking her for a nun, ducked his head and tugged his forelock.

"Sorry, sister," Amelia heard him mumble. "Nothin' meant."

If the neophyte replied, Amelia never heard it, and a moment later the little escort party had moved on through the crowd.

"I had forgotten the sharpness of your instincts, Baroness Righteous," she told her guardian. "Thank you."

"T'is only our duty, Your Grace," Righteous replied.

"Indeed, but as to your previous assertion, you are incorrect. You are a baroness now, and it is most definitely for you to say what your opinion is of our hostess. You may not be exactly equal, but you are the same rank. You are as entitled to have and to express your opinion on the matter as I am."

Righteous stopped dead in the street and stared at the arch-duchess. Even with the mask, her expression made it clear that the Lace Fang was only just now recognizing the truth of her new status. She shook her head slightly, as if to deny the fact, then whistled, her only unladylike gesture on the entire journey so far.

"Well, then...put it that way, Your Grace," she said, turning back to her duty, but keeping up the conversation. "I'd say Baroness Penny wants someone to understand her in the way of things."

"How is that?" Amelia asked. She paused as a mule cart backed into the street suddenly and the three escorts adjusted the points of their defensive triangle once again, keeping their mistress safe.

"You know I come up on the cobbles, runnin' like the boys and such," Righteous returned to her explanation once their journey was orderly again. "She's had something the same—well, the noble version like. Her Da's only child, him widowered and never remarried. She's only had cousins and what all and she's grown up with the boys. That's all fine when they were boys and girls, cause a littlun's a littlun, if you ken my meaning. But now the boys are all wantin' to be knights and they want her to be a maiden and swoon and all that. I think she wants some of that, but she don't want to give up the best bits of runnin' with the lads."

"She told you all that?" Amelia asked, her eyebrows wide with surprise but also with amusement. The more Baroness Penelope's story drew close to her own, the more the former street fighter's accent slipped back to the alleyway speech of her childhood.

"Not in words," Righteous explained. "A lot's just my feelin'. But she's so nervous, and so lookin' for an older woman to tell her it's all alright. No mam, no sisters, and sounds like she never had a Matron Bettina of her own. My thinkin' is that's prob'ly why she gave Lord Farringdon those boats in the first place. She's heard tell of this powerful duchess lady from the west who held her lands against monsters and enemies, turned out any nobles that wouldn't accept her, and even raised herself to a new spot in the world—an *arch*duchess. And you've got a pride of lionesses around you, all steel claws and fearlessness. Baroness Penelope's heard all these stories, and she can't decide if she wants to be *like* you or to *be* you, Your Grace. What she most surely wants is for you and she and me to be best friends, sisters in spirit against the world. She isn't a man, and she's scared she doesn't know how to be a woman, or even if she wants to be. That's why she's pinned so much hope on your friendship, Your Grace. And on mine, so it seems."

The Great Bridge Road crowd began to thin, and ahead, the open air of a span like the final bridge near Norgate came into view. A small company of orange- and gold-tabarded militia were holding back a handful of curious onlookers, but as they approached, the herald twins noticed Amelia and her ladies, and the women were ushered swiftly through the blockade. Ten or so paces further on, a group of horses were being held by bored-looking pages, and Amelia was sure she recognized her husband's mount amongst them. Then she noticed Prentice's Boots, the bay easily distinguished by his white socks. Ahead of the horses, a crowd of patricians and few nobles were flocking about behind the unmistakable figure of the armored baroness. Beside her, a standard bearer held aloft the lady's banner with its heraldic bear in gold.

"Thank you for your opinion, Lady Righteous," Amelia said quietly as they crossed the final distance to their appointment. "You have given me much to think about."

"It ain't...that is, it isn't, all my own thinking, Your Grace," Righteous said, nodding her head to accept her liege's thanks. "I had a lot of these notions sorted out for myself only a little while back by a very canny midwife in Fallenhill."

Amelia cocked an eyebrow, then put her hand on Righteous's in an earnest gesture of friendship.

"Thank God for true elders, My Lady," she said, and then turned to present herself for her morning appointment.

CHAPTER 18

"Archduchess Amelia," Baroness Penelope said merrily as the two noblewomen bowed to one another. "I hadn't expected you to be able to pull yourself away from your morning duties so readily, nor your knights commander and captain theirs."

Amelia looked askance to see Prentice and Farringdon standing slightly off to one side, both in their uniforms and armor. Baroness Penelope herself was surrounded once again by a dozen or so mostly young men in fine clothes and polished steel, but Amelia's two officers were still distinctive, even though they were dressed in much the same style. Amelia kept the main of her attention on the baroness, since that was polite, but in the back of her mind, her thoughts turned over the reason why her men seemed so shabby next to Bridgetown's predominantly youthful nobles. Was she not buying them the uniforms they deserved? Were they failing to respect them? With money once again of no concern for her, one of those should be simple to solve. The other possibility was even less of a concern. If there was one fear the archduchess no longer suffered, it was that these two men might disrespect her or the roles they had in her service. If any woman was better loved as a liege than Amelia was, history had not recorded the fact, of that she was certain.

"No doubt you are wondering if I am touring you through our fortifications," the baroness was saying, having taken the moment of Amelia's thoughtful distraction to greet Righteous as well. She then turned to look at what must surely be Sougate, guarding Bridgetown's southern entrance over a span nearly fifty paces in length. Whereas Norgate was little more than a symbolic defense, a mere barbican, it turned out Sougate was a true fortification, with a large gatehouse, curtain walls to the left and right, and impressive turrets sprouting like mighty pillars. Clearly this was designed with war in mind, not merely the mimicry of fortification which a long-peaceful town in the Grand Kingdom might have.

Well trade or not, we are still officially at war with the Vec, Amelia thought as she regarded the striking bastion. Vec princes had long ceased trying to assault Bridgetown, and this edifice made it obvious why.

"I am at your disposal, My Lady," Amelia said, turning from the fortification to the baroness once more.

"It shames me to admit that the Usurper's men have troubled me at both ends of my great town," Penelope said sadly and there were dutifully grim mutters from the gathered nobles.

"Daven Marcus' men?" Amelia asked, astonished. How could Duke Robant have men on this side of the river as well?

"The last of the rogues who terrorized our smallfolk so mercilessly," said a tall young man in silvered mail and a sky-blue linen cloak with a fur collar. "The cowards have shut themselves up against us." He sniffed and tilted his head back as he looked at Sougate, as if its very presence offended him.

"My apologies, good Sir," Amelia said to him. "I have not had the pleasure of your name."

The young man looked about to introduce himself when Penelope interposed.

"This is another of my cousins, Archduchess—Cyprian, from the other side of the family than Wilforn, whom you met yesterday. Beyond him there is his brother Cassian. They are the leaders of the Young Hopefuls."

"No more than first amongst equals, Your Grace," Cyprian said, and he bowed formally. Beside him, his brother, equally resplendent in mail but without a cloak, the sky-blue instead found in the slashes of his doublet sleeves, bowed less gracefully.

"The Young Hopefuls? What are they, My Lady?" Amelia asked, having heard the term more than once now since arriving in Bridgetown.

"Would-be knights, Your Grace," Penelope answered readily, and Amelia noticed a shadow pass over Cyprian's face, while his brother Cassian openly scowled. Amelia wasn't even sure she understood what Penelope was saying, but it was clear to her that neither young man enjoyed having their situation so described. Her uncertainty must have shown on her own face however, as after a moment, the baroness began to offer an explanation.

"The Usurper's night of blood was especially brutal for Bridgetown, Your Grace," she said, describing the feast at which Daven Marcus had publicly slain his father and any nobles who dared to object. "Most of our knights martial were present, having answered the call of King Chrostmer. We know little of the specifics, but we do know that Bridgetown kept its honor that night, and none knelt to the kingslayer. Some fought their way free of the massacre, only to be hunted down before they could reach home. By pure miraculous mercy, my father and uncle had been called away that evening to escort worthies from the king's court. An unremarkable duty that proved their salvation."

From the baroness's expression, it was clear she was deeply thankful that her elder relatives had not been slaughtered during the Usurper's rebellion.

"Since that time, any men who had been squires, or who would have become such, have had no knights here in town to take their pledge and no true king or prince to present them their spurs or longswords. Noble born but bereft of sponsors, they are rudderless in the stream of life."

"Bereft, but not without hope," Cyprian said smoothly. "Hence our title 'Young Hopefuls'."

If the baroness resented his interjection, she did not show it.

"They look forward to a day when a new king will be crowned, and they can again continue their journey to full knighthood. In the meantime, they maintain themselves as a kind of fellowship, modelled after the dueling societies of the Vec."

"A mere stopgap measure," Cyprian added. "But surely better than simple despair. At least this way we may still be of service to our town...and our liege."

His acknowledgement of the baroness came a fraction late, as if an afterthought, but Amelia hardly noticed.

"Are all these men Hopefuls?" she asked, noting that at least a few of the other men around her were grey haired and plainly too old to be squires seeking knighthood's spurs. Youths or greybeards only, the men of middle age present all wore the black robes of guildmasters and merchants, except for the haphazard Bridgetown militia, of course.

"Goodness, no, Your Grace," the baroness said lightly with a small laugh. If the men gathered around her shared her humor, it did not show. "These are the few others who have taken refuge here when their lands were conquered or were already too old to fight another war."

Baroness Penelope's eyes ranged over the well-groomed men. She raised a hand in the direction of one, her mouth open as if she meant to introduce him, then she paused, looking the small crowd over once again. Amelia wondered if the young noblewoman had just realized that she didn't know all the men present by name.

What would the Inquisition need of skin thieves in Bridgetown? the archduchess wondered. *The liege cannot even name her closest courtiers.*

"You know, there's to be a banquet soon in your honor, Your Grace," Penelope said at last, covering her failure, it seemed, by pretending to have just thought of something. "That would be the best time to make formal introductions, I think."

When you have heralds and stewards at hand to remind you of the obscure names? Amelia wondered and had to force herself not to smile. She understood the sheer effort a ruler had to make simply to show respect to their underlings and courtiers. It was a profession unto itself, and Amelia had always appreciated the efforts of her servants to help her with the duty. *Dalflitch, Turley, and Bettina. I have been as well bestowed as any peer, I do not doubt.*

"I'm sure, gentles, that you will not resent that my cousins have jumped the line on you," the baroness said to the gathering. "The Hopefuls are all young and courageous. Holding back is not in their nature."

As the men made muttered agreements, Penelope leaned in conspiratorially to whisper in Amelia's ear.

"Truth be told, I've known most of them only a handful of days. They knew my father, but while the Usurper's men were in charge, these all went into hiding lest they be dragged out and tried for not swearing allegiance to the kingslayer's throne. Even my uncle made an art of dodging the rebel knights, though he at least found ways to remain in public doing it."

All at once Amelia's confusion about these brightly attired nobles and the comparison with Prentice and Farringdon evaporated, like steam from a hot pan. There was the wear and tear of the march on her men's panoply—patches where stains could not be fully washed out of the cloth, scratches and minor dents that could not be polished out of steel and were too deep for a campaign blacksmith to easily hammer away. The men of Bridgetown were too young or too old to have fought in this latest and bloodiest of the Grand Kingdom's wars. The sudden juxtaposition brought an involuntary smirk to Amelia's lips. Her men looked the shabbier, but it was a shabbiness that spoke to power and experience that everyone else present lacked, most especially these two leaders of the "Young Hopefuls." She glanced at Cyprian and his brother, noticing that the disdainful Cassian was already watching her closely. Suspecting that the arrogant young man might be thin-skinned into the bargain, she quickly schooled her smile.

"So many injustices have been visited upon all our lands by the Usurper," she said to the baroness, to bring the conversation back on point. "What I do not understand is how his sworn men might be in this fortification to hold it against you, Baroness. Is this not the wrong side of the river?"

CHAPTER 19

"On the night of the late Earl John's death," the man named Cassian said, "we managed several successes, including capturing, trying, and executing the ringleaders of Daven Marcus' occupation. Nevertheless, our efforts fell short, and we were unable to prevent a clutch of his honorless dogs here in the Sougate from shutting the doors and gates to us. They have repulsed our assaults and have been holed up there like ferrets in a deep hole ever since. Of course, I accept full responsibility."

Prentice listened to the young man's explanation and found his opinion of the frustrated squire hardening. There was something about it that sounded like the typical young Grand Kingdom nobleman, feigning humility but actually feeling that nothing was truly his fault. At least that was Prentice's impression, which was only reinforced when Farringdon leaned in close.

"I would bet my own toes that not one of them thought to secure the gatehouses that night," the marquis whispered. "Men of action but not consideration, I would say."

"Young and unguided," Prentice whispered in return, nodding without looking to Farringdon, not wanting to seem impolite by having their own conversation in front of the ranking peers. He looked at the confident Cyprian and then past him to his brother. Cassian had been the confrontational young man who had brought Prentice the baroness's summons, and he could well believe the youth modelled himself on duelists from the princedoms. With a much more fluid social structure than the Grand

Kingdom, the Vec had significantly more complex pathways for martially minded men to rise and fall in status. Knightly tourneys were fewer in the south but opened to many more, even those of non-noble status. The dueling societies, and other martial academies existed to fill the gap in training and experience that the lack of strict knightly advancement provided. The Seven Rings Cross and the Three Streets Vipers, whose masters had taught Prentice and his wife respectively in childhood, were both fighting styles and schools which had originated in the Vec. It was an odd social context, which led to its own rivalries, battles, and civil strife. The rigid social structure of the Grand Kingdom might be a clear form of tyranny, but the dueling societies of the Vec could turn towns into battlegrounds, rivals challenging one another over every tiny slight. The young man Cassian was of that kind, Prentice was sure of it.

"Baron Prentice, you have a reputation as a gate taker," Archduchess Amelia's voice penetrated Prentice's thoughts. "What would you say?"

"Your Grace?" Prentice asked, hoping she would realize he needed her to repeat the question.

"In your opinion, what would be the best way for Bridgetown to evict the Usurper's mongrels and install good men and true?" the archduchess asked. "While the gate is closed, trade with the Vec is greatly reduced."

Choking off the tariffs which keep the nobility in coin, Prentice noticed Archduchess Amelia did not add, even though the notion could not be far from anyone's mind in this gathering, even the Young Hopefuls, whose attentions were ostensibly only fixed on matters of honor. He shook his head. No one here wanted his opinion on taxation and dispensations to the nobility. He turned to face the Sougate bastion itself, and as he did so, noticed that the bridge between there and the spot where everyone stood had been soot-stained and spiked in a number of places by fallen crossbow bolts. Prentice sought out the one nearest.

"I take it that is about the limit of their range?" he asked.

"Range?" the baroness replied, but the cousin, Cyprian, had Prentice's meaning.

"No one has been struck any farther out than that," he answered.

Of course not, Prentice thought. *Because even you green-blades aren't foolish enough to let your liege stand in the open like this if she was in range of a deadly shot. But if that is their range, they have no warbows or full crossbows up there.*

The point with the nearest bolt was no more than forty paces from the bastion, by no means long range for true archers. The companies of crossbowmen the archduchess and the Lion Banner had faced in Aubrey would not be challenged by that distance. Fey archers would likely consider it still in close range.

"And the scorching of the door and bridge?" he asked. This time the Hopefuls were not eager to answer, and when Baroness Penelope looked to Cyprian, he turned to his brother, who scowled as if he meant to refuse to speak. At last, he looked to Prentice.

"We tried to use black powder to blast open the door," Cassian said bitterly. "But it was too strong. We burned the bridge, and they mocked us while we had to put the fire out. Useless damned stuff!"

"We have heard that you have had some successes with new ways of war," Cyprian added. "Alas, we find that the proven ways are more reliable."

Smooth, Prentice thought, watching the older brother protect the younger's pride. *How many pointless battles have your swift words saved him from?*

"Can it be done, Baron?" the archduchess asked.

"Blasting the door with powder or taking the bastion, Your Grace?" Prentice responded reflexively.

"For a man who is supposed to have all the answers, your knight commander seems to ask many questions, Your Grace," Baroness Penelope commented lightly. There were some chuckles from the hangers-on, and the brothers both smiled, Cassian most contemptuously. "His reputation is for boldness, isn't it, not talk?"

Prentice ignored the sycophants and looked only to his liege. She smiled at him, but he was sure it was not with pleasure at hearing his reputation questioned.

"Baron Prentice asks many questions so that he may light upon the best and shortest path to his prize," the archduchess replied with a raised voice. "Boldness is admirable, but without wisdom to guide it, it only results in scorched boards and damaged bridges."

The Young Hopefuls' smiles froze on their faces, as if they had just been slapped, and several of the crowd chuckled quietly again. Baroness Penelope laughed openly and clapped her hands together, as if the archduchess were her jester.

Not another one who thinks this is all for jest, Prentice thought. When nobles played politics as a great game, too many ordinary lives were lost, swept away like pieces taken off a board.

"Black powder is the marquis knight captain's area of expertise," Prentice said, eager to keep the interchange on the core military matters. The more talk was drawn into social interchanges, the more likely it was he would say something that would embarrass his liege. Besides, Archduchess Amelia could more than hold her own with these amateurs. If there was a more astute politician in the Grand Kingdom than the liege of the Reach, man or woman, Prentice had never heard of them. He turned to Farringdon. "Could it be done?"

"Sappers' art," Farringdon said, considering the door. "It has to do with placement so that the force and fire are focused inward, not outward."

"Such a thing is possible?" the baroness asked, but her cousins only scoffed. Wisely, Farringdon ignored them.

"It is, My Lady," the marquis knight captain said soberly. "I have only a rudimentary understanding of the science, but I believe the best tool for the task is called a petard. Its manufacture is something of an art unto itself."

Baroness Penelope's lightly mocking expression transformed into one of burgeoning respect.

"Would you need such a device to reclaim Sougate?" she asked.

Farringdon turned to Prentice, deferring to military rank.

"No, My Lady," Prentice said, flattered by Farringdon's humility.

"You captured Dweltford's gatehouse back from rebels in less than one night, Baron Gate-taker," the archduchess said, giving Prentice a nickname he'd never had before. "Could you do it again?"

"We could, Your Grace," he told her.

"One night?" Cassian scoffed. "Go right ahead."

"Mind your tongue lad, these are peers of the realm you speak to," Farringdon said suddenly, and Prentice looked at him in shock. He hadn't realized the marquis's patience was wearing so thin.

"Is that so?" Cassian demanded, and his hands went to his blade. Prentice steeled himself, ready to interpose his body between the young man and the archduchess. He noticed that his wife, standing a pace behind their liege with the two neophytes, had her hands in her wing sleeves, also ready to draw if needs be. Thankfully, the young man's brother intervened once more.

"Forgive us, My Lord Marquis," Cyprian said as he put a hand on his brother's arm. "Bold, but not too restrained sometimes."

Most laughed at the pacifying jest, but Cassian himself only stared daggers at the two Reach men-at-arms.

This fool's going to make trouble for us no matter what we do, Prentice thought. It was an unpleasant notion, but what disturbed him most was how easy this kind of belligerence would make it for the Inquisition to get close. A cluster of fools would be the perfect distraction for an assassin to exploit. But that was a matter for later.

"Your Grace, with no insult intended to yourself, Bridgetown's Sougate is a significantly greater challenge than Dweltford's town gate," he said, and was about to explain why when Cassian cut across him, speaking out of turn yet again.

"So, you can't do it! Not in a night, not ever! Just a frontier braggart," the young man spat.

"You go too far, Cassian!" Baroness Penelope said, aghast. She looked back with a fearful expression.

For his part, Prentice held his temper, ignored the insult, and looked to the archduchess. She nodded, giving him permission to respond. The knight commander smiled in thanks and turned to Bridgetown's liege.

"My Lady, if it would please you, the White Lions will undertake to recapture the Sougate for you," he said.

Baroness Penelope all but beamed at him.

"Delightful, Baron," she said, managing not to clap her hands together again somehow, though it seemed a struggle. Prentice then looked to Cassian, still held back by his brother's restraining hand.

"It will likely take some days of observation yet," he told the brash squire. "But when the time comes for us to capture the bastion, I promise you it will be in one night."

"On your honor, Baron?" Baroness Penelope asked.

Honor? Prentice thought. *What do I care for "my" honor?*

Nevertheless, he nodded at the baroness. What else was there to do?

CHAPTER 20

"Fool's going to get himself killed," Farringdon said coldly in the night, speaking of Cassian.

"Likely so, My Lord Captain," Sergeant Nunel agreed quietly, "but word around town is that he's more than a dab hand with that sidesword. All the Young Hopefuls are the belligerent type, so it's said—giving and accepting challenges for the drop of a hat—but this Cassian fellow, he's their finest. Better even than his older brother, apparently."

"Silence, we're close," hissed Dahyoor, seated in the prow of their boat.

In the darkness, Prentice could not see how Marquis Farringdon felt being ordered about by a fey who was a mere squire, but he suspected the former prince would take no umbrage. The boat they were in was likely no more than ten or fifteen paces from the southern bank of the Murr. By any measure, they were now in enemy territory. Their hired craft shuddered momentarily as the keel struck bottom, but it lifted again almost at once.

"We are unseen," came the whispered announcement from the prow. Prentice hoped that meant they were literally not noticed on the south bank and not that his "squire" was merely reciting the proverb. They were trusting Dahyoor's superior night sight to watch for sentries. Prentice leaned over in the boat and put his hand on each man's shoulder—the agreed signal for silence from now on. Unless Prentice spoke to a man directly, no one was to talk.

"What if we get into trouble?" one of the picked men had asked as Prentice had outlined the night's mission to them earlier. "If someone comes on us out of the dark, like?"

"Then deal with him quietly," Sergeant Nunel had told the man. Since both were of the lancers, it was within Nunel's place to respond.

"That's well and good," Guillam had added, taking up the other grouser's argument. "But what if it's more'n one comes up on us? What if we can't take 'em quietly?"

"Then do your best to take the mongrels with you as you die, Sergeant," Prentice had told his insouciant officer with the cheeky grin. Both Guillam and Porth, the two senior corporals of the Gryphon banner, had been quietly and quickly promoted to sergeants after the meeting on the Sougate bridge. The rest of their ordering of ranks was still postponed. "That way, the rest of us will be able to sneak away safely."

Guillam had touched his finger to the side of his nose in the yeoman fashion of acknowledging a joke, but the lancers in the mixed team of militiamen had looked aghast. A squad of ten men, half Gryphons of Prentice's choosing, half Lions picked from the lancers by Knight Captain Farringdon, none of the second half had ever actually served directly under Prentice. They were unfamiliar with his battlefield humor.

"He's jesting," Farringdon had reassured them. "I swear it is we who will have to drag the knight commander from the fight, if it comes to steel in the 'partlight. He will not abandon us."

A pretty compliment, My Lord, Prentice thought, remembering the knight captain's words as the boat touched bottom a second time and then held fast. *But one I am unsure I deserve.*

Prentice never planned to leave any under his command behind, even at the cost of his own life, but nevertheless, he had, at times, and knew he would again if more men's lives depended upon it. In the dark watches like this he remembered Sir Gant's salute across the waters and the cracking shots of the loyal five gunners, who kept up their Roar fire until the deluge had swept them away. Then he remembered that they had had to drag him off the Redlander bridge to keep him from throwing himself into the water and swimming after his friend. And he had knelt on the back of the Serpent Witch and refused to flinch from the flood so that the blood she had shed, Reacherman and fey, could be avenged.

Troubling thoughts are for safer hours than this, he told himself and set his mind on the mission.

His original plan had been for Dahyoor and himself, possibly with one other, to sneak across the channel from Bridgetown into the Vec and around in the dark to look at the other side of the Sougate fortification. Baroness Penelope insisted that Sougate had no provisions for siege in it when it had been shut up. No one had seen the besieged men fishing or trying to escape, so that meant they would surely be hungry by now. They should soon be starving, in fact, unless they had found some other source of supply. They almost *had* to be buying food from the Vec side. Prentice wanted to see that side to know for certain.

As soon as he heard the plan however, Knight Captain Farringdon had insisted on coming along, and that had changed things. Both senior officers could not go alone, or even with Dahyoor. It was simply too great a risk. That meant that they had to bring an escort, and so a two-man mission had become a ten-man expedition. Prentice knew the marquis's insistence was not based in pride or folly. Farringdon truly was their greatest expert on black powder, especially now that Yentow Sent was dead. It made sense for the marquis to see the bastion from all sides to get the best understanding of how the explosive alchemy might be applied to the siege, if needed. Blasting away the door, for example, might prove fruitless if it risked collapsing a wall that, while it might look imposing, was only good for keeping men out, not for withstanding siege engines.

The picked squad maneuvered themselves over the sides of their boat, lowering their bodies into the water as quietly as they could. None were wearing armor in case it came to a swim for safety at some point, and all had their faces and any other bare skin smeared with ground charcoal mixed with tallow. The same blacking coated any of their metal and the blades in their scabbards—anything that might seem bright when the light of the Rampart or moon hit it. Up to their waists and sure of their footing, Farringdon's four lancers reached back into the boat, and each took out a bundle wrapped in waterproof oilskins. These contained their short wheellock firearms, usually fired from horseback.

"Their trigger mechanisms need no wick, so no tell-tale smoke before they shoot. They are fired by a spark scratched on a spring-loaded flint within," the knight captain had emphasized to Prentice when he explained why he had brought only lancers and no men more practiced at fighting afoot. "Each has a pair, and the shock of a powder blast close in the night will be no small advantage if it does come to combat."

Prentice had agreed, accepting the explanation of the triggers. As the lancers held their wrapped weapons high above the water-line, so too Dahyoor held his bow and arrows in their embroidered leather case over his head. The top of the bow poked out, but the horse archer had unstrung the weapon for the crossing to keep the string from any moisture at all, since a wet string could stretch and become useless all too easily.

We are still four times what I would have preferred, Prentice thought as they stalked up through the riverside reeds to find the edge of the fields. There was an old east-west road somewhere nearby, which followed the river off toward the tiny earldom of Longshepherds. The road was in some disrepair, and word was the prince of Town Sobridge, the Vec land they were currently prowling through, had fallen out with the earl and ordered the road closed. Nevertheless, the beaten path was a recognizable landmark for them to follow in the shadows, and when they found it, they turned toward the Sougate bastion, keeping their heads low so that the dark shape might be recognizable against the starlit sky. They needn't have bothered.

"Are they besieged or hosting a festival?" Farringdon whispered in an astonished tone as the infiltrators stopped on the roadside to see their first glimpse of the strongpoint from the enemy direction. Not that they were enemies, it seemed. Daven Marcus's holed-up knights seemed quite at peace with the Vec. On the Bridgetown side, Sougate and the bridge it guarded were in near-total darkness, with not a single light to see by. The besieged knights inside had lit none, and no lamplighters of Bridgetown had dared the enemy's crossbow shots to light the bridge's lanterns. On this side however, there were several lights blazing, including two braziers, one each side above the closed main gate, and what looked like an oil lamp hanging near the base of the far side turret. From that distant corner, there came the sound of raised voices—not in anger but calling back and forth, as if speaking at a distance.

"I want to see what that's about," Prentice whispered, and the line of skulkers moved off once more. They kept to the side of the old road near the reeds, but soon that relative safety failed them. They were nearing the intersection with the Great Bridge Road, which meant a sprint over open ground made worse by the fact that Veckander rural roads were often made of nothing more than crushed limestone and thus were white. In the night, the sneaks would be black shadows moving against the pale rock, and a vigilant sentry would have a fair chance of spotting them. Better than fair even, if the besieged garrison was canny and bold enough to have a sentry hiding out in the shadows of the field somewhere. Then there was the crunch their sodden boots would make. Prentice tapped Dahyoor on the shoulder and the two led the way across, crouching swiftly once they reached the grass on the other side. There was nothing long to hide in here, though. Unlike on the north side of the river, where Duke Robant's army had made planting and harvesting the nearby fields pointless, the farmers of Town Sobridge's lands had mowed the hay in the meadows and gathered it into stacks already.

Early harvest? Prentice thought as he kept watch while others sprinted the open road. *The prince of Town Sobridge thinks war is coming. Does that mean* he *has sentries posted on this road as well? Or post riders?*

He shot a cautious glance south, to where the dangerous pale road stretched away into the darkness. Even if the foreign prince had the trade route well patrolled, there should be little chance of any enemies coming so close to the Sougate bastion. If it had been daylight, Town Sobridge itself, the town from which the princedom took its name –the "Town South of the Bridge"– should have been visible on the horizon. Doubtless, there were lanterns there now, but the distance was far too great for anything but the largest signal fire to penetrate the night. If there were post riders out there, they were not using lanterns to see by either. Dahyoor's superior sight raised no warnings from the shadows.

At last, the ten infiltrators were across the road without any sign of Veckander might, and they began to work their way over the mown field to where the lamps were glimmering at the foot of the eastern turret. Careful to stay well back in the shadows, they watched the pool of light against the stone footings.

"Postern gate," Farringdon whispered, identifying the narrow single door they could see built into the base of the tower. Typically hidden away in a tight corner, a postern gate, also called a sallyport, was a common feature of many fortifications. Made so that it could only be approached single file and usually as awkward on the inside as on the outside, the postern allowed the defenders to sneak small groups of men-at-arms in and out of a besieged fortification for scouting or to sally forth, to flank an assault on the main gate. Their tiny size and relatively awkward positions made the openings all but useless for an attacking enemy to exploit. Even if besiegers could reach the postern with a sizable force, they would only be able to enter it single file, while from above defenders would hurl all manner of attacks down upon them. Looking to the overhanging parapet, Prentice was sure some version of the boiling water cauldrons on the roof Norgate were waiting there to punish foolish sorties if they were manned for defense. For now, though, the postern was open, with an iron lantern hanging hooked on the door's corner. A man-at-arms with a sheathed longsword to hand was lounging against the door jamb while a pair of farmwomen chatted with him, baskets at their feet. Likely they were selling bread and eggs, or similar victuals, to keep the knights inside well bestowed with food.

"Well, we won't be starving them out in a hurry," Farringdon observed.

"No," Prentice said, chewing the inside of his cheek as he watched.

"Could we do as you did with the Dweltford gate? Take them in a rush?"

There was a quiet scoffing sound from one of the militiamen in the dark. It was impossible to know whom, though Prentice was ready to put money on Guillam, just as a matter of course.

"I do not like our chances," he told Farringdon, agreeing with the scoffer, whomever he was. "We might get to the door before our friend there closed it, but even if we did, it would be beyond unlikely that we could take him in silence. Then we would have all the joys of a postern gate to experience."

"Tight confines and the defenders on the battlement showering their respects down on us," Farringdon agreed. "I wouldn't hurry to praise the builders of Norgate, but Sougate's architect knew his trade."

"I could bring all three to the dirt before the women raise an alarm," Dahyoor said in his usual flat tone. There was a soft creaking sound which indicated he was refitting his weapon's string.

"We are not women-slayers," Farringdon whispered in the dark, clearly horrified at the prospect.

"No," was all Prentice said, knowing that that was all Dahyoor would need to hear. The creaking stopped, but it was more likely the fey man had finished stringing than anything else.

The infiltrators crouched in the stubbled field, watching silently for a long space. The farmwomen chatted with the gate sentry, soft giggles echoing in the night now and again. At this distance, it seemed the man-at-arms was trying to entice one or both to a tryst and they were flirting with the notion. Prentice wasn't surprised by that. There would be more than one bored farmwife who married young and still dreamed of being swept away on a mighty destrier by a knight in armor, all flashing metal and glory of youth. And perhaps the women were happy to play, with no more dreams than flirting. Maybe they held the man-at-arms by *their* strings, extracting every coin they could for their wares before fading away back to their farms, to leave the besieged knights to dream of *them*. Either way, if this was a typical evening's trade, Prentice liked this as a possible way to exploit the postern after all.

"We'll come back a few more nights and watch," he said. "If this is the norm, we'll get ourselves ready and bring some of her grace's neophytes. They can play the part of the farmwives for us and put a knife to the sentry before he can sound the alarm. Then we can use the postern to breach the gate."

In the dark, Prentice could almost feel the men beside him nodding. Nevertheless, Farringdon still had an objection.

"I know the talk is that the Usurper's men are as arrogant as he," the knight captain said. "But if the knights inside know their business even half as well as they should, they will have other men positioned within at the head of the postern steps, at least, to raise the alarm should their sentry be overwhelmed."

"Of course," Prentice replied readily. "When the time comes, we will make sure our 'farmwives' have a heavy basket full of fresh butchered beef, something awkward that will take two men to carry."

"And the sentry will have to call his support down to the door to help?" Farringdon said, his tone making it clear he understood the cunning of the plan.

"When he does, we will send a signal to Lions on the bridge, have them make an assault on the gate to distract the watchers above," Prentice added. "That way, any alarm raised by the postern gate should be lost in the distraction from the Bridgetown side, leastwise long enough to get inside."

"Canny," someone breathed out of the darkness, but one of his fellows shushed him.

"Mayhaps," Prentice answered the unauthorized comment. However cunning the plan might seem in its bare bones, he had no doubt it could easily go utterly astray. If it worked, it would seem like genius. But if the garrison had more than one extra sentry, if there was a second lockable door inside the postern with murder holes in the ceiling and a manned chamber above, if the sentries on the battlement knew their business and were diligent to look in all directions even as they defended against an "attack" from one side? There were a thousand and one ways his "canny" plan could become a dog's breakfast, with Lions dead to pay the price for its failure. Now that he had seen the bastion from all sides, he would set other sentries to cross the river and watch from this side for a few nights. While they did that, he would polish his "canny" plan until he made it as close to infallible as he could. This was not the Dweltford gatehouse, and his liege's army was not trapped outside the town with winter coming, as they had been then. He could afford to be patient with this objective.

"Time to head back," he whispered, but as they raised themselves up to move off, a noise came in the night that made them all freeze.

CHAPTER 21

It was a resonant, low beat, barely audible in the dark. As anyone confronted with an unexpected noise when sneaking about, the entire infiltrator party held themselves taut, halfway between crouched down and standing to move, choking on the instinct to panic and run. The silence stretched on, making the darkness seem alive, every unseen shadow an imminent foe. Prentice looked to the two flirtatious women and the object of their attentions. The three were continuing their conversing in a way that made it almost certain they had not heard the noise Prentice's men had. Either that, or they were acting better than any mummers or minstrels he had ever seen, pretending to obliviousness to serve as bait for his men. Prentice was almost certain they were not such ingenious performers.

The sound happened again, and everyone strained to hear it. This time it was punctuated by a soft rattle.

"Bowshot, north, on the bridge across the water," Dahyoor whispered. "Not fey bows. The ugly wood and iron *kreff* ones."

Crossbow shots? Prentice wondered.

"Other side of the bastion?" someone mused—Nunel, by the sound of his voice. "What's going...?"

His rhetorical question was cut short by cries of alarm from the Sougate battlement. Those cries multiplied and mixed with a new noise—a heavy, rumbling, thumping sound, like an empty hogshead barrel being rolled over cobblestones. The sentry at the postern stepped out three paces to look up at the battlements overhead. The farmwives asked him questions, but he waved them away distractedly. He shouted for attention from the sentry above but was not given any response. He clearly decided whatever emergency was unfolding, he did not need to wait for clarification. Pushing both women away, giving one a rushed kick to make his meaning unmistakable, he darted inside, pulling the postern gate behind him. The two women stared at the door a moment and then looked up, no doubt hearing the growing clamor on the rooftop.

"Someone's assaulting Sougate," Farringdon said with a tone that showed he found the notion as inconceivable as everyone else crouched in that enemy field. "From Bridgetown? We gave no commands to attack, and Amelia trusts us enough to wait at least until dawn for our return."

She trusts us a long throw farther than that, My Lord, Prentice thought. He already had a strong suspicion who would be casting themselves upon the barbican across the burned and damaged bridge.

"It ain't that lacklustre militia of theirs, surely," Nunel muttered, clearly feeling bolder in the growing racket of combat coming from Sougate.

"If it is, then I will give you odds our brash young friends are with them, leading the charge," Prentice said as he watched the two farmwives decide to make themselves scarce, disappearing into the night, thankfully heading in a south-westerly direction. If the attack had come a few moments later, he and his scouts and those women would probably have run into one another in those fields. It would have been a disaster, leading to their discovery, or worse, the death of the two women just to keep the secrecy of their mission. The restraint he had placed on Dahyoor would have been for nought.

"The Young Hopefuls, you think, Commander?" Farringdon asked. "Why? They were there when the baroness gave the duty to us. Why would they do this now?"

"*Because* the duty was given to us, if I had to guess," Prentice muttered, but he was only half listening to the marquis knight captain at this point. Slapping Dahyoor on the shoulder, he gave the signal that they should move off but not back toward the boat. He was heading straight toward Sougate.

"They're tryin' to gazump us, you think, My Lord?" Guillam said easily, and from the sound of his voice, it was clear that he was keeping up with Prentice and his squire in the night. Trust the convict corporal to see what Prentice had seen—an errant rogue from his earliest years, in any other profession Guillam would have been an inevitable criminal. In the militia, he was one of the Gryphon Company's shrewdest.

"Knight Commander, where are we going?" Farringdon asked, likely using formality to cover his confusion.

"There," Prentice said and pointed to the postern, trusting that the lamplight would silhouette his gesturing finger for them all to see. The sentry and his farmwife flirts were gone, and the postern door was pulled but the lamp remained. And the ring it hung from was now jammed between the postern door and the wall, preventing it from being fully closed.

CHAPTER 22

Prentice could hardly believe the sentry had been fool enough to leave the postern door unbolted, but trapped men tended to think poorly, especially men-at-arms frustrated by being cooped up and waiting for rescue, unable to come to grips with the enemy. Again, it could be a trap, but with each moment that passed, Prentice was surer it would not be. A deception like that would take the kind of cunning displayed by a Bluebird or a skin thief to engineer, and if those servants of the Inquisition were so far ahead of him in plotting, Prentice might as well put the fetters on his own feet and march himself to the gibbet right now.

"What if there's another man on the inside, like you said?" Farringdon asked.

"Then he will be the first to die," Dahyoor answered.

Prentice held his hand up in front of the fey, stopping him short. Others came to a halt as well.

"This could all go completely astray," Prentice said quietly, tension making his whispering voice almost sound like a hiss. "We must be swift and tight together, but watch the battlements. If you see anything falling on us, anything at all, shout your warning and dash back out. Head to the riverbank as fast as you can and swim for Bridgetown—best will be the jetty on the east tip of Greenmarsh Island. Watch for the currents. If one of them sweeps you away, you will be done for. There are hostiles on either bank, so once you miss the islands of the town, your choice will be whether you want to run from Duke Robant's forces or the Vec prince's."

"Assumin' we don't drown," Guillam observed.

"Pleasant set of options," Nunel added. Farringdon clicked his tongue at these lapses of discipline, but both men had already said their piece.

"One last thing," Prentice added, already moving forward once more. "This is bandit work, no mistake. We are bushwhackers and cutthroats, but I want no murder tonight. Mark me, if a man goes on his knee and offers up his arms, you spare him, is that clear? If you can hold him prisoner, all the better, but if you cannot, shove him back out the postern and let him run for it. The Veckanders can handle him."

"Are none to die?" Dahyoor asked.

"What, no killin' at all?" Guillam asked, making it clear he could hardly believe such a command.

"I am saying I want no *murders*. If some fool will not yield and you have to fight for your life, then do whatever you must. We are not saints and sacrists on the way to holy prayers here. But if they will yield, let them."

That was that last thing Prentice said before he moved off again. On the parapet overhead, there was a growing sound of melee—shouts and clashes of arms. Still, Prentice kept looking from the crenulations to the unbarred door and back, ears straining for any slight sound that might warn of an ambush waiting to spring. He was sure Dahyoor would sense anything first, before anyone else, but that did little to relieve his tension. He nearly flinched from the guttering lamplight but forced himself into its full glow and put a hand on the door, eyes straying upwards. He felt like a field mouse, watching the sky for the plunging talons of a hunting hawk. Still there was nothing from above but the sounds of affray. The postern opened readily, and Prentice swung around it, drawn sword leading. Inside, the tight passage twisted almost immediately into a spiral staircase, exactly the kind of thing he had expected. Committed now, he moved inside just as a heavy wooden and metallic crash sounded.

"Someone just fell from the walls onto the bridge," a man behind him muttered, but any more sounds were instantly muted as Prentice snuck inward and started up the stairs. He had not bothered with a shield for this night's work, nor any armor beyond a buffcoat and gauntlets, since combat would have represented a failure and every man had instructions to flee, not stand and fight. The rising staircase twisted around to the right, to give the defenders the advantage in combat, but Prentice had already resolved to use his blade half-sworded in the close confines, holding it more akin to a short spear than a typical sword grip. It would make working around the center of the spiral easier for him as well.

Point leading, Prentice approached the main level of the bastion, watchful for the sweep of a lurking guard's blade, but none came. His eyes drew level with the floor above, which was lit by a feeble rushlight, and he leaned his head around the center column of the stairs. Ahead was a chamber, dark and empty, with torchlight coming from his left. The stairs here stopped rather than going up to the higher levels of the bastion, another security measure to make it harder for any assault. This chamber would have been a perfect point to mount a defense against men assaulting the postern, but there was no one here.

Quickly climbing the last stairs, Prentice turned to the torchlight and saw through a short passage that led to what was likely the main gate chamber an arched entry where all the traders and caravans would move into and out of Bridgetown in peaceful days. In sconces on the four corners of the arched chamber, large reed-bundle torches were burning, lighting the space. Creeping to the opening of the passage with taut steps, Prentice poked his head around the corner to survey the bigger main room. There were two men-at-arms there, both in the full white steel harness of knights in battle, though without their helmets on yet, just their mail hoods. They were watching the reinforced main door to Bridgetown. It was cross barred, with a further reinforcing bar laid at an angle and embedded into an iron-reinforced notch in the floor. It would take a battering ram hours to penetrate such a heavily constructed portal. On the south side of the room was a similar door, with the added protection of a portcullis, already in place. The two men-at-arms in the room were keeping watch on the north door, beyond which the attacking force was now somehow assaulting the walls, and all these men could do was watch the closed portal and imagine what was happening on the other side. Plainly this was the duty their commander must have set for them in the event of an assault. The leader of the garrison himself must have been somewhere further above.

Prentice handed his sword off to Dahyoor, drawing his poniard and signaling for Guillam to do the same. Once they were both ready, the pair of them snuck out behind the armored men keeping watch. Making sure not to move until they were both in position, sergeant and knight commander struck from behind at the same moment. Prentice planted his foot directly in the back of his man's knee joint, pushing forward and up at the same time, so that he buckled the man's leg and then rode him to the floor with his full weight. The enemy fell to his knees and then flat on his chest with Prentice's weight on his back. It was a conventional wrestler's trick, but with surprise, it was decisive. Before the man-at-arms even gathered his wits, Prentice's head was right beside his, with his poniard's edge at his throat.

"Yield or die!" Prentice commanded, risking his regular speaking voice in the midst of the clamor rising above. "Call an alarm and you will taste steel for the last time."

The man under him barely hesitated.

"I yield," he muttered, and Prentice looked to the man's partner, equally trapped under Guillam's crab-like form, who clung to the sentry by hands and legs. The felled guard also had blood flowing from his nose, which it looked like he must have broken in the fall. Knowing Guillam's fondness for affray, Prentice would not have been surprised if the corporal had deliberately smashed the man's face to the flagstones just for good measure.

"And you?" Prentice asked the bloody-mouthed knight. The man's expression fell as he realized resistance was futile.

"How did you even…?" he began to ask, but Prentice cut him off. There was only one discussion he was interested in having.

"What is above us? How many rooms and how many of your comrades?"

"Gate works and barracks above that. Open across the whole floor," the man explained.

Typical defensive works, Prentice thought, pleased.

"Are any men-at-arms in the gate works?" he asked.

"For what?" the prisoner demanded, but the uncooperative answer still told Prentice what he wanted to know for sure. Since these men had no intention of opening the gates to anyone, they had no one in place to open them quickly. It was a good sign. It meant one floor, at least, was clear of foes. Prentice pushed himself onto his feet and hefted at his prisoner's harness, helping the man up as well. Guillam did the same with his captured man, and when both were standing, they looked around to see that ten militiamen and one pointed-ear fey now had the ground floor fully occupied. If the two men-at-arms were relieved that they had not surrendered in shame to two mere thugs with daggers, Guillam put paid to their relief.

"Your mate there left the door ajar for us," he told his man, nodding at Prentice's prisoner. "Lantern hooked on the corner."

"You damnable fool," the man cursed his comrade, spitting out blood through his painful lips and teeth.

Prentice turned his prisoner to face Farringdon. "That is Knight Captain Marquis Farringdon of the Western Reach," he told the prisoners. "Give him your parole and you will be safe. You might even be ransomed back to your family before winter if you are lucky."

Other militiamen stepped forward to seize the prisoners' swords and daggers from their sheathes and the enemy men were forced on their knees to the marquis to give their official surrenders. Once that was done, Prentice was ready to turn his attention upwards. Above them, the conflict was still going on, dimly heard through the intervening floors. Whoever had scaled the walls was making a concerted effort to take the battlements, and the defenders must have been equally as committed to holding their posts.

"How many are you in total?" Prentice asked. The man with the bloody nose looked away without answering. His fellow prisoner sneered.

"A hundred," he said, and the knight commander smirked at him.

"You should have said forty; I might have believed you," Prentice told the prisoner, a man of barely twenty summers, looking down at him on his knees. "How many have you really got? A dozen?"

"More than you can defeat with this rabble," the man answered, glaring in contempt at the barely armored foes who had captured him in moments—no challenges, no possibility for glorious self-sacrifice. Prentice studied the fellow's expression, reading the truth from his face and eyes rather than his words.

"No more than a dozen and most of them on the roof, am I right?" he asked, and the man's surprise showed through despite his obvious plan to lie.

Not enough time playing cards, Prentice thought, knowing how well the laying of coin on the turn of a card tended to sharpen a man or woman's skill at the bluff.

From this main gate chamber there was the passage which they had entered by, leading to the postern, and another matching pair of passages that ended in spiral stairs upward. Two men were set to tie the prisoners' wrists and watch them while the rest of the infiltrators were split into two groups of four, one for each stairwell. Each group took one of the main chamber's reed torches for themselves to light the way on the otherwise pitch-dark stairs.

"Do you prefer the west or the east, My Lord?" Prentice asked, taking back his long blade from the man holding it for him.

"Does it matter?" Farringdon replied, and Prentice could not tell if he was jesting or genuinely asking.

"Not to me."

"The east then," said Farringdon, pointing to the stairwell that was marginally closer to him. "We'll see you at the top."

"Just make sure we clear everything in between as we go."

Farringdon saluted and led his little squad away. Prentice turned, and his three companions followed.

Time to capture another gatehouse.

Chapter 23

The stairs spiraled upward, tight confines making it hard to rush, and as they had been assured, the first landing opened onto the gate works. Mighty capstans were anchored to the stones of the wall so that the portcullises could be lowered and raised, while Prentice noticed that a third set of locking bars were slid through slots in the floor to secure the gates even further. No wonder the powder blast had done almost no damage. It might well be easier to batter the whole fortification to rubble than actually blast away these gates.

Whispers of the remaining torchlight in the chamber below lit the murder holes in the floor. There was a bucket set nearby full of iron darts—forged spikes, large as nails for a main beam or the planks of a mighty ship. Each spike was shaped like the fletching of an arrow, with an extra lump of iron weight in the middle of its length. If some force managed to breach one of the gates and found themselves confronted with the portcullis, these heavy iron darts would be dropped through the murder holes to kill men beneath. Even a foe in a well-forged helmet would feel like he had just taken a mace hit across his skull, assuming the dart did not punch straight through.

In the large room full of complex mechanisms, the air leapt with jagged shadows as Prentice carried the torch partway in, searching the corners for anyone hiding. Dahyoor followed him a few steps into the space, then shook his head confidently. There was no one and nothing unexpected. When Farringdon's squad's torch lit the opposite doorway, Prentice waved them upward, returning with his squire to their own stair. Handing off the torch to the man ahead, Prentice let someone else take the lead for a moment. Following on third, he nearly cursed when they passed a landing halfway to the next level on the left. It was a sentinel's niche, designed to let a man hold the stairs at the darkest point. Anchored to the wall on the sides of the niche was an iron-barred gate, barely visible in the wash of shadows. If the Usurper's men had had someone stationed there, the gate could easily have been swung closed against them.

"Lucky they keep leaving doors open for us, eh My Lord?" Guillam said when he saw it, half amused, half disgusted.

"This place is supposed to be a rat trap, and we need to keep our eyes peeled," Prentice replied tersely. "They could still catch us by our tails if they mean to."

Thankfully, the sounds of battle continued to echo from above, but as he listened, it seemed to Prentice that the intensity was fading. Not long and whoever was victorious on the parapet rooftop would be turning their attention to the levels below them. The barracks' room access was closed off by a wooden door, and Prentice had a flash of memory of himself and Turley hammering like madmen on the similar door in Dweltford's gatehouse. Was life repeating itself upon him? Pushing forward to try the latch, he was relieved to find the portal neither locked nor barred. Holding a finger up for silence, he pushed the door a crack and peered around it. Inside, the barracks room had been set for a siege, with all the beds pushed to the middle and oil lamps hanging from the central overhead beam where they could not be knocked over in the chaos. The rest of the floor formed a clear perimeter walkway, which would allow men at arms to move freely about to any of the bowmen's loops in the wall for shooting down at attackers in safety. There were three such positions facing north and another three facing south. Only one of the three was occupied, as far as Prentice could see—the one facing down onto the bridge, closest to his door, by a man in a black brigandine with a large hunting crossbow. The drawn string released with a clack and a thrum.

"Got the beggar!" the crossbowman shouted triumphantly.

"Good man! Keep it up," someone called from farther into the room, somewhere Prentice could not see. He waited until the man in black had reloaded his weapon and shot again. Then, as the shooter put the crossbow to the floor and his foot in the stirrup to pull back the bowstring with both hands and reload once more, Prentice rushed from the doorway straight at him. The fellow was so intent on reloading that it was not until he had latched the string that he looked up to see Prentice's sword pointing straight at his face.

"Quietly," Prentice warned in a low voice. "Yield or go now to the Judgement Day. The choice is yours."

Blinking in disbelief, the man leaned back, and almost as if he did not know what he was doing, lifted his crossbow, pointed it at Prentice's chest and depressed the trigger lever. The string released, but there was no quarrel in the groove. The crossbow was incompletely loaded. Even as the weapon triggered harmlessly, there was a matching hum of a string and an arrow shaft bit into the man's throat. Dahyoor had shot the man.

"Balden...," the man gurgled as his lifeblood rushed from the wound and his mouth. He managed to say no more before he fell, dropping his weapon so that it clattered on floorboards.

Not sparing time to admire the man's courage and dying loyalty to his comrades, Prentice sprang over his collapsing form toward the center of the room, looking for "Balden." There was the ratcheting sound of a crossbow string and then another man-at-arms stepped from the farthest loop, crossbow loaded and held at his waist. No more than three or four paces of distance lay between them, and Prentice knew he was too late. In a moment that was likely no more than a single breath but seemed to last for hours, he stared into his enemy's eyes. There was no hate there, no rage, and in truth, Prentice felt no enmity for this man either. There was only a determination to see the next task completed, and Prentice felt the same way.

Then he heard the click of the trigger and the thrum of the string's release. There was no time to dodge out of the way, and Prentice never even saw the quarrel shot from its groove. He simply flinched by reflex, and as he did, with his sword held in a habitual guard, he caught the head of the short missile with the edge of the blade, and the motion deflected the shot. The crossbow bolt flung itself at one of the beds, punching through the mattress into boards underneath, only a pace from where Dahyoor was already leaping across the bunks, bow held ready. Cutting an arrow or quarrel from the air was not an unheard-of skill, though it was rarely guaranteed. If the shooter had been twenty or thirty paces away, Prentice might well have tried it deliberately. At this close distance, it was simply a matter of pure good fortune, an act of God.

Prentice looked back to the crossbowman and found himself smiling and nodding to acknowledge the attempt, hoping to make it clear the man had no options left. Rather than yield, the enemy turned on his heel, doubtless thinking to rush to the stairs on the other side of the room and flee. He had gone no more than a step when Farringdon confronted him, longsword drawn, having come from those very stairs.

"Yield or die!" the marquis shouted.

The fellow barely hesitated. He threw his unloaded bow at Farringdon then reached for the rondel dagger at his waist while the knight captain flinched. The weapon wrenched free and was half raised to strike when Nunel, standing at his commander's left hand, pointed his wheellock and fired. From behind, Dahyoor loosed another arrow. At point blank, the bullet punched through the defender's breastplate and into his chest. The fey shaft hammered into the fellow's thigh. The man staggered, falling to one knee as the arrow's damage knocked his leg out from under him, and then he fell sideways, quite dead. As the sulfurous stink of powder smoke wafted through the room, an eerie silence seemed to settle with it, and Prentice listened intently for any sound that someone else was hiding in the barracks, ready to sell his life for one of his enemies'. His eyes met Farringdon's.

"Sorry we were so late. There's a sentinel's gate on our side," the knight captain said wryly. "It was shut and locked. Took us a moment, but the twits left the key in the lock, can you believe it."

"We had one, too, but left open for us," Prentice said. "No wonder we were a step ahead of you." He did feel the knight captain's disbelief, however.

"I'm sure that was the only reason," the marquis said with a grin. Then he looked upward. "They've stopped fighting above, I think."

Following Farringdon's eyes, Prentice looked up as well and realized it was true. There was a breath and then two things happened at once—the sound of someone hammering on a door and the scream of someone falling, ending in the heavy, metallic thump of a body striking the bridge boards.

"Yield the barbican to us, or watch your fellows try to fly!" a muffled voice called from outside.

CHAPTER 24

"That's not someone falling! They're throwing prisoners off the roof," Farringdon said, horrified as he followed Prentice up the final twist of the stairwell to a portal that was angled so that it was half door, half trap in the stairwell's roof.

"But which 'they'?" Prentice asked. Who had ended the combat in command of the parapet? Were those Usurper's men being thrown down or loyal folk of Bridgetown? As soon as he asked himself the question, Prentice was almost certain he knew. Cyprian, and likely his brother Cassian, were up there now with however many others of the Young Hopefuls. That would mean the parapet was Bridgetown's again, along with the tower he had just cleared. The battle should be over.

"My Lord," he said to Farringdon, "would you send your lancers down with the message to gather the prisoners in one place and guard them."

"You suspect they will attempt to escape?" Farringdon asked. "Some have given their parole already."

"And their comrades above are being thrown to their deaths," Prentice retorted. "If I thought that was my fate, I might not feel compelled to honor my pledge of parole." In truth, Prentice was more worried that if the assaulters had their blood up so much that they were throwing defeated enemies off the roof, then there was no knowing what they would do to any other prisoners if they got their hands on them.

Prentice also ordered Dahyoor to go with the marquis, as there was little use for his bow in the tight confines at the top of the stairs. Farringdon was replaced at Prentice's back by Guillam whose usual mocking grin was now a look of grim resolution in the sparse torchlight. The knight commander put his hand to the latch above him and carefully hefted up the door. It was barely open, with just enough space for him to look above the jamb, when a voice cried out from across the shadowy rooftop.

"There!" came the shout, followed by a crossbow shot which flew into the gap and deflected off the angled door. It skittered on the steps, drawing a curse from Guillam. Prentice reflexively pulled the door back closed, and the latch bar clicked in place automatically. A moment later there was banging on the other side.

"Do we know who that is?" Guillam asked, scowling.

As if to answer him, a voice from outside shouted through the wood.

"Open up in the name of Baroness Penelope!"

"We're Reachermen, daft mongrel!" Guillam shouted back, his voice almost oppressive in the echoing space. The banging and shouting on the other side did not stop.

"Seems they do not recognize us," Prentice said to him. Then he cocked his head and shouted against the banging as well. "For Bridgetown! For the baroness!"

The attacks on the door continued for a time, but when Prentice shouted his declaration again, Guillam adding his own voice as well, there came a halt.

"Bridgetowners?" a voice demanded.

"For Bridgetown!" Prentice and Guillam shouted back as one.

There was a long pause, and Prentice imagined the Young Hopefuls on the other side, consulting with each other. Another breath passed.

"If you're for Bridgetown then open the door and yield the gatehouse!" came the command at last. Prentice nodded and carefully unhooked the latching bolt, using the bolt's iron ring. Almost as soon as there was a gap, the thin point of a sidesword was thrust through it, scaping against the steel of Prentice's fighting gauntlet. Without those plates' protection, he would have lost fingers for sure. Even as that happened, other hands on the outside began to wrestle with the door to pull it out of the way. The blade strike caused Prentice to recoil, dropping his own sword so that it fell clattering down the stairs, but he kept his grip on the iron ring and all but hung there, his weight holding the door closed while those outside tried to get a grip to pull it open. But he could not latch it again because of the blade caught in the gap. It was a momentary stalemate. Those on the roof could not open the door, but Prentice and Guillam could not latch it fully closed either. The two Lions looked at each other a moment.

"I'll go get help," the corporal said at last. "We can tie a rope and pull it down."

Prentice shook his head.

"There's no time for that," he said. With the full force of his weight on the ring crushing awkwardly against his armor-clad fingers, he could feel his grip tiring already. If he slipped while he waited for others to locate some rope, it could be the death of him. He decided on a different course of action. "Go back to the sentinel's niche and close the gate behind you. Make sure it's latched and locked, then call up here to tell me you've done it."

"Behind me?" Guillam asked with a cocked eyebrow. "You're not plannin' on fightin' 'em all yourself, are you, Commander? You know your lady wife'll have my guts for garters if I leave you to die like that."

"I am planning on making a flying dash for Farringdon's stairs and the sentinel gate there," Prentice told him with a smile, though the twisting pain in his fingers cut the good humor short. "And grab my sword as you go. I will not have time to fetch it myself."

Guillam nodded, accepting Prentice's command, but before he left, he squeezed past to reach up and wedge his own gauntlet-ed fingers between the door and the trapped blade. Then he wrenched the thin length of steel sideways, bending and irrevo-cably ruining the weapon. The blade would have to be recut into pieces and those bits reforged in a layered billet, if the steel was to be saved at all.

"Give you a fraction's extra head start," Guillam said, and his grin came back a moment. "The fella on the other end of that steel's quick with it, no mistake. This'll slow him a hair, at least."

Prentice nodded his thanks and then Guillam was gone. Like a man twisting from gallows, Prentice kept hanging his full weight on the iron ring. His fingers did not especially ache yet, but he could feel the tension in them pushing that direction, and the fact that he dared not release them even for a breath of a respite only added to the growing discomfort. From the depths of the stairwell there came a metallic scraping sound followed by a curse and a loud clack.

"Got your sword, but that gate didn't want to lock up, My Lord," Guillam's voice echoed up like a ghost in the bottom of a well. "I think I got it shut tight now. You want me to head to the other side, bring you your sword?"

"Yes," Prentice shouted down and then he set himself for the sprint. He muttered a tersely whispered prayer. "Lord God, just let them not notice right away."

Then he released his grip and turned, shoving himself down the steps, using both hands to keep himself barely upright in the rush. He was thankful now that he had dropped his sword. Even sheathed, it would have been more hindrance than help in the tight twists of the stairwell. Above him there was a cry and the bang of the door being torn open. Prentice did not pause to look back.

At the barracks level he dove through the door, almost losing his footing on the wooden floorboards as he made a skidding turn around the beds and rushed for the portal on the other side of the room. He was barely past halfway when the shouts of the Young Hopefuls following him sounded through the open door behind him. Some likely continued on down the steps and would find

Guillam's locked iron gate, but the hammer of steel-shod footfalls on the floorboards told Prentice that at least one of them had diverted into the barracks and would soon be close on his heels. He did not risk even a moment to look.

Through the opposite door, Prentice slammed into the center pillar of the twisting stair and then cascaded downward, feeling like a child's wooden ball bouncing off every surface. He almost missed the sentinel's niche and had to wrench himself around to stop in time, hanging upon the gate itself as if it were a swing. He was only thankful it wasn't his weaker shoulder, the one that carried the old injury, that took the main of the force. The barred gate scraped over the stones with a whine like the cry of a dying animal, and the lock clicked into place. For a breath, he felt safe, then realized that the lock still had its key in place. Reflexively he tried to reach through the bars to retrieve it, but the narrowness of the gaps blocked his gauntleted fist. After bouncing off with a loud clang, he gripped the steel on his left hand and began to pull away the protective item. Made to fit well, so that they would not come loose in the turmoil of combat, gauntlets were not swift to remove. The leather pads of the palm and fingertips of his right gauntlet slipped on the steel of the left as he pawed at his hand like a trapped animal. The hand protection came loose just as he heard the metallic footsteps on the stone stairs above, as well as the clatter and scrapes of a man in steel pushing down the spiraling stairwell. Shoving his bare hand through the gap, Prentice ignored the feeling of vulnerability as his fingers twisted back to grip the key. He found it and had just begun to pull it loose when the armored figure of his pursuer crashed into sight, running right into the gate itself.

Prentice cried out at the sharp spike of pain as the man's breast-plate slammed against his arm, trapping it up against the bars with the pursuer's full weight. He had time to wonder if it was broken, or his wrist dislocated, when the weight was immediately removed. A muffled voice on the other side of the bars swore. The man-at-arms who was hunting him was still wearing a closed helmet which limited his visibility. That, along with the meagre light in the stairwell, meant the fellow appeared to have no idea what was blocking his passage. His hands began to feel about, and in the sudden gap, Prentice ripped the key from its lock and began to pull his arm free. The assailant felt the movement and tried to pin the retreating limb, but in the near-total dark, Prentice was able to slither it away through the bars. When it came out, he pushed himself backward, almost tripping and tumbling a short distance down the stairs. He only just stopped his fall by pressing bodily against the curved wall.

"Who is that?" the man on the other side of the gate growled through the bars. "Open this up and face me like a man."

"Cassian, is that you?" Prentice asked, thinking he recognized the man's voice.

"Who are you? Show yourself?"

There was a series of strange noises that took Prentice a moment to recognize, then a hateful eye peered through one of the gaps in the bars, just barely recognizable in the shadows. Cassian had removed his helmet to better identify his frustrating prey. He gripped at the bars and shook on them, as if thinking to tear them down with the might of his rage alone. The ironwork barely rattled on its hinges. It would take tools and hours of hard work to pull that barrier forth. As Knight Captain Farringdon had observed, the makers of Sougate had known their craft.

"Good Cassian, a pleasure to meet you once more, but if you will excuse me, I must take our prisoners to my liege and she to the Lady Penelope," Prentice said, the exultation of victory giving him a moment's humor. "As promised, the Lions have taken Sougate in a night!"

"We have the roof and the barracks," Cassian spat back. "And you owe me a sword."

"Owe you?"

"It was a gift from my father and now it is ruined, bent sideways!"

"That was yours? Well, you will certainly need a replacement," Prentice said with mocking geniality. "I suggest you not use the next one as a makeshift locking bolt. It will last longer."

The man Cassian screamed in unrestrained indignation and shook at the bars in his grip like a wild animal in a cage. Prentice ignored him, however, and made his way swiftly down to the ground floor, collecting Guillam at the door to the gate works. The newly raised sergeant had crossed after securing the sentinel's gate on his side to make sure his leader was alright.

"What'd you do, Commander, cut his manhood off?" Guillam asked as Cassian's voice followed them down the steps, inarticulate rage becoming a stream of invective. He handed Prentice back his sword.

"It seems he does not handle defeat well," Prentice told his corporal.

"Is that all?" Guillam scoffed, cocking a disdainful eyebrow. "Can you imagine him at dice or cards?"

CHAPTER 25

On the ground floor, Farringdon and his men had discovered another exit from the tower. Realizing that once the bars were emplaced for the main gate it would take some time and many hands to remove them again, the knight captain had gone in search of other possible smaller entrances, similar to the postern gate but working in reverse. He found one at the base of a short set of steps opening onto a narrow stone landing built into a spot where the tower met the bridge's footings. Just as the postern was designed to be out of the way, so this aperture was out of sight around a corner, invisible from the bridges and the town in general. Only someone on a boat in the river would be able to even see it. There was a good chance the Usurper's men, who had been holding the tower against the town's garrison, had not even known it was there.

"The footing looks slimy," Farringdon explained as Prentice poked his head out the door, "But there are solid bars for hand grips in the walls all the way around and then a good ladder up to the bridge height. I thought we might as well take our prisoners out this way, save us trying to bring them to the boat over the Vec ground. Who knows what Town Sobridge and its prince thinks of all the ruckus?"

Prentice nodded, and then, giving a signal for quiet, stepped out onto the ledge, fingers searching for the handholds. Following around the few paces at the base of the tower, he found the ladder Farringdon had mentioned and indeed it was strong enough to take several men's weight. Likely it had been built with the thought of possibly moving supplies into or out of the tower, although he had to wonder at the paranoid mind that thought the garrison defenders needed this many entries and exits. He considered that perhaps the garrison had once had its own boats and this door had let down to a jetty, even before the bridge itself had been built. Then he shook his head—yet another question for a quieter moment.

At the top of the ladder, he poked his head over the lip of the bridge and found himself perhaps eight to ten paces back from the tower's main gate, the one that was heavily barred and scorched by the failed explosion. It was in shadow, but not as dark as he had expected. The dimness was not being pushed back by the various lanterns and torchlights that glittered from the town and danced on the inky mirror of the water's surface, however. Rather, there was a much nearer source of light—a heavy handcart, such as the kind a wood cutting team might use to transport logs into the town. It had three lit lanterns nailed on its front, as well as a squad of Bridgetown militia standing by it, many with torches raised over their heads. There were a number of crossbow bolts stuck in it as well. Any of those who did not have a light in hand were working to keep the cart's two heavy wheels from rolling backward, wedging heavy blocks under and around them. The wheels were constantly being pushed against by a long ladder positioned in the back of the handcart and now resting against the tower all the way up to the parapet.

That was the sound of a "barrel" over cobblestones, Prentice thought, realizing it had, in fact, been the rumble of the cart on the bridge's boards. Seeing the makeshift siege engine, Prentice was impressed by its brilliant simplicity. The militia had pushed the cart with the ladder's base already in position. Then, once it stopped, the attackers could have levered the ladder upwards while the cart's haulers secured the wheels. By the time the defenders even knew what was happening, the ladder would have hit the stones and the first man-at-arms up the rungs would be coming over the top. Prentice was willing to bet Cassian had been that first man. Now that the battle for the roof was done, the militia that had acted as the draft horses for the cart had no duty, it seemed, other than to keep themselves safe and the ladder aloft. Since Prentice and his men had eliminated the crossbowmen, that was an even easier task than it might have been. The militia around the handcart were more like workmen at the end of a hard day, lounging around and not keeping any kind of watch or trying to engage in the conflict.

A voice from above called for mason's tools.

"You what?" demanded one of the militiamen, peering upward into the night.

"Mason's tools, and be quick about it!" the order was reiterated.

"Mason's tools?" a man on the bridge repeated in a disbelieving whisper. "What are they plannin'? To take it down stone by stone?"

"Just do what they say," whispered another. "Don't want to end up like Helders."

Helder's fate, whatever it was, must have settled the issue, as one of the cart attendants now trotted back down the bridge toward the town at an unenthusiastic pace. Prentice dropped back below the level of the bridge, pleased with the thought that the single-minded Hopefuls were planning on ripping the sentinel gates out of the walls on their brute-force path through the Sougate's now empty defenses. He made his way back to Farringdon and the other waiting infiltrators to explain the situation on the bridge.

"What do you want to do, Knight Commander?" the marquis asked. Prentice gave him a smile.

"I think we should escort our prisoners out this door, around the ledge here and into town across the bridge."

"Just like that?" Sergeant Nunel asked, obviously somewhat skeptical. "Straight past the men who just tried to kill us in the race to capture this pile?"

"Those men are above us, calling for mason's tools," Prentice explained. "I suspect they imagine we are cowering down here somewhere. By the time they make their way through those gates and find we are not, it's likely to be dawn already."

"What if the militia tries to stop us?" Farringdon asked.

"For what? We have their liege's mandate to recapture Sougate and to take the Usurper's men prisoner. Which we have done."

"And if some of them wish-to-be knights comes back down the ladder, their blood all up, then what?" asked Guillam.

"Then we show them a bit of brass. I am a baron and knight commander," Prentice said, then nodded at Farringdon. "That is the knight captain and marquis consort of Bridgetown's closest ally. If that doesn't stand for something, then we will just have to show them what service in the White Lions makes of a man. Surely, we can do that."

"Fair enough," Guillam answered with a grin, but Farringdon looked troubled by the notion of open conflict on the bridge with the Hopefuls. A confrontation between two forces who did not expect each other in a dimly lit gatehouse was one thing; a brawl between the Reach militia and the remnant nobility of Bridgetown on the other hand could scuttle the whole burgeoning relationship between the two liege ladies. Prentice was not unsympathetic to the marquis's likely concerns.

"All this is by the by," he said, his face becoming stern once more. "Best if we manage to get away without any fracas. Once we have these prisoners back to camp, we can send to her grace, announcing our success and asking what she would like us to do with them."

The scouting party arranged their prisoners, five in all, using a length of rope scared up from somewhere in the tower to tie each man by his left wrist, forming them into a prisoner coffle.

"The first few steps are a bit slippery, so we will leave you a free hand," Prentice explained. "Do not take that as an opportunity to make any foolish decisions, though, because if you slip, you will not just doom yourself to drown in your armor; you will take all your comrades with you."

The prisoners scowled back at him in the glimmers of torch-light, but it seemed that the fight was out of them, at least for this night.

They might even be thinking to honor their parole, Prentice mused. Having been hated by the peerage for so long and knowing that the vast majority of the Grand Kingdom's remaining nobility would despise him no matter what rank the archduchess raised him to, it felt odd to imagine that these knights would keep their pledge of peace.

Choosing to go first, Prentice sheathed his sword and took one of the captured torches, leading the way back around the ledge and up onto the bridge. Once his flaming brand crested the bridge level, he rushed up the rest of the steps, so that there could be no suggestion he was creeping about, torch or no. The militiamen on the wagon would be surprised enough by his appearance—no need to unnerve them into the bargain. As soon as his feet were on the bridge decking, he looked back down the ladder, not even sparing a glance to see what the Bridgetown militia thought of his arrival. Like a man going about his business with nothing to hide, he acted as if he expected not to be noticed.

"Right, you lot, up this way," he ordered the prisoners loudly, affecting a working man's accent. He kept watching as the first one on the coffle put his hand to the rungs. "Some of that wood is moldy and slick, so you ones in your steel sabatons take extra care. Like I said, if one of you falls, you'll take your mates with you. Sorry way to die."

"Here, what's this then?" a voice from behind Prentice called, but he deliberately ignored it, as if he was about the most mundane activity that could be. Obviously, anyone troubled by some nearby goings-on could not possibly think *he* was the one out of the ordinary. He kept his attention on the man climbing and watched to ensure the imprisoning rope did not become entangled.

"You! Stand and be named," another voice commanded, and now Prentice did stop. He straightened up and turned to face the militia, two of whom were approaching, one holding a torch taken from the ladder-cart.

"Prentice Ash, Reacherman," Prentice said with a puzzled expression, as if he were any other yeoman and the militia were rousting him in the street unfairly on the way to his day's work. "In service to the Archduchess of the Reach."

"Oh aye?" one of the Bridgetowners responded, as if Prentice had just claimed to have climbed down a rope from the moon. "Let me guess, you's a goatherd and this lot all tied together is your little herd of milkers."

Prentice pretended to be amused by the man's jest, smirking a little.

"No, mate. These are prisoners of her grace. We've to escort them to the militia camp in Runners Field."

"Where have they come from?" the other man in orange and gold asked, his voice filled with more wonder than belligerence.

"In there," Prentice said, cocking his head at the Sougate, and the two guards looked to the still barred door, as solid as any of the barbican's stone walls.

"Our Young Hopefuls are up there now, fighting their way in," the more aggressive man challenged. "How've you taken this lot without them knowing?"

"We come at the problem from the opposite end," Prentice answered. Before he could expand on that claim, there was a rattling sound from the ladder and suddenly Dahyoor appeared on the side of the bridge. With his bow and case slung over his shoulder, Prentice watched the fey man scramble up and around the escorted prisoners, and then a moment later he was standing on the bridge as naturally as if he had just walked there from the town. Not only a master horseman, Dahyoor was clearly also an expert climber, and given the agility he displayed, Prentice wondered if the fey were all part cat.

"The knight captain one tells me that you will need another to watch the captives as they come up," Dahyoor declared and immediately grabbed at the prisoner's rope, tugging to urge the next one up while he pushed the first out of the way.

"Hell's bells," the lead militiaman swore as he saw the fey man's ears, noticeable even in the poor light. "Who the hell *are* you that you got a devil in your service and knights on a lead?"

Prentice sighed. There was little chance of them getting away easily with their prisoners now. Time to switch from mundane and harmless to superior and dangerous.

"I am Baron Prentice Ash of Fallenhill," he declared, his voice hardening and rising in volume. "This is my squire and sworn man, a fey rider of the western plains."

Prentice almost gave the men Dahyoor's name, but remembering how reticent the fey were about revealing their names with *kreff*, he stopped himself. Of course, anyone who wanted to find out the name would only have to ask around the White Lions' camp. It was hardly a secret. Somehow though, Prentice felt it would disrespect the loyal Dahyoor to share his name with these strangers.

The two Bridgetown militiamen fell to a conversation of heated whispers while behind them their fellows still holding to the handcart were lifting up their own lights to get a better look at the "devil" man. Prentice didn't mind. With every passing moment, his team and their prisoners were gathering on the bridge. Soon they would be free to march away.

"Fey tales?" the lead militiaman said, his voice rising with disgust and disbelief, as if he was being taken for a fool.

"Yea, well I figured on it, the way you are, but look for yourself," the other man said, also raising his voice above a whisper.

"Marsden's a twat who spins tales when he's in his cups," the leader declared angrily, his voice rising once again despite trying to lower it.

"No denying," his man agreed and then pointed at Dahyoor, who had now pulled his bow from its case and scanned all points of the bridge, including the captives, arrow casually nocked to the string. "But there's one of 'em there, isn't it?"

"Pixies on horseback," the leader declared with a scowl and shake of his head. His expression was one of frustration and beleaguered doubt, as if he felt he was supposed to do something about the mythical figure that had just appeared out of the night but equally felt it was unjust for the world to lump this duty upon him here in the middle of Great Bridge Road. He looked back and forth at his own hands, as if weighing possible responses, and Prentice was sure the man would most like to go back to sitting on the cart and forget this whole strange diversion with prisoners and fey had ever occurred.

Too late for that, he thought.

Nevertheless, prisoners and White Lion infiltrators were now all on the bridge, with Farringdon himself coming last. Once he gave Prentice the nod, the knight commander turned toward Bridgetown, sparing a glance for the two uncertain militiamen.

"We will take our prisoners away now," he said. "Thank you for your assistance. We are going."

"No, you damn well aren't!" a deep baritone voice declared out of the darkness, as a richly dressed man marched up, accompanied by two more militiamen carrying poleaxes and a somewhat bewildered and sleepy-looking tradesman with a belt of tools around his waist and leather carry bag at his side. The group emerged out of the shadows from the direction of the town. "Now, who on earth are you and who called for a mason with his tools?"

CHAPTER 26

"I will offer you my name when you offer yours," Prentice said to the demanding newcomer.

Just by the man's self-possession and dress, it was clear the fellow was a patrician of the town, at least, if not a nobleman, although Prentice could not recognize him from the faces that had been around the baroness earlier in the day. In times gone by, Prentice would have played the polite servant to someone like this, recognizing the rights of the peers of the realm and other highborn ranks out of reflexive self-defense. Now, he was Baron of Fallenhill, ostensibly nearly equal in rank to even Bridgetown's own ruler. He would never have to tug his forelock to any man. Even so, he had to fight his own hand that twitched at his side, ready to give the humble obeisance.

"You think to demand my name?" the man said, swaying back as if he had been physically pushed. He was a stout figure of middling height, but there was a fitness to his limbs and movements that spoke of a physical life, perhaps in the saddle or at war.

A noble then, Prentice thought.

"I believe, My Lord, that you are Baronet Forsle," Farringdon said as he drew up beside Prentice. "Brother to the late Earl John. The baroness' uncle. My wife, the Archduchess Amelia, told me to keep watch for you as I moved about the town. Forgive me that I have not yet had a chance to introduce myself. I am Knight Captain, Marquis Consort Farringdon and this is..."

The knight captain paused and looked to Prentice, cocking his head ever so slightly. Prentice had to marvel at the man's courtly manners. The issue between them was that they were nobles who had not been introduced, and Farringdon was defusing the situation with an apology that offered no disrespect to anyone and made continued ill-will a rudeness. He was even pausing to ask Prentice for his permission to introduce him, though his rank as marquis made him still the most senior peer present, despite his forfeited princely status. Prentice nodded his head to his fellow militia commander and then bowed to the newly acknowledged Baronet Forsle. He had learned how to bow in noble fashion during his time at the Academy in Ashfield and had thought it a simple enough technique to master. As he bent at the waist in front of a real nobleman, not a fellow student, Prentice felt overwhelmingly awkward suddenly, certain some part of his manner would reveal how new he was to his noble rank.

"Baronet Forsle, may I present Baron Prentice Ash of Fallenhill, Knight Commander of the Western Reach," Farringdon said as smoothly as if they were meeting in their liege's court rather than on a bridge by torchlight.

"A baron with two names?" Forsle asked, his lips downturned.

"Ash is his war name, My Lord," Farringdon explained on Prentice's behalf. "Hard fought for and justly won."

"Hmph," was the baronet's only reply. Grand Kingdom nobles, especially those of high peerage, such as the rank of baron or above, prided themselves on having only their personal names and their titles. Surnames, which typically described a person's place of birth or their occupation, were a mark of yeomen. Amongst the lower born, they were a mark of respect. John the smith was called John Smith, and proud of the craft he used to serve his community and make his way in the world. Nobles disdained that notion for themselves, since it implied that they had to work to prove their value rather than having it declared by their birth. Of course, as with almost everything, there were exceptions, and a battle name was exactly that kind of thing, halfway between a surname and a noble title. Baron Caron Ironworth's name was of that type, like a surname given to an ancestor and then proudly lived up to by each succeeding generation. In a hundred years' time, would there be young men, great-great grandsons of Prentice's and Righteous's, who would drive themselves night and day, hoping to become man enough to earn the name Ash? Prentice wasn't sure how he felt about such a notion.

"Baron; Marquis Consort," Forsle said, suddenly taking a step back and bowing to each of them in turn. "Forgive me my presumption. I was not told you would be here tonight."

"No apology is necessary," Farringdon offered readily. "You are diligent in your niece's service, even as we are seeking to be."

Prentice blinked at the Bridgetown man's sudden change of posture, and then he remembered something his wife had shared of Lady Penelope's description of her uncle—that he was a hardline traditionalist, devoted to the right order of things. Even if this man loathed the very sight of Prentice, he would bow at this moment because that was what God and rank demanded of him. Recognizing the man's honorable acceptance of his place in the scheme of things, Prentice felt a sudden, unexpected respect for him in turn. The baronet had to know the stories of the convict raised to nobility, not to mention the tales of the woman from the Western Reach who was claiming hitherto unknown titles for herself, about whom swirled rumors of witchcraft, heresy, and adultery. And yet, here the man was, bowing. Even if he had no respect for them as men, he honored their rank. It was more than most Grand Kingdom nobles might do, more than the Young Hopefuls had.

"Baronet, may I offer you my and my wife's condolences on the passing of your brother," Prentice said suddenly, finding that he wanted to honor the man in return. "I never had the blessing of being presented to Earl John, but all reports are of a man who led his folk with diligence, righteousness, and strength. His passing is a loss to Bridgetown and all the Grand Kingdom."

"Thank...thank you," the baronet said quietly, his belligerent tone giving way to one of surprise and sincerity.

In truth, Prentice knew nothing of Earl John, other than the fact of his death, but he saw no reason not to praise the man's memory. Unless they had truly hated each other, or even if they had, it was probable the surviving brother was grieving and feeling regret at his sibling's passing. Even estranged from his own family as he was, Prentice could only imagine that he would feel like that in the same situation.

"We have not been presented as the days of mourning are only just coming to an end," the baronet told them. "I have been in vigil for my brother's soul this last while and have only just this past sundown completed my duty. I believe my niece plans to feast your liege lady in welcome tomorrow's evening, now that the days of mourning are at an end."

You said it twice, My Lord, Prentice thought, and as he did so, he noticed that the heaviness of Baronet Forsle's clothes—black cloth, fur-lined, with no jewelry or other adornment—was a mark of official grieving. *You have honored your brother's passing to the letter, but you are one of the only ones. And it offends you, doesn't it?*

Prentice's mind went back to the bright colors of the baroness and her entourage. No mourning black amongst that flock of popinjays. The baroness might be forgiven, since her town was besieged and the needs of war can outweigh even familial duties, but in that case, some of her courtiers should have taken up the weight of the duty for her. That only her uncle had was a telling factor.

But what tale does it tell? Prentice wondered. Before any other words could be shared, there were fresh shouts from the parapet, and the ladder started to groan and rock as first one and then several armored men started down it.

"Here we go," Farringdon said under his breath, and Prentice spared him a gallows' smirk. Whatever peace they had made with the baronet was about to be hacked at by the Young Hopefuls, no doubt. The knight commander turned to Dahyoor and gave a surreptitious signal that he hoped the fey would read as an instruction to stay calm but ready. He also looked the prisoners over once again to make sure there were no signs they were plotting escape. One was watching everything closely, but the others had the insistent disinterest of newly captured men, pretending to be too proud to care about their captors' doings.

"That's him! That's the damnable mongrel that ruined father's sword," the man leading the way down the ladder all but screamed. "I'll kill him! I'll have his eyes! Damn him to hell!"

"Cassian?" Farringdon whispered, and Prentice nodded, the extra light enough now to recognize for sure the man who had pursued him so hotly through the shadows inside Sougate. Behind the infuriated youth came his brother, seeming as equally enraged but keeping quiet. The pair were sprayed with blood from the melee on the roof.

"Seize him! No one let him get away!" Cassian commanded as he leaped from the hand cart to the bridge boards with a heavy thump that reminded Prentice of the falling bodies they had heard during the assault. These were wrathful young men who threw prisoners to their death as an interrogation technique. There was little chance now that this would not end in more blood.

Still, for the sake of his liege's alliance, Prentice set himself to try.

CHAPTER 27

As Cassian stalked toward them like a hunting animal, Prentice was surprised when Baronet Forsle stepped into the gap between.

"Nephew, what is this?" he said, taking hold of Cassian's shoulders and forcing the young man to look him in the eyes. There was barely restrained fury in that gaze, and Prentice was impressed with Forsle's nerve that he did not flinch, even though it was clear that the baronet had no hope to survive if Cassian lost control of himself.

"That bastard ruined my sword from father!" Cassian said, huffing like a bull about to charge. Forsle looked down at the perfectly functional blade in the young man's grip. When he saw the look, Cassian shrugged away his uncle's hold. "Not that one!"

He turned and looked over his shoulder at one of the other Hopefuls now descending and gathering as their own small force, facing off against the White Lions and their prisoner coffle. Cassian waved impatiently at one of his comrades, who stepped forward and offered up the bent sidesword like a page bearing a knight's chosen weapon in a tourney. Snatching it, the furious young man held it up to his uncle. The baronet looked from the weapon to Prentice and Farringdon.

"There was a great deal of chaos in the assault," Prentice said readily, determined to keep Farringdon from taking the blame before him. He was all but certain the marquis would, if given the chance. "It is unfortunate that a prized weapon was so damaged as a result."

"You did this, mongrel!" Cassian retorted and seemed ready to step around his uncle. The baronet did not let him.

"Actually, lad...," Prentice heard Guillam start to say behind him, apparently about to take the blame as well, and he hissed for the sergeant to be quiet.

I am the commander here, Prentice thought, feeling his own anger rise. *The rest of you just shut up, will you!*

"Are you saying that you did not do this?" the baronet asked.

"I did not," Prentice answered truthfully. He was about to explain the full context, but Forsle did not give him a chance. The baronet turned back to his nephew.

"There, you have your answer."

"He's lying!" Cassian shouted, spittle flying from his lips. "I challenge him!"

"You cannot..." Forsle began, but Cassian cut him off.

"He's a liar and he owes me an honor debt! I will challenge him!"

"Squires do not challenge peers of the realm, no matter the debt!" Forsle shouted back at his nephew, and Prentice guessed that the baronet was not typically a man who bellowed at his relatives, since Cassian's rage was momentarily quelled by surprise. He looked from the baronet to Prentice and back.

"What about in the case of treason?" Cyprian asked gently, but audibly, from behind his brother.

"What talk is this of treason?" Forsle said, looking past Cassian to the older brother but putting his hands back on the younger's shoulders so that he could not be stepped past in the distraction.

"We captured the Sougate, and inside we find these fellows waiting for us," Cyprian explained, his eyes narrow as they bored into Prentice with a colder kind of hate. Prentice looked from younger to older sibling.

Your brother's the passion, but you are the intellect, aren't you? the knight commander thought, watching the two. It raised an interesting question: was Cyprian the wisdom that kept them both out of trouble as best he could, or was he the one who stirred the pot, knowing he could shift the blame onto his hot-headed younger brother?

"*We* captured Sougate!" Farringdon declared. "You seized the parapet and would be up there still if we hadn't opened the doors to you."

"Liar!" Cassian spat again. Prentice tensed, ready to fall back and draw his blade if the young hopeful made to push past and attack. Dahyoor must have sensed the imminence of danger as well, as Prentice heard an ever so light pressure creaking on the bowstring. The fey was readying to shoot, and his first target would be a dead man. Suddenly, Prentice wanted nothing more than to step into the path of that arrow, so desperate was he to keep the peace for his liege's sake. Yet he feared even that motion might be read as provocation by Cassian in his knife-edged state.

"We were on the Vec side of Sougate this evening," Prentice explained, holding his tone calm. Baronet Forsle clearly had influence over his nephews and their cadre, and the older man no doubt also wanted to keep the peace, even if only for the sake of the social order. Prentice suspected the man wanted to protect his niece's burgeoning alliance as well. How would it bode for Baroness Penelope if her own cousins got into a brawl with the Reach's highest nobles?

"See, he admits his treason," Cassian said with a bloodthirsty grin, but the baronet only held up a palm and hissed for quiet. Then he nodded politely to invite Prentice to continue.

"We were there to scout all options for taking the bastion, as our liege promised the baroness," he explained. "We were considering our possibilities when the Young Hopefuls began their courageous assault."

"Courageous assault?" Forsle repeated. Prentice nodded. The Young Hopefuls wanted all the glory from the night's action, but the knight commander was not so hungry for praise. He could share the credit.

"Their attack on the parapet. It was swiftly executed and well done, there can be no denying. My only criticism was that they did not tell us of their plan first."

Prentice paused and looked at Cassian and then his brother behind.

"We could have coordinated better in that case. Nonetheless, the force of their attack so unnerved the occupiers that in their haste to defend the parapet, they left the Veckander side postern door unbolted."

There was a series of angry mutters amongst the prisoners at that revelation and a sharp thump as one of them clipped the delinquent postern guard across the back of his head, as if he were a disobedient child.

"More likely you were already in there plotting with the Usurper's men and are now seeking to take credit for our victory rather than being found out for your treason," Cassian said hatefully. Prentice looked at him but kept his expression carefully neutral.

You will have to do better than that, lad, if you want to needle me into making a challenge, he thought, knowing full well that Cassian was trying to provoke him to get his honor duel. If Prentice wasn't concerned by the imputation, Baronet Forsle was not so undaunted.

"You cannot make such a claim without evidence," he insisted.

"The fact they were in there isn't enough proof?" Cyprian pressed, backing up his brother's ploy.

"We have prisoners taken in honor," Farringdon declared. "Paroles accepted and observed to the letter. Ask any of them if we were in cahoots."

"Or you could ask your own prisoners," Prentice added. "You did take prisoners, did you not?"

Cyprian's and Cassian's eyes narrowed into hateful slits in the dark of the night. When Farringdon had suggested questioning the prisoners, he had left a door open to vulnerability, if the Usurper's men decided to try spreading dissension. They could lie and say that the White Lions were in fact conspiring with them.

Prentice shut that door by reminding the captive knights what had happened to all the Young Hopefuls' prisoners.

"We did not take any prisoners," Cyprian muttered, clearly annoyed at being out-maneuvered. "They all fought to the death."

"Or fell to it," Prentice added so that there would be no doubt between them. The baronet turned to the tied men-at-arms.

"Well then, what say you? Were you machinating with the Reachermen?" he demanded. The prisoners shuffled uncomfortably until one spat on the bridge planks.

"A pox on all of you, on the wayward bitches you all follow, and no doubt rut with through the night watches," he said hatefully. "The devil must have given them loins of leather to be able to service so many mongrels..."

The man seemed to be intent on going on, but his voice was stopped in his mouth by a gauntlet-clad slap from Sergeant Nunel.

"Have a care, sir," said the lancer. "Parole does not give you freedom to run your mouth so wild."

No one, not even the other prisoners, stirred at his intervention.

"It seems you have no witnesses and no evidence," the baronet said to the brothers, turning back from the disciplined prisoner. "You owe the baron an apology."

There's a first, Prentice thought at the notion of someone of rank being forced to apologize to him. He was not surprised when neither young man agreed, shaking their heads, but saying nothing further.

"Baronet, if I may," Prentice offered gently, thinking he might be able to see a path out of this mess and back to the victory for all that it should have been. The baronet stepped aside, watching sidelong for any sudden movement from Cassian. Prentice took a single step forward and nodded to the brothers.

"Gentlemen," he began, speaking loud enough for everyone on the bridge to hear, "there can be no doubting the courage and ingenuity of the Young Hopefuls' assault. You captured the parapet against fierce opposition. If not for the diversion you provided, the Lions would not have been able to take the other floors from the opposite direction. We will not speak of this victory to the archduchess or the baroness without remembering that it was built equal footed on your contribution and ours."

Prentice turned his eyes directly on Cassian.

"I apologize for the damage done to your father's gift blade," he said quietly. "While I did not do the deed, nonetheless, I understand the loss of connection with one's family. Let me pay to have it reforged, or if not, for another to be made, commemorating your father and tonight's victory for his sons."

"There you go," Baronet Forsle said eagerly. "A just resolution and generous."

Cassian stared at Prentice, seeming less out of control but no less hateful.

Take my offer lad, Prentice thought. *Let us all get our feet out of this useless bear trap.*

Cassian was not interested, it seemed, his lips pressed tight, face set like flint. Then his brother stepped up behind him and whispered something in his ear. The younger brother's eyes lit up with delighted malice. He looked down at Prentice's sword belt.

"You want to replace my sword?" he said, venom dripping from his words. "Give me yours."

"Mine...?" Prentice's hand went involuntarily to the hilt of his blade. In one respect, there was nothing Prentice would like more than to give the weapon over. Beautiful as it was, he loathed the thing for the blood he had spilled with it. It had become a symbol of him and his supposedly heroic actions, a part of his "legend." He knew that rumors flew about that it was magical, which was ridiculous. Enchanted or not, though, it had many layers of meaning, and so he could not simply give it up. The blade was from a champion who had not needed to die, the handle from the horn of a unique beast, whose beauty should never have been driven out of the world. It had a lion's-head hilt crafted of Reach silver, the only piece that Prentice felt truly reflected him, a lion forged in the west, and the unicorn mane tassel, the last of such threads that would ever be seen in the world. The fey of the far west called this sword a "death thing," and Prentice felt that to carry it was his burden, the one he had taken up when he swore to the archduchess to fight for the Western Reach in her name.

"This can never be given, lad," Prentice said sadly, but as soon as he did, he could see the fury spark again in Cassian's eyes. The young man had taken his words as a challenge, he was sure of it.

"Then let me take it from you, or suffer the blood between us," Cassian said, like a mummer playing a hero in a morality play. It was all Prentice could do not to smirk at the poor fellow, so desperate to be taken seriously, to act like the knights he had grown up watching and hearing about. Knights like the ones taken prisoner or thrown from above.

"No," was all Prentice said, shaking his head sorrowfully. "Knight Captain, escort the prisoners, if you will. We are leaving." There was nothing else good to do. Cassian, and likely his brother, would not yield this night.

Indeed, the pair blinked and looked to each other, momentarily bewildered that they had simply been dismissed, and in that gap, the White Lions moved away, escorting their captives. By the time Cassian had registered that his fury would go unanswered, Prentice was ready to turn away as well. Odds were good that the youth would not be able to keep his temper, but if he did make a foolish assault, it was a certainty he would fall with a fey arrow through his eye, dead before his time. Such was the fate of too many hotheads all over the Grand Kingdom these days. Prentice remembered Guillam's dead youth on the ground before Norgate, made a knight as the Young Hopefuls wished to be but slain all the same.

"Well, he sure got his gander up," Sergeant Guillam said as he moved beside Prentice, marching into the unlit portion of the bridge and toward the town proper. They were not safe from some kind of follow-up to the confrontation just yet, but it sounded to Prentice like the baronet was working hard to counsel his nephews to peace, at least for now.

"You think that's the end of it?" the Roarsman asked, his mischievous grin audible in his tone, despite the darkness hiding his expression.

"No," was all Prentice said. He was tired, thoroughly tired of the night, of the war and of watching good men, young and old, throw themselves at death to no good purpose.

"No, me neither," Guillam said. "I don't think that's all over, not by a long stroke."

"Quiet in the ranks, Sergeant," Prentice muttered wearily, and they continued the rest of the march back to Runners Field in silence. Dawn was breaking by the time he had the prisoners disposed and he returned to his own tent to rest.

CHAPTER 28

Amelia emerged from her curtained "bedchamber" to join the morning's bustle in the broader apartment. Neophytes with their veils pulled aside moved back and forth attending to many duties, though some were only standing attentively, like stewards waiting to fetch and carry or pageboys ready to run messages. Lady Dalflitch sat at the head of the main table, letters and account books spread in front of her, with two such neophytes in attendance at her shoulder. She placed a fresh-looking goose feather quill into a porcelain inkwell with a hinged silver stopper and took up the note she had just been writing. Pausing to blow upon the fresh ink to dry it somewhat, she handed the note to the trainee on her left. The girl accepted the small sheet with a bob and then walked away, holding the velum in front herself with reverence, as if it were holy writ.

"No summons this morning?" the Archduchess asked, approaching the table.

"Good morning, Your Grace," Dalflitch said, standing politely and curtseying. The maid behind did likewise. "If you mean to ask if the Lady Penelope has called for you, then no. The young baroness-elect has offered no invitation this morning. I have a request for an audience from an alderman concerning tariffs into Dweltford for his leather goods. He seems to think he deserves special treatment of some kind or thinks to ask for it. Mathilda's baker's boy doesn't speak for the entire town, I'd say. Now that the color of your coin is flashing in the sun a little, more folk will start to like our presence in the town. The conclave will be in the lead, I expect."

"I think we should invite some of the others to meet us as well," Amelia said as her lady-in-waiting stepped aside to yield the table's senior position gracefully. "Put it about that we are trustworthy and open to overtures."

"A good plan, Your Grace," Dalflitch agreed. "I will seek out some names that would be best to start with. No doubt Master Welburne will know who. In the meantime, would you break your fast?" she asked. Amelia nodded and Dalflitch moved to clear the documents away for space, but the archduchess stopped her.

"Leave them. My head aches too much to sit in leisure and eat. If I must have a sour mind, I might as well turn it to business while I have the strength," she said and stroked her belly that was slowly becoming pregnant. Having seen Lady Righteous's recent experience with maternity, Amelia had feared that the days of morning sickness might force her into seclusion. So far though, her stomach had showed little sign of trouble. Of course, she had spent most of her maternity so far in fear for her life while trapped with the Lion Banner in Aubrey, so she may have mistaken morning sickness for simple fear. Even so, it was settling these days. Her head was another matter. Headaches of a morning were something of a norm now. As Dalflitch moved aside, Amelia took the vacated place at the head of the table. Almost immediately, she was presented with a bowl of pease pudding so laden with fish that it smelt more like a chowder and a cup of tea that had an equally distinct aroma.

"What is this?" she asked, sniffing at the tea while the neophyte serving presented a silver spoon for the pudding, a clean linen napkin over her left arm.

"Licorice root tea, Your Grace," the girl explained readily. "With a spice called cinnamon mixed in."

Amelia sipped from the cup and found it pleasant, though unusual, and then accepted the spoon and took her first mouthful of the porridge. It was savory and fresh, flavored with river fish and fennel, which paired well with the tea. She had dipped her spoon for a second mouthful when she noticed the girl still standing by, attentively watching, as if she expected some further instruction from her mistress.

"It's lovely," Amelia said, and when the girl did not take the hint, she followed up with a direct dismissal. "You may go."

The girl curtseyed and then stepped backward, but Amelia felt she maintained a closer attention than normal. She looked to the serene Dalflitch, and as she did so, realized that a number of the other neophytes were also closely watching, and not just their liege lady, either. Some were studying the business of the table like prayerful monks meditating on an ancient iconic painting, seeking religious insight. Others were studying the girls around them as they moved about the room. Now that she had noticed it, a few quick glances told Amelia that the entire population of her chamber were watchful now, working to somehow simultaneously keep their heads politely bowed but their eyes on everything that moved.

Was that how I looked to Daven Marcus? she asked herself, remembering momentarily the near paranoia with which she had marched west under the Usurper's watchful and hateful gaze. If her bearing then had been similar to that of her maids around her now, she could almost understand some of the traitor prince's ire. Every one of the young women looked like shifty villains in a play, affecting good manners while their ranging eyes told the audience they were on the lookout for no good doings.

"Have our nuns turned into footpads and street thieves overnight?" she asked Dalflitch lightly.

"Your Grace?" Dalflitch answered with raised brows, but then her expression showed she caught her liege's meaning. "Oh no, Your Grace. It is something your Lace Fangs have devised. We know that the Inquisition has their skin thieves and that if such a one was to infiltrate us, intent upon your murder, we likely wouldn't notice before it was too late."

Amelia nodded. While other concerns had dominated her thoughts since arriving in Bridgetown, it was these shape-changing agents of the Silent Hand of the Church who gave her the most consternation, ultimately. How did one stop an enemy who could literally become anyone they wanted?

"Ladies Righteous and Spindle observed that..." Dalflitch began, then paused as several figures entered the Paramour's Chambers at that moment, including both Lace Fangs. "Ah, here they are now...I shall let them explain it, Your Grace."

Lady Righteous and Lady Spindle led the way from the streetside door to the table, accompanied by five more neophytes, all of whom turned back their veils as they entered. The small crowd curtseyed to the archduchess, and when she nodded to accept their entrance, the neophytes moved away to join the swirl of duties that the large room allowed. Two even sat down to sew in the light of one of the windows, as decorous as any ladies-in-waiting.

"Forgive my late arrival, Your Grace," Righteous said. "I was det...det...I was held up feeding my littluns. I hope you weren't...inconvenienced." She said the last word slowly, emphasizing every syllable, obviously intent on using the "correct" word despite it being unfamiliar to her tongue.

"A mother's duty is always first to her children," Amelia said with a benign smile, and Righteous bowed, plainly taking that as acceptance for her apology.

It's an apology you'll be making for many years, I suspect, My Lady, the archduchess thought. *Myself as well, soon enough.*

"And I have been about the cloth merchants with some of our flock of learners, Your Grace," Spindle said of her own delayed arrival. "I have some notions for dresses for yourself and the rest of your chamber. Lady Dalflitch sent them along to help me, but turns out none of the haberdashers wanted to laden such refined ladies as ourselves with burdens of cloth. They will send the whole of our purchases with their apprentices later in the day."

"Well, good that you all had some time about in the open morning," Amelia conceded. "But what is this plan you and Lady Righteous have devised?"

"Which plan, Your Grace?"

"'Which plan?'" the archduchess repeated. "The one that has my entire chamber so watchful, like long-tailed cats in a room full of folk in hobnailed boots."

The two Lace Fangs shared a momentary look, and then between them seemed to wordlessly decide that Righteous would take up the tale.

"Well, Your Grace, you know we have these tricksy spies that can look how they want?"

"Not just look but even actually become, I'm told," Amelia said, nodding.

"Tis true enough," Righteous agreed. "Well, when I was with my Prent...with my lord husband...in a private moment, me and the baron realized that there were some tiny signs, like spoor a hunter can follow, that only we would know about each other."

"As husband and wife, of course," Amelia said, holding back a smile at her lady-in-waiting referring to Prentice as her "lord husband" and "the baron." The woman's pride in her spouse was like a banner flying over a castle. The archduchess hoped she appeared likewise when she spoke of her marquis consort. Of course, discussing their love and devotion in terms of "spoor" put rather an unpleasant cast on the notion.

"Aye, that's the thinking of it," Rigtheous said eagerly. "I know Spindle would say that she has the same kinds of tells with her man, and no one here would doubt that Your Grace and Lady Dalflitch both have the eye on your spouses that would reveal the truths none else know."

"Thank you for the compliment, My Lady, but what has this to do with the extra watchfulness all about?" Ameila asked, but even as the words left her mouth, she was beginning to suspect. When Dalflitch took up the explanation, her suspicions were confirmed.

"We all live in such close proximity, Your Grace, not dissimilar to the closeness we married women have with our husbands," the beautiful woman explained, her voice sweet as the morning sunlight around them. "If we are watchful, it should take us all little time to find the 'spoor' Lady Righteous referred to, for each of us. The myriad little tics and traits that are so typical that whenever we think of that person, we remember those signs—signs no mere spy would think to counterfeit, so that even if a skin thief were to steal my voice, as the one in Dweltford Castle tried to do, everyone here would not be fooled because the other signs would not be present."

"What sort of things?" Amelia asked as she took another sip of the licorice tea.

"They could be anything, Your Grace," Righteous offered.

"The way I holds a darning needle," Spindle added. She waved a hand in the air, indicating a hypothetical woman, not pointing at any specific neophyte. "Or the way she says her placenames, with a little bit of Masnian accent. Or the fact that another always moves a little odd cause she can't get her slippers to fit right."

"You've been giving this some thought. I suppose you will be observing myself as well for my...what did you call it...my spoor?" Amelia said.

"Naturally, Your Grace," Dalflitch answered, although Spindle and Righteous both nodded readily as well. "If one of these sorcerous spies was to replace *you*, then the damage that could be done might be immense. The Lions could be commanded to the wrong place in the campaign, or all your most competent and loyal retainers could be rounded up and imprisoned. Your noble house could come undone in too short a time."

Dalflitch's words made a dire kind of sense to Amelia, and the proposed solution was as good as she could think of for herself for now. Nonetheless, she did not imagine there were too many ranking peers in the Grand Kingdom who would suffer themselves to be scrutinized by their own chamber servants and close retainers. Most did not even allow their lessers to look upon their faces directly. The whole point of tugging the forelock or bowing was visible evidence that the inferior person was forcing their head downward in respect. As she mulled these notions over, Amelia cast a glance at her porridge server, still standing by dutifully with her napkin over her left arm.

"So, what odd tics of mine have you observed, maiden?" she asked, and the girl's eyes darted around like a panicked animal. Before the neophyte could speak, Righteous called out in the girl's defense.

"Oh no! No, no, no!"

There was a pause as the Lace Fang seemed to recognize who it was she was talking to.

"Forgive me, Your Grace, but we must not ask it of each other to reveal our tells," Righteous went on, speaking quickly, her courtly manner slipping in her haste. "If we know 'em, then we can give 'em away to a spy like."

Amelia looked from Righteous to the others around her, and Dalflitch explained.

"These skin thief spies are cautious and watchful," Dalflitch said. "If we make a habit of sharing these little pieces of evidence, then there is a chance we might share them with a spy before we realize we have done it. Or, if the spy divines that we have this method, then he would only have to kidnap one girl and ask her, 'What do the others watch for in you?' and he would be able to mimic her completely. The fortress will be unlocked for him, as it were."

The lady seneschal paused and nodded to the Lace Fangs, giving them credit in the explanation.

"We decided that the wisest and safest course, at least until we learn how to undo their magicks completely, is for each of us to maintain our own lists of tells and to keep them utterly secret."

The archduchess nodded and scanned the apartment once more—a vast room full of suspicious young women at their work, snooping on one another like the worst village gossips.

"I have more than twenty people in my close chamber alone," she said, musing. "It would take nearly all my thought to learn a secret clue to every one of their identities. The notion is daunting."

"It should be enough for we to maintain the watch on your behalf, Your Grace," Dalflitch conceded. "After all, that is how bodyguards work. They keep you safe so that you may concentrate on other matters."

"Indeed." Amelia nodded, thinking through the proposed system. "And what happens if we suppose that one of us is a skin thief?"

"Then we seize 'em up before they can do any damage," Righteous said confidently.

"What if you suspect me?"

"Then we seize you up very gently, Your Grace," Spindle offered, and there was a savage glint in her eye behind the lace mask. "And if we are wrong, we apologize. If we are right, then we avenge you without holding back."

"It seems a...goodly...plan for the moment," Amelia agreed, and she drained the last of her tea.

A plan with flaws, she thought. *But better a house with a hole in the roof than one with no doors or windows of any kind.*

Looking down at the papers on the table in front of her, she began to think of the rest of her morning's duties. She took up a changer's receipt with her seal stamped in ink on the bottom. The document had been approved on her behalf by Dalflitch.

"I see by this that we have exchanged nearly enough gold for silver that we can pay our militiamen," she said.

"We have, Your Grace," Dalflitch answered.

"Excellent. That is an obligation I am looking forward to fulfilling. Let us see if we can complete the exchange this morning and move to paying the Lions even today."

"As you say, Your Grace."

The porridge bowl and spoon were cleared away and more tea was poured. As she sipped, Amelia allowed Dalflitch to walk her through the accounts as they pertained to the White Lions, especially to the rewards and extra dispensations she meant to make for those who had distinguished themselves. Prentice had requested permission to commission special dragonfly medallions for those who had campaigned with him in the far west to place upon their armor. Amelia had already agreed, and though the Baron Knight Commander had offered to pay the whole cost from his own funds, she was of a mind to shoulder some of the burden from the Reach treasury. Courage and loyalty had to be rewarded, especially if the rest of her life was to become one of near-paranoid watchfulness.

CHAPTER 29

With the oddness of the morning and a roomful of suspicious eyes around her, Amelia all but forgot to think of her husband's absence through the entire night. She and Dalflitch had almost finished reviewing their accounts, speaking with a money lender who promised them nine guilders on the Masnian, docking one from the lady seneschal's preferred exchange for the rush of providing them by the afternoon. The two were discussing the man's manner now that he had left when a note arrived from Knight Captain Farringdon outlining the previous evening's actions at Sougate.

"They have captured the other barbican already," Amelia said with a smile as she read the message to her ladies.

"In one night, just as Baron Ash promised," Spindle added, casting a glance at Righteous, who was smiling with satisfaction. Although only one was married to the knight commander, and he certainly had eyes for none but his wife, it was clear that both women were very proud of him. Why would they not be? Without him, they were nothing more than a scarred seamstress and a ragamuffin widow. By his hand, both were now respected ladies-in-waiting to the most powerful woman in the west and, in all likelihood, the entire Grand Kingdom.

That is who I am, Amelia thought. *I am that "most powerful woman."* She wasn't sure if the notion comforted her or terrified her. Scrabbling to get control of her lands, for all that it had been desperate, somehow felt purer and clearer than having the control and all the ease that such power would give to her.

As well as giving me yet a broader host of would-be enemies? Amelia could not help but wonder.

"We are essentially done here," she said to Dalflitch at last, then turned to Spindle. "Send to your husband and give him word that guards will be coming to fetch the exchanged coin for the White Lions' pay from his strong room this afternoon."

The Lace Fang curtseyed and left immediately, with two neo-phytes in tow.

"I will change my dress now, ladies," Amelia continued. "Dalflitch, if you would be so kind as to draft a note on my behalf. Tell the knights commander and captain that we will be bringing them their pay, so let them send a trusted escort to carry it through the town."

The archduchess withdrew to her curtained bedchamber and dressed for her day's affairs, spending the entire time trying not to be uncomfortable under the spy-detecting scrutiny of her own handmaids. It would doubtless come to feel like second nature eventually, but for now, it was an odd sensation.

Surely, I have been the center of attention in enough ceremonies and state affairs that I will become accustomed to even this, she told herself.

By the time she was dressed, the silver had arrived from Mas-ter Welburne's secure storehouse—five heavy coffers escorted by three times as many hired guards in their company's green livery. They stood sentry duty over the strongboxes in the little fenced yard of the Paramour's Chambers rather than bringing them in-side, awaiting the handover to the Lions' escort. The brightness of the early morning had turned slowly overcast as clouds came in from the east. Before the militiamen could arrive, a missive from Baroness Penelope was delivered by a steward in orange and gold.

"It turns out you are invited somewhere by the baroness today after all, Your Grace," Dalflitch said as she reviewed the note for her liege. Amelia almost cursed out loud at the young noblewoman's timing. She would not refuse their host's invitations, at least not lightly, but she likewise would not miss the distribution of pay and promotions that was now arranged for the afternoon. The coin was in the yard, waiting. To postpone now was to invite thievery, not to mention the prospect of eight thousand men-at-arms being told they would have to go back to waiting for the pay they were expecting.

"Now that the days of mourning are at an end?" she read from the illuminated page Dalflitch handed to her. She felt her brows furrowing. "I hadn't realized they were still observing the mourning at all."

"It seems the baroness' responsibilities have kept her from the more public duties of her father's passing," Dalflitch said with a neutral tone.

"Were they estranged?" Amelia asked. It was not unknown for nobles to ignore the debt of mourning they owed to their forebears as a kind of posthumous revenge, especially if there happened to be bad blood between them.

"Not to my knowledge, Your Grace," the lady seneschal answered. "All reports are that the baroness was the apple of her father's eye, as she herself said, and she doted upon him in return. As I say, the most likely explanation is that she has simply been too swept up in the needs of her domain."

Amelia could tell by Dalfitch's tone that the lady-in-waiting thought something else might also be at play.

"*Most likely*, but not the only explanation?" she asked.

"Quite so," Dalflitch agreed, nodding her head, but not expanding further upon the notion. There was a knowing look in her eyes. "After all, Your Grace, you had a demesne invaded by sorcerous barbarians, as well as a mindless brute harrying you for your hand, and yet you managed to maintain your rule and mourn your lost husband equally. If she were of a mind to, I cannot believe the baroness would not be able to shed some public tears on her father's behalf."

"A feast to honor the heroes who took back Norgate one day and Sougate the next, and to welcome me to Bridgetown formally. Introductions and the like," Amelia summarized from the invitation before she handed it back to Dalflitch, pairing it with her husband's missive.

"At least it is for this evening. It shouldn't interfere with the pay. We must make sure the prisoners captured from Sougate are ready to be handed over if the baroness wants them," she said, relieved at least that the coins would not be left languishing.

"Do you think she will...want them?" the lady seneschal asked.

"I wanted Duggan captured and tried," Amelia told her, referring to the mutinous rebel knight who had held her castle against her. "I imagine Lady Penelope will want to put these who opposed her on trial as well."

Dalflitch accepted the archduchess's word with a nod. Soon, a small corps of White Lions—four lines, forty men in all—arrived fully armed to take possession of the strongboxes. Amelia met them in the yard to supervise the exchange. With the Lions, acting in part as a guide or even a leader, was young Solomon, looking fine in a new gambeson that was a little loose for his lanky form but which he wore with the pride of any new recruit. A thumping chest salute punctuated his arrival, which raised more than one smirk from the other militiamen, the way the boyishness of youth often amused men who were older and, ideally, wiser. But there was a look of discomfort on his face that did not seem motivated by his fellow militiamen's amusement.

"What troubles you, Solomon?" Amelia asked.

"I...I'm learning to ride a horse, Your Grace," he told her. "It's made my...my...legs...awful sore."

"He walks bowlegged like a drunken chook," one of the militiamen joked, but that was a lapse in discipline too far for the line first leading the escort party.

"Quiet in the ranks," came the bellowed instruction, and all forty men snapped to attentive silence.

"Surely Baron Prentice is not teaching you to ride?" Dalfitch asked, and Amelia became momentarily indignant at her lady-in-waiting's own amused tone.

They've just been told off for laughing, Dalflitch, she thought. *You only make it worse if you make a jest of this as well.*

"No, My Lady," Solomon answered politely despite his discomfort. "The baron knight commander has set his squire, the fey man Dahyoor, to teach me the art. I could have no finer teacher."

Amelia nodded approvingly. Solomon was a bright learner and always seemed to have a knack for putting himself in the most respectful place in any situation.

"The sores will pass, Solomon," she told him kindly. "And if you attend to the squire's lessons, you will soon learn the knack."

Solomon seemed to take the words as the encouragement she intended.

"Now, young man, to your duties. Let us bring the men of the Western Reach the pay they have earned."

The coffers were taken up, two men to each box, while a neophyte brought Dalflitch's and Amelia's horses from where she was holding them in another corner of the yard. Then the escort party moved out, the densely filled streets making the short journey take three or four times as long as it otherwise might, all eyes on the wealthy and powerful woman from the west and her many attendants and soldiers.

CHAPTER 30

"It is one of the finest amphitheaters in the world," Farringdon enthused as he stood with Prentice on the solid stone platform at the bottom of the rising, semicircular steps of seating for an audience that could easily number ten thousand. Behind the stage, facing the seats, was a solid rock face, itself carved in a distinctive curve. "They call this monolith Great Dredgeman, though I have no idea why."

What Prentice had thought was merely a quarry at the far end of Runners Field was in fact this nearly overwhelming piece of geography turned architecture. Once it had been the quarry from which Bridgetown obtained the stones for its buildings, bridge footings, and roads. Over time, as the masons carved the rock away, they had created this space that could easily fit a quarter of the town's entire population at one time. Surely it would hold the gathered two banners of the White Lions. Prentice had never imagined he would have a chance to address ten thousand men at once, yet here was the perfect opportunity.

"We will yet have to shout to be heard at the back," he said.

"Not so much as you might think," Farringdon countered readily. He sprang from the stage and dashed up the steps to the middle of the seating. "Speak now," he called.

"What do you want me to say?" Prentice shouted, but Farringdon waved him off.

"No, *speak*. As if I were standing beside you. I will hear."

"Ridiculous," Prentice muttered, shaking his head.

"Not ridiculous," the knight captain retorted loudly as if he had heard. "It is the science of the curves in the walls and seating."

"You read my lips, surely," Prentice countered, speaking at a normal volume.

"Not so, My Lord."

"Then why are *you* shouting?"

Farringdon nodded and began to return down the steps once more.

"The curves send the sound out into the audience, but it does not work in the opposite direction," he said as he reached the edge of the stage. "It is an ancient technique especially remembered by the masons here in Bridgetown. There are similar smaller ones in the Vec, but they are all fashioned of wood and the performers must all work to project their voices, though they need not shout."

Prentice shook his head in wonder. He had never heard of such a thing. Educated he was, but the further knowledge wandered from the arts of war, the less he knew. Nonetheless, this amphitheater would allow him to do something he had not ever expected. He would be able to conduct all the promotions and divisions of the two banner companies at one time. Every militiaman would be a witness and would be able to feel a share of the pride of their company, from lowest to the highest.

A drummer ran up from the direction of the camp, saluting his commanders.

"Sergeant says I'm to tell you, Lord Commander, there's a escort comin' back with the Lioness herself and the whole of the company's pays. Even mine."

"Even yours, huh lad?" Farringdon asked, and he smiled at the messenger.

"Return to the sergeants and tell them to ready the companies. All but a provost force are to attend here. Every man will take his pay, and the knight captain and I will be presenting promotions. Do you understand?"

The boy listened, but it was clear from his expression that the whole message was too much for him to remember. The fair-haired lad could only have been all of ten years old.

"Just tell him I want both banner companies here in the seats within the hour," Prentice said with a smile. "Except for provosts. Can you remember that?"

"Yes, My Lord," the boy said and when Prentice dismissed him, he rushed off, likely as much from relief as eagerness.

"This was once the home of a revered troupe of actors, as well as an annual festival of travelling players," Farringdon said, still admiring the outdoor architecture.

"*Once*?" Prentice repeated, raising an eyebrow. Farringdon shrugged.

"From what I know, the festival drew from up and down the Great Bridge Road, and the acting company was made from the most renowned players of all types. Somehow they managed to offend the earl one year," he said and then waved his hand. "Not the late Earl John, of course. This was long before his rule. At any rate, I don't know the entire story, but the troupe was forced to flee after insulting Bridgetown's ruler. They tried to set up shop in one of the princedoms, but as players are wont to do, they broke apart further and returned to wandering. Which is how I come to know the tale, I suppose. Since they left, no actors have been permitted to perform here, hence the weeds. The tradition of Bridgetown theater is dead, and the grass grows over its grave."

Prentice looked about and realized that there were indeed weeds and tufts of grass tenaciously gripping the cracks and gaps be-tween many of the stones. He had not paid them much notice until this point—this was a quarry, and of course there would be weeds. As he looked, though, he wondered at the loss they signi-fied. How many hands had labored over how many generations to hack this space from the rock, to fashion its audiological wonder? For now, it was still here, but how much longer, if it remained untended, would it take for the grasses to crack the "wonder" apart, to turn the amphitheater back into a mere hole in the rock.

And all because a nobleman's pride was pricked. It would take no more than a pair of gardeners and perhaps a single mason to maintain this place indefinitely, even if no theater returned here. The wonder could be experienced by generations to come—political discourses, lectures and classes on natural philosophy, scripture readings. Prentice's mind swiftly made a list of possible uses for the fine but decaying space.

"But we have left it fall to ruin," he muttered to himself, having a sudden sense of the amphitheater being like so many of the magnificent things of the past—indeed, of the Grand Kingdom itself. It would have needed only a meager sense of stewardship, a handful of gardeners to tend the weeds. Instead, kings and nobles, Church and guilds locked knowledge and power away behind doors, fearful that to share it would be to lose it. And that was before the Inquisition stepped in, setting fire to the remnants of the ancient world.

Now, instead of a wonder that drew others from all over the world to admire, it was falling into ruin, worn away inexorably by time and the elements of life. He remembered the glorious statue of a dragonfly they had found in the far west, how its function had been corrupted by the Redlanders, and how at last it had fallen into the lake, its power dispelled, its glory smashed.

Would that I was a gardener, Prentice thought. *Instead, I am surely one of the weeds, unable to be fully burned or hacked away, slowly cracking everything great.*

It was a grim thought, not to mention self-piteous and not entirely true, Prentice knew. Nonetheless, the notion left a sour taste in his mouth, and he spat on the stones, as if to purge the flavor. He realized that Farringdon had just asked him a question.

"I am sorry, My Lord. What was it you said?" Prentice asked.

"Only whether you would like me to set some militiamen to clean the weeds," Farringdon explained. "It would take a cohort no more than a quarter of the candle to make the place presentable."

"A goodly thought, Knight Captain," Prentice agreed. "And I will fetch up our banners and standard bearers. We will place both here on the platform, so that they face the company. The quartermaster merchants will need some tables too. We will use them to disperse the seneschal's silvers. Their account books already carry most of the outstanding debts as it is, so they can take their due as the coins go over. I do not want Lions getting in the habit of buying on credit and then forgetting their debts come payday. We are not thieves any longer."

"Were you ever a thief?" Farringdon asked, though he knew full well that Prentice had been convicted of far worse than mere larceny. Prentice acknowledged the gentle ribbing with a smile and then the pair left the quarry together, parting soon after, going to their respective tasks. By the time the pay coffers arrived, with their militia escort and the archduchess herself, the Bridgetown amphitheater was purged of weeds and transformed with Reach colors, standard bearers holding the two great company banners aloft like icons in the apse of a great cathedral.

CHAPTER 31

"This is my army," Archduchess Amelia whispered as she sat on the wooden camp chair set for her on the stone platform, looking upward into the curved stone benches—row upon row of uniformed Reachermen. Almost none were in armor, save for their cream-coloured buffcoats, which looked more grey than white in the overcast light. Autumnal clouds overhead had crowded out the morning's brightness fully now, but it seemed there would be no rain, at least for the moment.

"Not quite as impressive as seeing them arrayed in the field, Your Grace," Dalflitch said equally quietly, seated at Amelia's side. With so many armed, loyal retainers around them, neither the Lace Fangs nor the neophytes had been seen as necessary companions at this time. "But no less inspiring, I would think."

Behind the paired noble ladies, the two great banners of the White Lions Companies, the Lion and the Gryphon, rippled in the light breeze. Placed in iron stands, their poles shifted and creaked as they were moved about. Amelia wondered if they would be safe should the wind pick up more, but each standard had an attendant to keep it safely upright. She had thought that the Lion banner's attendant would be the company's Banner Sergeant, Markas. During the campaign in Aubrey, Markas had served her faithfully and well. However, the two men with the duty at this moment were unknown to her.

"It's not the same as a conclave hall, is it, My Lady?" she whispered to her attendant.

"At least this time others come with their hands out to you," Dalflitch offered. "Far better than begging those skinflint prigs for money they were never going to offer."

The lady seneschal was referring to a meeting in the Counting Hall of Dweltford's conclave in the spring just passed, when she and Dalflitch had sat as they did now, whispering in front of a curious crowd. Then, though, she had been escorted by a mere handful of guards. Now the crowd itself was her escort, and it numbered nearer to ten thousand. She cast a glance behind herself, thinking that the Counting Hall, for all its wealth, had lacked the natural grandeur of Great Dredgeman that towered over them. Amelia's husband had already explained to her the wonder of the curved wall, that it projected the sound of any speech upon the stage outward to the audience. Despite the continuous murmur of a crowd of militiamen, the myriad noises any mass of folks makes except in the most exceptional circumstances, Amelia insisted that they only speak in whispers. Lady Dalflitch had seemed skeptical of the notion of projecting sound but was more than happy to speak softly all the same.

"Whispering is my native tongue, Your Grace," Dalflitch had mocked herself readily. "I am your glorious gossip, the wanton at large in your court. By the time my words are heard, the truth is already lost to mystery."

Amelia appreciated that this was the artfully crafted image her lady seneschal projected, but the archduchess also knew it was false to its last word.

"Your husband would not approve to hear you described as a 'wanton,' My Lady," Amelia chided. "Any other would suffer bitterly at his hands for such disrespect should they do so."

"Quite rightly, too," Dalflitch said primly. There was a hidden note of longing in her tone, Amelia was certain.

"It seems we will remain in the Paramour's Chambers at least until the end of winter," she said and put a hand upon her lady's sleeve. "The river traffic is running almost as before the drought.

It will be no matter to send for Sir Turley to come by boat for a time."

"He has his duties as castellan and head of your household," Dalflitch said with a proud sniff.

"And I will need his report on the progress of such things," Amelia pressed. "He is the anchor point of our chain of supply from Bridgetown all the way back west and north on the waterways. It should take at least a week for him to organize this end of the chain to his liking. You know how he feels about rats in his storehouses, nibbling at the grain."

"Rats in *your* storehouse, Your Grace," Dalflitch insisted, emphasizing her husband's loyalty. Then she turned from her serene oversight of the gathered men-at-arms and gave her liege lady a sincere smile. "I would like that very much, Your Grace. Thank you."

In front of the two regal women, five tables were arrayed, with black-garbed men in long coats seated behind—the quartermaster merchants, traders who had committed their personal businesses wholly to the Lions. Each table had a stack of codices, accounts for the companies, listing the pay owed to each militiaman, as well as any debts he had accrued or costs for replacing any lost equipment. It had amazed Amelia to learn just how many tools and weapons went missing until Prentice and Turley explained that the losses were often from men selling them off for grog or other favors. On the march to Aubrey, the command had been issued that any damaged or missing equipment would be paid from a man's owed wage, and the rate of loss quickly choked off to a mere trickle. There were few simple militiamen who could afford to have the cost of a quality steel sword or a good pair of boots deducted from their pay, let alone pieces of armor.

Next to each paymaster's table was one of the strongboxes containing her silver, converted from the gold of Masnian coins, and it filled Amelia with pride. She could pay her debts, especially to these men whose blood and sweat purchased so much of her domain's freedom and prosperity. The last report from the silvermen of the Miner's Guild indicated that it would take her mines another two years to recover this amount so that she could pay back the Masnian merchants who had sent her the gold in the first place, allowing her to circumvent the bankers' embargo the Inquisition had brought upon her. Unless, of course, the war brought some other unexpected burden upon her treasury.

Amelia was so lost in her satisfied thoughts that she almost did not notice one of the militiamen mount the side of the stage and approach the two women's seats. It wasn't until he was directly in front of her that she recognized the man—Markas. Amelia smiled at him but was astonished when he moved directly past her to stand in front of Lady Dalflitch. He reached up and tugged his forelock, as any yeoman would to a noblewoman of rank.

"My Lady, I know I ain't known to you, and forgive me, but I am Markas, Banner Sergeant of her grace's company," he said nervously, casting a look askance at Amelia, as if fearing her disapproval. "I know that you are her grace's seneschal and closest..."

He paused and seemed to be reaching for the right term—lady, handmaid, advisor, confidante—any of these would have done. Dalflitch regarded the man with her usual stately indifference, and Amelia felt her heart clench for the poor fellow. He had rendered too much good service to feel so overawed in their presence.

"I am in good standing in her grace's service," Dalflitch said, looking down her nose. "What of it?"

"Well, I was hoping to speak with her grace on a matter of my own like..."

"You wish to speak to her grace alone?" Dalflitch asked with a raised eyebrow, tone and expression withering in their disdain.

"Oh no...no, no, no! Nothin' so like that!" Markas stammered. "It's just a matter of my own, so it's important, but not to her grace. Just like to me, so."

"Of course you may speak to me, Markas," Amelia said, freeing the poor man from her lady-in-waiting's expert social defense. "What did you wish?"

"Well, Your Grace," Markas said, and he tugged his forelock again. He was working so hard to be polite that it made Amelia wonder what could be on his mind.

"You know I carried the banner for the Lions all summer?" he began, once he had swallowed a steadying breath.

"You did fine service," Amelia agreed with a nod. "I understand the knights commander and captain have arranged a specific reward for you."

"I know...I mean, I heard, Your Grace, and that's the kind of my problem."

"You don't want to be rewarded?" Dalflitch asked, her voice filled with disbelief.

"It ain't that! S'just that I..." Markas took another gulp of his nerves. "I had this deal, of a sort, with Captain Ash...I mean the Knight Commander."

"What kind of deal?" Suspicion narrowed Dalflitch's eyes, and Markas half ducked his head out of fearful reflex.

If the Inquisition had interrogators like you, My Lady, they would have no need of their instruments of torture, Amelia thought. Talk of a deal, though, put a better perspective on Markas's discomfort. He and Prentice might have made some agreement between them, but it was a bold yeoman who thought he could hold a nobleman to his word as if it were a sealed contract. Doubly bold for an ex-convict like Markas.

"The knight commander has already informed me of his plan to submit your name to me for a knighthood," she told the banner sergeant, thinking she understood his concern. "Promotions of many sorts will be distributed today. Have no fear. He will not renege."

Markas blinked as if his liege lady's words surprised him, which made her wonder if she had missed the point. As he explained further, she realized that she had, indeed.

"That's not the matter," Markas said earnestly. "Captain Ash is good for his words, every last one of them."

"Then what is this deal and the cause of your fear? Speak your matter! You waste her grace's time!" Dalflitch demanded. She was looking from Markas to the rest of the assembly, and when Amelia followed her gaze it became clear that the day's proceedings were almost ready to begin. Markas tugged his forelock yet again.

"Captain...that is, Knight Commander Ash, he made me the banner sergeant of the Lions, but when he did, he promised he would bring me back to the Gryphon Company once he was done in the west."

"Then I'm sure that is what he will do," Amelia said. "As you say, he is true to his word."

"Yea, sure and all, but thing is, I don't really want him to." As he spoke these words, Markas's shoulders sagged as if some tension had left him, like a guilty child forced at last to confess their misdeed.

"You do not want to be a banner sergeant anymore? Or you don't want to be a Lion anymore?"

In truth, based on his service to her so far, Amelia would gladly grant any clemency Markas asked for and let him depart with a mustering pay of many guilders. He deserved that much, at least. She would not allow any of that, though, without talking to Prentice first.

"I don't want to go to the Gryphons, beggin' your pardon," Markas explained. He lightly fingered the noose-like white lanyard around his throat. "I owe the knight commander my life, no doubt. But standing beside you, Your Grace. Keeping the shield over your head and holding your standard, well, that was just about the proudest moments of my life. Watching you face down them Heron beggars like the queen of lions. I beg you, please, let me keep as the Lions' banner sergeant. Square it with the knight commander, so he knows I don't disrespect him none."

Amelia smiled, tears welling in her eyes. She drew in a deep breath to keep her voice steady.

"Banner Sergeant Markas, you will end this day a knight of the Western Reach and remain my loyal standard bearer carrying the Lion, I promise you."

"Thank you, Your Grace," Markas said, and he bowed and tugged his forelock. He backed up a step, ready to head off, but Amelia stopped him for one last moment.

"Sergeant Markas, I am the Lioness, and you are of my pride," she said, meaning the word "pride" in multiple ways, though she had no idea if he would understand. "You never have to tug the forelock to me. As I lead, so you follow. A salute will always be welcome."

Markas furrowed his brow, thinking about her words for a moment, then stood tall and slapped a salute, which the archduchess accepted with a stately nod. When he was gone, she went back to letting her eyes rove over the crowd that was seated facing her.

"I hope they are all that loyal," she said quietly.

"I doubt they are *all* so, Your Grace," Dalflitch said. "But if even one in three is of such a mind, then Daven Marcus has no chance in this childish war of his."

"A goodly thought, My Lady," Amelia told her, even though they both knew that final victory was easier spoken than achieved. It was good to take hope that this was the force that would deliver that victory, and such loyalty was a perfect foundation for triumph, but there was still much blood to be spilled between that day and this.

And what will that day even look like? the archduchess wondered.

CHAPTER 32

"He genuinely feared to offend you, Knight Commander," Amelia said as she relayed the newly raised Knight Banner Sergeant Sir Markas's request after the ceremonies were concluded and they had returned to her chamber. On hearing the story, Prentice had broken into a broad smile and chuckle, which the archduchess did not understand.

"I am merely trying to reconcile that image with my memory of the day he and I met, Your Grace," Prentice explained, raising a hand in a gesture of apology. "I know you hate the noose he wears, but compared to the rags he was garbed in on the walls of Fallenhill in the rain, that lanyard is virtually jewelry."

"He was a convict then," the archduchess said. "If he can rise to a knighthood and leave that state behind, cannot he not put off its trappings as well?" Markas's lanyard, symbol of his status as a man twice spared from the gallows, was a sore point between Amelia and her knight commander. Because he was the Lions' first standard bearer, his "noose" had become a part of his uniform and possibly the uniform of every standard bearer to come after him. She did not like that thought.

"The trappin's is hard won, Your Grace," Righteous said, slipping into her vernacular, as if remembering her own past as a convict brought that way of thinking and speaking back upon her. "Traditions bind folk together, sometimes too tight, but no traditions is a worse way to be. Part of somethin' bad is bad; part of nothin' is sure worse."

"Well, he is a knight now," Amelia said and settled herself into her seat at the head of the table. "He will have traditional rights, including the right to attend tonight's banquet as a part of my retinue if he wishes."

"You might have to command him to it, Your Grace," Prentice added.

"You think him too overawed, Baron?" Dalfitch asked, but the knight commander shook his head.

"No, if I know our man, he will be at work now and all through the night, picking men for his new division within the company," he gave Dalflitch a knowing smirk through the candlelit gloom within the Paramour's Chamber. So late in the afternoon, not only was the setting sun on the wrong side for the windows, but it was also hidden behind the clouds that had closed in the sky like a blanket of grey sheep's wool. "He will agonize over every pick and torment them until they keep their new duties like holy writ, I promise."

The pay and promotions had taken almost all the afternoon to execute. First had been the announcements. Five lions were awarded knighthoods beside Markas, including Sergeants Gennet and Sedgemark for their respective services in the summer past, along with Sergeant Nunel of the lancers. It was made clear that these titles in no way adjusted a man's rank in the company, nor the term of his service. Every Lion served; every Lion marched. The Gryphon Company had taken a long portion of the afternoon, being reorganized as every man-at-arms who had made the westward campaign against the Redlanders was essentially moved one rank upward, to act as the complete command structure over the thousands of raw recruits who were now formally welcomed into the banner. A few positions for line first were drawn from recruits who had arrived with excellent reports of their conduct from Sergeant Franken, commander of the training detachments in Fallenhill. Though absent, the loyal sergeant was also awarded a knighthood, the writ to be sent to him on a boat upriver as soon as possible.

A number of men were given dispensation to muster out of their service, having lost the use of their hands or arms, or otherwise become too injured to continue. Prentice had promised each one his pension was safe, and a claim to a parcel of land was issued for them to show respective guild conclaves back in the Reach. Lady Dalflitch had descended the stage, escorted by a charming-looking young corporal, to stand beside one of the paymaster's tables and supervise the writing of the writs of land, sealed with the archducal signet. A forlorn flock of women had been presented as well—wives who had lost their husbands. Each was given their writ, along with a promissory note for a pension. Amelia had watched them gratefully receive her promise, and it nearly crushed her heart with grief. Their husbands died in her service. They should not be thanking her. If they bankrupted her treasury from here to doomsday it would not be enough for her to repay what she had taken from them.

"I know at least one of the fellas Markas is going to take under his wing. I heard it on the rumor mill," Lady Spindle offered enigmatically. Amelia looked to her and nodded that she should continue.

"He's takin' on… I'm sorry…taking upon himself, the fool who was caught dipping his hand into one of the strongboxes."

Glances were cast around the room, at least amongst the worthies. The many neophyte maids were always glancing and staring, working to fulfill Lady Dalflitch's instructions to memorize the identifying patterns of everyone around them.

"Was that the commotion at the far table when the pays were being handed out?" Amelia asked, remembering the minor incident. While lines were in front of the tables waiting for their guilders, there had been an offended cry and a swift scuffle. Of course, with so many Lions about, including every officer, it had been resolved before the archduchess had even had a chance to ask about it. Spindle nodded.

"I gave orders that he was to be disciplined," Farringdon said from his chair at his wife's left hand. "He's lucky not to hang, taking coins like that in full view. If he'd been one of Baron Prentice's reformed convicts, I'd have had no choice."

Spindle acknowledged the knight captain's words with another nod.

"Mar...*Sir* Markas will do the flogging himself, I'm told. He talked with the fellow, quiet and stern at first, and made clear the kind of bed he'd made for himself. He wasn't stealing from some fat merchant, he was stealing from the Lioness herself, and almost as bad, from each of his brothers in the militia. Then Sir Markas asked him, said the words loudly, so everyone around could hear him, what should be done with a fellow that steals from his own brothers? He asked the bloke, 'What would you do'?"

"And how did the miscreant respond?" asked Dalflitch.

"He said he'd never had brothers before, but like as not, he'd give them a good kicking."

Dalflitch cocked an eyebrow. "At the very least," she agreed archly.

"Sir Markas had the same thoughts, I'd guess," Spindle continued, "for he told him next that he had a choice. He could lose a finger for thieving and be put out of the militia for good, or he could take a flogging and then Markas would bring him on especial, like an apprentice standard bearer, watching over his reform. The fellow scowled and mumbled to himself a time, they say, but in the end, he accepted the banner sergeant's offer."

Many listening nodded their heads in approval, and Amelia made a point to look to Farringdon's reaction, since it was his command to discipline that was being fulfilled. The marquis knight captain nodded solemnly to his wife, showing that he would accept this outcome if she did. She was relieved that it was so, because she was especially pleased that the new *Sir* Markas had not had to begin his tenure as a knight by hanging a thief. Removing a finger was a typical punishment for petty theft, but as the man had sought to make off with some of her treasury silver, that constituted theft of taxes, which had always carried a death sentence.

"Why was he so foolish as to think he could dip his hand in such an obvious place?" she asked in wonder.

"He did attempt some subterfuge, my love," Farringdon explained. "He just wasn't very good at it."

"Force of habit?" Righteous offered. "For someone who's taken coin more than they've ever earned, that much silver in one place might've been temptation they couldn't resist."

"Indeed," Prentice agreed, and husband and wife shared a knowing look. Amelia could guess what they were thinking of.

"What then the risk of keeping such a weak-willed fool around?" Dalflitch asked rhetorically, her voice icy and disdainful. "Wouldn't her grace's realm be better served by packing the twit off a finger short?"

Efficient but heartless reasoning, My Lady, Amelia thought. It made sense to her that Sir Markas, the one Lion redeemed from the deepest condemnation, would be the one to offer the criminal another chance.

"Those who have been forgiven much can themselves forgive much," she said, attempting to quote the scripture, but almost certain she did not have the wording precisely correct.

"Quite so," Farringdon said approvingly.

"An astute observation, Your Grace," Prentice added. "Although I am not certain Markas would be pleased to have himself compared to a prostitute."

Amelia blinked as Prentice's words reminded her of the story from which she had drawn her quotation.

"I suppose not," she acknowledged, and the group fell to thoughtful silence for a long moment. At last, she looked back to Lady Spindle.

"Thank you for bringing this to my attention, My Lady," she said. Spindle nodded calmly, her expression still as enigmatic as it had been throughout the tale. Then she suddenly let out an exhausted sigh, as if she had just completed a long bout of exercise. Amelia wondered what could be wrong.

"Are you well, My Lady?"

"The Forever Countess says the best practice at speaking in a courtly fashion is to recite a story you've been told but aren't much familiar with," Spindle explained. "She says it forces you to watch all your words, because you don't know for sure, so you can't just make it up. You mustn't lie, she says, 'cause that's just gossiping. I've been looking for a time to try it, and it is not as simple as it seems. It's like being fussy with your threads, 'cept you can't unpick the wrong words like you can the wrong embroiding."

Everyone in the room chuckled at her words, and Spindle joined them.

"Gives me a new respect for folks like sacrists and whatnot, as well as some in this very room," she finished off. "Making an effort like that all the time."

"It, too, becomes force of habit soon enough, My Lady," Dalflitch said.

"If you say so," Righteous said with a tsk and shake of her head.

"You also should not judge yourself too harshly," Amelia added comfortingly to Spindle. "You spend your days in the company of two masters of the art. As with any craft, such folk make the skill seem as simple as breathing."

She lifted her cup and raised it first to Dalflitch and then to Prentice. Each accepted her word with a polite nod and then nodded to the other.

"And now, gentles, we must ready for the baroness-elect's banquet. She has sent no precise word what size or ritual of feast she means to set, but since I have yet to receive her formal welcome to Bridgetown, we may expect a night of some significance."

Everyone nodded, and Dalflitch stood from the table.

"Will you want to present the prisoners from the Sougate to the baroness tonight, Your Grace?" Prentice asked. It was a simple question and a necessary one, but it seemed to dim Amelia's mood within herself, like the snuffing of a candle. No matter how much her household might enjoy each other's company, they were still at war and still about the business of securing her lands and her ally's lands for the safety of all their people.

"I think it will be enough to present the names that gave their parole, My Lord," she told Prentice. "That will give the baroness the chance to decide what to do with them for herself. No need to parade them in triumph."

"I will have the list ready for you," Prentice said, and the archduchess dismissed them all to ready themselves for their first public dinner in Bridgetown. Not since the exiled Earl Sebastian had feasted her on his accession had Amelia not been the mistress and host of any banquet she attended. Even without that responsibility, she did not feel she would be able to merely relax and enjoy the meal. She wondered sometimes if she ever would again.

CHAPTER 33

Entering the feasting hall to trumpets and the bellowed announcements of the twins, Prentice followed the archduchess and her marquis consort husband into the large room, with his wife Righteous upon his arm. They were second in the double line order of procession, with Dalflitch alone behind them and then further back, Spindle on her husband Caius Welburne's arm, followed by the newly knighted Nunel and Sedgemark, wearing their uniforms and themselves each escorting a neophyte. As Prentice had predicted, Sir Markas had declined to attend, preferring his duties in camp. Lady Dalflitch had chosen two specific neophytes, apparently, to escort Nunel and Sedgemark, giving them instructions to observe everything that they could about the proceedings. Apparently, the lady seneschal intended to quiz the two trainees at the end of the evening. Prentice could only imagine they would make poor dinner conversation companions now, being too fearful of missing a detail for which their stringent tutor would take them to task. It seemed even more so when the knight commander remembered that Sir Nunel already had a young woman whom he favored with his affections. She was not noble, and they were not yet married, so the lancer sergeant could not invite her as his companion. Thus, Nunel would have two reasons not to enjoy his neophyte's polite company.

Lastly in the procession came Brother Whilte, stepping lightly on his pegleg as if it were the most natural way for a man to walk. Prentice had offered to find a suitable escort from amongst the

Lions for Lady Dalflitch, or even to allow Whilte to fulfill the duty himself, but she had dismissed the notion.

"If perhaps your own or Marquis Farringdon's hands were going begging, I might be persuaded to accept them," she had said, "But I will not sully my husband's place, even if only on my fingertips, by offering them to a lesser man."

Prentice did not remind her of the escort duty done by the corporal earlier in the day, deciding to appreciate her declaration of loyalty to his old friend instead. Of course, he also felt that referring to Brother Whilte, whom the Gryphons called "the Moses of the White Lion," as a "lesser man" was far from just. The chaplain himself made no comment on the subject and took his own place at the rear of the procession quite readily. By the time the group of guests entered the feast, Prentice was thoroughly sick of his marshalling duties. Leading a company of five thousand on the march felt less complicated than this.

"It's not even half the size of the Dweltford great hall," Righteous whispered as they advanced along the aisle between the tables of guests.

"But easily twice as grand," Prentice whispered back. It was true. While the feasting hall was significantly smaller than Castle Dweltford's great hall, it was much more richly appointed. More of a square shape than a rectangle, the walls were covered first in a row of polished marble along the footings, then rising from those to the ceiling were tall panels of richly stained cedar, which filled the room with a pleasant atmosphere. Above that, vaulted ribs soared across the ceiling, all perfectly plastered white, where they met in a gold finial carved like the head of a snarling bear looking down upon the center of the room.

Because of the room's square shape, the entry aisle was by no means as long as Dweltford's, or Griffith's for that matter, but there was a double bank of tables on each side, so that local worthies invited to their baroness's feast turned in their chairs or stood to their feet to watch the entrance of the ruling peer from the other side of the mountains and her closest courtiers.

"It's worse than gawpers at a hanging," Righteous muttered.

"It is like this for kings and nobles every time they leave their homes," Prentice told her. "Have you not noticed? You are one of the peers now. Eyes will be on you almost always."

"I'd rather be back with our babes," Righteous said.

"Petty fussing and filthy small-cloths under their covers?" Prentice joked. "I do not really see much difference."

Righteous smirked, then fixed her smile again in the false expression of serenity that she copied from Dalflitch.

"Mayhaps, but at least ours are ours by blood, and I can teach 'em to be goodly children," she whispered. "Can't well take this lot in hand and clip 'em all under the ear, can I?"

That made Prentice want to laugh, but there was no time, as the procession had reached the high table and the archduchess was presenting her entourage personally. A separate table had been set for the Reach guests on the right side of the hall, a place of honor for allies. As ranking peers, only Amelia and Farringdon, with Prentice and Righteous, were given seats at the high table. From Bridgetown, the only guests so highly placed were the baronets Forsle and Christmark. Forsle was alone, at his niece's right hand, while Christmark sat at the far end with his wife, a quiet and plump-looking woman. When all were announced, introduced, personally welcomed, and escorted to their seats by liveried stewards, everyone sat with an air of thankful relief.

"That mutton smells good," Righteous said as she surveyed the table. Taking the hint, Prentice served his wife generous slices of the roasted meat, which appeared braised in a rosemary sauce of some kind, his eyes wandering over the hall at every second moment. The high table was ever the best vantage from which to spy upon a feast, and though he was a baron now, he kept still to his first duty—the protection of his liege.

"Keepin' a watchful out are you, husband?" Righteous asked him quietly, as if making the most mundane table conversation. "A watchful," meaning a watchful eye—paying attention—was street-fighting slang, and it reminded him that he was not the only wary one in their company. "You'll have kenned to the table on the left here? All them young men?"

Righteous did not look in the direction she was speaking of, and Prentice did not have to check either. He had indeed already noted that the table on the left, corresponding to the Reach guests' table on the right, was populated entirely with young men, all well dressed and quite obviously wearing their sword belts, despite the inconvenience weapons posed for sitting at a feast.

"The Young Hopefuls," he said.

"Or a big part of them," Righteous agreed.

"Oh no, just about all of them, I would bet. Not one will have wanted to miss this. Not after their man Cassian's performance last night."

He searched the faces for the brothers, Cyprian and Cassian, and found them at the far end, fixedly staring at their meals as if no one and nothing else in the hall existed.

Pride still smarting lads? Prentice mused.

"They come with steel, too. You think they're of a mind to eat with cutlery tonight?"

Cutlery was another of his wife's street terms. If the Hopefuls were here to "eat with cutlery," it meant fighting and bloodshed, not polite dining.

"I left my own sword at home," Prentice said quietly to his wife while smiling to Nunel's veiled dinner partner as she passed him a silver pot with crystals of salt in it. "I take it you have come ready for dinner."

"I'm a Lace Fang, husband," was all Righteous said in reply, taking a pinch of the salt for herself and sprinkling it upon the lamb. "But I'm to thinking that they're wearing steel for brass, not to set to a 'meal.'"

I agree, Prentice thought, *but too many hot heads in life bring a weapon just for show and end up using it because they cannot control themselves. If nothing else, Cassian is exactly that sort.*

The mutter of conversation barely drew Prentice's attention through the banquet, being more like the buzzing of insects by the riverside to his ears—always there but for the most part ignored. So it was that he was not really prepared when he heard a question addressed to himself directly.

"I am sorry, Your Grace, my mind had wandered," he said, recognizing that it was the archduchess herself who had called for his attention. He turned his focus to the center of the table where Amelia and Penelope sat side by side.

"I was telling the baroness-elect that you have the prisoners from last night, as well as their names and pledges of parole, and are ready to hand them into Bridgetown's custody at her pleasure," the archduchess reiterated.

"I do, indeed, Your Grace," Prentice confirmed. He heard a low shift in the conversation at his left, and from the corner of his eye he thought he could see some of the Young Hopefuls leaning in close, listening out to hear conversation about the Sougate's prisoners. Prentice nodded his head to the young baroness. "I can provide either or both at any time, and you may dispense with them as you see fit. They are of course, Bridgetown's enemies and your prisoners. We hold them only in trust. I also want to mention, if I may, how well the young men of Bridgetown did in their role during the assault."

"Wilforn, did you hear that?" Lady Penelope called down to her cousin, sitting in the middle of the long table of Young Hopefuls. "Baron Ash tells me you lot contributed well to his victory in Sougate."

That's not what I said, Prentice thought ruefully. The baroness had just taken his attempt to share credit and made it sound to the Hopefuls like a veiled insult, damning them with faint praise.

"Thank you, Baron," Penelope told him, then turned back to her main guest. "Tell me, Archduchess, what would you or your knights commander and captain do with the prisoners? You've dealt with men like this before. Should I have them executed as traitors, or should I return them to their usurper master as prisoners ransomed? I doubt their weregelds would add much to my treasury, but I feel I should do what is best for my people, too. I can afford to be somewhat merciful to these particular men. The worst of the Usurper's brutes were all punished the night my father passed."

"By our hands!" an unseen voice from amongst the Hopefuls declared loudly, and the entire table banged their cups, saluting their own actions. The noise settled rather swiftly, not taken up by any other tables present. Those were all populated by what looked like the guild and mercantile class. It seemed to Prentice's eye that the Young Hopefuls were not the heroes to Bridgetown's people that they saw themselves to be.

Perhaps the folk of Bridgetown feel they have swapped one group of entitled, abusive nobles for another? he wondered. *Watch out lads. What you have taken by force can be taken from you the same way.*

The baroness's question remained unanswered, and Prentice looked to Farringdon, then both men nodded to their liege. The question had been addressed to all three of them, but protocol could only allow Archduchess Amelia to speak first. She seemed about to when Baronet Forsle leaned over from Baroness Penelope's other side and intervened.

"I think these are matters better left for later, niece," he said in an avuncular tone.

Chapter 34

Amelia watched the baronet's intervention closely. From Prentice's description of the man, she knew he was likely to be a stickler for every point of protocol, but it seemed he was happy to violate it to give his niece advice in public.

"I am baroness," Penelope told her uncle. "Can I not seek counsel and judge in my own realm? It is my peace that was offended."

"It was still your fath...," the baronet began, then paused, in the manner of a tutor judging which of a student's errors was more important to correct first. "Only a prince or a king may rule over a realm. As baroness, you could only judge in your own *domain*. Moreover, I remind you that you are not yet baroness. Until your accession, you are merely baroness elect."

"I have no siblings to make a claim. I am my father's heir," the baroness objected. "What difference does it make?"

"The difference is that by waiting for your accession to the title, you make certain that your judgements, when you do make them, are unquestionable in law, tradition, and righteousness."

The young noblewoman sighed heavily, a little like a frustrated child who can see their elders' wisdom but wishes they did not have to follow it. Penelope looked to Amelia.

"What do you say, Archduchess? The Lioness is known for delivering swift justice to her enemies. Do you think I should wait?"

Is that what I'm known for? Amelia wondered, but she nodded to her hostess and the baronet at her side.

"Right justice is better than swift justice," she said. "Your uncle is wise to encourage you to make sure your rule is above reproach. If wisdom calls for justice to be swift, then be swift. If not, why rush?"

"You would not rush?" the baroness asked.

"The men are your prisoners, secured at your pleasure. They will be no less guilty tomorrow. If you need to judge them then, they will still be there. But, as your uncle said, you will be more secure and your judgement more unchallengeable once you have acceded to your title."

Amelia did not think she was being a hypocrite counseling the young noble to patience, but she did wonder. After all, she had famously had the rebel Duggan killed right in front of her in the midst of her own feast hall the night he was captured. She told herself that was a moment when "wisdom called for justice to be swift" and hoped she wasn't deceiving herself. As she thought about it, Duggan was not the only one her swift justice had fallen upon in her years as a ruler.

The baroness nodded thoughtfully for a moment.

"Alright," she said. "They can live awhile longer, and I'll decide what to do with them after. But that only points us to the next, and even more important task ahead of me, and I also certainly want your advice about that."

"Niece...?" Baronet Forsle began, but Penelope ignored him.

"My time of mourning is officially over, and it is now time for my accession," she said. "In this particularly, I plan to follow her grace's example."

Amelia felt her brows furrow again as she tried to understand the young woman's meaning this time. Marne, Amelia's first husband, had been the Duke of the Western Reach. She had married into her title. She had had no claim of blood and thus could not have acceded to the position. What did Baroness Penelope mean? Forsle was similarly confused, it seemed.

"What are you saying?" he asked.

"I'm saying that it's silly that my father could be an earl but I am only a baroness, or baroness-elect," Penelope explained. "Why is his title higher than his heir's, just because he was a man?"

Amelia had a sudden premonition of the baroness's ultimate purpose, and she had to work hard to keep her misgivings out of her expression. She hoped the baronet would foresee his niece's intentions and head them off himself, or even just explain that an earl was not the same as a baroness, since an earl sat upon the nation's frontiers and was law bound to ride to its defense. The tradition was that an earl was always a knight ahorse and a man-at-arms. Since his wife, or daughter, would not ride to war, they could not inherit the same title. A small voice inside her did wonder how the situation might be different if the earl's wife was a Spindle or a Righteous, but she shoved that aside for later contemplation. For now, she focused her entire attention on the baroness-elect and baronet's argument.

"This is how it is, niece," Forsle was explaining. "It is the way of things."

"Well, it is a fool way," Penelope said with undisguised contempt, her usual light-hearted expression hardening. "It's the ways of fools that have gotten our kingdom into this bitter state in the first place. Only fools would think to let a monster like Daven Marcus claim a throne, any throne. Letting the coxcomb claim a chamber pot is too good for him."

Baronet Forsle hemmed and hawed for a moment, and Amelia could imagine the conflicting forces undermining his thoughts. If he was the traditionalist he seemed, he would at once agree with Penelope's assessment of Daven Marcus's character and at the same time object to hearing the king so described, even a king who definitely should be tried and executed. After all, only Mother Church had the authority to try a king, and the Usurper's actions had been spurred by factions within the Church. How could Mother Church judge Daven Marcus when it was itself divided by the politics of the kingdom? Even if he were utterly loyal to the old order, Baronet Forsle would still be a man conflicted within. Baroness-elect Penelope did not wait for her uncle to gather his wits out of that inner turmoil.

"No, I am finished with doing only the 'done thing' uncle," she said, and as she continued to speak, her voice rose in volume, so that everyone in the hall could hear it. "The 'done' thing has been to let livereaters, bedswervers, and old men ride our lands into weakness and then into war. To what end? Not only do I reject this folly, but I look to the example of another woman, one who has shown that she can defend her land not only against usurpers and traitors, but even against monsters out of legend. A woman who is *respected* by the men in her *realm*, for she *is* a princess in her realm."

Amelia was certain now she knew where the baroness was going, and she earnestly wished she could counsel the girl to caution. She looked to the baronet, but he seemed too confused by his niece's words to be any help any longer.

I may be respected by the men in my realm, the archduchess thought, *but I didn't gain their respect by insulting them. Be careful, girl.*

The Usurper might well be a coxcomb—the Archduchess of the Reach had said worse things about him, and in public—but to say that the entire rest of Grand Kingdom men were livereaters and bedswervers was far from fair. A bedswerver was an adulterer, and it took all Amelia's will not to look at Dalflitch at that moment. Truly, of anyone present, if the insult was deserved, it was by her, and Lady Dalfitch would be the first to admit it, to her normally concealed shame. Livereaters were folk greedy to enrich themselves, to gain fat and comfort by taking only the best. It was typically an insult for the merchants and guildsfolk, though usually only used by yeomen. Nobles often ate just as well as the mercantile class, both literally and metaphorically, and tended not to draw attention to the fact. Not because they feared to be seen as greedy, but because they never wanted to be taken as similar to the lower orders, no matter the wealth involved. When a noble insulted their lessers, they always emphasized birth not wealth.

"Seeing as she has protected her realm and her people when the men around her failed, I will follow her example for myself."

"The men around me failed?" Now you are insulting my husband and my closest friend, Amelia thought, and knew that she was struggling to keep from saying something. *No woman alive has had two such loyal and capable men in her life, never mind all the other faithful souls which they have helped draw to my service.*

Her mind went involuntarily to the recently knighted men sitting at the right-hand table, there in front of her. Every one of them had wounds in her service, scars in her name. And they were proud to have them.

And I have another eight, or more, thousand out in a field not leagues from this very room! Are you determined to insult everyone except me, girl?

The baroness had, in fact, moved on from careless offense and now seemed ready to top her words with a crowning shock.

"I announce tonight that at my accession I shall assume the title of Archduchess of Bridgetown," the baroness declared with the precise wording of a practiced speech. "The ceremony shall be held in Bridgetown Cathedral in three days' time."

"It cannot be in three days," Baronet Forsle said weakly, as if in shock. "The patriarch is not here at present. He is in synod, meeting over the dissensions within the Church. And he will not return for an accession that claims so much, surely. You know how the Church has named the actions of the woman from the west."

"I don't care what the Church has named," Penelope told her uncle archly, and the man recoiled as if slapped. Clearly troubled by flouting minor traditions, it was obvious that rewriting the social order and disdaining Mother Church fell on the man's heart like a millstone. Amelia felt no small amount of pity for him. Since the Redlanders came out of the west, too few of the world's old truths seemed reliable anymore. Even though she had accepted change was inevitable, and had even forced some of it herself, she still knew the loss to be felt at the passing of the old.

"It's only a blessing. Any sacrist can say it," the baroness-elect insisted.

"No sacrist of Bridgetown would dare, I promise you." Baronet Forsle shook his head, unable to imagine it.

"I don't need a Bridgetown sacrist! There's a perfectly service-able sacrist right there, and he is accustomed to following his liege's commands. I don't doubt the Lioness will lend him to me!"

The baroness looked down to the table of Reachermen where Brother Whilte sat now with a hunted look on his face. Amelia watched the man and knew he was feeling a similar uncertainty to her own. There was a truth to Baroness Penelope's words, but they were being spoken brashly, wildly even, and they scattered offense about like the autumn leaves falling.

"You will not deny me, will you Archduchess?" the baroness-elect—soon to be archduchess-elect—all but chal-lenged, and Amelia found herself suddenly as equally at a loss for words as Lord Forsle. She needed this young woman's goodwill to keep her men-at-arms safe through the winter until they were rested and ready to march again, but the girl's ambitions were running so far ahead, and Amelia wanted—needed—a chance to consider the implications. She just couldn't think of a way to make one.

"Brother Whilte is my knight commander's chaplain, My Lady," she answered politely. "He is not simply at my beck and call. However, if you wish, I will ask him for you."

It felt a cowardly thing for her to do, but it was the only thing Amelia could think to say quickly. She looked to Whilte, and if he understood all of the political implications, little of it showed on his face. With a solemn expression, the chaplain rose from his place on the bench seat and bowed awkwardly to his liege and then to Penelope.

"I will do whatever you ask of me, short of sin, Your Grace," he said.

"You see, respect and obedience," Lady Penelope said, obviously to her uncle but addressing the whole room. "And because I can trust you as I can no others, Archduchess Amelia, I will ask you for another favor, one I will repay in whatever way I can eventually, but for now something my estate's weakness shames me to have to mention."

Penelope paused, and Amelia wondered for a moment if the girl expected her to say something, to take some part in this performance, which she was sure the young noblewoman had been rehearsing for a good long while. Too long. As it happened, Lady Penelope was happy to carry the stage on her own.

"I trust that you will accept my accession as an archduchess, and because I have such trust in you, I will entrust my town to you through the winter. In a mere two days you liberated our dear Bridgetown at both of its mighty gates—the siege at the Norgate and the occupation of Sougate, both ended by the swift, unanswerable might of your army, Archduchess. With your men-at-arms' greatness so well attested, I ask you now to train my militia, so that the bears might become as mighty as lions. And until you have done this, please take up the duty of protecting the gates you have liberated. I have no other warriors so capable of the task."

The Norgate siege is lifted? Amelia thought. She had not heard any word of Duke Robant quitting the siege entirely. It made her wonder what Bridgetown even needed from the White Lions now, and she was again confronted with the complexity of giving an answer. In one sense, these requests were exactly the kinds of things she had expected from the young baroness. Her militia was paying for their winter quarters with training and service as allies in the field. Bridgetown's militia were a mere handful, it's knights no more than squires cut short. Amelia's army was the largest commanded by any one noble in the known world. But Amelia had also never wanted this sense that the White Lions were coming as proud elites to lord their might over the folk of Bridgetown. Even as Baroness elect Penelope, soon to be Archduchess Penelope, it seemed, claimed to want to overturn the coxcombs of the established order, she showed the same superior disdain for others that was the worst failing of the Grand Kingdom's nobility. One did not win respect with disrespect, no matter how justified it might seem.

And as Amelia looked about the hall at the perplexed and often scowling faces of the guests, from her own entourage to the least guildsman at the farthest table, it was clear that everyone present felt disrespected.

Chapter 35

"I half kenned on them young blades throwin' down right there and then," Spindle said, recalling her memories of the young baroness's announcement as Amelia and her own court sat together in the late-night hours, reflecting on the feast just passed.

"The girl did manage to offend just about everyone in the room, I would say," Spindle's husband Caius added. "Though, of course, I cannot and would not think to speak for the peerage."

Amelia appreciated the merchant's commitment to politeness and respect. The nobility of the Grand Kingdom tended to look down their noses at Reachermen, even Reach nobility, as rough and uncouth, but Amelia had never been as respected by any men and women as she had by those of the Reach. The courts of Rhales and Denay might not consider the Reach their peers, but it was they who seemed so often to fail in manners and courtesy.

"Master Welburne, in this company, I invite you to speak as a peer," she said honestly. "We of the Reach are known to be flexible with tradition. We might as well enjoy the fruit of the rumor, as well as the embarrassment."

"You are kind," Caius said, but his voice croaked. He was still weak from his travails in the summer, and the thin man's pale skin looked as papery as ever. He was sitting in a cushioned chair, while Spindle, his wife, sat upon the arm beside him. She offered him a cup and he asked her what it was.

"Carabost red," she told him quietly. "Warmed, with essence of echinae flower. The herbwives say it'll do your chest good. Sip it."

The merchant accepted his wife's instructions with a nod and a smile, but as he reached up to take the cup from her hand, his sleeve fell back, and the thinness of his wrist shocked Amelia. He was not a well man.

And what little health he has, he lost a goodly portion in my service as well, she thought. A sudden flash of fury at the young baroness's disdainful pronouncements made her frown, and she chewed the inside of her lip until it became painful.

"Well, our young hostess has managed to cast effrontery over her entire domain—soon to be her realm, apparently," Dalflitch observed cooly. "It's an awkward situation for Bridgetown, but if I may suggest, Your Grace, our first question must surely be: how does this affect you and what should we do about it?"

Amelia nodded, prompted from her angry thoughts. She cast her gaze about her gathered courtiers. There were two fireplaces in the main Paramour's Chamber—a large one in the central space and a smaller one behind the curtains of the bedchamber, as well as the stone and iron stove at the far end. In recognition of Master Welburne's weakness, as well as the gathering cool of autumn nights and her own growing pregnancy, the chairs had been brought so that they could all sit or stand around the main fireplace, which crackled with a warming orange glow. With all eyes upon her, Amelia nodded once more to invite her advisors to share their wisdom. After a moment, Farringdon offered his first.

"As far as I can see, militarily there's nothing much we need to do," he explained. "At least, for now. We are already committed to training the militia and defending the town. Robant's force marched away in these last days, and there's nothing in the fields of Sobridge. Both gates are secure, and when properly garrisoned, will be sound in defense. If someone comes to assault either again, the Lions can surely hold them as well as those we replace. And the militia freed from those duties can come live in camp with us. Surrounded by two banner companies, they'll soon learn and come up to scratch."

"Are we really so secure as that?" Amelia asked. Her White Lions had been invited to rescue a town beset. Could two swift actions, one morning and one night, have been enough to reclaim Bridgetown's safety?

"Well, it will depend upon what Duke Robant does," Farringdon continued. "But even if he returns with two or three times the numbers he had, we will be able to make the Norgate bastion secure without too much trouble. If we set to it from tomorrow morning, then in a week we can have better than we had to hold the bridge at Aubrey, and here we already have the barbican."

"As simple as that?" asked Dalflitch. "And at the Sougate?"

"Sougate is reclaimed and is many times the stronghold that the Norgate barbican is. The archduchess-to-be could very well throw open the gate to trade again, I'd say. Unless there was something I'm missing."

The marquis looked to Prentice and eyes followed his. The knight commander was standing beside the fire, his face half in shadow, but even so, when she looked to him, Amelia could see the serious, thoughtful expression that he so often wore at councils like this.

"The Town Sobridge fields already have their harvest in," he said simply, and Farringdon's expression changed almost immediately.

"Ah, I hadn't thought of that," he said.

"Does that signify much?" Amelia asked, perplexed.

"The prince of Town Sobridge plans to go to war," Brother Whilte said from his chair on the opposite side of the circle.

"How can you be so sure?" Dalflitch asked. "It could be he has some weather seer telling him that winter comes early."

"He's brought the harvest in to have feed for his army and to free his peasants for a levy," Whilte explained. "He will not be expecting an early winter. He will be hoping for a late one so he might march a swift campaign before the rains truly set in."

"No other explanation?"

The chaplain looked back to Prentice, allowing the knight commander to further explain their thinking.

"Bridgetown is a treasure house, and right now it has a civil war at its back," Prentice said. "Sobridge's prince knows that no matter what happens on the south side of the river, there is no united Grand Kingdom army coming to Bridgetown's defense—not this year and surely not before winter. Baroness or archduchess, Penelope is a sentry alone on the bridge. In all history, these bridges have not been this vulnerable, and the Vec princes have coveted this treasure house since the days of the rebellion."

"That is certainly true," Farringdon agreed.

"And there is already one army on that side of the Murr, hired, raised, and supplied for campaign," Amelia added from her own thoughts. "We might have left the Golden Heron's mercenaries behind in Aubrey, but it will not take them long to march from there. They could still think to arrive before winter."

"The prince of Town Sobridge will be more thinking of a swift campaign before they can even arrive," Prentice said, not exactly contradicting his liege, but not agreeing either. "Unless he already has a pact with the Heron, he will not trust the bankers. He will fear them handing Bridgetown over to a mightier prince from farther south with a larger army. He will have enough trouble holding Bridgetown by himself against other Vec princes as it is. Why let mercenaries in and risk losing the prize to their greedy fingers right from the start?"

Amelia thought all that made sense, but as she considered Prentice's reasoning, she found herself affronted on behalf of her militia's honor.

"Surely this prince of Sobridge, whoever he is, knows we have arrived by now though?" she said sourly and lifted her own goblet to her lips. She was drinking brandy—not the heated wine Spindle served to her husband, but the liquor warmed her all the same. It was said that strong liquor was not wise for women with child, but a little at night was not considered too great a risk. "Will the prince not change his mind now that he knows we are come?"

"Vec princes are no more known for changing their plans than their Grand Kingdom counterparts," Farringdon said with a half-smile.

"And consider what he knows of us, Your Grace," Prentice added. "You have heard what little Bridgetown knows of you and of the White Lions. There's a witch in the west who ensorcells men, and she has a troop of witless fools traipsing around behind her. He might have heard that tale. Or else he has heard the tale of Daven Marcus, kingslayer, who has slaughtered all of Bridgetown's knights and now a rabble of convict rogues from across the mountains has been brought over to wave sharpened sticks at his own levy. He will doubtless expect Town Sobridge's knights to put paid to any resistance such worthless men might raise. Or the Veckancer prince could have heard some other rumor, equally as mistaken but enough to persuade him that this is his main chance."

"Or he could just be a brassy fool with his blood up," Righteous muttered from the chair beside her husband. The group became quiet as they mulled over the knight commander's words. In the relative silence, the sound of the neophytes going about their chores could just be heard. Already, many of the young women were skilled enough servants that they could pass as household staff of any great house. Almost all were gaining in their courtly manners as well and soon would be able to act as true ladies-in-waiting, at least in the junior sense. Of course, Lady Dalflitch had yet to suggest that even one was ready for such a role, and Righteous and Spindle still found moments to continue the girls' training for combat. Of a morning, the Paramour's Chambers echoed with thumps of girls wrestling and sparring with short blades in the attics above. Righteous and Spindle had made spaces in the ancient stores of furniture specifically for the purpose.

"So that leads us back to the question of the first, doesn't it?" Dalflitch asked. "What does her grace's household need to do next?"

"The knight captain's original answer was ostensibly correct," Prentice responded. "We must hold both bridge gates, as we are commissioned to do, while we train Bridgetown's militia. And we can, but we must do so expecting attacks upon each bastion—the prince of Town Sobridge or some other army from the south, or Robant returned from the north."

"The duke's army is a spent force, surely."

"Yes, but it might be reinforced even before winter, either by the kingslayer or by a noble of one of the other factions persuaded to the Usurper's cause."

"Is that likely?" Amelia asked.

"Very, I would think," Prentice said firmly. "The marquis will no doubt agree with me when I say that as the Vec princes accept no king, so there is no higher loyalty or authority to bind them. They make and change allegiances with the seasons. It is why they invade so infrequently. They have no one to unite them."

"But that is the Vec. This is the Grand Kingdom," Caius Welburne surprised many by saying in a strong, if rasping, tone, revealing a parochial heart Amelia never expected could be hidden beneath his shrewd and calculating demeanor.

"Yes," Farringdon, former prince of Aubrey conceded. "But as Baron Prentice hinted, now the Grand Kingdom has no higher authority either, only pretenders with no loyalty to bind to *them*."

CHAPTER 36

"Come what may, you know you have my full support in matters of war, Prentice," the archduchess said firmly. "Make whatever provisions you think necessary."

She paused and Prentice took a moment to look to Righteous. Ever since the babies had arrived, his wife had found these late-night meetings more tedious and sometimes fretted to return to their children's side by this hour. Tonight, though she seemed a little more taken with the evening's dramas.

"Is there any danger of Robant's force choking off the river trade to Dweltford again instead?" the archduchess asked, reminding them that the duke's blockade of the River Dwelt was only recently broken. Prentice did not favor Duke Robant's chances of doing that either, not before next summer, at least.

"Not until he recovers his army's strength once more," he said confidently. "And even then, without Bridgetown at his back to resupply him by river, any thrust into the Reach now will leave his supply trains vulnerable and his flank open to attack. The further west he went, the more spaces he would leave behind him on the riverbank where we could land harrying forces by boat. We could use fey archer tactics, even without their great skill and stealth, and pick his forces to pieces like a flock of crows about an execution cage."

Prentice noticed his liege shudder slightly as he invoked the image of a crow's cage, the form of execution where the criminal was left hanging to starve, until the carrion birds came to peck his corpse apart. Intended as a warning to others who might contemplate criminality, it was a brutal way to die. In Prentice's mind, it was Robant's force that would perish that way if they tried another invasion around the south spurs of the Azure Mountains, and he was certain the duke was a canny enough strategist to see the risk for himself. However, knowing what the duke would not do was not the same as knowing what he *would* do, or even what he was doing.

"Your Grace, with your permission, I will send Dahyoor north up the Great Bridge Road a day or two to spy upon the retreated duke and his remnants. Perhaps he can range about to some of the nearby villages and farms as well to see the state of the land. Officially, Bridgetown's demesne extends leagues north from the Norgate, I understand, but no one from the town has gone into that land for a year or more. It might be good to know who still lives and how."

The archduchess smiled, but there was doubt in her expression as her eyebrows knotted.

"A goodly notion, Prentice, but why ask my permission for this specifically? You send men a-scouting often."

"I ask Your Grace because it has been King's Law and Church Law for almost a thousand years that no fey nor fell creature be permitted to live in civil lands. To foster them is treason, and to know of them but speak no warning is heresy."

"Of course, and if *you* send him, he goes in *my* name, which would put me in danger of an ecclesiastical court...again," the archduchess said, nodding solemnly. Then she smiled with a sardonic expression. "I do not have the education you do, Baron, and neither you nor I have Master Solft's wisdom at laws. Yet if the scholar were present, I am sure he would remind you that much the same conditions pertain to every convict transported over the mountains. The Church in synod, back when they could agree at anything, did agree to revoke your pardon from King Chrostmer. If I am to be charged for your fey squire riding civil lands, then

I am surely guilty of leading you to the same. But thank you for giving me the chance to decide for myself."

Prentice bowed his head and shared her smile. For so many years he and his liege had been running from one crisis to the next. It was easy to forget exactly how far they had run—far past social and legal boundaries that once would have been thought impossible to cross. Which turned Prentice's thoughts back to the evening's main religious question, and he was not the only one, it seemed.

"If Your Grace's military position is secured, and Bridgetown's with it, then the true question of the night must be the young baroness' plot for her advancement in the peerage," Dalflitch said. "The military implications are not trivial but raise no insurmountable obstacles. What, then, of the politics and, as Baron Ash has touched upon, the religious?"

"The baroness had the right of the ritual requirement, as near as I know," Brother Whilte said.

"A ranking peerage does not require a prince of the Church, a patriarch, or similar high sacrist?" Dalflitch asked.

"For a king or prince, certainly, but even then there is precedent for lesser clergy to take the role, especially in the chaos of war when an heir must inherit his slain forebear's title immediately in order to take command," the chaplain explained.

"Blannheim at the Battle of Grimschurch," Prentice said, naming the first and most obvious historical example that came to his mind from the lessons of his youth. Whilte nodded sternly with a throat-clearing cough.

"And at least twice in the War of the Rhale's Greens, as I can remember," the brother added, citing further instances. "I would expect the patriarchs will protest my doing the rites, but only from the perspective of prestige or political opposition. They'll have no theological grounds to object."

"Not that that's likely to stop them," Dalflitch added sourly, and while Whilte was clearly not comfortable with the implication that Church leaders made their judgements and then invented their theological justifications afterward, it was a characterization he seemed reluctant to argue with. Prentice could understand. Pleasant or not, it was not an inappropriate characterization of the Church at this juncture. For every true and faithful man of God like Whilte, it seemed there was a venal and self-serving churchman who saw religious orders as nothing more than his worldly profession and his flock as no more than customers, a captive market, whom he could squeeze for whatever prices their purses would bear.

"If my religious danger is no further increased by supporting our young hostess, then what do we say politically?" the archduchess asked.

"She's in the same spot you were, isn't she?" Righteous offered flatly, and when others looked to her, she in turn nodded to Spindle, who shared her shrewd expression. Sitting on the arm of her husband's chair in the firelight, Prentice was struck by how much he could see both the lady and the convict within her, just as he did in his wife.

"She can have all the titles and all the territories she wants," the scarred Lace Fang said with certainty, "as long as she has the steel and the brass to take them and hold onto them."

Street fighting logic, Prentice thought and smiled.

"The girl's got all the 'brass' she needs," Dalflitch said, shaking her head. "I'd say she has ticked off her nobles, her churchmen, her conclave, and her men-at-arms—would-be knights and militia both. Whatever steel she has left will be reluctant to raise itself in her service now, I would think."

"Seems she has never been told that one catches more flies with honey than vinegar," Farringdon observed. While many chuckled at the common aphorism, Lady Dalflitch rolled her eyes contemptuously, not at the marquis as it happened, but at the baroness they were discussing.

"Never mind vinegar, My Lord. She poured oil over the heads of every estate within her domain and tried her best to set it all alight. The only flies she'll catch are the ones feeding on the ruins of her rule if she's not careful."

Prentice found he had to agree with Lady Dalfitch's assessment, with the proviso that the men-at-arms were no great loss to the baroness. Her militia was like a traditional Grand Kingdom town militia—happy to wear some colors and carry a weapon but equally happy to leave any real fighting to the knights. To call them men-at-arms at all was generous. As to the knights of Bridgetown, old men and Young Hopefuls, they were all more likely to harbor a rebellious Sebastian than a loyal Gant or even an equivocal Gullden. Just the expressions on their faces at the feast when the baroness made her announcement told him that. Dalflitch was right; brass, Lady Penelope might have, but she had little steel, and what she did she was throwing away.

Then it is my task to give her more and better, he thought. To that end, he already had some ideas, and as he considered them, another occurred to him.

"Dearest wife, surely you are becoming somewhat frustrated at your recent forced inactivity," he said to Righteous, who gave him a sudden withering glare.

"Inactivity? Is that how you think of new motherhood, husband? You think I loll about all day, doing nothing?" she said, her voice rising so that it almost seemed too loud compared to the midnight softness the conversation had had up to now. "Is that all you think of me? I am sure that the marquis consort here or Master Welburne would never show such affront to their 'loved goodwives, 'specially in company like this. Even that lout sweet Lady Dalflitch is sadly hitched to would be kinder in open circles."

"Open circles?" Prentice repeated without thinking. The privacy of the archduchess's inner court was hardly a public forum, but that was not his wife's true point. From her expression, it was clear that Righteous was enjoying the play of chastising him, and as Prentice looked around the group, each woman present nodded with arch solemnity, pitying for their poor, mistreated sister. Even the archduchess managed it for a moment, before hiding an irrepressible smile behind her sleeve.

"Quite so, Prentice," she said, struggling to keep her voice steady. "A baron should know better."

With a glance to the men around the room, who appreciated his discomfort but were clearly happy to enjoy it without coming to his defense in any way, Prentice turned back to his wife.

"What I mean, wife, is that knowing your predilection for weapon play and training, you must be feeling eager to have some again, since you are now returning to your former strength."

"My pre...pred...what?" Righteous said, blinking at him. "What's that mean?"

Before Prentice could answer, she turned to the group.

"He always breaks out the big words when he's losin'. Like king's cannons in a quarrel. Tain't right."

At that, many of them did laugh, and even Dalflitch put her cup to her lips to cover her smile. Prentice chuckled with them but adopted a stern tone that was only part joking.

"Lady Righteous, if you would, I would have you go tomorrow to the baroness and, as a peer, invite her to a training yard that the pair of you might share tips on edgeplay. And at the same time share with her some thoughts about honey and vinegar."

Righteous did not respond immediately to his request, though he knew she understood from his tone that it was seriously meant. He enjoyed her thorny playfulness as a part of her dangerous beauty, but when he spoke straight with her, she knew his hard edges readily enough.

"You really think I'm the one for this?" she asked, looking first to the archduchess and then to Lady Dalfitch. Prentice could tell what she was thinking. She was used to those two finer ladies carrying the diplomatic duties while she and Spindle kept watch and looked deadly mysterious. Even in the context of the martial-ly-minded baroness, Righteous did not consider herself the first choice to try to counsel another noble. Her liege, however, seemed to have no such doubts, as Prentice had expected.

"I can think of no better candidate," Archduchess Amelia said sincerely.

"Neither can I," Dalflitch agreed. "And if you can't talk any sense into her, then see if you can't beat some through her thick skull."

"I'm not sure I could give a sister baroness a good kickin'," Righteous objected, using the commoner term. "Don't seem proper, no matter how she might need it."

"Assumin' you could," Spindle added, also dropping to a cobble runner's argot and accent. "Might be that she's better'n you. Leave you like a split sack o' grain."

Righteous snorted in derision.

"In 'er dreams!"

CHAPTER 37

At dawn the next morning, Prentice made his way out to the camp and found Dahyoor in a quiet corner of Runners Field with Solomon. The young man was bouncing painfully on the back of one of Prentice's gifted ponies, no more than a saddle blanket protecting his tormented legs and backside. He was riding in a haphazard circle around Dahyoor, who watched him with a sour expression. Taking care not to get in the student rider's path, Prentice made his way to stand next to his squire. For a moment neither said anything, simply watching Solomon's awkward practice in the cool of the morning.

"You thought to start him on a fey horse?" Prentice asked eventually, wondering at Dahyoor's choice.

"Did you want him to learn to ride tortoises?" Dahyoor said in response, and Prentice looked at him with a smirk. He wondered if the fey man meant all Kingdom horses were like tortoises compared to the fleet ponies of the Wind Rising, or if Dahyoor was specifically referring to knights' horses armoured for war with their heavy plate barding.

"How is he doing?" Prentice followed up.

"Worse than you, but he's younger."

Youth and mount rounded the space in front of them in another circuit and the pony tossed its head somewhat, as if frustrated at the pace her rider was setting, barely more than a walk.

"Hands. Knees," Dahyoor shouted, and Solomon gave his instructor a worried glance before turning his full attention back on the filly beneath him that clearly knew more about what it was doing than he did. Just that one look askance almost cost him his control as it was. Prentice pitied him, remembering his own fumbling attempts to acquire this skill that so many made to seem so simple.

"He is learning, though?" he asked.

"When the spring flowers next, he will exceed you," Dahyoor said with typical fey certainty.

Excellent, Prentice thought, though he realized that even by Kingdom standards of horsemanship, better than him was not a high bar to clear.

"Will he be as good as a fey?"

Dahyoor only snorted and folded his arms, eyes still on his pupil.

"Your children might, if you stop holding them back from the saddle," the fey said enigmatically, and now Prentice was truly astonished. His children were no more than a season old. They were literally still in their cribs.

"Holding them back?" he repeated, turning to face Dahyoor directly, his eyebrow raised in an expression of disbelief. Was the fey man jesting with him?

Dahyoor seemed to pointedly ignore his knight commander for another moment, or perhaps truly did not understand the implicit question in Prentice's posture. Then he sighed and turned so that they were face to face.

"Fey mothers return to the saddle as soon as they can and nurse as they ride," he explained. There was a look of pain in his eyes, but Prentice had no way to tell if that was because he was frustrated to have to explain yet something more to a *kreff,* or if he was troubled at having to reveal his culture to the foreigner. Troubled or frustrated—or was it both?

"Babes suckle feeling the flow of the ride beneath them," Dahyoor continued. "They know the trail even before they have the words to name it. They hear the hoofs and the silence, even before they can tell safety from threat. They pass unseen in their mothers' arms, so that by the time they sit a horse alone, it is walking that is the stranger action."

Prentice nodded, accepting Dahyoor's words, but inwardly he could hardly believe them. He was sure the fey was not lying, and he had to acknowledge that the average nobleman's son or daughter typically took to the saddle as a young child as well. It was just that he could not imagine even the most equestrian noble mother breastfeeding while in the saddle.

"I have another task I require of you," he said, changing the topic. Dahyoor waited for him to elucidate.

"North of Bridgetown is the army that recently tasted what Wind Rising arrows can do," Prentice went on, and now Dahyoor did speak.

"Tortoises," he interrupted.

"Yes. Well, they have withdrawn out of sight of the town. I need someone to go after them."

Dahyoor turned away again, watching Solomon bounce and sway.

"You want me to ride their trail?" he asked. "Do you want me to hunt them?"

"Only if they force you," Prentice said. In any other man's mouth the question would sound ridiculous, but for a fey rider who could move with uncanny stealth and shoot with an accuracy that champion bowmen might envy, it was a serious prospect. Dahyoor could easily make himself like a ghost, hounding Robant's forces, never doing much damage, but unnerving them with seemingly random assassinations from the unseen shadows. Even alone, Prentice had no doubt Dahyoor could tie up a significant company of Kingdom knights in a long hunt before they finally brought him down. But that was not the knight commander's plan.

"Ride north, shepherd the road, until you find where their trail leads," he explained to his squire. "Then turn toward the mountains where the wind rises. Ride the land marked by those two trails, between the mountains and the great southern water.

Take a week, pass unseen, and see what is to be seen. Then return with the truth."

Dahyoor nodded, his lips a line, his eyes still tracking Solomon. Prentice had the feeling he was also planning the area he was being sent to in his mind's eye, perhaps recalling the key landmarks or estimating the distances.

"When do you wish me to ride?" he asked.

"As soon as you can make yourself and the horses ready for the journey," Prentice told him.

"The boy has another ten circles to make. I will go after that."

Prentice blinked. Even for a fey rider, he had expected preparations for such a journey to take at least an hour or two. He did not question his man's assertion, though. Even if it would not be an insult to Dahyoor's honour, it would do no good to ask.

"Come by my tent before you go. I will give you a letter with my seal so that you can pass through the Norgate."

Now Dahyoor gave him a skeptical glance. "We pass unseen," he said.

Prentice could only imagine how the fey man expected to pass through the guarded gate without being seen.

"Nevertheless, in case some *kreff* gets a trick of the wind," Prentice insisted, using the fey expression that meant ill-luck, a trick of the wind on an arrow. "It will make it easier for you to return as well, if you come back with haste."

It looked like Dahyoor wanted to sneer at that possibility, implying as it did that he might be in retreat, just as all fey sneered at the *kreff*, but after a moment he nodded, seeming to accept that such a thing could well happen. Nothing that once was certain could still be relied upon in this age of upheaval—not for the Grand Kingdom and not for the Wind Rising fey.

"One week," he agreed with typical fey finality. Prentice knew his command was now like a law in Dahyoor's mind. Before his squire rode away, there was one more question he wanted to ask him.

"How long until the Wind Rising return with more word?"

If they were to face an enemy on each bank of the river, Prentice knew a contingent of fey horse archers would be invaluable to have at his command.

"The rains will fall and cease to fall before you see them," Dahyoor told him.

Not until after winter, Prentice thought. Not ideal, but not a time too long to survive. No army wanted to be in the field in winter at any rate, and though he was convinced that both the Golden Heron's mercenaries and the Sobridge prince would be looking for a quick conquest, he doubted they would want to camp out in the cold either. What Daven Marcus and Duke Robant wanted to do, beyond cling to the Denay throne by their fingertips, was anyone's guess.

CHAPTER 38

Righteous liked the twist of sending Lady Penelope an invitation for once, instead of the other way around, and she listened as Lady Dalflitch read the letter she had written on her behalf with delight. It was full of pretty phrases and language that the newly noble Righteous could barely understand, but that only made her love it all the more. Righteous knew she was a harsh woman by nature, made so by a harsh life—all wire and knife points. No amount of noble titles or motherhood was going to change that. But she also knew there was a tiny memory of herself as a young girl somewhere inside her that liked things that were pretty—pretty clothes, pretty words, pretty things. She scorned such as fripperies, of course, but she still felt that inner part's delight, and "her" invitation to the baroness-elect to meet on a sparring field and train together, written for her by Dalflitch's expert composition, made her feel ever so chuffed in the watery autumn morning's light of the Paramour's Chambers.

Her happy mood did not last as long as she hoped, however. Once the invitation note had been sent with a messenger and answered with an almost immediate acceptance and counter invitation to practice together in the Bridgetown castle itself, Baroness Righteous had retired to her own chamber to change to clothes better suited to swordplay, only to discover to her dismay that she had nothing appropriate to wear. She had returned to the main room cursing in a truly unladylike fashion, wearing only her shift-like underdress with a pair of striped trousers slung over her shoulder.

"They don't bloody fit!" she declared, throwing them on the table with disgust.

"What on earth are you speaking of, My Lady?" Spindle asked, using her courtly tones.

"Them trousers, of course!" Righteous retorted, ready to share her fouled temper with any who were available. "I been keepin' hold o' them in the bottom o' my chest since the Usurper's night, and now, when I best need 'em, they won't fit!"

Whispers and subtle shifts of attention told Righteous the neophytes were all watching her outburst, so she scoured them with a challenging glare, daring even one to smirk or snicker.

"What can have happened to them?" Spindle pressed, and this time Lady Dalflitch, who was working through accounts with her grace at the high end of the table did indeed smirk. Righteous saw it, and her eyes narrowed to slits. Angry as she was, she could not challenge the archduchess's seneschal to a knife fight, although it would not be the first time she had wanted to.

"I've become a heifer, that's what's happened!" she declared, and she thumped her fist upon her belly where the skin under her shift was still loose and, to her fury, somewhat lumpy.

Now Dalflitch smiled openly, though she did not look up from the document in front of her, and the archduchess audibly choked back a laugh.

"You are being foolish...," Lady Spindle objected, but Righteous cut her off. Her anger was in full flight, and she was not yet ready to call it to heel.

"Am I indeed? Used to be I was lean and swift, ready for the cut! Now I'm heavy and slow and fit to be slaughtered, like a fatted calf!"

"Oh tush, you bally twit!" Spindle said, and suddenly the elegant lady was gone. She was Tress again, just as the pair of them had been in the cold huts of Fallenhill's siege. "Sure'n you used to be lean, so lean you could pass for a boy. Solomon at his lankiest weren't as skin and bones as you! Now you got the body of a woman, is all. A woman with a good bed, good food, and a good husband. Stop wailing about havin' what every other maid in the room would kill to have!"

Spindle's words took the wind from Righteous's sails completely, and she poked her lip out forlornly, looking back to the tabletop.

"But me trousers…"

"Oh, I'll give you silvers to saddle soap all they need is takin' out a little. Or maybe a dart, but that's no demand. Do that in an hour. We'll have your trousers ready, no fear."

With that, Spindle Tress swept the garment from the table and summoned her two best seamstresses from the neophytes. Then she was Lady Spindle once more.

"May we have the use of your draperies, Your Grace? To guard the Baroness Ash's dignity?" she asked of the archduchess.

"I would be honored if you would, Lady Spindle," her grace replied, her eyes sparkling with delight.

"You're all enjoyin' this too much by far!" Righteous muttered unhappily as she was being led like a resentful child toward the curtained end of the room. "All of you!"

"I have no idea what you mean, Lady Righteous," Dalflitch said primly, still not looking up from the accounts. "We would never take the least pleasure in your misfortune."

Righteous scowled again, then stepped behind the curtains in the company of her dressmaking "attendants." As soon as she had, and the rest of the Paramour's Chamber was out of sight, Lady Dalflitch and Archduchess Amelia released their laughter. Righteous gritted her teeth at it, even though she was calming enough now to see the funny side of her predicament. Nonetheless, she was not about to release all her dignity.

"That had better be only her grace and the Lady Dalflitch chuckling I hear," she bellowed over the curtains as Spindle helped her out of her shift so that she could try on the trousers and the seamstresses could see the extent of the "problem."

"If even so much as one neophyte raises a smile, they better get ready to learn to count on nine fingers after their next training session with me and my knife!"

The two needleworker neophytes bowed their heads reflexively, and Righteous gave them fighting glares, knowing they were hiding smirks. They did not lift their eyes to her once as they tested the waist and fitting of the Lady of Fallenhill's striped trousers, once bought from a mercenary drummer boy on a prison barge in the Dweltwater.

"Why don't you just worry about the lesson you're about to give the silly filly of Bridgetown instead of threatening fearful young maids in her grace's chamber," Spindle chided.

"Silly filly," Righteous repeated. "I like that."

"I thought you might. I'm not calling her a horse, mind. Just that she's a prancer and certainly no she-bear, not yet. This is all a game to her, I reckon, like the village wildflower, who thinks she can tease all the boys forever and ends up a spinster cause they all wise up and realize any wife's better than waiting around for a flibbertigibbet. Well, it's up to you to wake her up. Steel cuts knights and nobles just as well as convicts and yeomen, and a winter with nothin' but a shirt and yer sticker, or your ear rotting off your head, is a bitter season no matter yer birth."

Righteous felt the remnants of her petty rage drain out of her like the dregs of an upturned cup. Her gaze flicked to Spindle's mask, where the missing ear's scars were hidden behind black lace. It was true. Whatever Lady Penelope had learned of fighting and war growing up, it clearly was not the same brutal set of lessons time had taught Spindle and Righteous, never mind the rest of her grace's men-at-arms—Righteous's own husband especially.

Time to give the flibbertigibbet a clip under the ear—at least the girl still had both of hers—and hopefully in some way that didn't put the mockers on the whole alliance between the Western Reach and Bridgetown.

CHAPTER 39

When Spindle's little team was finished, Righteous's old trousers fit comfortably enough, though she hated the feeling that they were tighter than they used to be and would only contain her flopsy middle with a belt. It made her feel like some pot-bellied convict overseer, overfed stomach spilling out of his waistband, and she did not hesitate to say so. Her friends ignored her, and by the time Spindle had the girls fetch the rest of her garb, including a blouse, her midnight blue gambeson, her gauntlets and her gorget, Righteous had let her grousing drop to no more than inarticulate mutters.

"Did you wish to leave your mask, My Lady?" one of the neophytes, a little bird of a thing, asked her politely.

"What for?" she demanded.

"I just...just know that you prefer to spar without it, My Lady," the neophyte said, clearly a little nervous at being challenged but not shrinking from the question.

"Good thought," Righteous said, but then she looked to Spindle with her own black lace visage—the pride and mystery of the Lace Fangs, to which every one of these neophytes aspired. Some of them were coming close, if Righteous was any judge. "No, I will wear it, thanks. The lace is our honor, and we paid for it in blood. If I'm to have it, I'd best learn to defend her Grace's household while I'm wearing it, wouldn't you say?"

"Yes, My Lady," the girl said, smiling with the confident pride that any member of a strong gang had when they had their mates about them. The way the Young Hopefuls smiled when Cyprian or Cassian was around, she was sure. Righteous returned that smile.

"You're Agatha, aren't you?" she asked, recognizing the slender-featured girl through her own memories from their special study of each other. Agatha, the little one, a bit shy like every smaller person but with a little tic of crinkling the right side of her mouth just before she smiled. That was her spoor.

"Yes, My Lady."

"We're done," Lady Spindle declared, stepping back and smiling.

"How do I look?" Righteous asked earnestly, her displeasured bravado slipping to reveal her true insecurity for a moment. She was about to meet a noble ruler as an equal, while dressed the way she had when she had been no more than a freed convict with a penchant for flouting sumptuary laws.

"Cutter Sal may be gone, but her ghost haunts men's nightmares still," Spindle told her, smiling with the same pride Agatha had shown a moment before. Righteous nodded her thanks and then noticed curious looks on Agatha and the other seamstress's face.

"Thanks Spindle," she said, then raised a finger to her friend. "But that's enough talk of Cutter Sal. You'll have the neophytes all beggin' you to tell 'em tall tales, and that you sure as doomsday will not do!"

"As you say, Baroness Ash," Spindle answered, curtseying as if her fellow Lace Fang were any other noblewoman. It steeled Righteous's confidence no end to realize that she meant every word without an ounce of sarcasm. With a final sigh and taking up her gauntlets, Righteous parted the curtain and emerged into the main room. Dalflitch and Archduchess Amelia looked up without comment, giving their own approval with wordless smiles.

"Will you not wear your brigandine?" Amelia did ask at last, as if the heavy piece of torso armor was the most natural wear for a baroness.

"We're to be sparring, Your Grace, not taking the field," Righteous responded. By preference she always eschewed the heavier protection, favoring her speed without it. Only when a large or unpredictable combat was likely would she go to the leather- and steel-plate chest piece. For sparring, her quilted gambeson and the plates of her neck protection were more than enough, to Righteous's mind, especially since for most of her life she had had no more than rags to clothe her hungry bones and she'd done alright with a knife through all that, not to mention the years fighting half naked in back tavern pits for cheering crowds.

"What I *will* do, with your permission, is borrow one of your cloaks, Your Grace," she said, curtseying to Amelia. "I have none, and I do not think it would be seemly for me to be seen traipsing through the streets like this. Baroness-elect Penelope has tweaked the nose of the sumptuary hawks enough for all of us noble ladies of late, wouldn't you say?"

The archduchess looked at her with a quizzical expression, smiling as if uncertain that what she was seeing was funny or strange. She blinked and presently her smile became full, the muscles of her cheeks lifting in a recognizably distinct way—especially distinctive now that her grace's face was glowing with growing pregnancy. Another spoor.

"An excellent thought, My Lady," Amelia said and looked past Righteous to one of the neophytes standing by. "Fetch Baroness Righteous my linen cloak, the one lined in blue. That should do well for a cool autumn day, I would think."

The neophyte left obediently.

"Will you take some attendants with you?" Dalflitch asked matter-of-factly.

"I was thinking Daisy and Beth," Righteous said. "They're both of a level in the art to appreciate a lesson with another master, as well as to not shame me if the baroness invites them to join us."

"Is it likely that she will?" Dalflitch asked, finally turning her full attention away from her ink-and-quill work. "And is she a master?"

"I wouldn't think so, but I wouldn't put it past her to have her own tutors present. A nobleman's girl doesn't learn steel craft in an open school where any old ruffian might make free with her. She'll have private tutors, I'd say."

"I'd well and truly say!" Spindle agreed from behind Righteous's shoulder. Looking back, Righteous had a fresh thought.

"I'll take Agatha there with me as well, if three is not too many, Your Grace," she said.

"Of course," the archduchess agreed. "Will three be enough?"

"I would say. Don't want Lady Penelope thinking I'm trying to show off."

"No, of course. Three then."

The order given, Beth emerged from the neophyte's bedchamber where she was attending to chores, while Daisy left the stove area. Soon the three neophytes were in a line, presented to Lady Righteous, Baroness Ash of Fallenhill, to serve as her attendants in today's engagements. Beth was a nondescript girl with a squarish face and eyes as dark as Dalflitch's. Daisy was sturdy and moon-faced, with freckles and a belligerent pout. She was also a skilled midwife for one so young, as Righteous knew from personal experience. The pair were by far the best students of the dagger that she and Spindle had amongst the neophytes and would benefit most from observing or participating in whatever happened between the two baronesses today. Agatha was not up to their standard, but that was no reason to leave the girl out. They were all here to learn.

"Ready to put your veils in place, my fillies," Righteous told them as she pinned the archduchess's fetched cloak about her shoulders. "Let's go see how good the lady's teachers are and whether the silly filly she-bear of Bridgetown is better than your mistress."

"Not a chance," Daisy said with conviction, and the other two nodded. Righteous felt that same street-gang pride and loyalty and looked to the door. Then she paused and whirled on them, her mood turning just as suddenly.

"No. You aren't coming today to cheer me on or shine my brass," she said in deadly seriousness, looking each girl in the eye as if peering into their very souls. "I don't need that, and you won't gain nothin' by it. You're comin' to learn. Watch close. Even if Lady Penelope moves like a sick cow, she might still know something you don't, and better to see it now than before you have to face it. I promise you, when it's steel to steel, days will come when you face somethin' you ain't never seen before. No way to prepare for it, no way to see it comin'. The more you see before you have to face them days, the fewer of them times will be in your future. And when they do come, you'll have a better idea what to do 'bout it. You must never forget, when the day comes that you have to do this in earnest, it will be ugly and bad in every way, even if it goes perfect right from first to last. Do you understand?"

"Yes, My Lady," the three answered in unison, bobbing and bowing their heads.

Satisfied, Righteous led off once more, wondering how she of all people had ever come to be a teacher, a mother, a lady-in-waiting, and a noblewoman all at once. God had a sense of humor, that was right and sure.

CHAPTER 40

"Which would you prefer, Norgate or Sougate," Knight Captain Farringdon asked as he and Prentice finally had a moment to address their combined officer corps. Prentice had his three sergeants—Sir Gennet, Porth and Guillam of the Fangs, Claws, and Roar respectively. Farringdon's sergeants were Sir Sedgemark, Sir Nunel, and Sir Markas, who served as both banner sergeant and leader of the Lion Banner's Claws, at least for the moment. The leader of Farringdon's Roar had perished during the battles around Aubrey and in the rush had not been replaced. Nunel had also been serving double duty in that regard.

"I'll need to promote someone in the next few days," Farringdon had said as he met with Prentice privately earlier in the day. "Do you have any recommendations for me?"

"Only that your judgement is sound, and you should trust it, My Lord," Prentice had answered him. "They are your men, and your word is law." He wanted there to be no misunderstandings between them. With any matter that did not concern the combined command of the two banners, the knight captain did not answer to the knight commander for a thing, not even "advice." The two-banner structure was not going to work any other way.

Two others were present at the start of the meeting—Lyrach, former squire without sponsor and now a line first of the Gryphon Roar, and Solomon, who seemed to sprout new height with every passing week. Already he was closing in on Prentice's tallness, his limbs long and lanky as a result.

"Lyrach I wanted you here to give you a choice," Prentice had told the line first in front of all his seniors. "You are skilled with horse, sword, and shot. As good as most standing here."

"Good as some, mayhaps," Guillam muttered, but Lyrach ignored the man. The pair mocked each other mercilessly but would have each other's backs in the face of hell itself.

"I planned to ask Knight Captain Farringdon," Prentice went on, ignoring the interruption, "to give you a horse of your own and a place with the lancers, though it would mean a demotion as they have no line firsts yet."

With only a single cohort and a horseman's more independent mindset for combat, Farringdon had yet to need to appoint line firsts or even a corporal. Nunel had been officer enough up until now. As the lancers grew, which they would be doing through the winter if weapons could be acquired for them, line firsts would surely be named soon. Knowing Lyrach's performance during the campaign in the west, Prentice was certain he would reclaim his rank swiftly through service.

Lyrach looked to Farringdon, who endorsed Prentice's plan readily.

"You would be most welcome amongst us," he said. "The knight commander speaks well of you indeed."

Lyrach's eyes widened with surprise, and he looked to his knight commander, clearly pleased by the thought of being praised so.

"However, the Gryphons require a standard bearer," Prentice said before the young man-at-arms could speak. "The place belonged to Knight Banner Sergeant Sir Markas, but since he has fallen in love with his liege lady, he cannot bear to give up his favored place in her closest company on the field."

"A purely courtly love, I trust, sir?" Farringdon said to the knight banner sergeant whose face was turning a bright shade as the men around him chuckled. "As her grace's husband, I would hate to have to replace you after putting you in your grave on a dueling field."

"I only…only…" Markas stammered, like a panicked apprentice caught damaging his master's tools.

"Only from afar, Knight Captain," Prentice said in a mock-reassuring tone. "Isn't that right Markas?"

"She's like my queen," the man said at last, protesting innocence.

"Quite right," Farringdon soothed him. "I trust every man here to protect my lady wife and my marriage both. I will impugn not one of you."

Many of those present, especially the ones who had wives themselves, or women they already favored for that place in their lives, nodded like advocates agreeing with the decisions of a wise magistrate or sacrists affirming holy law.

"Well, Lyrach, what's your answer?" Prentice said, turning back to the line first. The young man looked him direct in the face and straightened his back.

"I would be honored to be your banner sergeant, My Lord Knight Commander," he said clearly. "As honored as the Lion's banner man, I'd say, and for similar reasons. But, if it won't offend you, I will go to the knight captain's company. I am not ready to be a sergeant."

That answer surprised Prentice and impressed him, he had to admit.

"You already strut about like a sergeant as t'is," Guillam told him. "Might as well put the lion on your shoulder to go with your brassy ways."

"And the whole Gryphon saw you on the march," Knight Sergeant Gennet said in a more serious tone. "We know your mettle. If it's your youth, then that's naught to fear."

"With respect, Sergeant, you're wrong about that," Lyrach told him. "Those of us who marched west, they know me, but that's only a fraction of the Gryphon now. Nine out of every ten of our men are new, and all they see is a fresh face that only learned to shave yesterday, by their reckoning. I'll be proving myself every day just to have a dinner order obeyed."

"We all have to prove ourselves, lad. Only takes some effort and time."

"Sure enough, but it's extra time the Gryphon doesn't need to waste. The newcome militia need to see officers with the dust of the high plain in their beards and stories of blood and fire in their eyes. Not young lads still making their bones. If I have to prove myself, better for all of us if it's in a company where we're all in the same saddle, as it were."

Prentice marveled at Lyrach's new maturity. After the one campaign, the ambitious former squire he had been was a man transformed. Of course, given the brutality of that one campaign, it was perhaps little wonder. The knight commander almost regretted giving Lyrach the choice.

"Go to the Lions' Lancers, Lyrach, with our blessing," the knight commander said.

"And don't forget you were a Gryphon first," Guillam added with pride.

Lyrach saluted Prentice and then his new commander, then left the meeting, considering himself dismissed. Which led naturally to the other promotion Prentice had wanted to do privately. He turned to Solomon, younger than Lyrach by more than half a decade and not yet begun to shave, the lad's cheeks and lip being dusted with a peach fuzz that did not quite need a razor. Nonetheless, his days as a drummer and messenger had to come to an end, and Dahyoor was ridden off already on his solo mission, so keeping him around for riding lessons was also pointless.

"Solomon, it has come time for you to step up in service as well. I want every man here to know I am appointing you to the Gryphons as a Fang."

"I'd prefer to begin as a Claw," Solomon said before Prentice could continue, clearly attempting to mimic Lyrach's previous show of humility. "I'd hate to be thought of as a jump up."

Prentice did not respond, but paused, looking sternly down on the youth. Then he nodded to the gathered officers.

"He ain't offerin' you a choice, Duelist," Guillam said first. "And truth is, you ain't built for the Claws."

"It takes a bigger man than you and broader, my lad, to heft a pike or a halberd in the lines," Sergeant Porth explained. "You'd be no use as a Claw at this age."

"And Fangs aren't some elite, above the Claws for you to jump up to either," said Knight Sergeant Sedgemark, speaking as a Fang. "We're all in the company together—Claws, Fangs, and Roar. No one above another. Don't get the wrong notions in your head at the start."

Prentice could see the officers' criticisms knocking into the eager Solomon but forced himself to resist the urge to defend him. Solomon was about to step into full manhood, or at least onto that ladder's first rung, and he had to face others as his own man, not Prentice's adopted son, or else he would never become who he could be. Also, this was a necessity for Prentice and Solomon's relationship. Because of the circumstances of Solomon's service, the young man had friendships and contacts that no other White Lion drummer enjoyed. For that reason, Prentice wanted to nip any thoughts of nepotism in the bud, either in Solomon or the men around him. The whole point of the Lions was for men to rise on merit, not favoritism.

"You are too small yet for the Claws, Solomon, for all that you're old enough to sign on the barrel," Prentice told him, bringing the criticism session to a close. "So, you will go to the Fangs where your size and skill with a short blade will be an asset. Also, that is the last time I want to hear of you talking back to a superior. Orders are for you to obey, not to mull over. Understand?"

Solomon snapped to salute, maintaining it for Prentice to return it in the fashion of all White Lions, junior to senior. Prentice let him hold there a moment.

"You are a White Lion of the Gryphon Banner Company now, Duelist Solomon Ash. Go and wait for Sergeant Gennet by the standard. He will come to you after this and tell you who your line first will be. You will report to them and from now on follow their every order to the letter. Do you hear me?"

"Yes, My Lord, Knight Commander!" Solomon bellowed, parade ground fashion, his voice cracking ever so slightly, salute still taut against his chest. At last Prentice returned the respect and Solomon was dismissed. Prentice watched him go with a momentary flash of concern, such as he expected a loving father might feel handing a beloved son over to his new apprenticeship.

CHAPTER 41

"He'll be banner sergeant of the Gryphons himself before he's done, mark me," Sedgemark said of him as he marched off over the grass toward the central tents of the camp.

"Bugger that," Guillam retorted, and he sucked on his teeth. "He's got his sights set on bein' knight captain, at least. I'd lay all the silver in my purse on it."

The officers around the circle all nodded their agreement or gave some sound of assent. Solomon, the Duelist, had the respect of all the Lions, their earlier criticisms notwithstanding, and every man present either thought of him as the son they wished they had or the boy they would have liked to have been when they reflected on their misspent youths. Of that, Prentice had no doubts.

"Until that day comes, I am still looking for a banner sergeant for the Gryphons," Prentice said, turning the conversation back to the true purpose of the meeting. "And then we need to decide which banner will garrison which bastion, Norgate or Sougate."

"I can give you a list from the corporals best suited and best served to take the duty, My Lord," Gennet offered, and Prentice noticed that none of the three Gryphon sergeants present put themselves forward. In truth, the current Gryphon Banner Company structure had worked well enough without the role filled, but Prentice did not think that should continue, not now that the banner was up to its full strength. A fourth senior sergeant was needed just to manage a body this size.

"Before the dinner drumbeat, Sergeant," he said and Gennet nodded.

All of which led the meeting to Knight Captain Farringdon's inquiry—which banner did Prentice prefer for which bastion?

"I am not really sure I have a preference, My Lord Knight Captain," Prentice said in answer to the question. "Norgate is the smaller, less secure, but it also faces to the north where we have recently been victorious. The south is bigger and stronger, but as we proved, not invulnerable. Of course, signs and portents aside, we have no reason yet to fear an attack from there either."

"Well, my first impulse was to suggest Norgate for you and Sougate for myself," Farringdon offered. "Vec for the Veckander and Kingdom men on the Grand Kingdom side. Except, of course, and you'll forgive me I trust, Baron, you and your banner are not typical Grand Kingdom men. Your uncertain status with the Church might make your command on the Kingdom bank something of an affront to some of the folk north of here."

"And you? As the Veckander prince who surrendered his princedom, you might not find yourself so welcome on the Vec side either," Prentice extended from the prince's thoughts. The considerations were not irrelevant, but he could see no simple way around them.

"And yet the south will see you as a Grand Kingdom invader and the north will yet regard me as a foreign Veckander lord, surrendered princedom or no. It seems we have no good choices—damned if we do, damned if we don't."

"That's 'cause yer both neither of the sort no more," Guillam said, staring at the grass at his feet and kicking at it nervously, as if fearful of risking offence for once in his life. "You're Reachermen now. We're all Reachermen, and you're our lords. Not Kingdom, not Vec, not no more." He looked up with a cheeky grin, cocking his head to one side.

"My Lords," he added, as if just remembering. No one else around the circle spoke, but it was clear from their expressions they agreed with Guillam's sentiment.

"Well, if we are giving offence either way," Prentice said at last, "the Gryphons will have Sougate and you My Lord Knight Captain will command the on the north bank. Go this afternoon and garrison the bastion as you see fit. The Gryphon will do the same for themselves. Send the Bridgetowner militiamen back here to take up places with our tents. We will have to double them up a while until their own archduchess-to-be buys them new ones."

Farringdon saluted in response to Prentice's order, turning to face his officers.

"We could build it up with some extra works, like the bridgehead at Aubrey, eh sirs?" he said happily, clearly ready to turn his mind to his preferred subject—the engineering side of warfare.

"Me and Markas and Nunel...sorry, Sir Markas and Sir Nunel, we have some figurings of our own on that score, My Lord, if you'd hear them?" Sedgemark offered his company leader.

"Gladly," Farringdon replied, but before any more could be said, Guillam had yet another impertinent observation to make.

"'Ere, that's another matter, how come this lot's three 'sir' sergeants and we only got Gennet 'ere?" he demanded. "You got somethin' you'd like to say 'bout Porth and my service, Knight Commander, *My Lord*?"

"Because, you insolent lout," Prentice said without a trace of anger in his voice or posture, "Sir Gennet has been with me longest and served best. The three knight sergeants of the Lion banner recently did heroic service, holding back certain defeat in a doomed campaign in Aubrey and preserving the life of our liege the archduchess. You and Porth have yet to do anything of equal worth."

"We preserved your life in the west, didn't we?" Guillam protested.

"Exactly," Prentice answered, and even the quick-witted gunner sergeant struggled to catch the implicit joke in his answer.

"Never you mind who's got what, Guillam," Gennet rebuked his subordinate. "Just you set your small wits to helping plan the defense of this southern gate like the knight captain's loyal men are doing for him."

Guillam accepted the reproof with the usual cheeky grin.

"I reckon I'm lookin' forward to sittin' in that battlement and shootin' down on some Veckander nonces, like when we ambushed them fey and Redlanders, ay," he muttered.

"You ambushed Redlanders and fey?" Nunel asked, obviously impressed more than disbelieving.

"In the west," Guillam told him. "Sweet as a harvest fest bride."

"Truly?"

"Buy us a stoup in a tavern one night and we'll tell you the tale," Porth said.

"Enough!" Gennet cut across them. "Stoups in taverns are for later. We get the standard flying over the Sougate first!"

Porth and Guillam accepted that last correction and silence fell across the cadre of commanding officers. Prentice thought he could see some misgivings in the Lion sergeants' eyes. Perhaps they were shocked by Guillam's free speaking.

Why would they not be? he thought. Prentice had specifically given Guillam permission to run his mouth on the campaign west as a way to hold himself in check, to force him to test his own judgements against common sense. Since then, he had begun to wonder if he might have made a mistake.

"Tongues can wag and even run wild *here*, gentlemen," he addressed the whole group. "Knights and sergeants need that freedom in moments like this. Elsewhere—in garrison, on the field, anywhere else the White Lions find themselves—we are one voice or else we are silent as gravestones. Especially in front of the Bridgetowner rogues when they get here. Am I clear?"

"Yes, Lord Commander," Farringdon answered without hesitation, and every sergeant concurred. Needing honest subordinates without fostering grousers and malcontent was a balancing act that seemed to become more difficult with every step as the White Lions grew. Prentice knew it was not a tightrope he wanted

to slip from, or the fall would surely break him, the archduchess,
and most everything they had striven to build.

Chapter 42

Bridgetown's castle was named Earlsbastion, it turned out, which Righteous learned as she approached the fortification's main gate. Having long since been superseded as a defensive work, the town and its roads were built right up to the old castle's walls, some of the taller buildings almost high enough to let a person step from their roofs to the battlements. A nimble enough individual could make a climb of it easily. Righteous was sure she would have been able to do it in her youth, as would any of her crew from those days. She imagined that they would likely have dared each other to it without doubt. They had all been that kind of brassy rascal, issuing dares and taking risks. Which was probably why, as far as she knew, they were all dead now.

Except me, she thought as she stared up at the gate.

"It says Earlsbastion," a voice said from her left, and she turned to see one of the baroness's heralds standing just inside the shadows of the open portal. It was the first time Righteous could remember seeing one of them by himself, and she took an immediate dislike to the sneeriness she thought she saw in his expression.

"What's that?" she demanded in a voice like a challenge, her mind still half in her knife-edged youth.

"The words," the man replied, pointing to the carved marble arch that was too pretty for a castle gate that ever expected to be assaulted again. "They say 'Castle Earlsbastion.'"

"Do they indeed? I don't recall asking."

"You were staring," the man told her. "Looked like you were having trouble."

Righteous bit on her inner lip, ready to give the man a serve for his cheek, speaking to her in such a manner and failing to respect her rank. He should have addressed her as 'my lady' at the very least, never mind the presumption of assuming she could not read. Of course, Righteous was not able to read, and it made her more than a little ashamed in the higher circles where she now moved. But the herald had no right to his disdain. She was about to correct him, as she herself had done many times with impertinent or ignorant servants on the archduchess's behalf, when she stopped. She was a baroness. It was beneath her to correct an inferior in such a fashion. As she did it for the archduchess, so an attendant should be doing it for her. Except she had already told the neophytes to stand silent and keep watchful. And besides, the girls still were not quite ready. Soon, but not today.

So, what do I do? she asked herself. The answer presented itself quite swiftly as it turned out. She would ignore his ill manners. They were beneath her. She straightened her posture and looked at the man the way Dalflitch looked at dirt upon her clothing. Righteous affected her best copy of Lady Dalflitch's tone of voice, or even that of Lady Spindle, with her new courtly manners.

"I presume Baroness Penelope has you waiting for my arrival, to escort me to her?" she said coldly. She did not wait for him to answer her question. "If so, then you can dispense with the unnecessary lessons in castle history and do the duty for which you were sent. I certainly wouldn't want to keep My Lady Penelope waiting while I watched you play the jackanapes."

The herald blinked at the courtly rebuke, and Righteous merely stared at him in turn, like something on her shoe. It was clear he had not expected a true noblewoman's response from someone he did not consider a "true" noblewoman. That was Righteous's read of him at least, and people were something she *could* read. Of that she was confident.

The chastised twin held out a hand to usher Righteous and her party through the gate, then stepped ahead to lead the way. Behind her, Righteous heard one of the neophytes whisper, "Showed him," but one of her companions quickly shushed her, as it should be.

The herald's path into the castle led them across a main bailey paved with marble flagstones. There was no separate keep, as the rest of the castle, like the town outside, seemed to have grown against the original walls and encroached on the great yard itself. It now more resembled an enormous rich mansion with an excessively stout perimeter fence around its portico garden. They passed small evergreen pines growing in stone pots in a row and entered a long building that looked like a windowed gallery along the southern side of the bailey. No sooner were they inside, though, when the herald led them through another door to an open garden with a carefully manicured lawn. Twisting pillars that seemed inlaid with gold formed some kind of decorative structure in the midst of the grass. It was not a fountain, as no water spilled from it anywhere Righteous could see, but what its actual purpose might have been eluded her.

I am truly a lady amongst ladies now, she thought and reminded herself to keep every kind of watch on her tongue, her bearing, and her behavior. The archduchess was depending upon her. The herald ahead of her party was moving swiftly—too swiftly it seemed to her—and she wondered if it was because he feared to be slack after her rebuke or if he was trying to make her rush to keep up with him as a petty point of revenge. Righteous found herself quickening her steps to keep up, and she forced herself to slow down. *She* was the peer of rank in this situation, and *she* set the pace for others to follow. The notion put a mischievous smirk on her face for a moment, and she crinkled her nose under her mask.

That's right, I'm in charge here now, she thought, talking as much to enemies in her memories long past as to the petty functionary escorting her. *Get that.*

Passing through a hedge into yet another courtyard, the open horizon suddenly burst into view, glorious even in the moment of late autumn sun. Flocks of clouds were scattered across the deepening blue sky while the river glittered beneath where it could be seen between the crowding buildings of the town. Looking south, the land swept away, a vast gold carpet punctuated by small woods, and in the distance beyond the harvest farmlands, Righteous thought she could just make out the shape of a town.

Town Sobridge, she thought, but it could as easily be the distance playing tricks on her eyes. For all she knew the *Town* of Sobridge itself was in an entirely different direction.

"The Vec," Baroness-elect Penelope said, stepping up beside Righteous before the herald even had a chance to announce her. The young noblewoman looked south at the magnificent vista. "My father used to bring me up here when I was a little girl. 'Once this was all ours, young Penny-drop' he would say."

Lady Penelope sighed and then looked to her guest.

"Not our family's personally, of course, but it was the Grand Kingdom's—dukedoms, earldoms, and counties all the way to the Masnian frontier." She affected a deep, mock-masculine voice. "'And it will be ours again one day, daughter. God and king will lead us, and we will reclaim our kingdom's rightful possessions.' He had such hope and faith. It...it broke his heart when Daven Marcus rebelled."

It didn't do the king's heart much good either, Righteous thought with reflexive snark, but she managed to bite her tongue. If only Dalflitch and Prentice could know just how many such swift arrows she drew her bow for and never loosed. Would they respect her or just be angrier?

Lady Penelope turned away from the view and invited Righteous to follow her with an open hand. Thus, the Baroness of Fallenhill noticed that the rest of the hedged space was to be their training yard. A border of perfectly manicured grass surrounded an open square of equally perfect sandstone flags that were not so bright in the sun as the marble of the bailey had been but made the area seem rich and civilized to Righteous's mind all the same. Fight training for her was a hidden peasant thing, secreted away in the backroom of some dusty warehouse or the illegal tavern rooms with their shallow pits and baying crowds, all drinking, betting, and hoping for blood.

At one edge of the square, two elegant stuffed chairs, carved of dark wood, were set beside a table on which were goblets and a silver ewer. To the right of that, if one were seated there facing the square, was a long table akin to the main table in the Paramour's Chambers. Righteous could see an array of weapons, wooden and metal, the sun raising a few glints on the steel polished to a mirror sheen. If these were practice weapons, they were of a quality the former pit fighter had never seen for such tools. Beside the table, two men in Bridgetown livery tabards stood at firm attention, each holding a quarter staff with ribbons tied to their ends—one end gold, the other orange. From the same door Righteous and her ladies had been led through, a third man, a nobleman Righteous knew she had seen before but whose name she did not remember, arrived. He was wearing a short gambeson, undyed and showing signs of being comfortable and well worn. He had leather gauntlets in his left hand and moved with the air of a man ready for his day's exercise. It struck Righteous that she had not noticed that Baroness Penelope was similarly attired in an elegant gambeson sewn with leather panels down its sides and orange and gold threads embroidering. It looked as if it had had use in its time but was not so worn, and its colors were still bright. It was nothing like her husband's campaign gambesons with half their dye washed out. Even cleaned and repaired, its rivets polished, his brigandine was nowhere near so bright. As usual, Penelope wore this garment over her skirt, although this one was slightly shorter than normal, revealing boots on her feet. Looking, Righteous had the impression the skirt itself was of a sturdier material than typical for a lady's garment—more like a leather butcher's apron.

That'll be good for keepin' down the bruises, she thought.

"Please forgive me, ladies," the newly arrived nobleman said as he bowed to them both. "I hope you have not been inconvenienced by my lateness."

"Not at all, Baronet," Lady Penelope replied. "We weren't inconvenienced, were we, Baroness Righteous?"

"Uh...no. We were just admiring..." Righteous said, trying to sound courtly and finding the right word refused to heel when she whistled.

"The view," Lady Penelope completed the thought for her. "I was just telling Lady Righteous how much father used to love this place for its view."

"Indeed, he did," the baronet agreed, nodding but frowning with a sorrow that seemed genuine to Righteous. The man missed his lost liege. He had the bowl haircut and pointed goatee, with flashes of grey, that made her think of bankers crouched like avaricious spiders over their accounts, but there was an openness to his expression that gave her a trustworthy feeling. With a loud sigh, he seemed to put his sadness down inside himself, and his previous smile returned. He bowed to Righteous. "We have sat at table together but have not formally met, My Lady. I am Christmark, Baronet of Dell Island. A pleasure."

"I am Lady Righteous Ash of Fallenhill," Righteous said trying to be equally formal but thinking she must have made some mistake when the baronet cast a doubtful sidelong glance at his liege lady. Whatever it meant, the doubt evaporated in an instant.

"Well, we've come for an afternoon of swordplay. Shall we to the matter at hand?" he said happily.

Again, Lady Penelope turned to her guest.

"Well, we have refreshments set forth, of course," she said, gesturing to the two chairs and table. "But I wasn't sure if you would wish to sit and chat first or begin immediately, My Lady. Oh, and I have no chairs for your ladies-in-waiting. Would you like me to send for some for them?"

Righteous looked behind her at Daisy, Beth and Agatha, the three neophytes clothed from head to toe and as patient and anonymous as faceless statues. Nonetheless, their eyes ranged in every direction. The trio was working to make sure not a single detail escaped their notice, as they'd been told to.

"They know their place," Righteous said simply as she turned back. "And my old master, Elmantin, used to always say that you had to work up a thirst before you got to take a drink."

"A stern man, Master Elmantin," Baronet Christmark said approvingly, which was something Righteous understood, at least. A soft fighting master produced soft students, and soft students were soon to be dead students.

"My masters, Frederick of the Whitmore School and Vrest of the Narrow Vec style, are both here with us today," Lady Penelope said, pointing to the two staff bearers by the weapon table. "They will magistrate for us, if you are happy."

Magistrate? Righteous wondered, unfamiliar with such a use of the term. A magistrate was a petty court judge, wasn't he? The one time she had ever met a magistrate, he had ordered her branded and transported for murder, brawling, and affray. She had never heard of neither the Whitmore School nor the Narrow Vec style, for that matter, but she recognized lowborn fighting master names when she heard them. She gave each man the respectful nod that she would have afforded them if they had met in the street. If either man noticed, he did not return the gesture.

Two masters? Do Bridgetown high-born folk do everything in pairs?

"Is that acceptable to you, My Lady?" Penelope asked again.

"My Lady?" Righteous felt her brow furrow beneath her mask. "That they magistrate?"

"Of course," she answered at last, not knowing what else to say.

"Excellent. And blades? I've had a selection laid out, if you please."

The baroness led the way to the table and its array of practice steel. Righteous studied the options on offer. One of the blades was a blunted longsword, lying at the top of the table by itself. The former streetfighter had no interest in that. She was no knight, not by birth and not by training. The rest of the blades were slender sideswords, like those carried by the Young Hopefuls, with small variations in length and hilt or knucklebow shape. There was half a dozen or so, and all had blunted tips and likely dulled edges, perfect for training.

"I brought my own with me," Righteous said absently as she stood at the table. She waved to the neophytes, and Daisy and Agatha stepped forward, each slipping a cloth bag from her shoulder. Daisy's was long and slender, carrying Righteous's sword. Agatha's was squarer and held the Baroness Fallenhill's buckler shield. Righteous had been surprised when Spindle had presented her with the bags for her kit as she made to leave that morning.

"You've got your armor under a cloak to hide it from the busybodies," the seamstress had said. "What kind of fit do you think they'd pitch if they saw you strutting down the street with a longblade on your hip like one of them Hopeful twits?"

Righteous accepted the sword bag from her attendant.

"Mine's sharp for proper cutting," she said absentmindedly, opening the bag's drawstring and allowing the hilt to come out. "Probably better I not use that. I will take one of these, if it suits you."

"Oh, happily," the baroness answered, and her enthusiasm confused Righteous for a moment. It reminded her of something—something inappropriate—but she could not think what. There were so many things in her mind that she was trying to keep track of at once.

"May I?" the baronet asked politely, reaching for the hilt. Righteous offered it to him and he drew the blade from its scabbard, still in the bag.

"Hmm," he said, holding the blade up to examine its edge. He gave it a few testing swings. "Weighted for swift movement, single edge and false edge. Fine steel by the look, and you keep it sharp."

He put a naked thumb to the edge and flicked at it.

"Very like the sideswords we favor here in Bridgetown, though much shorter."

"Indeed," Baroness Penelope concurred, looking at the weapon with the same professional air, though it seemed more affected on her. "A handspan shorter at least, I'd say."

"We fight in tight amongst the halberds and pike of the Claws," Righteous said a little weakly, not sure why she felt the need to explain her weapon of choice to this pair, or anyone for that matter. If she wanted a longer blade, she'd get herself one. And how was one handspan "much shorter"? How much length did they want?

"Masters, if you would take up your points," Lady Penelope said to her two silent instructors. The men bowed and moved off to each stand in opposite corners of the square, staves in hand. The baroness took up one of the training weapons, which was significantly longer than Righteous's "live" blade. As Righteous received her sword back from the baronet, she handed it hilt-first to her attendant, along with the scabbard still in its bag. Then she unpinned her cloak, absently handing it off to Beth while she looked for a sparring weapon of her own. Suddenly a girlish squeal burst from Lady Penelope.

"See Christmark! I told you a woman can wear trousers!"

She clapped her hands together as if Righteous was a minstrel acrobat who had just performed an especially impressive trick. The Baroness of Fallenhill looked down at her striped pants, fitted tighter against her than she liked, and tried to cast off memories of Bluebird, the minstrel assassin and the acrobatic tricks he'd used to lull all around him into the sense that he was a harmless jesting fool.

"I have never denied it was possible, My Lady," Christmark said with an affectionate weariness. "I have only ever pointed out that it cannot be done without the ire of Mother Church and any number of scribes at law."

"Well, perhaps those same scribes at law could turn their minds to the question of how to bring a usurper kingslayer to justice instead," Penelope retorted. "And as for Mother Church, let them figure out between themselves what they think before they worry about me. Aren't they supposed to remove a plank from their eyes before they nitpick?"

"If you say so, My Lady."

"I do say so. We both do, don't we, Lady Righteous?"

"I wear skirts and dresses mostly," Righteous said, feeling ever more numb by the moment. How did the archduchess or Dalflitch track these changing moods of high-born folk? One minute they were all serious and dignified, then next the baroness is squealing like a girl playing in the street with her friends and their toys. That caught Righteous's attention. That was the inappropriate feeling she had been receiving from the baroness. Penelope was behaving like a girl at play. It made Righteous very uncomfortable.

"I only wear trousers on the field these days," she went on, her thoughts still as distracted as they had been. "Not so much troubling over sumptuary laws in a battle, 'specially now there's more paid men and it's not all knights and pomp and what all."

Baronet Christmark looked askance at Penelope once again, this time with a scowl, but Righteous hardly noticed, and the liege of Bridgetown certainly didn't. Lady Penelope had taken up her blade and stepped away onto the flagstone square.

"Shall we, My Lady?" she asked happily.

Righteous looked over the remaining options and chose a weapon of a length with her own blade and with a guard that fitted the sparring gloves she was already wearing well enough. She followed Lady Penelope, and as her host stopped at a seemingly random spot, Righteous noticed that she was, in fact, standing on a mark—a straight line graven in the stones. Looking about, she then noticed another mark in the opposite half of the square and took that as her own commencement point.

"All very formal, this Bridgetown training," she muttered before turning to face her sparring partner, hoping she would not be heard. As she turned, the young baroness's smile took on a calculating cast, which put Righteous on her edge.

"I'll be gold and you be orange," she said. Righteous had no idea what that meant. The two masters in their corners suddenly struck their staves upon the stone like heralds calling for attention.

"Begin," they shouted in unison, and Baroness Penelope surged forward.

CHAPTER 43

It was a perfectly executed lunging thrust at the end of a swift, skipping dash. In the back of her mind, Righteous's internal Master Elmantin approved of the form. The blunt tip of her sword struck Righteous right on the back of her glove, a precise blow, which would have been all the more impressive if Righteous had had her weapon fully at the ready, but it was not even yet in guard, only held lightly, since she hadn't had any indication of when the duel would start.

Fearing a knave's trick with her two "masters" in cahoots, Righteous pushed herself backward, stumbling as much as stepping in her haste, expecting a range of follow up blows to the surprise attack. The thrust had been a kind of attempt to disarm, she guessed, though it hadn't caused much pain. The metal plate riveted to the back of her leather gauntlet happily absorbed most of the impact. As it turned out, she need not have bothered.

"Point gold," the two masters shouted in unison, and both raised their staves so that the gold ribbons were high in the air. The baroness stood from where she had not yet moved, remaining until then as if frozen in her perfectly executed lunge.

Right, so that's what being gold and orange means, Righteous told herself. *But what's with this point talk? Are we fighting for...points?*

Penelope turned and walked back to her starting spot and then faced her opponent once more. She had a calm, proud demeanor that immediately broke into a grin.

"Sorry about that," she said gleefully, not sounding much sorry to Righteous's ear. "I had to have the first point off you. For my pride, you understand. I'm sure you'll beat me soundly with all your experience, unless of course your legend is all smoke and tavern talk."

Unless my legend...? Righteous wondered. Between memories of her childhood, doing her utmost not to embarrass the archduchess with her bad manners, and thinking to improve her friendship so that she could bring up the issue of Penelope's brash speech the night before, Righteous's head was already swimming. Talk of legends and scoring points only added to her confusion.

"Fair enough," she said, only just keeping herself from thrusting out her lip like she would have once if someone had done something similar to her in a back alley. "But why'd you stop? You had the noose in place. Why not kick me off the gibbet?"

"What?" Penelope asked, clearly not recognizing the expression.

"Why didn't you follow up, I was wrong footed, after all."

"I'd already won the point," the young baroness said, as if the notion was self-evident. "Master Frederick always says that unnecessary effort is wasted effort."

She nodded to one of the two men with their staves, and he returned it politely.

That's what magistrating means, Righteous thought as it dawned on her. These two men were the judges, like seconds and witnesses at a duel. *You two'll be judging who gets these "points" will you? Best score fair. Favoritism's next to roguishness by my ken.*

"Of course, Master Vrest says to always be ready," Lady Penelope continued. "Once your foot is on the line, you're in the fight."

This time there was a shared polite nod with the other magistrate master. Righteous absorbed the rule as she returned to her own starting position. Taking care to make sure she had her blade in guard first, she placed her foot on the carved line in the stone.

The baroness came on again, as swiftly as the first time, and in the same straight line. Righteous deflected and defended, falling back again. The sideswords they were using were lighter and faster than the backsword she carried as a Fang corporal, but she wasn't overwhelmed, trusting more to her reflexes than trying to out-think her opponent just yet. Get her measure and then go on the offensive.

"Point gold," the two masters shouted again, and Baroness Penelope stood once more from her stance to return to her start mark.

"What? You never touched me!" Righteous protested.

"You put your foot on the grass," Penelope said over her shoulder before wheeling on her heel to face Righteous again from her start mark. "Stepping out of the square is the same as leaving the field of battle. Leaving the field of battle is a retreat, and a retreat is the same as a defeat. You yielded the point."

The words had the ring of a saying to Righteous, and she wondered which of the masters had hammered that little bit of wisdom into their noble pupil.

"Tell a girl *all* the rules, why don't you," she muttered as she also returned.

"You don't have that rule in the Reach?" Penelope asked her, again in her stance. Righteous looked from the baroness to her two instructors and then quickly at the baronet, who had taken up one of the goblets and was now standing by the table, sipping at it and watching proceedings.

You're a bloody knight, she thought. *Are you at peace with all this nonsense points and rules talk?*

She tried to imagine Prentice or Farringdon or indeed any White Lion just standing up and walking back after a single touch. Master Elmantin had slapped his child students with a switch, sometimes 'til they bled, until they learned that a fight wasn't over until it was won.

"Better I cut you with a switch than an enemy does with a actual blade," he used to say. "Cause odds are good you won't have a chance to cry about it afterward." A stern man indeed, at least sometimes.

Righteous took up her start position again, and when "Begin" was called, she fell back a third time, taking care to evade with sideways steps right from the start. Penelope followed her and even smiled, it seemed, to see that her easy first victories would not be forever. As the passage of blows went on, Righteous found herself adapting more and more to the less familiar blade and finding a measure of the style the two masters had taught the young baroness.

You're all stabs and thrusts girl, she thought. *Let's see if I can't get inside your point.*

Luring her opponent into an overcommitment, Righteous stepped to the offside of the baroness's guard to her own right rather than back so that the attacking point sailed past her. Then she half-stepped back in to swing her own sword overhand. Of course, she did not actually want to clout the lady on her exposed scalp, but she let the blow go as close as she dared before withdrawing it. To her own way of thinking, she never came close to actually hitting. Nevertheless, Penelope recoiled as if physically struck and staggered away, wrong footed by her rush to get out from under the attack.

"Hold!" both magistrates cried at once with no small indignation, and even the quietly watching baronet slammed his goblet to the table and took a half step toward the field with an inarticulate grumble of disapproval.

"I am bare-headed, My Lady," Penelope said with horror.

"I never struck you," Righteous replied. "I hoped that would be enough to take the point. You weren't in danger, I promise."

"You cannot take points from a head strike if we are not wearing masks or helms," Penelope explained. "If you wished to be so free in our match, you should have said so. Is all fighting in the west so boorish?"

Boorish? You should be so bloody lucky, Righteous thought, feeling the retort dance eagerly on her tongue but managing to bite it back. All these rules and talk of good manners were turning her nervous mood well and truly sour. Fighting was to the death unless you fought back enough to make it otherwise. If Lady Penelope thought this was what a fight was like, no wonder she squealed like a little girl at the prospect. *You're almost as bad as the mongrels that used to cheer when we were in the pits, loving the sight of blood. Except you can't even do that. Waving a blunt edge near your head frightens you and all your hangers-on as well. Masters? Pfft!*

"I am wearing a mask," she said, touching her finger to the lace.

"Not like that," Penelope retorted. "Proper sparring masks made of wire to protect the face." Her mood was plainly souring as well.

"With all these rules, it's a wonder you Bridgetowners can fight at all," Righteous muttered, not really under her breath, and Baroness Penelope's mood took a full turn to the annoyed.

"By God, you sound just like the boys," she said, her fury rising openly. "Just like Wilforn, Cassian, and Cyprian. My cousins won't train with me anymore because they can't face losing."

Losing? How could they win when all the rules prevent them? Righteous wondered if she might have some sympathy for the Young Hopefuls after all, if this was how their liege treated them. How could someone claim to win when the rules never permitted anyone to even face them in a fair fight?

"I ain't afraid of losin' nothin'," Righteous said, and later, when she recounted the day to her husband and the archduchess, she would realize that this was the moment she lost her self-control and reverted to the basest part of herself. "If you're not afraid, why don't you let me show you what the boorish west can really be like? Unless you really aren't up to bein' a fightin' girl."

"My Lady?" Christmark called from the sidelines, his concern obvious in his tone. Righteous knew he was talking to his liege, but she could see by Lady Penelope's expression his uncertainty fell upon deaf ears. Now Righteous did stick out her lower lip, using her sneer to make sure she pushed the baroness over the edge.

"I've scored upon you repeatedly!" Lady Penelope shot back with furious disbelief. "Alright then, if your reputation is not false, unleash your boorish west-of-the-mountains fighting. I'll not hold myself back either and we will see who is afraid."

Righteous couldn't help but smirk. She knew the baroness was unafraid, but it was the fearlessness of someone who had no idea how much danger they were in.

And as for holdin' back? she thought. *You ain't held yourself back one single moment since her grace arrived in Bridgetown, you daft prancer. Silly bloody filly indeed.*

As they faced each other, Righteous slid one of her secreted daggers down inside her sleeve, a small stiletto, hiding her left hand behind her back as she did so. She realized that there was a good chance the magistrates might notice it, but it was out of sight of both Lady Penelope and Baronet Christmark, at least for now. Righteous only needed it for one pass—she would make certain of that. With a dramatic stamp, she put her foot upon her mark and the baroness flew forward with speed like a diving eagle. Exactly as she had at the first, and exactly as Righteous assumed she would. Make your best attack. Even knowing it was coming, it took all Righteous's skill to deflect it, and this time the blunt tip was aimed not at her hand, but at her chest. As it was, Righteous's deflection was slightly late and the thrust still managed to catch her on the shoulder, but she didn't care. She made a defensive step that put her in exactly the right place, with her sidesword blade on top of Penelope's, free to strike. It was the same position from which Prentice had broken Sir Liam's jaw all those years ago in the upper bailey of Dweltford Castle.

To her credit, Lady Penelope recognized her vulnerability, and since Righteous's positioning made it too difficult for her to bring her blade around to defend herself, the young noblewoman did the next best thing, seizing Righteous's blade and holding it from flicking upward. It was a perfectly legitimate technique, and many a trained knight would not hesitate to use it, even against a live blade if he was wearing his gauntlets. But it played straight into

Righteous's hands. Now Penelope was using two hands to control only one of Righteous's and old Cutter always loved a free hand with a dagger in it. Having Penelope already slightly off balance, Righteous shifted her step a little farther into the girl's leg, and with a light barging, set her to topple sideways. Except instead of letting the girl fall flat, she caught her with her sword arm, all while keeping the two blades engaged, and twisted her around slightly so that Penelope went to one knee, tangled a little beneath her heavy skirt. She landed with Righteous's other arm over her shoulder, stiletto point to the young woman's throat. She let it press in just enough that it could be felt. It would likely draw blood but only a pinprick.

"Feel that?" Righteous demanded, loud enough to be heard over the whole yard. "That's my best sticker at your throat. You like thrusty blades? I promise you this one's been inside more bodies than all the blades you've ever held in your life."

Both magistrates lowered their staves to use as weapons, growling, and Baronet Christmark seized the practice longsword from the table, a serviceable club, even if it couldn't cut.

"Hold your horses, gentlemen," Righteous shouted at them. "Your lady is in no danger from me, unless she does something right foolish! So stay back and where I can see you."

The three men hesitated, and Penelope struggled to get some advantage for a moment, unable to raise her blade still. If she released her grip on either her own sword or Righteous's, all she would do would be to grant her opponent a greater advantage.

"See where you are? There ain't a man in this castle, not in your entire town, could help you now if I wanted to take your life. I'd have this little stiletto dagger up in your cloth head before anyone moved an eyelid. Makes your bowels turn to water, don't it? What you're feelin' right now, that's what a real fight feels like. No one and nothin' between you and death except your steel and your skill. And look where yours has put you. On your knees. You ask your masters, both of 'em, how many men they know as could make a fight of it from this spot? I'd give my Prentice a fightin' chance and the champion bloke Ironworth. Likely was he could've done it. But you? You're finished lass. One pass, not even a whole pass, and I've got you on your knees waiting to be butchered like a beast."She cast her eyes over the yard once more, noting that her neophytes all looked poised and ready, their eyes not on she and Penelope, but each with one watching one of the male threats around them, ready to come to their mistress's aid if needed. As they should. She turned back to Penelope.

"I'm going to offer you a hazard. I'll bet any silver you want your Da loved you ever so much and thought the world of you. He doted on you and thought everything you ever did was special. I know because all these fellows around you, his loyal men who did what he told them, act like doting uncles. And the secret they would never reveal to you is this—you aren't nothin' like as good, powerful, or dangerous as you think. Your mates? Your cousins, the young bucks that won't play no more? They figured it out when your 'uncles' wouldn't let them win. Now they don't waste their time. They're lookin' for real challenges to conquer, which you would be, too, if you were half the bold warrior woman you seem to think you are. So, take a quiet moment here on the ground with a deadly point at your throat, and see if you can understand the part of your lessons you've been missing up until now."

Righteous fell silent but did not release her prisoner. No one moved and the clouds seemed to be scudding more swiftly overhead. It would rain soon, most likely.

"I hit you first," Penelope protested weakly after a long moment.

"That you did," Righteous conceded. "Good swift thrust that almost beat my guard. But look what it cost you to get that hit. If this had been a real fight, I'd have gone home with a nasty poke in my arm. Maybe it might've got infected. It could've made me crippled in the arm, and it could even have rotted the thing right off my shoulder. But you would still be just as dead. There's no magistrates and no point scoring in real fights, and wars are as real as it comes. No points, just alive or dead."

CHAPTER 44

"I'm right sorry, Your Grace, I promise I am. I know I made a dog's breakfast of it all, but she's a little girl who thinks steel to steel is like playing with dollies and braidin' each other's hair. She's worse than the neophytes when they were all just come to Fallenhill with me."

As Righteous made her earnest apology, Prentice cast an eye across the various neophyte handmaids around the room, wondering if they resented the imputation that they, too, had been like little girls when his wife had begun their instruction. He doubted he would be able to tell, even if they did. Many of them were still readable, but most were learning the harsh, cold reserve for which their mistress Lady Dalflitch was famed and feared—their liege as well, for that matter.

"I was working so hard to get it all right," Righteous said miserably, her voice trailing off.

"Yes, well, what is done is done," Archduchess Amelia said without emotion. It was clear that she was deeply disappointed. Righteous's relationship with the baroness had seemed a perfect anchor point upon which to build their alliance with Bridgetown, but now it looked smashed for sure. The entire partnership between the two domains might now be in question. In fact, it was entirely possible that Lady Penelope could turn the White Lions out of Bridgetown within a day, forcing a winter march home through hostile territory—not an overwhelming prospect but by no means desirable.

Prentice took a step to come close to his wife, and as he did so, he was a little surprised how firmly she pressed herself into him, hiding her face against his chest. He put his arm around her, ignoring the breach of protocol. She felt so small in his embrace, like she did when they were alone in the night, tender and fragile. He stoked her hair over her veil, his finger tripping softly over the ribbon that tied her mask in place. She looked up at him.

"I never meant to be all gutter rat like that, I swear," she whispered. "I wanted you all to be so proud of me."

"I am so proud of you, Righteous," he said just as quietly, as if the rest of the room was empty and they were completely alone. "You are my beloved wife and there is no other like you in my sight."

He held her tightly again for a moment and then looked over her head to his liege.

"Your Grace, I have just remembered that Amy and Gant were fretting for their mother when I arrived," he said. "Would you release my wife to their care? They need their mother's care. She will doubtless be available again once they are settled."

"Of course, Baron," the archduchess replied, eyes turning to the window she was standing near, looking out into the evening dark of the town. Light rain was falling, and the few lamplights visible were scattered by the circular patterns in the glass panes of the window, so that they were like bright stars seen from just under the surface of a pool of water. Prentice bowed his head to his liege and then turned to look down to his heartbroken wife once more.

"Go, my sweet, see awhile to the beautiful children you made for us," he whispered. "Gather yourself in their company and remember who you are. Your triumphs outnumber your mistakes. You are yet Baroness of Fallenhill and my queen in here."

He awkwardly threaded his hand into the small space between them and tapped himself on the chest. Righteous looked up at him.

"I will kill for the chance to die in your arms," she told him, as if they were two young cobble runners thinking to live and die by their twentieth summer. Then she turned back to the archduchess and curtseyed. "Thank you, My Liege."

She turned to leave, but just as she did, Lady Dalflitch spoke from where she sat in a quiet corner.

"One last matter if I may, Baroness?" she asked. "In this unfortunate endeavor, was there anything I should know about the three sent to attend you? Just because your own mission was unprofitable does not mean that they are exempt from review."

Righteous paused and looked to some of the neophytes, although Prentice had no idea which ones specifically had accompanied his wife to Earlsbastion. It occurred to him that he could identify very few of them by sight as it was and did not know any of their names for certain. It was a gap in his knowledge he would have to address.

Along with a thousand others, he thought ruefully. There were never enough hours in his day.

"Flawless," Righteous said of her attendants, as if assessing the quality of a fine sword. "They were poise and attention every step outside this door. Quiz them, of course, My Lady, but don't fret you none. They watched, saw, and acted just as you would wish. I'd hazard odds that they even can give you a better picture on this day's failures."

"I will put that to the test," Dalflitch said with a tone that sounded as if a glacier had been given a voice to speak. "My thanks."

Righteous made to move off again, but the archduchess called one more command after her.

"Also, put those trousers off again, would you, My Lady?" she said without looking in her lady-in-waiting's direction. "You are yet a member of my chamber."

"Yes, Your Grace," Righteous said, curtseying again, and then she was gone. The room became almost silent, with only the susurrating movements of neophytes, like an unseen river flowing in the corners of the chamber. Prentice stood patiently, watching his liege as she in turn watched the nighttime town through the windows. The autumn rains would be putting a dampener on the evening markets, but Bridgetown was a trade settlement like no other, buying and selling being the main business of all those folk, such that even foul weather was no great impediment to commerce. Prentice doubted if the depths of winter would stop it. If Baroness Penelope did not send them packing first, he would find out.

"It's been hours and there is no word from the castle," Dalflitch said eventually. "She doesn't strike me as a patient brooder. Silly filly or not, she's no Daven Marcus. As long as we have no enemies in her court to push her farther away from you, Your Grace, I think our alliance might be safe, at least for now."

Prentice could well imagine the kind of tantrum that might have resulted if someone like Righteous had done the same sort of thing to Daven Marcus. Distant relatives would likely have been gibbetted or burned at the stake before his murderous, petty rage was sated.

"Silly filly?" Amelia repeated, and her voice sounded more weary than angry.

"Your Grace, would you hear me speak in my wife's defense?" Prentice asked. Normally, he would not be so reticent, especially in relative private like this, but the unknown neophytes made him feel a touch warier than usual.

"Of course, Baron Ash. I...," the archduchess began, then paused and sighed, turning back from the window. "I am not angry at Righteous, Prentice. Disappointed, but not even really in her."

"Her provocation was dire," Prentice said. "And you and Lady Dalflitch have both observed how free with disdain the young Baroness of Bridgetown can be. She is not flighty, exactly, but she certainly does not understand how much darkness her shadow casts upon her underlings, let alone her peers."

"Of course, Prentice," Amelia agreed. "I just...Righteous...Baroness Righteous...has come so far, and I had such hopes. I never paused to consider that Lady Penelope would be so..."

"Silly?" Dalfitch offered, and the archduchess smirked. What better way was there to describe her.

"She's lost in her private notions of the chivalric dream, Your Grace," Prentice observed.

"Save that she thinks that she is the knight on the destrier, riding to everyone's rescue and receiving all the glory," Dalflitch added. "Someone should have explained some things to her by now."

Prentice nodded. Having heard his wife's account of the day's "sparring" session, he did not disagree. If Baroness Penelope wanted to put sword and harness on, mount her charger and ride to war, he did not care in the least. The problem was that she had seen "war" only from the training hall and the castle solars. She still thought it was a simple matter of stepping out the door in armor and then returning in praise and victory. She had never ached at the end of endless days of marching, sleeping on merciless ground. She had not smelled the blood and sweat, heard the tears and screams nor tasted the mud and bitterness of the battlefield. Men glorified battle because it was easier to remember it that way than through the nightmares of the quiet hours. Better to sing and drink and carouse than to awake in sweat, crying and praying that their souls would not forever be trapped in that hell. This was a truth all veterans knew, to a greater or lesser degree, and why raw recruits learned to stay silent while the tried and tested spoke. Something the Baroness of Bridgetown had yet to discover for herself.

"It wasn't Righteous' fault, Prentice," Amelia said at last. "Make sure she understands that I know that."

He bowed to her, and she shook her head with a sad smile, stepping away from the window and coming back to her chair at the head of the table.

"Oh, Prentice, sit, would you," she said, waving at a place near her at the table. "You're not on trial. No one's losing their title over this. As I said, what is done, is done. So, what do we do now? Apologize?"

Prentice took his chair and raised an eyebrow to Dalfitch, who he felt sure would share his opinion on the matter.

"You could apologize, Your Grace," he said. "But I think it would be a mistake."

"You do?" his liege asked noncommittally. As Prentice hoped, Lady Dalfitch took up his line of reasoning for him.

"It won't do any real good, not in the long term," she explained. "It is the politest course, but it will also help the flibbertigibbet to think that she's in the right and needs do nothing to change her ways. Better for us to say nothing and act as if all is well. It shows we have no doubts in her or her alliance, despite her embarrassment. She invited a master swordswoman to her castle for a lesson in the blade and that is precisely what she got."

"She invited Righteous for a chance to show off her skill and be told what a true woman warrior she was," Amelia countered, but Dalflitch only shrugged her shoulders.

"Of course, but she will never admit that publicly, and why should she? Who was the last liege you saw admit to humiliation? None that I can remember."

"Not in the age of Liams, Robants and Daven Marcuses," Amelia agreed.

"So, we protect her dignity and trust in turn that she keeps the alliance," Prentice added. He and Dalflitch nodded to each other and then stopped for a moment to let the archduchess digest their thinking. Then an extra notion occurred to him. "Remember, Your Grace, that she needs us easily as much as we do her. In two days, we accomplished what her sparse forces could not in weeks. Could not have done, even if she had ten times the men-at-arms."

"They are really that bad?"

"Their militia certainly are. The Young Hopefuls are armed and trained, but young oxen gore one another for want of a ring through their nose. They have no one strong to lead them. They are as much a danger to each other and to Bridgetown as to Lady Penelope's enemies."

"You said they almost took Sougate without you," Dalflitch countered.

Prentice shook his head.

"They captured the battlements by themselves, but that was no more than a useful diversion for our infiltration," he explained. "If not for us, the rest of that garrison would have fled easily. Not to mention the number of prisoners they slaughtered out of pure bloodlust. In gentler times, they would have relatives riding from up and down the Great Bridge Road to be avengers of blood. Every one of the Young Hopefuls would have lost what little wealth they had paying weregelds that any half-just lord would have awarded against them."

"Fair points and true, Baron. Thank you," Dalfitch conceded.

"And a reminder that we should not embrace every new way simply because of the tyrannies of the old," Amelia mused. "Removing a heavy rock from the ground can let weeds grow just as well as grass and flowers."

Poetic, but not wrong, Prentice thought.

Again, the trio was silent at the table.

"We will do nothing for now," Amelia agreed at last. "We will proceed as if all is as it was at dawn today. What next, then?"

"Both bastions are now fully garrisoned, Your Grace," Prentice said. "The Lion flies over Norgate and the Gryphon in the south. Knight Captain Farringdon and Knight Sergeant Sedgemark already have their plans to reinforce the north bank, and Sergeant Guillam is all but praying that the Veckanders attack so he can give them a taste of what we learned in the far west."

"Knight Sergeant?" Amelia repeated, as if the phrase was of a foreign language. "Are we hypocrites to want the "archduchess-elect" of Bridgetown to keep to old ways when we are inventing new institutions out of whole cloth?"

"Perhaps, Your Grace," Dalflitch acknowledged, "but we live in strange times. If hypocrisy was our worst sin, I, for one, would face the judgement with little fear."

Both women looked to Prentice for his opinion.

"Not the way I might have phrased it," he said, "but close enough to true."

"And what of the Bridgetowner militiamen?" the archduchess asked, pressing for the rest of Prentice's report. "We have our commitment to train them yet. Will that be a burden when you have the new gryphons to bring along as well?"

"The new gryphons *are* trained, Your Grace," Prentice assured her. "Franken and his men know their craft. No one marched out of Fallenhill unready."

"*Sir* Franken," Dalflitch corrected him but with a light smile on her lips, and they chuckled at the ironic humor.

"*Knight Sergeant* Franken's recruits only need to learn their place in the full order. Just by being in camp they are five sixths of their way to that," Prentice continued, taking up the humor. "In comparison, the Bridgetowners are slugabouts, coasting by on hereditary militia commissions, some awarded to ancestors centuries ago, I would guess. Half could not pick one end of a halberd from the other. If they were horses, we would be slaughtering them for meat and leather."

"Are they really as bad as all that?"

"You should have heard them grousing about having to march out to Runners Field and live in camp. Most of them are used to going home to their own houses and trades. They only serve the town's militia a few weeks out of every year. It is far short of what they need to be."

"How did you respond to their complaints?" Dalflitch asked.

"I am Knight Commander," Prentice said, drawing himself up and affecting a puffed pride he would never have shown normally. "*I* do not lower myself to listen to the grousing of mere recruits. That is my underling's duty."

"Well, how did they respond?"

"Knight Sergeant Gennet was quite direct, I hear. He told them that if they shirked, they would feel his wrath, and if they left the camp, as some threatened to, they had better run farther than just back to their homes in town because he would be sending his tricksy fey friends to hunt them out in the dark watches to fetch them away in secret and bring them back to where a deserter's gibbet would be waiting for them."

The two women smiled at the gallows humor, though Prentice knew they were aware how true every word was.

"Ever since the day we arrived, when Benjamin's *keshiyaa* put Robant's steel-clads to flight, there have been rumors of our fey rider friends flitting about the lowborn folk of the town, apparently, making us seem both mysterious and a small portion of terrifying in the light of ancient legends," he concluded. "Useful allies to have, the fey."

"When we do have them," the archduchess added grimly, and Prentice felt he had to concede that point. The meeting ended and the knight commander took his leave to look in on his wife. As he was exiting, Lady Spindle entered from the door to the street. They passed each other in the doorway, but when Prentice acknowledged her, she hardly even noticed him. It was an uncharacteristic rudeness, which Prentice ignored. His mind was on his own lady's wellbeing. Spindle was obviously agitated, and the four neophytes that trailed behind her had troubled expressions when they flipped back their veils.

"Your Grace," the Lace Fang said as she approached the archduchess's chair. "Some...things have happened."

"Things?" Amelia asked, sitting up. "What things?"

CHAPTER 45

"It weren't nothin' at first," Spindle began but then trailed off, her eyes looking in every direction at once. She was rocking back and forth from one foot to another like a thoroughbred eager for a race, and under her mask, Amelia could see the lady-in-waiting's skin was flushed, as if she had been running.

"My Lady, sit," Amelia urged, indicating the chair Prentice had only just vacated. Spindle headed towards it, but as her hand touched the back, she pushed away again.

"Not just yet, if I may, Your Grace," she said and set to pacing instead, back and forth near the table. "I'm ropable. I'm fit to stick someone, I swear."

Amelia looked to Dalflitch, wondering if she might shed some light on Spindle's distemper. The two had once had a set to over a comment taken amiss a year ago, and the archduchess wondered if that might be something like this, involving someone else other than Dalflitch, she assumed. For her part, the lady seneschal seemed equally at a loss, and she looked to the neophytes. One of them caught her gaze.

"We was fitted up for a bushwacking, or near enough," that wimpled girl began, but Spindle cut her off.

"I can tell me own bloody tales, Seskia!" she snapped. Almost immediately, Spindle hung her head in frustration and disappointment. "Sorry lass. That's old Spindle Tress speakin' out of turn again. Come now girl, get your 'plomb back. You can do it."

Amelia watched as her ireful lady-in-waiting breathed deeply and worked to reclaim her courtly calm, her aplomb. It was a discipline the archduchess knew well. Slowly, Spindle became her better self, and with a polite nod of her head, pulled out her offered chair and finally sat down.

"Come closer, ladies," she said to the neophytes over her shoulder. "You will likely have reflections to add to my story once I am calm enough to ask for them."

The women stepped closer to the table but still kept their polite, deferential postures. Amelia turned to the neophyte attending her at this time, Beth.

"Fetch something for Lady Spindle to drink," she told her, and Spindle thanked her mistress.

"Start your tale at the beginning, My Lady," Dalflitch urged, and the entire chamber waited while Spindle found the words.

"I guess it started with that note this morning, Your Grace, the one Lady Dalfitch had from the haberdasher," she began.

Dalflitch looked to her papers gathered on the table.

"I can show it to you, if you like, Your Grace," she said readily, clearly a little puzzled as she fetched the individual note out. "It seemed perfectly normal to my eyes."

"Oh, sure and certain it was, My Lady," Spindle agreed. "There's one tricksy bit in it, but I didn't spot it and I'm not surprised it slipped by yourself as well."

"What…'tricksy'…bit?"

"They asked you for *one* girl, didn't they?" Spindle told her. Dalflitch looked to the note and then handed it to Amelia. The archduchess scanned it quickly and then reached the pertinent line of text.

"I have found another quarter bolt of that lace brocade you so admired," Amelia read out loud. "If you can send a girl for it this morning, it will be yours as a gift to your liege from our cloth house."

She looked up at Spindle.

"That seems perfectly ordinary and generous," she said.

"In a 'currying favor and future custom' sort of way," Dalflitch added, as if fearful they might forget to remember that merchants always had one eye on profit in all their public dealings.

"Yea, Your Grace. That's how I took it. I could well have just sent Seskia or Beth along to collect it, with no thought," Spindle said, acknowledging the neophyte who was pouring a silver cup of wine for her. She took it from Beth's hand and looked of a mind to down it in a swallow. Then she stopped and forced it to her lips in a slow deliberate manner, sipping gently and returning the cup to the table.

"As it happened, I had a thought to select some new fabrics, ones I thought I'd seen last time I was there," she continued. "Some of your ladies-to-be are fierce canny with needle and thread, Your Grace, and they've made us some finery already. Near used up the best of my first shop's worth, if you can believe it. What with that and a whole clutch of new silvers burning a hole in my purse, now the Masnian's is exchanged, I was of a mind to make another proper shop of the morning, make sure we've got a good load of fabrics in afore winter so we can sit and sew without having to go out in the rains for more. We'll keep good and busy through the cold days to come."

"Your diligence is creditable," Dalflitch said while Spindle took another sip. When she put her cup down again, Amelia could see her forming the words with her lips, as if checking she was able to pronounce them before she tried to speak them out.

"That is a compliment, isn't it, My Lady?" she asked quietly, choosing not to repeat the words.

"It is indeed," Dalflitch said, and Amelia nodded as well.

"I took it as such," said Spindle. "Thanks to you, Lady Dalflitch.

So much for the two who went at each other with daggers a year ago, Amelia thought, though, in truth, it was only Spindle who had flashed any steel. Righteous had been the one to put her on the back foot that day. Dalflitch had been glad to come away without a permanent scar.

"At any rates, I took these four with me, Your Grace, and went shopping. The haber', his place is just around a corner, down a narrow street like, on a place they call Greenmarsh. One of the islands, I'm told. Not a dark alley, quite, but out of the way, that's for sure. When I rounded the corner, there were two louts out the front—skips' ruffians for sure. I knew that as soon as I laid eyes on them. All the girls kenned 'em for what they were."

Behind the dagger-seamstress, all four neophytes muttered and scowled, and in an instant, her nun-like trainee ladies were all dockside maids again, sharp-eyed and furious at being so misled.

"Could they have been there for other business?" Amelia asked, more to follow the story than to doubt it. "Standover men collecting for a debt owed to a skips' boss?"

"Nah, Your Grace," one of the neophytes said. "Standovers don't hang about. They come, they rough you up, and then they clear off. Less chance of runnin' into the bailiffs that way."

Dalflitch gave the girl a stern glance, but Spindle did not disapprove of her involvement.

"Joan's got the right of it, Your Grace," she said. "And even if they could've been on the up and up, their first words told us what they were about. They stood when they saw me and pulled out belaying pins."

"Belaying pins?" Amelia asked, unfamiliar with the term.

"A boat tool, Your Grace," the girl Joan explained. "'Bout a third the size of a bailiff's cudgel and useful like a sap—hide it under a cloak or like and bash a head in with it."

Amelia's eyes went wide. Since the beginning of her time as ruler of the Reach, she had learned so much of the surprisingly mysterious riverfolk culture, through reports from Prentice and Dalflitch mostly, yet she still had much more to learn, it seemed.

Is there nothing that cannot be made into a weapon? she wondered. Prentice had captured a man once with no more than the manacles on his wrists to wield. Perhaps anything could be turned upon an enemy or a victim if the fighter was cunning enough.

"Soon as I saw 'em standin' up, all swagger and sneers, clouts in hand to give us a thumpin', I knew we'd put our foot in a trap, Your Grace," Spindle went on.

"And you're sure that that was exactly their intention?" Dalflitch asked, her gaze now shrewd and calculating. If someone had used one of the Archduchy's business contacts to arrange an ambush of some sort, that was absolutely within her purview. She would not suffer it to go unpunished, that was certain. Amelia had a moment of wry amusement as she wondered whose ire she would less like to face—Spindle's or Dalflitch's.

"One of 'em said as much," Joan told them. "There was only s'posed to be one of us, he said. They were only paid to take one, and we should pick who was going and who was gonna stay behind."

Well, it doesn't come clearer than that, Amelia thought.

"How did you respond?" she asked.

"With skinned steel, of course, Your Grace," Spindle said as if offended that Amelia might think anything else.

"We flashed blades at 'em, and while they still sneered, it didn't take us long to show 'em up for fools," Seskia said proudly. "Lady Spindle and Lady Righteous know how to teach fighting, I promise you, Your Grace. They thought we was little fluffballs, but a few choice cuts and they were running like chickens from a butcher's block."

Spindle and Righteous are good teachers, but thank the Lord Almighty you girls are good students, Amelia thought, remembering Righteous's disastrous "lesson" with Baroness Penelope only earlier today.

"They surely ran," Joan took up the story, the most outspoken of the four clearly feeling more confident or more enthusiastic to tell this part. "And Lady Spindle here, she wasn't worried much about them. She wanted the haberdasher. She was in his shop like a harridan, threatening to burn his whole stock with his own lamp. It was wild beautiful to see."

"That's enough of that talk, Joan," Spindle chided, and the girl bowed her head once more, though it seemed her smile did not fade. Spindle looked to Amelia. "I was something of the shrew right then, Your Grace. I don't think it's like to reflect bad on you, though."

"What happened to this haberdasher?" Dalflitch asked. Amelia could see the lady seneschal crossing his name off every contract the archduchy had with him in her mind, like a sovereign signing a traitor's name to a death warrant.

"He's all water washed downriver," one of the other neophytes explained. "Gone. Prob'ly afore we even showed up."

"I will give his name to the Conclave," Dalflitch said conclusively. "He will not trade openly in Bridgetown again, and we will have a good claim on his stock as compensation. A share of it, at least."

"Well, that sounds like a dire day's events, but the outcomes seem better than they might have, at least," Amelia said.

"With respect, Your Grace, the outcomes are not even truly known at this stage," the lady seneschal corrected her. "We have no idea who did this or why."

"And that's only the half of it," Spindle said.

"Half? What else was there?" Amelia asked, wondering how many impressive adventures her Lace Fangs could have collected in one afternoon.

Chapter 46

"After we left his shop, I confess I wasn't of a mind to let the matter sit, even for a breath, Your Grace," Spindle continued. "I remembered how Baron Ash captured that traitor leather merchant years ago in Dweltford, when he was still just a convict captain. Lady Righteous has told us the tale more'n once. She's still livid he went to that task without her, but I think mostly 'cause she was already gettin' sweet on him at that point and just wanted to be around him."

Amelia remembered that night's work. Prentice had only been recently freed and had hunted down a man named Folper as a member of the conspiracy that Duggan the traitor had arranged to overthrow her rule. Folper had tried to run from Dweltford in the night, and Prentice and Sir Gant had chased him through a dark storm.

"Like the baron, I wanted to run the haberdasher down, but I had no idea where to look for him if he wasn't in the shop," Spindle explained.

"I said we should wait for him to come back," Seskia put in, "but Lady Spindle didn't think he was comin' back and she weren't of a mind to let him go so easily as that."

Spindle raised her hand for quiet.

"That's enough for now, maids," she said. "I have my wits back to me enough to carry the story. Unless you are asked, you'll hold your tongues from now on."

The four neophytes curtseyed.

"I wanted him like a drunk wants a drink, Your Grace," Spindle said, her tone suddenly like that of a penitent sinner. "I'm a little shamefaced to say I raged about it some, but only in the shop, not the street. I remembered your dignity."

"Thank you, My Lady," Amelia told her.

"For a moment I was on the path to do as Lady Dalflitch suggested, going straight to the Conclave house and list the fiend as a front for smugglers and cutthroats, but then I figured on a longtime trader like this haber' having friends in the Conclave, so I decided on a different course. I went to my husband's trader's house. I knew he was there—spends most of his days there while I'm here and her Grace's gold has been in his strongroom. I knew he'd have an ear to where to find this crooked-dealing clothier. Nothing happens 'mongst any town's merchants that my Caius doesn't make a point to learn when he's staying there."

"Then I will make it a point to consult him," Lady Dalflitch said, "with your permission, Lady Spindle. If he has intelligences on these matters, I would like them in my hands as well."

"I think he'd like that, My Lady," Spindle said back. "He speaks highly of you, though not frequent, and he's always spoken of your canniness and good judgement. I have never heard him mention your beauty once."

"Well, now, I don't know whether to be complimented or insulted," Dalflitch retorted, her facial expression once again the haughty bedswerver of king's and princes rather than the shrewd spymaster she truly was.

"Be complimented," Spindle didn't hesitate to tell her. "My Caius has no time for fripperies, except to sell them."

Dalflitch accepted the un-courtly praise with an amused smile.

"Did your husband know the man's contacts, or where he might go to ground?" Amelia pressed, hoping for good news. If someone was plotting to kidnap one of her neophytes—which was certainly what the skip thugs seemed to mean—then it can only have been to discover their secrets. The most likely notion was that they had thought to grab a maid and interrogate her before replacing her with a skin thief. How many such agents did the Inquisition have in Bridgetown?

"It never got to that, Your Grace," Spindle said, continuing before Amelia could ask what that meant. "Caius was attacked this afternoon, right there in his own trades house."

"What?" Amelia asked, her personal concerns swiftly overridden by her fears for her lady-in-waiting's husband.

"In his own trading house?" Dalflitch repeated. "With his guards about him? Trained men-at-arms with stout weapons and mail shirts?"

"That's only one fool part of a whole fool plan," Spindle assured them. "It was three cutthroats, maybe the same skip captain's blokes, but these one's hadn't come to take a hostage or nothing. They had steel under their wimples."

"Wimples?" Dalflitch and Amelia asked both together. Spindle's angry expression turned to a sardonic smile.

"Aye, wimples. They figured they had themselves the finest disguise. They was mocked up like neophytes—dresses, wimples, veils, the lot. They tried to pose as our girls sent from this very chamber. Course, how they kenned to pass as women, unless one of them was a castrate soprano, I'll never figure."

Amelia shook her head in wonder at the brazenness of the attempt.

"My Caius' said that they fronted up all heads down and veils in place and just handed over a letter, s'posed to be from Your Grace. It said they were there to collect one of the Masnian strongboxes on your order."

"My order?" Amelia asked. "Why would I send ladies-in-waiting, even provisional, to fetch strongboxes?"

"That was part of what tipped Caius to what was happening," Spindle explained. "He asked why the archduchess was calling for the monies again so soon, and which changers they were being taken to. These three just stood there silent for a long while, apparently, which only made them look all the more suspicious, then bang, whack, they were skinning steel and shouting for the keys to the strongroom."

"A robbery in daylight hours in a public business on a street full of traders?" Amelia wondered. They were inviting disaster, even if their poorly conceived disguises had worked.

"The only hours Master Welburne is trading, Your Grace," Dalflitch offered with a speculative shrug.

"So, what happened in the end?" the archduchess asked and Spindle's smile broadened further, then she turned to the neophytes.

"You can tell this bit if you like, Seskia," she said, and the young maid's dark eyes glittered with a delighted menace.

"The blades they brought were too long to get out of their dresses quickly," the neophyte said, and all four smirked happily. "While they were shouting and pushing Master Caius to the floor, two of them got their edges tangled up, and that was the end of them. The merchant master's hired men took them down with clouts of their maces. The third tried to run but never even reached the door. By the time Lady Spindle led us in, an apothecary was seeing to Master Welburne's cut forehead and the three fools had already been marched off with the bailiffs. They never even saw the strongroom."

Amelia found herself smirking with her maids, amused at the failed banditry, but underneath that was a deepened concern. Their fears of lurking enemies in the shadows were confirmed now, but even with that clarity, they were no nearer to knowing who or how they were being opposed. The first incident had all the hallmarks of the Inquisition and its patient plans—a setting move, building a hand for the winning play. The second was so haphazard that it could almost have been opportunistic, a clutch of fools with more greed than wits. Except that both had the look of riverfolk, skips' men. Of course, in Bridgetown, that was everyone who wasn't a conclave merchant or guildsman. These could be two completely separate incidents, linked only by their timing, but far from a comforting notion, that only suggested that they had twice the number of secret enemies, plotting against them.

"I would have you write to the Conclave immediately, My Lady," Amelia told Dalflitch. "We must petition for a chance to question these three captives. Perhaps they know something of the haberdasher's plot as well, or if not, we can ask how they came to devise their ill-conceived theft."

"As you say, Your Grace. The Conclave could not dare to refuse you, I would think. Between your rank and being the affronted party, they could well simply hand the men over to you for your justice."

"Better not," Amelia insisted. "The day's other events mean we will have to be extremely careful not to tread on the baroness's toes in the next while."

"Yes, of course," Dalflitch conceded and then looked to Spindle across the table. "May I suggest that Lady Spindle and Lady Righteous accompany you to the questioning itself, though, when we receive permission. We all know how persuasive they can be, and I am sure My Lady has some choice words for the men who knocked her husband about in his own place of business."

"I think that an excellent idea, My Lady," Amelia said. Spindle sipped her wine and nodded politely, as if she had just been offered a gift. Her smile gave the archduchess a momentary chill.

Whoever you are, lurking in shadows, she thought, *best for you if you stay there. Once my Fangs hunt you out, your lives will be short and unpleasant.*

CHAPTER 47

For the next two days there was no word from the castle, and despite Prentice and Dalflitch's confidence that things would return to a natural equilibrium, Amelia felt herself fretting. Part of that was accentuated by the fact that the letter to the Conclave, reporting the haberdasher and insisting on a chance to question the robbers before they went to the magistrate, had received a disturbing reply. The haberdasher was dead, found the next morning entangled in fisher's nets near the island known as Bell's Hummock. The aldermen apologized and swore that a "substantial portion" of the man's stock would eventually be given over to the archduchess's ladies in recompense for the attack, but until the cutthroats had also been captured, no dispensations could be made. The Conclave would have to hold onto the cloth merchant's wares in the meantime.

"By the time the skips' ruffians are captured, the entire store will have been purloined by unseen hands and somehow, mysteriously, found its way into the back rooms of other Conclave member's storehouses," Dalflitch had declared, cynically. "Do not hold your breath for your compensations ladies."

As calculated as that outcome surely was, there was nothing more than mere venality behind it, Amelia was convinced. Every Conclave was a brotherhood of wolves, protecting each other's interest because they were stronger together but falling on the weak amongst them as soon as chance presented an opportunity.

The fate of the three thieves was a far more troubling propo-sition. During their first night in the cells of Bridgetown's petty courts, the arrested men had taken their homespun disguise dress-es and torn them into lengths from which they wound nooses to hang themselves. Three men brave enough to front a rich mer-chant and his hired guards, right at his strongroom, were appar-ently so grief stricken or fearful of conviction, that they chose to immediately commit suicide. If venality explained one part of the Conclave's response, then this part beggared imagination.

"They must surely have been murdered," Amelia had said, shaking her head in disbelief. "That is how it seems, doesn't it? There's no piece of this that I'm missing, is there?"

"Not that we can see, Your Grace," Dalflitch had said, having already discussed much of the note with Spindle and Righteous. All three were certain someone of great influence must have been behind the robbery and the murders, but was that a problem or a comfort? The Inquisition had almost infinite influence, it seemed, but to get someone into the jail to slay the men on their first night and make it look like suicide—that made them seem like the whole power of Bridgetown itself. If the Inquisition could reach anyone in the town so easily, Amelia herself should already have had multiple attacks on her person directly.

"I would bet it was a bold skips captain, Your Grace," Right-eous had declared. "Too much brass for his own good."

"Or *her* own good," Dalflitch had added, reminding them all of the power of the only recently deceased Ragmother. "And we must remember that while it might have been the plot of a skips crew, it might yet have been at the Inquisition's instigation. A gang of bravos to act as hired mercenaries."

"They wouldn't need to have paid them either," had been Spin-dle's opinion. "Just given them the good word about gold in the strongroom and let them go to it."

For his part, Prentice had taken the events as mostly a good sign.

"Our guards and defenses all worked as we would want them to, Your Grace," had been his summation. "No neophytes were captured, and no coins were stolen. Also, this is not the plan of someone who has unlimited skin thieves to send against us. If they have any, they must not be many and are being held back, so we need not give way to terror just yet."

"I am to be reassured that our watchfulness and preparedness have not failed us yet, but we will have to remain at least as equally vigilant?" had been Amelia's sour conclusion.

"Unless Master Solft has uncovered a method to reveal skin thieves directly," Prentice had added. In fact, the scholar had not, though he claimed it was still early days.

And so, with the shadows thwarted for now, the archduchess found her mind turning back to the disaster between Righteous and Penelope. She compared it with her other memories of the Baroness of Bridgetown and discovered that she had gathered quite a catalogue of impressions in the short time they had known one another. Very little of it felt reassuring, either.

Headstrong was the word that recurred in Amelia's thoughts, bringing a smile to her lips when she recalled Dalflitch's term—a *silly filly*. The problem was that headstrong was exactly the kind of derisive term arrogant nobles would use of Amelia herself—or at least would have some years ago. Now she had moved far past headstrong, through wayward, and all the way into over-ambitiously heretical. "Archduchess-elect" Penelope was still well short of that heinous level of bad reputation, and Amelia imagined if she tried to explain it to Penelope, the young girl would only hear the voice of tradition, the voice of calcified convention, seeking to hold her back for no good reason except fear of old men's disapproval.

And that is not an untrue way to view it, in a sense, she thought as she sat quietly, watching Spindle supervising neophytes at embroidery and Dalflitch examining the girls Agatha and Daisy for their numbers and mathematics. Both were more well educated than anyone expected, it seemed, though neither had any skill for reading or writing.

The problem is that reputation and approval are necessary, like them or not. Not one of us, not kings, not patriarchs of the Church, not nobles or conclaves or guildmasters or even headmen and over-seers—none of us rules by the might of our hands alone. If we must lead others, then we must win their good report. And it is theirs alone to give or withhold. A noble who demands the respect of others without fulfilling the requirements of the social order becomes a Daven Marcus—an infant brat in the body of a man.

"I do not envy the girl," she murmured, and Dalflitch looked up from her work attentively.

"I'm sorry, Your Grace?"

"Lady Penelope wants to rule in her own right," Amelia said. "She doesn't understand how much that requires the goodwill of those around her. It's a...a minstrel's balancing trick, I suppose, loath as I am to use such a picture."

The whole room grew a fraction more still. Since Bluebird's attempted assassination, and the revelation that he was merely one of an array of possible spies and assassins, all with magickal powers, mention of minstrels had become an unpleasant matter in the archduchess's chamber. Amelia went on to explain her metaphor, laying out her thoughts as much for her own benefit as for her ladies.

"Too far on one side of the balance and one falls into tradition that locks around your feet more tightly than the strongest iron fetters," she said. "Look at Sebastian."

"Hidebound," Dalflitch added by way of agreement.

"But tip the trick too far in the other direction and we have nothing but chaos, all previous bonds dissolved. Then the only power anyone has is the sharpness of their own steel and the strength of the arm that wields it."

"Civil war, or warlordism. As in the time after the mountain was cast into the sea. From the birth of the Grand Kingdom 'til now."

Amelia gave her lady seneschal a raised eyebrow.

"How come you by that reference?" she asked.

Dalflitch waved a sublimely indifferent hand over the parchments and folios.

"A seneschal's yoke carries many a document with it, and some are informative on history, theology, and even genealogy."

"Truly?" Amelia had thought she was the only one who read for learning. She knew Dalflitch was extremely literate but assumed that came mainly from her past. In recent years, the lady-in-waiting had seemed to have time only for accounts. Dalflitch nodded politely and then flashed the sincerely charming smirk that she hid from almost everyone in the world except her husband and most trusted friends.

"No, Your Grace," she explained. "In truth, Master Solft asked recently for access to a tome in your collection, which has some history of the pre-Kingdom era, apparently. He explained his interest to me during a swift conference between meetings with moneychangers' factors. He reports that he is hard at work searching out our mysteries for us. And as custodian of your purse, I can report that he is doing so with commendable thrift."

That's pleasing, Amelia thought, though she wondered why she had not been asked directly for one of her books. *Because I was taking a rest at that time, no doubt.*

She stroked her belly, knowing the cause of her need for more rest than a mere night's sleep. Already, it felt like her waist was twice its usual size and she was barely halfway through her pregnancy. Size aside, though, she felt quite healthy, she realized. Her husband had already told her that she was glowing more than once—a nearly cliché compliment for a pregnant woman but which secretly pleased her all the same.

At that moment, Farringdon entered the Paramour's Chambers and she smiled as he marched straight to her and bowed. With so many new attendants, most of them still considered probationary, he had taken to being respectful of her place even in her inner chamber. Now, she was archduchess first and wife second in almost every part of her life. Yet his love was so clear to her that she did not mind.

"Beloved liege," he said warmly, stepping up and taking her hand to kiss it. "Are you well this morning?"

"Quite, and our growing heir with me," she said. "And you, dear husband, how goes your day?"

"I am still wracking my mind over a sergeant for the Roar," Farringdon admitted ruefully. He scratched at his cheek. Amelia wondered if the recent attacks in the town had made him more doubtful of the loyalty of the men under his command. It would be a bitter side effect.

"Is it such a difficult choice?" Amelia asked. Her husband tilted his head and gave a shrug.

"In one sense, not at all," he admitted. "The man Prentice offered the Gryphon banner to, this Lyrach, he's commanded Roarsmen and has a head for the role. He'd be ideal, except he happens to be a talented horseman into the bargain and a good sword as well. I would much rather have him in the saddle with the lancers. He could be second to Nunel tomorrow, and likely once he's settled in and shown the rest of the company his mettle, I'll give him the role."

"Oh, well all you need is another one like him," Amelia joked, and Farringdon smiled.

"I'd be glad of someone only three quarters as good, if I could have ten of them," he countered happily. "What I need now is to find a Roarsman who is close. I've set Knight Sergeant Markas to help me with that."

"Then the matter is three quarters resolved," Amelia said. Her tone was light, but she meant what she said. Markas was not a Prentice or a Farringdon, nor a Turley for that matter, but his reliability had become unquestionable in her mind. She turned to her attending neophyte. "Tea."

The girl left silently to fetch her a cup.

"Would you join me, husband?"

"I would like that, but forgive me, I cannot," Farringdon apologized. "I have actually come on a matter of Lions' business."

His expression turned earnest so swiftly that Amelia wondered for a moment if another vile attack had happened. Worse, she imagined that Baroness Penelope's silence had turned out to cover some kind of trouble with the alliance. Problems from Prentice's and Farringdon's perspectives were more likely military than nefarious, after all.

"What worries your mind?" she asked, sitting forward. Her handmaid returned with a porcelain cup, which she accepted, holding it by the rim so that the hot sides did not hurt her fingers.

"We've commenced to dig the trenches and embankments in front of the Norgate bastion," Farringdon explained. "I've given Sedgemark a rotation of two cohorts for the purpose—a fresh two out of camp each day so that no one is exhausted. And his progress is excellent. Two hundred hale and hearty men with picks and shovels can move mountains in short order. We'll have almost all of it in place, with wood shelters and reinforced palisades, before the heaviest rains of winter come. If we design it right, we could probably turn the outer ditch into a water-filled moat."

"That all sounds excellent. So, what then is the problem?"

"The Conclave came to us with some questions this morning, and an offer."

"They're afraid we'll choke off the reopened trade?" Dalflitch asked from the table. "Do we need to meet with the selectmen? They cannot keep prisoners safe for us but will criticize how we protect their town?"

"No, we were able to assuage their fears on the account of trade, thank you, My Lady," Farringdon reassured her. "What they offered us was a winter contract for their convict chains."

Again, the room grew still. Other than Farringdon and Lady Dalflitch, every person in the room had been low-born, to some degree, and everyone knew the Archduchess Amelia's disgust at the abuses convicts suffered in the Grand Kingdom. One of her first acts upon becoming archduchess had been to abolish the practice within her lands.

"A winter contract?" Amelia repeated, feeling her ire rise. "They lost the three prisoners we wanted and so they think we will accept any others in recompense?"

"To help us dig the fortifications, so they say."

"And to give us the burden of feeding and housing them through their most unproductive months," Dalflitch mused, turning her eyes back to Agatha's novice attempts to write the numbers that went with the arithmetic she already knew. The lady pointed to something on the neophyte's page, and Agatha began to scratch away again.

"You haven't accepted, have you?" Amelia asked.

Farringdon shook his head. "No, but they are most persistent," he explained. "The Conclave has moved a number of men in fetters to the fields beside the gate, ostensibly to search for any unsecured loot from Robant's retreat but truly to have them ready to hand to us, I think. Their presence is raising the Lions' disgust. There's already been one confrontation between a line first and a convict overseer that nearly led to blood."

"Overseers'll regret that mismatch," Spindle said from her corner of the room, and a small mutter of agreement sounded from many of the neophytes, though not from any one in particular so the ill-discipline could hardly be punished.

"They want as much of your gold as they can get, Your Grace," Dalflitch observed.

"And simply gouging me on the exchange rate is insufficient for them, it seems," Amelia added, agreeing and grimacing at the thought.

"Gouging?" Farringdon asked. He rarely discussed finances with his wife.

"Since the attempted theft, all the negotiations have begun at five guilders on the gold," Lady Dalfitch complained airily. "Even a contract already inked was rewritten yesterday, so that when it arrived for her Grace's signature, nine silvers had been rewritten as seven, with an apology that such was all the money changer in question could afford at this time."

"Incredible," the marquis muttered.

Amelia's mind was focused on the question of convicts rather than the exchange rate of gold to silver. If the archduchess never saw another man or woman on a chain again, it would still be too soon. She sipped her tea and considered the problem. The easiest thing would be to order the Lion company to send the convicts back into the town on the pretext of maintaining the defensive strength of Norgate. Such a high-handed action would only make her enemies in the Conclave, driving the exchange rate further down and likely adding to the prices she would have to pay with the newly acquired silver. According to Dalflitch, no one was ready to be paid in gold directly yet—curse the Golden Heron and the influence they had on trade from Masnia to Denay. She took another sip, and a fresh notion lit her expression with a smile.

"The merchants want my gold at extortionate rates?" she mused. "Why not let them have it but without the changers' involvement? I have to spend it on something. Knight Captain, please inform the Conclave that I would be pleased to accept their offer of convict labor at whatever price they deem worthy, so long as I am free to pay in Masnian coins directly."

Farringdon's face showed clear surprise, but he stood waiting, obviously trusting that his wife had a twist in her tale.

"And on the further proviso that they sell me the entire contracts," she continued, and her husband returned her smile, though a little more quizzically. "I don't want them for the winter; I want them for good. They will come to us, and we will make use of them as we see fit."

"Offering them the Lions' contract?" Farringdon asked, more rhetorically, as he saw the meaning of her words.

"If the convicts wish. Or if they refuse, they can yet serve as auxiliaries to the banners—fetch and carry while we are here in Bridgetown."

"And when we return to the Reach?"

"We will take them with us," Amelia said. "Do make it clear that we expect full contracts, and we won't require any cadre of overseers. The Lions will be sufficient to supervise these 'bad' men."

The ranking members of the chamber all chuckled at that. The worst belligerent convict Bridgetown had would be of no concern to one of the Reach's proven militiamen. After all, the truly brutal cutthroats would already have been hanged, and whatever kind of criminal a convict was, Lions were as well, with militia training, equipment, and experience on top.

"The Conclave aldermen may not like that." Farringdon said, more as a matter of form than as a genuine objection.

"Then they are free to retain their convict charges and I will keep my money. But if they want my gold, then this is what I wish to pay for. After all, my Lions have the silver I owed, my chamber is warm, and my domain is secure. What else is there to spend my gold upon?"

Farringdon executed a courtly bow that made the straps of his breastplate—the only piece of armor he was currently wearing besides his gauntlets—creak in the otherwise quiet room. Then it was drowned out by a thump heard through the ceiling of neophytes training above, soon followed by a cry from one of the twins in their room below. The Paramour's Chambers were rarely quiet for long these days.

CHAPTER 48

"The accession is announced for tomorrow? Have you heard what part I am to play?" Brother Whilte asked Prentice as the knight commander shared this news while they watched the new recruits to Farringdon's lancers being taught the company's basic practices. The knight captain had managed to find a merchant with ties in Masnia who promised to supply him with more triggers and wheellock pistols for the new riders, as well as word that the Fallenhill workshops were turning out as many as they could manufacture. And so, the unique company of shooting riders was going to expand through the winter quite effectively.

"A sealed announcement was brought, formally inviting the archduchess to attend the ceremony," Prentice said. "Accompanying it was a terse note explaining that your services would not be required after all. Another churchman has been found to speak the blessing over the young noblewoman's rise."

Whilte nodded solemnly.

"As a rebuke to her grace?" he asked, and Prentice was not surprised Whilte had heard about the falling out between the two lieges that Righteous's actions had caused. Even if every member of the archduchess's chambers had kept silent as the grave, he imagined the baroness's servants would not have. They did not show the kind of discipline Lady Dalflitch demanded of the neophytes. Not even close.

"I recognize the affront," Whilte went on, "but I must say I am pleased to be left out after all. I find I abhor politics now. I will steer clear whenever the Lord permits me."

The humble chaplain scratched at his rough, shaven tonsure for a moment, smoothing his wispy blonde hair around the bald patch at the same time. Prentice watched him and remembered the fair-haired summer child he had met at Ashfield all those years ago. An arrogant third son of a mediocre noble family, easy with friendships and bitter in his hatred of the young jumped-up merchant's son who had beaten his brother in a fool's duel. Prentice was not the only one who had travelled a long distance from his beginnings.

"My Lord, Knight Commander?" a militiamen asked for Prentice's notice, saluting as he trotted up and brought himself to attention.

My Lord, Knight Commander, Prentice repeated in his thoughts. *We have both travelled a long distance, indeed.*

"What is it?" he asked of the messenger.

"I'm to tell you there are some of them cocksure Hopeful fellows come asking to see you."

"Where are they?"

"Waiting at the west edge of camp, My Lord. Our sentries held them there and called for extra bodies. They're a brassy lot—quick to look for a barny. The provost didn't want to risk any trouble."

"Excellent," Prentice told the militiaman. "Go tell them I am coming."

The man ran to give his superiors the knight commander's answer.

"You're not in a hurry to attend them yourself?" Whilte asked as Prentice looked to the part of the field where the Hopefuls were said to be waiting, not moving off to meet them immediately. "You're not becoming like old Rallings, are you?"

Rallings had been one of the instructors at Ashfield, infamous amongst students for making them wait, never being in haste, ostensibly to teach patience in his young charges but most suspected it was out of either the exhaustion of age or merely pure cantankerousness. Prentice had not thought of the old theology teacher in many years. A difficult man but not petty or hateful, as far as he could remember.

"No, Brother, I am not, but if you were to walk with me, I would be justified in being late, having to match your crippled pace," he said quietly as he set off toward the west boundary of the camp.

"'Crippled pace'?" Whilte repeated indignantly. "I've not slowed the Lions' march, nor the Gryphons', not in all my service to you."

"True, but the Young Hopefuls do not know that. It will be what they think, even if some fluke of good manners causes them to hold their tongue. Let the young fools feel the inconvenience of their poor behavior. Perhaps they might even learn something from it."

"They will learn to hate you all the more for making them wait," Whilte assured him, though not sternly. "Just as we learned to hate Rallings."

"Then pray they will not need to be put on a chain or lose a leg to learn the better lesson," Prentice told him, and Whilte nodded quietly. For a long pause, they walked together quietly past rows of tents and men about the business of an army in camp. The bump and sucking sound of Whilte's pegleg as he planted it in the mud and then used half his body to pull it forth with a wrench gave their steps an odd rhythm, but true to his word, the chaplain's pace never slowed Prentice even half a step.

"Do you mean what you said?" Whilte asked at last. "Would you see these Young Hopefuls taught? Or are you just wanting to put them in their place."

Prentice scratched at his beard a moment, thinking before he answered. In truth, he had been musing about children and parenting lately, in his one spare moment each day, and not merely because the wondrous and overwhelming duty had come to him through the gift of his own twins. Solomon's coming soon into his manhood, after years as a loyal drummer lad, was another tributary feeding the river of Prentice's thoughts. His overwhelming drive in the campaign west had been to make the Reach safe for his archduchess and for his family, but considering his own experiences growing up and seeing now the situation in Bridgetown with so many orphaned youths, he felt there had to be something more to fatherhood than just protecting his family, as important as that would always be.

"They have lost their fathers," he said to Whilte at last. "In as wrong a way as they could imagine. Not just the Hopefuls, the baroness—archduchess-elect—as well."

"Archduchess Amelia, too, when you think about it," Whilte added, and Prentice had to acknowledge that that was the case. The archduchess's father had passed away before she and Prentice met, but his legacy and absence had always been a force in her grace's life. Nevertheless, even though the archduchess's father had been killed by bandits on the road, his passing was still not quite the horror that the slaughter of the Bridgetowner knights at the kingslayer's coup must have been. All murder was ugly, but bandits were always a possibility for merchants. The Usurper had overturned the whole of upper society in his petty rage.

"The Hopefuls have lost their guides into manhood right at the last step," Prentice explained, ordering his thinking for himself as he outlined it to Whilte. "You know it is the step that for a knight is impossible to take alone. A squire needs a noble sponsor to make his final transition to the knighthood, and now none are available. Daven Marcus killed them all. Add to that the myriad subtle truths that a wiser older man imparts to a fellow newly raised to his full status, whether that was as a knight in court or journeyman at his craft. Even the best students, like Solomon, need that guidance—how to speak as a man, how to respect and be respected."

Whilte nodded quietly, and it was clear he understood his commander's thinking. Despite his awkward gait, his face was somber and pensive.

"And the situation is worse by far for the Baroness Penelope," the knight commander continued, pausing only a moment to salute two militiamen who jumped up from sharpening their halberd blades and snapped to attention at his passing. "Since her father allowed her to grow in unconventionality, her path is so much the harder. As Archduchess Amelia's journey to power shows, it is not impossible for a woman to oppose the presumed 'natural' order of things, but it is a much more treacherous road to travel. Doing it without her father or mother almost guarantees she will trip over her own feet sometimes, more times than once."

As he spoke, Prentice felt the notions coming into order, settling some issues he had been allowing to go unresolved while he focused on the needs of the White Lions. Whilte's next observation knocked all that settled feeling askew, like a game of pub skittles.

"You want to avoid making your own father's mistakes for your children and the Young Hopefuls both, would you say?"

Prentice stopped dead in his path and turned to face the chaplain.

"What has *he* to do with any of this?" he demanded, surprised at his own forcefulness. He did not think he was as angry as he sounded. Whilte smiled at him, a pastoral expression, with a deeper touch of sympathy than Prentice had even known in the religious counselor's face before.

"You talk about the Young Hopefuls bereft, the baroness and the archduchess, too," Whilte explained. "I suspect if you were pressed you would feel the same for Solomon and even your goodwife, Lady Righteous. But in all you ignore the fact that you were orphaned younger than all of them."

Prentice cocked an eyebrow and gave Whilte a doubtful smirk.

"My father and mother both live yet," he said. "At least so far as I know."

"So far as you know," Whilte agreed, nodding, then the motion turned to a mournful shake of the head. "But the man was barely a father to you, and I ask you to hold with me as I say so, for I mean no insult. In truth though, the man who should have been your father was merely the one who saddled you with a near impossible burden and paid instructors to force you to carry it, like convict overseers with a lone, fettered rogue. In so many ways he was merely the chief taskmaster of a cadre of taskmasters, and when you were crushed under the weight of the burden he put upon your shoulders, he cast you off with the same level of compassion. In too many ways he was no more than a—what did you say the fellow's name was—Druce? Forgive me my bluntness or call it a privilege of being of the cloth, but your father was little more than the first Druce in your life and no better for all that he was not as cruel. He was the coldness; he entrusted the cruelty to your instructors."

There were sometimes moments in Prentice's life when someone came to him with an insight into his own character that he had never considered. As a man of thought himself, he knew his mind turned much more readily to the problems outside himself than within. Nevertheless, he had never imagined a moment like this one. Of all the things he had ever experienced, he had never thought to question the rightness of his childhood, harsh though it unquestionably had been. Was Whilte correct? Were his father's actions as cruel as the chaplain made them sound? And was that something driving his thoughts and emotions, something pushing him in directions he might not recognize until it was too late, like a horse with blinders on? The thought did not please him.

"My Lord Knight Commander," a Gryphon line first said as he saluted, leading his ten-man line on what looked like a practice march in full kit through the camp. Prentice returned the salute absently as each of the nine following militiamen slapped their fists to their chests.

"You are father to more than you realize, My Lord Knight Commander," Whilte said quietly, so that no one nearby might hear. "Solomon might be the first of them, in a way, and no doubt your twins will ever be your most precious, along with all the others I pray the Lord blesses you and Righteous with. But there are many others. I urge you to be careful to take on no more than you can carry. Your father, un-fatherly as he was, did teach you to shoulder impossible burdens. Just be wary when it comes to the Young Hopefuls. They may be Sebastians—good but led astray by poor counsel—or they may well be Liams, and no amount of good treatment will deliver them from their wild ambitions. Or they might be like me—only able to be rescued after a stern rebuke that many might resent."

Prentice wanted to answer Whilte's concerns, but the truth was, they were sound, and he knew he had not fully absorbed their wisdom. Instead, he thanked the chaplain, and they both finished the short journey to the camp boundary in silence. It was easy to find the exact spot they were looking for as, yet again, the small deputation of Young Hopefuls had not deigned to dismount to speak their piece. Amongst the well-dressed young men on horseback, Prentice readily identified Cassian and Wilforn from the other anonymous faces, six in all. They watched him approach, accompanied by Whilte, and showed exactly the scornful expressions he had expected, but perhaps because of the chaplain's conversation, he found himself feeling less hard toward them than he would ever have expected. Looking them over at this moment, he saw not the arrogance of the social order, peers of the realm despising the lower born as if they were no more than clods of dirt on their feet. Instead, Prentice saw misguided boys, working their hardest to copy the men they so admired and wanted to be like. He saw Solomon, trying to mimic Lyrach—not wrong, only misguided. Even the hateful Cassian's contempt took on a new cast in his eyes.

"At last, the *baron* graces us with his presence," Cassian declared, sighing theatrically with a wave of his hand to his companions, as if Prentice's lateness would have exhausted the patience of a saint.

"If you had been worthy of my haste, young Cassian, you would have received it," Prentice replied in the way many a teacher had spoken to him in his youth. "This is Brother Whilte, chaplain of the White Lions."

Whilte made to tug the forelock, but Cassian was not interested.

"Worthy?" he demanded. "I am worthy of...of more...more than you, that is certain!"

"If you say so," Prentice told him. The knight commander looked to the young man's sword belt. "I see you have not replaced your lost blade. Have you rethought my offer to have it replaced for you? I will spare no expense. I can even have the new one made from the pieces of the old, preserve the hilt and knucklebow, so that the new feels almost like the one that's lost."

"I threw that useless thing into the river," Cassian retorted, his expression twisted to almost a snarl, like a furious animal. "It was good for nothing else."

"Then a new one of Reach steel. I could send to the Fallenhill workshops. Our great master is sadly perished, but his journeymen have no small skill. You could have a best blade come by the rivers before midwinter."

"Reach steel? Better he wield a sword made out of a chamber pot!" Wilforn declared, and his fellows all laughed. There was a shift amongst the watching sentries and provost, but thankfully none of them broke discipline enough to express their umbrage.

Prentice sighed heavily. His compassion for these orphaned young men was wearing thin very swiftly.

"If you have not come for that matter, then what is your business here?" he asked.

The other Young Hopefuls all looked to Cassian, who leaned forward on the pommel of his saddle in the classic pose of a relaxed and contemptuous nobleman—a bully fully confident in his power, at least at this moment.

"My cousin accedes tomorrow, *Baron*," he said, as if revealing a secret flaw in an enemy's plan.

"We have heard," Prentice replied, wondering where this was going.

"Once she is anointed an archduchess, she will have the power to bestow knighthoods, just like in your own little frontier town," Cassian continued. "We will all be created knights, and you will no longer be able to hide from my challenge. Bridgetown will have its rightful military commanders back."

"You think the knight commander hides from you, lad?" Whilte asked, and though Prentice did not look to his face, the disbelief was unmistakable in his voice.

"I doubt Baronet Forsle will any more appreciate a knight challenging a baron than he would a squire," Prentice said calmly. It seemed for all his growing understanding of the Young Hopeful's motives, there might be no turning them from their wild course. He had a sudden image in his mind of these young men gathered in taverns, drinking, and complaining, feeding each other's resentments with no one to cool their hot heads, as Brother Whilte and his friends must have after Prentice defeated Whilte's brother Khalte in their duel and Khalte killed himself in disgrace and despair. He wondered what burdens Khalte's father had laid on his lost sons' shoulders.

"It doesn't matter what Forsle says," Wilforn was saying while Prentice hardly listened. "Penelope is ruler, and when she's fully an archduchess she *will* permit this. You watch. Your dumb wife made sure of that."

Have a care lad, Prentice thought. *My patience has limits as well, and misspeaking of my goodwife can cost more than you can pay.*

"Forsake your anger, I urge you," Whilte said earnestly. "I know from experience that it leads to no good place. The knight commander has been profuse and generous in his apologies, and the Sougate capture was a significant victory, worthy of enough praise for everyone. Can you not share the glory and forgive the debt you feel owed?"

"What do I care for the experiences of a cripple?" Cassian said savagely, and he seized his reins so with such violence that his mount whickered and tossed its head. "Put your affairs in order,

Baron. Come tomorrow evening, your days on this earth come to an end, old man."

With that, he wheeled his horse and rode away at a trot. His companions were a little surprised at the suddenness of his departure and kicked their own mounts to catch up with him. Prentice watched them go, wondering if he felt as sad as he wanted to. It seemed Cassian was intent on being a Liam more than a Sebastian, and it just made Prentice weary. He imagined Cassian with the same deformed jaw that his fight with Liam had given the rebellious knight. He was jarred from these sour considerations by an unexpected voice.

"That young fella don't seem to like you very much, Baron Ash."

CHAPTER 49

"Turley!" Prentice all but shouted, delighted by his friend's sudden appearance. He crossed the short distance between them and seized him in an enthusiastic embrace. The two men were not so typically effusive, but the pleasure he felt after the bitterness of recent dealings and the sheer amount of time since they had seen one another released more joy than he expected. "When did you come to town?"

"Just off the boat this morning," Turley replied, and as Prentice released him, he reached his good hand to rub at his crippled arm, wincing.

"It pains you?" Prentice asked, surprised.

"Coming winter weather sets it off somethin' fierce," Turley explained, waving at the sky and obviously biting the inside of his cheek against the discomfort in his arm. "That's why I'm dressed like a popinjay's popinjay. Soon as you tell a tailor you want velvet for its warmth, he thinks you need to be prettied up like a maid with a crown of wildflowers."

"Well, sorry for my roughness," Prentice apologized, remembering his own injured shoulder, and looking his friend up and down, seeing the source of Turley's other complaint. He was indeed wearing a doublet of deep green velvet and long sleeves, with slashes revealing a dark Reach blue underneath. His breeks were equally fine, doeskin dyed the color of mahogany, and his boots were likewise darkly stained and polished to high sheen, with silver buckles.

"Do we say sorry to each other now?" Turley asked, his smile coming back, but slowly, as if he had to force it. Then it faded a moment once more, and he rubbed at his arm again. "If only it didn't make me feel like half a man half the time. Half the man I used to be, at least."

Prentice smiled sympathetically at his friend.

"When we are young, we feel we will be hale and powerful all our lives," he said, remembering some of the things he and Whilte had just been discussing. "Growing to manhood means learning your strength is not unlimited, and as you spend it, so its level is slowly lowering. Eventually the well must run dry."

"Dry and crippled," Turley muttered.

"Says the man with the wife who is the envy of all other men. And you surely know *she* does not see you as crippled?" Prentice cocked an eyebrow, disdaining his friend's dalliance with self-pity. None of them were the young men they had once been, and truth was they were blessed beyond words to have come out of their convicthood with any strength left in the well at all, never mind the rewards they had spent their strength upon—loving wives, places in the world, titles and wealth. "Speaking of which, have you even seen Lady Dalflitch yet? Surely you have not neglected her to come here."

"Lord, no," Turley agreed. "I went to her a-first, of course. I miss her fiercer than my arm aches, don't you worry about that."

"She misses you the same, no doubt, though of course she burdens no one with complaint."

"My fine lady," Turley said lovingly, eyes glittering and a sincere smile on his face. "I was with her, but she has so much work to do with the local conclave. It seems they haven't come to recognize her superiorness with moneys yet like the Dweltford patricians have. She'll win them around or whip them to it. In the meantime, she released me to follow after my own desires. I thought I'd use our short time apart to call in with my wretched old friends who she doesn't approve of. And who can blame her? Look at the company you keep."

Turley cocked his head at the trees on the edge of Runners Field where the Young Hopefuls had disappeared, returning to the town proper.

"Your wife disapproves of me not one whit," Prentice said without hesitation. "And as for the quality of my friendships, she knew I was friends with you before she married. If I would lower myself that far, nothing else should shock her. The writing was on the wall, if she had cared to read it. She was too seduced by your rough ways and handsome smile."

"*She* was seduced?" Turley laughed at that and then noticed that Brother Whilte was standing quietly nearby. He bowed his head, and the chaplain tugged the forelock in return. "Greetings, Chaplain. You keeping my fellow here out of trouble?"

"Greetings, Sir Turley," Whilte replied. "Keeping the knight commander out of trouble is a fruitless quest, I think. It seems to seek him out. Thankfully he's quite accustomed to foes who wish him dead, no matter where they arise."

"Yea, well you never managed to kill him when you tried, for a start."

Prentice winced. It was exactly in keeping with Turley's character to shoot a jest right into the midst of a potentially painful spot like that, and while he was not offended himself, he wondered how Whilte would feel being reminded of the worst matter between them. As it happened, the chaplain showed no displeasure, though there was a shadow on his expression for a moment.

"I have thanked God many times since that day, Sir, I was not successful," Whilte said at last.

"Believe me, you ain't the only one," Turley responded earnestly. Then he turned back to Prentice. "You busy? Only the boatman I came down with turned me onto a house with what he says is the finest lager known to man, and I mean to test the claim. You'd be welcome to join us, Brother."

"My thanks, but I have my duty," Whilte answered.

"As do I," Prentice began but realized that an hour or two with his friend in a tavern was no great indulgence. The camp would not stop without him, at least for that long. "But I would benefit from news of Dweltford and the Reach. Come share your insights with me over a mug of this famous lager."

After giving the provost the tavern's name so that he could be quickly located, Prentice let Turley lead him until, a quarter of the candle later, the pair were ensconced at a small table in the back of a more reputable taphouse, with small pewter tankards of a foaming amber that looked and smelled like it could well be the best beer in Bridgetown. As the stout and pleasant barmaid left their table, Turley handed Prentice his stoup, and the knight commander was surprised that where once the act of bringing beer would have earned the woman one of his friend's famous charming smiles, now Turley hardly saw the woman. He was a man reformed, it seemed.

If anyone had the power to tame his wandering eye, it would surely have to be Dalfitch, Prentice thought, happy for his friend.

Turley lifted his mug. "To your newborns, to wet the babies' heads," he said in toast. "May their days be long, their loves deep, and their purses never empty."

"Amen," Prentice said, clinking his cup with his friend and they both took deep drafts. The lager was cool, clean, and slightly bitter—a fine brew, indeed. "So, tell me, when are you going to do your duty as a man and give *your* wife a child?"

A shadow passed over Turley's face, and he took a long swig of his beer.

"A sore point?" Prentice asked, wondering why it would be but not surprised. As two folk from wildly different origins, not to mention important duties that took them away from each other, Sir Turley and Lady Dalflitch had a complex relationship that he only inquired after at times like this, when there was space to unravel a tale.

"When she was a young girl and playin' the hussy," Turley began, his usual jovial demeanor replaced with soberness. He paused, took a deep breath, and then dove all the way in. "When she was like that, a babe was the last thing she wanted. It's hard to seduce your next noble when your belly's swollen with the last one's bastard."

Prentice nodded over his cup. He could well imagine. Curiously, as his friend relayed the story, there seemed no sign of jealousy, little enough of anger—just a kind of bittersweet resignation.

"What she tells is that she couldn't name the number of times she swallowed some vile apothecary's concoction to keep her womb empty," Turley continued. "She said it was almost akin to her breakfast drink—like the cup she took with her porridge, year on year. Then she said she stopped taking it, 'cause she felt something different in herself, something changed. All the time she was with Daven Marcus, she wasn't using it. Course getting *his* bastard was a different matter too—that she did want. But nothing. Could be he was the one without the life in his loins. Mongrel that he is, it wouldn't surprise me. But Dalflitch says she thinks she's done too much… too much sin, too much alchemy brew, whatever it was. She don't think she can have babes no more, no matter what we do."

"That is a sorrowful thing," Prentice said, his heart clenching a little at the thought that his friend would never know the joy he had discovered as a new father.

"We do try, don't you doubt," Turley said, suddenly lifting his head and forcing another smile. He downed the rest of his mug. "And if it don't work out, I figure I could do like you did with Solomon. There's more than one war orphan floating about these days. I could bring one in and sort him out."

"A noble thought," Prentice said, as Turley stood to order another beer. He offered Prentice another shout as well, but the knight commander waved him off, with his own cup still half full.

"Suit yourself," Turley said and sauntered toward the bar where the barmaid's husband, a pox-scarred man with only a finger and thumb on one hand, drew another pot from a tapped keg on the properly carved bar. Guilders clinked on the wooden surface, but the sound was swallowed by a sudden roar of voices from around a corner out of Prentice's sight. They were sounds of disappointment but not anger, and, curious, Prentice stood with his mug and made his way around to where a corner of the floor was encircled by a crouching crowd made up of merchants, two senior rivermen in the typical sleeveless vests, but well-made and maintained, and Prentice noticed, two men in White Lions' gambesons. A pair of ivory dice rattled over the floor to bounce against the wall of the corner and then fall still. Men shouted again and coin changed hands, winners cheering themselves while losers scowled and shook their heads. The dice were gathered, and in the interval until the next set of throws, one of the White Lions reached for his tankard on the floor next to him. As he took his drink, he looked up and saw Prentice watching from the back of the crowd. As if suddenly pulled taut by a string, he shot upward, dropping his tankard and spilling beer to the curses of his fellow gamblers. His fist slapped to his chest.

"Knight Commander?!" he said, voice loud like a drill order. His fellow Lion looked at him as if he had suddenly gone mad, then he, too, noticed Prentice's presence, and he also shot upward and saluted. The two men held their position while around them merchants and rivermen stared, bewildered.

"Are your tents pitched farther from the standard than all the others?" Prentice asked them quietly. It was a false question really, since all Lions knew they were never to billet amongst a populace by order of her grace. She was resolved that her militia never exploit the common folk and had been from the beginning. Now that there were known enemies stealthily preying on her grace's household, Prentice had issued a command that not even the lowest ranked Lions were to travel alone in the town, though this pair were obviously not in violation of that order. One of the duo, a line first by his uniform, answered Prentice's question's true inquiry.

"We just finished three days' straight sentry and haulin' duties, My Lord," he explained, swiftly but with confidence. "Sergeant Sedgemark said we was worthy of a reward for our hard work and give us a day to ourselves, a personal holy day, as it were, long as we stuck together. We got freedom from the provosts and come here for a drink and a throw of ivories. Spend some of our new silver on some innocent pleasures, like."

"I see," Prentice said, and he realized he had no way to know that these men were telling the truth until he returned to camp and asked around the provosts.

We should develop some kind of sign of passage, he thought, *so that men can be given their leave legitimately and shirkers or deserters can be sniffed out, not to mention frauds or skin thieves. Heaven help any fool who tries to get his hands on some Lions' uniforms to play the same trick as the "nuns" in the strongroom. Getting the provosts to sweep the town's inns and taverns regularly will be a wise move as well.*

He looked the two men over and from their behavior did not think they were malingerers, but legitimate. He hoped so. The longer the Lions went on, the more their ranks were comprised of standing men-at-arms and fewer convicts one step from the noose. He could not keep treating them like rogues 'foot forever.

"Alright, then carry on," Prentice told them. "Just make sure you are back in camp soon enough to sleep it off before you return to your duty."

He turned away to see that Turley had come to join him, watching proceedings. Prentice was about to usher them both back to their table when he had a thought.

"Are you up?" he asked the two men. The line first blinked in surprise, but his militiaman comrade smiled, gap-toothed.

"Ten guilders, My Lord," he said happily. "Seems God knows a White Lion's life is short and hard. He's blessin' us for our service."

Some of the men still crouched about muttered at that statement.

"I doubt the sacrists would think too much of that theology, militiaman," Prentice said with a smile. "But you are right about the hardships the Lions endure. Enjoy your winning until the dice turn on you. But if they do not, remember to share a taste of your joy with the barkeep and his wife before you come back to camp. And may God continue to bless you."

Prentice saluted them and the two men smirked and nodded, then crouched back down to their dicing.

"You didn't want to join them?" Turley asked as they returned to their table.

"Would you want to drink and gamble in the presence of your lord and master?" Prentice asked.

"I don't see as it would be a problem."

"Oh truly? As steward you would have been glad to have the archduchess with you in the kitchens, sat at one of the tables, watching every move as you flirted with the scullers?"

"I don't flirt with servant girls," Turley protested, like a sacrist accused of sinning.

"Before you were married," Prentice clarified.

"Oh, well no, that wouldn't 'ave felt like much pleasure," he acknowledged, sitting back on his chair.

"And so it is for those men," Prentice said. Turley nodded thoughtfully, apparently mulling over his friend's words.

"I still forget how wise you are about some things," he said at last.

"No surprise," Prentice told him, "since you forget the wisdom as well."

"Well, never had much use for it, myself," Turley said, straight-faced, and Prentice chuckled. They settled to their drinks and Prentice soon ordered a second stoup. They talked of Dweltford and the Reach, the sightings of fey that were becoming gradually more frequent, and the progress of the workshops in Fallenhill. Prentice told Turley of Righteous's training session with the baroness and that made the burly man lean his head back and laugh, mop hair flicking about like the shaggy fur of a friendly mongrel dog. He gave an abbreviated account of the march into the west, focusing as he had always planned, on his adventure climbing the ancient obelisk and the vision of the dragonfly lake that resulted.

"So, blood and that mask took you all the way to the end of the Murr by magicks?" Turley asked, astonished, but not denying the truth of his old mate's tale.

"Only my mind, my thoughts and perceptions, as it were," Prentice explained. "My body remained behind, sinking into that pool and nearly drowning."

Turley took a thoughtful swig of his lager.

"Did I call you wise?" he asked, almost rhetorically. "I meant dumb as a post."

Prentice laughed. The whole session of drink and company was refreshing to him, like the spring sunshine after a long winter, and he was reluctant to leave. Nevertheless, after his second lager, he stood from the table.

"My Dalflitch said she won't have the time for me until nearer to sundown," Turley said, explaining why he would not be going with his friend. "I figure on having one or two more of these and maybe looking to insert m'self in that dice game. See if I can't add to the silvers in my purse."

"Just as long you know where to stop, as well," Prentice told him. "If you come back to your lady wife deep in your cups, I am certain she will not appreciate it and will let my lady wife know. Then *I* will be in trouble for not keeping *you* out of trouble."

"I know how to hold my drink," Turley protested.

"Since when?"

Turley clutched his good hand to his breast, as if offended, then waved Prentice away.

"Get back to your camp, old man," he said. "Leave us common folk to our pleasures."

"You are a knight now, remember?" Prentice told him, enjoying their banter.

Turley cocked his head as if surprised to just remember his own social status. "So I am. Who would have thought?"

With that, they parted happily, and Prentice returned to camp, planning in his mind what preparations might be necessary for the celebration of the baroness's accession on the following afternoon.

Archduchess', he corrected himself in his thoughts. It was odd that he had such trouble remembering. Accepting his own liege's increase in status had felt almost instantaneous. He wondered if it boded something. Only once he had passed the picquet and provosts did he realize that he had violated his own order for no Lions to be abroad in the town alone. If anyone else noticed, nothing was said.

CHAPTER 50

The clouds of the overcast sky were the lighter grey of autumn rather than the heavy rain-bearing storm clouds of winter. Even so, the day was so much less bright than it might have been and as Archduchess Amelia looked around the crowded square in front of the Bridgetown Cathedral, she could not help but feel a moment of sadness for the archduchess-elect. There was no way to guarantee the weather of any day, but the grey pall seemed so much like the coolness that had come into their alliance and that touched Amelia with regret. For all that she felt Lady Penelope foolish, she only wished the best for the young noblewoman this day.

"At least the bunting is bright," she said absently as she looked at the long streams of orange and saffron-colored cloth strung from posts and buildings around the square. She was impressed by the sheer volume of it. "No expense was spared, it seems."

"The Conclave provided the decorations," Dalflitch observed. "They begged permission to shoulder the cost, so I have heard. Even for the flowers."

All around them in the crowd, women wore marigold blooms, yellow and burnt orange-colored varieties, so that while the sun might have been hidden, there was a sunlight color to the festivities at least, not to mention being the Bridgetown chivalric colors. Militiamen standing guard along the path that the baroness would walk in procession to the cathedral had strings of the flowers twined around their ashwood poles. True weapons were rare in the square, since only those with a peerage and a few other exceptions had the right to carry them to a festival day as this.

"Must've set them merchants back some," Righteous added. "Wonder how the tight fists felt about that?"

Amelia cocked an eyebrow at her, and Righteous tilted her head, clearly not understanding her mistress's displeasure.

"You know that my father was a merchant and a selectman of his conclave? And let us not forget Lady Spindle's loyal, good husband" she chided, and Righteous immediately ducked her head apologetically.

"Sorry, Your Grace."

Amelia let the matter rest with a benign smile.

"Word is that the cloths are all to be sold afterward," Lady Spindle offered. "In bolts of a size for women's clothes. Goodwives and maids will be wearing their prized 'accession day' dresses for years to 'memorate the fact that they were there this first day of its kind when Bridgetown got its first archduchess. Caius has already laid down a reserved order for us, Your Grace. You, Lady Dalflitch, and me and Righteous will all have our own marigold dresses. Each will be its own, too, I promise. I see a lioness proud over flames of orange and gold for yourself. I think Lady Dalflitch will be most glorious with a dress of that deep green that works so well with her mien but with sleeves of the Bridgetown colors, like a bird with wings of fire."

"My mien?" Dalflitch asked with a quizzical expression.

"Is that not the right word, My Lady?"

"Oh no, Lady Spindle. It is precisely acceptable, and the dress you propose sounds perfect."

"Well, the conclavers won't end up out of purse after all, I guess," Righteous summed up, and much as Amelia disliked the contempt implied in her words, she could not deny the truth of the observation. The Conclave would have offered to fund the decorating with at least one eye on the profit of selling the bunting afterward—a tidy profit without any doubt.

The conversation lapsed as around Amelia's entourage the crowd began to press a little closer, as more and more spectators crowded into the square for the ceremony soon to begin. Archduchess Amelia had been informed of her role in the coming ritual only that morning—a small part that amounted to little more than standing to one side, witnessing Baroness Penelope's rise to the new, higher title, and formally acknowledging her as an ally and fellow senior peer. For that role, no one had thought it necessary to attach Amelia and her close attendants to the formal procession, likely another small snub expressing the displeasure of Righteous's "lesson" at the castle. They were told the militia would keep the procession way clear for the Reach delegation to join at the very end after the Bridgetown worthies passed, then they would corral the crowd, falling back and ultimately allowing as many visitors as could crowd in behind to fill the nave and witness the ceremony. Amelia was also not invited to bring an escort of White Lions to the square or the church, but she felt safe enough accompanied by the Lace Fangs, along with two chosen neophytes, Beth and Mathilda. Not to mention Prentice, Farringdon, and Turley, all present and armed by right as nobles, as well as Brother Whilte, who for all his humble appearance was a veteran man-at-arms and still had his prophet's rod—the staff made from a broken spear. Together these members of the archduchess's court formed an effective cadre of arms that kept the crowds at a polite distance around the formally dressed ladies of her grace's chamber. With them also was Caius Welburne, standing as proudly as his ill health and recent assault allowed. The blow to his scalp taken when the "bandit nuns" had attacked him had left a pronounced bruise on his forehead and around the side of his left eye. It was a dark purple color, yellowing at the edges. Next to the younger and healthier men around him, he seemed more akin to a scarecrow under a bearskin cloak, the heavy fur clutched tight against the cooling weather.

"It will be a pity if it rains," Amelia said, imagining the processional party having to rush to get into the cathedral ahead of a cloudburst or else arrive drenched and bedraggled. There was a sudden hush rippling over the crowd, and Amelia turned to the entry to the square, a short road overshadowed by buildings, coming from the main thoroughfare that ran like a crooked spine through the center of the town. She expected to see that the procession had arrived, but there was no one there.

"That's the fella they got to replace you is it, Chaplain?" Turley asked, and Amelia looked in the opposite direction to the cathedral steps where a humble-looking sacrist with a bright red stole over a plain, homespun cassock had come out of the open doors and was now standing on the top step, sternly surveying the crowd with his hands in his sleeves. He looked to Amelia like a poor village clergyman given a single piece of a rich patriarch's vestments, as if to tidy him up for the cathedral. She wondered where Baroness Penelope's people had found the man. Perhaps they had indeed had to dredge up a rural sacrist, if Baronet Forsle's prediction at the feast had proved true. Maybe there was no sacrist from the town's clergy prepared to take the duty.

And so one of God's humblest servants is snubbed by another, she thought, sparing a disappointed moment's glance for Brother Whilte.

The crowd's excitement took on an air of anticipation and heads craned from the cathedral steps to the square's main entry and back. A collectively held breath seemed to freeze the day in place for a moment. Then a trumpet was sounded, clarion clear, echoing over the hush. The twins appeared at the end of the diligently maintained aisle through the crowd's middle. Folk pressed forward almost without thinking, and all up and down the path, guardsmen's poles rapped on the stones before they fell like barriers to hold folk back. In truth, if the crowd had been determined, even the hundred or so militiamen could have done little to restrain them, but the folk of Bridgetown had come to cheer and celebrate with their new young liege, not to riot.

"Make way! Make way!" the twins bellowed with voices that seemed too loud for their chests. "Hark and bow for the coming of

Her Grace to be, Archduchess-elect Penelope, daughter of John, scion and rightful heir to the seat of Bridgetown."

The crowd erupted in cheering, arms waving, and marigold blooms were thrown into the air to fall upon the processional path. The trumpeter blew again, seeming much less loud now, and he led the way, followed by the twins, each bearing orange and gold pennants from long rods. Behind them followed the archduchess-elect, leading her procession of worthies—Baronets Forsle and Christmark, along with Forsle's lady wife and the aged-looking Sir Nencet, whose expression made it seem as if had no idea why there was a crowd or what they were cheering about. In his own way, he seemed to Amelia even more frail than Master Welburne. Nevertheless, he was dressed in fine, polished mail, not quite straight-backed under the weight, with a gorget sitting heavily around his neck and a polished leather baldric holding his longsword in a jeweled scabbard. Following these ranking folk came two lines of Young Hopefuls, each wearing similar harness to Nencet, all polished so that it was bright despite the lesser daylight, and each wearing their sideswords from their own baldrics.

Soon to be longswords, no doubt, Amelia thought. Prentice had told her of the young man Cassian's threat, and she found her eyes strayed to him automatically as the train of worthies drew nearer. He and his brother were recognizable as the ones at the head of each column of Young Hopefuls, and she wondered if the Hopefuls were in two columns because neither had been willing to yield the preeminent position to his brother. Of course, they also formed a more imposing pair than they would have as two individuals, and she suspected they knew it. She imagined they would exert their influence over the martial culture of the new archduchy for years to come. In spite of the young man's threat, Prentice had reassured her there was little to fear from Cassian since, even knighted, there would be enough rank between them for Prentice to disdain any challenge.

Unless she raises him straight to baron, as I did for you, Amelia thought warily, watching the young man, who, even in the light of this occasion, looked more hate-filled than proud. The new archduchess of Bridgetown would have to skip over her own uncle and all the remaining senior nobility of her domain to create a barony for Cassian, but that was precisely the kind of rash action she seemed to favor. *Lord let her not become a female Daven Marcus.*

Amelia shook her head at that last thought. It was unjust. Although Penelope was youthful and impetuous, perhaps even a little childish, there was none of the vile malice in her that characterized the Usurper. To compare them was simply not right. Penelope drew near, wearing her typical skirt of house colors, with her polished breastplate above and finely wrought steel gauntlets on her hand. The sleeves of her doublet, visible from shoulder to wrist, were slashed, and underneath showed gorgeous cloth of gold that seemed to glow. She had a salet tucked under her arm, like a knight on the field, and it made Amelia shake her head again, despite herself. That was such an exaggerated gesture and a pointless weight to carry through a ritual all day. Perhaps she would hand it off to someone once in the cathedral. Doubtless, one of the Young Hopefuls could be persuaded to act as a squire for her, knowing there were knighthoods coming by the end. Amelia met Penelope's eyes as the procession drew level with her place in the crowd, and the Reach archduchess inclined her head politely, while all her ladies curtseyed more formally. If Penelope noticed, she made a clear point of not showing it and in a moment had moved on.

"The girl plays politics like a cat plays dice," Dalflitch said quietly as she rose.

Amelia cocked an eyebrow at her. When her lady noticed, she explained.

"It can't roll the dice properly, and if it even realizes it's playing a game, it doesn't know the rules well enough to tell if it is winning or losing," Dalflitch explained.

"True as true can be," Lady Spindle concurred solemnly, and the whole moment filled Amelia with a nearly irresistible desire to laugh, to throw off the ill taste of her soured friendship with the young noblewoman. By the time she felt fully in control of herself, the procession had mostly passed, and she had to be ready to follow behind.

"Penelope of Bridgetown," someone shouted, loudly but shrill, as of a male voice not strong enough for the volume it was seeking. It echoed from the cathedral end of the square, and all heads turned to see. The procession stopped. The ritual was going to begin outside the church, it seemed, though Amelia noticed the expressions on the Young Hopefuls toward the end of their columns, the ones she could see. They were so obviously surprised by this that if it was part of the planned ceremony, they could not have been briefed for it.

"Halt, foolish Penelope, for the church door is barred to you, daughter of perdition," the sacrist went on, and shocked whispers rushed through the crowd like a wind over long winter grasses. Everyone spoke in the most hushed of tones, no doubt thinking not to miss any further words of the challenging cleric, but a thousand whispering voices were almost enough to drown out his wild speech all the same. Through the craning heads, Amelia caught a glimpse of the man with his right arm raised high, a preacher delivering a sermon of judgement and rebuke.

"Your father rebelled against the rightful king, Daven Marcus of the Denay throne. Since childhood you have been a sumptuary seditionary, indulged by your father the rebel. Now you become a sister to heresy and an apprentice to witchcraft, inviting all the worst sins of the west into your house. Do you think to exalt yourself to equal depravity in the very house of God? It will not be."

"Bollocks to that," Amelia heard Sir Turley mutter grimly, doubtless indignant at hearing of the "worst sins of the west."

"The man's just signed his own death warrant," Farringdon said, almost breathless with the audacity of it. Beside him, Whilte nodded.

"Though likely spoken out of earnest belief," the chaplain said. "He does not look like a wolf feigning shepherdry to prey upon the flock. I wonder who has put him up to this."

"He'll be dead all the same," Turley concluded, and when Master Welburne moved closer to ask what was happening, the knight castellan leaned down to explain to the pale and wan merchant. Amelia felt a stab of pity for Caius. He had never seemed a healthy man, but his recent decline felt too sudden and too steep, nonetheless.

Of all the men about her, only Prentice said nothing, and when she looked to him, Amelia realized that he was silently directing the members of her entourage to respond to the tense situation with clear responsibilities, tapping shoulders and pointing. Already Spindle and Righteous had taken up posts at either side of their liege, and in short order Amelia found herself and Lady Dalflitch in the center of a small armed cordon, with the Lace Fangs and neophytes on either side, as well as front and back, and four armed men at four offset points on the outside of that formation, hands on the hilts of their weapons and looking in all directions at once. Trying to understand everything that was going on for herself, Amelia noticed that many of the Young Hopefuls had also put their hands to their weapons, though they seemed to have a different purpose to the Reachermen. They all had angry eyes for the sacrist on the cathedral steps.

The man's sermon continued, and Amelia found herself being referred to less obliquely and more directly. She was the temptress, heretic sorceress again, being blamed for everything short of the crucifixion itself. To hear him speak, it sounded as if the sins of Jezebel had come alive from scripture and embodied themselves in her person. It would be laughable but for the life it was about to cost.

"You have no right!" Penelope shouted, and even her feminine voice sounded deeper than the preacher's cracking speech.

"I am Mother Church's will manifest," the sacrist retorted, not missing a beat. "Oppose my words at the peril of your soul."

"To hell with this!" Cassian said loudly enough for Amelia to hear and drew his sword with a flourish so wide that the crowd near to him shied back reflexively. He pushed past the knights and baronets ahead of him and even bumped into Penelope herself as he strode forward in a fury, along the aisle in the crowd. The sacrist saw him coming and stopped shouting, lowering his arm and clasping his hands together serenely once more. Amelia had a sudden, shocking insight.

"Good God, the Inquisition!" she said in horror, and Prentice turned to look at her. When their eyes met, she could see that he understood her meaning.

"A sacrist slain on Church steps," he agreed tersely and then turned away, not to watch Cassian or the preacher, but the crowd. Wild violence was all but inevitable now. To oppose the Church's judgements or condemnation was one thing. To slaughter one of the clergy on the steps of a major cathedral was the kind of act that could curse an entire noble line. Kings had been toppled by such events in the past. Even in this time of a kingslayer king, it was likely that an action such as this would have damaging reverberations over Penelope's rule for however long it lasted. No Grand Kingdom noble would ever accept her as an archduchess, that was certain. And Amelia was equally certain that this sacrist had been positioned to make this stand for exactly this purpose.

To die for their conspiracies? she wondered in horror and immediately chastised herself inwardly for her naivete. *Is it the first time? Of course they have suicidally devout sacrists in their employ. False the Inquisition may be, but their false faith has no lack of zealots. And as Whilte said, this one may simply be an earnest fool, serving evil while thinking to do good.*

"Do you come to repent, boy?" the sacrist screamed suddenly at Cassian as the young man closed the gap. "Or do you think mere steel can halt the judgement that comes from heaven? No sword forged by man could wound a servant of God without heaven's approval, and my blood is no bar to the will of heaven."

The man was goading Cassian, all but daring him to attack.

"Strike if you will, servant of slatterns, but look now and see, God will unleash judgement upon you and all of this den of iniquity. Hell will open up and the demons will be sent to drag you down."

God sends angels to work his judgement, fool, Amelia thought, suddenly furious. *I have seen them and the true majesty of their power. Hell is a prison, and if devils are ever unchained from its confines, it is never at the will of God.*

A sudden desire to see Cassian strike gripped Amelia as she felt anger at this perversion, but it was broken almost immediately when she remembered the power the pronunciation magicks of the Inquisition had had over her during the summer. Could this man's words conceal such supernatural control, forcing even Cassian and the crowd to take their part in this morality play writ large? An ominous growl sounded from somewhere across the square, followed by mutters of unease.

"We must get the archduchess to safety!" Prentice commanded and as one her entourage began to crowd into the aisle, pushing past the distracted poles of two bewildered militiaman and aiming straight back toward the square's main entrance, away from the cathedral and its religious drama. Confusion already reigned in the crowd, and the low growl they had heard suddenly erupted into a savage bellow, as towering over the heads of the mass, a man looked to be standing up but as if he were a giant, double the height of any man. It made Amelia wonder if the fellow had been crouching the whole time, to have been unseen so long in the crowd. Even as she watched, though, the figure's proportions began to change, and his face contorted in agonized fury. Fangs more suited to a beast sprouted in his mouth, tearing the flesh of his lips into bloody ruin, and then his nose pushed forth, to become more like an animal's snout. Drool sprayed about as flailing arms seemed to grow more muscles even while Amelia watched. Remembering Prentice's account of a cultist becoming a mantis under the power of an enchanted mask, she suddenly realized what she was seeing—a *brakkis effar* transforming from human to beast man right before her eyes. But a beast man unlike any they had met before.

A bear man.

CHAPTER 51

P rentice had not expected the *brakkis effar*, or even anything similar in fact, when the sacrist had started his sermonizing rant. With only one whispered sentence between them, he and Righteous had immediately gone on the lookout for hidden assassins in the crowd, assuming the judgmental preacher to be a diversion. When the growl sounded amongst the throng to his right, his eyes were searching in the other direction. As he turned to seek the source, his gaze ranged over the steps of the cathedral just in time to see Cassian make his thrust while the Inquisition's planted martyr opened his arms to the blade point, as if welcoming a long lost relative. The sacrist collapsed, and Cassian's blade wrenched free with a spray of blood. The main of the crowd, transfixed by the drama, groaned in horror, and that sound all but drowned out the first snarling growl of the transforming beast man. Prentice located the growing giant just as his face was developing its snout and fangs, sprouting thick growths of stiff, dark hair, like tufts of water grasses at the riverside. Looking into the tormented victim's eyes just before they became fully animalistic, Prentice was dumbfounded to recognize the man now become the beast.

"Inxyphos?" he breathed, scarcely able to trust the evidence of his own sight.

"Good Lord, what have they done to him?" Whilte muttered beside the knight commander, and Prentice could have no doubt. The Inquisition knight had been transformed into a *brakkis effar*. It seemed the merciless preachers of mercy had no mercy even for their own. With sudden certainty, Prentice knew that they were in even greater danger than anyone imagined, perhaps the greatest they had known since the night of the Red Sky.

"Her grace must be seen to safety now, no delay," he said, risking turning to the archducal party only for a moment. "Turley, you go with the Lace Fangs, Master Welburne, and her grace's ladies. Neophytes, your training faces its fullest test today. Do my wife proud."

"Where are you going?" Knight Captain Farringdon asked, recognizing from Prentice's words that the knight commander would not be accompanying the archduchess.

"Her grace has undertaken to protect Bridgetown," Prentice explained. "I am going to stay and bring that monster down if I can." Given its stature, easily as tall as any *brakkis effar* he had faced, Prentice assumed he would be facing a bull man or another horned man—something mighty enough that it could make a ruin of this crowd who still had no idea how much danger they were in.

"Then I will stay with you," Farringdon said at once, but Prentice shook his head vehemently.

"The Lions cannot risk both leaders to a fight like this," he told his second-in-command. "If I fall, you must be in place to take up my role. Moreover, you must go now and fetch your lancers into the town. This crowd is about to become a panicked mob, and we all know what that can do in tight confines like the bridges. They will need you to herd them, like stampeding cattle, else they will be their own worst enemies. You know the Bridgetowner militia will never reclaim order once they lose it. Forget your dignity, My Lord. Run like a boy in a foot race. Good folks' lives depend upon you!"

Farringdon did not hesitate, even to salute, but turned on his heel and sparing only a passing glance for his beloved wife, rushed down the aisle in the crowd that was already starting to collapse into the morass of a confused mob.

"I am with you," Whilte said to Prentice.

"I was about to ask. Are you ready?"

"As ready as our first day at Ashfield," the chaplain replied resolutely, "when we swore our lives to end malevolences like this."

"Then we all have our purposes. Go to!" Prentice instructed the whole group and was about to lead off when Turley caught him by the shoulder. He turned to see his friend's hand drop to the handle of his flanged mace, hanging from the knight castellan's belt.

"Don't send me away. Let me fight with you, please," Turley protested. In all the time they had known each other Prentice could count on one hand the number of instances he had heard his friend plead for anything. Even with his withered arm, the castellan was still a burly man and the taller of the pair, but looking into his friend's pained expression, Prentice felt he overshadowed Turley for the first time ever. For a fraction of a moment his eyes dropped to his friend's disabled limb, and he had to scowl just to keep an expression of pity off his face.

"There is a wild, terrified mob brewing between the arch-duchess and the safe harbor of the Paramour's Chamber. You are the only one I have with the strength to part that raging sea and lead her to safety. I trust no one but you and Righteous to pilot the ship for me. I would gladly have you with me, to our dying days, but we all have duties our liege needs us to fulfil."

Turley nodded as he absorbed Prentice's words, then he too turned to face the square's exit, the aisle now dissolved into a confused crowd—many frightened but most still bewildered enough to not think to flee just yet. Any moment now.

"I am the prow, ladies, you are the boat," Turley told the archducal party. "Stay close and follow me. If the boat breaks away from the prow, then they all sink to the bottom."

With that, he led off, almost immediately confronted by a militiaman of Bridgetown, his ash pole loose in his hand as if he did not remember what it was for. Without instructions, many of the militiamen who had been maintaining order for the crowd now stood as members of the burgeoning mob, as aimless as the common folk. Turley shoved the man roughly aside just as a bellowing roar, as thunderous as the trumpeter's blast, echoed from not too far away in the crowd and the horror of the sacrist's murder was at last overwhelmed by the greater horror of the *brakkis effar's* appearance.

"He's a bear!" Whilte declared as he followed behind Prentice, pressing through the crowd that was now trying to scatter and pushing against the others behind them. The knight commander unhooked his scabbarded blade from his belt and used it as a baton to shove the crowd clear. He was none too gentle, but a clout on the shoulder was nothing compared to what the claws or bite of the transformed Inxyphos would do. Even as he barged through, Prentice saw the now hairy limbs, more forelegs than arms, swinging about, and the former Church knight truly did resemble an enraged bear.

Cunning mongrels, he thought, shoving and thumping his way toward the monster. He had no idea how they had done it, but he was sure the Inquisition had somehow taken the mysteries of the Redlander Cult that Inxyphos had learned in the west and used it to make a beast man of their own, and they'd made him a bear deliberately to mock Bridgetown's ambitious first lady.

Almost as if the crowd had melted away, Prentice suddenly found himself in the open, a space forming around the raging beast, as much left by the slain as by the escaped, and many folk lay bloodied and broken on the flagstones, the moans of those not yet dead mingling with the bear man's growls. As Prentice watched, the *brakkis effar* lifted a screaming man two-handed above its head, then lowered him to bite into his side, tearing away a hideous chunk of flesh. The creature pulled its arms apart, as if intending to rip the man's body in twain. It was the poor wretch's limbs that failed first, however, and the beast man's grip slipped such that while he did not wrench the victim apart, claws shredded so much of his flesh that he was dead before he hit the ground. Watching, Prentice felt all the fear and confusion, along with what little warmth there was in the day, wash away. The blood in his veins was cold with fury, and there was almost nothing in his sight save this thing that he must slay.

"Inxyphos!" Prentice shouted, his parade-ground voice echoing off the houses and other buildings around the square, even over the chaos. The beast turned to look at him, and there was that spark of mortal intellect inside the bestial gaze that Prentice had first seen long ago in the nameless village of the Reach—the look of a mind behind the madness. It recognized him. Even as a beast, Inxyphos remembered the one who had derailed so many of his plans.

Good, Prentice thought. *Now let us end this.*

Bear Inxyphos bellowed again, and Prentice readied for a charge, planning his own rush to the assault. He was caught by surprise, however, as the creature seemed almost to sneer at him with its fanged mouth and then turned to a woman who was crouched, weeping, not far from where it stood. She seemed to be crying over one of the slain, and part of Prentice's mind wondered if she had just lost a husband or child. She would hardly be the only one. He thought to call out a warning, but his focus was on slaying the beast, not on saving the innocent. It took him longer to switch intents, and so he said nothing as, with almost casual disdain, Inxyphos the bear reached out one clawed hand, now with talons longer than any natural creature of its kind would have, and seized the mourning woman by her head. Lifted bodily into the air, her crying became a wail of pain that was suddenly cut short as a simple flick of the creature's mightily thewed grip snapped her neck. Then, rather than attack Prentice, it threw the body at him before charging at some other folk who were cringing against a wall on the fringe of the square.

"No!" Whilte cried out as he and Prentice were forced to dodge aside, the brother's disgust unmistakable at the lazy evil of such an act, as if a mortal woman was no more than an ant to crush.

"Send folk to the cathedral. Get the doors open and get them on holy ground," Prentice told him, realizing that while much of the crowd was now clearing the square, those nearer to the cathedral end, with no minor roads or alleys to escape by, were virtually trapped. To flee, they had to come into the open space and let the rampaging monster see them and hunt them. Like panicked sheep, the crowd were flocked together, not safe, but safer than alone—and also easy pickings. At least they would have sanctuary if they could be urged into the church.

"They just slew a sacrist on the steps," Whilte answered tersely, making no motion to leave Prentice's side, and the knight commander shook his head in disgust and grudging respect for the infernal cunning of the Inquisition's plan. The cathedral was profaned by murder—murder of a sacrist, no less. It would not be holy again until it was reconsecrated, assuming such a thing was even possible, and Prentice had no clue on that score.

For another day, he told himself with the icy resolution that was born of the frozen depths of his soul, the unyielding parts of him that had been fed on a diet of suffering and purpose, at his father's insistence, from the earliest days of his life. *For now, we do this the hard way.*

Chapter 52

"Inxyphos, you coward," he shouted at the beast, which was done harrying at stragglers on one side of the square, leaving their bodies behind it, and was now sauntering on four legs toward the main crowd pressed back to the cathedral steps. It turned its head to him and then looked back at the crowd. Something there had its attention, Prentice could tell.

"For God's sake, either help us or get your liege to safety!" Whilte shouted, and Prentice risked a swift glance back to see that Baroness Penelope was standing at the edge of the crowd, flanked by her town's remaining nobility and the Young Hopefuls. While the would-be knights all had their blades drawn, neither lost squires nor full nobility were doing anything other than watch. Even the baroness was standing, frozen in horror. It was not surprising. Only the knights and noblemen present would have had any experience of the true chaos of massed battle, which this was closer to than any dueling school's lessons, and even they would have known nothing like this. In the short moment of his glance, Prentice saw the elderly knight Nencet collapse to one knee and suspected the man's heart had just failed him. Whilte shouted his instruction again, but still none of Bridgetown's worthies moved or even seemed to notice his call.

Inxyphos did.

If a bear could be said to smirk, the *brakkis effar* did so, and its saunter became a focused stalking. It had sighted its best prey. Prentice shook his head slowly, eyes narrowed to slits as he saw what was about to happen. For one long moment, it felt as if he, the beast man, and the Baroness of Bridgetown were all connected by taut cables, pulling tighter and tighter, like the strings of a lute or harp. Then the tension snapped, and Inxyphos the bear was charging straight for Bridgetown's liege. At the same moment, Prentice felt the release of the breaking string, and then he was throwing himself forward, feet hammering the stones, leaping over the fallen, desperate to cut across the charge and intercept the monster. Penelope and her attendants all tried to press back, to retreat, but the crowd behind them was too tightly packed already. There was no space to make for them to push through. To their credit, Forsle and Christmark stepped into the creature's path, their liege behind them, longswords drawn as they set to receive the charge. Not one of the Young Hopefuls joined them.

Inxyphos beat Prentice to the crowd, and with its shoulders hunched, the bear tossed its head to the right as it barreled into the two guarding noblemen so that its mass drove into Christmark while it bit at Forsle. Christmark crashed into one of the Young Hopefuls, and the two armored bodies crumpled together in a metallic cacophony. The bite managed to punch through the mail on the baronet's hip and he screamed in agony but retained his wits and strength enough to slam his longsword down on the creature's back, hacking fur and flesh away in a weakening strike. Then Prentice reached the *brakkis effar*, coming up from behind. He leaned all his weight and momentum into a strike that swept horizontally at its back leg, more like the swing of a stick at a ball in a yeoman's game on a village green than any kind of legitimate sword technique. The blade bit deep, and with a spray of blood darker than a natural creature's, Inxyphos the bear bellowed with rage. A swipe of a forepaw struck at Prentice, and with his blade slowed by being drawn cut from the wound he'd given the bear, he took the hit square upon his chest. It knocked him from his feet and ripped the leather of his brigandine so that the overlapping, finger-sized plates underneath were torn apart as well. Bits of steel clinked as they fell to the flagstones while Prentice rolled with the force as best he could. The blow drove the breath from his chest, and he came to his feet sucking air. His ribcage felt like he had been smashed with a sledgehammer, but there was none of the sharpness he would expect from a broken bone.

Thank God for small mercies, he thought, keeping his eyes on the monster. For its part, the bear had backed away and at last some of the Young Hopefuls had thought to join the baronets in protecting their liege, although notable in his absence was Cassian, and Prentice's swift glimpse did not pick Cyprian amongst them either. A hedge of uncertain swords now stood between the *brakkis effar* and its highest prize. Also, it seemed to have learned, or relearned, caution when it came to the knight commander of the White Lions. Gingerly, the creature tested its back leg. Prentice had managed a similar cut on the mighty stag ridden by the champion of the Verdant Fey in a battle in the west, and that had hamstrung the majestic beast. Inxyphos's sorcerous bestiality was of sterner stuff, it seemed, as he managed, slowly, to put his weight on the two legs and rise up rampant once again. Prentice watched and barely registered as he heard Whilte hobble up from somewhere behind him. Perhaps in any other context, the lamed chaplain could keep up with the rest of the militia, but in the square scattered with the slain and trampled, his disability had slowed his arrival, short though the intervening distance had been. As it turned out, though, he was not late. As might be said in a calmer moment, the timing of God is always perfect. Just as the rampant *brakkis effar* opened its wretched snout to roar again, Whilte—the Moses of the White Lions—lifted his prophet's rod, and light from its shattered blade blazed like the sun right into the beast's eyes.

"Be stunned and amazed," Whilte shouted at his hellish foe. "Blind yourself and be sightless; be drunk, but not from wine; stagger, but not from beer."

Inxyphos the bear swatted at its own eyes and snout, as if the light was a painful, bothersome insect that it could bat away. It swayed on its hind legs as it did so—so like a drunkard it was almost unbelievable how precisely the words of scripture Whilte had quoted at the beast were being fulfilled. Prentice had no idea how long the prayer might hold the fell power at bay, but in that moment, staring at the impeded monster, he was reminded of all the fey slain for Inxyphos to learn the dark secrets of the serpent witches—fey of the Azure Mountains, Wind Rising fey, Prentice's adopted kin.

"You owe us blood, merciless man," he growled at the staggering monster that seemed already to be fighting its way back into self-control. Then he drove forward, his single-edged blade turned in his hands to that the sharpness of the curve was on the upside. The point bit deep, and Prentice kept forcing with his full weight, like a butcher thinking to cut an animal carcass all the way up the belly and through the sternum. The *brakkis effar* screamed, a horridly human sound, and then toppled backward. As it fell, Prentice felt the weight dragging at his blade, but he refused to release his grip, and so as the beast tumbled, his rising cut became a circling sweep that erupted from the ruined chest in a spray of gore. Even with the wet muck in the air, the light of Whilte's staff seemed to glow upon the steel so that the edge flashed for one moment, as if in the brightest of sunshine. Then the motion swept the blade back to a guard and the light faded. The bear body thumped like a dropped sack to the ground and there was a sudden breathless pause. Then the Young Hopefuls surged forward, stabbing at the beast, apparently to make sure it was dead. Prentice stepped back, exhausted, and let them have the moment for releasing their own fear and anger however they might. A benign smile lit his lips, and in his sudden fatigue, he slipped in the blood on the ground, going down on one knee.

He knelt there a long moment, trying to get a comfortable breath into his badly bruised chest. Whilte came to him and put a hand upon his shoulder, praying softly. A moan drew his attention, and he turned to see the wounded Baronet Forsle lying mere paces away. From the nobleman, he looked to the baroness, who was still standing, staring at the scene, mouth open. The helmet she had been carrying so proudly now hung in her hand by her side, as if she had forgotten it was there or even what it was. The crowd behind her were clearly all as shocked as she was.

"My Lady, your uncle needs the help of a healer," he told the baroness and waved Whilte over to the badly wounded baronet. "He must be taken somewhere safe to rest, and you also must be seen to safety. Your enemies might yet have other ambushes planned for you. I urge you to go to your castle immediately. The White Lions are coming to help restore order to your town. We will police these bodies and see that folk are named and prepared for their burial rites. It will likely take time to bring order back, but once things begin to settle, we will provide you with a proper escort so that you may see to your people's needs more safely. We will tend to Baronet Forsle's needs in the meantime."

In the manner of shocked and panicked people who do not know what else to do, Baroness Penelope allowed herself to be led by Prentice's instructions. Nodding and then quietly gathering the Young Hopefuls around herself, she headed away. All sense of the glory of her planned accession was gone now. The grey day would soon be darkening to evening. The bright bunting seemed pointless frivolousness now. As the crowd began to leave quietly, they skirted Prentice and the monstrous corpse, as if fearful the awful battle was not truly concluded, the thing not truly slain. For a moment between the moving figures, Prentice caught a glimpse of Cassian, still standing on the steps of the cathedral, his own blade dripping blood, staring in incensed disbelief at the scene before him. Then the crowd blocked Prentice's view, and when there was another gap, the Young Hopeful was gone.

Another problem for another day, Prentice thought, and he forced himself to his feet. Whilte had already secured the assistance of some of the rescued townsfolk, lifting Baronet Forsle on his own cloak as a stretcher, and was now readying to lead them to a better place for the baroness's uncle to rest.

"I will return once he is indoors," the chaplain said as he moved past. Prentice nodded, then smiled wryly.

"Scripture lessons, Brother?" he asked, referring to the passage Whilte had quoted.

"The prophet Isaiah. It was the only thing I could think of to say," the chaplain explained sheepishly. "I trust by the outcome it was the leading of the Lord."

Prentice almost said that he wouldn't have cared if it wasn't, as long as they received this outcome, but he stopped himself as he realized that was not true. That was the Inquisition's flaw, thinking they could use evil to fight evil. Once the compromise was made with evil, it became increasingly impossible to pick evil from good in the first place. It was a temptation to care only about the hoped-for outcome and not realizing that the path to one's goal was just as important. A kingdom built on sin could not be the kingdom of God. Years of watching all manner of evil justified in the name of a good land or a good cause had at least taught Prentice that.

He waved the stretcher party on its way and started to survey the square. The Inquisition was here in Bridgetown. If there had been any doubt left, it was gone now. Time to see what breadcrumbs the twittering birds had left behind. Hopefully a trail they could finally follow and hunt them by.

Chapter 53

The grey sky was almost fully dark, and Prentice was looking for someone to fetch him a lantern as a cohort of the Gryphon Banner marched into the square to occupy it and begin the work of cleaning up after the slaughter. The knight commander had already spoken with Farringdon, who had ridden back swiftly and reported that he had dispatched the lancers to restore order before returning to command them in that duty. He said he had paused on his ride only to reassure himself that the archduchess and her party had reached the Paramour's Chambers safely. They had, although there had been some altercations, especially when the hired guards of a Conclave merchant had thought the crowd had come to loot the caravan they were hired to guard and had interposed themselves between the archducal party and their goal. The archduchess had managed to persuade the mercenaries of their honest intent without Sir Turley having to make good his threat of caving in their thick skulls.

"That being said, I suspect it was the sight of four masked women with drawn fighting daggers that likely gave them most pause," Farringdon had said with a smile, and Prentice smirked at that thought as well.

In the meantime, the baron knight commander had moved amongst the corpses, trying to find the exact position that Inxyphos had been hiding in the crowd before he transformed, and from that, perhaps locate some witness still alive or some other clues to follow. Several of the newly arrived militiamen had lanterns or torches, and one was quickly lit for their commander. A Fang held it aloft as Prentice went from corpse to corpse in the twilight. There were men, women, and children all dead on the stones, some mostly whole and others mere fragments of bodies, ripped apart by razor claws and inhuman strength. Prentice himself had felt that power, saved from death only by the strength of his now ruined brigandine. One of his first acts when the Gryphon cohort arrived had been to doff the damaged piece of armor and hand the remains to one of the militiamen. Several of its straps and buckles had been torn apart by the force of the blow, but with one, the metal fixer had been so twisted by the impact that it would no longer undo. Prentice had had to saw through the leather of the strap with his dagger.

Having only a vague idea of the location he was seeking amidst the carnage, Prentice had marked out a rough space and commanded that no bodies be moved from there until after he was through, so that while the rest of the square had begun the return to peace and order, even now, he still stood in an expurgated field of blood and filth.

"I have someone for you to speak with, My Lord," Prentice heard Whilte say as he was looking more closely at pair of dead young men in practical workmen's garb. One had a cheap tin guild pin on his breast—young workers given the day off to witness the momentous ceremony that now might never take place. Even if it were rescheduled, these two would not see it. Prentice stood and turned to see Whilte had brought a young woman, a fishwife by the look of her streaked apron and deeply tanned face and hands, who was standing, leaning on a walking stick.

"You were hurt?" he asked the woman and she nodded.

"Got knocked 'bout and trampled some," she told Prentice. "The sacrist 'ere got me 'ealed up mostly, but 'e says I'll likely limp awhiles. 'E said I could use this stick, since the old owner's...got..."

"No use for it now," Whilte finished, likely not meaning to use battlefield humor, but apparently trying to put the woman at ease. Prentice thought if he had tried such a comment, it would have come out brutal and mocking, but the chaplain managed to use it to relieve some of the woman's tension. She flashed him a small smile.

"Then keep it with my blessing," Prentice told her, and he glanced at Whilte, raising an eyebrow. The chaplain looked in turn to the woman and nudged her gently. She nodded, resolute.

"I was near to 'im, that thing," she said and swallowed visibly as she did. For a moment she looked down, as if trying to hide her eyes from her recollections of only a few hours past, but the paved ground at their feet was awash with the brutal memories of it. Bodies were close by, some still in the place where they fell, at Prentice's instruction. Blood ran and pooled in many places, and where it did not the stones were still crimson, smeared as bodies or body parts were dragged away to be given their rights and be burned or buried. That part of proceedings had already been handed over to the local clergy. Bridgetown was at least coming back to itself enough to tend to its dead.

"'E was 'unched under a cloak, 'eavy and dirty, but it looked like it was sewed of burlap. Like a poor riverman's thing that'll keep the sun off, but ain't nothin' if it's cold. I figured 'im for a mad beggar," she said, lifting her head to Prentice again.

"If it was such a common thing, then why did you notice it? What made you notice him?" Prentice asked, studying her expression as he listened to her answer. He wanted to see if there was anything she was not saying as she unfolded her story.

"'E was drunk," she explained readily. "Leastwise I thought so, bent over, moving with a stagger and muttering to 'imself. I took 'im for havin' been at the drink to celebrate early and gotten ahead of 'imself. Some charitable soul must have fronted 'im a few guilders for a cup or three and 'e got his hands on somethin' too strong for 'im. I thought it a waste. 'E was so far gone 'e weren't goin' to remember none of the great day, and what else 'as a beggar got to enjoy in life?"

She sniffed and then snorted, as if disgusted by her own naivete, surrounded by the tragic remnants and human wreckage of the "great day." Her speech was an odd mixture of accents, so that some of her words were mispronounced and others were softly said. She was of the rivers herself and traveled, by the sound of it.

"Did he say anything in his mutterings?" Prentice pressed. "Or was he carrying anything? Anything at all? Something wooden or metal perhaps?"

"Not as I seen, but 'e could've 'ad something under 'is cloak and I would never've seen it, so 'unched over 'e was."

"And what did 'e say?"

"I didn't 'ear, nothin' but just mumblin'. Made me right twitchy, so I moved away. I was thinkin' 'e might be trouble and wishin' there was a militiaman to sort 'im out if 'e was."

"Was there?" Prentice asked, sure he already knew the answer, but refusing to get ahead of himself. A stone he skipped as he crossed the river might have been the one he needed not to fall in the water. Patience was his watchword now.

"Nah. All the militia was guarding the baroness' path," the riverwoman said. "They wanted to be part of the ceremony, didn't they?"

"So, he was wandering through the crowd alone?"

That notion troubled Prentice. What little he knew of Inxyphos told him the man was not the kind to volunteer himself as a sacrificial servant. A solo mission of suicide such as this one was not in keeping with his character. Perhaps he had brought the power of the magick upon himself to use it as the Redlander champions did, and it had overwhelmed him.

"Wait, no, 'e weren't by 'imself," the woman said suddenly. "'E had 'is uncle with 'im."

"His uncle?" Prentice asked.

"I figured 'im for an uncle, or maybe the one who'd plied 'im with all the drink," the woman said. "I remember as I moved away some grey-haired fellow—old, with a limp—come up beside 'im and took 'im by the shoulders. I remember I was relieved. I mean fool or not, a fellow shouldn't be drunk like that in the street alone. It ain't safe. I'd just moved to near a house where some fellows were sittin' on a 'igher windowsill. I was about to ask 'em to give me a bunk up so I could see when the growlin' started, just about the same time the crowd all got antsy about what was 'appenin' at the cathedral door. I never saw either thing for true, but just before the blood started to fly, I saw that burlap cloak. It slipped off as 'e...as 'e...st...stood up, so tall, so...Oh God in heaven, 'e was so tall and so wild. 'E was just a monster, a mutterin', killin' monster."

The woman began to sob, the day's memories overwhelming her, and Whilte put his arm around her shoulders. She hung her head a moment and then looked up at him fearfully.

"They're sayin' someone killed a patriarch or someone in the door of the cathedral."

"A sacrist was slain on the steps, yes," Whilte confirmed with a soft, sad tone to his voice.

"Oh, they're saying that's a curse. The whole town'll be cursed, and the monster came from 'ell to punish us. God'll 'ate us for killin' a 'oly man or being there when it 'appened. Monster's will comin' for all of us."

Is that what they are saying? Prentice wondered, but he did not think to respond to the notion. Whilte held the woman from the side, giving her a pastoral hug.

"None of that talk," he chided her gently. "God delights not in the death of *any* man or woman; and you said it yourself—that mad fellow was muttering in the crowd long before the murder was done. Even if the merciful Lord in heaven is angry with us, this is hardly the worst thing to happen in these sad days, and he will not keep his anger forever."

The woman nodded, accepting the religious man's consolations more because she needed to than by actual persuasion. At least that was how it seemed to Prentice. With a nod, he gave Whilte permission to escort the woman out of the square away from the carnage, and by the time the chaplain returned, Prentice had found the discarded piece of burlap, half entangled with the bodies of those who must have been amongst the earliest slain.

He was crouched down and lifting one edge of the cloth out of the blood with the tip of his dagger, directing his lantern-bearer to shine the light closer at points.

"What do you seek?" Whilte asked as he stood beside Prentice, unable to crouch with only one good leg.

"Any of the Redlanders' written sorceries," Prentice explained. He had no idea if their words could be embroidered or painted on cloth, but they had shown themselves carved, forged, and written in blood so far, so he was taking no chances. Flipping the burlap up in the light, there was no such thing to see in the parts not covered by gore, but did that mean it was safe?

"You think this acted as his mask? A cloak in place of a mantis face?" the chaplain pressed.

"Or it might have used magicks to restrain him until the correct moment," Prentice mused. "That fishwife was made of stern stuff, and her witness has helped us. You made sure she knew, I hope."

"I did," Whilte said. "Gave her some coins from my alms purse."

Prentice muttered approvingly, but his mind had been drawn by the thought that the woman was a fish wife, and his nose told him of a smell he hadn't realized he was noticing. In amongst the tang of blood and the waste smell of emptied bowels and bladders that was the odor of every battlefield, he smelled fish. He lifted the burlap on his dagger point again and sniffed closely. It was there for certain—fish and ...

"Salt water?" he muttered.

"My Lord?" Whilte asked, not understanding.

"It smells of fish and salt water."

"Well, she said the man looked like a poor fisher," the chaplain said, clearly not seeing the potential significance. "And the Murr runs from here all the way to the Tassasim Ocean."

"Precisely Brother," Prentice said as he stood and sheathed his blade. "All the way to the ocean, leagues away. How far does a river fisherman's range take him? Especially a poor one."

Whilte scratched absently at his tonsure, which he often did while that he was thinking, Prentice knew.

"You think he must have come from somewhere downriver, not local," he said pensively, catching Prentice's own thoughts. "We know that Inxyphos cannot have come into the town over the bridges, so he had to arrive by boat." He paused, then his eyes lit up. "If he came to unhorse the baroness' ceremony, he had to have arrived recently, too, on a boat recently arrived itself, perhaps newly today and still at its dock. Should we send word to the knight captain to have any boats or crews from the Tassasim seized for questioning?"

"A fair thought, but there would be little point now," Prentice said ruefully. "Any such boat and crew would have put back out already, I have no doubt. They would know what has happened and made their escape. And that assumes they are even aware of any of this plot."

He looked up to the darkened eastern sky, as if to see all the way to the far ocean.

"Where exactly does the river flow to before the salt of the sea turns the water brackish? There is a point where the one becomes the other in every great river, from the Ramat to the endless runs of the Vec. Inxyphos could have taken a boat from any such place on the riverbank. And for the whole journey he might have been nothing to them but another riverman."

"I doubt he would have been too plausible in that role. More like our robber nuns," Whilte said, cocking his head to the side. "We both know Inxyphos. He would have struggled to keep his pride in check in the face of kings and patriarchs, let alone fisher-men. I can't believe he could keep up the act."

"He would not be the only one these days," Prentice retorted, but the chaplain's point was well taken. Inxyphos would make a poor spy. Whatever else the man had been before he ended his life as a monster, it was prideful. The irony of such a self-important fellow dying as a contemptible beast was not lost on Prentice. He was still contemplating all the evidence when a loud altercation arose near the church steps on the far side of the square. Puzzled, Prentice led the way to where the only other body that he had ordered remain in place still lay upon the stones—the body of the monster himself.

CHAPTER 54

"I come with the will of Bridgetown," a lone figure berated the two sentries Prentice had set to watch the corpse. "You will obey my command at once!"

In the sparse torch and lanternlight it took Prentice a moment to recognize the Baroness of Bridgetown's cousin, the petulant Squire Wilforn, one of the lesser Young Hopefuls.

"What passes here?" he called as he approached, and the two sentries saluted reflexively, free hands on their halberds, while Wilforn's eyes searched against the approaching lantern glow behind Prentice's head. When he finally realized it was the knight commander of the White Lions, his already contemptuous expression took on an even deeper sneer, if such was possible. Having been despised by kings and princes, this abortive young knight's disdain almost made Prentice laugh with his own contempt in return. He managed to keep a straight face, however.

"You? They tell me you're in charge," Wilforn said with raised voice that reminded Prentice of the preacher who had died before the door only paces from where they were. "My cousin demands your report. When will the cathedral square be cleansed and the bodies removed? The ceremony will need to be rescheduled. She also commands that this...thing...be taken. and after it has been confirmed safe, hung in a cage at the crossroad market so that her people may know that she has returned peace and safety to her land."

"*She* has returned peace and safety?" Brother Whilte repeated, plainly indignant on the White Lions' behalf, not to mention likely somewhat annoyed to hear his own role in the affair disregarded. Even for a man as humble as the chaplain, that was no small insult. However, it was not that news which caught Prentice's attention.

She wants to reschedule the ceremony? he thought, studying the cocksure young nobleman's shadowed face in the flickering light. Surely someone had explained the significance of the day's events to her. Even if the question of curses on her rule and noble line were ignored, there was the question of the sanctified ground defiled. If clergy had been reluctant to have a ceremony here before, they would absolutely refuse it now. No sacrist who wanted to keep his cassock—or his soul for that matter—would risk such an affront to Mother Church, even in these divided days. For himself, damnation at the judgement of the patriarchs was little enough to fear, doubly so in the light of the ecclesiarchy's conflicts, but Prentice also conceded that he had never taken clerical vows either. Knowing that, his mind put Wilforn's demands in another light.

"Does the baroness even know you are here?" he asked.

"Of course!" Wilforn blustered, his voice just a little too shrill, even for a green youth trying not to be intimidated by men obviously blooded and accustomed to battle. "I am her cousin and carry her authority. Now do your duty and finish this housework, rogue. Tell your inferiors to heft this thing and bring it to the crossroads, as her grace commands."

"She is not her grace yet, lad," Prentice told him, and as Wilforn opened his mouth to argue back, he stilled him with a raised hand. "But you may go to your cousin, *Squire* Wilforn, and take her word that Baron Knight Commander Ash has almost concluded his investigation of the monster, to confirm that it is truly dead, that the magicks will not bring it back to life at the new moon, and to find out how it came to be here in *her* town."

Wilforn bristled at being reminded of his lesser status in the peerage and made an offended noise with his open mouth, gawping like a caught fish, but also shied slightly, giving the dead monster a nervous glance. Prentice was not finished.

"Marquis Knight Captain Farringdon assures me that peace will be fully returned to the town before midnight, and no great acts of looting or affray have accompanied the panic. Most folk are happy to return to their homes safe and hale. You may pass that along to your cousin the baroness as well, with the Western Reach's compliments.

"When all that is done, return here with as many workmen as you think are needful for the task and you may haul this corpse away for yourself. I will have finished my inquiries by then, I would expect."

For a long moment Wilforn continued to gawp, as if unable to believe anyone had spoken to him in such a manner. Prentice and his men only watched him, impassive as stones. Then the young man did something utterly unexpected. He fetched a leather cup of some sort, with a lid that could be tied tightly in place, out from his doublet vest. Then he squatted quickly and dipped it into the thickening pool of the creature's blood. He collected as much as he could and stood again, replacing the lid. When he noticed the White Lions all about staring at him, he shrugged, a little shamefaced.

"The beast bit my uncle," he said, more humbly than Prentice had ever heard him speak before. "If the bite had a venom, an apothecary might need some of the blood to make a mithridate. I must take it to him immediately."

That explanation made a kind of sense to Prentice and put the young man's pushy demands in a different light. Of course, if Baronet Forsle was Penelope's uncle, then he would be Wilforn's as well. Cassian and Cyprian were also cousins, so Prentice had heard. Was the baronet uncle to them all, or were some his direct children? What a challenge for the aging man, seeking to guide so many unruly orphans across the last threshold of youth. Even so, it annoyed Prentice that Wilforn had not bothered to be upfront about his needs. All the bluster and subterfuge only wasted everyone's time. Wilforn gave no obeisance as he turned to leave, and Prentice made no point of criticizing his rudeness.

"Cocky little snot, callin' us rogues," one of the sentries said, shaking his head with a sneer of his own. The man had a long scar on his chin that left a line of bare skin through his beard.

"Did I ask for your judgement, militiaman?" Prentice asked him quietly, and the man snapped to attention.

"No, My Lord."

"Quite so."

Prentice turned from his underling to the monster's corpse. It seemed a little smaller than he remembered now, and he wondered if some of the Redlander magick had fallen away when the creature died. He had not seen that sort of thing with other *brakkis effar*, but he had also never seen a bear man before.

Not much of a bear, he thought, studying the form. Now that the rush of battle was passed, he could see a misshapenness to its transformation. Other beast men were akin to perfect mergings of mortal and animal, as if they were the creature itself, just with a different skeleton and mortal minds and souls. A wolf or a serpent, even a mantis, was unmistakably like unto its archetype. This thing was bent in odd places. Some human skin showed in patches amongst the fur, and its claws were more like those of an eagle than a bear. The fingers were elongated, hardly like paws at all. This was nothing like one of the beast men whose models formed the heads of the great serpent he had seen so many times in holy visions.

"The hounds," he muttered as he remembered the one other kind of Redlander shape changer he had seen in the invasions, though rarely since the earliest days in the time of the Horned Man. Hounds, like hunting dogs, but usually misshapen and often looking as if melded from a combination of odd beasts, including beaks and feathers amidst fur and fangs. Like the mythical gryphon he had adopted as his heraldry—eagle and lion in equal measure. Was there a gryphon man somewhere in the wider world, awaiting his own chance to assault the Reach and the Grand Kingdom?

"Beggin' yer pardon, Brother," the other sentry who had not spoken out of turn muttered quietly, clearly trying not to disrupt his commander's contemplations. "But is it true what the knight commander says, that the monster might come back at the new moon?"

"Fear not, militiaman," Whilte answered in a calm tone. "I think you'll find the knight commander was only tweaking the youngling's nose."

"For sooth?" the man asked, his tone a mix of hope and pleased surprise. His companion snickered a moment before getting himself under control yet again. It clearly tickled both their fancies that their leader might have invented the notion on the fly just to put the willies up the arrogant Wilforn.

"You didn't march into the west with us, did you?" Whilte asked, and Prentice saw out of the corner of his eye that the militiaman was shaking his head. "Well, you ask around. Whether it's Roar shot, Fang's sword, or Claws halberd .."

The chaplain paused and pointed to the polearm the sentry had in his hand.

"...once a beast man is put down, he stays down. That is the power of the White Lions."

"Not to mention the power of God on our side," the sentry added, and he nodded at Whilte's own staff.

"Just you look to do the right thing and fight with your own weapon. Leave the things of God to God," Whilte chided, sounding more embarrassed than angry to Prentice's ear.

"But you turned the waters with that rod," the man protested. "Like the Moses from sabbath scripture. Everyone knows the tale."

"That is enough, thank you militiaman," Prentice said sternly, not angry himself, but to save his friend from discomfort. Claiming a share of the battle's victory was one thing, but a prophet's mantle was far above the humble Whilte's ambitions. During the conversation Prentice had been pretending not to listen, focusing his eyes on Inxyphos's corpse in the poor light, but try as he might, all he could see was an abomination that he was glad was dead—not to mention a justice delivered when he considered the Inquisition knight's former crimes.

"That is all I need to see," he said, feeling ready to go from the square and find a drink to wash the metallic tang of blood from the back of his throat. The air around them was so thick with it that he could almost taste it. "I do not trust Squire Wilforn to actually return for it, now that he has what he truly came for. We will dispose of it ourselves."

"You want we should hang it like he said, My Lord?" asked the free speaker. "Don't s'pose there's a crows cage big enough for that in the whole town. The whole world even. We'd have to have one made special, I reckon."

"No, we will not," Prentice said. "That talk of the baroness' orders was a fey tale, I do not doubt. Fetch some oil and wood and burn the thing right here on the stones. Then have the ashes taken somewhere away from folks and gardens and bury them."

"Ay, My Lord."

"Beggin' your pardon again, but what about the charm?" asked the nervous sentry.

"I told you man, dead is dead, even for Redlanders and their magick," Whilte said, a little exasperated, but the sentry shook his head.

"Not spells or nothin'," he declared. "I means the bracelet."

"Bracelet?" Prentice asked, his head jerking up.

"There on its wrist, like," the militiaman said, pointing with the butt of his weapon. Prentice waved a lantern over, and in the brighter light he saw that there was indeed a bracelet on the monstrous wrist, pulled tight by the swollen flesh and bone transformed. In the poor light and long hair, Prentice had missed it completely.

"Good spotting, militiaman," he said earnestly, and he crouched down, drawing his dagger again and poking at the string of beads. Not a charm bracelet per se, it was in fact prayer beads, of the kind illiterate folk used to track their prayers. It was sometimes called a wrist rosary, though where that name came from or what the beads had to do with roses, Prentice had no idea. Most such strings were wood pieces threaded upon twine, but there were some sacrists of status who carried jeweled ones of gold or silver, though rarely. It was sometimes seen as a mark of deficient education in writing and reading. A peasant's tool was not a profitable thing for an ambitious cleric to be seen in possession of in most contexts. This particular string was of the humble persuasion, and Prentice wondered for a moment if the beads might have been carved with the Redlander symbols that had been absent from the burlap. Was this the "bear mask" to start the transformation?

With great care, he slid the tip of his poniard under the string to try to pull it away from the hairs for easier examination, but the already taut thread wanted no more stretching, and the blade's edge cut the twine easily. The beads rattled as they scattered on the stones or else plopped straight into the puddle of drying blood. The sentry danced out of their way, as if the tiny wooden balls were hot coals spilled from a blazing hearth. Prentice ignored the pieces as they fell because as the string snapped, it revealed something else tucked tightly beneath it—a little folded wad of parchment. It tumbled into sight, and he snatched at it, catching it before it fell into the blood. He stood up and unfolded the small sheet, looking at what was inside.

"Fetch a broom and sweep those things up," he told his men absently. "Don't pick them up. Just sweep them up against this thing and burn the lot. I have to take this to the archduchess."

CHAPTER 55

"A bear?" Amelia asked, staring, perplexed at the piece of parchment in her hands. Prentice had delivered it to her only moments before and immediately summoned extra lights for her to see by. There were a number of images on the sheet, like illuminations in a fine book but much simpler—roughly fashioned, in fact. Even her husband or Master Solft's roughest sketches had a more refined appearance. These were more like pictograms than full drafts. In the center, immediately recognizable for all its unrefined hand, was the heraldic bear of Bridgetown, rampant. Amelia handed the page off to the others for their opinion.

"A bear bearing a bear?" Sir Turley joked when his wife handed him the page after her own examination. Lady Dalflitch tutted at her husband's simple wit, but her glance at him was unmistakably affectionate. She approved even when she disapproved.

"What does it mean?" Amelia asked.

"I think we should hear Master Solft's opinion," Prentice said, and all eyes turned to the scholar who had been summoned from his studies especially for this meeting, quietly seated in his preferred place at the bottom of the table. Prentice insisted the man was not as timid as he appeared, which made Amelia wonder if this preference was some kind of exaggerated humility. Timid or not, Master Solft studied the document with the same focused attention he seemed to bring to every academic activity.

"Crude," he said, confirming the archduchess's own opinion of the images. He pointed to different parts of the parchment as he spoke. "Well...I'd say that is the cathedral, and that is a sacrist in a stole, if I had to guess."

"As the preacher wore a distinctive stole on the steps?" Dalflitch asked, and the scholar nodded.

"Yes, I would say, or at least as like as they could make it."

"They, Master?" Amelia pressed.

"Whoever created these drawings," Solft explained.

"And any clue to who that might be?"

"No one trained, that is certain," he said with confidence. "I'd bet these were done with proper compressed charcoal, not just a burned stick from a fire, but not by a skilled hand. The bear itself tells us that. It's heraldic but only just. They certainly meant it as Bridgetown's bear, though."

"How do say that?" Prentice asked, clearly most interested in specifics, as usual.

"If I look closely, right up to the light," Solft said, drawing one of the table's candlesticks to himself so that he could peer at the image. "I'm sure I can see some color smears. Certainly, an attempt at ochre and possibly some gold or yellow. Whatever they used was not proper paint, which is why it's so faint, I think. If I had to guess, I'd say they just took marigold blooms and tried rubbing them straight on the page. If they'd taken even a day to steep the petals in some hot oil or vinegar, they could have improvised a stronger pigment. Whoever did this was unskilled or rushed—in fact, I'd say most likely both."

Prentice nodded solemnly, as if Solft's words confirmed his own suspicions. Amelia had long since ceased marveling at the breadth of Prentice's knowledge, so she looked to him to add his own reflections.

"What do you suspect, Baron?"

"I think whoever unleashed Inxyphos's final crimes against Bridgetown did not ensorcel him long ago, or else if they did, they held his final transformation back somehow, until they had a proper use for him. Like saving their best arrows for the right target on the hunt."

"Sure, if you're hunting nobles, the baroness would be only second to her grace here for a trophy," Turley agreed. "And both were in that square this day."

"The baroness was not the trophy, old friend, nor her grace," Prentice said confidently. "Bridgetown was."

Turley blinked and rocked back in his chair, clearly not understanding the claim, but Amelia thought she did. The preacher's denunciations were the clue.

"Our alliance is already rocky," she said, and everyone turned to look at her. "Now, would-be-Archduchess Penelope has been soundly, horrifically rebuked before God and all mortal men for seeking to 'follow my path.' They—and by 'they' I think we can assume agents of the Inquisition—seek to split us fully apart."

"They seek to keep Bridgetown weak and isolated," Prentice corrected but gently. "But yes, Your Grace, breaking our alliance is a part of that."

"Well, that can leave us in no doubt that it is the Inquisition behind this," Dalflitch concluded, her voice sour, as if the words tasted bad. "A weak Bridgetown will be ripe for the wretched Duke Robant to return and pluck it for his master."

"Unless they want the Heron to have it," Prentice offered, and that set every face at the table to scowling. Somewhere to the south and west, the Golden Heron's mercenary army was likely still on the march toward Bridgetown at this very moment.

"Why on earth would they want that?" Dalflitch asked, the notion stretching even her insight into politics beyond its limits.

"I have no idea," Prentice admitted. "But that army the Lion Banner faced in Aubrey will have cost them a fortune, even if the Inquisition opened its own coffers to help cover the bill. If Aubrey was the prize, they have it already. If what little word we have from the Vec side is true and they are marching eastward, what other target do they have? What *other* target would the Inquisition pay so much for?"

"For Bridgetown or myself, personally?" Amelia asked.

"Either or both," Prentice said with a shrug.

"They got to take the one to get to the other, if they aren't going to use this bear thing 'arrow' for the job," Turley added. "Take the town and get her grace in the bargain."

"But why do they hate me so?" Amelia asked, suddenly overwhelmed by the prospect. Bridgetown had not ended up in flames, which the panicked crowd had made seem possible for a moment earlier in the afternoon, but Farringdon was still not returned from his mission to restore order. She missed him suddenly, fearful for his safety, though she had no fresh cause to be so. "And is it me they truly fear or a strong Reach? Or just a knee jerk in defense of the sumptuary order? A resentment of a jump up?"

"For a long time, I assumed they were Daven Marcus' arm of vengeance, I must admit, Your Grace," Dalflitch offered. "But increasingly, it is you and your rule they seem to abhor. If our guesses are true, they have already expended huge resources to undermine you—undermine us—and today only adds to the bill."

"To what end?"

Amelia wanted to pursue this line some more, but at that moment Lady Spindle entered the room. When they returned from the chaos of their flight from the square, the archduchess had released the Lace Fang to care for her husband, whose frail form had not seemed to cope well with the jostling of the crowd during the retreat. As she entered, it took Amelia a moment in the candlelight to realize that Spindle looked like she had been crying.

"Is something amiss, My Lady?" she asked earnestly.

"My Caius, Your Grace," Spindle told her, swallowing loudly. "He...he collapsed, just as I almost had him in bed. He just dropped, half in and half out. It was like he was punched cold. When I rolled him over, I couldn't be sure he was even breathing. When I leaned close and could hear it, it sounded like his chest was full of gravel. He's fearsome sick."

"Have you called for a healer?" Amelia asked. She turned to her knight commander. "Prentice, send to Brother Whilte."

Prentice stood without hesitation, but Spindle waved him back toward his seat.

"No need, Your Grace," she said. "Caius' family has 'emselves a goodly healer they call on, lives here in the town. I also sent to a herbwife I knows well. Both are with 'im now. They say he's got the pneumonia on his chest. Fearsome sick, like I said. Oh Lord, I can't lose 'im so soon. I knew he was much older, but not so soon."

That thought was too much for the Lace Fang and a tear rolled down her cheek, glittering in the candlelight. Amelia's heart went out to her lady-in-waiting, and suddenly all the other horrors of the day faded in the archduchess's mind. Everyone knew there was a significant age gap between Master Welburne and his wife, Lady Spindle, but it was not unknown for wealthier men to marry later. Amelia's own first husband had been more than twice her age when they had married. Nevertheless, before this moment Amelia had not considered that in a real sense this was a near-inevitable event that Spindle had likely been preparing for in her mind since the day Caius had begun to woo her. And yes, it was still too soon.

"My Lady, you must go back to your husband immediately," she said with a heartfelt smile of sympathy, rising to cross the distance between them. Spindle was shaking her head as Amelia approached.

"I am your Lace Fang, Your Grace," she protested.

"As is Baroness Righteous," Amelia told her as she drew close.

"She has her babes to attend to," Spindle persisted. "She's with 'em right now, ain't she?"

"Rightly, too," Amelia said, and at last she reached out and took her companion in her arms. "She is with her babes, and you must be with your husband. And still I will be well bestowed with protectors."

She waved her hand around the Paramour's Chambers to the neophytes attending to their duties in the corners, though many had gone to their beds early. They would rise in the small hours to take a second guard shift and allow their sisters to rest. There were never fewer than a half dozen women awake in the archduchess's chamber at any time these days.

"Look at all these you have helped to train, to fashion for my protection," Amelia continued. "You and Lady Righteous will ever be the first and finest of the Lace Fangs, but you are now far from the only ones. I believe the time is soon come for some others to shed their wimples and take some lace for themselves. Whatever else today's events prove, it is that, surely."

She looked to Lady Dalflitch.

"Would you concur, My Lady?"

"I will never be completely satisfied," the finest of ladies-in-waiting said imperiously. "Nonetheless, I think your judgement is correct. It might indeed have come time for the *Lace* Fangs to have a promotion ceremony of their own—the first of its kind."

"See?" Amelia said to Spindle, hugging her again. "And that is thanks to your efforts. You have earned your time with your husband, even if it was not your right. Go you now to his side. Keep me informed of his condition. You lack for neither wealth nor friends, from my household and his, but I have authority that Caius does not. Whatever his wealth lacks to produce, my influence will provide."

"Thank you so much, Your Grace," Spindle said, producing a lace-edged kerchief from her sleeve and wiping her nose. Amelia smiled and turned to escort her to the door. As they went, she heard Turley ask his spouse an indignant question.

"Never completely satisfied wife?" he asked in his classic tone of mock umbrage.

"In matters of her grace's chamber," Dalflitch answered him icily, sucking in a loud, offended breath. "In matters of our own chamber, we will not speak of them in present company, or indeed in any company."

"Quite right," Turley said, as if he were the offended party, not the one being cheeky with his humor. "I only ask because of our pasts..."

There was a loud thwack that Amelia knew meant Dalflitch had slapped her husband, likely straight across his bearded face.

"Right," he responded, without the least sound of shame in his voice. "We won't mention that in company neither."

Close together in the shadows by the door, Spindle and Amelia's eyes met, and the archduchess rolled hers theatrically. The sight made Spindle suddenly give a small, sniffling giggle, and that relieved Amelia's own heart. A laugh was good medicine for a sick heart, so it was said, and as she let Spindle through the door, Amelia was almost certain her knight castellan had said what he had deliberately, hoping to relieve some of his friend's pain. She only hoped that his wife would understand it the same. Before she had returned to them at the table, there was a dull thump echoing in the sky outside the windows.

"Thunder?" Turley asked. "Looks like the winter rains've come. That'll make cleaning those flagstones in the square much easier. Sluice 'em right off."

Another thump sounded, muffled and distant.

"That is not thunder," Prentice said, and he looked to Amelia with obvious unease.

CHAPTER 56

"There, Knight Commander, off to the southwest some," Sergeant Guillam said, pointing into the darkness from the bastion roof where he stood beside Prentice, looking into the night-shrouded fields of the Vec. Suddenly, a gout of flame erupted, lighting a blast of smoke like a cloud of fire as another cannon shot was fired. In the dark, there was no sign of the ball itself, but a whistling marked by a heavy thud told them that it had landed somewhere nearby, and then there was a splash, suggesting the shot had bounced into the river. Thankfully.

"They come up late afternoon while the lancers was all runnin' about after the monster attack," the sergeant went on. "They was diggin' and heapin' up the earth in patches for a while. I didn't know what it might be for, so I never made much of it. Then there was trains of men with torches in the evening and the creak of what I took for wagons, but looks like it was these things."

There was another gout of flame and smoke and a whumping sound, followed by the thud of a bouncing strike and another splash. Prentice stroked his beard and tried to mark the spots that were lighting the inky space. He realized it was a redundant exercise as dawn would reveal the cannons' locations readily enough, but he thought to use it as a discipline of the mind—to begin to put together a picture of his enemy, their strength and their intent. Already they posed a mystery which Guillam's next comment articulated very well.

"What I can't figure is what they think they're aimin' at," he said around his chewing, sucking his blackened teeth. "First guess was us, o' course, and I just read 'em as bad shots in the dark, but that makes no dog's sense. I mean, we ain't doused our torches or lanterns. Sougate's the only thing lit up on this bank o' the Murr. How hard is it to point at? And if it is that hard to hit, why not wait until dawn and take a proper shot?"

"Knight Captain Farringdon tells me that shooting a big barrel like that is not so much different than loosing an arrow from a bow or even a ball from a Roarsman's matchlock," Prentice explained. "The shot drops away, only over a much longer distance. The cannoneers must find their range, lean their barrels back enough to shoot the shot long but not too high or they shorten the range again."

"With that much powder and them big iron shot? I scarce can credit it."

Prentice could well understand his sergeant's disbelief. Cannons, whether they were the monsters of the Denay Bronze Dragons, whose construction was a secret lost to history, or the newer, humbler-seeming types created by inventive men like the late Yentow Sent, were a tool of warfare to boggle the mind. It was little wonder the founders of the Denay throne called their weapons "dragons." What other name could capture such raw power? Another shot was belched forth and this time the whistle was not punctuated by any thumps, only a loud splash.

"Saw that one," a sentry on the battlement further along called and pointed to a part of the river lit by boat lanterns on some of the docks. The splash had already fallen back to the river by the time Prentice moved to that side of the barbican roof to see.

"It's like they're *aiming* at the river," Guillam declared, shaking his head.

"No sergeant, not the river," Prentice told him tersely. "The town."

"For sooth?"

Prentice was not yet ready to say he was certain, but as he thought about it, he realized it made ready sense of their tactics. What other reason would they have to start firing in the night when they could hardly aim true and would have no way to see where their shots fell and adjust that aim when it was awry? Only if their target was so large that it could not be missed once they reached their range. Only if the town itself were the true target.

"If that's their play, then why set themselves up so far back from the water? Why not line 'em up right on the bank?"

"So they have time to retreat or organize some other defense when we go out to get them," Prentice said.

"Are we going to go get 'em?" That prospect seemed to appeal to Guillam.

"Eventually, we will have to," Prentice told him, and he turned away to look toward the firing positions still cloaked in ink, revealed only by the thunderous flames and smoke. He stood there for most of the night, quietly watching and contemplating, only speaking to answer the occasional question from Guillam. The firing continued, though at a diminished rate. Near dawn, Farringdon joined him, returning from the completed peacekeeping in the town, along with Sir Nunel and Sir Sedgemark.

"Markas has the Norgate command at the moment," the marquis explained as the trio arrived, "but I thought I'd bring you my sages of shot. Between the three of us, we might add up to the expertise of one Yentow Sent, God rest his soul."

"Your thoughts are welcome, sirs, My Lord." Prentice said, and just as the eastern horizon was lightening to cloud-drenched grey, the first whistle that ended with a crash of wood drew fresh shouts of alarm from Bridgetown. Across the simple river channel from the south bank of the river, the nearest island, called Greenmarsh was lined with a stone wall, from water line to above the level of any reasonable jetty. It was part of the town's defenses against the Vec. As Sougate was a bastion, so Greenmarsh's bank on this side was a castle wall, of sorts. Above that talus however, the island was the same mass of wooden structures leaning upon one another – warehouses and businesses amidst tenements and other civil buildings. It was one of these that the ranging shots of the Veckander cannons had now finally reached.

"That's a bullseye," one of the sentries facing the town called out of turn, but even as Guillam was moving to rebuke the man, a second shout sounded from somewhere downstream on the riverbank. Prentice and the other officers moved to that side and looked into the ground that was still lost to dawn shadows. They could not see who called, but they did locate a light, as of a lantern suddenly unhooded, waving back and forth in an obvious signal.

"Spotters," Nunel said simply, equating the men to the wide-ranging scouts who accompanied hunting parties, locating the game for the nobles to bring down.

"They'll have been waiting for that moment, I'll wager," Sedgemark added. "Holding the lit lantern closed all night just for this time. They know they have their range now."

"Which means those fisher boats in the channel had better take to the open water or their owners will lose them for good," Farringdon concluded. Within the hour his prediction was realized as the fortified channel cleared of every craft, a panicked flotilla rowing and poling its way desperately clear of thunderous iron. Even with the rapid response, three boats—one of them a large, flat-bottomed barge that could be used to haul vast amounts to and from the town—had been sent to the bottom. Prentice wondered what bold captain had thought to sail his cargo straight through the contested channel in the first place. The fishers he might understand—the day's catch on traditional runs being too valuable to give up easily—but the cargo vessel surely could have tried to reach its berth by some safer route. It made him wonder exactly how difficult it was to navigate the narrow, bridge and jetty congested paths of Bridgetown's other channels.

"It's not quite Robant's blockade, but they mean to choke off trade," Farringdon observed as yet more balls fell amongst the fleeing vessels.

"Can they, My Lord?" Sedgemark asked with a tone of dubiousness. "I mean, it's only one channel. There's plenty of docks on other islands. Maybe they just want to batter spots in the wall to land their own boats."

That sounded like a lot of effort for a small return to Prentice and it seemed Farringdon saw the enemy's plans the same way.

"With one gate blocked, and the other letting out onto a troubled road, even one channel cut short might be a fatal blow to Bridgetown, Knight Sergeant," Farringdon explained. "You only need to wound a man's heart to win against him, not smash every limb and organ into meat."

"Pleasant image," Nunel muttered, smirking, but no one laughed. They had all seen something like it in their time.

"What do you say, Knight Commander?" Farrindon asked Prentice.

As the night wore on, Prentice had become more acutely aware that the men around him were looking to him and listening out for any comment he might make. When he arrived, his mind had still been occupied with Inxyphos's appearance and the murders in the cathedral square, chewing it all over and trying to see what connections there might be with the previous attacks on the Archduchess's neophytes and Master Welburne. It had taken the knight commander time to come to grips with this new development. Then, he realized that his own uncertainties were not helping build confidence in his men's minds. He could share his thoughts with his senior officers, letting them air their own reflections. His rank-and-file men-at-arms had to see their leader sure footed, with a plan for victory and the confidence to see it carried through.

"I think, My Lord, that we should take a full report to her grace," he said at last. There were enough implications for them to consider, so that watching any more now would not help. He looked to Guillam.

"Keep watch and send to Sir Gennet to ready a force in case they turn their attention on our gatehouse," he told the sergeant as he gestured for the other officers to head to the nearest stair-well. "If they start to do something significant, fetch me from the Paramour's Chambers."

"Signif'cant, Knight Commander?" Guillam asked him, no doubt knowing how broad such a description could be. Any number of enemy actions could fit that bill.

"You will know it if you see it, Sergeant," was all Prentice could think to say. "I trust your judgement."

"Just do me the favour of rememberin' that fact when next comes time to hand out those honors her grace likes to bestow," Guillam sniped, his pensive expression giving way to the more usual impudence.

"You are impertinent, Sergeant," Farringdon said, half shocked and half amused.

"Guilty," Guillam responded. "And that's not the least of my true crimes, I promise you, My Lord Marquis Knight Captain."

In spite of his reckless insouciance, he still stood to attention and saluted with perfect discipline. Farringdon shook his head as if in disbelief before giving Prentice a sidelong look.

"I would have sworn there could only be one Sir Turley in this world," he joked quietly. Prentice chuckled and nodded.

"An unsettling thought, isn't it?"

And then they were off the roof, descending to return to the town down the same steps they had used to capture Sougate on a night not so long past—an age ago.

CHAPTER 57

Archduchess Amelia was already well informed of the attack on Bridgetown's southern warehouses and workshops, as almost immediately after dawn she had been called upon by a trio of finely dressed Conclave merchants, including a gold-pinned master of the Carder's Guild, lords over all things of wool, traded or woven. Forced to rise earlier than she would have preferred Amelia, was pleased that she felt no morning sickness at least.

"You're reaching the best part now, Your Grace, if I may say," Daisy had told her as she brushed her mistress's hair and helped her dress. "Your hair's getting thicker and beautifuller. Your cheeks'll blush with life soon and all."

That idea appealed to Amelia, and despite the harrowing recent days, she felt confident as she sat to receive the Conclave selectmen while she broke her fast on curds and licorice tea. The three men had bustled in with neophytes acting as escorting stewards, their hands clasped as if in earnest prayer, golden rings glittering on their fingers.

"They mean to ruin us, for it is we who are most affected," the carder master, whose name was Herrimans, declared with the passion of a player pledging his love in a romance. "Greenmarsh Island is called the wool island, everyone knows this. All our trade comes to Bridgetown there, and it is we who cover all the dock fees and tariffs. I cannot think why the Veckanders would hate us so that they would single us out for such treatment."

"Perhaps because yours are the only places they can target easily from their side of the river?" Lady Dalflitch ventured in a tone of impatience, as if having to explain the obvious to a dolt. To anyone else, the lady-in-waiting was ever the picture of perfect poise and beauty, but Amelia was sure she detected an air of weary impatience in her friend. The previous day's horrors, the long night awake, and worry for Spindle and her husband had not made for an easy passage of time, and it might be beginning to show. The notion of Dalflitch with frayed edges could almost be an amusing curiosity, if the causes were not so dire. The prospect that her pregnancy might lend her vitality while her famously beautiful lady-in-waiting was harried and worn was a cruel irony that nonetheless had a momentary appeal as well. Whatever the three Conclave men thought of Dalfitch's archness, they made no comment.

"However the cause," Master Herrimans continued, "it is we who are suffering. You have pledged to protect our town, and we thank you for the great service your forces have done in that—both at the cathedral and through the night. Despite what some are saying, we know who our savior was against that accursed assault on our peace. We do not fear to trade in gold."

What who are saying? Why would anyone "fear" to trade in gold? Amelia wondered. A number of possible whisperers presented themselves immediately—other members of the Conclave, the Young Hopefuls, the baroness herself, perhaps? A combination of all three? No, most likely agents of the Inquisition, following up their attack with confusion and misdirection. Like Bluebird as he had juggled, tumbled, and jested, seeming harmless, while all the time undermining her at every turn. As to fear? Of gold? That was a bewildering notion indeed. Amelia did not like merchants all being thought of as grasping livereaters, but that didn't mean they weren't profit-motivated men.

At that moment a neophyte curtseyed and announced Prentice and Farringdon, the two marching into the room with the echoing volume that men in armor inevitably made on floorboards. This time, though, her husband was the only one fully armored. Prentice was wearing just a gambeson on his chest. It was in a sense a wonder that he was still standing, knowing the power of the bear man's strike and how it must have hurt. Another debt owed to the belated Masnian master smith, never to be repaid. Amelia turned from the two commanders' arrival to the three men hunched in their pleading postures in front of her.

"See, gentles, my husband and knight captain, along with my knight commander, arrive to give us their report of the attack on your island and its holdings," she said. "Hark, and they will reassure you."

She gave Prentice a meaningful nod, trusting that he would be able to discern who her visitors were and what reassurance they would need. For herself, she wanted nothing more than to return to her bed. The sickness of early pregnancy seemed to have mostly missed her, but her freshening "glow" seemed to be coming with a desperate need for more rest and fewer late-night conferences. Instead, she contented herself with a sip of tea and prayed inwardly that Prentice would assuage the selectmen's fears and help them leave quickly.

"The houses on Greenmarsh Island are the current target, Your Grace," Prentice said, bowing as he did so.

"This is no news," one of the lesser merchants protested, but Prentice ignored him.

"Now that dawn is come, it is clear they have a full company of cannons, perhaps of a similar size to the ones that were lost to you at Aubrey."

Lost to me at Aubrey? Amelia repeated inwardly, noting that Prentice did not say "that you lost," because that might imply a failing on her part or Farringdon's. He was ever defensive of her honor.

Their loss was not my fault, Knight Commander, she thought, *but certainly I did not handle them or their destruction well.*

"A company?" she asked.

"At least eight, perhaps as many as twelve," Farringdon explained. "We have been judging by their fires in the dark, but some are more hidden behind the earthworks of their firing positions. Whoever commands them, he has a significant company of hands with shovels with him. Sedgemark could not believe how swiftly they put their embankments up, given his recent works at Norgate."

"What is to be done about them then?" Amelia continued.

"We will have to sally at some point, Your Grace," Prentice averred simply. "Knight Sergeant Gennet is already preparing a force for the task. It will be a simple command when the time comes."

"Then why, sir, have you not already done so? Why do you delay while we are tormented so vilely?" the merchant Herrimans demanded, also showing a strange readiness to become annoyed with men who should be seen as his superior. Was it his emotions or a touch of the more flexible manners of nearby Vec culture infecting this province literally in the border between the two great nations? Or something else? Did he think of the White Lions as of a caliber with Bridgetown's miserable militia?

If he does, it's a vile mistake, Amelia thought, not to mention making his earlier praise of her forces look like nothing more than insincere flattery.

"The *Baron* Knight Commander has not ordered a sally yet, Master, because as awful as the bombardment might be to you and yours, it might also be no more than a feint," Farringdon explained, clearly insulted on Prentice's behalf, even if the knight commander himself was showing no umbrage.

"A feint?" Herrimans repeated, as if the word were of a foreign tongue to him.

"Yes. In the darkness there was no way to know if Sobridge had a force poised and ready to ambush a sally, or even to rush the open gatehouse, seize it and then usher in a full conquering force. What of your precious businesses then, as Bridgetown was sacked by rapacious mercenaries? Aubrey was, only this last summer!

Sougate has been seized and recaptured in the past season. Would you have it risked to a third assault? Do you wish some kind of legacy of failure upon your town? Is yesterday's horror not enough for you?"

Amelia watched as Farringdon's beratement made Herrimans quail, the merchant turning visibly pale at his words. The other two clenched their hands together so tightly the joints went white, their attitude of prayer more desperate than ever.

"No, of course not, My Lord," Herrimans said, and he bowed to Farringdon, then turned to Prentice and bowed to him as well. "Please forgive me, My Lord Baron. I let my fears for my people run away with my tongue. I meant no insolence."

It wasn't much of an apology, but Amelia was not surprised when Prentice accepted it with a slight nod of his head.

"Gentles, be reassured that my forces will be turned to the protection of all of Bridgetown's folk, lowest to highest," she said, taking back control of the conversation despite her wishes. "As it was in the cathedral square yesterday, so it will be in front of Sougate and for your island. Please go so that I may consult my captains in private, but know that while there might seem to be some delay, we will act as soon as victory is certain. If you do not see the Lions, it is not because they are not there but because they are already crouched in the grass, stalking their prey."

"Bless you, Your Grace," Herrimans said, and the three dark-robed men bowed as they backed away from Amelia's chair, as if she were a monarch upon the throne. Once they were gone, she arched her back and yawned in a most unladylike fashion. As she fully expected, no one in the Paramour's Chamber took the least notice. She was the ranking peer after all, and from Prentice and Dalflitch down, no one here lacked for the right etiquette in such matters.

"Is it truly as simple as you say, Prentice?" she asked after sitting straight again and sipping some more tea. She waved to a neophyte to refresh her cup.

"There are some uncertain matters, but essentially yes," Prentice told her—a typically thoughtful and guarded answer, not lacking confidence but too honest to speak as if utterly sure.

"Such as?" Dalflitch asked as Amelia sipped the fresher fennel tea, thanking her attendant with a nod.

"They don't have enough men-at-arms on that field to stop a sally," Prentice said. "The last thing we did before coming from Sougate was to make a swift survey of the force the Town Sobridge prince is fielding. It is not large."

"'Tiny' was the word Sergeant Guillam used," Farringdon added. "Lucky if it's even a thousand, and over two-thirds are peasant levies, more equipped to dig the earthworks than to fight. I'd guess they were still bringing in their harvest not a week ago."

"Has the prince no knights?" Dalflitch asked.

"There are banners and pennants enough for fifty, or a hundred at the most. It is a small force, barely enough for the lesser wars Vec princes fight amongst themselves. It could never threaten Bridgetown with capture, even if they had three or four times the number of cannon."

"Do you suspect it must be an ambush? That he has some greater force in hiding?" the lady-in-waiting pressed.

"That makes the most sense, my love, but where? Every field from here to Town Sobridge proper itself is denuded. What woodlands he has are tame and tiny as well," Farringdon explained to his wife. "The nearest village is leagues away. There is simply nowhere to hide them."

"Then why attack?" Amelia asked, looking to Prentice, knowing he would have a suspicion and that it would be more trustworthy than most leaders' certainties.

"I think Town Sobridge's prince expected to assault a Bridgetown in confusion, bereft of its baroness and already turning on the heretic witch its populace had been told to blame," he explained, referring obviously to the previous day's cursed events and attempted assassination. If Inxyphos had managed to slay

Penelope, with her cathedral defiled into the process, there would have been no better time to attack her town.

"The Inquisition put him up to it?" Amelia asked but shook her head before either Prentice or her husband could answer. "No, of course they did. It is exactly in keeping with the kind of tactics a man of theirs, like Bluebird, or even those skin thieves, would use. If this liege of Town Sobridge is as weak in his own seat as his army makes it appear, then a swift campaign for the juiciest of prizes would have been easy bait to dangle."

The archduchess shook her head at the fact that the Inquisition must have agents not only inside Bridgetown's walls, but also just outside them, whispering to the Veckander enemies.

Unless the bold spies simply row back and forth in the night, she thought. Bridgetown's gates were shut, but its docks were always open, of course. If they were strong swimmers, they could make a nightly exercise of the waters, even if they had to swim all the way around Greenmarsh's high stone footings. Her teeth ground with frustration at the thought.

"Speaking of Bluebird, my love, Farringdon said, "am I the only one who recognized his presence in the fishwife's tale? The 'kindly uncle' with Inxyphos before he transformed? We know him by sight. I've not spoken of this with Baron Prentice, but I want to put some cohorts into the streets now to seek the mongrel out. We know he's here, and if he's engineered all this in the short time since we arrived, there's no knowing how much more trouble he will stir for us if we let him."

"An excellent idea, husband..." Amelia began but then, again, shook her head. "No. No we cannot send Lions. He will see them coming all the way from Dweltford. He escaped the castle with a crippled and bleeding knee, with Sir Turley hunting him like thunderous judgement. We need to spy him out or he'll find boltholes that we never will, and the trouble will be worse."

The archduchess reached out and touched her lady-in-waiting on the arm.

"We said yesterday that it was time for some of the neophytes to take their full place in my chamber. It is also time for them to take up their whole mission as my anonymous eyes and ears abroad in the world, and messengers to the former skips who now swear to us. We need to set the neophytes to find Bluebird."

"Your Grace, no," Dalflitch responded immediately, clearly aghast with more sincere emotion than she normally ever showed in public. "They aren't ready! They..."

She stopped and then gave a rueful chuckle.

"Look at me. I play the heartless witch with them day and night, but actually suggest they go to the duty for which we have been training them and suddenly I am their protective mother bear. One or two are most definitely ready, Your Grace, and others are good enough to give some support, at least in a riverside town like this. We could not send them to Rhales or Denay yet to pose as great ladies from lesser backgrounds, but for fishers and smugglers, they will fit in better even than most of Bridgetown's actual maids."

"Sending them to the docks is the right move," Prentice declared. "That burlap cover stank of seawater, and Bridgetown is a river community first and foremost. Whatever Bluebird or his equivalent is doing, the docks will be a part of it."

Perhaps we will learn word of spies crossing the water in the night as well, Amelia thought hopefully.

"We will devise a strategy for them to follow, My Lady," she ordered Dalflitch. "And as for Sobridge's diminutive force, Knights Commander and Captain, I will send to Earlsbastion with word that the White Lions will yet again rescue Lady Penelope's seat from its enemies. Let her dislike our alliance in the face of that."

Her retainers all nodded their acceptance, but before they could go to their respective duties, a neophyte entered swiftly, turning up her veil to reveal Seskia's face.

"Your Grace, I had to bring this to you, straight quick," she said, rushing to the table and stopping with a smooth curtsey. In her hands was a sheet of some kind of paper, obviously cheaper and flimsier than vellum, and by the look, block-printed rather than written upon. A handbill perhaps? "I can't read it proper, of course, but the picture's easy enough to understand, and a butcher's boy read it me when I asked. It's bad—no, it's wrong. Wrong is what it is."

Amelia received the sheet from the girl's hand and turned it around to read it. There was a picture of the bear in the center, fallen and bleeding, with a pair of dashing-looking young men standing over it, stabbing it with sideswords. The archduchess read the banner over the picture and the commentary underneath. With a sour frown, she flicked the sheet at Dalflitch, barely able to restrain herself from crumpling the document in fury.

"Well at least now we know what 'they' are saying about me," she muttered darkly. Dalflitch held up the paper and read it aloud.

"Praise be to God for the Young Hopeful squires, loyal sons of Bridgetown. Our beloved Baroness lives this day only by the swift, courageous intervention of these orphaned knights. If not for them, Lady Penelope would have fallen in front of the cathedral, slain by disgusting sorcery and beasts from the west. How long will we endure the witch from across the mountains in our home? Could we hope upon the Hopefuls to put an end to her threats as well?"

Farringdon looked at his wife with a pained expression, clearly hurt for her by the slanderous words. Prentice only scowled, expression more thoughtful and as furious-seeming as Amelia felt.

"Our whispering enemy, whoever they exactly are, has limitless cunning and energy, friends," the archduchess told them through clenched jaws, her hands gripping the arms of her chair tightly to keep from slamming them on the table. "Let us be just as canny and even more industrious. Go to your tasks and let us make an end to the Bluebird's songs. I have heard them enough for a lifetime."

CHAPTER 58

Despite the urging of the Conclave merchants and the arch-duchess's promise to render swift aid, Prentice did not lead the Gryphon Banner Company out of Sougate that day. Watching through the afternoon, he was still not convinced that the bombardment was not bait to a larger trap. As sundown approached, the rate of fire began to slow and then died away completely when the sun touched the horizon.

"Thank the Lord," Sergeant Porth said on the battlement, having relieved Guillam earlier in the day. He rubbed at his jaw. "Was starting to make my teeth ache."

Prentice could understand that. There was something about having cannon fire even nearby that twisted the nerves. Likely, Porth had been clenching his jaw for some time and not even realized.

Darkness fell over the land like a cloak, and still no additional forces had appeared. More than once in the preceding hours Prentice had thought to regret having sent Dahyoor north on his scouting mission. A few hours in the dark southward fields and the uncanny sight of the fey would have found out any lurking ambush force.

"Perhaps they are coming up now in the dark," he muttered.

"I reckon they must have a mountain of black powder down there, if they was prepared to throw so much iron and fire at us," Porth observed. He looked back at the town, so much of the near island dark now, the harried sections of Greenmarsh clearly hoping to hide themselves in the night. Not like the bustling docks and suspended wooden walkways of the previous evening. Bridgetowners scarcely slept, it seemed, but now the vulnerable island warehouses were as black as the night sky and silent as the grave. Pity the warehouse guards trying to stop sneak thieves in that environment. No doubt men like the skips bandits would be out now, thinking to exploit the damaged walls on the waterfront.

"And what was it for?" Porth continued, studying the darkened island. "Four boats sunk, only one of them a significant-looking thing, that one poor fellow smashed about and killed, and a some pockmarks in the stone footings. A lot of powder for a little fire, if you ask me."

A cannon ball had struck a riverside worker by sheer fluke in the day, killing him instantly, but he was the only one.

"They are certainly no Bronze Dragons," Prentice agreed, but that was not their true purpose, he was all but certain now. Perhaps they were not the bait he feared them to be, but once the dozen artillery pieces were turned on Sougate directly, even the stout bastion would not last more than a few days. Perhaps this was a prelude to drive away any militia that might wait on the nearby island to help defend the Sougate from serious assault. If the Inquisition was prompting the prince of Town Sobridge to the attack and was also helping to finance the Golden Heron's army, perhaps the Veckander ruler had slipped his leash a fraction early. Perhaps the Heron was supposed to be here by now but had been detained unexpectedly. The rains were still infrequent but would break out fully any day now, so if they were coming, they had not timed their march well.

"What is the prince of Town Sobridge's name, Sergeant? Have we learned?"

"No idea, My Lord," Porth responded. "I heard some fellows were asking about for you, but none of 'em come back with any answers."

"We fight too much of this cursed war in the dark," Prentice said and released the bastion roof to his sergeant's command.

Come the dawn, if the Golden Heron or another Vec force had not made an appearance in the night, he would lead a sally and put as many of those guns out of commission as he could—or, better yet, capture some for his own use. Knight Captain Farringdon would dance for joy at the prospect of turning cannon back on their enemies, revenge for the Inquisition's sabotage at Aubrey.

Prentice returned to spend the evening with his wife and children, enjoying the simple pleasure of holding each of his twins in his arms, one at a time, then both together before handing them back to the nursemaid.

"You'll be needing a new brigandine," Righteous said quietly, staring at the flames as she breastfed little Amy.

"I have Gennet scaring up a temporary replacement for me," he told her.

"Pah, it'll fit like a wine barrel, for sure," she told him dismissively. "That plate shirt of yours had been made 'special for you. Any old other's just not going to fit right. You need another special made."

"Even if Master Sent were not gone, there is no time for something like that. My gambeson is thick enough to protect from anything that pinches, at least for the hour or so that this battle should take."

"Oh ay? As if our enemies is so polite as to stick to our candle's hours." She looked away for a moment, cooing encouragements to Amelia, softly rocking. Then she turned her face back to Prentice. The orange firelight cast her face in profile, so that the shadowed side was like her lace half mask, though the sides were reversed and her brawler's brand was plainly visible.

"I hate your brigandine's been ruined, but mostly I hate that I wasn't there to see it," she whispered.

"You wanted to see me nearly gutted?" Prentice asked her.

"I wanted to see you gut that Inquisition coxcomb," she responded with a vehemence that caused their daughter to grumble at nearly being dislodged before she was finished feeding. "From stomach to sternum, someone said. Butchered the beast but good. My man."

"You are an odd mother, wife," Prentice said, smiling at the juxtaposition of her loving care for their child and the savage, bloodthirsty expression on her face.

"I am the mother of your children, Baron Ash, and perfect for the role. I'll put a knife to any that calls that to question."

"You are, indeed, darling," Prentice said, and he leaned forward to kiss her gently on the forehead. "I will take some rest now. We will be readying to march out as soon as dawn shows."

Righteous nodded happily and turned back to gently rocking Amy.

CHAPTER 59

Dawn was delayed by the densely overcast sky, but in the greying light, two things were plain enough to see. The first was that whatever force Town Sobridge may or may not have been waiting upon, it had not arrived. The other was around half the Gryphon Banner Company, lined in the Great Bridge Road at the far side of the river's southern channel next to the buildings that had yesterday been smacked at by cannonballs. The columns were ready for the order to attack, when they would rush across the bridge and swift-march to the cannons behind their embankments and long ditch to engage the Sobridge footmen and the few knights that accompanied them. The plan was for the Gryphons to make for one of the flanks of the dirt constructions as swiftly as possible so they would spend as little time in front of the cannons, exposed to shots, as they could.

"We will sweep around the west side, Knight Captain," Prentice gave his final orders. Today, for the first time ever, he would be riding a horse into battle, looking to command rather than to fight from the front. This was not a field of his choosing, and he needed to see more than his men needed to believe he was right in amongst them. He also did not want to spend the next hours on foot with his ill-fitting replacement brigandine. Despite his objection to his wife, the piece was quite uncomfortable to move in, pinching under his shoulders. The bruising ache from the bear man's hit was not much diminished, either. In all, he was in significantly more discomfort than he cared to admit. He wondered if he could scare up some apothecary's remedy for the pain—like the gum with willow bark essence in it—but there was no time to go looking now.

The Gryphon standard had been given to a man named Gerrindon—a stout, broad-shouldered corporal whom Gennet assured his knight commander was ready to step up to the role of banner sergeant. Prentice placed the man into the ranks of the company's first cohort and planned to ride beside that square during the start of the battle. He looked over his shoulder to Gennet standing in the Bridgetown side doorway of Sougate's main chamber. The heavy wooden door to Bridgetown was open, and the moment Prentice gave the order, the sergeant's chosen drummers would beat it out, summoning the company. That was when the Vec side door would be opened for the first time in almost a year, and not for trade. This would also be the first time in over a century that a Kingdom army, albeit a Reach army, would invade the Vec from this fortification. It felt to Prentice a good sight more risky than historic.

"That's as light as we need, Sergeant Gennet," Prentice said, noting the overcast sky. "Give the order, and remember, take only the time to form the columns into cohort squares. We need fleetness of foot more than massed ranks at the first." He turned to Farringdon, seated on his own mount beside him. "If you will bring your lancers out to the left flank, My Lord. Watch for any oblique marches."

Farringdon nodded and put his helmet on his head, riding back to join the lancers waiting behind the Gryphons. In a quarter of the candle, three hundred horsemen and over two thousand men-at-arms afoot would be formed up and bearing down on the cannon's insufficient escort force. At least that was the plan. Prentice was just about to signal for the drumbeat when a militiaman half tumbled out of the stairs that led to the rooftop.

"My Lord!" he was shouting even before he came out the bottom. "My Lord Knight Commander! Word from the sentry corporal. There's fresh troops on the move."

The Veckanders had arrived, but were they the Heron or a new force?

"From which direction?" he demanded. "The Town Sobridge road or from the west?"

"Neither, My Lord," the messenger said almost out of breath even from the short journey from roof to tower floor. "They're crossin' in boats on the west side of the bridge."

"Boats? On the west side?" For a moment Prentice could not credit the report. The west side was upstream, the Murr going back to the Dwelt and then all the way into Radengon-Beyond-Dwelt. There was no boat floating on those waters that did not owe allegiance to Archduchess Amelia or Baroness Penelope. Except...? For a long, horrifying moment Prentice thought the Redlanders had returned, that they must have found some way to repair the toppled dragonfly and were traversing their boats through mirrored skies once more. Then his mind lit on the one word he had not noticed.

"Crossing?" he repeated, and the messenger nodded vehemently.

"They's comin' across from the islands," the militiaman confirmed, "in every kind of boats they might find, I'd guess. Must've taken 'em from other docks. It's the Bridgetowner militia by its colors, almost the whole of them. It's gotta be!"

The Bridgetown militia? Prentice's mind raced as he tried to factor in this new development. The handbill was the key, he realized. Could the town hope upon the Young Hopefuls to save it? That was the Inquisition plan, he was sure. There would be no reinforcements arriving to save Town Sobridge or its cannons. The Young Hopefuls would rescue Sougate from the sieging war engines and so save the town "again," proving that Bridgetown had no real need of the White Lions. For sure, the Bluebird's song was being whispered in Lady Penelope's ear right now, pressing her to abolish the alliance. And the proud and resentful Hopefuls would gladly play the heroes, regardless of how treacherously their glory might be won. Prentice wondered if they even knew they were being used. Surely Wilforn and Cassian would not care, even if they did.

"Hold the drums, Sergeant, and let's get that door open," he commanded loudly, and soon the complex bolts and bars were slid back, an entire militia-line of ten men operating the mechanisms in the room above. The oaken boards of the doors, a handspan thick, swung as lightly on their complex hinges as curtains in a breeze.

The first time in over a century, Prentice thought, and he geed Boots over the threshold. Hardly was he even onto the ramp that led the road up to the barbican than he could see the Bridgetown militia forming up on the riverbank to his right, not far from where he and his infiltrators had come ashore the night they took Sougate from the Usurper's men. Behind them, a dozen or more lighters and heavy barges lolled in the shallows, and sure enough, it looked like the entire of the militia, all three hundred or so. Already lined up in front of the men afoot were about thirty or forty young men on horseback, dressed from head to toe in white steel plate—more Young Hopefuls than Prentice had realized there were. It seemed they had decided they were knights enough to fight in the traditional Grand Kingdom manner, and even as Prentice watched, someone in their force blew a challenging trumpet and the whole body began to move forward, heading to the western flank of the cannon embankment, the side Prentice had intended his own men to take.

Very well.

Prentice turned in the saddle to look back into the shadows of the main gate chamber.

"Gennet, up here!"

The sergeant trotted forward, and Prentice scanned a finger across the entire developing situation.

"Change of plans. I will take command of the lead cohorts and form them up on me," he said quickly, trusting Gennet to follow his thinking. "We will march to the left side of the embankment and trap the Town Sobridge force on the opposite end. I will put the squares together and set them straight to the fight. You run back and tell the knight captain what you see here. Then return to find me with the banner. You are going to have to be my runner for the first part of the morning."

Gennet accepted the change without question and saluted before heading back down the bridge to the waiting columns. The drumbeat commenced, and the main gate reverberated with its echoes so that the two lads chosen for the task sounded like twenty. Double time, long polearms tilted back to fit under the high roof that was still too low for pikes five paces in length, the first columns rattled over the bridge and emerged from the gate, trotting down the ramp, Prentice and Boots at their head. As soon their feet reached the level of the fields, they veered left off the road, aiming for the eastern end of the heaped-earth fortification, so rough and swiftly built that the Sobridge force had not even begun to put wooden stakes or a palisade in place. Perhaps the prospect of a counterattack had not occurred to the Vec prince. If so, the man was even more unready to lead an invasion than it appeared.

Regardless of Town Sobridge's unreadiness, Prentice kept his eyes on the heaped earth and the places where the cannon barrels could just be made out, poking over the top, leaning back on the reverse slope for maximum range. This was the moment of greatest danger, and if there was to be an ambush, this was where they would spring it. A ready force, out of sight somehow behind the barricade, could ride around the side he was aiming for, pinning his company in place and bring it to a halt right under the guns, ripe for a hammering. With the whole Gryphon Banner coming double file across the bridge at once, there would be no possibility to retreat. The way back would be blocked. And it would be next to impossible to form their strong squares under cannon, not so close. Even a single shot would rip a file to carrion, as Marquis Farringdon had once remarked when he first proposed these weapons for the Reach. Town Sobridge had twelve pointed at them. In fact, there was no need for an ambush. If the cannoneers were even merely watchful, they could react now, and the same problem would beset the Gryphons.

Pray God they are still abed, he thought. *But if they are not, we will have to assault that ditch and embankment straight up and over, in column.*

An attack in column could be a disaster in itself, since it meant only two men would be at the front. Like feeding a string of sausages into a hungry dog's mouth, the beast would only have to keep biting. Maybe it would choke, eventually, but it would swallow a lot of sausages before it did.

"Form the front from here," Prentice bellowed, and one of the drummers left his marching beat to run up the side and stand beside Prentice's horse. He drummed a new rhythm, and for a moment the first eight men in each paired column came to a stop, marching in place. Behind them the next eight stepped to the right and came up beside them so that two short columns of eight men became four. Then, the next eight pairs of men stepped further to the side and four lines became six, then eight, and finally ten, forming a square block of eighty men, ten across the front and eight rows deep. Two smaller blocks of ten men each formed at the front corners of that larger square—the Roar, with their long-matches smoking readily and their powder horns hung from baldrics across their chests. They would fire from the flanks, ready to flee into the main body for protection if they were suddenly charged. That was one cohort, one hundred—the Lion's basic battlefield unit. With time and space, each successive cohort would form up next to its precedents, as close or distant as needed for safety or flexible maneuver, until they were one whole battlefront. This field's peculiarities allowed them no time or space, however, and Prentice sent the first hundred to sweep around the enemy's flank immediately and begin the assault while the second cohort began to form itself up from the marching columns.

A trumpet sounded again from the west, and the knight commander looked for a moment at the Bridgetowner advance, already sweeping into the field around the west side of the earthworks. Compared to the precision of the Gryphon Banner Company, the town militia was little more than a rabble—a crowd of armed men moving en mass but with almost no structure at all. The Young Hopefuls, as proud and mighty as any formation of knights ahorse, were already charging ahead, long streamers of orange and gold trailing in the wind of their gallop. Prentice thought he recognized the Bridgetown bear on one standard near their middle and imagined the rest of the pennants were cut from the accession day's bunting. He wondered idly for a moment if the would-be knights had bothered to pay the Conclave for the cloth.

The sound of matchlock shots drew Prentice's mind back to his side of the field, just as the third cohort was marching away and the fourth was forming up. The first cohort, already past the edge of the embankment, had found at least one cannoneer crew trying to bring their gun to bear in defense and had started to shoot to clear them away.

"The Bridgetowners are going to get themselves shot if they ain't careful, My Lord," Sergeant Porth said, appearing at Prentice's stirrup as his chosen cohort began to form.

It was a fair point. The earthwork defense was barely two thirds of a league from one end to the other, no more than six or seven hundred paces. With the Gryphons shooting along its length from one end and the Bridgetown militia attacking at the other end, the Roar were essentially firing directly at them. If the two groups closed too quickly, allied militiamen were bound to be hit by errant fire.

"When you get into the thick of it, be sure to pass the word that the Roar should take care," Prentice told the sergeant, who was already moving off with his cohort. "But conquer the guns first. I'll not curse a Roarsman whose duty caught a fool ally unawares."

"As you say, My Lord," Porth shouted over his shoulder. The sergeant knew well, as all the officers down to the line firsts had been told, that the cannons were their absolute first tactical priority. If they could be seized, the rest of the battle was a different prospect. Barring the possible ambushing force, which was becoming increasingly an unfounded fear, Town Sobridge had nothing like the forces to resist the Gryphons.

For what felt like no time at all but must surely have been close to half of the candle, Prentice watched the company go one cohort at a time around the flank. Then Sergeant Gennet came up with the final hundred, followed swiftly by the hoofbeats of the lancers as they rode out of Sougate and off to the farther left flank to sweep around the cohorts already engaged or marching to battle. The sounds of Roar fire were still only sporadic, but a small cloud of powder smoke was rising now from behind the eastern end of the earthworks. Occasionally, some sounds of shouts or clashes rang in the air, but it was nothing like the full cacophony of battle, at least not as Prentice and his men had known it in their time.

"I leave you to anchor the tail, Sergeant Gennet," Prentice told him as the last cohort formed up. "I want to see what's happening behind that wall."

"You should have an escort, My Lord," Gennet said, and Prentice smiled at the truth of it. One man alone on a horse might be spared as a messenger, or he might be trapped and taken down as an easy target, ripe for a ransom.

"I will go with the lancers," he said. "My squire is still away."

Gennet saluted and marched with his unit while Prentice wheeled Boots to canter towards the lancers, satisfied with their initial progress. The first part of the battle had gone exactly as planned, even with the Young Hopefuls' unexpected involvement. For the sake of his militiamen, he prayed the rest was as smoothly done.

CHAPTER 60

"Welcome, Knight Commander," Farringdon called, his helmet visor tipped open as he led his cantering force to a slower walk, watching the ground behind the cannons and looking for the most useful place for his horsemen to deploy. "It seems the Lord has blessed us with the run of the field."

"So far," Prentice said, sounding less confident than he felt at that moment. His own helmet was still on his saddle, though, and while he had yet to have need of it, he realized it was foolish not to put it on. He tried to fit it one-handed, needing the other for his reins, but the awkward motion almost tipped him from the saddle. Knight Captain Farringdon watched po-faced as Prentice righted himself, but the knight commander could see the amusement in his eyes.

"None of you mongrels better smirk," he declared, casting a scathing glance over the nearby horsemen of the formation, any one of whom was ten or twenty times the rider Prentice would ever be.

"No, My Lord," one of them protested loudly. "We've all had troubles with our gear at times. Especially with an *old saddlebag.*"

You have been speaking to Dahyoor, lancer, Prentice thought, scowling, but actually pleased to think that the exiled fey man might be gaining some friendships amongst the White Lions in general.

"The phrase you want, militiaman, is *palpalon* elder," he said coldly. "And if I ever hear you using it, you will be shoveling my two horses' dung from here to doomsday. Am I clear?"

"Perfectly, My Lord," the man replied, seeming more pleased to have scored a secret point off his leader than chastised by the threat. Let him be. Prentice had more pressing concerns than his own deserved indignity as a horseman.

"How well do we look, My Lord?" he asked Farringdon, buckling his helmet strap and wishing he had taken the time since coming back from the west to get himself an arming cap. The poorly padded steel still felt uncomfortable on his head.

Too bad, he told himself and listened to Farringdon's assessment of the field.

"The Gryphons are doing so well, I think we will be unnecessary," the marquis reported with an almost disappointed air. "It looks to me as if we've used a one-ton block to drive a single nail, a team of draft horses to drag no more than a pound sack of grain."

Prentice looked, standing in the stirrups, and surveyed the field as it stood beyond the earthworks. The cannons already had Reach militiamen standing on or by them from one end of the digging to the other—two or three cohorts by the look. The rest of the Gryphons were in a single mass, apparently engaging with the Town Sobridge levies. Even now, the volleys of Roar fire had died away, which made Prentice think that, despite the continued shouts, his sergeants judged the battle almost concluded there as well. A trumpet blast drew his eyes southward.

"That was their camp, I would guess," Farringdon said, following Prentice's gaze. Not more than three hundred paces back from the cannons, a small cluster of bright tents, typical of knights on campaign, was gathered, surrounded by what must have been the cookfires and bedding of the Vec princedom's foot troops. The poor levies must have slept the night in the open air, as they had no tents of their own it seemed. Unpleasant in the autumn weather.

The trumpet blast that had caught Prentice's attention came from the open space between the camp and the cannon bastion, where two forces of knights ahorse did battle in the traditional fashion over the stubbled field.

"Would you say they are both about the same numbers?" Prentice mused, watching the companies clash, then withdraw from the melee and reform for another charge. It was an ancient and outmoded tactic he recognized all too well.

"Sobridge has about fifty to the Young Hopefuls' forty or so, by my count," Farringdon said. "The princedom of Town Sobridge has never been known to be powerful, being mostly content to buy its enemies off with shares of the trade taxes from the Great Bridge Road, but I never had any idea their forces were this small. And poorly skilled as well, by the look of it. The Young Hopefuls have their measure."

It seemed true, from this distance. The Hopefuls' charges pushed the Town Sobridge knight force back farther and farther with each clash, slowly whittling their numbers down.

"Perhaps he has other knights tied down elsewhere," Prentice wondered out loud. "But then why attack Bridgetown? Why commit himself to two conflicts at once?"

"Excess trust in his cannons?" Farringdon offered.

"Indeed, though not everyone has the advantage of having been forced to hold the field while Baron Ironworth and the Bronze Dragons rained hell upon them."

"That is true, My Lord."

"Well, Marquis Farringdon, I think our allies have the Town Sobridge prince's measure, but I would have you wait here in case things turn poor for them. Ride to their rescue if they need, but otherwise let the orphans have their moment of glory. Perhaps it will cool their ardor for praise. In the meantime, I am going to see this last fight of the foot up closer. Would you loan me a line of your lancers? My fey riders have not returned yet."

It felt almost too easy to Prentice to be upon this particular battlefield, and even though he joked as he always did to seem fearless to those under his command, this time he really did feel unafraid. Even so, men were dying while he jested, and it left an unpleasant taste in his mouth—the bitterness of disgust.

"Line First Lyrach?" Farringdon shouted, "the Gryphon requires your service once more—you and your line."

From the body of the lancers, ten riders trotted up, Lyrach in the lead, his helmet's visor raised as most of the lancers' were.

"My Lord, Knight Commander," he said, slapping his gauntleted fist against his chest.

"You are my escort for now, Lyrach," Prentice said simply. "I mean to ride up onto that poor rampart and along until we can see the fronts of the men afoot. It sounds like we are not far from victory, but I want to see for myself."

The line of lancers took up flanking positions beside Prentice and Boots, and they trotted the short distance to the cannon emplacements, quickly mounting the embankment to see a cluster of men in plain tunics kneeling amidst a cohort of Gryphons acting as guards. When the Reachermen noticed their commander approaching, a cheer went up, and it progressed to the other militiamen standing over captured cannons and ammunition. Even some of the cohorts standing at the rear of the fighting took up the praise and celebration, making Prentice hope it was not premature.

"Make sure to secure any fires, Corporal," Prentice commanded a junior Roar officer whose cohort appeared to have seized the cannoneers' supply of cannonballs and barrels of black powder. Not quite the mountain Sergeant Porth had imagined but an excellent addition to the Lions' stores. As long as it survived the battle.

"Already ordered, My Lord," the corporal said proudly. "Powder's a wild bitch not one of us trusts with a loose flame."

"Good man," Prentice said and then geed Boots along behind the cannons. The normally placid mount shied once or twice when confronted with a fallen body or blood, but she accepted his hands on the reins and did not really rebel. Soon, the ride along the raised earth beside the massed footmen brought Prentice to the front of the fighting, expecting to have to be wary in case his little escort became dragged into the fray. What he found made him nearly curse.

"What in God's name?" he muttered.

CHAPTER 61

"The battle's over, My Lord," Gennet reported as he detached himself from his cohort once more and moved behind the front ranks to Prentice's position on the cannon barricade, what was essentially now the right wing of the Gryphon's formation. The banner was currently raised in the middle of the line, and Gennet had been near to it when Prentice had sent one of the lancers to fetch him out. It was a simple enough matter because, as the sergeant said, the battle was over, or at least it should have been.

"They come out of their camp at us in just a crowd," Gennet explained. "We formed up and commenced to fire, but they ignored that and tried for the cannons. My guess is that they had protecting these guns as their first aim, but that was already too late. The First Cohort was up on the mounds, driving back the gunner men no problem. We had those ones wrapped up sweet in no time."

He pointed to the clustered prisoners being held near the middle of the line of earthworks, close by to the captured supply of ammunition and powder. Prentice was not surprised to hear that the Town Sobridge footmen had tried to defend the cannons. From a tactical point of view, that would have to be their prime mission in the siege. If they had been under his command, they would have been stationed at either end of the barricade, even camping there, so that sweeping around them to attack the cannons would have been so much more difficult, especially if they were sleeping in the open anyway. And they should have been digging all day and night to extend the front of that defensive work around the sides so it was more like a fort of its own.

"By the time they knew it was a fool's errand, they were already caught between our boys and the Bridgetowners," Gennet continued to explain. "They're just levies, My Lord. Not a one of them's got a weapon worthy of the name, just billhooks on sticks. It's like a rogues 'foot all over again. A couple of volleys from half the Roar and they were throwing down their weapons and we were taking prisoners. They never even dared our pikes, let alone needing the Fangs into the fight."

"Then what the devil is happening?"

Prentice asked because from where he was standing on the Gryphon's side of the battle, Gennet's story made perfect sense. Barefoot peasants wearing no more than the clothes they would wear any other day and carrying tools turned to makeshift weapons were being taken prisoner by the front ranks of the company. They were being disarmed, the levies seeming almost eager to surrender, which made an uncanny sense because on the other side of the battlefield, the Bridgetown militia were hacking their way into the ranks of Sobridge levies as if it were Armageddon and no man thought to survive the day.

"They surrendered, My Lord," Gennet said with a shrug. "Every man jack of them, but the Bridgetowners wouldn't have it. They just started in at them. The fellas that threw down their weapons, they were the first to go. Others have been picking them back up and trying to defend themselves, but the orange and gold? They're like men possessed. They ain't giving any quarter. We're takin' prisoners, but it's like rescuing men out of the raging floodwaters, not taking pledges of parole."

Even as Prentice watched, the crowd of Town Sobridge levies was shrinking under the horror of the advancing massacre. Already, a force that should have outnumbered the Bridgetown militia three to one looked to have shrunk to a roughly equal number. The screams and cries of the wounded were being cut short as any who fell were hacked apart on the ground, and more and more were turning to flee toward the refuge that being a White Lions' prisoner would offer. It would be moments before the crowd of rogues 'foot would be dissolved completely. On the opposite flank, some tried to escape south, but the Bridgetowners saw them and ran to interpose themselves.

"They've gone mad," Lyrach said at Prentice's side, the horror in his voice as clear on every man's face. Wherever the knight commander looked, his men-at-arms were appalled and disgusted by what was happening only paces in front of them. Most were still green. The only battle they had seen previously was the almost casual march to lift Robant's siege, not counting the equally easy action that had fallen on the small force that Inxyphos had abandoned on the shore of the Dwelt when he escaped from the dragonfly lake. Even so, the experienced militiamen amongst them were also markedly unnerved. Line firsts urged Claws to keep their pikes and halberds ready, recognizing that bloodlust like this could easily spill over allies if it ran out of enemies to slay.

"I reckon they want revenge for the firing on the town," Gennet said.

"Or for the attack on their baroness," Lyrach offered.

"Or just for the vexation of being cooped up in their homes for months," Gennet went further, but Prentice did not care what motivated this obscenity, only that it be stopped. But how? He was all but certain the Bridgetown force would not listen to him. Even if they were of a mind to be calmed, who were their officers to begin the process with? In all their days so far, working near to them and then taking them to the camp for training, no militia leaders or officers had ever been named, other than the long-slain knights and nobles for whom the Young Hopefuls served as poor stand-ins.

Any moment now and we will come to blows ourselves, Prentice thought. What would that mean for the alliance between the baroness and the archduchess? How else could he stop them, though?

"Lyrach, bring me whoever the captured cannoneers have by way of a leader," he said, following a hopeful thought. Perhaps they could get the gunners to turn one of their cannons around and fire a shot with powder, no ball. Musket fire would not slow the maddened militiamen, he was sure, not without firing straight into them, which he could not order. Perhaps a cannon shot would frighten them a moment long enough to restore order. "Swiftly man."

Prentice was thankful Lyrach asked no questions, only wheeling his mount in place and riding back the short distance to the prisoners. As it was, he would be too late. A trumpet blew from the south, a long fanfare, as of a victory, and it resounded again, yet still the killing continued. Knight Captain Farringdon rode up at a gallop with two lancers beside him behind the front, between the first line of cohort squares and the second, who would have been used as a reserve if the first had experienced a real fight.

"The Young Hopefuls have their victory," he shouted, flipping up his salet's visor. "It was hard to see, but it looked like they captured the prince of Sobridge's own standard. They're taking parol...oh, good God!"

His report choked off as he saw the slaughter happening not twenty paces away. The harvested grainfield was littered with bodies and crimson with their blood. Wherever a fallen man lay and moved, a murderous militiaman pounced upon him with a dagger. Suddenly, like a tiny puddle of water boiling on a hot skillet, the Town Sobridge levies evaporated as a body of men. The last few who hoped to survive were still trying to fit in between the Gryphons' pike points, fearful of stabbing themselves, with their empty hands raised high in surrender. Some of the Bridgetowners saw them being delayed, and like a pack of slavering dogs moved to attack them, but they were confronted by the Claws themselves and pulled up surprised when the Gryphon Banner did not yield to let them pursue their prey. Some of them snarled or hissed, seeming yet more like wild animals.

"Back away!" someone in the front line shouted clearly in the rapidly gathering quiet. There was something like a collective growl from the enraged Bridgetowners, and it was answered by a drumbeat for ready arms, and as one, the Gryphon Company stamped one step forward. With both he and Gennet not in the line, Prentice felt an instant's pride at his militiamen's self-possession and discipline.

Pity it's not like to stop anything now, he thought, though it looked it could if they let it. The Bridgetowners could see their enemy being taken prisoner and cowering behind the White Lions, who now looked more like enemies than allies. All that was obvious in their expressions. It would still take only one wild fool to leap to the attack and a hundred allied madmen at least would throw themselves to their death on Reacher pikes. Prentice had no fear for his men. Even if his company didn't outnumber the remaining Bridgetown militia nearly ten to one, he favored the wild louts not one whit to win a fight against even one cohort of the Gryphons or the Lion Banner.

Before the seemingly inevitable could happen, the entire contingent of the Young Hopefuls charged into the no-man's-land between the two allied forces, their heavy destriers kicking up ruddy clods of earth and smashing the bodies of the fallen beneath their iron shod hoofs. At their head were three men in full steel harness, anonymous behind closed visors. One carried the rampant bear standard, and another had a different cloth, this one predominantly red, bundled on his saddle in front of him. At the back of their small company, a string of knights—all on foot, their helmets removed, and their hands tied together—were forced to run hard to keep up with their captors. Bridgetown's men-at-arms ahorse had thought to take prisoners this time, at least. As the riders reined in, the standard bearer flipped up his visor to reveal Wilforn, his expression exultant.

"Rejoice, we are victorious," he shouted, and beside him the rider bearing the red cloth hefted it over his head, revealing it to be what Prentice took as the captured banner of the prince of Town

Sobridge. As it fluttered from one hand, the third rider fished into a bag hung on his pommel and dragged out a severed head, which he held aloft as triumphantly as the other had the banner. The blood-maddened militia erupted into cheers that sounded to Prentice more like the baying of wild dogs.

CHAPTER 62

Bridgetowner militiamen spat at the captured Veckander knights as they were led past, the riders that held their ropes already leading them off to the west around the cannon bastion and back to Bridgetown. Some of the other Hopeful squires followed them, perhaps as an escort, and some of the militiamen went as well. Most, though, stayed watching, as if expecting something more to happen. It seemed they had no idea how to tell when a battle was concluded. Prentice walked his horse forward, Farringdon with him, and was not surprised when the two other leaders ahorse lifted their visors to reveal Cassian and Cyprian. It was Cassian who had the Sobridge prince's head.

"Did you come to witness our great victory?" he asked, and he looked as drunk on success as the militia had been on blood.

"You seem to have done well, Cassian," Prentice said loudly. "What little I saw of your charges showed courage and might."

"Ha! Faint praise," the Young Hopeful scoffed, and he waved his trophy again, ugly droplets falling from the wound. "I took the head of a Veckander prince! The first Kingdom man to do it in who knows how long?"

"Seventy-six...no, seventy-eight years," Farringdon muttered out of the side of his mouth. Prentice nodded without looking to his second-in-command. As a former prince himself, it was the kind of historic detail Farringdon was likely to know well.

"You are to be congratulated on your remarkable achievement," Prentice told the young man. "I am sorry I did not witness it myself, but I was distracted, leading my men to bring your unruly gang of cutthroats to heel."

"You say what?" Cassian demanded, as if Prentice's words were a challenge. It seemed the hot-headed squire could take anything that way.

"They were slaughtering prisoners rightly surrendered," Farringdon shouted in a sudden burst of fury, and Prentice realized just what it meant to him to see men he once thought of as countrymen, of a sort, murdered in front of him.

"*We* took the prisoners," Wilforn objected, looking benignly bemused, as if he was talking to a drunk or a fool.

"Not your ransoms, boy!" Farringdon spat, ready to give full vent to his feelings now. "These you see fallen around you."

Wilforn and Cassian both looked over the field, as if only now noticing the hundreds of corpses and the stained earth. Cyprian also scanned the gathered militia, quieted at last, but drenched in blood such that their gold and orange colors were now lost to the crimson.

"These are levies," Wilforn objected, his brow crinkling, but his eyes lit with amusement. It looked like he was struggling to keep himself from laughing in contempt at the man challenging him. If he did laugh, Prentice would not be surprised if Farringdon charged him right there—not the way the knight captain sounded by the emotion in his voice. The alliance was not safe yet.

"They were men surrendering," Farringdon said, lowering his tone a little, showing he was at least trying to keep his composure.

"Knights and peers surrender," Cassian said, having once more stuffed the prince's head into its trophy bag. Cyprian had likewise lowered the captured banner, perhaps to rest his arm. "A rogue cannot offer parole or accept it. It is a matter of chivalric law."

The three Young Hopefuls looked at each other and smirked. Farringdon tensed on his saddle, but Prentice put out a hand to hold back his friend's arm.

"Knights and peers, you say?" he asked coldly. Whatever sympathy he might have had for these young men trapped on the threshold of their adult lives and titles was bleeding away like the lifeblood of the many slain. "You are neither, *Squire* Wilforn, so I wonder how you came to accept so many paroles, including the prince's, of course. Did he try to surrender as well? Did he offer his sword before you took his head?"

"I took his sword as I will yet take yours in open combat," Cassian said savagely, and he drew a longsword from where its scabbard hung by its belt on his saddle. In taking the prince of Town Sobridge's head, he had also taken the time to loot the fallen ruler's sword. It had a disc pommel of graven gold that was brightly polished. Cassian would come away from this day's conflict with his coveted symbol of knighthood, at least, if not the title itself. All three Young Hopeful leaders scowled hatefully at the White Lions' commanders, as did some of the others still on their horses who had removed their helmets or lifted their visors now.

"No, you will not," Prentice declared flatly. "You failed in your duties as leaders of your towns' forces. You rode off to glory while your militia committed bloody murder behind you. The honor of Bridgetown is as stained as your militiamen."

"We rescued Bridgetown, while you watched, baron-from-beyond-the-mountains," Cyprian said. He cast his gaze over the Gryphon Banner cohorts, still standing in their ranks, weapons ready, and then over the Bridgetown men. "One need only look at who bears the day's baptism to see who did the work. Take as many levies as captive as you like, we have the true prisoners that matter and the trophies that matter. The Young Hopefuls, the hope of Bridgetown, have triumphed again, rescuing their liege-lady as they did before and will once more."

Prentice recognized the reference to the handbill Seskia had brought to the archduchess. It impressed him that the young Cyprian had the brass to speak its words to his face, though. Cyprian knew that Prentice was the one who had slain Inxyphos, and only with Brother Whilte's help. Both Cyprian and Cassian had seen it as it happened, after all. There was a good chance that every one of the Bridgetowners standing now in the bloody wreckage knew.

"If you have your trophies, then ride back to your liege and make your boasts," Prentice said, making no effort to hide the dismissal in his tone. Cyprian sneered, still enraptured with the confidence of victory, it seemed, but both Wilforn and Cassian started, pushed to fresh indignance. How did these wild fools ever keep themselves out of pointless fights? Did they even know how?

"Have a care, old convict...," Wilforn began, but a growl from the nearest cohorts caught him by surprise, it seemed, and he looked at the pike and halberds pointing at him as if suddenly recognizing them for what they were.

"Have a care yourself, boy," Farringdon shouted, also doing nothing to hide his contempt for these wild, sneering youths. "Lest you face the wrath of real men-at-arms, blooded in true battles—not this monstrous crime."

"You dare threaten...?" Wilforn's mouth hung open, an expression that Prentice was coming to think he must use most of the time. Several of his following riders looked shocked and concerned as they realized how dangerous their leaders' contempt might prove for them. Flush with victory or not, there was no possibility that they could actually survive direct conflict with the Gryphons afield before them. "We are allies."

"Allies who want no part in this shame of yours," Prentice told them. "Quit the field or help us clean up after your folly. Make your choice."

Wilforn's mouth opened and closed as his expression went through a series of poor emotions, all backed by a not very well-concealed fear of actually coming to blows. Prentice was impressed that Cyprian had reclaimed his calm swiftly, for the older brother now sat with a shrewd look in his deep blue eyes. He, at least, knew he wanted no fight on these terms, that was clear.

"Let us go, gentles," he said calmly. "Let us leave the baron and his levies to the tasks they are so eager to perform. We have the day's trophies."

Wilforn still had some fight in him, or at least the pride to object to being threatened.

"They are guests of our lady," he stammered, flabbergasted. "They cannot threaten us like this."

"Let it go, Wilforn," Cassian said, his tone sounding mild but his eyes flashing challenge as he glared at Prentice. He still had the bared, captured sword in his hand. "What else can we expect of barbarians from across the mountains? Like slattern wife, so heretic husband."

"You slander a better man than you could hope to be!" Lyrach suddenly snapped, returning from his ride to fetch the gunner commander to speak out of turn with as much indignance as Farringdon a moment before—more, if that were possible. "There isn't a man on this side of the field would not thank God Almighty for the chance to give his life for the knight commander. Can you say the same of even one of the slug-abed manslaughterers you lead?"

Prentice raised his hand, and Lyrach fell silent at once. Cassian had been trying to provoke violence with that parting jab, and there was little point in answering it. In truth, now that the blood-lust was sated, he wanted the Bridgetowners gone quickly before one of them realized the value of the loot and trophies they were proposing to leave behind—a "small mountain" of black powder and twelve functional guns unlikely to have been sabotaged by any Inquisition agents. If he could just get these fools off the field, the White Lions would restore their lost cannon cadre in a single morning. After all, it was not the first time he had been despised to his face by a noble, nor the first time he had heard his wife's honor called into question.

His calm thoughts stopped dead, and like a rogue storm wave in the depth of the dark sea, his own icy rage rose up and demanded to be unleashed, if only for a moment. Almost before he knew to stop himself, he called after the Young Hopefuls who had begun to lead the Bridgetown militia off the field at last, back around the west end of the bastion.

"We will leave the gate open for you, Bridgetown-men," he shouted. "Save you recrossing in those boats. But Squire Cassian, perhaps you should get yourself to prayer after this. If your murder of the sacrist on the cathedral steps yesterday did not damn your soul, then your butchery of a prince surrendering honorably certainly did. In fact, best hope they reconsecrate the building swiftly. All your men have souls in danger of damnation for this day's work."

Cassian almost wheeled back at that, but his brother caught his rein and stopped him. It made Prentice smirk. The anger in his soul wanted nothing better than for the arrogant squire to make his try, but the leader and father in him still saw a youth adrift in the world, trying to cling to anything that helped him hold off the fear of it. It was a strange doublemindedness he did not fully understand. It also annoyed him, that having kept his temper the whole way through this monstrous morning, he let it off the leash now of all times. Beside Prentice, Farringdon spat upon the ground loudly, though the Hopefuls were now so far gone that they would not have heard.

"You know that I never met Liam, but I have heard the tales," he said venomously. "Was even he ever that bad?"

"Worse," Prentice said reflexively, glad for the distraction, then shook his head. "No, not worse, just with more power and less excuse. If ever you wonder what Liam was truly like, then Cassian is a good mimicry."

He turned to his side and saw that next to Lyrach's horse was a man in an unusually cut tunic of dark color, sleeveless over a linen shirt with the cuffs rolled up to the elbows. He had long black hair, tied back in a braid that reached down the length of his back. A Masnian by his appearance. Prentice looked the man over, blinking in surprise.

"My Lord, Baron Knight Commander Prentice Ash," Lyrach said, presenting his leader in the fashion of a full, courtly introduction. "I present the leader of the Town Sobridge cannoneer force, a nobleman of far Masnia, apparently."

The cannon commander straightened his shoulders and leaned his head back, as if trying to look up at Prentice and down his nose at the same time.

"I am Master Benlow Sent-Fane," he declared proudly. "Master of large guns, weapon and armor smith to kings and princes. You are familiar with my great-nephew by low marriage, I understand. We have received word that my nephew has died. Is that true?"

CHAPTER 63

"Yentow Sent's uncle is a Masnian noble?" Amelia asked her husband once he was finished relaying the events of the morning.

"So he says," Farringdon answered and accepted her unspoken invitation to sit. "He's Masnian, that's for certain, as are more than half his crew of cannoneers. He says that he is not a great uncle by blood but by 'low marriage,' whatever that means."

The archduchess could scarcely credit the claim, although the longer she thought about it, the more it made a kind of sense. Yentow Sent had always had the kind of airs of superiority typical to nobility the world over, but even as this news explained that fact, it raised the further question: why had he been working as a weaponsmith in a far country?

"And this Benlow Sent is younger than his nephew?" she asked.

"Benlow Sent-Fane, and yes, by a decade at least, I would say," Farringdon confirmed, waiting as a neophyte filled a cup with watered wine for him. He received it from her hand and saluted his wife with it before taking a sip.

"What was he doing working for the prince of Sobridge?" Amelia asked him once he had had his first drink. "Do Masnian nobles regularly travel to work, like some kind of merchant tradesmen?"

"I couldn't say, my love, but the cannons we captured are his for sure. They even have Masnian writing cast on their sides. They are quite impressive as works of artifice, if you'll forgive me saying; I know your distaste for the deadly engines."

Amelia nodded benignly, then softened her expression to smile gently on her beloved husband.

"I yet have my disgust and misgivings about the wretched things—Denay, Masnian, or Fallenhill construction," she said. "That hasn't changed, but now that the odd spell is gone from my mind, I am not so loathing that I will hate you for mentioning them once more. I know you value them as prospective tools to defend our lands and our people. Your expertise with the lancers is proving its value, and I will trust you with these things as well. But please, reassure me that they can be made safer. Let us not have entire hilltops blasted away in our future."

"I cannot guarantee, my love, but I can tell you these are a cut above Master Sent's sabotaged constructions at the very least. They are cast in bronze, just as the ancient Denay Dragons are, though they are still much smaller than those monsters. It appears the Masnian smiths have recovered the secret of their making, or else devised a facsimile of their own."

That answer only puzzled Amelia on a different level—one of craftsmanship that put her in mind of her conversation with the smith in the camp outside Aubrey.

"Is bronze not weaker than iron or steel?" she asked. "How can bronze cannons be stronger than Yentow Sent's iron ones?"

"Because of the forging," Farringdon explained, his usual enthusiasm for matters of craftsmanship making him smile and speak more eagerly. "The bronze is melted completely and then cast into its shape, something far more difficult to do with such a large amount of iron and impossible with steel, though legends of the Bright Age say that there was a secret known then. If it was, it is another mystery lost at the fall of that age."

She was about to ask what difference that would make, but he was already carrying on to explain, like an excited tutor. He was not the stern teacher Prentice was, forcing her to find her own answers, and his enthusiasm was infectious.

"Being cast in single pieces, the bronze guns are so much the stronger as a whole because they have no seams, no weak points."

"No possibility for the skin thief sabotage," Amelia added, seeing an additional advantage.

"That I cannot guarantee, my love, but I think it must be very much harder. There would be no welds or forgings to easily and secretly make weak so they fail during firing. And we have seen them used already. They work well."

Amelia accepted her husband's opinion. She would never have more than grudging respect for the horrid engines of destruction, no matter how much they appealed to her husband, but she would not deny their usefulness, especially if both Farringdon and Prentice judged them as valuable.

"Prentice has seized them as prizes of war, this Benlow Sent-... I am sorry, what is his name, husband? I know you have told me twice."

"Benlow Sent-Fane," Farringdon told her, sipping his drink again but waving off the attendant neophyte when she tried to refill his cup. "And that was the intention, especially when the Young Hopefuls made it clear *they* could not care less about them. As it turns out, Master Sent-Fane claims he has come north from Masnia seeking *us* out, if you can believe it—or yourself at any rate."

"What, why? And how does he know who I am?"

"Our order of wheellock triggers," Farringdon said with an amused expression. "Apparently there is a long-standing rivalry between our two Masnian masters, or at least there was when both lived. Though they are relations, they had little respect for each other, and when Master Sent-Fane learned that his nephew by low marriage was here providing iron cannons and perhaps inferior triggers to our militia, he felt compelled by family honor to come investigate. He brought his cannons to sell to us, along with a supply of handguns, convinced they would be superior to whatever Yentow Sent had produced."

"But he was serving Town Sobridge!" Amelia objected. At every turn the tale twisted ever more in fantastical directions her mind balked to follow.

"The prince compelled him, apparently. The Master Sent-Fane, his crews and their guns, were all seized and, with promises of shares of the booty from a captured Bridgetown, The prince of Sobridge all but forced the Masnian guns to fire on the town at sword-point."

"The prince genuinely thought to capture the most heavily defended town in all the south? The gate to the Vec that has stood for centuries against almost all assaults?"

Amelia shook her head, leaning back in her chair.

"Master Sent-Fane seems to think that the prince had little respect for Bridgetown or its militia. He felt the Sougate was the only thing preventing him from sweeping them out the other end of Bridge Road. He was also expecting some allies soon in support, apparently. It was only word of the baroness' death that gave him the confidence to rush the attack on his own."

"Penelope is not dead," Amelia protested reflexively, though as Farringdon nodded, she realized that in the immediate aftermath of Inxyphos's attack, reports were naturally likely to be unreliable. The prince heard a rumor and thought to strike while the iron was hot, as it were. Either that, or agents of the Inquisition prompted him, giving the Young Hopefuls the easy victory they took from the day and making the White Lions seem ever more redundant, as the little paper posts around the town were pressing folk to believe. Already, her handmaids had found two others in various quarters.

Just how many ears is the bluebird singing into? she wondered, sighing.

"Well, if we hold his cannons as prizes, what is this master's intention?" she asked. "I have no desire to hold men forced to fight as prisoners, and I doubt they would be well received if they returned to Town Sobridge, whoever is next in line to succeed the prince."

"Having learned of his nephew's passing, and its manner, Master Sent-Fane is insisting...yes, insisting...that he take over Yentow Sent's role, both as smith-master of our captured guns and rightful heir to the workshops in Fallenhill."

Farringdon paused and then chuckled at the raw audacity of the story.

"Fallenhill is mine...well, Baron Ash's...as are its workshops," Amelia told her husband, as if he did not know. He nodded again, his smile not diminished for an instant. He was finding this entire strange twist of fate nearly hilarious, that was clear.

"He lays no claim of possession on the shops themselves but on the fealty of their apprentices and journeymen," the marquis explained further, clearly loving to tell the impossible tale. "Apparently, it is the crafts' way in Masnia. More than that, he not only has no disappointment at our capture of his guns, but he expects no compensation for their loss and insists that he take service with Your Grace as recompense for his uncle's failure. It is a stain on his family's honor, apparently."

That revelation was almost beyond Amelia's comprehension, and she shook her head in bewilderment.

"Unfathomable. He came north to sell us his finest creations, had them captured out from under him, and was pressed into service. Now that we have captured them and him in turn, he means to accept the forfeit and insists on indenturing himself to make more and other such weapons, for the sake of *his* family's honor?"

"So he says."

Amelia stared at the heavy tabletop, waiting for her disbelief to ease, but when it did not, she turned to Lady Dalflitch, sitting nearby overseeing two neophytes at needlework. No one had ever seen the lady herself take up thread, but she happily stepped into Lady Spindle's supervisory role while the Lace Fang cared for her sickly husband.

"Does this make any sense to you, My Lady?" the archduchess asked.

"I have never visited Masnia, Your Grace," Dalflitch answered readily. "Nor have I ever desired to. Whatever are their ways, I cannot say."

Amelia nodded, but her lady-in-waiting was not quite finished.

"I will say that given the deeds done in the name of pride, honor, and family here in our own Grand Kingdom, nothing the marquis says surprises me. Men are ever strange creatures in their way."

"Men, My Lady?" Farringdon asked, twisting in his chair to look back at her. She did not even raise her head from the sewing neophytes.

"I mean of course, mankind, My Lord," she said contentedly. "While it is men we discuss in this case, we women have our own forms of honor and pride and can be every bit as twisted in our pursuit of them."

"Words of great wisdom, Lady," Farringdon said, turning back to share a smile with Amelia. The archduchess shook her head in amusement.

"In the light of all this, Knight Commander Ash has sent me here to request you approve our new 'replacement' Masnian master, as harsh and unworthy as such a notion truly is, and allow him to take the cannons and their crews into your service."

Prentice, ever alert to my place in things, Amelia thought.

"If he were free to decide for himself, they would already be in our camp by now, wouldn't they?" she asked rhetorically.

"If it were up to Prentice, my love, they would already be mounted on Norgate and Sougate, six at each bastion, to truly secure the town," Farringdon averred, vehement but still with a pleasant expression.

"Tell him yes, he has my permission to take them, but there are twelve guns in all, correct?" Amelia paused and her husband nodded. "Then we will offer six to the baroness. The day was her victory as well."

"Politic, Your Grace," Lady Dalflitch said.

"As you say, but I suspect she will not want them," the knight captain responded and his pleasant expression fell to a bitter frown, his eyes on the tabletop. "The Young Hopefuls will already be proclaiming their great victory over the Veckander rebel prince of Town Sobridge."

Amelia watched as the horrors rose in his eyes, the fresh memories that he had been holding off gaining dominance over his thoughts. She had seen men come from battle before, victors and defeated—the exhaustion from terror mixed with the relief of survival or the elation of victory. This emotion was none of these things. Her husband had never been in danger this morning and he had seen no true victory. His eyes were filled with disgust and shame, as of a good man who comes upon the scene of a heinous crime.

"It was truly terrible, wasn't it?" she asked earnestly, awkwardly shifting forward in her chair to take his hand. He looked at her, and the anger in his eyes softened. It pleased her to have that effect.

"It was murder; there is no other word for it," he said. "They were drenched in the blood of surrendering men and still they fell upon them like rabid animals that killed not for food or fear but as if they knew nothing else. Men pleaded and wept. They threw themselves at the Gryphon company and begged to be captured. We pulled as many out of the maelstrom as we could, but the knight commander dared not break the formation or we would have found ourselves in melee with our own allies. God alone could say what that would have brought upon the Reach. And the Young Hopefuls, strutting about on prancing ponies like squires at their first parade and joust. They boasted. They called it a great victory."

"It is a wonder Knight Commander Ash did not order the lot of them killed," Dalflitch said as lightly as if picking up one of the neophytes for a dropped stitch. "Sir Turley says that he would rather face an enraged bull than the Baron of Fallenhill when he gets the battle-chill in his eyes."

"Battle-chill, My Lady?" Farringdon asked.

"My husband's term. He says there is no other name he can think to give it," Dalflitch explained, looking up for the first time with a gentle shrug. "Like the gleam of a sharp sword—clean, cold even, in the bright sunlight."

"A goodly description," the knight captain conceded. "But Baron Ash—Prentice—never forgets his duty. Ever."

Amelia knew exactly the kind of cold fury Dalflitch's husband, Sir Turley, Prentice's oldest friend, had named a "battle-chill." She had seen it in his eyes, an icy rage that laughed in the face of death and blood.

"I am thankful Baron Prentice indeed never forgets his duty. He is a man forged of a hard life, and the fact that he accepts duty's leash at all is a surprising and precious blessing to the Reach and to me," she said.

"He does it out of love for you," Farringdon said, clearly not thinking before he spoke. "I sometimes wonder if I should be jealous of his devotion and fearful lest you fully understand its depth one day."

No sooner were the words out of his mouth than he snatched his hand from his wife's fingers and clapped it to his lips, as if to stop the words too late from leaving.

"My love, forgive me!" he said, aghast at himself. "That was cruel to you and unjust to the baron. His love for you is loyalty and fealty, nothing more, I know. You he obeys, but Righteous he adores. She is the queen of his heart. He would never turn from her nor undermine our marriage and love."

Amelia smiled and nodded to her husband, reaching for his hand again to show she did, indeed, forgive him. In truth she had more than once secretly asked herself the question, wondering whether she might have wanted Prentice for a husband if their circumstances had been different, but she was sure she would not want that match at all. Proud as she had become of her own strength, she did not feel a rider of sufficient skill to mount up on the furious marriage such a man as Prentice would make.

"You are not my second prize, dearest husband," she told the marquis and drew his fingers to her lips. She was sure he already knew it, but it did not hurt to say.

"And My Lord," Dalflitch added by way of a final observation, "the baron's loyalty may be absolute—I suspect it is—but I would fear for our liege's safety if she thought to interpose herself in any way between Prentice Ash and the true love of his life."

"Truer words never were said," Amelia agreed and kissed her husband's hand again. "I am thankful that we each have our blessed marriages now. The ladies of my chamber are old maids and widows no longer."

At least this war has yielded some joys, she thought, and her hand strayed again to her belly, as it did frequently these days. In the midst of the happiness it gave her, though, she could not shirk the images in her mind of Farringdon's description of the massacre.

CHAPTER 64

Lady Dalflitch composed a formal letter outlining the archduchess's offer to share the cannons as spoils of war with the barony of Bridgetown while also politely but strenuously protesting the massacre and urging that public reprimands be made lest the event stain the honor of the town and the Western Reach both. For another two days there was no reply, but a new handbill was circulated on the second with a woodcut celebrating the "ever-victorious Young Hopefuls," savior squires of Bridgetown.

"Why emphasize their status as squires?" Farringdon had wondered as he read the bill the evening it was discovered. "It undermines their claim to ransoms for the Town Sobridge knights, doesn't it?"

"They are strengthening their hands before playing their next full gambit," Prentice said.

"How so?"

"Put the idea about that these *squires* are doing the work of full knights and then the question will become why have they not been raised to the status of full knights yet? The Hopefuls will not have to ply their own cause one whit. The honors will come to them by public demand."

Every one of the archduchess's court was present that evening, except Master Solft. Even Lady Spindle, whose husband had begun to rest easily, it was said, and they all nodded, though several had uncertain expressions in the candlelight. It was Sir Turley who voiced the question.

"But why are the Inquisition so intent on raising the Young Hopefuls?"

Many looked like they could answer the question, but they waited on Prentice, and as he scanned the table, he had a notion that he could use this moment for an additional purpose.

"Lady Dalflitch, Lady Righteous, Lady Spindle," he said, addressing each one in turn, "of all the neophytes, whom would you say is most ready for the half mask? Which ones should step up to become Lace Fangs first?"

The three trainers of the archduchess's bodyguards consulted each other wordlessly and then deferred to Lady Dalflitch.

"Daisy, Agatha, and Beth," she said confidently. Prentice recognized the names from Righteous's day with the baroness.

"Very well, My Lady, if you would summon them."

He turned to the archduchess to allow her to object if she wanted to, but she only gave him a nod and a smile of curiosity. The neophytes were called, and the unveiled three all came from some corner of the main of the Paramour's Chambers to stand at the end of the table.

"You three have been hearing our conversation?" Prentice asked, his tone as much a statement as a question. It was convention that servants were expected not to listen in, indeed, not to even hear the conversations of their betters, but only a fool actually thought they walked around selectively deaf.

The neophytes nodded.

"So, tell us, if you ladies-to-be might know, why would the agents of the Inquisition support the Young Hopefuls?"

This was an important test to Prentice. He was certain Spindle and Righteous already had it deciphered, but he wanted to know if their students had the same instincts. They would need them in order to fulfil their duties properly. He watched as the three looked between themselves without speaking and wondered if they were overawed for a moment. That was not a good sign, if these were the readiest of the candidates. Then he noticed their hands, fingers flowing, half-hidden by their sleeves. They were communicating by signals. He had no idea their training had that level of sophistication. Could his wife speak silently like this? At last, they lifted their faces to the table. It was the freckled Daisy who was nominated to speak.

"They don't support the Young Hopefuls, My Lord Baron. Not really," she said.

"No?" Prentice prompted, impressed with the direction they seemed to be heading right from the start.

"What are they doing, then?" the archduchess asked, ready to join Prentice in the interview. He suspected she understood his true purpose now.

"They want Bridgetown ripe for the Usurper to come take, Your Grace," Daisy said simply.

"And how does raising the Hopefuls help with that? Bridgetown has no knights or nobles at present. If the Young Hopefuls rise to the titles, won't that solve their problem?" Archduchess Amelia pressed.

The neophyte Beth scoffed, and Daisy prompted her to take up the explanation.

"The Reach don't need...sorry, doesn't need nobles for its defense," she said, and Prentice was struck by the throaty depth to the girl's voice. He knew from his wife the girl also had dark, thick hair that naturally fell in waves when she removed her wimple and brushed it. With that voice and mahogany hair, once she had a mask on, she would be a figure of beauty and mystery to make young men swoon in any court of the land. "But if they do become nobles, that would be worse than none because they're like sliver shavers."

"Shavers that boast about doing it," Agatha added.

Good girls, Prentice thought, certain they were on the right track.

"Ah, yea, of course," Turley said, but his wife touched her hand to his, quieting him.

"Your reasoning might not be clear to those here who were born into the peerage," the archduchess said. "Explain it for them.

"Well, a merchant who shaves is a cheat. He gets to make some more money for a while, but over time his fellows become suspicious. No matter how well he tries to conceal it, it'll come out eventually," Daisy took up the explanation again.

"And if he makes it known abroad, then his clients dry up in a day," Agatha added again.

"So, it doesn't matter how strong the Hopefuls become, there aren't enough of them to make Bridgetown strong enough on their own, otherwise Your Grace's force would never have been invited in in the first place. They have few victories and claim ones that aren't even theirs. They like to think they're invincible, but they're just like virgin boys in the street, boasting about how many maids they've kissed but never having bedded a one."

All the women at the table smirked at that characterization, and Prentice and Turley rolled their eyes at each other.

"Are we being mocked, good fellows?" Farringdon said by way of a joke.

"I wouldn't think so, My Lord," Turley answered with his mischievous grin. "After all, we all only kiss one good woman each, and I for one would never discuss the bedding of any lady. Such a crass thought."

Now it was the knight castellan's wife's turn to roll her eyes.

"So, you think the Hopefuls are buying Bridgetown victories with shaved coins?" Prentice asked.

"We do, My Lord," Daisy answered with polite confidence. "They win but never by themselves, and they let affray go on. Word is they still stalk the taverns, looking for duels and challenges, even with their 'victory' over Town Sobridge. Whatever they win only adds to the shame of Bridgetown—covers the orange and gold with blood. The markets and docks are full of mutters of curses for the death of the sacrist in the cathedral, and while most are happy to see the Veckanders take a bloody nose, they talk of how it was too much blood for good folk to bear. The washerwomen who saw the militia uniforms after the battle say their tubs ran red like blood, and some had to throw theirs away with the water. They feared the ill luck of ever trying to wash in those basins again. And that's just the small folk. What will proud nobles or Mother Church say, when time comes?"

"The Hopefuls win battles, or claim wins, but do not understand wars," Prentice said, rounding out Daisy's astute analysis. "They love the fight and the flash of the killing strike, but they do not know how to take prisoners or make peace after the battle, and they cannot share the glory. They are costing their liege many potential allies, and, if the Inquisition have their way, will cost it the alliance it already most depends upon."

"With my foolish help," Righteous muttered bitterly.

"We have spoken of that matter already, Baroness," Amelia said gently. "There is no need to revisit it now."

"Thank you, Your Grace," Righteous answered, and Prentice felt for his wife. He had urged her to forgive herself more than once, but he knew she had not reached that peace in her mind quite yet.

"Do you young ladies have any notions of a solution?" the archduchess asked, and the question even caught Prentice off guard. The three looked to each other's hands and the signals seemed to fly. Prentice raised an eyebrow in Dalflitch's direction.

"Just how sophisticated *is* this signaling system?" he asked.

"It grows daily," she said, and there was an unusual sense of satisfaction in her tone—not the typical defensive reserve with which she kept the world at bay. Something more genuine, and Prentice had a sudden sense of insight.

You are proud of them, My Lady, and well you should be, he thought.

After a prolonged moment of silent consultation, the three women looked up, shamefaced.

"We don't know, Your Grace. We're sorry," Daisy said.

"No need to apologize," the archduchess told them. "In my chamber I will invite any wisdom I can find to answer open questions like this one, regardless of its place of origin. Even my Lace Fangs, as Ladies Spindle and Righteous will attest."

"That does not mean you will be welcome to speak out of turn though, my girls," Spindle added. "The Lace Fangs do not forget themselves, and the private chamber is not the open court or, God forbid, the public square. You remember that, won't you?"

"Yes, My Lady," the trio said in unison, curtseying to Spindle as one.

"Well then, if you have no further questions, Baron, I think we can conclude this interview," the archduchess said with a smile, and Prentice found her good feeling infectious. He looked around the table and knew that every one of the inner court recognized what was happening. He had no plan for ceremony but perhaps ceremony was not the right thing for a moment like this amongst bodyguards trained to have concealed identities and to work as spies as much as ladies-in-waiting.

"Did you want to say anything, My Lady?" he asked Dalflitch. She shook her head politely.

"The tutor might assess the student," she said, "but cannot graduate them. It falls to the founder of the school to do that. The Lace Fangs were always your notion first, Baron Ash."

"Very well," Prentice said, and he stood in place, looking to the three at the end of the table. "You girls, remove those wimples."

The three raised their hands hesitantly, reaching behind their necks to undo the ties and release their headdresses. Soon, each held the pale, winged covers in their hands, their previously covered hair now bared and frizzing as it came out. They looked suddenly like young girls who had been out playing in meadows, and they lowered their heads sheepishly.

"Go now and find for yourselves lace masks and dresses worthy of ladies-in-waiting," Prentice went on.

"I've had them at sewing such things for some time now," Spindle said. "Glory boxes for ladies of steel and lace, as it were."

"Excellent," Prentice added. "I trust you each have blades?"

"Yes, My Lord," they said together, their expressions showing gathering excitement as they no doubt were growing to realize what was happening.

"Can we perhaps get them something commemorative, husband?" Righteous asked, apparently sharing the feeling. "A proper stick...a proper stiletto for each girl. Something a lady can carry in her sleeve and trust to guard her honor?"

"I think so, Baroness Righteous," Prentice agreed smiling proudly at his wife. "It will come from Fallenhill's treasury, a last expenditure before they are presented to the archduchess's chamber."

"Yes," the archduchess agreed. "From tomorrow, you three will draw a stipend from my lady seneschal, and you will use it to buy what you need. You carry my dignity with you now, and I will expect you to keep up your clothes and other chattels."

"Yes, Your Grace." The three bobbed so energetically, they were like wooden floats on the river when the wind tossed it.

"So, Agatha, Daisy, Beth," Prentice addressed each one in turn, "from this moment you are neophytes no more. You will wear the lace mask and accompany her grace in public, being watchful for her enemies and protecting her dignity. You will attend her here in the chamber as well, as you have trained to do. Your training is complete, but you will not stop learning yet, as those who come before you have not."

He stopped to nod at Righteous and Spincle.

"One day, perhaps, you will even have the right to sit at this table and be counselors to her grace in full, as the first Lace Fangs have become. In the meantime, serve as you have trained and you will do very well. Congratulations."

He had not planned to, but suddenly had the thought to applaud the three women and did so. He was not surprised when the archduchess pushed herself up from her chair and joined him. That was signal enough, and soon the entire table had stood and was gently applauding the three graduate fangs. Prentice let his eyes range over the room at the rest of the neophytes in their places in the candlelight.

Be diligent, not jealous, young maids, and you will receive your applause soon enough, he thought.

CHAPTER 65

It was another day before the archduchess received Baroness Penelope's reply to her letter, a formal document issued on vellum and illuminated with crimson inks and gold leaf. The Bridgetown crest took up the top quarter of the page, and the bear upon the shield had a sword held upturned in its paws, a new item in the heraldry.

"Gold disc pommel?" Farringdon said as he studied the image after Amelia handed him the document, having read it herself. "That's Town Sobridge's sword, looted by Cassian. Clever of the little butcher. He's hungry for his own longsword but smarter by far to hand that one off to his liege lady. Much more the knightly act to surrender it for the honor of the earldom."

"Still, not an earldom for long," Lady Dalflitch added as she perused the letter after the marquis. "She still styles herself archduchess-elect."

"Perhaps she has someone to reconsecrate the cathedral," Farringdon wondered, but Dalflitch did not agree.

"It takes a patriarch to consecrate a high church seat, and while I do not doubt the Inquisition has even its own pet patriarchs, none of them are close to Bridgetown as I know. Not close enough for invitations to have gone out and been returned yet, even if they were favorably received."

"Perhaps they are that many turns ahead of us in the game, My Lady," Amelia worried.

"I would give you Baron Ash's answer to that thought, Your Grace," Dalflitch said in response. "If they *are* that far ahead, they would have other cards than these in their hands to play. Unless they have another hateful trump card, like their man Inxyphos-turned-bear, we need not worry about them doing the incredible, only the undesirable."

Even after all this time, watching the Inquisition's whisper-campaign unfold against her, Amelia still felt that her enemy was made of smoke and shadows. No one had yet laid eyes upon Bluebird, though the neophytes now were going about without their uniforms often, posing as girls off the river, seeking work or trading from upriver fishing villages. No one had heard tell of anyone like Bluebird. Prentice had said that Inxyphos's clothing smelled of the sea, so perhaps the Inquisition's main agent had left the town for a time, retreating to the ocean again, with underlings watching over his plots for him in the meanwhile. Perhaps he was sailing to fetch a patriarch or a skin thief or another bear man. If he could bring a senior noble to acknowledge Penelope's accession to archduchess or a promise from Daven Marcus to do it, for all that was worth, then the alliance between Bridgetown and Dweltford would be all but useless. Amelia wondered if the time had come for her to make some kind of concession to keep Bridgetown on her side against the Usurper, although she also wondered if she really needed to. Now that her militia had had some safety in which to rest, a march back to Dweltford, even in winter, did not seem such a dire prospect.

"Except that that would leave Bridgetown back in the hand of the Usurper and us both fighting for control of the rivers again," she muttered.

"My love?" Farringdon asked and Amelia shook her head.

"The baroness denies any claim that Bridgetown's militia acted improperly on the field outside Sougate," she told them, "and releases us, as Bridgetown's liege, to dispose of any prisoners we have as we see fit."

"That's because the Young Hopefuls took all the prisoners they think might have a ransom to pay," Farringdon said bitterly. "We only have Town Sobridge's levies. They're scared and cold and desperate to get back to their homes before the full rains come. It must surely be any day now."

"Any pledges of honorable peace they offer us will be useless," Amelia said, and she waved to Lady Agatha, standing at her right hand to fill her cup with tea once more. Now that the Lace Fangs were more in number, Dalflitch had made it clear that the honor of serving the archduchess directly would be reserved to those in half-masks. At present it was Agatha. Both Lady Daisy and Lady Elizabeth were at large in the town, each accompanied by two neophytes, ostensibly shopping for woolen cloaks, but in fact gathering what intelligence they could from the gossips, beggars, and tradesfolk.

"We might as well simply let them out the Sougate," Amelia finished off, sipping her tea. "They will be forced to serve whatever lord replaces the dead prince."

"I suspect the baroness...archduchess-elect...thinks it is herself," Dalflitch observed. "Incorporating that sword might be a claim of sovereignty over Town Sobridge."

"It'll be worth less than that sheet it's printed on if she does," Farringdon observed. "The princes are jackals when one of them falls like this. Word will have reached the princedom's neighbours even by now, and I'd warrant Longshepherds is already on the march. His domain is small, but so is Town Sobridge. If he can get here fast enough, he can combine the two and make a proper Vec prince of himself."

"Unless the Heron is on the way still, as Baron Ash fears," Dalflitch added. "Another thing worth noting is this rejection of your offer of the six cannons, Your Grace. It makes me think Baronet Forsle might be recovering, the way it references King's Law in the repudiation. 'Only the throne in Denay is at liberty under Heaven to retain such weapons.'"

"Is that true?" Farringdon asked. It looked to trouble him that he might have been pushing his wife and liege into difficulty politically because of his drive to adopt the powerful weapons.

"Not strictly," Amelia told him, hoping to relieve his fears. "What King's Law actually says is that the Bronze Dragons belong unto the king and that any attempt to make one's own will be treason against the throne."

"And so we thread a needle between law and rebellion by having our own smaller cannons?"

"It was an easier needle to thread back when the Lions' cannon were to be made of iron, husband," Amelia conceded. "Silly distinction, but more than one legal case is built on such things. Nevertheless, since we acknowledge no legitimate king in Denay to commit treason against, we might as well keep them and use them. If it comes to a question for the sake of peace, I will not hesitate to give them up as an item of trade in negotiations."

"Using them to win battles and then differently to win the war and peace," Farringdon said, using Prentice's ideas from the previous discussions. Amelia nodded, and Dalflitch also agreed. The lady seneschal laid the document in her hands onto the tabletop and then ran her fingers over its surface.

"This illumination is fine work. It represents many hours' effort, so the substance was decided yesterday at least, perhaps earlier. Whoever is advising the archduchess-elect, and I suspect it is more than just a twittering bird, they have her jumping to decisions quickly."

"They're exploiting her youth, pride, and wounded feelings," Farringdon said, seeing the implications.

"And no small amount of fear, I would wager," Amelia added. "Let's not forget that a monster tried to kill her only a handful of days past."

"Well, Your Grace," Dalflitch said with a dismissive tone, the way she used the nickname silly filly, "it's not as if no one at this table has ever been through something similar."

CHAPTER 66

"**I**t's becoming a problem, Knight Commander," Knight Sergeant Gennet told Prentice, standing out the front of his tent. At least half the nights the baron spent in bed with his wife, beside his infant twins, while the rest of the time he was forced to be here, matters of camp occupying him late into the early morning hours. He never had enough time to sleep.

"The Bridgetowners think they are above us now," Prentice said, acknowledging the problem as he understood it. It was more than a week since the cannons had been captured, and the Bridgetown militia still strutted about as if they had conquered the whole Vec and were marching on to take the Masnian emperor's surrender. "We'll bring them to heel soon enough."

"Begging your pardon, My Lord, but it ain't just them," Knight Sergeant Gennet said quietly. The loyal officer was plainly uncomfortable to have to raise the issue with his commander.

"What is it then?"

"The Gryphon Banner, My Lord, the whole company to a man. They refuse to have anything to do with the Bridgetowners. Won't train 'em, won't talk to 'em, look the other way when they walk by."

"Insubordination?" Prentice asked, not as angry as he thought he might be. He could understand his militiamen's feelings, though he could not condone them.

"Well, sure it is, My Lord, but I can't say as I blame 'em," Gennet said, and the pain in his expression grew acute, his eyes almost closed to slits as if in physical discomfort for his emotions. "You were there. You saw what it was like. It weren't right, not by any stretch. Even if they were the worst rogues—convicts with bloody histories and a list of rapes and murders long as your arm—it wasn't how it should be. It was like the Redlanders."

That was something Prentice could not deny. In all the years since Prince Mercad's crusade, he had never imagined he would fight on a side as hateful as the Blood Sects' brutal warlords. Even Liam at his most ruthless was not so murderous. Prentice had to snort a small laugh at that thought—someone or something Liam was not as bad as.

"I understand your feelings, Knight Sergeant," he said quietly, absolutely watchful to not be heard discussing insubordination in compassionate terms. Men who thought their rebellion sympathetic would never be turned from it. "But regardless, White Lions obey commands, or they are punished. It is that simple."

"Oh, I've handed out the punishments, My Lord, I swear, but I'm running out of possible things. Making examples only makes them rally around the more. Thousands all refusing their duty? I'll never find enough tasks to set them all to, and even if you want to bring back flogging or hanging, who'm I going to set to do it?"

Since the earliest days in Fallenhill, Prentice had kept flogging out of his discipline repertoire because of the memories it evoked. Whips were the tools of convict overseers. White Lions must aspire to something more.

"I will speak to Knight Captain Farringdon," Prentice said with a sigh, rubbing at his wearied temples. It was only a short while after dawn, too soon to feel this tired. Perhaps a mouthful of something for breakfast would help.

"Knight Commander, come quick," a militiaman shouted as he sprinted up, nearly breathless with his effort at haste. "It's something bad. Truly bad."

"You don't give the knight commander orders, son," Gennet rebuked the young man-at-arms, but Prentice was more concerned with what "truly bad" thing had happened.

"What is it?" he asked and pointed for the messenger to lead him wherever he had to go.

"It's Sergeant Porth, My Lord. He's hurt. He's hurt bad."

That did indeed sound "truly bad", and Prentice followed the militiaman to the edge of the camp, with the knight sergeant in tow. Soon enough they found a small group clustered around three men on the still dew-damp ground. Two—Brother Whilte and Sergeant Guillam—were kneeling down beside Sergeant Porth, who was laid out, his face pale and his breathing coming in gasps.

"What in God's name is this?" Prentice demanded before he even realized he was saying it. Porth's right shirt sleeve had been torn away, and strips had been used to bandage the same arm. The limb was in ruins, and at first glance looked as if it might have been savaged by a wild animal, but the wounds were longer and cleaner than a beast's claw strokes. They were sword cuts, deep ones and numerous. In two breaths, Prentice knew these were not wounds sustained in a fight, at least not all of them. Any two would have been combat-ending wounds, making it impossible for Porth to hold a weapon. There were eight at least, and maybe more than a dozen. They ran together in his ravaged flesh. It was a miracle he had not bled to death, and as Brother Whilte prayed and ministered his healing, Prentice tried to imagine how long ago the wounds had been made. From the bloodstains down the right side and front of Porth's body, quite some while.

"I'm sorry, Knight Commander," Porth said suddenly, sighting Prentice and lifting his uninjured arm pleadingly. His face was drenched with sweat and pale as morning milk. "We were only mouthin' off a bit, and they deserved it. We should've given a better account of ourselves, but we only had daggers and they had swords. We never meant to leave Monteath behind, but he was already gone. Had to be dead."

"Lie still, you bloody idiot," Whilte said, an uncommon tension in his voice as he held onto the horridly wounded limb. "I'm not baking biscuits here."

He pushed Porth back onto his back and returned to praying.

"Guillam, do you know what this is? Who's this Monteath he's talking about?"

Guillam snapped to his feet and surprisingly saluted formally. Prentice wondered if it was out of guilt or an attempt to get himself onto a level footing within. His own hair was sweat-plastered to his head, and he had blood smeared all up the sides of his clothing and over his hands. It was almost certain he had tied the makeshift bandages, and it looked like he had then walked his wounded comrade back to camp. Both men were out of uniform, which was allowed as sergeants if they had permission from Gennet, so Prentice knew they had likely come from somewhere in the town. He suspected an ambush by some servitor of Bluebird. A skips crew, perhaps? Since the three false nuns had "hanged" themselves, no word had been seen of any others, not even the standover men, for news of whom Lady Spindle kept an eager ear out.

"He's a relative of Porth's, My Lord," Guillam said. "Seems this Monteath and him have a cousin in common, or something. They were joking about her all night. She's got a pair on her, apparently."

"Did this Monteath fellow meet up with you in the town?"

"No, My Lord, he's a Lion, a Fang actually. Porth only found out a day or two ago, and we got him off duty for the three of us to go drinking."

"Tell me, sergeant, that you did not get yourselves into a tavern brawl."

Prentice felt his jaw clenching. Bad enough that there were enemies in the shadows, but a fool drunken stoush would be almost as much trouble. With every power but the Conclave trying to paint the White Lions as worthless interlopers, smashing up the town would only help that false cause. As it happened, Guillam's story was even worse.

"Truth tellin', My Lord, we almost did," the Roar sergeant explained. "But I swear it weren't our fault. We picked a nice place, somewhere quiet where we could keep out of trouble, and then some of them Young Hopefuls come in. We said nothin', I swear, and at first, they didn't even know we were there. Then one of them spots us and it started."

"What started?" Prentice could imagine, but he needed the details. He would have to have them before he could decide what to do next. Beneath him, Porth groaned in agony and Whilte's muttered prayer continued.

"The poking talks—you know the sorts of thing, My Lord," Guillam said, his face as pained as Gennet's had been only moments before. "Fool things at first. Loud comments 'bout how the Lions should be named the puppies. Too afraid of the sight of blood. March in pretty lines but couldn't fight their own grandmothers already dead in the grave. Fool things."

"And how did you respond?"

"Mostly, we didn't."

Prentice cocked and eyebrow, but Guillam protested his innocence.

"Truly, My Lord. They was twits, and we'd been there. They were four and we were three. It wasn't a tight contest if come to a contest. Monteath, he had his sword and was up for a barney, but Porth said he was too old and had marched too many miles to care what a bunch of pups thought. 'Cept he said it just that bit too loud, and they took it as a challenge. They thought they weren't going to let us out without a fight, but after a moment we kenned they wanted us to have a go first. Well, that was easy enough to ignore, and Porth, I think he regretted sounding off like. He said best if we just find another tavern. Had to be others still open. Bridgetown merchants trade all night."

Another groan drew Prentice and Guillam's eyes downward. Whilte's prayers now had a desperate tone, and Prentice realized the injured sergeant was sure to lose his arm.

"Keep going sergeant. What happened next?"

"We left. They jeered some, and once we were out on the street, they followed to give us a sour send-off like, but we figured that for all there was. We were wandering the streets, trying to find a shingle with a lit light out the front, when they jumped us from behind. Monteath shouted like he'd been stuck, like that was the first he knew of it. Porth got his poniard out, but there were more than one, and like he said, they had them sideswords they like so much."

"And where were you?" Prentice asked, sensing a gap in the tale. "How is it Fang Monteath is somewhere likely dead, and Sergeant Porth is here, like that, and you have no more than scratches?"

Guillam looked askance, and for the first time he could ever remember, Prentice saw shame on the former convict's face.

"I was over by a wall, takin' a slash," he said. "They didn't even see me at first in the dark. They went for Monteath, and Porth tried his heart out, but they got him down and one of 'em started to go to town on Porth's arm. They even fetched Monteath's sword for the job. They kept askin' where I was, and Porth said I'd gone off to fetch some mates. They told him that was good, 'cause they all wanted a trophy from the night. That was all I could listen to. I had thought to run for help, but the hell with them, torturing him like that. I charged 'em out of the shadows yellin', 'Let's get 'em lads! They're only like four of 'em. We got 'em two to one.' That frighted them and while they backed off, I just grabbed Porth up and rushed him down an alley."

He drew in a long breath before going on.

"Then we were playin' peekaboo, tryin' to stay out of sight while they hunted us up. It was clear they wanted it all secret, cause they never fetched a lantern, but I heard 'em for an hour or more as I tried to figure my own way in the dark. We got near one of the working docks at one time, and I could see enough to try and patch Porth's arm, but it weren't much. You can see that for yourself."

"Did you sound off, too?" Prentice said, his eyes cold on the sergeant's. Guillam nodded reluctantly and frowned.

"Yep, I did," he said, clearly ashamed to have to confess. "Just the once, when we were leavin' the tavern. I told 'em that we'd been there, and we'd seen what was done. Any time the Young Hopefuls wanted to fight something braver than Town Sobridge rabbits they only had to skin their blades and we'd show 'em what war was."

He stopped and looked away again.

"Those is fightin' words, no mistake. It's my fault, ain't it?"

Porth groaned, and Whilte's prayers drained away.

"Of course it's not your bloody fault, Sergeant!" Prentice said, venting his fury as the chaplain rose to his feet, his own hands now bloody from his attempts at healing.

"He will have to surrender that arm, Knight Commander," Whilte said soberly. "Sooner the better. He'll sicken from the pain and the open wounds if I'm not swift."

"Go to, Chaplain," Prentice commanded. "You men, take the sergeant to a tent where the chaplain can work out of the rain. Smells like we might have some before noon." He rolled his aching shoulder that also spoke of rain. "Gently, he's a veteran of Gryphons, worthy of honor."

The men around leaped to do the duty, and Prentice stood by as they took Porth away, groaning. In their swiftness to move, some of the wounded sergeant's blood smeared on Prentice's hand as they struggled past him. He rubbed at it absently while his teeth ground in fury. Soon, the promised rain began to fall, heavy droplets that drove him to shelter but did not wash the blood from his hand.

CHAPTER 67

"Seven men? Seven?"

"Yes, Your Grace," Prentice told his liege, his voice terse and filled with tension. He had remained in camp all morning, occupying himself with mundane duties, chewing on his fury and awaiting word of Sergeant Porth's fate. Not since his days upon the chain had he felt such anger burn in his soul, such murderous hatred. At one point he thought about the past in that context and recalled that, in fact, his convict days had been less energetic in their raging emotions. It took him a moment, but he realized that he had lost the resignation, the acquiescence to the vagaries of fate that had helped him accept the injustices of those years, and there had been *many* injustices in those years.

Now, having risen in the world, he had hope. And not just hope—a wife, children, and place, a life and duty worthy of the name. All this had given him a belief in justice once again—not the naïve sense of fairness he had dreamed of as a youth, even with the harshness of his childhood to bear. This was a conviction that it would be possible to forge a juster world, or at least a more just time, if only for the years he had the strength to wield a weapon. Seeing all this laid out in his soul, he understood why this particular injustice made him rage inwardly so. This was not his "battle-chill"; there was nothing calm and purposeful about this, and as much as he strove to understand and restrain himself, he was a taut rope again, twisting tighter and fearing he would snap. Most of all, he felt any sympathy he had for the Young Hopefuls was gone. His full wrath was directed at them now. When the archduchess appeared in camp, throwing herself from the saddle and striding forward like an avenging angel seeking whom God had marked for death, he could see his own fury reflected in her eyes.

"Word has been coming in through the morning," he explained to her. "In three separate taverns, and a line first with a mate, buying a new apron for the washerwoman he means to woo. The Hopefuls went looking for fights all through the night. Some of the Gryphons gave them one, but as many tried to walk away, and they were jumped as they did. Two died—the man Monteath and another, the line first. The only name anyone knew for him was the Old Jack."

"Another woman widowed before she had the chance to marry and love," the archduchess muttered.

"Give us the word, Your Grace," Lady Righteous said at her liege's right shoulder. On her left, the newly masked Lady Elizabeth nodded sternly as well. Her black lace face covering was shaped like a butterfly so that it seemed as if a dark and foreboding insect had landed upon her face. Letting it sit there made the Lace Fang all the more intimidating and mysterious to Prentice's eye. "Give us the word and we'll have their blood over the cobbles like the morning's chamberpots."

"And we would have war in the streets of Bridgetown. What good driving away the enemies without, then? We might as well hand the town to the Bluebird, wherever he roosts," the archduchess demanded, spinning on her lady-in-waiting. She whirled back at Prentice.

"Counsel your wife, Knight Commander," she told him, her voice cracking with emotion that Prentice knew was not directed at him or his spouse. The archduchess stared at him intently, as if willing him to speak, and when he did not, her eyes grew wide. She had seen something unexpected in his face. "Good God! You agree with her?"

Prentice looked past the archduchess to his wife, and despite her mask, nothing was hidden between them. Righteous had trained many of the men of the White Lions. As far as Prentice knew, none of the attacked were ones she had taught personally, but her love for them and pride in them was as strong as his in so many ways. He knew she wanted to avenge them. And he could not deny that he felt the very same. Even if he did not, he would do it just for her. If she wanted it this much, he would not as her husband deny her. She was that important to him.

But then he thought of their children.

He could not bequeath them vengeance and hatred, blood-shed without restraint. What he longed to do now might satisfy his lust for revenge, but it would only seem like a crime to the folk of Bridgetown, an act of murderous hatred. He could sound the trumpet now on a blood feud that might last generations. His children's grandchildren could grow to maturity fearing Bridgetown and the fierce warfare they had no responsibility for, tit-for-tat reprisals stretching back so far that no one remembered why. Like the Redlanders with their hatred so old that even the chronicles were forgotten and the fey with their fears so great they would rather let their land die of thirst and live as slaves than hear of another way. Like biting down on shards of glass, he forced himself to speak.

"No, Your Grace, Lady Righteous, we will not fly into the streets and hunt them out like carrion crows, dogs though they are and deserving," he said, and his chest clenched, the last of the bruises from the bear-claw strike aching for a moment. "But two men are murdered, and another three will likely never march under your banner again. Sergeant Porth certainly will not. Brother Whilte and an apothecary fetched from the town are treating his amputated arm as we speak. These are crimes that cannot go unanswered."

Prentice saw the archduchess blink, and he knew she was recognizing how rare it was for him to speak so bluntly to her in public. The calmest part of his mind trusted she would not take it amiss, but knew in her current state, she could. They were all enraged to a greater or lesser degree, with no one to hand to vent their feelings upon except each other or underlings who were as wronged as they were. His wife's eyes scoured him with a demand that he release himself from his own personal chain of discipline. Cobble and alley justice was what she wanted. It was all he could do to refuse her. He met her gaze though. He would not disrespect her, or himself, by looking away.

"I...I will...write to the...to the baroness," the archduchess was stammering, and Prentice could see how impotent she felt as well. At every turn, their attempts to keep Bridgetown an ally were stymied. The Inquisition was winning, and in the Young Hopefuls it had the perfect tool for the task. They were so deeply fitted into the life of Bridgetown that their every misdeed was all but approved, their lies accepted as greater truths, their vanity as justified pride. The Conclave might claim they knew who truly saved the town, but how long before they were converts to the cult of the Young Hopefuls, too—like a drunkard who does not understand that the drink was what was killing him? How do you save the drowning man who thinks he can swim? And do you let him drag you down with him?

"I will request that she..." the archduchess cut herself off mid-sentence. "No damn them! I will *demand* that she bring justice for my militiamen and for the slain of Town Sobridge."

"She will refuse," Prentice said.

"Then she will lose the friendship of the Lioness and the protection of her pride," the archduchess retorted, and even though they were arguing, it was surely clear to all around that Amelia of the Western Reach and her baron knight commander were both as angry as each other, and for the same cause. The indignity of it mattered not at all at this moment. The camp was as far from the privacy of the lady's chambers as could be, but they were both surrounded by family, as much as if they stood at the hearth of their own homes.

"If that happens, then the Inquisition will have won," Prentice said, finding his calm in the face of his liege's fury. She needed him to be the voice of reason for her now, and loath as he was to douse the fire, he would try.

"Let them!" Amelia spat. She reached into her sleeve and snatched out a small scroll, a letter it seemed. She waved it like a rod of authority. "The Golden Heron has been sighted at last, south of Town Sobridge and on the road, marching north. An old friend of Caius Welburne sent word this morning, a swift rider. It seems that the Earl of Longshepherds' hope to claim Sobridge has been gazumped by Everard, Prince of Sunbury. He and his knights are marching with the Heron's mercenaries up the Great Bridge Road. We can expect to see them within days. Whatever else the prince's expectations, we must surely know he will join them in attacking Bridgetown. Why steal the throne of Town Sobridge and not try for the jewel in the crown as well? We have days to prepare or to decide to throw the doors open and leave the brats to their fate."

In all their years, Prentice had never seen her grace so at the mercy of her anger. In her youth he had seen her overwhelmed with grief and occasionally, though rarely, with fear. There were stories that some kind of melancholy madness had overtaken her in Aubrey, but given the hardships and cruelties of that campaign, not to mention her growing pregnancy, it was unsurprising that she had taken some time to regain herself after being caught in the carnage of the cannons. There were men in his ranks who might lose themselves to fear after that. But this was not fear; it was fury, and if he did not act for her, it would carry her into damage that could not be repaired. Before Prentice could speak, though, two men rode up swiftly on horses—Farringdon on his charger and Dahyoor riding his fey pony, leading its partner behind. Farringdon dismounted swiftly and bowed to his wife while the fey man sat his saddle. His people did not dismount in front of strangers without cause.

"Dahyoor has returned with news, Your Grace, Knight Commander," Farringdon reported. "Urgent. I brought him through the town immediately."

"What news? Returned from where?" the archduchess demanded. She looked up at the fey rider as if she thought to command him to dismount and show her the correct respect. Knowing her current feelings and how well the instruction would be received, Prentice moved to intercede.

"Speak what you have seen," he told Dahyoor. When the fey man cocked his head slightly, showing a moment's suspicion, Prentice added. "What I know, the Lioness knows."

Dahyoor shrugged.

"*Kreff* in steel, riding under colored flags, are coming, a day behind on the trail."

"A fey day's ride or a Kingdom ride?" Prentice asked, knowing the two were far from the same.

"A *kreff* day," Dahyoor explained.

"Two armies?" the archduchess all but cried out. "The Inquisition springs its trap, and we are dithering here trying to keep this village of children from playing in the road and being crushed under their marching feet. No wonder the Heron has been unseen so long. They were waiting to time their arrival with their allies in the north."

Prentice's eyes met Farringdon's, then slipped to his wife before going back to the marquis. He nodded, giving the knight captain the signal to explain.

"It cannot have been that, my love," he said, stepping closer and risking taking her hands in his own. As his gauntlets closed upon her fingers, she pulled back, as if to resist his comfort and maintain her rage. He caught them again and pulled her close, speaking more quietly, so that even Prentice barely heard him. "It is not possible to coordinate so many men so well over such distances. It might have been their hope, but it is pure luck that they achieved it. Also, if it is Robant's force returned, then we have little to fear. He was driven off once already."

The archduchess nodded gently, looking into her husband's face and allowing herself to be comforted some, at least. Prentice's ear caught on one particular word, though.

"How say you 'if', My Lord?"

"Your fey man there says they are not coming by the Great Bridge Road," Farringdon explained, looking over the archduchess's head as he continued to hold her close. She had placed her palm on his chest now, intimate despite the hard steel of the breastplate on his torso. "The army he observed is camped at a village somewhere between the Azures and the Rose Carabost woods. The men coming to us now are only a fraction of that. By the description of the banners, it sounds like a delegation. I think they are the nobles who have not bent the knee to Daven Marcus, the loyal peers of the Grand Kingdom, the Usurper's enemies in the civil war."

"Potential allies?" the archduchess asked, her voice softening at last. It seemed the surprise of the revelation had helped save her grace from the runaway steed of her own emotions. Prentice was impressed but not surprised. Feminine though the Lioness of the Western Reach surely was, she was not called the Lioness by accident.

"We can hope, my love," Farringdon agreed with her softly. "But whoever they are and whyever they come, we must send word to the baroness. And we must be the first. If she learns the news by other hands, it will suit our needs not at all."

The archduchess nodded, then looked to Prentice and he forced himself to nod as well but was unable to soften his own expression. For all that circumstances had stilled the cries for vengeance, his militiamen were no less dead or wounded.

"The knight captain's judgement is sound," he managed to say.

"Then I have two reasons to send to the silly fi...to the baroness," the archduchess said, and she straightened her shoulders, her baby bump suddenly becoming pronounced. If any Reachermen had not yet heard the rumors, they would learn within the hour, surely. Their liege was with child and soon to have an heir.

"I will go to at once, and we will be first with the news. Perhaps yet more evidence of our service to the alliance will prompt the baroness to do what is right and bring the Young Hopefuls to account."

"And if she does not?" Prentice heard himself ask and cursed inwardly. The archduchess was calming to a more level-headed decision making. Why would he risk stirring her ire once more? She looked at him and sighed heavily. Perhaps she understood what prompted his question better than he expected, perhaps better than *he* did.

"I am yet the Lioness, Baron Knight Commander," she said. "I will defend the pride, and if that means we fight the Inquisition alone, then pray God he blesses us in that endeavor. We can all only do what we can and trust to the Almighty."

That word would spread with news of her baby bump, Prentice was sure. Any Lions who did not love her yet would find it hard not to now, once it became clear she would shatter her own political ambitions on their behalf. Prentice bowed to her as she left, and the militiamen standing nearby—badly pretending to be about some duty but no doubt listening like curious gossips—all saluted. The archduchess and Farringdon mounted up and rode away.

You chose well when you picked her, Lord God, Prentice prayed inwardly and then smirked at his own ridiculousness. If he trusted that God was there, and he had met the Almighty's messengers enough times to have no doubt, then surely he must trust in the Almighty's greatness and right judgement. Anything less would be utter foolishness, or despair.

CHAPTER 68

T he arriving force was indeed no army, but a collection of dignitaries, nobles of a dozen major banners and twice as many minor, perhaps seventy men-at-arms in all. They had been sighted in the dawn light camped a short distance from the town, coming from the west along the riverbank. Forewarned by Dahyoor, Amelia had been prepared for word of their arrival, and so, by the time Lady Penelope and her entourage stepped onto the roof of Norgate to watch the delegation approach, Amelia was already there with Prentice, Farringdon, Dalflitch, and two Lace Fangs—in this case Spindle and Agatha. It was decided that Righteous's presence might be too provocative, although Lady Amelia had to be persuaded. She was becoming tired of tiptoeing around the Bridgetown liege's fragile sensibilities. Nevertheless, the highest worthies of the Western Reach were already awaiting their ally to watch the arrival of yet more peers to Bridgetown.

"Welcome, My Lady," Amelia said pleasantly, bowing her head to the young baroness. "Kind of the rain to hold off for us."

"It is a poor day to welcome so beautiful a sight to my town, Your Grace," Lady Penelope responded, not quite cold but aloof enough that the term of respect sounded almost like an afterthought. Amelia was not surprised. Her letters to the baroness had been direct and full of implicit consequences. She doubted the younger noblewoman would ever again treat her with the enthusiastic friendliness of their first meetings, certainly not for a long while. "Even so, it is fine to see so many peers and men of rank come to Bridgetown."

Come to you, you mean? Amelia thought, schooling her expression. After the hopeful start here in the southernmost domain of the Grand Kingdom, she was back to the guarded watchfulness of courtly life she had known in the first days of her peerage, keeping her face a mask and her thoughts to herself.

"What are *they* doing down there? Do you mean to try to hold them off?" the baroness's cousin Wilforn asked. The ruler of Bridgetown's entourage was nothing like the mass of men it had been when Amelia had arrived, but it was also now made exclusively of Young Hopefuls, that was clear. The proud loud-mouth Wilforn was present still, but the archduchess was pleased that Penelope had brought neither Cassian nor Cyprian with her. Perhaps she was trying not to be too provocative, either. Amelia could only hope. She did not need to look to see where Wilforn was indicating, however.

"They are an honor guard, set out to receive Bridgetown's guests," she explained sweetly. "Given the banners approaching, it seemed appropriate."

Fifty White Lions with their panoplies polished and cleaned were lined on either side of the Great Bridge Road immediately behind the Norgate's additional earthwork defenses.

"An honor guard?" Penelope demanded, not of Amelia but of Wilforn, and then the other Hopefuls standing behind her. Their smug smiles slipped some in the light of their liege's clear displeasure.

Careful boys, Amelia thought. *The approval of uneven nobles is a tough horse to ride. It is never fully broken to the saddle.* Their discomfort was a petty pleasure, however, and she put it aside in her thoughts.

"We only thought to stand by their entry into the bridge, of course," she said politely. "Their escort through the town belongs rightly to Lady Penelope and the guard of her choosing. We can offer our assistance, but I did not want to presume."

"Did you not?" Penelope asked coldly.

"You presumed to put those illegal, humorless bronze noise-makers out the front of our town," Wilforn snapped. "What welcome does *that* give? And you've defiled the baroness' fields to do it."

Amelia had to smirk at that. Prentice and Farringdon had divided the twelve cannons between them, deploying six to each gatehouse, south and north. The Sougate guns had been mounted on the bastion's roof and on two lesser towers, covering not only the Great Bridge Road as it wended its way from Town Sobridge but also the south banks of the Murr on either side. When the Golden Heron's army arrived, if they thought to bypass Sougate and simply try to cross to the town by boat, the cannons would be able to punish them, even shooting over the river itself some way.

By contrast, Master Benlow Sent-Fane had declared Norgate's roof too weak to take the force of cannon shooting, and so the other six guns had been incorporated into the embankments and trenches Sir Sedgemark had been building to defend the northern bridge. Long before any assaulting men-at-arms reached the Norgate barbican, they would be forced to traverse over fifty paces of rises, dips, spikes and pits. The road itself had been redirected so that it snaked through the defenses, making a direct charge impossible as well. Short of building a curtain wall and an actual moat full of water, the small northern fortification could hardly be more protected.

"We have garrisoned the Norgate and done whatever we can to make it secure," Amelia told Wilforn. "Far from making them feel unwelcome, I think this will show the coming delegation just how unassailable Bridgetown has become, now that she has thrown off the shackles of the Usurper's occupation and set her own course."

A course marked by childish ambitions, she did not add. It would not hurt to flatter the flailing baroness a little at this point. After all, it might be a near impossible task, but if the Young Hopefuls could be used to drive a wedge into the new alliance, why should she not try to drive a wedge between the fool Hopefuls and the leader they were leading astray? Now that her hurt for her people was less raw, Amelia recognized that the alliance *was* worth saving, if it could be.

But only if you punish the savages that hunted my militiamen, little girl, she thought. Amelia turned to regard the approaching men on horseback. Their polished steel seemed greyer in the overcast morning light, but they rode with straight-backed pride nonetheless. Searching their pennants and banners, she did what she could to recognize any she might know. She was sure some had been hanging in King Chrostmer's audience chamber back before the Red Sky. That chamber had really been a hall of another noble's manor-house, loaned to the king for his use. *What had been that man's name?* Amelia found she could not recall, though she wondered if he might be down there somewhere amongst the enemies of her enemy, Daven Marcus. Of the banners themselves, she knew some names—Kelberrin, with his crossed gold keys, and surprisingly, the ship and mermaid over hatched blue and white of Gawestead. The last time she had seen Earl Gawestead, he had been supporting Daven Marcus against her in King Chrostmer's court. The earl must have fallen out with the Usurper at some point since.

As the column drew closer to the gate, it circled around the single road leading through the earthwork defenses. In amongst the fine men in armor, Amelia noted at least two distinct sets of fellows in darker robes, though no less gilded and adorned with finery—ranking members of the clergy, peers of the Church. Were these from the men who had been meeting in synod recently? And was that a true synod, or was it a faction? Just as the nobles represented a part of a shattered nobility, so the clerics must be a part of the shattered Church hierarchy. Daven Marcus's one great act of petty hatred had broken all of higher society, from the Azure Mountains east to the Tassassim Ocean.

The riders in column paused just before they reached the part of the path where the White Lions were lined up on the sides. At the twin column's head was a herald bearing a trumpet, which he put to his lips, blowing a resounding b_ast with a varying tone.

"The trumpet call of peace," Penelope said, a little breathlessly. Amelia had never heard of such a thing, and she looked to her captains. Farringdon shook his head in confusion, unable to confirm or deny. Prentice shrugged.

"Old tradition," he said, leaning close to whisper in her ear. "I could not say if this was exactly it, but it is a close enough guess. Our hostess is supposedly a lover of all things chivalric. If anyone would know…"

Amelia nodded and waved Prentice away again but gave him a swift smile of thanks. The trumpet blew once more and then the herald let it rest upon his knee.

"Ho, the gate," he shouted in a voice so loud and clear that it might even have put the twins to shame. "What troops are these and whose flag flies over Bridgetown? We have word of the death of Earl John. Who sits the seat of the earldom?"

It was a formal question, and as it rose to the barbican roof, Penelope rocked on her heels and back, looking again like the enthusiastic girl she had appeared to be the day Prentice's Gryphon Banner of the White Lions had arrived.

This is what you had hoped our coming would be like, isn't it? Amelia thought as she regarded the young noblewoman, feeling only a sad pity. The stalled baroness turned to one of the twins on the other side of her from Amelia, and the man stepped to the battlement, leaning over to shout through a crenel in the battlement. Despite his awkward physical position, his voice was clarion clear.

"Lady Penelope, heir of Earl John, Archduchess-elect, rules here," he bellowed. "Name yourselves and state your purpose in coming armed to her door."

The herald looked over his shoulder to the front of the column. Words were exchanged, unheard at this distance, and the herald turned back to the barbican.

"We are the emissaries of the Forberest Compact, sworn to oppose the false king and to see a true king crowned in Denay," came the cry. "If Bridgetown and her liege would welcome our cause, we come in peace and ask leave for an audience."

Amelia was doing her utmost to see what was happening on the ground without the indignity of leaning over like the herald twin, but out of the corner of her eye she noticed Penelope bringing her hands up as if to clap with delight, then stop herself just in time, pressing them together beneath her chin as if in thought instead.

At least she's making an effort at dignity, Amelia thought, then noted the woman's gleeful smile. *Not a great effort, granted.*

"Tell them the gate will be opened to them soon," the baroness instructed her herald, and then she turned toward the stairwell. Wilforn didn't notice her movement at first and so she called after him impatiently.

"Where are we going now?" he asked in his usual impertinent manner, but his cousin's mood let her ignore his failing this time.

"To the castle, of course," she said happily. "I will receive them in my great hall." Then she headed down the stairs and the rest of her entourage followed unquestioningly, while the twin shouted down the instruction to the waiting knights and nobles. A moment later, the barbican roof was empty of all except Amelia's own entourage and the White Lion sentries, holding watch as their brothers below held post as the honor guard.

"Well, it appears we are not invited," Amelia said simply, more bemused than offended.

"We must attend regardless, Your Grace," Dalflitch said naturally. "I, for one, have never let being uninvited keep me out of the places I needed to go."

"Indeed, My Lady," Amelia said with a smile and shake of the head. "And perhaps my invitation is implicit. Perhaps I have simply moved from honored ally to least favored member of the new archduchess' entourage."

"An intolerable demotion, if true," Dalflitch declared. "A misstep the young filly must be made to realize, lest it cost her dearly."

Lady Dalflitch's tone remained as light and cool as it always was when she was in public, but Amelia knew her well enough to know that she was infuriated on her liege lady's behalf. When Dalflitch spoke of a misstep and making Penelope realize it, Amelia suspected the lady seneschal was already plotting possible revenges of the courtly form, the game she was a past master at playing. The archduchess wasn't sure if she wanted to restrain her lady-in-waiting or to unleash her. It was a similar feeling she had with Farringdon and Prentice when thinking of Bridgetown's defenses.

Strange, she thought, marveling inwardly. *Now that I am strong, almost unassailable in my status, with the mightiest warriors and weapons—both military and social—at my command, the greatest challenge is knowing when to hold them back and when to release them to conquer.*

The sound of the gatehouse doors and the portcullis being drawn rumbled up through the barbican while the baroness's gold and orange skirts flew to the other end of the bridge and disappeared under the keep on the island side. Soon, the clop of the first horses coming onto the bridge could be heard. Amelia looked to her husband, but he misread her expression, apparently thinking that she was asking his opinion on their invitation, or lack of.

"I cannot say, my love," he said with a shrug. "Kingdom politics is still something of a mystery to me. If this had been the Vec, with all that's happened between us and the Bridgetown folk? Well, you can be sure there would have been four duels to the death and a minor war by now."

"The day is yet young, My Lord," Dalflitch said quietly, and there was a sense that it was not entirely a jest between them.

Amelia smiled nonetheless and then looked to Prentice. He was not smiling. His manner was sober, and the archduchess was sure she could read his thoughts easily enough.

I am your sworn man, she heard him say in her heart. *Only pursue justice for our slain and I will shed my blood to the last drop for you.*

She nodded to him solemnly, and he returned the gesture. He knew full well she would do just what he wanted, for it was what she most wanted as well.

CHAPTER 69

"Daven Marcus is dead!"

Amelia felt her heart skip the moment those words rang through the air of Bridgetown's now crowded great hall. Leaving time for the emissary company to cross into the town and feeling no desire to lower her dignity by rushing, Amelia and her closest advisors had arrived at Earlsbastion some while later. By the time they did, the mass of men in steel plate had been ushered within, their horses filling the castle's small bailey like a breeder's corral. Wending their way through the many mounts being attended by a handful of squires, they had found the way into the castle proper completely unimpeded. All its stewards and servants were now rallying to formulate the proper reception for so many worthies at once.

"There probably has not been a gathering of peers and lesser nobles like this in Earlsbastion in their lifetimes," Prentice observed as they passed without objection through halls crowded with many moving bodies, half too distracted to even think to bow or curtsey at Amelia's passing.

"It must be many years since Bridgetown was a stop on any royal progress," Dalflitch agreed. "It certainly was of no interest to either prince when I was a part of the Rhales court."

History lessons were all well and good, but Amelia was stopped when her party reached the doors to the great hall, where for the first time they were delayed by attendants. However, lacking any instructions to the contrary, the delay was primarily concerned with whether the guards at the door should allow the Arch-duchess of the Reach into their mistress's presence unannounced or not. In the end, Lady Dalflitch persuaded them with a glowing smile that it would be simpler for all involved if her grace entered quietly. Amelia had not quite snuck into the hall after that but was reminded suddenly of the horrid night she had had to force her way into Prince Mercad's forfeits council—the night Liam had threatened her for the first time and Prentice had taken him in hand like an unruly child. That part at least gave the unpleasant memories a cast of grim satisfaction. As it was, the guards seemed to change their minds about letting her into the chamber unannounced and even before the Reacher contingent were ten paces within, they bellowed her name and title so that every face turned upon them.

Nothing for it now, she thought, and beside her she heard Dalflitch sigh under her breath, a sound of unmistakable exasperation. Baroness Penelope, seated alone on the dais, as if a princess or queen upon a throne, was receiving the highest ranking of the emissaries. She had looked up immediately at Amelia's being announced and made the excited exclamation about Daven Marcus. A room full of martial men all stared at Amelia as her mind struggled to incorporate the impossible news.

Dead? Is it over?

It took all Amelia's will not to shake her head in disbelief. Like a monstrous troll said to be lurking in the mountains, or the witch in the deep forest, the far Usurper had been the monster lurking at the eastern frontier of her domain for years. It seemed inconceivable he had simply passed away. Who was the mighty hero who had slain the horror?

"How?" she managed to force out, certain her voice sounded weak, as even the lightest shifting of the crowd filled the air with minor creaks and clashes of metal that together added up to a true din.

"In the north…" Penelope began to explain, but a handsome, dark-haired young man with fluted armor edged in gold, coughed politely.

"With respect, Lady Penelope, if I may," he said, and his voice was smooth and well formed. He seemed familiar to Amelia, and her mind searched for his name. "Reports of Daven Marcus' death have not been confirmed, but his army is routed, taken to ships and fleeing from the Quenland frontier lands to return to Denay."

"I did not even realize he was so close to the far north coast," Amelia said as she forced herself forward, continuing to approach the dais. The knights and nobles in armor watched her, and she was sure there was a mix of expressions on their faces, but her thoughts were fixed entirely on the baroness and the leader of her guests.

"That's the most delicious part, Lady Amelia," Penelope said, stripping the archduchess of at least one rank of peerage, though whether intentionally or not was hard to say. Even more than usual the liege of Bridgetown looked like an excited young girl. It was disconcerting in a ruler. "The kingslayer was besieging Lastermune's castle on the edge of the Quenland forests, and that's leagues from the coast. In order for his army to flee by boat, they must have been broken and driven away."

"Which is part of why it is said that Daven Marcus might himself be dead," the emissary leader explained and suddenly Amelia recognized him.

"Sir Marken?" she said without thinking. He heard his name and smiled, bowing his head to her.

"Count Marken Lark-Stross, now," he said politely. "I inherited the title nearly two years ago."

"I am sad to hear that, My Lord," Amelia said sincerely. "I knew your father but little, but in all my dealings with him I found him to be honest, courageous, and worthy. His passing is a loss to the Grand Kingdom."

"Only one of too many, I fear," the young count said philosophically, then he cocked his head. "I am sorry, but I do not know how to address you. I understand you style yourself an archduchess now, but I do not know the forms for that peerage."

Style myself? Amelia thought. *What a polite way to tell me you do not agree with my title. You really are your father's son.*

"The Archduchess of the Western Reach is still her grace," Lady Dalflitch explained, fulfilling her role as lady-in-waiting. "Within her own realm she sits a throne and reigns as a princess. Amongst the other peers of the realm, she is yet of the same rank and makes no new claims of authority or reverence."

"As you say, My Lady," young Lark-Stross said to Dalflitch with an inclination of his head, then turned to Amelia once more. "Your Grace."

"My Lord," Amelia answered him with a similar motion and then turned to her husband. "May I introduce my husband, Marquis Consort Farringdon, former prince of Aubrey, now returned to the bosom of the Grand Kingdom through the Western Reach."

"Lord Count," Farringdon said, bowing as rank required, playing the polite nobleman at his wife's side. Amelia was sure he would not mind her using him in this way to remind them that while she had adopted a new Veckander-style title for herself, in doing so she had brought fresh honor to the Grand Kingdom as a whole and not only to herself. She was hoping to head off any jibes or pre-emptive questions of legality. She was not as successful as she desired.

"Is Aubrey in Reach hands?" an unnamed noble standing near to one of the clutches of clergy asked with a cold expression. "We had heard it was reclaimed by a Veckander army almost as soon as you married."

"Oh, not so, My Lord," Farringdon said to the fellow before Amelia could answer. "The army that beset my homeland is gone from the territory, and the former rebels of Veckander Aubrey have embraced Archduchess Amelia as their liege lady. They are free Reachermen in their hearts and lives, faithful to Grand Kingdom and a rightful king, when he is crowned. As am I."

The snide noble scowled and looked away, annoyed at the simple rebuff. Amelia kept herself from smiling. Farringdon was no fool when it came to the ploys of courtly life, but his earnest demeanor was more disarming than many would expect.

"These are not the matters at hand, surely," Lady Penelope said, sitting forward on her "throne." No doubt she wanted to steer clear of matters about titles. She had not relinquished her own ambitions to the same rank as Amelia, after all. "If the kingslayer is broken, then why have you come in force, gentles?"

Count Lark-Stross paused and looked at two or three of the men standing closest to him. By their armor and its accoutrements, Amelia guessed they were high peers themselves—counts, earls, or dukes. How many were only recently raised to their stations by their fathers' or other relative's deaths, Amelia wondered. Were these what the Young Hopefuls could have been? Regardless of new statuses, they had accepted Lark-Stross as their leader, that was clear at least, as they gave him unspoken freedom to address the baroness on their behalf.

"Our war against Daven Marcus's forces is not concluded, even if the kingslayer himself is, in fact, dead," he explained to the liege of Bridgetown. "We heard word of your defeat of Duke Robant's army here and came to see if you were ready to join the compact, to finish the war and put a new king, a righteous king, on the Denay throne."

Penelope looked to Amelia, meeting her gaze directly, and for a moment Amelia wondered what the young woman was thinking. Penelope began to explain to the count before she looked away.

"We put the kingslayer's men out of Bridgetown," she said, clearly phrasing her words carefully. "We also leant our aid to the archduchess in a moment of her need. In return, she helped us finish off with Robant's army. It gave us space to ready a bloody nose for the Vec prince of Town Sobridge. Perhaps you heard of our victory."

That's one way of putting it, Amelia thought, doing her best not to sneer at her increasingly petty ally who was now almost certainly working to not look.

"I fear we have no word, My Lady," the count said. "But any victory over a rebel prince is to be welcomed. Perhaps at a later time you might share the tale with us."

"Gladly," Penelope gushed. "If you think to put a rightful king on the Denay throne, you must have a candidate in mind. Is it you, My Lord?"

"She wishes," Dalflitch whispered, just loud enough to be heard by those closest to her, lifting her sleeve to discreetly cover her mouth and pull out a handkerchief. "Take watch, Your Grace, she means to skip archduchess and princess completely now, moving straight on to queen. Trust one who once had the same ambition."

Amelia thought her lady seneschal might well be correct. Even in her most immature moments, Penelope had never seemed quite this girlish. As she leaned toward the handsome count, he shook his head with a polite, self-effacing laugh.

"I fear not, My Lady," he said readily. "My connection to the royal line is far too distant and too thin to be considered. There are heirs with better claims. As to a picked candidate..."

He paused and looked to his fellows, his pleasant expression dropping for the first time since Amelia entered the hall.

And that is the crack in the foundation of your "compact," isn't it, My Lord? Amelia thought. There was more than one faction here, regardless of their united appearance, and they had different claimants they foresaw upon the throne. Even if Daven Marcus was indeed dead, the civil war might yet go on.

"Of course, My Lord," Penelope was saying when Amelia turned her thoughts back to listen to the conversation. "A throne is not something one can simply claim and try to force upon their peers."

"Fool thing to say, girl," Dalflitch whispered, dabbing at her mouth again with the kerchief. Amelia had to agree, and a moment later the assessment was vindicated as a short but stout clergyman in a black robe of deep velvet pushed himself forward. On his chest he had a gold cross, but as she recognized him, Amelia thought it was less ornate than the one he had worn when she had first met him—Reverend Master Faldmoor, Primarch Elder of the Academy at Ashfield.

"It is pleasing to hear that you do not approve of lesser nobles claiming thrones by force," the reverend master said with an imperious voice, as well spoken as Prentice's or the newly acceded Count Lark-Stross, as well as projected with the skill of a gifted orator. A great preacher by training and talent, that was clear; pity he was such a pompous, self-righteous twit. "There has been much fearful talk of late. Use of words like 'archduchess-elect' put us in mind of mistakes made in other quarters of the Grand Kingdom. We would hate to think the opportunism seen in those parts might have infected thinking here in Bridgetown."

Cur, Amelia thought, and for a moment she wondered if Faldmoor might be in the service of the Inquisition. He could be, even though he ostensibly stood with Daven Marcus's enemies—the Inquisition seemed to be forever playing many sides against the middle, as it were. Amelia watched Penelope's mouth open and close mechanically as the girl reached for something to say. The young noblewoman was about to be thoroughly outclassed in conversation in her own court. Amelia knew what that felt like. In her first meeting with the reverend master she had barely escaped without being formally branded a heretic. He had been in the company of a Lark-Stross count that night as well. She looked to the new count and was surprised to see Marken did not seem to approve of the learned sacrist's intervention at this moment. When she glanced back at Faldmoor, Amelia found her own attention suddenly drawn to a man standing behind him in a mail byrnie and tabard of a Church knight order because she recognized him. It was the exiled former-earl, Sebastian. Just how many of this Forberest Compact were enemies of hers? Amelia shook her head.

Fool question, she thought, chiding herself. Without doubt there would be an array of men in this room with cause to hate her, justified or not, and that before the question of over-ambitious claims to titles was even raised.

"With respect, Reverend Master Faldmoor, this is not the time for such matters either," Lark-Stross said, and Amelia did not envy him his task of mollifying all the sides of his possibly shaky alliance. "I remind you that for now we have come ask Lady Penelope into our compact, and now that we have confirmed that the archduchess is here, to invite the Western Reach to join us as well. It has already been decided that we will make the invitations first."

"And I remind you, young count, that those invitations must be accepted, if they *are* accepted, with certain assurances," Faldmoor replied.

"What assurances?" Penelope asked. The count turned to answer her, but the reverend master got in first.

"Amelia of the Western Reach must cease from styling herself as an "arch" duchess," he pronounced, turning his disdainful gaze on Amelia, while behind his shoulder Sebastian glared at her with equal loathing. The archduchess felt her eyes narrowing in hatred as she returned their gazes, but then she schooled her expression to neutral and straightened her shoulders. No need to reveal her own emotions at this moment. It would gain her nothing.

"Further, she must immediately present herself before Mother Church and recant her heresies, including her ungodly marriage. She must beg forgiveness and accept a true husband, appointed for her by the elders of God's people. This is the decision of the patriarchs in synod. You have been told that these matters must precede your political negotiations."

Amelia stiffened, and beside her she felt her husband do likewise. It was only that the man's audacity was so breathtaking that she did not offer an immediate retort. It was as if the last few years, the chaos and killing, did not even register in the sacrist's mind. He still talked as if he and his ilk had an iron grip upon the moral character of the Grand Kingdom. Did he not realize how stained the reputation of the Church had become? Behind her, she was cheered to hear an unknown voice from the other side of the room make a none-too-quiet, whispered comment.

"What synod? Half the patriarchs are preaching Daven Marcus' kingship and sending Church knights to kill you lot. Without us, you'd all be hung in crow's cages by now, tongues cut out and bits burnt off with hot iron. That's the only reason you're with us, to save your own hides."

Amelia did not look to find the speaker and hoped that talk of torture was more of a metaphor. The slaying of the sacrist on the cathedral steps had been shocking enough for her. The thought that members of the Church hierarchy had resorted to brutalizing their "rebellious" fellows and then executing them made her sick to her stomach. Were all the clergy like the Reclanders or the Silent Hand now? Had any ever been men of faith and mercy? It was surely an unjust question, but a difficult one to banish from her thoughts.

If the reverend master had timed his objection poorly for the other members of the compact, he had completely misjudged the liege of Bridgetown. When Amelia looked back, she saw that Penelope was already on her feet, the archduchess-elect's face a mix of fury and disappointment that certainly did not bode well for Faldmoor's cause within this new alliance.

"This audience is concluded," she all but shouted. "Get out of my hall, all of you. I will not hear any more of this talk today." As soon as Faldmoor had denounced Amelia's status as archduchess, he had shown himself an enemy of Lady Penelope's dreams as well. As the ruler of the Western Reach already knew, the young noblewoman did not take having her dreams damaged at all well.

With her simple dismissal, Penelope left the dais at pace and exited the hall through a side door, which was quickly closed behind her. Lark-Stross watched her go, too dignified to call out but clearly disappointed by her exit. Then he turned his gaze upon Faldmoor. Amelia could not hear what he said, but she could read his lips, as likely everyone in the hall could, if they were looking.

"Bloody fool."

Amelia did not disagree with the assessment.

"Poor girl is disappointed at every turn," Dalflitch commented calmly, her tone expressing not the least bit of compassion or concern.

"About time she learned to play the game properly then," Amelia said, equally coldly. Most of her anger was in fact directed at the sacrist not ten paces from where she stood, but it spilled over in her mind at least some upon the girlish noblewoman who was not managing her new duties at all well. Looking about, the archduchess saw that she was not the only one who had an angry face to show the reverend master, which was comforting. Count Lark-Stross even gave her an apologetic frown for the one moment their eyes met. For his part, Faldmoor appeared serene in his self-righteousness, not the least concerned with whatever ire he had aroused around himself. Slowly the emissaries left the hall, and Amelia wondered what they would do now.

CHAPTER 70

The archduchess retired to the Paramour's Chambers for the rest of the afternoon, explaining that she planned a nap, since no other urgent matters awaited them. She released her senior ladies-in-waiting to their own concerns, trusting the three newly raised Lace Fangs to guard her in her own dwelling. Prentice looked in on his wife and children and had a chance to introduce the babies to Sir Turley.

"I'm your uncle, little tots," the Knight Castellan of Dweltford told the infants, hefting up the swaddled Gant like he was testing the weight of a sack of flour or sugar, then winked at baby Amy still in her crib. "Whatever your stuffy old da and ma won't teach you, come and ask me. I know all the best secrets. Oh, and I'm the one who knows how to get the booze, so when you figure on yourselves as old enough, I'm your man."

"No, you are not!" Dalflitch said as she looked up from cooing over the little girl. She turned back to Amy. "Don't you listen to that mop-haired lout. His head's as woolly on the inside as it looks on the outside. You listen to your parents and obey them. They love you and will put you to right every time. This jackanapes will ruin you, just like he's tried to ruin me."

"I have not ruined you," Turley protested.

"I said you have *tried* husband, not that you had succeeded."

"I don't know who you two are putting this act on for, but it for certain isn't my children," Righteous said archly as she took Gant back from Turley's hands, as if frightened he might be about to toss him like a sack as well. She passed her son to Emma, the wetnurse, and then moved to stand beside Lady Dalflitch.

"For ourselves, 'course," Turley asserted. "I tell you, every night in our house is like this."

He looked at his wife as if to garner her agreement, but she regarded him stone-faced.

"At least, I *could* tell you," he said swiftly under her stern gaze. "Except I am not the sort of man that speaks of the private things what happen in our good home. I am not so un...so un..."

"Uncouth, husband," Dalflitch finished for him.

"Quite so. I am not an uncouth man, no how. I am a knight, a castellan, and a respectable man, possessed of great whopping stores of couth, in my inner-most. My good lady wife says so, and I trust her word impl...im...no question."

Dalflitch sighed and rolled her eyes before looking to Righteous for sympathy, but all the baroness could do was laugh. Prentice chuckled with her.

"I am afraid our children are doomed to become wastrels and gadabouts, my darling," Prentice said, smiling as he did so. "Their uncle's example is sure to lead them astray."

"Not if I have aught to say about it," Righteous replied without malice.

"And you shall have my support in that as well, My Lady," Dalflitch assured her. "It is the least I owe you for not keeping my husband on a tighter leash."

"Any tighter and I'd howl like a dog with a thorn in its paw," Turley protested.

The conversation paused at a knock upon the door, and Farringdon entered to say that he was going to the camp to review the evening's orders and dispositions and to ask if Prentice wished to accompany him since even the White Lions' two commanders should not travel about alone, following the knight commander's standing orders. As the twins were dozing and she had been cooped up all day, Righteous decided to go with them. Turley seemed about to volunteer to join them as well when his wife mentioned that she had no business planned for the afternoon and that she felt her grace's treasury needed no attending at this time. Turley cried off to have the company of his wife. Thus, the two leaders of the Lions and the first Lace Fang walked together through the streets of Bridgetown, talking in the darkening hours of the late afternoon.

"Do we yet know exactly how many of our lads got jumped?" Righteous asked. "Names and all?"

"Almost, My Lady," Farringdon confirmed. "We have two men yet at large from the Lion Banner and one from the Gryphon, but all three are men with family in Bridgetown and official leave to be abroad. If they were in trouble, or badly injured, we would expect their relatives to have come to us."

Righteous nodded. Prentice let the conversation range without much input. Between deciding the best use for Benlow Sent-Fane and his gunners, wondering whether to restart the Bridgetown militia's training, and thinking of ways to reinforce Sougate against the soon-to-arrive Heron army, he had enough to occupy his mind. And that was before considering what to do about the Young Hopefuls and the ambushed Lions. That last matter he was happy to leave in the archduchess's hands, at least for now. The crowds around them, trading on the streets of the town, were readily standing back, either out of respect or fear, and their chatter blended into a background noise, like the flow of the river whenever they drew near to a channel or a bridge. It was simply always there. That was why he stopped in surprise when he thought he heard an oddly familiar voice call his name from down a side alley. He looked and saw a retreating figure he might have recognized but could not readily identify.

"My Lord?" Farringdon asked from a few paces ahead when he realized that Prentice had stopped.

"Somethin' wrong, husband?" Righteous also asked, stepping back to him.

"I thought I heard..."

"Heard what?"

"My name," Prentice said, struggling to order his thoughts. His mind struck upon the identity of the person he thought he had seen, but it seemed so far-fetched that he couldn't quite believe it.

"We didn't call on you until after you stopped," Farringdon said.

"No, from down that gap between those buildings there. I think...it sounded like my brother."

"Pallas? What would he be doin' here?" Righteous demanded, more skeptical than concerned.

"Not Pallas," Prentice said. "My eldest brother."

"Could it have been him?" Farringdon asked, peering down the alley. Now that his companions had joined him, Prentice could see that it looked like a potters' row, with at least one obvious brick kiln and numerous craftsmen sitting in front of their workshops, crafting in clay or painting already fired creations.

"I suppose, but I doubt it," Prentice said, feeling his thoughts start to arrange themselves back into order. "My head felt strange for a moment, similar to the way the archduchess described when the Inquisition man read his spell over her in Aubrey. I think they might have been trying to summon me by it. Perhaps if you had not been here, I might have been more encharmed."

Farringdon and Righteous looked at each other with some concern.

"Good thing we were here then," she said earnestly.

"Although it might also be that the charm was simply not strong enough," Farringdon added encouragingly. "My love was not affected at first. The charm only overtook her with the added shock of the hilltop explosion."

"Then they've wasted another good arrow this time," Righteous concluded. "Did you want to go after 'em, see if we can catch us a agent of the Quiet Hand?"

"Silent," Prentice corrected his wife, reflexively.

"What?"

"Nevermind. No, I do not want to go down unknown alleys or across the planks in this foreign town, unsure if it is my friend or foe that I seek. Besides, what I took for Xavoer might well have been a skin thief, posing as my brother. If that's so, we will never find him. He could have had three new faces and two new sexes by now."

"Worrying though that the Inquisition might know your brother's appearance well enough to falsify him to you," Farringdon observed, and suddenly all three looked at the crowd yet swirling around them. "Do you know him well enough to pick a true brother from false?"

Prentice shook his head.

"It took me a long moment to recognize the voice at all. The last I saw him was before I left home for Ashfield. I doubt he even looks as I remember now."

Even as he spoke the words, Prentice realized he was not telling them the truth. He *had* seen his eldest brother one more time, some years later, but that was not a memory he wanted to unfold on a street like this. The uncaring crowd continued to move about them, just as the river itself flowed around the shores of the islands and the footings of all the bridges and piers.

"Well, we would do well to remain watchful," Farringdon said. "They might have come at you now, but they could yet go after any of the least of our two companies and work their way up to someone more important. I've already ordered men back from all leave in the town for my banner, especially if the Young Hopefuls are yet upon the prowl. I urge you to do the same, Knight Commander."

Prentice nodded. It was a sound notion.

"Unless that's what they really want," Righteous observed. "The folk thinking our lads are afeared of the Hopefuls. That'll bilk our credit with them merchants and craftsfolk, right quick."

"I hadn't thought of that," the knight captain conceded.

Damned if we do and damned if we don't, Prentice thought. His mouth twisted into an angry sneer.

"I am tired of fencing with invisible opponents," he said coldly. He started marching away, his anger helping him to throw off the last of the malaise the strange encounter had laid on his mind.

"We need our fey boys back," his wife muttered, and he thought that would be a good start but too long to wait.

We cannot delay until spring to find these foes out.

CHAPTER 71

A storm blew up out of the southeast in the night, but by dawn it had passed on, leaving the town drenched and shivering under a slate-grey sky. The fields of Town Sobridge were a sea of mud, but that did not stop the long-awaited Golden Heron army from finally marching into them in the sodden light of morning. Prentice and Farringdon watched from the roof of Sougate as the various companies of the mercenary force broke from their marching columns and began to set up their camp.

"I wonder if Prince Tarningcrest is still with them. I see the Sunbury banner—Prince Everard's standard—but no sign of Tarningcrest's yet. Rosedale's a long way from here, or perhaps he is still back in Aubrey, trying to secure his conquest. Amelia won't let him hold it long, I think, but that is for another day. In the meantime, Everard has a large cadre of knights ahorse, as I recall, for a Vec prince. See, that's some of them there," Farringdon said, pointing to a triangular pennant with a large red sun emblem on a green-and-white background. It was carried by an advance force of riders who had mounted the old cannon earthworks and no doubt discovered the wretched end of Sobridge's levies. With so many dead, Prentice had not ordered his men to the vile ordeal of burying them, and no one had come from the nearby villages, so the bodies rotted in the open. When the wind blew from the south, the sentries on Sougate said the stench was almost overwhelming.

"If they were inclined to mercy or restraint before, they will not be any longer, now that they have seen Bridgetown's handiwork," Prentice said as the men who had clearly ridden to scout the gate's defenses were instead distracted by the horror of the fallen.

"We should go down and tell 'em it weren't us," Sergeant Guillam said, not quite his usual sardonic self. He had returned to his duty after Brother Whilte had finished his ministrations to Sergeant Porth, but the whole experience had hardened his attitude to the world, at least for a time. Porth would live but never fight with the Gryphon Banner again, and Prentice was on the lookout for now for yet another new sergeant. The man Gerrindon, who had taken the banner and was to be the Gryphon's new standard bearer had been one of the other men wounded in the Young Hopefuls' ambushes. Word was that he had walked in on the fight and rushed to his comrades' defense, pure bad luck. Prentice was not so sure. He would not be surprised if the most recognizable officers of his banner had been deliberately targeted. Whether the prospective new sergeant would recover from his wounds was still an unresolved question. The whole incident had left Guillam in a vengeful mood, it seemed. "Or better yet, grab the filthy swines that did it and chuck 'em out."

"That's enough of that talk, Sergeant. Bridgetown is still our ally," Farringdon said, speaking slightly out of turn to rebuke one of Prentice's officers, but the knight commander did not object. Sergeant Guillam saluted as readily as ever, as well.

"Of course, I do hope to see the little bastards strung up by their own mistress before all is said and done," Farringdon went on. "And if she chose to exile them for their crimes instead, I would happily march them to the Vec side of the river and feed them to our friends out there. I'd even invite you to help me do it."

"Very good, My Lord," Guillam said, giving a black-toothed smile and spitting on the slick, wet stones of the parapet.

For his part, Prentice let them go on, focusing his mind on doing a rough count in his head as the enemy deployed to various parts of the field. They were still too distant to say for sure, but making some assumptions, what he saw was not comforting.

"They have more than either of our banners by themselves," he said. "If we have to meet them afield, we will need Gryphon and Lion both."

"They'll have those crossbow companies with them, no doubt. If they've learned their lesson from Aubrey, we can expect them to be put to good use," Farringdon added. Prentice was about to ask for a fuller explanation of the experiences in that campaign when the door to the stairwell was thrown back and two different sets of men climbed out of it. The first was the Masnian man whom Benlow Sent-Fane had set to lead the Sougate contingent of the new cannons. Slight, with an odd-looking topknot, the man was otherwise similar to his countrymen. He emerged and, looking about, moved straight to Prentice, bowing to what seemed an exaggerated depth.

"I check. All powder in oilskin in boxes," the man said, apparently explaining the disposition of the ammunition. Ball shot was stacked by the guns, but powder was stored in rude wooden boxes, lined with waterproof oilskins, and lids with rope hinges, not metal. No metal was allowed anywhere near the powder magazines, as they were called, for fear of striking a spark. The gunners were even forbidden from wearing boots in case the hobnails scratched on the flagstones. Instead, they padded about in soft leather slippers. With the rains, Prentice doubted there was much chance of a stray spark, but the cannons themselves were already under wood and oilskin shelters that sluiced the rain away from them, so the floor stones around them could have been somewhat dry. Even so, he did not envy the gunners with their sodden feet in the cold of winter. Two of Sougate's six guns had been moved inside to be mounted down on the barracks level behind arrow loops that had been brutally expanded with hammers and chisels. Prentice expected the duty of tending those guns, out of the winds and the rain, would be highly sought after. The Masnian crew commander continued his report.

"More powder in the base...base-room."

"Basement," Prentice corrected.

The man bowed his head again, happy to be reproved. "Basement is powder store. Tell men...only gunners to carry. Best if only key is in me."

"I will see to it," Prentice reassured the foreigner, and a moment later the man was walking along the battlement, checking each gun and crew in turn, his wet foot coverings squelching as he walked.

"Don't salute or speak like he can put two thoughts together," Guillam observed. "Hope he can at least shoot straight."

"He is a foreigner, Sergeant," Farringdon said. "Kingdom speech, even Vec styled, is not his native tongue."

"Just as long as it don't affect his aim," the sergeant replied straight-faced, though Prentice could tell he was doing it to give the knight captain a wind-up.

He moved away in case his own passing grin was taken as an encouragement and found that the second group who had emerged from the stairs were two men—Sir Turley and, to his astonishment, Count Lark-Stross. Pausing only to make a mental note that he must command his own sentries to steer clear of the cannons if they were wearing boots, Prentice moved to this odd pair who were standing right at the edge of the ramparts and staring at the arriving army.

"My Lord, Baron Ash," Turley said readily, acting the herald as he had been learning to do ever since he had risen in the archduchess's service, as if he and Prentice had never been friends. "May I present Count Marken Lark-Stross, leader of the Forberest Compact, first among equals, and guest of the Baroness-elect of Bridgetown. My liege lady bids us welcome him and tour him our defenses of the town."

Prentice had to force himself to not shake his head in disbelief. Where was the roguish horse thief he had had to keep out of trouble for so many years on the convict chains in the west? Here was a junior nobleman, dressed in a warm velvet doublet beside an equally warmly dressed senior peer. He even had the cunning to name Penelope "baroness-elect" rather than "archduchess-elect", a more politic move with the leader of the contentious Forberest Compact. Lark-Stross himself had doffed his armor, and now only wore a short tabard with his noble insignia as a marker of his military mission. Next to them both, Prentice felt distinctly chilled in the cold wind. The gambeson he was wearing to replace his lost brigandine was thick but stiff, so that it did not fit cleanly, and the cold tickled its way in through sleeves and under hems. He bowed to the count politely.

"My Lord."

Lark-Stross accepted the gesture with a polite nod.

"Master Ash..." he began but cut himself off with a scowl and shake of his head. "Oh, this is a nonsense!"

"My Lord?" Turley asked, casting a look askance at Prentice. Was the leader of the White Lions about to receive another disdainful rejection? As it turned out, the opposite was about to happen.

"They counsel me that to even acknowledge you is a mistake," Count Marken said. "They say that we must disdain your accession so that we make it clear that this title of archduchess will not stand. For the life of me I cannot see why."

"'They,' My Lord?" Prentice asked, warily curious.

"The members of the Compact, well one of the factions at least," the count explained. "The other two main ones are more interested in victory first, though each see victory to mean their lad on the throne, so even in that they do not agree. But when I said that I meant to begin sounding your liege-lady out, since Lady Penelope has withdrawn from discussions, they were insistent. If I even used her new title, or granted yours since it derives from hers, I will be making a grave error."

"I see," Prentice said, looking again to his friend, who shrugged with a puzzled look on his face. Behind him, Prentice heard the knight captain approach, and the count looked to him with a more natural smile.

"My Lord, Marquis Consort, a pleasure to meet you," he said readily, and Farringdon bowed in response.

You do not hesitate to recognize him, do you? Prentice thought wearily. Because although he had a new title, Farringdon had been born a prince, even if of a rebel, foreign land. If the young count was growing tired of Grand Kingdom politics, Prentice knew he was personally thoroughly sick of it. The heir to the throne had put his own father to the blade and set the kingdom ablaze, but heaven forbid a woman who has ruled her own land with absolute brilliance and devotion take a fraction more honor than the old ways would allow.

"So, what do we do about this, My Lord?" Prentice asked, and the count looked back to him with a sad smile that brightened suddenly despite the greyness of the day about them.

"Well, My Lord Baron Knight Commander, I think I shall do what makes the most sense and leave legal matters to the lawyers," he said, and he bowed his head to Prentice, the amount of respect a count would normally give to a baron. "You've raised your liege an army worthy of any nobleman or royal, and if even the least stories of your achievements are to be believed, you have led it well in her name. If we still had a legitimate king, a petition would have been made on your behalf, and either a rightful prince or the Denay throne itself, if it was even half committed to righteousness, would have bestowed you some kind of accession. When he was still a prince, Daven Marcus threw titles about like they were bones for his dogs."

"Still does, from what I hear," Turley said. "And dogs might be the best word for them."

Lark-Stross smiled, shaking his head indulgently, the way Archduchess Amelia might at one of the knight castellan's jests.

"My father always said, 'Listen to what a man's enemies say about him but judge him by his deeds, and judge a ruler by the men he allows to swear to him,'" the count said.

"A wise man, your father," Farringdon offered.

"I regret my one interchange with him was so difficult," Prentice added sincerely. In the light of all his new experiences with fatherhood, he found himself feeling for this young man who had lost his own father but carried the elder's wisdom with him in his heart. This was how youths were supposed to become men, and the difference showed.

"He liked you, Baron Ash," Count Marken said, surprising Prentice further. "He said so after that night, the way you took all the shame for your lady while she struggled with the reverend master's insults. He said it was something I should remember. That was the sacrificial service every knight owed their liege, and he wished he had a man like you in his service. When word came that you had beaten Baron Ironworth, my father wept for the dead knight marshal, and he refused to believe it when the later story was circulated that you had slain him through treachery."

The count stopped and pointed to Prentice's sword, the one he had claimed that day in the duel with Baron Ironworth.

"He knew, he said he just knew, that you would never shame your lady with such a foul ploy. He heard what your enemies said, but he watched what you did. He would not want me to disdain your success and your rise just for political expedience."

CHAPTER 72

Prentice felt an unexpected lump in his throat and wondered at it as he swallowed. He had received compliments before, but for some reason this tale of respect from a man he barely knew touched his heart. Was it the fatherliness of the man or just the possibility that not every noble had hated him?

"Thank you for your kind words, My Lord," was all he could think to say.

"Kind, but true," the count insisted, and then he looked out over the battlements once more. "Would you share your thoughts with me, My Lord? Marquis Knight Captain?"

Accepting the senior noble's invitation, Prentice and Farringdon stepped to the stone ramparts, facing the Vec fields. Sir Turley chose not to join them but moved around and stood beside the watching Sergeant Guillam a short distance away.

There's trouble, Prentice thought, though not seriously. Out of the corner of his eye he saw Guillam offer Turley something, perhaps some of his chew, but Turley waved it off. For sure his wife would not approve of him blackening his teeth as the sergeant did. Guillam hawked and spat loudly on the stones, and as the three nobles turned to look at him momentarily, he saluted and bowed his head in mock sheepishness. *Oh, trouble indeed.*

"They come in force, My Lords," Count Marken said. "They mean to make history."

"We will have their measure," Farringdon replied confidently.

"I do not doubt. I have seen your camp."

"You have?" Prentice asked, not happy that the recently arrived Kingdom nobles might have been sniffing around his company camp. It was yet another complicating factor they did not need. The Young Hopefuls' night of hunting had both companies looking for blood. A scornful peer could easily provoke an incident from his sentries without even thinking.

"Yes, Sir Turley escorted me there first from your liege's chambers, seeking for you or the Marquis," the count explained readily, which eased Prentice's concerns somewhat. "We learned you were already here and came to seek you out."

"You must have been at my lady's chambers at the crack of dawn," Farringdon said, looking up at the sky momentarily. It was still early morning as it was.

"Indeed, My Lord. Any earlier would have seemed impertinent, I thought," Lark-Stross answered. "I feel the only lady's chamber a man should call upon before dawn is that of his good lady wife. Would you not agree?"

"I do," Farringdon said in a tone that made it clear that even dawn was too early for him to have anyone calling upon his wife, in any capacity. The count turned back to the Veckanders. The mounted scouts had withdrawn now, and the enemy camp continued its slow birth in the muddy fields. Almost certainly they would not attack today.

"If Bridgetown is their ultimate target, they will surely take to boats eventually."

"They might, My Lord Count," Prentice conceded, "but they will have to build them themselves. Bridgetown and Dweltford have the rivers secure all the way west of here to the far escarpments."

The count looked surprised at that statement, but whether it was the claim of control or the mention of a far land feature he would never have heard of, Prentice could not say. He also did not bother mentioning that their control of the rivers was built in part on the loyalty of turncoat smugglers who had only just survived the shadow war on the river against preachers and converts of the Redlander cult.

"There's wood aplenty down in Eden Bay, I'm told," Count Marken went on. "If they are resolved to cross, they could build rafts down there and ship them up here."

"Eden Bay is a long way to go for a raft."

"And one raft is not enough for an army that size to cross the river," the count explained. "They're already here in the rains of winter and paying good silver for the privilege, so I'm told. If they are so resolved, then Eden Bay is not so far to go."

Prentice had to credit the man's assessment. There were myriad woods and thickets visible in Town Sobridge's lands, even from just the top of Sougate. Those were all small, though, well harvested already, and in the midst of farmlands that had been civilized for centuries. If this army wanted the kind of wood needed for large rafts in the amount they would require, then Eden Bay would be simpler, for all the distance was farther to go. Any crossing would have to be a single, overwhelming assault, or else it would be doomed to failure. The White Lions' experiences with Redlanders made that clear. In ones or twos, landing boats were too readily overwhelmed when they tried to come ashore, even with the painted men's craft with their excellent construction and sorcerous sails. En masse though, they could sweep around Greenmarsh's southern defences and put an army ashore on the other islands in an hour. Even though the Golden Heron's force was surely less adept at that kind of action, they would know that massed assault was their only hope, or else they would be feeding their men like sausages into the hungry lion's mouth. The White Lions would eat them for breakfast. In the meantime, it was more likely they would try to seize the Sougate, and Prentice meant to hold the bastion for as long as it took for Prince Everard and whoever else joined the Golden Heron to realize this was a fool's errand. Bankers might have the money to hire an army, but they only spoiled their own business putting one in the field. Any prince with them had to know they could turn on him once he helped them attain their first conquest. A canny prince would not wait for that to happen. He would move first, and hired men did not make the best bodyguards, not like sworn retainers. If he could make the cost too high, the delay too long, Prentice thought there was a good chance the Vec army would fall to infighting. It had happened the last time the southern princes tried to invade.

"Will your liege lady sign on with the Compact, do you think?" the count asked without preamble. It caught Prentice by surprise, and he looked to Farringdon. The marquis seemed equally nonplussed but happy to answer the question.

"I think she would like to," he said. "She sees that the Grand Kingdom must be brought back to peace. If Daven Marcus is dead, she will be less inclined to compromise concerning her rights and titles though, My Lord. Her archduchy has been hard won and secures the Reach's protection on multiple levels. As the knight commander has already observed, the rivers are hers, as are Halling Pass and the Azures entire. The Western Reach has walls and defenses on all its borders. She will welcome a rightful king in Denay but will not be forced if that new royal will not acknowledge the realities of the world after the Usurper's rebellion."

"Belligerence will not help the making of peace," the count said, his pleasant demeanor shifting to a sterner cast for the first time since he had mounted the Sougate steps.

"Then someone of your compact should put a muzzle on the reverend master," Prentice answered readily. He met the young peer's unhappy gaze with a steely glare of his own. Every time Ecclesiarch Faldmoor had met with his mistress, the man had been hateful to her. Prentice had no compassion to spare for the proud churchman or his positions, political or religious. Count Marken held Prentice's gaze for a moment and then shook his head ruefully.

"Damn, I wish you were wrong," he said, conceding the knight commander's point. "The man's knowledge of laws, Church and throne, is prodigious, and he can preach the four legs off my best warhorse, but he never shuts up. Even if his judgement is perfect, we won't make allies by slapping them in the face with his superiority of thought."

"Do you think him superior of thought, My Lord?"

The count sighed.

"My father taught me to believe in God and respect and love Mother Church," he said and now the weariness in his voice showed pain as well. "And I do…I mean I believe…but how can I…how can I love…?" His voice trailed off and he stared out over the battlement again. Prentice doubted he was seeing the Veckander army, though.

The knight commander looked to Farringdon, but before either of them could speak, the count turned back to them.

"They're killing each other," he said, and his voice was anguished. There were tears in his eyes. "Worse than the worst of the Usurper's excesses. They tear at each other like wild dogs. Meetings are set between factions and become bloodbaths. I have seen it myself. Nuns—some old women who surely were nearly blind with their age—I have seen them stripped naked and hanged from wagon-wheel gibbets on the road to their nunnery. Hanged like pieces of meat on a butcher's hooks. How can this be? And neither side is pure. The Inquisition did the murders of those nuns, the three crosses seen on the men-at-arms' tabards, but another order of church knights, the ones who back Faldmoor and his ilk, came upon a village sacrist in a little church who was preaching fidelity to Daven Marcus as the rightful king. They barred the church doors and put the whole congregation to the torch."

"The merciless preachers of mercy," Prentice said simply.

"What was that?" Count Marken asked, as if the simple expression might be a saving line to pull him out of his grief.

"Something some allies of ours say," was all the explanation Prentice wanted to give at this time.

"We have seen our own share of churches and churchmen defiled," Farringdon said quietly. "The Reach has not been spared. But we have also seen the hand of God at work. Many take faith that there is a lit path out of this darkness, though it seems narrow."

"Enter by the narrow way," the count said, recounting scripture, it seemed. If he thought it applied to this situation though, his expression did not show it. He looked from knight commander to knight captain. "You should hear what is said of your lands, the tales told. That exiled man of your liege's—the former earl, Sebastian—he has recanted much to earn himself his title as a Brother Elder of Faldmoor's preferred militant order, but he still speaks of things too strange for many ears."

"Give us a night to sit by a fire together and we will tell you tales to outstrip his," Farringdon told the troubled man. The count looked from him to Prentice, obviously suspecting the claim was a jest or a boast. Their serious expressions seemed to persuade him otherwise. He drew in a long, calming breath.

"Monsters or no, fey tales or simple mortal enemies, it matters not. We need your army, your grace's army, the one you have built for her, Baron Prentice, and I will need to hear otherwise from God himself before I believe aught else. You have more men-at-arms than our forces combined, and we are too fractious to be fully combined. At least half the Compact is terrified that Archduchess Amelia means to march for Denay on her own behalf and make herself queen."

Prentice blinked, too astonished to say anything. Farringdon made a better response, but he almost stammered, reaching for the words.

"We have discussed it, My Lord," he said, which was news to Prentice, "but she is adamant. She has one throne, and she does not sit that by might or force alone. She will not seek a greater throne if might or force are her only path to that."

Count Marken Lark-Stross nodded, and his expression returned slowly to its more thoughtful and diplomatic cast as he clearly took control of the grief that lay under his other motivations. It was an impressive display of self-control, and Prentice felt it was good to see. This man was no hothead, even when sorely provoked. Perhaps he could be persuaded to take some of the Young Hopefuls on as his squires.

"I believe you, Marquis, and am glad to hear it," Lark-Stross said. "I know her grace has made a pact with Bridgetown, and to see its girlish liege giggle and smile like this is all a game is disconcerting. To know the other and stronger half of the alliance is in the archduchess' hands is reassuring. But looking out at the Veckanders here, I realize that it does not matter. Heresy or no—law, theology or tradition—none of it matters in the face of this. We need your army. Any price short of our souls is not too dear to pay."

"I am heartened to hear you say so, My Lord," Prentice said earnestly. "The marquis knight captain and I both are, I am sure."

Farringdon nodded. The count gave them another sad smile.

"Do not be too comforted yet, My Lord Baron," he said. "If I spoke these words openly, the Forberest Compact would be ended that very hour and the factions would be scattered to their own preferred versions of justice, all of them merciless in their own ways."

"Like herding cats," Farringdon said, but it was clear the count was not familiar with the saying.

CHAPTER 73

On the basis of Prentice and Farringdon's report of the arrived Vec force, Amelia composed a letter to Lady Penelope in her own hand, outlining the danger in the most strenuous terms.

"Did you think to mention the Young Hopefuls' crimes again, Your Grace?" Dalflitch asked as she helped her liege draft the letter. Amelia had begun to shake her head, then stopped.

"No, I will," she answered resolutely. "It offends me to think I would make defense of Bridgetown contingent on a matter of civil law, even one this heinous, but it seems little else has penetrated the lady's fluff-filled skull. I will not threaten outright, but mentioning it should at least connect the two ideas in her head."

"And if she decides her boys have the brass to hold her territory without us?" Lady Righteous asked, sitting at the table and nursing Amy, whom she had brought with her on a short walk to get out of their room for a while.

"Then she can try getting her murder militia to hold Sougate for themselves," Lady Spindle interjected.

"By the description, simply having her go to Sougate herself should be persuasive enough," Dalflitch said, passing the archduchess a freshly trimmed goosequill.

"Indeed. That is what I will do," Amelia decided. "I will invite her to see the enemy at Sougate for herself, urging her to be quick."

"She should be seeing it from the castle by now, but sure she'll come hasty enough once those cannons start firing, which they will if the Veckanders attack," Righteous declared, lifting young Amy to burp her. A neophyte stepped forward to lay a cloth on the baroness's shoulder in case the little baby was sick on her clothes.

"Or if you tell her the young count's already been up to look," Spindle suggested, smiling under her mask. "She's only met him the once and I swear the girl is carrying a brightly lit torch already."

"He is fine enough to look upon, I suppose," Dalflitch said in the tone with which she would compare the breed of two horses. "It might do us well to encourage such a match, if the count can be persuaded to accept a wife who'd much rather duel with him than lay with him and give him an heir."

"They can do both, can't they?" Righteous objected. "Me and Prentice can. Turley would too, if you wanted him to."

"No doubt about that," Spindle agreed.

"What my husband would or would not do is of absolutely no concern of yours, Baroness Ash," Dalflitch sniffed and looked to the yet undrafted letter on the table in front of Amelia. All the ladies in the room chuckled, and even the two new Lace Fangs standing attendant behind the archduchess, Daisy and Agatha in this case, risked quick smiles of decorous amusement.

In the end, Amelia did mention Count Marken Lark-Stross in her letter but was careful to make no intimations of a marital nature, only that he had seen the Veckander army and expressed concern at its size. She also asked for the liege of Bridgetown to soon make a decision concerning trials for the Young Hopefuls, or at least a release for Amelia to bring her own charges to the magistrates under the Conclave laws.

"There is no point the Reach militia defending the safety of Bridgetown if the White Lions are not safe within the town's walls," Amelia read as she blew away the fine sand she had used to dry the ink on the page.

"Bridgetown hasn't really got any walls, not truly," Righteous said as she stood to take her now sleeping baby back to its crib downstairs.

"It is metaphorical, My Lady," Dalfitch told her, though the young mother's expression made it clear she had no idea what "metaphorical" might mean and was suspicious, as she so often was, that the lady seneschal was insulting her in some secret high-born fashion.

"The baroness-elect will take my meaning, Lady Righteous," Amelia reassured her, and so the letter was sealed, rolled in a scroll, and sent with Lady Agatha and two neophytes to find a messenger to take it Earlsbastion. When a letter was delivered from the castle in return not a half an hour later, they were all astonished.

"What does it say, Your Grace, if I may ask?" Spindle inquired as Amelia read. "Has she decided to give the Hopefuls what for?"

"No, My Lady," Amelia replied quietly. "I don't think she had read my letter when she wrote this. Or it was written for her, however it went."

There was a long moment of silence as she continued to read, and Amelia knew her not speaking was raising her ladies' sense of concern, but she could not help it. What she was seeing was simply so dumbfounding.

"What silly thing has the filly done now, Your Grace?" Dalflitch asked at last.

Amelia shook her head.

"There's to be a banquet," Amelia said, handing over the letter. "A banquet and dancing in Earlsbastion's hall. The White Lions will not be required as escorts or guards of honor."

"Will they not?" Dalflitch asked, obviously catching the implied insult in the phrasing. "Are *you* even invited, Your Grace."

"There at the bottom," Amelia said. "The worthies of the Western Reach."

"You are not even mentioned by name?" Dalflitch asked, scanning the invitation. "This is intolerable."

Amelia was almost inclined to agree. At another time she might think to spurn the entire event, to pointedly remain in her chambers and make no apology. Her presence might not be missed, but her absence would be noted. The rebuke to Lady Penelope would be considered obvious. The problem with that maneuver was that if Amelia did that, she would miss out on the politicking of the evening and, strong as *she* was, the only peace that could come to the Grand Kingdom would have to be forged by the men in that hall. Amelia had to be there, working the nobles and factions of this Forberest Compact for the sake of her own realm and the good of the Kingdom as a whole. If Daven Marcus *was* already dead, or would be in days to come, whoever took the throne after him must not have a divided kingdom under them.

"I have found, My Good Lady, that the things which I am able to tolerate are far greater than simple slights like this," she said to Dalflitch. "Let us go to this banquet. If the music is good, I might even dance."

The archduchess was deeply pleased that Dalflitch appeared to understand her implicit double meaning.

"Oh, Your Grace, when you dance, especially amongst the kinds of courtiers sure to attend, then even vultures float in the air like turtledoves," declared the lady seneschal. "The words of your song are rhythm enough to set the entire hall to dancing."

"I hope so, My Lady."

From her seat with the other seamstresses, Spindle was watching the two senior ladies converse. Her expression beneath her mask was one of puzzled curiosity.

"I don't understand," she said openly. "Are we going to a dance or not?"

"Indeed, we are, Lady Spindle," Amelia said, feeling suddenly shrewd and eager, though not in the girlish fashion she imagined Penelope likely was at this moment. A night of courtly gambits awaited, and actual dancing was the least thing on the archduchess's mind.

CHAPTER 74

"After asking about, it seems there's one duke—a Lord Sestmanmark—and one son of a duke, Duke-elect Brennham, not raised 'cause there's no true king to do it," Turley reported to the archduchess and her entourage as they waited before entering the great hall. "They're both in one o' the factions, but not the one that that snooty Faldmoor bloke is in. He's part of something that calls 'emselves the True Sons o' Mother Church, and they're mainly made o' Church orders and sworn knights, like what Baron Ash was trainin' to be years ago. The third faction is the smallest, but they're all on that Lark-Stress's account, and everyone agrees he's their best leader—on the battlefield and in the conferences. It's him that's keepin' all the peace. That's what I know to tell you."

"In less than an hour you learned all this?" the archduchess asked with an awestruck expression.

Sir Turley had gone ahead much earlier than the others, acting in his old role as chief steward to find out the lay of the land and what the archduchess was expected to do at this dance. He had clearly kept an open ear during the process and it had collected him a nearly astonishing amount of information.

"He's as canny at all this as you are," Lady Righteous whispered to Lady Dalflitch, though still loudly enough for those nearest to hear.

"You didn't think I married him for his looks, did you?" Dalflitch retorted.

"I did, actually."

"Yes, well," Dalflitch muttered, her expression one of grudging confession. "That was a factor, and not an insignificant one. But it is the bright pennant flying over a castle built upon much sterner stone, I assure you."

"No doubt," Righteous agreed, but she and Lady Spindle shared a smirking glance. Sir Turley groaned quietly.

"I thought, wife, that we weren't discussing private matters in public," he said in an aggrieved whisper. "Wasn't that what was said?"

"An empty corridor outside of the great hall is hardly in public, husband," Dalflitch replied.

"And you might be surprised what counts for private in her grace's chamber," Spindle added, teasing, and Turley groaned again.

"Is there any protocol we must follow?" Marquis Farringdon asked, clearly looking to return them to the issue at hand and cease from standing in a hallway, whispering like mischievous children.

"There's only the high table, My Lord, not like the earlier banquet, so I'm told," Turley explained. "No one's been invited to sit there. It's just the baroness-elect lady, her cousin and her baronet relative. He's not looking too flash either, I'll say that for him. I reckon they had to carry him from his sickbed."

Poor Baronet Forsle, Amelia thought, feeling for the wounded man. *He will have insisted on being present to protect his niece, perhaps even from herself.* He struck her as the kind of man who would cling to life with the skin of his teeth for the sake of his family. If only he could rein the headstrong girl in, even a little. Then Amelia had an unhappy thought: *Perhaps he is already, and this is the best he can achieve.*

"There's food on a couple of long tables to one side," Turley continued, his common accent falling off again now that the subject of conversation had moved away from gossip. "Stewards are bringing wine and some other drinks from casks in the kitchen. There are some chairs around the edges of the room, pushed up against the wood walls with their fancy smell. The rest of the space is opened for the dancing and musicians, as you can hear."

Indeed, music was filtering through the closed hall doors.

"I've silvered some palms to make sure there's a spot for yourself, Your Grace, and you, my love," said the former chief steward, acknowledging his wife along with his liege. "It's not exactly right up next to the high table, but I figure them chairs is to be full of Bridgetown muckity-mucks anyways. Yours are a handful down the wall to the right of the high table. Nice spot, no food table nearby. You can see and be seen, but if you want to be discreet, that should be doable as well."

"Excellent work, Sir Turley," Amelia said sincerely. "Now, the only question that remains—do we enter humbly and quietly or with pomp and circumstance?"

"We're all set for either way, Your Grace. I found how to get to a side door, if you wanted to go in sly and shifty like, but if you wanted to make a big rattle, I slipped a purse to the musicians' leader, the head of the ons-momble, to go quiet for us on my signal."

"Ensemble, husband," Dalflitch corrected. "Musicians are an ensemble."

"That's the word," Turley agreed happily.

"So, which should it be?" Amelia asked, and she looked about to her entourage, which included all five of her lace fangs, though no neophytes were here this time. The ladies all stood with reserve and dignity, offering no opinions. Dalflitch had little more than a wry observation.

"You know how I have attended such affairs, Your Grace," she said, "and I do not think your husband would approve of you dressing like *that*."

Amelia laughed and nodded, thankful for the moment of humor. For himself, her husband showed only loyalty.

"Whatever you decide, my wife, I will be at your side," he said with an earnest smile. She took his hand and squeezed it lightly. That left only Prentice. As with the other two noblemen with her this night, Prentice was not in armor since the White Lions had not been invited. Instead, he, Farringdon, and Turley were all wearing surcoats in chivalric colors over trews and shirts of linen. Farringdon had his wife's lion on his tabard, with one of its paws discreetly lowered from rampant, to recognize that he was only a consort and not a husband with the full rights of his new noble family. Sir Turley, likewise, had the lion of the Reach on his surcoat but only on the upper breast over his heart. He was a bannerman, a retainer knight. Both were in blue edged in cream. Prentice was different.

The Baron of Fallenhill had a Reach blue 'coat, but his heraldry was the rampant gryphon, with lion's forepaws rather than eagle's claws. Around the gryphon's throat was a crown made of bricks, signifying that his family held a warranted, fortified town in their domain. If he had wanted it, Amelia would have allowed him a unicorn asleep at the gryphon's feet, a stag's horns for the gryphon's head, a red X-shaped cross to signify a defender of the realm, or a horse rampant, marking his role in bringing the Wind Rising fey into an alliance. There was also a dragonfly or a broken ship, perhaps. Many were the symbols Prentice's service could claim for her, and she would gladly have bestowed them all until his coat-of-arms looked like a wall full of awards and trophies. Instead, he chose only these and seemed all the more noble for it, in her eyes.

When she looked to him for his opinion, Prentice was typically direct.

"You are the Archduchess of the Western Reach," he said bluntly. "The Lioness. Even before you acceded, you were higher than all but Brennham, and since he has not acceded to his own seat, you would technically be his superior as well, at least until the Usurper is thrown down. If they want to return to the old ways, they can begin by honoring the old ranks. In that room, not one is your superior. Why shirk that, Your Grace?"

Such friends I have, Amelia thought, and she nodded to Turley.

"As the baron suggests, through the main doors with the pomp my rank entitles," she said, glancing over her friends one last time. "We will go in, but decorously everyone. Remember that. Rightful grandeur, not smug."

"Yes, Your Grace," the ladies all replied, and Sir Turley returned to the main door, slipping through swiftly. Amelia led her close companions up to the entry and nodded for Prentice and Farringdon to take posts, one at each door to open once she had been announced. The music inside faded and muffled through the wood panels, and she heard Turley's strong voice calling for the gathered company to be upstanding for the arriving archduchess. She nodded to Prentice and Farringdon, and the doors were pushed wide, the heat and light washing into the corridor.

This is hardly the first time you've done this, my girl, Amelia chided herself inwardly as a flash of nerves snapped at her thoughts. *And as Prentice said, even if you were not now more than you have ever been, you still have every right to be here.*

She forced her feet to move and led her mysterious, masked entourage into the great hall of Bridgetown to meet with the men and women who would save the Grand Kingdom, if they could.

CHAPTER 75

"You've seen them, I take it?" Marquis Farringdon asked Prentice as the crowd whirled to a stop in its formal dance, the name of which the baron did not know and whose steps were a mystery to him. While at the Academy in Ashfield, he had trained in a myriad of the common arts of the knighthood and peerage, but since Church knights were men of religious orders and expected to remain celibate, dancing was not one of the things pupils were taught. As it was, it was not the dancers to whom Farringdon was referring.

"The cocksure children over in the corner, My Lord?" Prentice asked without looking in that direction. Except for Squire Wilforn, who had somehow claimed one of the rare places at the high table beside his cousin the baroness, the Young Hopefuls here at the dance were all clustered in a corner on the opposite side of the hall, far enough away that their jests and conversation could not possibly be heard. Sir Turley had picked her grace's position in the room exceedingly well, it seemed.

"They know enough to give their seats to their lady guests, at least," Farringdon observed, and Prentice saw that it was true. While the Hopefuls had ignored the nearby table of the female guests at the previous banquet, now they were quite attentive, it seemed. In fact, save for the fact that he knew them for murderers, or footpads at the very least, Prentice thought them quite the benign-seeming group of young courtiers.

"Cassian is not with them," he said as he realized it was true, and his eyes began to range about the hall to see if the young hothead was present. He paused a moment when he noted that Count Marken was not with others from *his* faction but standing before the high table, conversing pleasantly with the baroness. Lark-Stross had a tabard with his family colors, as did most of the nobles present—his was a deep green shade. Prentice noticed it because, for the first time, he realized that Baroness Penelope was not wearing a breastplate or any other form of armor in public. Instead, she had an overdress in the usual orange and gold, and beneath that, an underdress of the exact same green as Lark-Stross's tabard.

"Not very subtle, is she?" Lady Dalflitch said as she noted the focus of Prentice's attention.

"It is only a color," he replied, not really meaning his words.

"Oh yes, and the Gryphon Banner is just a cloth," the lady-in-waiting said archly.

"Point taken, My Lady," Prentice conceded, and he turned his attention back to seeking out the missing Cassian. Perhaps the youth was not even here. Perhaps he had even been injured himself in his murderous misadventures and was now holed up somewhere, healing.

We can only hope, Prentice thought. He was surprised when a steward in Bridgetown livery appeared before him and bowed.

"Baron Ash, I am bid by Baronet Forsle to invite you to the high table," the steward said, looking back to the head of the hall and indicating where the baronet was sitting. "If you are amenable, he would speak with you."

If I am amenable? Prentice had to keep himself from smiling since it could be seen as rude. He wondered if he would ever become used to such politeness. He held up a finger to indicate the steward should wait for his answer, then turned to the arch-duchess, who was seated with her five Lace Fangs arrayed around her—a better honor guard for this affair in their way than even a cohort of White Lions would have been, especially in this fine company.

"Your Grace, Baronet Forsle has asked to speak with me," he told her with a polite bow.

"You have my permission, Baron," the archduchess said with a smile. "Please convey my compliments to the baronet and inquire after his health. Tell him he is in my prayers."

"Yes, Your Grace," Prentice agreed, and then he nodded for the steward to lead the way through the dancers who had begun a new dance to a new piece of music. Whether the steps themselves were new or different, Prentice could not have told, even if he had wanted to. The steward led the way to a place in front of Lady Penelope first, and Prentice bowed as he was introduced, according to polite protocol. The young noblewoman was clearly annoyed at Prentice's arrival but was surprised, it seemed, when the count welcomed him readily.

"A pleasure to see you again, Baron," Marken said and nodded his head as Prentice bowed to him in turn.

"Do you know each other, My Lord Count?" Penelope asked, blinking at the revelation.

"Indeed, My Lady," Marken told her. "The baron and I met just before the tragedy of the Red Sky and the kingslayer's crime, and we became reacquainted this morning on your southern battlements. He was very helpful in explaining the dangers you face from this new Vec army encamped across the river. You are to be commended on the strength of your Sougate Bastion. Rumors have abounded that the kingslayer's sworn blades tried to hold it from you and that you took it back swiftly. If that is true, then those men did not understand its strength as your current garrison does. It will surely never be taken swiftly again."

"Yes, Sougate fell in one night," Penelope said slowly, making Prentice think that she would much rather talk to the count about anything else. Marken's words had complimented her but by implication had covered Prentice in glory as well. All the things the lady had just been praised for, she had by his hand. Also, the mention of a previous relationship between Prentice and the young count would be at odds with the kinds of stories of a heretic convict raised above his station, which the twittering birds would have been singing in her ears. Prentice appreciated the count's kindness, though as he thought about it, the man was really praising him in order to rehabilitate the Archduchess Amelia's reputation. Whoever it was this wise young man thought to put on the throne in Denay, they would reign with a masterful advisor at their side as long as they recognized Marken Lark-Stross's usefulness.

"My Lord Count, My Lady Baroness," Prentice addressed them in turn. "I give you my compliments. I am requested by your uncle, My Lady. May I speak with him?"

The older man was literally sitting at his niece's left hand, not two paces from where Prentice was. He had to be able to hear every word spoken, even though he was clearly almost lost in his physical pain, his skin pale and sweating. Nevertheless, as he had asked leave to come to speak with the baronet, so Prentice asked the baronet's liege permission to have the conversation in her presence. She nodded and then turned pensively to look at the count once more, leaning forward to rest her chin on her hands, elbows on the table. Lark-Stross was clearly the only thing in the room that actually mattered to her at the moment. Prentice took a step toward the baronet, more a gesture than an actual change of position, but as their eyes met, Forsle waved him even closer so that the knight commander was leaning over the table to speak very quietly with the Bridgetown nobleman.

"You didn't bring that one-legged sacrist with you?" Forsle asked as an opening question, and Prentice shook his head. The baronet's voice was a strained whisper, and his brows knotted with the pain he was bearing.

"No, My Lord, I am sorry," Prentice said to him, feeling compassion for the man. Inxyphos's bite had been a savage wound, taken in defense of this nobleman's liege. Despite Prentice's distaste for many of the ways of the Grand Kingdom peerage, the brotherhood of the battlefield was one he found he rather liked. "I can send for him if you need a healer."

The baronet waved that away.

"I am past a healer's care now, even one with a reputation for miracles like yours."

"Likely, things you have heard are exaggerated, My Lord," Prentice demurred politely, hoping to protect Whilte's preference for humility. He had sat with the chaplain a moment as the exhausted man wept over the standard bearer he could not save only that morning. Gerrindon had not survived his wounds. Three dead Gryphons. Talk of miracles would only make Whilte angry for many days yet.

"I don't believe you, My Lord Baron," Forsle said but without anger. "You forget that I took my wound at the same time your brigandine saved your life. I was there that day, and I owe you an apology."

"An apology, My Lord?" Prentice asked. The most paranoid part of his heart wondered if Forsle was confessing complicity in Inxyphos's attack. He dismissed the thought as implausible, but he struggled to think what else the baronet might reveal with an apology.

"Yes, I am sorry," Forsle continued, every word rasping from his lips and making him sweat and grimace all the worse. "We had heard the stories of beasts from the west. My niece adored them for a good while, but I dismissed them as fantasies. Fey tales. Even when your allied riders arrived and they seemed to be clearly fey, I denied it in my heart. Then that beast erupted out of the crowd, exactly like a demon out of hell, as the sacrist said. My heart stopped in my chest, I am ashamed to say."

"None of us believed until we saw it, My Lord," Prentice said firmly but with a kind undertone. "Even though we have seen much of the Redlander's evils, days like that one bring a new beast we have never seen, and it stops all our hearts in our chests for a moment."

Forsle shook his head.

"Not you, Baron," he said. "I was slow to come to my niece's defense, but I saw you. And your chaplain. A devil had come to Bridgetown, and all ran from it or stood transfixed in its power. But you and your chaplain, you dispatched your liege to safety and charged at the beast. They say you defeated Carron Ironworth in honourable duel, and I believe it now. More than that, Baron Ash. I saw the power of God about you both. I saw the light and the flash of your blade, like the sword in the hand of righteous Michael himself."

"I am not so divine a man," Prentice protested, but the baronet cut him off.

"Oh, shut up! Take the praise when it's offered. I know you put your every breath on the line to stop that monster, and God honored your risk. The chaplain's prayers held the beast, and you put a sword to it. Did you know that every one of the Hopeful's blades that were stabbed into it took damage afterward? Six of them are now carrying about their old youth blades, not their slain fathers' blades they were so proud of. The beast's blood rotted the steel, as if corroded by years of rust. But not your blade, I'll wager."

He looked at Prentice's sword hanging from its swordbelt at his side. The knight commander shook his head. In fact, the bear man's blood had done nothing to it, so far as he knew, and his blade had been soaked in the ichor. The baronet leaned back in his chair and closed his eyes, pinching at the bridge of his nose, as if his head ached along with all his other infirmities.

"When I close my eyes, I can hear the trump calling me home," he said, so quietly Prentice had to all but lay himself over the table to hear. "The wound has sickened and will not heal. Nothing the apothecaries try will purge my blood of the poison. It will not be long now."

So much for Wilforn's hoped-for mithridate. Forsle's eyes flickered open, and he looked at Prentice earnestly, seeming almost mad with the pain.

"I am sorry," he said. "I know you will want to abandon her, but please, my niece needs protectors like you."

Forsle's eyes strayed to Count Lark-Stross and the baroness, still in deep conversation.

"That gives me hope," he said. "I only fear that she aims too high. Is Bridgetown enough of a dowry for such a man?"

"He would make a worthy husband, I think," Prentice said. "I cannot guarantee I will be able to do much for your niece personally, Baronet. Please be comforted by the knowledge that my liege lady has no desire to abandon Bridgetown, or your niece."

"I believe that. She has weathered so many provocations already, and if she was of a mind to become offended, she would have." The baronet paused and then looked at the table for something—his cup. Before he could reach for it, a hacking cough wracked his chest, and his face contorted in genuine agony. Prentice was surprised when no one thought to come to his aid, though his niece did give him one concerned glance. He waved her away and took a deep swallow.

"My fear is that she will find the next provocations to be an arrow shot too many at last," the baronet went on softly after another moment. "I urged my niece to grant the archduchess's petition of law for your men, but she waved high law in my face, as if the girl had ever read a line of the King's Law. Some fool had told her that it took many witnesses for an accusation by yeomen to be brought against any of high birth, even squires. And since your militiamen were not even yeomen, but convicts, they had no standing to accuse at all. If the Young Hopefuls had wanted to, they had the right to line your militiamen up and run them through just for the practice. She actually said that, to my face."

He shook his head and closed his eyes again. Prentice tried to focus on his concern for this man and his sufferings, because if he did not, the things he was learning of the baroness were only hardening his heart towards the young woman. The baronet opened his eyes again, slowly.

"She didn't mean it, you understand that?" he pressed. "She said it as a matter of rights, not acceptability. Do not hate her; her head is full of her father's stories. Ooh..." he paused as a groan escaped his lips. "How did the young come to this pass? Were we this foolish when we were their age? I know we sometimes ran wild, and I am ashamed to say I have a bastard son somewhere whose mother received no more honor from me than a payment to go quietly away. But we did not slay our fathers or butcher rogues and levies for our own delight."

Prentice wanted to object to that. As a former convict rogue himself, he had seen many men butchered for little more reason, and more than once. Perhaps Baronet Forsle and his friends had been some of the "better ones," the not-so-bad nobles who refrained from excesses but did not know how to stop them in others, either. How many had stood by and then bowed the knee to Daven Marcus, even as the brat had his father's blood on his hands? All because they had no idea how else to react.

"I hear the trumpets calling, Baron Ash," Forsle said, and he closed his eyes once more. "I doubt I will see another dawn. I have counseled my niece as best I can, and tell your lady wife that her lesson was the best and clearest that any have tried to teach Penelope in far too long, wrong as it was for her to threaten her with a dagger like that. I want you to know all these things so that you believe me when I tell you how sorry I am for what is coming next."

"What is coming next?" Prentice asked, grabbing the man's hands and wondering if another Usurper's night was about to befall the Grand Kingdom. The majority of the nobility that opposed Daven Marcus was in this hall right now. If the Usurper's men had not been fully driven out, if somehow they had conspired to hide in the town all this time, they could break in now and make another bloodbath. The Grand Kingdom would be finished. It would never again be what it was. What had the baroness even done with the prisoners he and the archduchess had turned over to her? Without releasing the baronet's hands, he scanned the room behind him over his shoulders, trying to find any sign of an ambush waiting to spring. The main doors were closed again, but the sides were open, and servants flowed back and forth unimpeded. The musicians continued to play, and the dancers circled and promenaded according to the dance and the tune. At least half the men around the room were armed and would be able to mount a defense if there was some kind of ambush coming. Of course, the same could have been said the night of Daven Marcus's regicidal patricide, so that was little comfort.

If it is anyone, it will be the Young Hopefuls, Prentice thought, searching out their corner of the hall.

"He is fast, watch for that," the baronet was whispering, sounding almost incoherent now. "He likes to hit first and hold the initiative, but he hates to take a hit. He's all blade and no armor. Remember that. I'm sorry it comes to this. I love him. Be merciful if you can, but do not blame yourself if you can't. I'm sorry, but I love him."

Who, damn it? Prentice wondered. Daven Marcus? Robant? Who should he be on the lookout for. Releasing Baronet Forsle's hands, he turned on his heel and almost staggered down the one step of the high table's dais, pushing dancers aside rudely as he pressed his way toward his first duty. Her Grace had to be informed. Ignoring the indignant mutters around him, he burst into his liege's presence.

"Take warning," he said not quite louder than the music, but loud enough for every one of the archduchess's entourage to hear. "I have word we are in danger."

CHAPTER 76

No sooner had the words left Prentice's mouth than the Lace Fangs had moved, their already watchful gazes matched by their hands going swiftly into their wing sleeves, ready at an instant's notice to draw forth hidden daggers.

"Should we leave?" the archduchess asked, not questioning Prentice's word, even for a moment.

"I do not know," he told her honestly. The baronet's warnings had been cryptic, but they seemed sincere enough. However, it was also possible that the words had been crafted to cause the archducal party to react in just this fashion and leave. Perhaps there was an ambush awaiting them somewhere out in the corridors or in the dark streets of Bridgetown. It could be that the warning was a ploy to get them into a more vulnerable position. As much as many of the Forberest Compact might hate Archduchess Amelia, few of them would actually stand by and let invading men-at-arms turn the hall into a slaughterhouse, even if those invaders only aimed themselves at the ruler of the Reach. Out of their sight, Amelia would be so much more vulnerable.

Prentice scoured the crowd with his eyes. Farringdon came and stood beside him, his hand straying seemingly of its own accord to his longsword, a provocative enough gesture in this noble company, though no one else seemed yet to notice.

"The baronet gave you some dire warning, My Lord?" he asked, and Prentice half shook his head. He hardly really understood what the baronet had said at all. The man had seemed to confirm the archduchess's opinions of Lady Penelope, which had been comforting, but his talk of dying soon, mixed with the enigmatic apology he kept trying to make, left Prentice uncertain. His eyes found the duke Turley had pointed out earlier, and his closest flunkeys. What was that man's name? The heat in the room was suddenly almost unbearable, and Prentice blinked the sweat from his eyes.

"The music is too loud," he muttered. His gaze went to another corner of the hall. Where was the danger?

"My Lord?" Farringdon persisted.

Out of the corner of his eye, Prentice could see the look of concern on the marquis's face, but he hardly registered it. The whirling colors of the dancers swam in front of him, and his mind refused his commands. He could not bring his thoughts into order. He had to defend her grace, but against whom or what? Suddenly the over-loud sounds of the music were mingled with, and then overwhelmed by, the sound of laughter. Not mocking or hateful chuckling, as Prentice might have expected—the sound of evil pleasure that would have fitted with previous visions he had known—but rather a fresh, joyful sound, as of children at play. As he looked about, the dancers were all at once children, capering and skipping as the young in the streets outside would do. The little girls had their hair in plaits and ribbons; the boys wore short tunics and had bare feet. They clapped and laughed and threw brightly painted balls between them. Astonished, Prentice then saw that not all the children were playing. Some were to one side, seated at little tables, like scholars' desks, reading and writing. They were studying, but what?

What was all this?

Candles upon the desks lit the pages at which the diligent children stared, and by their light, Prentice noticed the shadows in the room—moving wisps of darkness that took on new shapes as he watched. Some were ghosts and others wolves or hounds that began to stalk the playing children. Yet others still flitted into the air to become carrion crows of smoke and darkness, singing war.

Few of the children even noticed the animals, and those that did only clapped and laughed the more, thinking to play with them as if they were pets.

"God in heaven, what is this?" Prentice cried out, looking upward to the ceiling's vault, feeling suddenly trapped, oppressed by the heat and tormented by the sights and noise. So many of his visions had led him outside. To be trapped like this felt wrong somehow, or at least undesirable. While he watched, the vaulted roof fled away, as if falling into the sky the way the mantis magicks had linked waters above and below. The horrifying notion that this was Redlander power caught Prentice's breath in his chest, and the pain of the bear's strike flared again, as brutal as when the mighty claw had landed the first time. He almost fell to one knee under the agony of it. Instead of water above, though, rain started to fall, dark drops that turned to crimson when they struck the ground or the dancing children. The sky was raining blood, and only the studious children to the side were not soon drenched in it. The others only splashed in the gore, as if it were summer showers to delight on a hot day. Prentice was reminded of the Bridgetown militia and their hateful massacre. Somehow this childish joy reflected their bloodlust on that vile morning, to his mind.

"What is this?" he begged God a last time, feeling an overwhelming desire to weep for the wrongness of it all.

"Their grandfathers betrayed the first white lion in the eagle's name," the lion angel's voice rumbled through the air. Prentice looked for the transcendent being, but it did not appear. Only its voice was there, as if heard from some distance away—thunder from a far-off storm, approaching but not yet arrived. "They betrayed the lion at the first and were themselves betrayed by the hateful bird and his shadowed unkindness of ravens."

The birds of smoke and shadow rose and were flocking and circled over the whole assembly.

"The young eagle thinks they serve him because he has grown so large, but they serve themselves, as they have since they ceased to serve the prophets whom they betrayed. These children's fathers grew and dwelt under the shadow of the eagle's wings as the ravens protected his nest, and the blood has dripped upon them all. Now, the children play in the blood, even if they throw stones at the eagle as he comes."

"The eagle is coming?" Prentice asked, shocked, wondering at it. Was he being warned of Daven Marcus's approach? Or was there a new "young eagle" marching in the Usurper's footsteps. Not a few kingslayers in history had been in turn slain on their own purloined thrones.

Prentice looked up and saw that there was a texture to the darkness above. It was not clouds that dripped crimson through the missing roof, but enormous wings, as if of a bird so vast and mighty that it was larger than the castle. Now, some of the children noticed as well, and they had begun to pick up rocks and throw at the wings, but this, too, they did as if it was a game.

"They are only children," Prentice protested, thinking of his own children, and strangely, his own childhood. "Must they be held responsible for their grandfather's sins? Does the Lord Almighty truly hate sinners to the third and fourth generation?"

Prentice knew that particular line from holy scripture, and in his quiet moments it troubled him. It was the kind of holy writ favored by merciless preachers, he thought.

"God visits the iniquity of the fathers upon the sons of those who hate him," a softer voice replied from beside him on the opposite side to Lord Farringdon, whom he could no longer see amidst the chaos. It was a voice Prentice remembered well from his last days as a convict—the savior himself, or so Prentice was convinced he was. Before, the vision had come as a convict, dirty and chained as Prentice was. Now he was wearing steward's garb, but without any heraldic colors to mark him as belonging to one noble house or another—only a doublet of bleached white. It had a crown embroidered on the breast, and his hands were yet bandaged.

"His love is steadfast to those who seek him, to a thousand generations," said the Lord in his vision. "Not all the grandfathers of these babes hated God, and for their sake, the wrath has been held back. But these have stored up a deep cup while that wrath was waiting, and the eagle has drunk of that cup until the blood drips from his wings. See, the ravens are his cup bearers."

Prentice looked, and some of the birds of smoke flew through the rain to land on desks amongst the studious children, whispering in their ears. Some of those children stood up and snuffed their candles, dancing out into the blood to play with the others. The metallic stink of the gathering puddles made Prentice want to retch. He was suddenly afraid for his wife and his liege, and he looked back to see that they, too, were sheltered from the rain, seated or standing amidst a pride of mighty lions. The angels had arrived in his vision at last. Many of those glorious creatures had paws that rested in the puddles, stained by them, but only on the paws and claws. Amelia was sitting well clear of the rain, as was Righteous, with their two swaddled babies in her arms. Then Prentice realized that he was not with them. He was alone amidst the unruly children, jostled by their play and sometimes struck by the rocks they threw over their heads. The blood from the eagle's wings dripped on him until he, too, was soaked in it. He could taste it on his tongue, and suddenly he felt chilled, furious at the injustice of it all.

"Do I hate God that I am outside in this wretched rain?" he demanded of the servant king. "Have I brought two babes into this world so that they might be accursed by my iniquity? How can that be justice for them?"

CHAPTER 77

Prentice could not deny the passion he felt as he challenged what he thought was being laid upon him, but somehow it was disarmed within him. He looked into the calm eyes of the man beside him who miraculously stood clean in the blood-fall, his clothing brighter the more the cursed deluge washed down and felt his own rage break. Prentice wished he might face him with the cold fury he had for the battlefield, but it simply was not within him for this—not for when he faced God.

"David was a man after God's own heart, and beloved, but by the blood upon *his* hands he could not build a house for God," the steward said softly, sadly, yet with such power that Prentice felt the words quake in his injured chest. "Are you a man with less blood upon your hands?"

He looked away from Prentice to the playing children, filthy with gore and delighted with it.

"In service of my land and my liege," Prentice protested. "In hope of right outcomes!"

"Is that so? Speak the truth, If the whispering birds had not put you out of the care of the flocking ravens, named you as a heretic, would you have ever disobeyed them? Were you not resolved to be a prized pupil?"

Prentice opened his mouth to answer but said nothing. That question struck to the heart of his objections and undid them in an instant. He looked at the children and saw himself in them, saw them and himself as his Lord saw. In his own way, Prentice had been foolishly playing with blood when he had provoked Whilte's brother Khalte to a duel. If he had not ruined the fellow Ashfield student's sword hand in that contest and set him on the path to his death—the first of many to follow—Prentice would certainly be a church knight himself by now, perhaps a servant of the Inquisition. Would he be hanging old nuns from wagon-wheel gibbets or putting church congregations to the torch? He had held no service back from his liege lady. Would he have done less for the venal ecclesiarchs if they had asked?

Knowing the dedication with which he had studied, Prentice could imagine he might have drawn the Inquisition's favorable attentions, if he hadn't drawn their other "mercies" first. He could have been an Inxyphos by now, or worse yet, a Bluebird, playing good folks against each other to serve hateful ends. He could have been marching in the perverse service of the Usurper. The notion disgusted him more even than the vision of blood.

"I was spared that fate," he protested, feeling a sudden, unexpected compassion. "Can they not be spared as well?"

He pointed to the playing children. They were filthy with blood now, and the stones they had thrown at the eagle had dislodged many feathers that now stuck to their gluey skin. Yet, still, they laughed and played. It was sickening to watch. Could it ever be washed clean?

"I thought you wanted them punished?" was the reply to his entreaty.

"I did...I do," he confessed. "But I..."

He trailed off. There had been a moment, not so long ago, when he had been willing to accept that the Young Hopefuls were only confused—orphaned and meaning little true evil. After the massacre at the Sougate and then the hunting of his men, his heart had completely hardened to them. Now, faced with his own history and the one twist of fate that had turned him from becoming the kind of man he loathed, he wanted to see these wretched children receive their own impossible deliverance.

"Some will be spared," he was told. "But just as your path out of the shadows' grip and into the light was long and steep, so will theirs be, and many will refuse to put even one foot upon it. They were born into shadows, deep under the eagle's wings, and are intent on digging deeper still. Though they hate the young eagle, they love his feathers and would wear them for themselves."

"What can be done?" Prentice asked. "What can I do about any of this?"

"You have been chosen to teach the harsh lessons you have learned," was the answer, and there was a compassion in the steward's voice that set Prentice trembling worse even than the power of the angel lion when it spoke. "Your steps were set on the path to bloodshed long before you even learned to walk. The blood that drenches you is not the blood you shed, and you hate it, which is all to the good. You will slap their faces, and it might stop their laughter long enough for them to see their wretchedness for what it is."

"Why? Why me?" Prentice asked, not feeling resistant, exactly, but burdened. The answer shocked him

"Because you asked."

"When?"

"Every night in your prayers," the servant said. "From your earliest youth. You knelt and asked God Almighty, begged him, to make you a knight in his service."

Prentice remembered. It had been his nightly prayer from childhood. His father had instructed him to it. To beg God to make him successful—first in preparing for the Academy, then to pass the test for entry, and finally throughout his training. He prayerfully craved any service God might require of him all the years of his young life, every night before he went to sleep. He had not ceased until the day he had been handed over to Khalte's avengers and then to the Inquisition. Those three days in the earth under the ministrations of the Inquisitors—that had been when he had stopped praying.

"I did not know what I was asking for," he whispered quietly.

"Children seldom do," came the answer. "They do what they are told or mimic what they see and are led astray. Your childhood ended and you found yourself in the darkest pit known to men of your age. Now comes the time for *their* childhood to end, and if they will not see they need to be washed clean, they will sicken of the blood they have reveled in and die. It is the only way it can be."

Tears came to Prentice's eyes, and he felt relief mingled with sadness of such an agony as he never imagined was possible. He reached out and grabbed someone—he suspected it must be Farringdon, but in his vision state he could not say for sure. It didn't matter, for his attention was still on all these children dancing and laughing and splashing in the lifeblood of too many slain.

"They are orphans," he said through his tears, his voice barely a whisper. "They do not know."

"They know enough. Much is hidden from their eyes, but the wings of the eagle and the ravens do not overshadow all truth. They have not apprehended the light because they love the shadow better."

"Must it be harsh?" Prentice asked.

"Blood must be repaid in blood."

Prentice nodded at that, and his eyes looked at the servant's bandages.

"If they will not let me pay for them, then the debt falls on them in this life and the next," the regal steward went on. "If a child puts its hand to the fire, a loving parent must correct him with the rod so that he will learn that the lesson of danger is not to be disregarded. If the child refuses to learn, then the fire will teach him instead, and the parent will comfort the child, for the fire was always a harsher teacher than a strike from a loving father."

One of the playful, bloodied children skipped close to a study table and reached out to touch the candle upon it. A tutor appeared, recognizable in his scholar's robe, and seized the child's hand, stopping him from burning himself and rapping the child over the knuckles with his rod of instruction—a harsh strike but not an unusual level of discipline for a boy in the Grand Kingdom.

The child ran off but returned a moment later with others, one of them a little girl but dressed like the boys. The symbolism was unmistakable. Bridgetown's liege was that little girl. Now the first willful child sought to touch the candle flame again and urged his friends to do the same. This time, the tutor was unable to discipline so many children, and though he flailed with his rod, they pushed him off and his blows became weaker until they ignored him altogether. At last, the children all stared at the flame, and it began to burn much larger, like the fire in the main fireplace of the great hall, red and overwhelming.

"If a child will still not learn, or worse, try to feed other children to the fire or help others to do the same, the fire will consume the child, for that is what fire does. God is a loving father, and fathers, mothers, and tutors have all been sent to these children, orphans though they now are. They listen to none anymore."

The children played with the candle, letting themselves get burnt and laughing as they sucked their burned fingers. Then the shadows at the edges of the candlelight took on form once more, and those figures escorted a group of blindfolded men into the candlelight. The children hardly noticed, though the original rebellious child did, and he began to speak with the unseeing newcomers. They offered him one of the raven's cups and he drank from it.

"See the tutors the orphans prefer," the steward said, and his tone was devoid of patience now. It was a frightening notion to Prentice, and it chilled him, mingling with the familiar cold fury in his soul but also hurting him, making his heart ache. It was the chill of the night deeps between the stars—ancient—and the birthplace of the mountain that was thrown into the sea. Many preachers spoke of the fires of God's wrath. For Prentice, it was as it always had been—agonizingly cold.

"This is their last chance," Prentice heard himself say, remembering that the chance he had been given had led him into the depths of the earth and then to lay in rejected fields of night-dark cold. He wondered if this was what the man Abraham had felt when the pronouncement was made against the ancient twin cities of iniquity, though God had sent the fire that time. God's fiery wrath was terrible to imagine, but the frost of God's indifference was greater terror to the man who had been exiled as a heretic. For if God turned his face from a man, if the light of life was taken away, there was no life in the umbral fields under the eagle's wings.

"One last chance will be given, different for each child, but it cannot be a gentle lesson. It must be harsh, for they have refused all other forms and have loved the lies of blind teachers. They must be dragged out from under the eagle's wings or they will be crushed beneath it when it dies. Be resolved, what comes next will be as cold and steel-edged as everything seen in the west. It has been given to you to cut the fangs from the serpent and throw it back across the sea. There is nowhere to throw the eagle."

The rain ceased and the pools of blood upon the floor were gone. Adult dancers no longer splashed in gore, and the music was its usual, tuneful self. Prentice looked and realized that he was, indeed, holding the marquis's arm, steadying himself. Farringdon was staring at him, brows knotted in concern.

"Are you well, My Lord?" he asked. "Has something you have eaten or drunk turned your stomach? I have said to Amelia we must be watchful for poisons, especially in public moments like this."

"Thank you, My Lord, but no," Prentice said, smiling at the irony of calling this man lord after the supernatural conversation he had just had. "I never drank the poison. The cup was knocked out of my hands before I could."

Moving his hand from Farringdon's arm to his shoulder, he gave him an appreciative shake, as between men who are good friends. For his part, the marquis looked utterly bewildered. Prentice could not blame him. He felt an overwhelming thankfulness that though he must walk through blood and cold lands, he did not walk alone, and it was not the blood he had shed, and it did not stain him by merciful twist of fate. Then he looked over the archduchess's entourage, seeing so many whom he loved, including the one he loved most.

"I had a moment's turn, brought on by compassion for the baronet and the heat of the room," Prentice lied to the marquis, nodding in the direction of the high table where Forsle still sat alone. His lidded eyes seeming to be watching Prentice even at this distance. The knight commander then had a sudden moment of actual pity, seeing in the baronet the failed tutor of his vision, overwhelmed by the wayward pupils he had tried to teach. Prentice knew he still did not understand the specifics behind Baronet Forsle's warning, but it did not matter now.

He at least had a clear sense of what must be done, harsh though it would be.

Scanning the crowd once more, his eyes lighted swiftly on the spot he expected to find, the place that had been concealed from his sight in the confusion before the vision. In a point near the back of the room, Reverend Master Faldmoor was standing with an imperious look on his face, disapproving of the entire gathering at once, no doubt for myriad good theological reasons. It was a wretched fact of the world that evil men might still be right in some of their judgements, even if their hearts were dark with shadows and hate. Prentice was astonished to realize that even the truest words could be woven into blindfolds.

Let me never blind myself to truth with true words, he thought.

Beside the reverend master, the former earl, now Brother Elder Sebastian, looked equally contemptuous, and *his* gaze was clearly reserved for the archduchess and her companions. Prentice had a sudden memory of his younger brother Pallas standing in a similar manner at Faldmoor's side, led astray into evil by his own hatred. That memory revealed the identity of the third man standing with the two religious men—Xavoer, Prentice's oldest brother. He *was* here. As incomprehensible as it felt, somehow it made sense to Prentice. His eldest sibling was grey-haired and half bald now, but his black merchant's robe, embroidered with gold lace along the hems, indicated that he had been successful in the years since Prentice had last laid eyes upon him.

Just as our father planned, Prentice thought, and it filled him with a sad kind of joy. He had no hatred in his heart for his family at this moment, his brother especially, or even for the father who had made his childhood a torment. What would be the point? His father's decisions had ironically helped keep Prentice alive in the face of a fate none would have predicted, and all they had cost the man was everything he had dreamed of for his son. Prentice had the title and wealth now, and his father could connect himself to none of it.

It was the last of the four men stood together, and the youngest, that drew Prentice's main attention, however. Finally, he had located Cassian, and he noticed that the Young Hopeful had yet another new sword at his belt, which he was proudly displaying to the seemingly fascinated Faldmoor. The blade was drawn, and Cassian waved it about as if flourishing it in battle but with exaggerated movements no trained swordsman would ever waste time with.

"You really are playing in the blood, aren't you?" Prentice said to himself quietly.

It saddened him a little to think, but the boy had drunk from the cup and would not stop putting his hand to the flames.

CHAPTER 78

Prentice took two steps back toward the archduchess and bowed as he drew close. He did not rise from the bow, but kept himself low, meeting her eyes directly in a most impolite manner as she sat upon her seat.

"Do you trust me, Your Grace?" he asked. "I mean, truly trust me, even at this very moment?"

"I do. Of course, I do," the archduchess told him earnestly, but her expression made it clear she was becoming nervous about his behavior. "Are you quite well?"

"Your husband only just asked me that himself," Prentice said, feeling strangely buoyed by having full control of his own thoughts once more, even though he knew the grim moment that was coming. "You fear that I am not myself, Your Grace? Perhaps a spell has been read upon me, like Robant's when you were at Aubrey?"

"It was not Robant's, exactly," the archduchess whispered, and Prentice could see it troubled her to recall the effect of the hateful magick upon her mind. The little of confusion he had just experienced was more than he wanted to repeat. He would not blame her grace if her own memories troubled her soul. "*Has* someone spoken a spell over you, Baron?"

Prentice looked back to Baronet Forsle, who had slumped in his chair such that at last a steward had thought to look to his wellbeing. A man in livery was fanning the baroness's uncle, and even Penelope had managed to lift her attention from Count

Lark-Stross to inquire after his needs. It seemed impossible to Prentice that that man with failing health might have spoken some kind of spell, disguised as the cryptic warning, but he knew so little of arcana that he had to admit it might have happened.

But a vision of God sings over the mutters of every sorcery of men, I have no doubt, he thought confidently.

"Your Grace, we have jumped at shadows for weeks while we waited for the bear cubs to grow up," he told her. "They are too stubborn, and we are running out of time. I have just seen a path out of the shadows."

"A path?" the archduchess repeated.

"Like Count Marken's narrow way?" Farringdon asked, having drawn close to listen in.

"Yes, My Lord," Prentice said. "A narrow path to the future, but I cannot guarantee it leads to the alliance you have been working to build, Your Grace. The way and the door are narrow, and we may have to leave the baroness and her fellow children outside, in the rain."

The archduchess met his eyes, and they held each other's gazes for a long moment of silence. Prentice knew she could not possibly understand the true meaning of all the things he was saying, but this was almost as intimate as anything he had ever known, save the sweetest moments with his wife. He felt a sudden twitch of discomfort, knowing how hard it must be for Farringdon to witness something like this. If his Righteous experienced even one such moment as this with another man, he thought it could well break his heart.

"You have *seen* this path, Prentice?" she asked, and he knew that she at least understood enough. At different times, both of them had seen visions or dreamt dreams that pointed to true things. The archduchess wanted reassurance that this was one of those moments, that he was speaking from a divine madness and not a curse upon his thoughts.

"Yes, Your Grace," he told her earnestly, resisting the temptation to reach for her hand. The archduchess nodded, and he could see her make the decision to trust him written in her eyes.

"Our friends are harried, our loyal men ambushed and slain," she said. "The enemy mocks us from the shadows and besets us on every side. Find me this path you have seen, and I will follow you though it leads through fire. Let us be Meshach and Shadrach to one another. We have seen angels enough to expect to find one in the furnace."

Prentice wanted to laugh. He would indeed follow this woman, this Lioness of the Reach, into flames. More than everything he had ever asked for in his childhood prayers, God had given him a liege worthy of dying for, and a wife and family even more precious still. He stood up and stepped to Righteous, reaching out and taking her hands. She allowed him, but her eyes showed uncertainty.

"I do not know what the next few days or even moments hold, darling wild rose, but you are my gift from God, better than all the others," he told her, fearful that the loyal moment of intimacy he had shared with his liege might make her feel troubled. "Nothing and no one delights me like you."

She only smiled at him, her eyes glistening.

"Knight Commander, what exactly is going on?" Lady Dalflitch asked, obviously disconcerted by Prentice's actions—perhaps for no other reason than for the uneven and undignified impression it must be making, Prentice was sure.

"What is happening, My Lady, is that I am inviting Marquis Knight Captain Farringdon to accompany me as I pay my respects to the gentles in that far corner over there," Prentice said, the cold in his soul now stirring playfully, making him smile his battle smile. He nodded in the direction of Faldmoor's little faction.

"Respects? Why, who are they...?" Righteous asked, and then her voice trailed off, until she realized what and who she was looking at. "That's a Fang's sword! That's Monteath's sword!"

"Most likely, my love," Prentice told her.

"I'm coming with you," his wife declared, but he put a gentle hand upon her shoulder, holding her back.

"No. Her grace requires your service here. Besides, as Monteath's banner captain, Lord Farringdon has the right."

Righteous looked as if she meant to argue, then she curtseyed to her husband, lowering her eyes as she did so, the perfect courtly wife. It set his heart alight with warmth that made him feel like he was aloft on wings of fire. Yet still, the cold storm was brewing, demanding its time.

"My Lord, if you would accompany me as I go to these men," he asked Farringdon. "I expect I will need the company."

"The company of a *second* man?" Farringdon asked, recognizing the import of Prentice's invitation. "You think to pick a fight?"

"I would much prefer not to, My Lord, but that choice will not be in my hands. Having a second there with me is simply good preparation."

Prentice turned to go, but Turley suddenly stepped up to him, the pleading look in his friend's eyes once more.

"You don't want me, do you?"

"Not for that part, but how good is your silver with that musician leader of yours?" Prentice asked him.

"I slipped him a fair purse," Turley said, brows knotting in confusion. "Should let me call the tunes all night if I want."

"Then that is where I need you," Prentice told him.

"Surely, but to what end?"

"You will know," Prentice said and then stepped away.

"What is your purpose, Baron Ash?" Amelia asked.

"Is this going to be a barney or not?" Turley added as well, but Prentice pretended not to hear either of them. How could he tell his liege lady that Cassian had drunk deep from a cup of wrath, and it had come time for him to find out what it was like to awake from drunkenness? It had come time for him to feel the hangover and realize that his playing with fire had burned his fingers, perhaps too badly to ever heal. Turley wouldn't understand, certainly, and the archduchess would likely struggle. Prentice had had the vision, and he barely understood it himself.

CHAPTER 79

It was only a short distance to the far corner of the hall, even as Prentice and Farringdon deliberately skirted the dancers in their lines and circling formations. Nonetheless, it was one of those short journeys that time played games with, so that Prentice felt he had an age to consider all the implications of his coming actions, enough to wonder what he would say and how it would be received. Within him the cold fury he so often depended on had returned, not killing the compassion of the vision or even holding it at bay, but focusing it to a resolution, like the fine knife of a chirurgeon when cutting out a tumor or lancing a boil. For a moment, it almost seemed as if he would never reach the clutch of enemy church folk, and then he was there, walking the last few steps under their contemptuous gazes. As he met their eyes, Prentice smiled and could not help but think of the moment at the start of any battle, be it between armies of kings on historic fields or gangs of streetfighters in back alleys—the moment when foes resolved to do battle meet each other face to face.

Righteous would love this, he thought, sorry for her than he had had to leave her behind.

"Reverend Master Faldmoor," he said with a gentle nod, as if meeting an old acquaintance. "Brother Sebastian. Xavoer."

Of all the men present, only his eldest brother's expression actually mattered to him, as it was the only one that was not a mask of pure hatred. Xavoer clearly had no desire to speak to Prentice, but the older man's expression showed a complexity of emotions, including some guilt, Prentice thought. It was not to these men he had come to speak, however.

"Squire Cassian," he said sternly, "that sword in your hands does not belong to you. It is a Lion Fang's sword, earned with service—service you have not done."

"I won this sword fairly in a duel, Reacherman," Cassian replied with his usual disdain, returning the bared blade to its sheath as if that alone would deny Prentice any claim upon it. "Not every man from the west is frightened of a fair fight, though they should be."

Sebastian and Faldmoor snickered, and Cassian smiled hatefully, proud of his little jest.

"You took it from its owner after you ambushed him in the dark, you and your companions, because you were too cowardly to fight a Lion of the Reach openly," Prentice insisted. Cassian's eyes narrowed, but Prentice could not care less if the young man felt insulted. His words were the truth. It was time the lad saw the blood he was playing in for what it was.

"An accusation of cowardice from a twice rebellious heretic is worth less than the breath it took to speak it," Faldmoor pronounced, and Cassian's smile returned. Sebastian snorted in derision. Xavoer looked glum, and Prentice had to credit his brother for his honesty. Every man here knew they had plotted this moment. Why else would Cassian have made such a show of his purloined blade? Faldmoor had not vented his full contempt yet, though.

"What are you doing east of the mountains, yet again, convict? Is your soul not blackened enough with sin yet?"

"I was pardoned my conviction by the liege of the Reach," Prentice replied, his voice still light. "And my heresy was judged purged. That pardon was signed by you yourself. Unless you signed it falsely?"

Faldmoor bristled at Prentice's reply, and Sebastian's loyal smile turned to a scowl. Xavoer's discomfort shifted to pure confusion, as if he had just learned something new, and Cassian's bravado slipped a little as well. None, it seemed, had expected Prentice to come armed for a fight with words, as well as with his sword.

Oh, come now, Prentice thought. *You did not think to bait me to rash action with your first gambits, did you?* Rash action was still likely to come, and he knew it was what they wanted, but he was going to make them work for it first.

"My hand was forced to that signature by the late king's folly," Faldmoor said through gritted teeth. "It was revoked by the synod soon after."

He seemed ready to continue with his denunciation of Prentice, but Farringdon cut him off.

"So, you admit that you used your Church authority falsely at the urging of the king? Is your devotion to God so shallow that you forsake truth so readily? Hardly a faith that counts its own life less than service to the Almighty."

Faldmoor's eyes went wide, and Prentice wondered if the man had ever been accused of being faithless before.

"That is an excellent point, Marquis," Prentice said, enjoying himself more than he expected. "How can anyone trust the judgements of an ecclesiarch, or indeed any man of the Church, if he can be swayed to sign false warrants of pardon by soft words in the most genteel of circumstances. It was not as if good King Chrostmer threatened the reverend master, after all."

He turned from Farringdon back to the hostile group facing him.

"So, which is it, Reverend Master? Are you a faithless weakling or does my pardon stand?"

"God curse you, worthless mongrel," Faldmoor said and then clamped his mouth shut, as if fearing what else he might say.

Whatever other victories I have ever had or will have, Prentice thought, *that may well be my greatest achievement.*

He cast a swift glance at Xavoer, wondering if his brother felt insulted by Prentice being called a mongrel. After all, that was a slight on their father and mother as well.

For his part, Cassian had no patience for conversation that was not leading to steel, it seemed. He sneered at Prentice.

"You are never getting this sword back," he declared. "I will never relinquish that which is my right, and I will claim the others, as well. All of them."

His eyes dropped tellingly to the sword at Prentice's side.

"It's pretty," the Young Hopeful said. "But I know the story of how you took it now. You're just a treacherous coward who's been using the magick of a blessed blade to make himself look like a hero. You're a fraud, heretic, and I will unmask you."

"Even if it were true, are you not afraid to face a magick blade?" Farringdon asked, his tone making it sound as if he were genuinely puzzled by the strange assertion.

"I have a blade anointed to face magick with magick of its own," Cassian replied, and he shook the Fang's sword in its sheath.

Anointed? Prentice wondered, and he looked over his shoulder to the high table where Wilforn sat beside his cousin still, staring down the hall straight at this corner. *That is what you wanted the bear's blood for, isn't it?*

Knowing that all other blades touched by the slain beast's lifeblood had rotted, Prentice wondered what alchemy had been used to concoct the anointing, since Monteath's sword was plainly undamaged. He shook his head.

"Are these the kind fey tales you have been filling the lad's head with?" Prentice asked Faldmoor. He was surprised to see that both the reverend master and Sebastian seemed troubled by the accusation, making the knight commander think that it was not these churchmen who had proposed "enchanting" a blade for Cassian. How could it be? They had not arrived in Bridgetown when the Young Hopefuls went hunting. The Bluebird's song, then? That was the most likely alternative. Suddenly Prentice had a clearer notion of the meaning of Baronet Forsle's warning. The uncle knew of Cassian's plan to provoke Prentice this night.

"It is no fey tale, the shame you brought upon our family," Xavoer said suddenly, his voice a bitter brew of anger and anguish.

"Surely Pallas shamed you all far worse than my failures," Prentice retorted, hearing his father's rejection in his brother's words and unwilling to accept even one part of it. That was all done and finished in his life. He no longer slept in the night-dark fields. If his father's family still retained the aftertaste of drinking from the ravens' cups, that was not his burden.

"Pallas took the crosses to his tabard and swore to Mother Church," Xavoer defended their brother's name, fruitlessly, for Prentice knew the truth.

"Pallas slew his own commander on a battlefield in sight of hundreds of witnesses, Reach and Kingdom. It is nowhere contested, except by liars who were not there."

"Pallas suffers for his mistakes," Prentice's brother retorted.

"As have we all," Prentice answered, feeling the fury rise within him. When Cassian's impatience caused him to intervene, the knight commander found it almost a relief. He did not really wish to unleash his anger on his brother. Especially not since the main of it was deserved by Pallas. Xavoer was a man of commerce, not war, and just this level of confrontation between armed men was plainly making him shake with nervousness. Prentice almost pitied him, but Cassian was demanding his full attention now.

"Shut up, merchant," Cassian hissed venomously at the man more than twice his age. "This is a matter between higher men than you, even if one of them is your heretic brother here."

He turned to face Prentice fully, so that they were little more than a pace apart. The knight commander remembered the baronet's warning suddenly, that Cassian loved the swift stroke, and wondered if the young man had been trained in the art of drawing and cutting in one move. It would be a deadly technique at this close distance, and Prentice was about to turn aside in hope of deflecting Cassian's hand, but it proved an unnecessary precaution. Cassian thrust out his lip.

"I know your secret, now, old man," he said quietly. "You want your dead man's sword back? You'll have to offer me that one, because it's the only way you'll ever get it. Except you won't, because I'll have both in the end and you'll be as dead as those rogues outside Sougate you loved so much. So run away or make your challenge. Whatever you do, I promise you'll die on the edge of my new sword. It is foretold."

Oh God, lad, they really have twisted your soul, haven't they? Prentice thought. He bowed his head a moment, sighing as if with exhaustion. The vision was correct; there was nothing now but hard roads ahead, and bitter. *I have slept in the cold fields, lad, so long that the chill entered into my very soul. I wish you had let me spare you.*

He looked up and fixed his gaze on Cassian's, staring into pools of contemptuous triumph that suddenly seemed shallow and lifeless.

"Knight Marshall Baron Carron Ironworth surrendered this blade to me at the end of an honorable duel more challenging than anything I had ever faced in combat before," Prentice said quietly, putting a hand on his hilt, thinking that those around him could hear but intending his words only for Cassian. "Since then, this sword has faced horrors and slain legends, and been carried farther than you even know exists in this great world of our Lord's. In the far west are a fey people that call it a 'death thing,' and they fear it as you crave it. But I swear to you it is not the leastwise magickal. Knowing that, Cassian, tell me, is there anything you would not risk to claim this 'death thing' from my cold, slain hand?"

"Nothing," the Young Hopeful replied, investing the one word with more passion than everything else Prentice had ever heard him say before. Prentice shook his head sadly.

"You really do not understand the game they have you playing, do you? You are not a player, lad. You are just a card in their hand, and not a particularly high one."

As if expecting a fight at that very moment, Cassian's face showed surprise when, instead, Prentice stepped back and looked to Farringdon.

"We have no other choice, My Lord," he said, not as sad as he might have been, but regretting that things had come to this pass all the same. Before any of his enemies watching even knew what he was doing, he turned to the high table and bellowed with his parade ground voice.

"Lady Penelope, ruler of Bridgetown. I, Baron Prentice Ash of Fallenhill charge you now that one of your liegemen and cousins, the Squire Cassian, is a murderer and a thief. He has all but boasted of the murder of Monteath, a Fang of the White Lions and sworn man to my liege, Archduchess Amelia of the Western Reach. He flouts Monteath's stolen sword here in this very hall. As the slain man's knight commander, I call upon you now to do your duty as rightful ruler of Bridgetown, under King's Law and the laws of chivalry. Judge this Cassian as a murderer, a thief, and a fomenter of violence, and have him punished. If you are of a mind to be merciful for the sake of your relations, then I believe the Lioness of the Reach would accept exile as a sufficient punishment. Let him be banished from Bridgetown. Her grace has shown such mercy in the past, even to rebels against her own rule, as some here can attest.

"If, however, you are of a mind to refuse to do justice, you will show that you are no true ruler and the White Lions will march from your town, not to return and not to fight at your side, or even at the side of those with whom you fight. Even if your enemies are the Reach's enemies, you cannot be trusted as an ally."

CHAPTER 80

S ir Turley had already moved to stand near the musicians with their tabors, lutes, and a fyfe, and as soon as Prentice's voice began to ring out, he gave the lead player a signal and the music died as if snatched from the very air of the hall. The dancers continued a moment, confused by what was happening, but their shuffling steps soon stopped, and before the Baron of Fallenhill's pronouncement was half finished, they had begun to shift back from his part of the hall so that it became easier to identify him as the source of the shouted words. Nevertheless, Amelia stood to make sure she could see Prentice and Penelope at the high table at the same time.

Prentice's words ended, and there was silence in the entire space. One of the players lowered his lute, and the strings made a soft musical sound. Those around him glared as if he had disrupted a state funeral.

You brilliant man, Amelia thought, watching her sworn retainer stand proud in his denunciation. The baroness-elect was pinned in place now. While the diplomacy had been all in letters between nobles, Penelope had been able to sop her pride by vacillating, letting matters simply play out since the base circumstances favored her. She had the White Lions protecting her town regardless while the Young Hopefuls pranced about like invincible champions, taking credit for victories they had never won. Perhaps the young noblewoman, , was even growing to believe them, despite that she should know better.

But Count Marken Lark-Stross knew better, as did at least two of the factions of his compact. The so-called Sons of Mother Church might loathe Prentice and Amelia on principle and allow that to blind them to the realities of the war at this moment, but neither Marken nor the dukes would have any doubt. Bridgetown could not defend itself without the White Lions, and their own alliance could not be sure to win the Grand Kingdom without them, either. And if the Western Reach would never march with any who allied themselves with Bridgetown, then the Forberest Compact could not ally itself with Bridgetown. Maybe Bridgetown might think to face the future without the White Lions, but only one small part of the Compact suffered such delusions.

Amelia looked to the baroness-elect, who was now standing, glaring down the hall at Prentice, but at least once casting a pained, frightened glance at Count Lark-Stross, who had stepped back a pace or two from the high table. The archduchess had a moment's pity for Penelope, no longer a silly filly but a young noblewoman realizing she was far out of her depth and with her last wise advisor expiring in the chair right next to her, all but ignored in his death throes. A moment ago, she had been building her future, hoping to invite a high nobleman to woo her for the good of both their domains. Now, she was shamed by a dread accusation against a close kinsman that threatened to cost her the hoped-for marriage, the allies that defended her town, and her honor in the eyes of all the peers of the realm. Between this moment, the massacre before Sougate, and the death of the sacrist on the cathedral steps, Bridgetown's reputation was becoming stained beyond cleansing, even in these times when the bloodshed of war stained the whole of the Grand Kingdom to one degree or another.

Thinking that it was probably unnecessary but wanting to support Prentice all the same, Amelia reached out and took Dalflitch's hand. Her lady seneschal did not fully understand what she was doing and almost recoiled in shock as Amelia did not, in fact, lead off anywhere but used her hand as a support as she stepped up onto her chair, kicking the simple cushion out of the way first so that she could stand stable on the wood. Dalflitch looked at her liege's pregnant belly, perhaps fearful for the baby's safety, but Amelia was happy. Now she would be seen above the crowd.

"I am Amelia, Archduchess of the Western Reach," she shouted, hoping as she so often did at times like this that her voice was not as shrill as it sounded in her own ears. "I affirm that every word he speaks is true and of my will. The baron is a true witness, and his word is the most trusted in the Western Reach, exceeded only by scripture itself. See, my husband stands by him and will bear witness as well."

"I do, Your Grace," Farringdon said, and Amelia loved him. She had just called Prentice's word more trustworthy even than his, and though she meant him no insult, he could easily have taken umbrage. Instead, he stood by her word without hesitation. Having made her declaration, Amelia decided to step down before she lost her balance and her dignity. As she regained the floor, she noticed Dalflitch giving her a raised eyebrow. She shrugged, and the lady-in-waiting nodded philosophically.

"It is hardly to your usual standard of subtlety, Your Grace," she said. "But since gentle diplomacy *has* failed, perhaps a mace through the stained glass will let some clearer light in."

Amelia certainly agreed, but as some of those closest to her turned back to watch the general proceedings once more, she decided to move off through the crowd. All this fancy talk was useful, but there was clearly a judicial duel brewing, and she had no intention of witnessing that while standing on a chair. With a quick signal of her intentions, the Lace Fangs gathered around her, two in front and three behind, Lady Dalflitch close by, and they began to make way for her in a barely polite fashion. Doing her best to keep watch on her husband and her loyal retainer through the crowd, Amelia heard more than saw Cassian's reaction to Prentice's denunciation.

"Bastard! Heretic! Useless cur! Convict mongrel!"

The Young Hopeful's insults flew from his lips like spittle, and they were punctuated by the sound of a sword being drawn and a sheath being thrown to the floorboards.

"I'll gut you like I did your rogues! I'll paint my father's tomb with your innards!"

Amelia had to wonder what Cassian's father had to do with this as she imagined the wild youth fulfilling his threat, but just before she reached the edge of the crowd near the confronting men, she heard her husband's voice again.

"Have a care, Squire Cassian," the marquis commanded with the same stern tone Prentice had used making his pronouncement. "The matter is now before your liege. The next move is hers, not yours."

"I don't need her!" Cassian shouted just as Amelia's escort brought her to the edge of the crowd. About a quarter of the hall was open space now, in the midst of which Prentice stood unmoving, radiating calm, while the red-faced Cassian ranted, waving the plundered Lion's sword around, causing even some folk on the edge of the crowd to flinch away.

Most were now looking to the high table, perhaps prompted by Farringdon's words, so they heard rather than saw the slap that Cassian delivered backhanded to Prentice's cheek. As they turned back, Prentice was straightening himself to face forward again. He had not flinched from the strike, but other than a mark on his jaw, it did not look like he needed to. Clearly incensed by Prentice's impassive response, Cassian followed up by spitting directly in the knight commander's face.

"There's no going back now," a resonant voice said to Amelia's right. She turned and saw Count Lark-Stross now watching from just beyond the perimeter set by the Lace Fangs. He had moved away from the high table during the interchange. When their eyes met, he acknowledged her with a nod.

"I'm sorry it has come to this," she told him.

"Are you?" he asked as if it did not matter anyway. Then he shook his head. "No. That is unfair. Your provocations have been many, and in the eyes of more than one of the Compact, your man has acted with admirable honor and courage this day, I'm sure."

"It is his way," Amelia said. "I will always be able to rely upon him."

"Assuming he survives the combat that is coming."

Amelia had not thought of that. She so trusted Prentice that she had almost unquestioning faith in his abilities as a man-at-arms. He had survived and triumphed in so many battles, after all. She had a sudden flash of compassion for Lady Righteous, and as she looked, she saw the Lace Fang watching her husband pensively, chewing upon the end of her fingernail.

"He'll be right fast," she heard her lady-in-waiting bodyguard whisper. "Watch for that. He'll do what he can to make it quick. They love that here in Bridgetown."

Oh Lord God, bless him, Amelia offered an inward prayer. She still favored her knight commander to win, but she remembered now just how brutal what was about to happen truly would be.

CHAPTER 81

Prentice felt the spittle drying on him and ignored it, choosing to remain impassive in the face of Cassian's wildness. He kept watch on the high table, where the Lady Penelope still looked trapped in indecision. He wondered if she had ever imagined that it might come to this, her cousin against her ally's champion, of sorts. Much as he hated the characterization, he had to accept it was how the story would be told. That, of course, would capture none of the true desperation of the moment and would make noble-seeming what would, in fact, be ugly, harsh, and murderous.

"If matters of law concern you, My Lady, may I reassure you that King's Law would permit you to allow your cousin's challenge, if you were so inclined," Reverend Master Faldmoor called from behind Prentice, offering his legal advice unsolicited. "Squire Cassian has been direly wronged by these public accusations, after all."

Penelope looked about the crowd for a while, and Prentice wondered if she was searching for Count Marken. He had lost sight of the nobleman himself, but a moment later caught him out of the corner of his eye, not surprised to see him near to Archduchess Amelia and the Lace Fangs. The baroness-elect now turned to her uncle's chair beside her, but the baronet was gone. In the hubbub, he must have been escorted back to his bed. Perhaps he had even passed away, unnoticed in this dramatic moment. It was a sad end.

"What is required?" Penelope asked, her voice seeming weak, barely carrying over the distance. This was not quite what her chivalric dreams of knights dueling for honor were supposed to look like, Prentice was sure of it. Of all of Bridgetown's bear cubs, she was the least blood-soaked, but he still felt little sympathy for her. There had been many tributaries she could have turned her boat down before it ran aground here.

"All that is needed is a time, a place, and terms," Prentice shouted, still using his pronouncement voice, speaking before Faldmoor had a chance to put his own colors on it.

"Here! Now! He has a sword and so do I!" Cassian shouted, his face still red.

"And the terms?" Farringdon asked.

"To the death! Victor takes the loser's blade as trophy and his woman, if she's not too heartbroken!"

"You wretch!" Farringdon said loudly, and he took up a stance, longsword point aimed at Cassian. The Young Hopeful likewise fell to fighting position, ready to defend himself.

"My Lord Knight Captain!" Prentice shouted, still having not moved. "I hope for you to act as my second. Please do not shame me by doing something rash!"

Farringdon stood straight immediately and bowed to Prentice.

"Forgive me, My Lord," he said, and Prentice nodded. Then the marquis turned to the still fight-ready Cassian. "She'd feed you your manhood at any rate, boy. Then it would be up to your brother to give your ashamed dead father an heir."

That was a comment too far for Cassian and he surged at Farringdon, who stepped back and brought his weapon once more into guard. Since Cassian was ignoring Prentice in his attack, the knight commander came to his friend's aid and planted a kick on the Young Hopeful's hip from the flank, pushing as much as striking, and sending him sprawling sideways. Cassian was back on his feet almost as soon as he struck the floorboards, but in that short space of time Prentice drew his own sword, the hero blade that brought such contention.

"At last," Cassian said like an eager bachelor receiving his paramour's pledge to wed.

"You have not nominated a second," Prentice countered before the Young Hopeful could charge once more. A figure pushed its way out of the crowd from the direction of the high table or nearby—Cyprian, coming to his brother's side. It was someone else who spoke first, however.

"I will second the lad," cried Sebastian, stepping forward. "With Mother Church's blessing."

"There, he'll do it," Cassian said, eager to get to the bloodletting.

Prentice wondered if his brother would be hurt or relieved. Nonetheless, he turned to the Brother Elder who had once thought to seek Archduchess Amelia's hand in marriage.

"I am sorry, Brother Sebastian," he said sadly. "You used to be a more honorable man than this."

"He does have Mother Church's blessing," Faldmoor declared loudly, his mellifluous voice drowning out Prentice's heartfelt comment.

"Which half of Mother Church?" an unseen wit called from the crowd. "The burning half or the hanging half?"

"Who said that?" Faldmoor demanded, infuriated, his face going as red as Cassian's. No one claimed credit.

"Who cares? Face me and face your doom!" Cassian yelled. Prentice turned cold eyes on the Young Hopeful at last and felt the steel in his own soul.

They sowed the wind for you Cassian, and now you must reap the whirlwind, he thought, and all the pity was gone from his heart.

CHAPTER 82

Prentice had only just brought his blade into guard when Cassian charged. It was not the wild charge of a madman, like when a *brakkis effar* gave full flight to its bestial nature. It was not Inxyphos's onslaught as a bear man. It was not even the rapid thrust that Righteous had said Lady Penelope favored, a reach for quick points. Almost instantly, Prentice could see that Cassian had training, excellent training, and that built upon a foundation of natural talent. He wielded the Lion Fang's sword expertly, thrusting and slashing, driving Prentice back and then away to the right. No sooner had Prentice made the sideways move than Cassian's point flashed through a fractional gap in his defense and caught him on the shoulder, slashing his sleeve but not quite cutting the skin beneath.

Prentice played for distance, and Cassian kept up the pressure, adroitly giving his opponent no time to reset himself. It was an impressive display, and the dispassionate part of Prentice's mind registered a deep respect for the young man's skills. He might be wild and hateful, but Cassian was a swordsman worthy of renown. Even this early in the duel it was obvious.

Now to only outwit and outfight the little orphan, Prentice told himself.

Again, Cassian pushed Prentice to the right and then a short while later did it a third time. The second time he tried the original thrust but didn't beat Prentice's guard. The third time he seemed to be repeating the technique but left a half beat delay, and when

Prentice moved to parry that strike like the previous ones, Cassian flicked his wrist and turned the thrust into a draw cut with the tip. It struck slightly lower than the previous time on Prentice's left arm, and the knight commander grimaced as the blow bit into flesh, leaving a slicing line of crimson that immediately dropped red spots on the cloth of his sleeve. It was not enough of a cut to truly wound him—it certainly did not penetrate to the muscle—but almost instantly the ache of his old wound from the duel with Baron Ironworth flared and was worse than it ever had been before, even on the day he had received it. His arm felt suddenly heavy and slow, and the throb of it pulsed through his veins to his head, where the ache began to press on his temples like a vice.

Poison! No wonder he was in such a hurry.

That was almost as much as Prentice could think through the hammering in his mind. All the talk of enchantments and magicks had made him miss the so much more mundane possibility. Anointed—that had been the word Cassian had used, and Prentice thought he should have seen it. Judicial duels, genuine legal duels over matters of law, often involved specific and binding oaths to avoid the use of tools like magick and poison. Tales of envenomed blades were the stock of morality plays, an act of villains of the stage. Prentice had never seen a poison for blades in all his life and had never heard of it actually being proved to be used in a duel. It was so rare and dishonorable that even to accuse an enemy of it was taken as virtual proof that the loser could not accept his own failure. It was a dishonor to even suggest your opponent was so dishonorable. There could be no doubt now, though. Cassian had pushed and prodded and provoked so that he could come to the combat itself before any of the typical oaths could be extracted.

Prentice blinked his eyes against the gathering shadows, and watched Cassian's blade tip, trying to see if there was any sign of an alchemical concoction there. Even with the whole hall lit with every possible torch and candle, he could see nothing but steel.

Unless my vision is already failing, he thought.

Now that he had made his tainted cut, Cassian began to hang back a little, appearing to all the world as if toying with his opponent, but Prentice was sure he was waiting to see how effectively the toxin was working.

You won't want to leave it too long, though, will you? If I drop dead of a little slash to my shoulder, questions will be asked.

"See how he runs away! The roaring lion shows himself to be nothing more than a wailing tomcat in need of spaying," Reverend Master Faldmoor declared loudly. "To the duty, my lad, with Mother Church's blessing, and let's be done with this thrice damned heretic."

Despite the arrogant cleric's urging, Cassian still held back some, watching, flashing the blade every now and then while Prentice shied and made weaker defensive movements. He knew how he looked, but if Cassian was half the swordsman he appeared to be, the Young Hopeful would be on the watch for a ruse, a gambit of some kind. It had taken three full feints, the last one suicidally committed, to fool Carron Ironworth, and while Cassian was by no means such a noble sword, the young squire was close to that great champion in talent. Like the fallen knight marshal, Cassian was not going to be easily fooled.

So, outwitting you is not an option, Prentice thought, *since you have already caught me out, like a scorpion under its rock.*

Cassian strayed in close a moment and Prentice erupted in a series of high cuts, aimed at the head, strong enough to drive him back. The blades rang, but the Young Hopeful showed no discomfort, deflecting each cut and then almost lazily riposting and forcing Prentice to sidestep yet again to get away, his own deflection so light that if Cassian had meant to hit him, he would have.

Playing with me, are you? Prentice watched as the squire even paused to receive the applause of a young lady standing at the edge of the crowd. Cassian bowed and blew the maiden a kiss. He turned back and Prentice felt his left leg half buckle at the knee so that he almost toppled sideways. Cassian saw it, too, and they both knew the final moments had come. The Young Hopeful smirked. He would make his last charge at any moment.

Prentice could see it would be soon, and he felt a moment of warm resignation. Death would be a relief, to allow the darkness gathering at the edges of his vision to enfold him like a blanket. Then, like a snap, like the crack of an overseer's whip, he remembered what the cold night fields were truly like, what it was to lie down in the aching chill, alive only because you were too despairing to even take your own life—too fearful that whatever lay beyond death might have the power to be worse even than this. Perhaps the flames of hell were never quenched, but they might never warm the icy depths of an empty heart, either. It was not beyond the power of damnation to burn and freeze at once. Even as he looked into the triumphant gaze of his enemies—Cassian and the treacherous men who backed him—Prentice remembered all the sufferings these children who grew up in the shadow of the eagle's wings, playing in the raining blood, had laid upon his flesh. He remembered the cold, skin-rasping ache of the fetters around his ankles in the depth of winter. His back recalled afresh the flensing sting of the overseer's lash. Most of all, his chest ached, and he remembered the burning for breath as he had driven the Horned Man down to the bloodied water of the brook, nearly drowning. They had clutched one another, determined to slay, even if it cost them their own lives. These were not even all of the things Prentice had feared, faced, and survived. For all Cassian's skill, this was a moment of a kind the Young Hopeful had never known, preferring instead to duel as his cousin the baroness did, in a world of rules and trophies.

Cassian's back foot twitched, eager for the spring, and he began his final pass. As he did, Prentice also surged forward, a primal growl erupting from his gasping chest, the roar of a lion that would die before failing the pride, the growl of one who knew if the children would go hungry, it was only because the fathers and mothers were already spent to their last breath and last drop of blood. As Prentice came on, Cassian adjusted his step and moved to get outside of his opponent's line—a classic defense. It would allow Prentice's momentum to carry him past and leave him open to a passing cut from the Young Hopeful.

"You have him now, young Cassian," someone cheered from the crowd. Prentice thought it might have been Sebastian, but he did not really care at this moment. Cassian's evasion was excellent and would have made him completely safe from Prentice's sword if Prentice had actually been striking for him, but that was not the knight commander's purpose. He was aiming for the Young Hopeful's stolen blade, managing for just a moment to engage the two swords, edge biting edge and putting them into a bind. It was something Cassian was trained to disengage from, of course, but as he did so, Prentice reversed his movement, his own feet almost slipping out from under him. As Cassian drew his blade slightly away to disengage it, Prentice all but dove at him, following the inevitable withdrawal of Cassian's guard. Suddenly, the talented squire found the flat of his own blade pushed up against his chest by Prentice's, and he staggered backwards reflexively, no doubt thinking to get it clear, but that only let Prentice press even further into him bodily.

A draw cut here at this moment might have slashed open the Young Hopeful's chest or perhaps bitten through his sword arm, but that was not Prentice's intent. Nothing short of utter defeat would diminish this hot-headed youth's love of battle, Prentice had neither the time nor the strength remaining to win a battle of cuts and thrusts. This had to be all or nothing. So, he let his left hand leave his hilt to grab at Cassian's belt while he cocked his right arm for an uppercut and smashed the lion's-head pommel up into the Young Hopeful's jaw. Cassian's teeth clashed and Prentice punched again. This time there was a louder crack, and a tooth flew loose. Then they were collapsing, dropping to the floor.

Both swords went sprawling, metal crashing and scraping over the boards, while their bodies tumbled. Prentice was the larger and stronger of the pair, but Cassian was fresher, blow to the jaw notwithstanding, and also not poisoned, either. So, as they clutched at each other's falling forms, it was the Young Hopeful who came out on top, one hand pressing at Prentice's throat while the knight commander was laid out flat on his back, momentarily vulnerable. Then Cassian's other hand went to his belt to pull out his reserve weapon, a rondel dagger of the kind almost all the noble men-at-arms carried with them everywhere. But that was his undoing.

Cassian loved his blades and always thought them the path to victory and glory—a knight *was* his weapons, in the Young Hopeful's mind. Prentice hated his sword, not because it was a bad blade but precisely because it was the opposite. It was one of the finest weapons in the room, for all that its magickal legend was utterly false. Victory was desirable to Prentice only as the path to the end of the fight. Glory was for tales and the dead.

In the fractional moment when Cassian reached for his rondel, he had to shift his weight to get it from its sheath, and Prentice exploited that movement, locking the young man's free arm in a bar that pushed him over and face first into the floor. Cassian smashed into the boards with a resounding crash, like an axe striking a tree branch, and as he slithered out from the stunned body, Prentice followed up with an elbow across the side of Cassian's head, knocking his face back into the floor and ensuring the squire's jaw was well and truly broken.

Sucking hot breaths into his burning lungs, Prentice staggered slightly as he pushed himself to his feet and stumbled to where the fallen blades lay, still near each other, as if they had never broken from the momentary bind during the duel. He picked up both and returned to the fallen Cassian who was groaning and nursing his jaw, having rolled over onto his back. Prentice put his foot on the young man's chest, being none too gentle, as much because his failing strength had him lean forward automatically as out of any pettiness. He held both blades at Cassian's face, and the Young Hopeful spat blood. It only went as far as Prentice's boot.

Compared to the drenching deluge of crimson from his vision, this seemed mild and modest to Prentice's eyes.

"Give me my sword and we'll finish it!" Cassian slurred through his broken jaw. The pain he was in must have been immense. Prentice remembered Liam, suddenly, trapped by his fallen horse and demanding a last duel for honor's sake, through his own half-healed broken jaw that Prentice had given him as well. The Knight Commander of the Western Reach could not give a damn about that kind of honor.

"You are beaten, Squire Cassian, the matter is settled," he said, thinking his own words were slurring as well. The poison was doing its job. He could feel the strength ebbing from his limbs, and his chest clenched, as if his ribs were crushing his own heart and lungs. Soon, he would be unable to even hold himself up, and Baronet Forsle would not be the only one to die this night. Prentice had one more duty, though, and he would not shirk it. The light had to shine the path out of from under the eagle's wings.

"I do not yield!" Cassian was shouting, bloody spittle flying. Another tooth came loose, and he spat that out as well.

"No need for that," Prentice told him. "The Lioness only needs a little blood to seal the judgement in her favor."

He pushed the Fang's sword forward, as if to nick Cassian's cheek with it. The beaten Young Hopeful cringed away, plainly terrified.

"No," he screamed, almost incoherently. "It is an agonizing death."

"A cut to the cheek? A little scar to remember me by?" Prentice mocked. He would have the treacherous youth confess if he could.

"It is poisoned!" Cassian admitted in a cracking tone. "You should be dead already, you hell-spawned bastard. They promised I'd see the light leave your eyes. It was prophesied to me!"

"False prophets say all sorts of false things, young Cass..." Prentice said, hearing his own voice trailing off. The shadows were almost fully closed around his vision now. It would not be long.

There were mutterings in the darkness, and Prentice wondered if those were the demons come to take his soul to hell, but in his thoughts he remembered the contempt of one of his Ashfield tutors at such peasant theology.

"Devils are God's enemies, and he does not send them anywhere on any errand but to be imprisoned in the earth to await his judgement! When God judges men, he sends his angels."

What was that old tutor's name? He seemed a wise man, as Prentice remembered him, for all that he was a crotchety old boot.

"Do you confess, boy?" the tutor was saying, but with Count Lark-Stross's younger and more pleasant voice now. Cassian answered the tutor's demands with some kind of protest Prentice could not understand. He felt himself collapsing into supportive arms. The swords were removed from his grip, which came as a relief. His hands were aching, he realized.

"It is done, Baron," someone said to him. "You have won."

"That is good," he said, thinking he should be smiling but unable to tell if he was. "Tell my wife to raise our children...to raise them...they have to know how to use the blade...but not to love it. They must never love the blade, for it will never love them back."

Then it was quiet and dark.

CHAPTER 83

There were voices muttering around him in the shadows and Prentice thought it was the demons again. Then he remembered the dank cell under Ashfield and the matter-of-fact cruelty of the Inquisitor and his nun healer. Terror that he was back there leaped awake within him, and he started, trying to sit up. Something was holding him down, and he rapidly became entangled in it.

"Stop, brother, cease," one of the demon Inquisitors told him, and a prayerful hand was laid on Prentice's shoulder, stilling his panic. Demons didn't pray, did they? Did the Inquisition? Would God listen to them? The whispered petition continued a moment, and the fear slowly went back to sleep, but nausea awoke in its place, and he felt himself retch like a drunk who has chucked so much that his stomach held no more than bile any longer. Someone hissed and clicked their tongue, muttering in the shadows.

"True," the praying voice agreed. "But better that muck is on the sheet than on his chest, rotting him from within."

Prentice lost them then and it was quiet around him. He knew he was still alive, because he was in pain, but it was dull. If he was dead and damned to hell, then surely the pain would be more acute, whether it was the bite of cold or the burn of flames. He wasn't weeping or wailing or gnashing his teeth.

A time later, Prentice did hear wailing, but it was the demanding cry of a hungry child, and when it stilled, he rolled over to see his wife, seated in the light of an oil lamp with one of their twins pressed to her breast. She looked up at the sound of him moving and peered at him.

"What do you see now?" she asked, as if it was not the first time she had.

"The most beautiful woman in the Grand Kingdom tending to one of the most beautiful children in the world," he said, smiling weakly.

"Oh, so you're still mad with the poison and fever, then?" she asked contemptuously, though from the glimmer in her eyes he knew she loved the compliment all the same.

"It is the truth I speak, as true as I know before God, and I will duel with any man who disagrees with me."

"I'm not a man," Righteous argued.

"Still, I would duel you, too, if you demanded it," he told her, and he laid back on the pillow with a groan. His wife snorted good-naturedly.

"No more duels. Besides, you'd lose a duel with a bowl of soup, way you are right now," she said, then cooed to the feeding baby.

Prentice lay listening to mother and child together for a while, his eyes closed.

"It was a strong poison then?" he asked when he realized that he was not going to fall straight back to sleep.

"Whilte said it was hell-spawned for certain," Righteous explained. "Took him days by your side just to break the fever of it."

"Where is he now?"

"Right there, in the nursemaid's truckle."

Prentice turned and looked to the other side of their chamber, and there was Brother Whilte, dirty and disheveled, sleeping in the narrow, box-like cot, his arms hugging his legs close in the awkward space. His wooden leg was removed, and it stood beside the bed, its straps dangling free.

"Moved in with us, has he?" Prentice asked wryly.

"Near enough. He tended you like a brother, you know. Prayed until his throat was hoarse. More than once I found him slumped next to you, exhausted and asleep."

Prentice lay back and nodded. "Not like my brothers. But I do owe it to him to be a brother," he said. "I took his first one from him, after all."

"That is simply untrue, My Lord Knight Commander," Whilte protested, having awakened now. His voice was hoarse, just as Righteous had said. "My brother Khalte's own pride took him from me. And mine almost carried me off with him, not to mention costing you your ambitions and almost your life into the bargain. How goes my patient?"

"Impatiently," Prentice joked, but his forced laugh hurt his chest. It made him wonder if the poison made from Inxyphos's blood had reconjured the pain of the wound the bear man had made with his claw—a sympathetic magick of hatred.

"This is the most coherent you have been for days," Whilte told him, smiling as he hopped over to Prentice's bed, not bothering with his pegleg.

"How many days?" Prentice asked.

"Since the duel? Eight."

"More than a week?" The knight commander laid back again with a frustrated groan.

"Be thankful," Whilte told him. "Cassian refused my help and did not survive."

"He died?" Prentice could hardly believe it. "How?"

"Well, you done his jaw in good, worse'n Liam's, if you can believe it," Righteous told him, detaching the baby and tidying her bodice. "But it weren't that what did it."

"The squire rolled on the edge of his own blade as you fell together," Whilte explained. "It cut his sword arm—poetic justice, I suppose. They say it blackened within a day and that by the time they finally amputated it, it stank with the rot, and he was weeping with the agony."

Prentice reached over to touch his own left arm, searching with his fingers to find where the envenomed blade had cut him. He discovered a bandage holding a poultice there, but even through the cloths, his own touch was painful.

"You still have your arm, if you're worried," Whilte told him. "The wound itself blackened a little, but it wasn't deep enough to penetrate your whole being too swiftly. I was able to fight the poison off with prayer."

"It certainly felt like it penetrated swiftly," Prentice retorted, remembering the duel and the power of the toxin in his limbs and stomach.

"You have an indomitable constitution," Whilte told him, "stronger than Cassian's at least, it would seem."

"Too angry to die," Prentice said, remembering the battle-chill and the compassionate hope to turn the Young Hopefuls away from the night-dark fields. He would not send even Daven Marcus to that place, if the venal Usurper's blood debt to the Grand Kingdom could be paid somehow. What weregeld did a king's life demand?

"So, Cassian died of the poison," Prentice muttered as he lay his head back on the pillow, marveling at the twist of fate.

"Not quite," Whilte countered. "He dragged himself from his bed and threw himself from Longbridge in the night, so it's said. Dragged a length of boat cable and a heavy block up from one of the docks to weight himself down. He must have been almost delirious with pain and fatigue by the time he got there, if your experience under the poison is any guide."

"Pity," Prentice said sadly.

"Pity? Deserved is what it was," Righteous snapped, and she lifted her sleeping babe back towards its cot.

"Is there anyone in this room not asleep who has received what they fully deserved, even for all the things we have suffered that we did not deserve?" Whilte asked, picking up on the underlying motive to Prentice's comment.

"Maybe not," Righteous replied, clearly ready for the argument. "But let's look at us, Chaplain, since you bring it up. Have we three suffered less than that fool boy? Batterings? Beatings? Limbs cut off, even?"

She nodded at Whilte's wooden leg, still sitting by itself.

"Weren't one of us walked an easy path, and maybe we needed judgement for our sins, but we faced it and chose to rebuild from the ruins rather than run away and chuck us off a bridge."

"Perhaps he lacked the strength, my love," Prentice said wearily. Already the conversation was draining what little reserves his healing body had gathered.

"He had strength enough to drag himself and a block and tackle all the way out onto the longest of the bridges, wrap it all around himself and throw himself in. How much more strength did he need to start the climb out of the pit he dug for himself?"

Prentice remembered the vision's promise, that the path out from under the eagle's blood-dripping wings would be steep and difficult. Perhaps his wife's harsh assessment was not as far from truth as he might want. Was it just that he was too tired to be firm in his beliefs?

"You could show more compassion, Lady Righteous," Whilte said quietly, and Prentice thought he sounded troubled in his soul more than this subject warranted.

"I could, Master Chaplain," Righteous said archly, standing and straightening her skirts. "And if one of them Young Hopeful twits wants to come and beg my husband's forgiveness for the wrongs they done him, or her grace for that matter, then I might well give them my pardon. But right now, I have no time for this moping on behalf of the treacherous little gutter rat bastard who tried to poison my husband and called it courage and skill. I hope the flames are tickling his toes and the stump of his severed arm right now. In the meantime, I will fetch some of this evening's pottage for my husband's meal. He needs to regain his strength."

With that, she left the room.

"She is resolute in her condemnations," Whilte said, sadly, it seemed to Prentice's ear.

"Her life has been as harsh as any I can think of," Prentice replied, head still on his pillow and eyes closed. "She is not merciless, only...as hard as her life has made her."

There was a long moment's silence between them, and Prentice felt the bed shift and Whilte's one foot thump on the floorboards as he hopped back to retrieve his pegleg.

"I do not begrudge her, Prentice," the chaplain said as the jingle of the prosthetic's buckles sang a sad tune. "I think I even agree to an extent, but I find my mind drawn back to Khalte and what he must have been thinking in those final moments."

Prentice's eyes flew open, and he sat up.

"Oh, damn, Whilte, I never thought," he said earnestly, looking at the chaplain's pained expression in the dimness. "Surely Righteous did not mean any criticism of your brother. I doubt she even connected his circumstance with Cassian's. I did not, and I knew them both."

"I did," Whilte said, sighing. "I have thought exactly the things that your goodwife just said but about my brother. He was so proud and strong. Why did he not use that to rebuild himself after he..."

"Lost the use of his hand?" Prentice asked. Having received many injuries and brutalities in his life, the knight commander had to admit that he was fortunate, indeed, to have suffered so few permanent infirmities, and none so significant as so many others suffered. Fortunate, or blessed.

"He could have fought back from even that. I did. He didn't have to leave me alone like he did," Whilte insisted, and though his voice showed hurt, there was an undertone of anger in it as well. Prentice realized the betrayal the young chaplain had felt when his brother took his own life rather than live as something other than a Church knight. No wonder Whilte had so fixated on destroying Prentice's life in the immediate days after his brother's death.

"Perhaps he had less choice than it seems," Prentice wondered. The notion confused Whilte, whose expression shifted to quizzical.

"How so?"

"I am lying here trying to think of any man I have faced in single combat, a proper duel, since that first one with your brother, who did not go to their death."

"You didn't kill my brother," Whilte insisted, but before he could go on, Prentice waved him quiet with an exhausted gesture.

"I am not so sure, Chaplain," he said. "I was not merciful to your brother, you know that. You were there. You saw the upstart brat staring down at Khalte, smug in his victory. I must have looked something quite like Cassian at that moment. But I did try to spare others. Not Liam, but Ironworth certainly, the Verdant fey champion as well, and even Cassian, if he had been willing to simply turn away from his pointless anger."

"The boy thought to fight the whole world and punish it," Whilte countered, "probably for his father's murder. He sought out excuses to love death and it paid him for his devotion with the currency it pays to all. As for the others, you defeated them but did not kill them. Others did that to them."

"Yet they are still dead. Perhaps I am as the Verdant said—a death thing." Prentice thought about how the Lord had said in his vision that he had been on the path of bloodshed since before he could walk, like Dahyoor's fey babes beginning to learn the saddle while they suckled and slept.

"No!" Whilte said with such vehemence that it was as if he shouted in the small room. He stood up and clomped an awkward step to Prentice's bedside. "You are a man, hard-forged like a sword, to be sure, but straight like one as well, swift to action when swiftness is required. Yet that is where the similarity ends. You do not live for bloodshed, and given a choice, you would be pleased to never draw a blade in anger again. Cassian, Khalte, even your younger brother Pallas, they all loved the blade. It was their preferred answer to every question, so much so that the truth of it was diluted in their minds. They made their choices, and even when you showed them mercy and tried to teach them the better way, they chose to love death. Death is a whore—it comes to everyone with open arms and loves none."

"I don't love it," Prentice said, not sure at the end of the sentence what he was even speaking about. A moment later, he was asleep.

CHAPTER 84

When she heard from Lady Righteous that Prentice was awake, Amelia moved quickly as she could to visit him. Even so, by the time she reached his chamber, he was already asleep once more. Brother Whilte reassured her that he was mending well and that his body showed no sign of permanent infirmity from the venom. Although it had cheered her to hear of Prentice's recovery, Amelia also felt her fury rise again at the entire circumstance, so much so that when she returned to the main room of the Paramour's Chambers and had taken a sip of her tea to calm her nerves, she inadvertently slammed the cup to the table after she drained it, smashing the small piece of porcelain. Lady Daisy moved swiftly and instructed Mathilda to clean the pieces away, which the neophyte did without comment.

"She beat me this morning when Lady Spindle had us at knife training, Your Grace," Daisy said about Mathilda once the smashed cup was removed and time had been taken to ensure that Amelia had not cut herself on the shards.

"Is that why you set her to clean up?" Amelia asked, wondering if Daisy had been getting some measure of petty revenge, commanding Mathilda to kneel to fetch the pieces from the floor.

"Lord, no, Your Grace," Daisy protested, her expression horrified under her lace mask. The new Lace Fang's face covering resembled a crescent moon, and given that Daisy was already what could be generously described as moon faced, Amelia wondered if it were not a cruel jest, of sorts. Since the girls each made their own masks for themselves, she also wondered if it pointed to some inner self-doubt. She hoped not.

"No, I only say, Your Grace, 'cause it's starting to not seem quite fair, that's all," Daisy explained.

"Fair?"

"Yes. Mathilda can hold against me with a shanker, and she's as craftwise in all the ways that Lady Dalflitch teaches. She ain't...sorry, isn't...as canny with other folks as Agatha, but she's a little oracle witch, we all swear, so Mathilda's as good as the rest of us, at least."

Amelia moved to her seat, blinking as she tried to follow Daisy's meaning.

"You think she's ready to become a Lace Fang as well?" the archduchess mused as she hit upon the maid's intent.

"Well, it isn't mine to say...," Daisy began, then she stopped and straightened herself, as if gathering her inner resolve. "The decision, of course, belongs to those above us, but if our thoughts and words are to be counted as sound, then yes, Mathilda is ready. The 'when' and the 'how' are always in your hands, Your Grace, but as to ready, then yea, she is."

"Thank you, Lady Daisy," Amelia said. "I will consider your words seriously and speak with Lady Dalflitch."

"Yes, Your Grace. Thank you," Daisy said, and she curtseyed as she had been taught.

Two days later, when Prentice was recovered enough to take breakfast with his liege lady, Mathilda had been promoted and there were now six Lace Fangs in the archduchess's entourage.

CHAPTER 85

Once word began to filter out that Prentice was up and about, small groups of White Lions—singly at first, then in twos and threes, and once an entire ten-man line—began to come to the door to the Paramour's Chambers, ostensibly with important news about some militia matter but mostly to see for themselves that their leader was indeed alive and recovering.

"It has been nearly two weeks since they last laid eyes upon you, Baron Ash," the archduchess said indulgently as she sat with him in the increasingly wintry afternoon light, candles lit as if it were already evening.

"I was at death's door, Your Grace," Prentice answered her. "A fortnight is hardly an unending shirking of duty."

The last trio of line firsts, all men who had marched west to the dragonfly lake, had not even bothered composing an excuse for coming knocking. They had simply waited for Prentice to appear in the building's little yard and asked for orders. Prentice had laughed at them, then told them that he would be returning to camp soon, and when he did, he would have so many orders for them that they would wish he was back in bed for another month. They had laughed with him and saluted before returning to their duties. Now, he sat with the archduchess, and it was her turn to laugh at his circumstances.

The boom of cannon shot rang through the air outside the window, and Prentice looked up like a hunting dog catching scent of the prey.

"Sougate again?" her grace asked him. He cocked his head and listened for the next shot. While he had been unconscious during his convalescence, the Veckander army had made its first full assault against the southern bastion. Knight Sergeant Gennet had been commanding and had sent for Farringdon as the most senior officer available. Even so, by the time the marquis had arrived, rushing as best he could down the crowded Great Bridge Road, the Sougate cannons and Roarsmen were already raining death on the southern army. After an hour or so, the Golden Heron force had withdrawn, bloodied and frustrated. They had men-at-arms afoot try to bring up ten scaling ladders to assault the main fortifications, but only one of them had even reached the outer trenches that had been dug in recent days. Sergeant Guillam had declared it a good day's fighting, though it was over before midday.

"I cannot say for sure, north or south, Your Grace," Prentice said as the second shot resounded. The thunder seemed to bounce from many of the town's roofs and walls before it blew in through the open windows, so telling its direction was beyond him, at least for now. The archduchess cocked her head herself and looked to his chair.

"Eager to go?" she asked, and Prentice realized that he was indeed poised to stand up. If the Gryphon Banner was fighting, it felt wrong for him not to be there.

"I am, Your Grace."

A third cannon shot rang out.

"If you feel yourself strong enough, Knight Commander, then I will not keep you," the archduchess told him.

"Strong enough to mount the steps of Sougate and at least watch, Your Grace. Unless they have developed some unexpected tactic that will overwhelm our garrison and reserves, there will be little chance for me to do more than that."

Prentice was fairly certain that he could make the climb to the parapet now, although he had a moment of nervousness, imagining himself reaching the top steps sweating and pale—not the impression he wished to project to his militiamen.

"Are you certain of your safety? Remember that your lost brigandine is not yet replaced. I only sent word to the Fallenhill workshops a week ago. Whatever journeymen they send for the task will not even know they are summoned yet, most likely."

With that thought, the archduchess turned to Lady Dalflitch, who was seated at the table, scowling at a ledger.

"Speaking of nobles in armor, My Lady, we should compose another letter to Lady Penelope, perhaps, once more inviting her to visit Sougate."

"As you wish, Your Grace," the lady seneschal replied without looking up from her troublesome account book. "I suspect it will receive the same treatment the others have received."

"Nevertheless," her grace said in turn. "But what is it that so vexes you this day?"

"Another money changer's letter," the lady seneschal said.

"Have they revised their exchange rate again?"

"Worse, Your Grace, they are refusing outright to exchange another Masnian coin. This one mutters that maybe even Reach silver might not be welcome. He is the last still doing business with us, and he talks about the dire threats and portents that are circulating."

"Circulating? Or being twittered in his ear?" Amelia asked. Prentice knew they all saw the whispers of the Silent Hand behind this. He stood up, grateful that the ache of sickness had mostly left his limbs now, though he still had nothing like the vitality he had taken for granted in recent years.

"Has Lady Penelope truly not been seen since the feast?" he asked before he left for Sougate.

"So far as any who will speak to us know," the archduchess told him. "There was a rumor that she was seen near Norgate when Count Lark-Stross and the members of his compact quit the town, but that was only the day after, and it has not been something our Fangs and neophytes can confirm."

Prentice knew there were also rumors that Faldmoor's support of Cassian, with its treacherous use of poison and possibly sorcery to boot, had set the Forberest Compact on very shaky ground. It could well be broken already, though there were no official reports.

"I say the girl is sulking like a child, Your Grace," Dalflitch said, pulling a sheet of vellum from a folio full of them. Each piece had an illumination at the top of the Reach coat of arms. Apparently, Master Solft had persuaded a scriptorium to provide the partially prepared documents to the archduchess as a gift and precursor to other business. It was all part of some complex exchange he had worked out that would also provide him with some of the ancient texts his research required. Apparently, the Inquisition had not yet intimidated the scribes of Bridgetown as it had the financiers.

With an adroit hand, the lady seneschal trimmed a quill and set to composing a letter with wording she had already written many times since the archduchess's chamber had arrived in Bridgetown. Prentice was sure the archduchess would prefer to go to the baroness in person, even with her growing pregnancy, but the gate to Earlsbastion was shut to all Reachermen at this moment,

"With your permission, Your Grace, I *will* see to Sougate," Prentice said at last. "Even if our defenses are yet 'invincible,' I would prefer to know for myself rather than simply trusting to reports."

"Then go to, Knight Commander," the archduchess said, dismissing him, and Prentice left the Paramour's Chambers, glad to be back to his duties even if he was not yet sure he was ready for them.

CHAPTER 86

Leaving the yard, Prentice turned to head toward Great Bridge Road when he was suddenly fronted up by Turley, accompanied by three young men who seemed vaguely familiar.

"Ay up! Here's the man himself, lads," Turley declared, and while Prentice was not unhappy to see his friend, he was aware of the continuing hammer-blows of cannon shot echoing over the town. He noticed that several of the traders and craftsfolk on the street looked up with every shot, as if fearful the cannonballs were about to rain from the sky directly.

At least it isn't blood from a giant eagle's wings, Prentice thought, the revolting image from the vision still troubling at the fringes of his mind. He scowled and looked over Turley's companions, not quite fully registering their presence, but he did notice that they seemed to shy from his gaze, as if ashamed. That stirred his suspicion while Turley made something of a presentation out of their meeting in the street.

"Are you of a strength to be wandering about?" he asked.

"Whether I am or not, you can hear the guns," Prentice replied, not meaning to be as sour with his friend as he was. "I am on the way to Sougate now."

"Well then, let me and my good men accompany you," Turley offered readily. "You Reacher militiamen ain't supposed to be abroad alone, is you? What with spies and assassins, not to mention sorcery and beast men, all at large on the streets these days, it's sure not safe for a man of your weakened condition to walk alone."

Prentice thought to snipe back at his friend, but another cannon shot split the air and he let the jest go unanswered. Heading for the crooked spine of town, Prentice walked through the crowd with his finely dressed friend, while the three anonymous young men followed. For some time, they walked in silence, though Turley enjoyed playing cock-o-the-town, waving to merchants and washerwomen as they passed. It was impossible that he could know even a third of them by name, but he smiled at any who met his eyes, as if he was an old friend with a long history between them. It was an easy manner that Prentice had always admired in his mate, a kind of simple charm that made everyone see him as a possible friend, or less frequently, hate him on sight as an obvious rake. Lady Dalflitch's place at his side had diminished that half of his character, so that this Turley was every man's friend. With his wife as the shrewd dealer and he as the irresistible rogue, Prentice doubted there was any conclave or merchant anywhere in the world that would not be vulnerable to their plans on behalf of their liege. With no more than a single hint from Prentice's own wife, a mere messenger-bird's missive, the pair had even recently sniffed out a skin thief assassin in Dweltford Castle in time to thwart the sorcerer agent's plans. That story impressed all who heard it.

"My Lord Baron, if I may?" one of the trio following behind asked timidly. "Is it true what Sir Turley says, that you know all about the monstrous men, like that bear thing? He says that you are the Reach's greatest expert."

Prentice turned to look at the youth who was so fresh faced that he might as well have still been a pageboy. His hair was styled in a simple bowl cut, and what little beard he did have was a wispy brown affair—bumfluff, as cruel maids might say to mock a boy struggling to cross into manhood. The young man was surely a year or two older than Solomon, at least, but the ex-drummer's own beard was already coming thicker and stronger than this poor fellow's.

"Is that what he told you?" Prentice asked and the young man nodded, his two companions joining him hesitantly. A glance to Sir Turley showed him to be beaming like a proud father, and Prentice felt his suspicion take on an annoyed edge. Was his old friend having a laugh at his expense?

"Tell me, *Sir* Turley, are we going to have introductions at some point, or do you have an unfair guessing game planned for the afternoon?" Prentice asked, and his friend's smile acquired its classic mischievous cast.

"Well, it weren't our plan, My Lord Baron, to meet with you in the open street like this," Turley said, ushering the others across to a less crowded part of the thoroughfare. In a gap between a basket weaver and a cloth merchant—a section of blank wall that smelled like many of the locals used it as a privy—the knight castellan of Dweltford outlined why he had not yet presented his young companions. "My plan had been to take you to the Dog's Leg, which a man of your sober disposition will not know is one of Bridgetown's finest drinking establishments, better even than that alehouse I took you to when I first come. Until recently frequented by only the highest born of the town, the Dog's Leg is seeking a new set to make up recent falls in its business, and a reputable knight and his squires are welcome there."

Years of practice let Prentice pull the key detail out of his friend's loquacious explanation.

"Squires?" he asked with a raised eyebrow.

"I'm a knight, isn't I? Knights take squires to themselves and help 'em become knights too."

"I know how knighthood works," Prentice said. "I almost became one myself, remember."

"So you did. So you did. And now, you've purged your soul of your sins, real and imagined, and you're risen to a much higher status than that. Do you begrudge these fellows the same possibility?"

Prentice looked the three fearful and earnest men over as Turley's words swirled around him like the crowd at its endless mercantile dance.

I should not be out like this, he thought, feeling his strength starting to flag and his mind becoming a fraction slower. The repeated, intermittent booming of cannon shot reminded him that he still had a duty to fulfil. Then, all the pieces of Turley's comments fell into place.

"You are Young Hopefuls," he said, and he felt the fury stir within him, not to mention a fear that somehow these three might have somehow persuaded his old friend to help in his assassination. Was this even Turley? Had a skin thief replaced his mate? It seemed to be the same charmer, but perhaps Prentice's mind was being clouded by magicks again. His hand went reflexively to his sword, though he knew it was a fruitless gesture at defense. If even one of these three was half the swordsman Cassian had been, Prentice knew he would soon be dead.

"Whoa, hold up there, old chum," Turley urged, and Prentice realized that far from seeming ready to do violence, the trio had actually flinched away. If they had come for a fight, they were terrified by the prospect. Maybe he could use that to escape.

"What is this?" he demanded, his eyes searching the crowd around them, watchful for a cutthroat or skips' thug posing as a merchant or customer. These four might not be the only enemies.

"This is a presentation, you twit," Turley told him. "I'm about introducing you to my new squires, who are no Young Hopefuls anymore. God's honest! Now I know I ain't never won a proper stoush 'tween us, not once since that first day when you stopped me slipping the chain and trying to run off. But given how you've been these last days, I favor my chances for once, so don't make me knock your head about to make you see sense."

Prentice nodded slowly, not removing his hand from his sword's hilt. Few enough people knew the tale of how he and Turley had met that he was willing to believe this was no skin thief.

"Alright," he said warily. "Make your presentation."

Turley smiled, then sniffed and screwed up his nose.

"Gahh, I hope it smells better than this in the back alley behind the Dog's Leg," he said. "If the drinks always as good as it was last night, I'll be back there quite some in the days when I come to town."

"I fear not so, sir," one of squires said with a smile.

"Oh well, I'll get used to it, I s'pose." Turley removed his hat and used it to point to each young man in turn as he named them. "Baron Ash, these three young gents are Squire Aldous, from a farm estate somewhere on the north side of the river that was burned by Duke Robant's mongrels. Squire Florian, son of a baronet whose estate is a small island some ways downriver from here but owes allegiance to Bridgetown. And this fellow who asks questions is Squire Piers, who was born and raised right here on the islands."

"But I'm not named after Piers Island," the young man insisted.

Prentice knew that Piers was the name of the one of Bridgetown's islands, but that was all, and he could not think why the man would want or not want to be named after it.

"Alright," Prentice said. "Why did you want me to meet with them?"

"What? Not even a hale and well met young gentlemen?" Turley said, a look of mock consternation on his face.

"As you have implied, I am not fully recovered," Prentice answered, harsher than he intended. "I am tired, still in some pain, and in more haste to reach Sougate before the Golden Heron overruns it."

"Why? It's not like you could help stop 'em if they were of a mind to," Turley said but then seemed to notice his friend's expression. "But fair enough, play's a good'n, but times come for work. These three *were* Young Hopefuls, like you kenned. But since Cassian was shown to be a treacherous little coward at heart, not to mention not your equal, even when he put the venom to you, they can't count'nance 'emselves that way no more."

"Cyprian and Cassian always seemed the best of us," the squire introduced as Florian explained. "They were the best swords and had the ear of the baroness, and could keep that snot Wilforn from being a bastard as well. They came up with all the plans. We just went along 'cause they said they could make a path for us all to make our pledges and become knights—glory and rank."

"Just went along?" Prentice repeated coldly.

"To our shame," said Squire Aldous. "And not just for your duel, My Lord. Even before, some of us were speaking together in our quiet moments. The blood in the fields before Sougate, it was sickening. And the foolishness of claiming it was we who slew the monster at the cathedral? We were all there. We saw what you did. How could we all just follow the brothers and pretend it was us? I pray nightly that my father will forgive me for that when I get to heaven, if I get to heaven."

"Now, young squire, don't fear you none," Turley said comfortingly, putting a hand on his shoulder. "You're back on a righteous path now, and you'll have your chances to do your father proud. Pay his memory right back."

Prentice was not fully persuaded, and his eyes narrowed as he saw a different interpretation to this apparent change of three hearts.

"The liege of Bridgetown has gone into seclusion and your leaders are in disgrace, one of them at least," he summed up as his penetrating gaze surveyed the three. "She will not be an archduchess anytime soon, and Daven Marcus will not have you, even if you were that base in your ambitions. So, you are forced to seek service with her grace, Amelia of the Western Reach, as the only path to the titles you long for? Is that it?"

Two of the squires lowered their heads in shame, but Aldous met Prentice's eyes.

"Yes, My Lord. That was a true part of our plan, but not in calculation or dishonesty, we swear! We have stains on our honor now. How can we purge them if we do not seek service somewhere?" He straightened his shoulders, but his face was still open, and his misgivings seemed unhidden. It was a distinctive show of character, strong and penitent at the same moment. If the lad was being false, he was a genius at acting.

"We went to your camp," he went on. "We thought to sign up with the Bridgetown militia. We heard that your lady raised men to the knighthood for militia service and thought, if she was commanding Bridgetown's men afoot as well, then perhaps we could serve there, purge our souls and rise. As you yourself have done."

"She's your liege lady now, as well, Squire Aldous," Turley corrected, serious for the first time since Prentice had met them in the street. Aldous accepted the instruction with a short bow.

"But the Bridgetown militia's all washed downriver," Florian added to the story. When Prentice cocked his head, Turley explained.

"They're in the wind. Washed downriver's the local talk for the same thing."

"They're gone, My Lord. We assume most back to their homes somewhere here in town, but no one's even thought to seek them out. And we couldn't go to sign on with the Lions, not after Cassian's hunt. They'd cut us up the moment they learned who we were. It was sheer dumb luck we ran into Sir Turley, seeking a finer tavern more suited to his tastes."

Touring the drinking houses of Bridgetown, more likely, Prentice thought, though he kept his face stern.

"And what?" the knight commander asked his friend, turning fully toward him. "You thought to present them to the archduchess? How do you think that will be received?"

"It's already been done," Turley replied, and now the knight castellan was almost as serious as Prentice. "I presented them a couple of days ago, and her grace has received their repentance and their pledges with welcome." He paused as he no doubt could see the surprise on Prentice's face. "What? The world goes on when you ain't there, you know. I'm her knight, and who I take as squire, or squires, is 'tween her grace and me. You don't need to have a say."

"Then why bother with this presentation, if my word matters so little?"

"Cause my lads insisted," Turley said, gesturing to the three earnest squires. "Tomorrow I'm taking 'em back with me to Dweltford on the boat. If they're to be Reach knights, then they'd best learn their service in the Reach, don't you think? Even so, they wanted to meet you before we pushed the boat off."

"Why?"

"To apologize My Lord and beg your forgiveness," Aldous said, and he and his comrades all bowed their heads. "Cassian *was* the best sword we had, and we thought he was the best of us, but we saw how that was a lie long before we admitted it, even to ourselves. Daven Marcus killed our fathers, and with them the knighthood of Bridgetown died as well, or near enough. We thought to replace them, but we...we became as bad as the Usurper."

The three shared rueful looks—angry, but at themselves. They nodded, accepting the condemnation between them.

"Bridgetown has no knights, not anymore, and precious little nobility. Even if we wanted it otherwise, we stood and watched like cowards while older men and foreigners saved our liege's life, and then we hunted honest men through the streets like footpads. Now all I long for is a last chance to purge my soul and make my life worthy of my father's memory. For years, nobles sent convicts over the mountains to purge their souls. I'll go there and maybe I'll find the same for myself in the west."

"That's not enough for me, My Lord," the youthful Piers said, shaking his head. "I want to do all that in the west, but I hope one day to return and to bring with me what you know. The White Lions are mighty, and they say they began from convicts and rogues. Even you yourself, Baron Prentice, if you'll pardon me saying. Aldous is right, Bridgetown has no knights anymore, but she needs them. If I can make good enough in the west, then maybe your...our...lady will release me, and I can bring the same genius back here. Rebuild what Daven Marcus has demolished with wisdom and service instead of anger and pride."

Prentice had to admit to himself that the three squires seemed to mean what they were saying, but he found he really did not want to accept it. He tried to shake his head, to deny the obvious, but then he remembered the studious children from his vision. He had watched some be led away from study to bloody play. Could others be returned from the crimson deluge to their desks and the possibility of cleansing themselves in service and repentance? Were these the ones with their feet on the hard and steep path now, having learned the lesson that killed Cassian and now coming out from under the eagle's wings?

"You led murderers and thieves into service as the finest army in the world," Turley whispered, leaning in close. "Made a steward and now a knight castellan out of this lecherous horse thief. Can't you let me try for these pups. They ain't rebels, just a bit wayward and led astray, is all."

"You made a knight castellan out of yourself," Prentice objected quietly.

"Bollocks to that. If I'd never met you, I'd be burnt on that pyre we made out of the others that tried to run that day. And even if not, how many other times did you pick the impossible road and fight our way through, hmm? Give the lads a chance. We'll do you proud."

Prentice looked at the three squires like plaintive children, fearful of punishment but standing still to receive it, longing most of all to be good.

"Do your *fathers* proud," he told them, correcting Turley's comment. "As to matters between you and me, or you and the White Lions, you can do this recompense. Serve the archduchess sincerely, utterly, completely, as all Lions and nobles of the Reach do, and I will count all our debts settled."

The cannon blast resounded again.

"Now, either walk with me to Sougate, or if you would do me some other service, run to the camp and seek out my squire—a man with pointed ears named Dahyoor. Tell him to fetch my horse to the southern gate. By the time I've climbed the barbican and come back down, I will not want to walk back to my bed."

"Yes, My Lord," Piers said, and Turley shepherded them away as Prentice turned toward the south once more. Just as they were almost out of earshot, Prentice heard one of the squires ask.

"So, they really do have fey in service, Sir Turley?"

Then they were swallowed by the trading crowd, and Prentice made for Sougate.

CHAPTER 87

"Good shot!" someone on the parapet shouted as Prentice stepped up through the door to the Sougate roof. The short climb had not been quite as difficult as he had feared, but a light rain had begun to fall from the slate sky, and he was pleased that any sweat on his face would be as likely to be taken for raindrops. As he wrapped his cloak about himself, he realized that the cold rain would present its own problems for his health. If any battle ran long, he would have to stay close to the braziers the cannoneers used for their linstock wires so he could keep warm.

Looking southward, he was surprised to see that the Golden Heron was not in the fields. Their tents were still visible, and the original earthwork wall was almost washed away now by the weather. None of the mercenary force was arrayed against Sougate, however. The sound of a cannon crew at work, loading and aiming a single gun drew Prentice's attention to the eastern turret of the gate fortification, slightly lower than the main parapet, and reached by a short flight of steps from the roof. Of the six cannons mounted in Sougate, this was one of only two that could be easily aimed any direction other than south, in this case east, and that was the direction the gun was being fired. Prentice pulled his hood up and moved carefully down the slick wet steps to where Sergeant Guillam was commanding the action, though it seemed for the most part his role was simply to call out targets. The Masnian gun commander was giving the real instructions in his homeland tongue.

"How goes it, Sergeant?" Prentice called. Guillam turned and the rising wind whipped droplets from his sodden fringe.

"We're gettin' to play some more, My Lord," the sergeant said happily.

"Guns are not toys, Sergeant."

"Mayhaps not, but when they come at us so daft as this, well." He shrugged happily.

Prentice moved forward, up beside the active gun under its rain shelter. An inch or two of the muzzle was protruding from under the little roof, and the hot metal sizzled as the raindrops steamed upon it. He peered down at the river, already half obscured in the gloomy weather. The whole world to the east was grey with falling rain, as if being seen through dirty muslin. He did not envy the gunner's the task of tracking their shots in these conditions.

"What am I looking for, Sergeant?" Prentice asked as his eyes searched for a target.

"On the river, My Lord," Guillam explained. "Them boats comin' up in a column from the east. After we slapped the smiles off the Veckander's faces last week, Knight Sergeant Gennet said to keep watch for boats havin' a go, just like that Lord Mark Sparrow fellow said when he was up here."

"Count Marken Lark-Stross, Sergeant," Prentice corrected.

"Yea, well, whatever his name, looks like he was right. They're bringing boats up from the east to come across at the town without the bridge here. Gennet said that if we saw boats that had armed men in 'em, we were free to give 'em what for."

The Masnian gunner shouted something in his own speech and then began to gesticulate at Prentice, continuing to shout, apparently forgetting that the knight commander did not speak the southern empire's tongue.

"Ah, My Lord, that's a warning to keep back," Guillam explained, waving for Prentice to step away from so close to the gun's lethal end. "The blast is well nasty on the ears when you're that close. A couple of us only made the mistake once and now we listen out for that shout of his."

Prentice nodded thankfully and walked back to the other end of the cannon. When the gun leader shouted his foreign warning again, every man on the parapet put his hands to his ears and Prentice joined them. The linstock wire was put to the touchhole and a moment later the powder ignited with a blast that rang in Prentice's chest and limbs. He was only glad it did not hurt. Even a few days prior, the bruises would likely have ached afresh at such a thunderous vibration. The metal beast rocked on its wheels, stopped from moving backward too far by immense wedges of solid-seeming wood. When the shot was done, the crew set about cleaning out the barrel and touchhole, put the linstock back into the coals to heat it, and fetched new ammunition. As the cannon rocked backward, it had pushed itself wholly under its shelter, and the last flames of the blast set the shelter roof to smoldering, but the rain smothered that so swiftly that the crew simply ignored it.

"Missed that one," Guillam said, having stepped up to assess the shot. "We don't get quite the extra range from this height that the ones up on the main barbican can, My Lord. Should've seen it. We were pummeling them even before they cleared that old earth wall o' theirs. Put the fear o' God's own thunder into 'em, no word of a lie!"

"Sorry I slept through it," Prentice said absently, staring down into the grey weather. With some effort, he could definitely discern the little trail of boats that was making its slow way upstream toward the southern bridge. In fact, if they were minded to, they were already in a position to turn aside to land on the east end of Greenmarsh Island, where the carder's guild warehouses had been cannonaded before. It seemed likely though that these boats would be aiming straight for the Sougate Bridge itself, which made sense. If that could be captured, the gatehouse could be assaulted from both directions at once and the main of the army let into the town through the gate after its capture. A sound enough strategic aim, but something about this left Prentice confused. Where had the Veckanders found this many boats so soon? He and Count Marken had thought it would take the Golden Heron army most of the winter to build boats enough to make a crossing assault. This smaller force was not a poor compromise, hoping to take the bridge first, but that seemed a gamble, doubly so as they were bringing the boats up in the daylight. Having been rebuffed once by cannon and matchlock fire alone, surely they would have thought to approach by night. They were sailing into the Gryphon gunners' shots like they were on an idyll cruise.

"Are we sure they are enemy vessels, Sergeant?" he asked as he contemplated the uncertain evidence of his eyes and his own thoughts. "I would hate to think we have started sinking a convoy of merchant vessels bringing exotic fruits, salt, and grain to Bridgetown for sale. We are unpopular enough with the Lady Penelope as it is."

One of the nearby sentries scoffed quietly, perhaps thinking to remain unheard, but clearly not taken with the young liege or her approval. Guillam clicked his tongue at the fellow, and then turned to answer his commander's question.

"It's harder to see now, My Lord, but when we spotted the lead boat it was clearer, and even in the grey their white plate was like silver on the water."

"Are you certain it wasn't a trick of the light on the water itself?"

"Sure as I can be," Guillam answered. "And when that first one went down, we saw fellows diving off in armor, trying to swim and not doing a very good job."

There were mutterings around the cannon that Prentice realized were the Masnian commander translating for his crew and then the gunners chuckled to themselves. The grim humor of the battlefield knew no language barriers, it seemed.

"And I figure them all for the same mob, 'cause their boats is all the same built type, and they ain't riverboats. That's for sure."

Prentice could see the sergeant's point on that immediately. These boats were of a significantly different design to a river lighter or skiff. They had pronounced keels that rose in front and back, forming the prow and stern. For a moment they put Prentice in mind of the Redlander's vessels, though they were clearly different, and coming under the power of rowers rather than sails. If they had any sails at all, those were furled in the weather. Knowing as little as he did of seamanship, they looked to Prentice as if they were ocean-going craft. Perhaps the Golden Heron had hired these boats at some Vec port on the Tassassim coast and sailed them up the Murr. It was known that Bridgetown essentially marked the absolute western point beyond which no sea-going vessels could safely sail. But that still left the question of how swiftly the Heron had brought them to service. If they had them so close and coming, then why waste time with the initial assault that had been thrown back last week?

"If you're still troubled, My Lord, they *were* flying flags, when the wind let them. It's swirling more now and not always strong enough to lift the cloth against the rain, but those masts they've got no sails on have pennants at the top. All the same ones—golden birds, the Heron sign them Veckanders is fighting under. They're a martial fleet bringing men-at-arms, I promise, My Lord."

Prentice absorbed Guillam's words and peered at the boats still coming upriver. The call to cover their ears was given and the cannon fired again. For a moment, smoke and flame obscured everything. The cannonball flew true this time, and as if its hot iron path through the air cleared away the grey rain for a moment, Prentice saw the craft where it was struck. The high gunwale of the seaworthy vessel was torn out on one side and as the whole craft shuddered, the flag flapping free on its mast.

And Prentice cursed himself for a fool.

"Sergeant Guillam," he bellowed, turning from the crenelations and already rushing back to the steps up to the main parapet. "Send a runner to Knight Sergeant Gennet right this very moment. Tell him to turn out the whole Gryphon Banner Company onto Sougate Bridge."

"My Lord?" Guillam asked, clearly caught out but rushing behind Prentice to keep up and receive his orders.

"All along the bridge, as many as the damn thing will hold," Prentice insisted. "The rest are to array on Greenmarsh. In fact, put the Roarsmen in the windows and under the eaves of the warehouses. That way they will be able to keep out of the rain and fire on the river. And see if you can't get those cannons on the main parapet moved to fire on those boats as well."

Prentice doubted that last order would be easily achieved, since it would mean either shifting the guns' shelters with them somehow or else wheeling them out into the rain, creating the same problem for them as the Roarsmen, whose longmatch wicks would never stay alight in this downpour.

"Surely, at once, My Lord," Guillam said, and by his expression it was clear he was obeying out of pure reflex. "You'll have the whole banner here in half a candle."

"I will not be here in half a candle, Sergeant," Prentice retorted.

"Where'll you be?"

"At Norgate, at least for awhile."

"Why?"

"Because, Sergeant Guillam, those pennants you saw are red, not black," Prentice told him, pointing westward downriver as he reached the door to the stairs. "The golden bird you saw there is not a heron. It is an eagle, with a crown over its head."

"A crown, My Lord?" Guillam asked.

"The Usurper's army is here!"

"Oh, hells bells," the sergeant muttered, and then Prentice left him behind, rushing down the steps and risking his wet boots slipping on the way. Even so, Guillam's runner caught him up before he reached the barbican's "ground floor." Prentice stepped aside to let the young militiaman bolt toward the camp, while he went looking for Dahyoor, hoping the fey squire had already brought him a mount and was waiting for him. He had to get to Norgate as soon as possible to know what was happening at Bridgetown's other entrance, and he also had to check every bridge and island on the way, because if the arriving force meant to capture one bridge, then it might well be planning to assault them all at once. Every defense they had planned against attack was about to be challenged by the one eventuality they had not even envisaged for a moment, a massive fleet coming upriver.

Chapter 88

"Still no sign of the Lady Penelope?" Amelia asked from under the broad hood of her heavy cloak as the flickering torches around her lit the roof of the keep-like gatehouse across the first bridge from Norgate itself. At Knight Captain Farringdon's request, she had not gone to that final bastion because of the threat of fighting. Even as the grey sky darkened to night, he was still insistent. Instead, she consulted the officers of the Norgate Bastion—Farringdon, Sedgemark, and Nunel—atop the more ancient keep on the first of Bridgetown's islands, Loncastel. Knight Sergeant Sir Markas had command of Norgate by himself for the moment.

"They were landing their monster guns, Your Grace," Farringdon had told her by way of explanation. "It was an impossible-seeming task and likely they will not be ready to fire on Norgate this night, but I would much prefer not to take any risk. Daven Marcus is infamous for his impatience, after all."

Now that the sun was going down, the rain had ceased, but the night air was chilled and turning bitter. Amelia knew that she would have to seek a warm fire soon for her baby's sake, at the least.

"No word from Earlsbastion, or any other quarter of the town," Farringdon explained, to the archduchess's chagrin. When Prentice had sent her word of this army's arrival, Amelia had seen the implications immediately. This was not the game as it had been played up until this moment. Bridgetown was in imminent danger like it never had been before.

"And we know for a fact that it is him?" she asked. "It is definitely the Usurper?"

"We managed to capture some overeager scouts, Your Grace," Knight Sergeant Nunel informed her. "They seemed to think the rain made them safe from all forms of shot, despite the sound of Sougate's cannons all afternoon. With our enclosed triggers, the wheellock is a different beast. Short of dropping it straight in a pool of water, she's a good chance to shoot for us. The lancers felled several horses and took the riders in. When we questioned them, they readily admitted to being knights sworn to Daven Marcus' service."

"Damn him. How can he be here?"

"The story Lark-Stross and his compact fellows had was incomplete and twisted to the wrong direction, my love," Farringdon explained, forgetting himself in the grimness of his tale. "Earl Lastermune did break the siege of his castle, but not in a manner we ever imagined. The newly acceded Duke Lastermune of Inverel and Greycastle has made peace with the Usurper, whom he once swore he would see dancing a gibbet before being drawn and quartered."

"Duke of Invernel and Greycastle?" Amelia repeated, almost breathless at the cunning of the plot.

"Indeed, lord of all the north, in effect," Farringdon continued. "And grandfather to the new queen."

"Queen?" Amelia felt herself almost stagger with the overwhelming revelation. Lastermune had married his granddaughter to that monster? For a dukedom and his descendants on the throne? Amelia's stomach turned with disgust at the very thought.

"Well, at least this should put paid to his claim to be married to me," she joked, not feeling the least bit humorous. "Does Knight Commander Ash know about this?"

"We couldn't say, Your Grace," Nunel reported. "Word was sent some hours ago, but the baron is said to be in a dozen different places at once. After he came here to bring us word and see the plans for the north bank for himself, he went back into the town."

"He fears for the bridges, Your Grace," Farringdon told her, remembering his rank and role once more, it seemed. "They are vulnerable to this many vessels. While there was light, the fleet stretched back as far as we could see down the Murr. There has been a battle for the Sougate Bridge already, so we have that word. The cannon firing on the boats was the opening of that conflict."

"We also heard that some had tried to put ashore at Runners Field, but that was just as we rode out under orders to come here, Your Grace," Nunel reported.

"There's no chance Gennet wouldn't swat them straight back into the river," Sedgemark added confidently.

"So, we are holding, at least until the dragons of Denay begin to breathe their own fire and stones?" Amelia asked, and they nodded. "What reason was there that Norgate's guns did not fire on the approaching boats?"

Her voice was not accusatory, but Sedgemark looked down shamefacedly for a moment.

"That was my fault, Your Grace," he said, but Farringdon cut him off.

"We built the defenses for a landward assault, Your Grace," he said. "It simply never occurred to any of us that Robant's army would try some kind of boat crossing or assault. His force was too small. In truth, even six cannons for Norgate was starting to feel heavy-handed, to my thinking. I was contemplating offering two back to Prentice to reinforce Sougate further since they were facing the heavier assault. It was a lapse in judgement, and it was mine."

"I do not care where blame falls, knights of the Reach," Amelia told all three of them, meaning every word. "None of us imagined this assault or this army—not I, not Count Lark-Stross and his compact, and not the baroness-elect, certainly. No man-at-arms can fight an enemy on every side. You prepared against everything that could be foreseen. Now we will adjust and turn our defenses to the new threats."

"With your permission on that count, Your Grace, I would like to move some of our cannons back here onto Loncastel Island," Sedgemark suggested.

"You need not my permission, Sir Sedgemark. You have my confidence already," Amelia affirmed for the knight sergeant, though she did want to understand his reasoning. "Is the roof of this strong-house sturdy enough for them? And won't bringing them back across the river reduce their range?"

Sedgemark shook his head.

"It will be reduced some, but my plan is not to put them up here, Your Grace."

He looked to Farringdon, who took up the explanation.

"We want to secure them at separate points on the island's riverbanks. That way, we can direct some to fire easterly and others to cover the banks to the side. We'll leave two at the gates of the bastion against direct assault, but this way we'll have better firing on a large swathe of the north bank. Even if it won't be as telling as the Sougate's guns, it will harry Daven Marcus and keep his dragons back from pummeling the town. We know how he loves them. And it will give us some shots at his boats, stop them thinking they can sail at the other bridges come the new day."

That all sounded excellent to Amelia's mind, though she was sure she recognized only about half of the tactical and strategic implications of their plan.

"Very well, men of the Reach, we have our plans for this side of our fortress of islands. The situation without our walls of river channels may have changed, but our place within has not. We yet have our commitment to Bridgetown and to its wavering liege. I trust you to steel our defenses, and I will make every effort to steel her will. The Usurper has come to us at last, and while I will not send one militiaman to a worthless death, I swear, I have longed for this battle like no other ever, not since the first day the Horned Man's raiders stalked out of the west."

The three officers saluted her, and she nodded to them in return before turning and waving her escorting Lace Fangs to lead the way back down into the keep and then out onto the Great Bridge Road, where the bustling trade was subdued for the first time since the White Lions had arrived in the town.

"What word of the knight commander, Lady Agatha?" she asked.

"Only that he has several cohorts on each of the major bridges and is with a further three cohorts of Gryphons, chasing a company of men-at-arms that came ashore somewhere on the north side of Greenmarsh, Your Grace."

"Let us pray and hope for his success, then," Amelia said.

"Back to the Paramour's Chambers, Your Grace?" Lady Spindle asked, eyes on the strangely empty street ahead, lanterns lit for evening trade but with so few customers about their business. Amelia sighed heavily.

"I would much prefer to go to Earlsbastion and box the ears of our hiding hostess, but I suspect that tonight, of all nights, the castle gate will remain closed to us."

"Yes, Your Grace."

For safety, the three ladies made a swift journey back to their liege's rooms. Occasionally they heard the sound of clashes on the wind, echoing over the windswept roofs, but soon enough they were in the relative safety of the Paramour's Chambers once more, waiting for the next day and the new challenges. The civil war had at last come fully to the White Lions' door, and it had arrived in power.

The battle was about to begin in earnest.

Epilogue

"We cannot get close to her now," the resentful young man told Bluebird in the back of the tavern where they were both sheltering from the weather and the conflict in the streets and bridges. The rain that had failed near sundown was back now as the hour drew past midnight, though the running battles over the cobbles and waterways were definitely continuing. Bluebird could have told Daven Marcus's twit captains, whoever they were, that his boats would never land enough troops to snatch the town away in an afternoon, not that he had any opportunity to tell them. He even wondered if the Inquisition had a high-ranking agent in the Denay court anymore. He himself had spent several months in Daven Marcus's execrable presence, feeding the brat king secret funds to hire the mercenaries he had used to attack Earl Lastermune's holdings on the Quenland border in the first place. It was inconceivable that Sanguine had not replaced him in the time since, but he had no idea who the new agent was.

"You will not get a better chance than this chaos," the Inquisition servant urged the miserable young swordsman who was probably too drunk now to do the job in any case. With his pride, resentments, and personal relationships, the youth had been a perfect-seeming resource for Bluebird to cultivate, but he was proving an increasing disappointment.

"The place is shut up like a merchant's strongbox," the young man countered. "Even if I wanted to, there's no way to do it."

"You cannot talk your way in? I thought you were clever."

"And be instantly suspect once the deed was discovered?" came the retort. "To hell with your 'thought you were clever'!"

"A fair point," Bluebird conceded. "You could climb up and use that sneak's way you spoke of. Make a proper attempt at subterfuge."

"And slip on a tile and break my neck? No thank you."

"No, I suppose that would be a risk on a wet night like tonight."

Bluebird was doing his best to project the right combination of eagerness to have the assassination performed and trustworthy acceptance of the lad's objections. Except, of course, that he did not give a tinker's cuss what the young man actually thought. If it weren't that he had so few other options to hand, Bluebird would quietly encourage this twit to slip and break his neck on the way home tonight as it was. However, since Inxyphos's final failure, the Vault Above the Pit was probably unlikely to expend many more fresh resources on the Bridgetown problem. He still had the one lyre to sing with that had arrived in the confusion of the Compact's visit—but that was a useful tool he did not wish to waste on a rush action. He had already lost too many other tools in that one noble summit. The Young Hopeful's failed duel had always been something of a gamble, though the murderous fool himself had been a small stake to wager. Nonetheless, Bluebird was certainly rueful that in the end it had cost him the whole of the little gaggle of forlorn squires with it. He might have found more uses for them yet.

The Inquisition's lyres were another matter entirely—patient instruments, and ultimately even one should be decisive. Notwithstanding the western bitch's clever chambermaids had sniffed out the two in the west, Bluebird was sure the one he currently had at his command would be all he would need to finish the whole Bridgetown question in the end. A stormy, portentous night full of warfare like this was simply another windfall opportunity to get some of the work done quickly but it seemed he would not be allowed any more "cheap gambles". Probably just as well—his gang of rowdies was also in the wind—washed downriver as the locals liked to say. The smuggler crew he had managed to recruit were another inept tool, but they also had kept the witch from the west jumping at shadows well enough until his real plans could be put into action. Except of course, having lost several of their members to prison and "suicide", the hired thugs were becoming reluctant to continue their "service" to their mysterious employer. And naturally the rivermen were too canny to poke their heads out of their dockside holes on a night like tonight when whole armies were turning the bridges and piers into battlegrounds.

He sighed again, more honestly than he usually expressed any emotion. He was stuck for now with greedy, venal twits like this one. When tools were rare, even the poor ones had to be husband-ed with some care.

"Let's get another bottle, a brandy this time, and we'll keep the cold out, toasting to future hopes of success."

"I'll drink to that," the young man slurred and tried to stand, apparently thinking he was the one expected to pay for the brandy. He slipped back to his chair with a chuckle and Bluebird stood.

"I'll get this round," he said, like a kindly uncle, and reached into his purse, which only had a single gold Masnian left in it. At least his other plans were coming to fruition. Soon there would not be a single money changer in the whole town who wanted to touch this currency, even to melt it down for its base gold. Between rumors and threats, that was working out to Bluebird's satisfaction. Of course, if the men set to shepherd Froster and the Golden Heron had done their jobs right in the first place, there would be no need to fear foreign denomination, and the bitch from the west would still be a pauper begging crumbs from her conclaves. It was another matter that irked him no end. The one thing Bluebird wanted more than anything was for the war to be over at last so that the Vault Above the Pit and the Silent Hand could return to the competent running of the Grand Kingdom. A hundred vile kings like Daven Marcus were nothing to be feared, just like the fool sinking into a stupor at the table behind him. Bluebird knew tyrants and monsters were in many ways the easiest of all to lead by the nose. But as the war cut its undiscerning swathe across all levels of society, from royal to rogue, it left fewer and fewer reliable folk in its wake, and if there was one thing Bluebird loathed, it was being forced to work with cowards and incompetents. At least the ones like Inxyphos could be put to good use, but then they were expended and gone as well. He put the last gold coin on the bar in front of the weary tavernkeep, who clearly wanted nothing more than to close up, and ordered a bottle of brandy.

"Some of us have homes and beds to go to, you know," the man said as looked around the otherwise empty establishment before moving to fetch the liquor from his small cellar.

Be thankful to God and the Inquisition that you do, ingrate, Bluebird thought. *Some of us do not.*

He leaned down and rubbed at his knee that ached so when the weather was like this.

GLOSSARY

The Grand Kingdom's social structure is broken into three basic levels which are then subdivided into separate ranks: the nobility, the free folk, and the low born.

The Nobility

King/Queen – There is one King, and one Queen, his wife. The king is always the head of the royal family and rules from the Denay Court, in the capital city of Denay.

Prince/Princess – Any direct children of the king and queen.

Prince of Rhales – This title signifies the prince who is next in line of succession. This prince maintains a separate, secondary court of lesser nobles in the western capital or Rhales.

Duke/Duchess – Hereditary nobles with close ties by blood or marriage to the royal family, either Denay or Rhales.

Earl; Count/Countess; Viscount; Baron/Baroness – These are the other hereditary ranks of the two courts, in order of rank. One is born into this rank, as son or daughter of an existing noble of the same rank, or else created a noble by the king.

Baronet – This is the lowest of the hereditary ranks and does not require a landed domain to be attached.

Knight/Lady – The lowest rank of the nobility and almost always attached to military service to the Grand Kingdom as a man-at-arms. Ladies obtain their title through marriage. Knights are signified by their right to carry the longsword, as a signature weapon.

Squire – This is, for all intents and purposes, an apprentice knight. He must be the son of another knight (or higher noble) who is currently training, or a student of the academy.

The Free Folk

Patrician – A man or woman who has a family name and owns property inside a major town or city. Patricians always fill the ranks of any administration of the town in which they live, such as aldermen, guild conclave members, militia captains etc.

Guildsmen/townsfolk – Those who dwell in large towns as free craftsmen and women tend to be members of guilds who act to protect their members' livelihoods and also to run much of the city, day to day.

Yeoman – The yeomanry are free farmers that possess their own farms.

The Low Born

Peasants – These are serfs who owe feudal duty to their liege lord. They do not own the land they farm and must obtain permission to move home or leave their land.

Convicts – Criminals who are found guilty of crimes not deserving of the death penalty.

Military Order

Knight Captain, Knight Commander & Knight Marshall – Every peer (King, Prince or Duke) has a right to raise an army and command his lesser nobles to provide men-at-arms. They then appoint a second-in-command, often the most experienced or skilled soldier under them. A duke his Knight Captain; a prince his Knight Commander; and the King his Knight Marshal.

Knights – These are the professional soldiers of the Grand Kingdom. All nobles are expected to join these ranks when their lands are at war, and they universally fight from horseback.

Men-at-Arms –A catch all term for any man with professional training who has some right or reason to be in this group, including squires and second and third sons of nobles.

Bannermen – This is a special form of man-at-arms. These are soldiers who are sworn directly to a ranking noble.

Free Militia – The free towns of the Grand Kingdom have an obligation to raise free militias in defence of the realm.

Rogues Foot – A rogue is a low born or criminal man and so when convicts are pressed into military service, they are the rogues afoot (or "on foot") which is shortened to rogues foot.

Other Titles and Terms

Apothecary – A trader and manufacturer of herbs, medical treatments and potions of various sorts.

Chirurgeon – A medical practitioner, akin to a doctor or surgeon, especially related to injuries (as opposed to sickness, which is handled by an apothecary).

Ecclesiarchs – ruling members of the Church. Their ranks correspond (very roughly) to noble ranks. The ecclesiarchy refers to the power of the Church where it rules with its own power, like a nation within the nation. Monasteries, churches, cathedrals and the Academy in Ashfield are all part of the Church lands, where religious law overrides King's Law.

Estate – A person's estate can be their actual lands, but can also include their social position, their current condition (physical, social or financial), or any combination of these things.

Fiefed – A noble who is fiefed possesses a parcel of land over which they have total legal authority, the right to levy taxes and draft rogues or militia.

Frater – brother (from the Latin word)

Hoi Polio – the common folk

King's Law – This is the overarching, national law, set for the Grand Kingdom by the king, but does not always apply in the Western Reach.

Magistrate – Civil legal matters of the Free Folk and Peasantry are typically handled by magistrates, who render judgements according to the local laws.

Marshals/Wardens – Appointed men who manage the movement of large groups, especially of nobles and noble courts when in motion. They appoint the order of the march and resolve disputes.

Physick – A term for a person trained in the treatment of medical conditions, but without strict definition.

Proselytize – Attempt to convert someone from one religion, belief, or opinion to another.

Pugilist - A professional boxer.

Provost – (short for provost marshal) junior officers assigned to sentries or patrol for the purpose of military discipline. In the case of the White Lions militia, the typical rank of a provost is a Line First. Roughly equivalent to military police duty.

Republicanists – Rare political radicals, outlawed in the Grand Kingdom and the Vec who seek to create elected forms of government, curtailing or overturning monarchical rule.

Seneschal – The administrative head of any large household or organisation, especially a noble house of a baron or higher.

Surcoat – The outer garment worn by a man-at-arms over their armor. Typically dyed in the knight's colours (or their liege lord's colours in the case of a bannerman) and embroidered with their heraldry.

Te tree – A tree, known for its medicinal properties.

The Rampart – A celestial phenomenon that glows in the night across the sky from east to west in the northern half of the sky.

About Matt Barron

Matt Barron grew up loving to read and to watch movies. He always knew he enjoyed science fiction and fantasy, but in 1979 his uncle took him to see a new movie called *Star Wars* and he was hooked for life. Then *Dungeons and Dragons* came along and there was no looking back. He went to university hoping to find a girlfriend. Instead, the Lord found him, and he spent most of his time from then on in the coffee shop, witnessing and serving his God. Along the way, he managed to acquire a Doctorate in History and met the love of his life, Rachel. Now married to Rachel for more than twenty years, Matt has two adult children and a burning desire to combine the genre he loves with the faith that saved him.

Learn more at:

mattbarronauthor.com

Also by Matt Barron

Rage of Lions

Prentice Ash

Rats of Dweltford

Lions of the Reach

Eagles of the Grand Kingdom

Serpents of Summer

The Mantis and the Mirrored Sky

Bears of Bridgetown

Dragons of Denay

More from Publisher

Be sure to check out our other great science fiction and fantasy stories at:

bladeoftruthpublishing.com/books

9 781642 480467